TO[barcode]

OF FIRE

A Novel

The Story of an American Demagogue

ERNEST FRANKEL

HITHER LANE PRESS
LOS ANGELES

TONGUE

OF FIRE

A Novel

The Story of an American Demagogue

ERNEST FRANKEL

SATURDAY REVIEW OF LITERATURE: "A true creation. A one-man story surrounded with abundance of detail, accurate, painstakingly precise, often pungent detail..."

CINCINNATI INQUIRER: "Almost an epic. Ernest Frankel has written magnificently of a man and his ambition and he has written well, too, of a Washington that is both comic and tragic."

MILWAUKEE SUNDAY JOURNAL: "A fascinating study . . . a book that makes it possible for readers to relive one of the most divisive periods in recent political history. It deserves a wide audience in a nation that finds entirely too much ease in slipping back into the bland assumption that politics can safely be left to the politicians, and that everything automatically turns out all right in time for the closing commercial."

NASHVILLE TENNESSEAN: "An exciting dynamite-laden book—well-written, dramatic, hard-hitting and blood curdling. A powerful, compelling portrait that deserves wide and careful reading. . ."

BOSTON SUNDAY HERALD: "A writer of power and meaning, a book with the potential of dynamite. . .a wide-ranging, intimately-detailed novel. . .scenes that are pageants and scenes in the back rooms and in brothels and bedrooms, in committees and across the world. . .the author explores with thoroughness and insight. . ."

"The lying tongue is like a fire that consumes everything around it, and then, in the end, must consume itself."
—Congressman Shepherd Reade of Alabama

Published in the United States of America

ISBN-13: 978-0-692-94908-5
ISBN-10: 0692-94908-9

Editing/Formatting: Cary Editorial & Book Consulting

Cover Design: Jade Design (Fiverr.com)

Hither Lane Logo: Tahir (Fiverr.com)

Author photo: Adolfo Banos

Originally published by THE DIAL PRESS * NEW YORK
© 1960 by Ernest Frankel
Library of Congress Catalog Card Number: 60-9401

The House of Representatives of the United States is peopled in this novel, as in fact, by a few great and wise men and many good and capable men, by some who are selfless and some who are self-seekers.

On the roll of that House have been men like Kane O'Connor, men who have come from Manton and its hundred counterparts to take their place on the national scene and leave their mark on the times. But the characters and committees and incidents in this story are imaginary. They exist only in the mind of the author.

DEDICATION

For my mother and father—and always, for Louise

BOOK ONE

1

WELCOME HOME KANE O'CONNOR. The red-on-white banner—surmounted by a cardboard replica of the Distinguished Service Cross—hung limply above the shirt-sleeved crowd waiting behind the Manton Airport guardrail.

"Welcome Hooo-m, Kane! Welcome Hooo-m, Kane!" the group chanted listlessly.

Manton High School's head cheerleader wiped his damp palms on the seat of his white flannels. "Hold the 'hoooooo-m' and clip the 'Kane' short. We wanna make him really hear it when that plane comes in, so give it all you've got!"

"All you've got!" the three assistant cheerleaders on each flank repeated.

"'Welcome Home, Kane.' You hear that and we go into the Army Air Corps song." Viola Eden faced the Manton High School band, and taking off her visored cap, wiped the sweatband with cleansing tissue. "You clarinets are out of tune," she said, dabbing at her neck with the frayed paper.

"You gonna be Lieutenant O'Connor's mother-in-law, mam?"

There was a ripple of laughter from the saxophone section that spread down the straggling rows of blue-and-white.

"If a certain saxophone player had his mind where it belonged, he wouldn't be blowing so many wrong notes." Then, unable to restrain herself, the plump little woman laughed. "Just don't you all disgrace me, Mr. Biddle's here — and he'll see his new uniforms; and if he likes the way we look and the way we sound, we might just get that bus we're after. And we're on the radio. And our picture's goin' to be in *Life!*"

WELCOME HOME KANE O'CONNOR — The sign painter from Manton Mills tacked the placard, still wet, on a wooden pole. "Never fails," he said. "Damned if folks don't always want somethin' yesterday. . ."

The *Life* photographer placed the poster between a dressed-to-the-hilt, eight-year-old white girl and a dour-faced Negro boy of ten, and had them support it between them. "That's fine. Now you kids hold that a minute and I've got some gum for you. Hold it!"

On the platform facing the crowd, the welcoming committee had gathered. Off to one side, watching the preparations, Tod Sands, Secretary of the Manton Chamber of Commerce, lit a cigarette from the stub of another. Though he was in his early forties, and his hair was prematurely gray, the short, slight man wore the look of youth. His head was cropped in a crew cut. His ruddy face was unlined. His eyes were bright, aware of everything around him.

There were the cheerleaders, bellowing hoarsely, and the resplendent band, polishing brass buttons with the sleeves of their blouses. There were the magazine photographers, pockets bulging with used flashbulbs and tom cartons, seeking unposed shots from the always posing subjects who considered *Life* men minor celebrities.

There was the radio engineer uncoiling cable and a newsreel crew shining reflectors on the platform and enjoying the effect like children playing with mirrors. There were the veterans of World War I clustered around their color guard, half-listening to a loom fixer at Manton Mills, a marine hero of Belleau Wood, retell an oft-embroidered tale now twenty-seven years old.

There were airport attendants leaning on the waiting ramp, throwing pocket knives into the baked red mud, and an aging Negro in a sweat-striped panama standing beside a wheelchair, holding a paper cup of water while a shrunken, chalk-faced man gummed at two limp straws. And there was a spastic peddler selling balloons and a grandmother holding a sputtering baby up to the drinking fountain and two boys playing catch with a beer bottle.

Tod saw Judge Wesley Barrett, the returning hero's uncle, struggling with a loaded tray of cokes. The old man's white-maned head rode high out of his wing collar as he moved down the line of Girl Scouts and Brownies, Boy Scouts and Cubs that made a living border around the platform.

Luke Biddle, owner of Manton Mills, joined Judge Barrett as he served the last drink. Biddle fluttered his bony, work-tempered hands in emphasis as he spoke, his squat, heavy body weaving like a wrestler's.

Cy Woodward, the heir to the Manton Bank and Kane O'Connor's good friend, relieved the judge of the empty tray. Then, standing there fanning himself with a sailor straw, he pulled loose the bow tie under his round, boyish face and pushed it into his rear pocket where the strip of polkadot hung precariously.

At the rostrum the mayor bent over his typescript, glasses in one hand, following each line, mumbling the same words the whole town had heard before at merchants' banquets, church dedications, tourist breakfasts, supermarket openings and election campaigns. ". . . Our magnificent hills and valleys, our good, God-fearin' native stock and our unequaled climate . . ."

The engineer from WWMG—"Watch Wonderful Manton Grow"—grabbed at Tod's elbow. "When's he due? We'll have to go to tape if the plane's much later."

"Any minute," Tod promised, glancing at the sky. "O'Connor's going to be shook when he sees this. Doesn't know what's coming off."

"Kane'll manage," the engineer said, grinning. "Hellfire, never was a time he couldn't come up with a speech that'd make you laugh or bawl, 'cordin' to the time and place."

Tod climbed back to the platform. The cheerleaders clapped in rhythm. Three white skirts pirouetted. Three boys did flips in the dust and landed squatting. With fists clenched, they pounded the air to left and right, and queried the restless crowd.

"Who's the hero from the sky?"

"Kane!" a dozen youthful voices responded while the adults in the group fidgeting, grinned in embarrassment and mouthed the hero's name.

"Who came up from Manton High?"

"Kane!" Louder this time.

"Who's the Air Corps' greatest guy?"

"Kane!"

"Who's the apple of our eye?"

"Kane!"

The sound swelled as the cheerleaders rose to their toes. "Welcome Hoooooo-m . . .Then, finally, a clipped, triumphant, "Kane!"

Tod called the head cheerleader. The youngster, brushing rivulets of sweat from his flushed face, ambled to the platform. "Just knock off that question-and-answer bit," Tod said. "Pure ham. Strictly from Smithfield."

"But we had a contest, and that won first prize," the boy told him. "Mr. Biddle's givin' a bond to the winner."

"Just drop it, son," Luke Biddle said, coming up beside Tod. "It's fine, has real spirit." He reached down to pat the boy's shoulder. "We'll give the winner his prize all right, but the program's runnin' a little long."

"Yes, sir."

Biddle smiled as the cheerleader turned back to his charges. "Tod, if you can manage it, wish you'd do me a little favor."

"Sure, Mr. Biddle."

"I kinda half-promised . . . well, my people elected a Miss Manton Mills this year. And some of my boys asked could she bring up the key to the city to give the mayor so he could give it to O'Connor." He grinned broadly, abashed.

"Welcome Hoooooo-m, Kane!"

Tod waited until the chant died down again. "The way we planned it, Laurie Eden—I understand that's O'Connor's girlfriend—was going to bring the key up to give to the mayor, and that would let the photographers have another good shot. . ."

"Well, I don't want to hurt the girl's feelings, Tod. She's a sweet little thing. Her mother's my band director, you know. I say, I don't want to hurt the girl's feelings, but couldn't you get O'Connor and her together afterwards for pictures?"

"Let's ask Cy. He's the one who worked it out with her." Luke Biddle called Cy Woodward and explained his predicament. "That's how it is, Cy. You know me. Never know how to say 'no' to my people."

"Okay," Cy said. He pulled his handkerchief from his rear pocket, and swabbed the full circle of his face. Grunting, he stooped to retrieve his bowtie which had fallen out. "Hate like the devil to do this," he said to no one. Then, leaving the platform by the steps, he saw Laurie Eden standing at the far edge of the crowd. He worked his way toward her, coming up from behind. "I swan, you're a pretty little thing!"

She turned at the sound of the familiar voice. Her auburn hair, which usually lay easily on her shoulders, was piled high above the dainty oval of her face. There was just a hint of mascara above the wide violet eyes; and beads of perspiration clung to it. Her soft, full body was trim in a handsome white linen suit. And she wore a navy cartwheel straw that threw a lattice of shadow across her face and shoulders.

"Gosh!" Cy said in surprise.

"Cy, I'm so nervous I could die. They fooled with my hair 'til the last minute. And it won't do right. And this hat . . . it's proper, I know. After all, I'm part of the ceremonies. But nobody else here's got a hat on . . ."

Laughing, Cy broke in on her. "Laurie, you're a picture in that picture hat. Sure are." He leaned back as if to get a better view of it, confirmed his original opinion that it looked like a scarab's web, and whispered, "If all these other women here want to look like yokels, why that's no call for you to look that way!"

She stroked his jowls. "I know. I just needed someone to tell me so." Tucking a wisp of hair behind one ear, she said, "I was about to send somebody after you. Isn't Mr. Biddle supposed to escort me to the plane?"

"Well, that's what I came down to talk to you about."

"And on the platform, when I hand the key to the mayor, you want me to go around and stand beside Kane?"

"Laurie, I don't know . . ."

"You see, if I'm just standin' there alone, I'd look out of place."

Cy, embarrassed, plunged into the speech he had already rehearsed in his mind. "Laurie, you mind waitin' 'til the big doin's are over to get together with Kane?" He saw her expression change, heard her catch her breath. "There's a little mix-up in the plan. Some girl from the Mill's supposed to take the key up. And we'll get you with Kane for the pictures."

The band reached the sixth measure of the Air Corps song, and stopped abruptly while the director berated two trombonists.

Laurie's hat was drooping in front now. "But I . . . Cy, you told me. It's been set for two weeks . . ."

"I'm sorry, honey." Clumsily, he put his arm about her waist. "If you say, I'll . . . I hoped you'd understand, and help us out." She swallowed visibly, and Cy was afraid she'd blink and tears would come. "Whose idea was that, the Great White Father's?" she said, taking his arm away.

"Just a mix-up, Laurie. Wasn't really Biddle's fault."

"Don't you go lyin' to me, Cy!" Her pouting lower lip trembled, and she cleared her throat. "It's all right," she said, unconvincingly. "I'll wait here out of the way."

"Cy!" Judge Barrett was calling, and Cy grasped Laurie's arm momentarily, then took the cardboard key and lumbered back to the platform.

"You the hero's girl, miss?" a young man beside Laurie asked. "Engaged," she said dully, still watching Cy's retreating back. "Ever expect to see him coming home. . . ?" He stopped in mid-sentence and removed his straw hat. "I'm with *Life,* miss. We're doing a spread on this thing. 'Smalltown, U.S.A. Welcomes a Hero.' Mind some questions?"

"Go ahead."

"Did you think he'd wind up a hero?"

"He's always done everythin' good." For an instant she saw Kane projected on the screen of her memory: Kane wearing a uniform, Kane in football togs, Kane in dinner jacket, Kane in gym clothes, Kane in swim trunks. "Always," she said.

The young man unslung his camera. "Mind if I get a shot of you?" He winked. "The food's bad and politics are uncivilized here, but they do grow good-looking women in the South."

She smiled, wetting her lips as he stooped in front of her. "You better save your film for Kane."

"It's okay. Mr. Luce is lousy with film."

"Mr. Luce?"

The photographer cocked his head quizzically. "Mrs. Luce's husband." She gave no sign of recognition, so he went on. "What is it our hero always does so well?"

"He was an all-state halfback in high school. And captain of the gymnastic team in college. And a champion debater. You want me to stop talkin' so you can get the picture?"

He stood again and checked his lens setting. "No. Go on."

"Well, Kane worked his way through law school, and still came out near the top.

"When are you two getting married?"

"Soon," she said, holding herself stiffly as the photographer watched her in the finder.

"You mind taking off that thing?"

"What?"

"The hat. Mind holding it or something?"

As she removed the hat, trying to keep her hair in place, a cheer went up from the crowd. A plane was lining up with the runway, coming in. The mass of people moved forward, swarming past Laurie and the photographer, leaving the guardrail for the field. "See you later, miss," the Old Man said.

"But the picture?"

"Later," he said, scurrying away.

She stood there, her hat trailing in her hand, the onlookers jostling her aside as they rushed for the plane. Two policemen held the surging mass back, and Laurie found herself shunted to the rear, unable to see anything but a forest of heads before her.

The plane taxied toward the ramp and swung around beside it. Luke Biddle and Miss Manton Mills waited patiently. "Hello there, Miss Eden," Biddle said, tipping his hat as he saw Laurie for the first time.

She was pressed back beyond the ropes. "Why, how are you, Mr. Biddle?" And then, angry, seeking some way to retaliate, she said, "Hope Mrs. Biddle is doin' fine."

Biddle's face paled, and he turned away without acknowledging Laurie's thrust. No one ever mentioned Mrs. Biddle while she was "away." Manton whispered and gossiped about her frequent drunken lapses, her trips to a sanitorium for "the cure." But to openly acknowledge what everyone had known for years was an affront to The Old Man.

As the crowd fell back, and Laurie was shoved along with them, she regretted her remark. It wouldn't help Kane to have a wife that The Old Man disliked. Backs turned against the gusts of wind from the whirling propellers and Laurie lost her hat and saw it trampled in the blowing dust.

Then the ramp was pushed into place. Luke Biddle and Miss Manton Mills were shepherded through the crowd to join the welcoming committee. The hatch opened.

"Welcome Hoooooo-m, Kane! Welcome Hoooooo-m, Kane!"

"Off we go, into the wild blue yonder . . . The band nearly in tune played the Army Air Corps song.

A shadow appeared at the hatch, bent over, stepped through and stood erect. The thunder of the crowd rolled out above the band as Kane O'Connor, blinking in surprise, his right hand shielding his eyes, the other arm in a sling, smiled at the tumult.

And then, shyly, his strong, lean face alight with wonder, he raised his one good arm in a gesture of salute.

2

KANE O'CONNOR drank in the wild scene before him, momentarily intoxicated by his first taste of fame, savoring it, as if this one heady draught might satisfy all his cravings, all his thirsts. In that moment his whole life stretched invitingly before him, like a highway, straight and smooth and clear, with easy, banked curves and the glowing city ahead.

From the plane he had looked down at the sprawl of Manton—the complex of The Mills, the company houses with their hundred identical chimneys, the old, columned mansions in Sunset Hills, the huddled oaks and pines of Biddle Park, the golden dome of the courthouse, the stark outcropping of Tower Rock, the white arc of tourist hotels beside Willow Lake, the glaring concrete "T" of Myra Biddle Memorial Hospital. But all that was the familiar, remembered Manton. Before him he saw a new Manton, its arms outstretched, its voice shouting his name.

Waving, flashing his broad smile, he looked out over the swarm of people below him, searching for Laurie. But he couldn't find her. He saw Judge Barrett at the foot of the ramp. Old Uncle Wes, he thought, still dressed like a Ham Fisher senator, still wearing the white carnation in his lapel. He saw Manton's four-term mayor watching him, applauding. And Luke Biddle fanning both himself and a vaguely-familiar girl with his broad-brimmed straw. And then, Cy Woodward, a little pudgier, but otherwise unchanged. And the perennial commissioners, the chief of police, the chairman of the school board, the hundred nameless, but unforgotten faces. His smile embraced them all. Then he stepped down the ramp to be one with them.

"Good to have you home, boy!" Uncle Wes pumped his hand and clouted his back. "I'm proud of you—proud, proud!"

"You're a credit to us all," Luke Biddle said. Then, to the girl beside him, "You couldn't want a handsomer hero to kiss." Kane was all but smothered by Miss Manton Mills's bouquet, her cloying perfume and her seeking lips which landed damply on his nose and slithered over his mouth to rest finally on his chin.

The mayor saved him. "Should have kept the best for the last," he said, laughing. "But come on up to the platform, and we'll do this real formal!"

Kane called to Cy, but his friend was already out of earshot, leading the way through the crowd to the platform. There, flanked by Miss Manton Mills and a new Catholic priest he did not know, Kane was enthroned in a carved black armchair from which he had once presided over Manton High's student council.

The mayor tapped the microphone, blew in it, frowned at the radio engineer's protests, asked his audience, "Can you hear me back there?" got no reply, placed his pocket watch before him, and began in unhurried prose to extol the climate, scenery, industrial progress, post office receipts, birth rate, blue laws, water resources, bank deposits and "fine, friendly people that make our city a veritable kingdom of plenty . . ."

Hidden behind the line of scouts that flanked the mayor, Kane relaxed, cupping one hand over his eyes and closing them against the glare. My buddy Matt left me in fine shape for a deal like this, he thought, and grinned over the wild reception Matt Fallon had given him in New York, a celebration that had started at 11 in the morning and ended twenty hours later in a siren-shrieking, police-escorted ride to Newark in a Universal Broadcasting limousine. Discharged six weeks ago, Kane thought, and that operator's already on his way. . .

Stifling a yawn, Kane nodded when Miss Manton Mills spoke to him. He found it wasn't necessary to answer. Occasionally, during the infrequent pauses she used for breathing, Kane would slip in an interested "oh?" or an agreeable "sure." Then he would lapse back into semi-awareness of the girl's whisper and the counterpoint of the mayor's monotone.

"But what is our most important product?" His Honor asked.

Tax-free corn liquor is our most important product! Kane answered silently.

"Our children!" the mayor insisted. "Our children are sent out into the world . . ."

Kane felt his khaki shirt clinging to him under his blouse. Wiping his neck with a handkerchief, he stuffed the damp cloth into his sling.

"Many are the sons we have sent off to protect their country. In the Revolutionary War," the mayor told his restless audience, "the founders of Manton."

Kane retrieved the hand Miss Manton Mills had managed to clasp in her moist palm. He was disturbed Laurie had not come, and could not understand it. *Maybe I was a little rough on her in my last letter. But, dammit, I don't want the money she's saved.*

"Your arm hurt you?" Miss Manton Mills was asking.

He assured her it was just a fracture that hadn't healed properly, but would be as good as new. Pretending to be intent on the mayor's words, he concentrated, recalling a single paragraph of Laurie's letter, the last one before he left London: ". . . *and Kane, dearest, you'll be proud of me yet. I've gotten some of your college books from your Aunt Mady; and I'm reading them every night. Well, not the big ones, but the literature and the history ones. I'm starting on George Eliot. You know, I never knew she was a woman. But I don't think I'm going to like her. She gives me the feeling her people never have a chance. . . .*"

"The War Between The States saw us send off the cream of our young to join the gallant gray legions," the mayor said. And giving that information time to sink in, His Honor clinked the ice in his glass and had a swallow of cold water. The crowd watched thirstily.

So like Laurie, trying futilely to read herself through four years of college . . . as if that made any difference.

Miss Manton Mills jogged Kane's elbow. Apparently the mayor had little to say about the Spanish-American and First World Wars. He had turned, and was calling Kane to the rostrum.

The reigning queen of Manton Mills, still carrying key and flowers, followed the hero, and handed the golden pasteboard key to His Honor. "How about givin' it to him already?" *The Manton Argus* man yelled.

Disdainfully, the mayor said, "In time! In time!" Then, turning solemnly to Kane, he looked up at the young man who stood a full head over his own five-nine. "You've distinguished yourself in combat; and you've won for yourself a place in the hearts of us all."

Kane was amused. Ten years before, Aunt Mady had caught him in the garage with the mayor's daughter.

"'As ye sow, so shall ye reap'" the mayor was quoting. "What we have taught our sons about life's responsibilities . . ."

Tod Sands muttered to Cy Woodward, "Can't somebody shut the old boy up? He's been at it twenty minutes."

Kane shifted his weight, retrieved his handkerchief from his sling, and patted his neck while trickles of perspiration ran down his sides.

"When I look at this young man I see an expression of God's will. Through fire he has passed, even as the captives of the Babylonian king. From the jaws of death he has escaped, even as Daniel."

Yea, verily, Kane thought, but nothing tops this! He took off his cap, mopped his face, ran his fingers through the thick, black wave of his hair. Below him, he saw that a few people on the fringes of the area were drifting away. An infant was crying, and the mother's "hush, hush, now!" punctuated the mayor's speech. One forlorn Cub Scout had obviously wet his pants, and was trying to hide the outrage behind Kane's leg.

"And now," the mayor said, and stopped for another glass of water, "and now, I want to remind you, Kane O'Connor, that you can always feel free . . ."

Another plane was rolling in, and the noise of its engines obscured forever just what Kane might feel free to do. The mayor lifted the key to the city, and handed it to the hero even as the final blast of wind from the plane's propellers caught it and swept the traditional symbol down the runway.

In the excitement, a policeman chased the key as it cartwheeled in the dust, the damp Cub Scout was banished by his scoutmaster, and a Brownie scout tripped on the mayor's foot and fell from the platform.

Kane jumped down and lifted the sobbing girl in his arms. Then, dipping his handkerchief into the mayor's water pitcher, he bathed the bruised shin. The crowd applauded both the desecration of the mayor's refreshment and the tender act of healing.

The policeman handed Kane the broken, scuffed key; and before His Honor could add any postscripts, Manton's hero stepped before the microphone. He kissed the little girl on the forehead, and she, enjoying herself hugely, said, "You got lipstick on you!" Kane laughed with the crowd, and allowed the child to wipe Miss Manton Mills from his face. Then, balancing the

Brownie on the edge of the rostrum, he began to speak. "Like all of you," he said, "I'm dusty and hot and a little bushed. And I know you'll forgive me for not making a speech. Everything that might possibly be said, has been said." He winked at the little girl. She winked back. And the crowd, loving them both, laughed.

"Let me say only this: I've gotten a medal for something I did for a few minutes one night six months ago. But, I don't want to masquerade as a hero. I didn't have time to reason when I went to the controls of that burning plane." His graceful hands fanned out before him as he shook his head. "If I had, I would have remembered that I was just a deadhead who flunked out of flight school because he cracked up two planes, who was a bombardier by the grace of my Manton math teacher and an Irish instructor who liked my name. No, I didn't think about what I did. I just saw my trapped buddy there, and moved by my heart and not my mind, I couldn't leave him."

His tone was warm, conversational. And his audience was still, listening intently, eyes fixed on the tall, lithe young man.

Kane smoothed the little girl's face, and then turned back to his listeners. "So, please understand that I rate no hero's welcome. There's still a war being fought in the Pacific; and others, more worthy than I, are dying there at this moment, though few will know their names or praise their deeds.

"What happened in that split second of decision over the English Channel is in the past. My interest is in what is yet to be. We all have a great job ahead of us—a job more difficult even than winning the war—and that's the job of giving life and strength and meaning to the principles for which the war is being fought." He smiled at them. "If I may paraphrase a wiser man than I, 'the successful speaker should be brief, be concise, and be seated.'" Caught off-guard, his audience waited in silence, as if they expected him to go on. Then they responded with cheers and applause. While Kane returned the bruised Brownie to her troop, and the priest stood to pronounce the invocation, the tribute to their hero continued.

Tod Sands turned to Cy Woodward. "When's the guy going to start running for office?"

Cy grinned. "Hell, Kane's been runnin' since he was twelve. He just hasn't announced it yet!"

After the invocation, Kane finally broke away from the well-wishers who crowded around him, and found Cy. "You ole tub, how the devil are you?"

Laughing, recognizing the cue for the "passwords" the two had coined when they smoked rabbit tobacco in a shaky treehouse behind the judge's home, Cy answered, "I'm fine as wine; I'm smooth as cake."

Kane finished the singsong chant: "Then let me have the ole handshake."

"I'm ready with the key!" the mayor told a *Life* photographer who was snapping a picture of the two boyhood friends.

"Never mind. I've got a shot of O'Connor holding it."

"But you didn't get the presentation," the mayor insisted. "Don't you think you oughta . . ."

"No more film," the photographer told him, walking away. Judge Barrett stood with his arms around Kane and Cy. "Come on! You two can do your talkin' when we get home. Your Aunt Mady's havin' a big dinner tonight, boy. And we might let it set a spell so you'll have time to pick up Laurie."

"How about that! Why didn't she show up?" Kane asked.

"Just a little misunderstandin'," Cy said. "I'll explain it later."

Kane frowned. "Looks like she could have gotten out here."

"I'll get your luggage," Cy said. "Meet you at my car."

Uncle and nephew plowed through the remnants of the crowd, shaking hands, the judge inching up on the toes of his shiny hightop shoes to whisper names as more people closed in on them.

Cy was waiting for them beside his Lincoln sedan. As Kane hopped in and slammed the car door, the mayor arrived, breathless, and handed the battered key to the city through the open window.

Uncle Wes leaned over the front seat and squeezed Kane's shoulder. "Quite a shock to you, wasn't it, boy? That's what I call a surprise!"

"Surprise hell," Cy said, laughing. "I wrote him what to expect three weeks ago!"

3

CY DROVE THROUGH the airport gates. Weaving past the maze of traffic—the Manton Mills van with its cargo of furniture and debris, the open-shelved Coca Cola truck, the magazine and newsreel and radio crews loading their equipment, the snarl of honking cars trickling from the parking lot—he turned the car toward town.

"Kane, your room's still waitin' for you, and your aunt and I'll be pleased for you to come back to it," Judge Barrett said.

"Well," Kane began, thinking of Aunt Mady, "it would probably be better for me to check into the hotel for a few days until I find something."

"The hell you say!" Cy slowed the car as they entered the city limits. "I've got a place of my own now. You're movin' in with me."

"Okay!" Laughing, Kane pinched the back of Cy's neck. "You talked me into it." No need of going through the amenities of protesting with his old friend. He settled back. The blue-green mountains ahead formed a majestic cyclorama for the remembered setting that rolled by; and Kane saw only a few glints of newness to remind him that time had passed, and that he had been away.

As the lush, green hills rose on either side, they sped past a cluttered mile of squat, gray concrete-block warehouses, a coal yard that sold ice and heating oil, a billboard with a mammoth armpit and a giant deodorant jar, the deserted Southern Railway water tank, three motels—one where you didn't need luggage—and a welter of filling stations.

The judge leaned over the seat and tapped Kane's shoulder. "Same old town, eh?"

"Same old town," Kane said.

Now sycamores and tulip trees began to emerge from the coagulum of feed stores, fruit stands and Negro shacks, used car lots and farm equipment showrooms, gradually forming a leafy bower as the car climbed Hillside Avenue and turned into Manton's business district.

"I'll give you a spin around The Square," Cy said. "Hasn't changed much."

The Square. Kane thought he might close his eyes and still recall every foot of it: The Gothic battlements of the County Courthouse in the center with its encircling moat of glaring concrete, the "U" of the two-story buildings on three sides, and then Biddle Park. My Olympus, he mused. My Everest. "Well," he said, thinking aloud, "I guess you've got to start with little mountains."

"What?" his uncle said.

"Beautiful mountains."

"You bet. No prettier ones anywhere."

They drove by the park—wide green lawns and vine-covered oaks and pines and a garish billboard listing the county's war dead; winding white gravel paths bordered by mountain laurel and rhododendron and the slate gray shuffleboard courts of the tourist league; the Wishing Spring, its icy water gushing from a grotto of silvery rock, and the Jaycee-sponsored refreshment stand, a leaning, rust-streaked structure, imaginatively shaped like the spool-and-loom trademark of Manton Mills and painted orange-and-blue, in faithful reproduction.

They swept on, passing the forest of meters in the municipal parking lot, the pebbled stucco garage of Drake's Ford Agency, and then the handsome redbrick Colonial firehouse, with its shiny American LaFrance ladder-truck glittering in the open doorway. "Skinny Faircloth's chief now," Judge Barrett said.

Cy stopped for a red light. "He's still tellin' the story 'bout how the three of us fed that cow mineral oil and parked her in the principal's office overnight."

"Uncle Wes laughed like mad," Kane said. "Cussed me out, but didn't lay a hand on me." Turning, he shook a finger at his uncle. "And then you went home and swore to Aunt Mady that you'd tanned me good!"

The store buildings were on their right now—a line of weathered brick buildings with the same glaring tin cornices, broken only by the handsome Georgian facade of the Manton Bank and Trust Company, the neat fieldstone trim of Blue Ridge Billiards, and the identical black-glass fronts of Mangel's and

Lemer's, the rival women's wear stores with their identical summer clearance signs. Only a few shoppers had braved the heat; and a single tourist lounged on one of the green benches that lined the sidewalk.

Kane looked out at the yellowing, ivy-clad courthouse, at the Civil War monument before it, the pitted cannon that was supposed to have fired on Sherman's men, and the irregular pile of cannon balls, still missing the one he and Cy left on Luke Biddle's lawn one Halloween.

"Newell's drunk again," Cy said, pointing to the flagpole. "Commissioners been threatenin' to fire him, but he's got all those kids . . ."

Kane saw the flag drooping from its mast, the union inverted in the traditional signal of dire distress. "A symbol," he said, winking at Cy.

The judge patted Kane's arm. "You're home, boy."

"I'm home," Kane said.

A few minutes later, Cy turned into the driveway of a sprawling ranch-style home. "I'll take your things in. You drop the judge off and go over and see your gal before you collapse from hunger pangs. I'll call a cab and see you all for dinner."

"New, isn't it?" Kane said, studying the house appreciatively. "Nice to have rich friends. Thanks, Tubby. See you later."

"Okay," Cy said, and reached for Kane's hand. "Good to have you back, fella. And don't call the V.P. of the bank 'Tubby!'"

Kane said, "While I've got this warm feeling for you, Tubby, and before our first fight, I'm moved to say that you're a nice guy."

"And you're a stinker!" Cy pulled the last suitcase out of the rear seat, let the judge in beside Kane, and slammed the door.

Kane managed to drive with his free right hand. Turning the car up Biddle Avenue, he remembered to avoid Manton's only one-way street. "Cy's the best," he said. "And I *am* going to stop calling him 'Tubby.'"

"Doin' well," Judge Barrett said, bouncing on the seat to arrange the tail of his coat. "He'll be runnin' the bank himself one of these days. Been like a lost soul this past year since he got back from the Army and you were away."

Kane smiled, remembering Cy Woodward sixteen years before.

The two boys had complemented one another since their first schoolyard battle when both were twelve years old. Kane, tall, aggressive, husky, had little trouble knocking the short fat boy to the ground. Cy had survived the pummeling, holding on, crying and pushing at the bigger boy's nose.

"You take it back, Woodward, you sonovabitch!"

"No I won't. And I'll tell your aunt you used that word."

"What word?" Kane asked fiercely.

"Sonovabitch!"

"You used it too! I'll tell your old man. And I'll tell him you called me a Catholic bastard, too!"

"I did not."

"I'll tell him you did."

"You're a liar."

"Take it back," Kane said, putting his fingers around Cy's neck. "Take back what you said at first about my father."

"It's so!" Cy gasped. "Your Aunt Mady told my mom your—"

Kane pressed harder. "You take it back!"

"You take back callin' me a sonovabitch," Cy insisted, scratching Kane's face.

"You take it back first."

"All right. I take back that your dad was a drunk!"

"I didn't mean you're a sonovabitch," Kane said grudgingly as he let him up. "But if you tell my aunt, you are!"

The next day, Cy called to Kane on the street before Uncle Wesley's home. "My dad says I got to 'pologize 'cause you're an orphan."

"Well?"

"I didn't know you're an orphan." Cy hesitated, then put out his pudgy hand. "I'm sorry."

Kane turned away from him; and when Cy walked around to face him, he saw the taller boy dab at his eyes. "You're cryin'. I said I'm sorry."

"Okay."

"Gosh, Kane," Cy said huskily. "I didn't mean to say anythin' wrong." Then, searching for some way to square things, "Go on. It's okay. You can call me a sonovabitch!"

+

Kane stopped the car before the green hedge fence that encircled the Barrett home.

"Come in to see your aunt, Kane?" There was something of a plea in the judge's question—the unspoken, "Why can't you two get along?" that Kane had seen in his uncle's eyes so many times. Why? Kane thought. After so many years. . . .

It was a cold, rainy day when the three of them—Aunt Mady, Uncle Wes and Kane—stood beside the upturned mound of sooty earth on a Pennsylvania hillside. The trembling ten-year-old walked past the bier, watched it lowered. Then, refusing to leave, he stood there as the first clods were thrown down, thumping against the plain pine box. There were only the sounds of the shovel scraping loose dirt, the sprinkling shower and then the hollow bump of a wayward rock.

"It's going to be mud," Kane said.

Then restraint left him. Then the shaking heads, the whispered words, the strange bed, the first night without his father—all these things rumbled through the child. He sobbed. He looked up at his Aunt Mady and grasped at her skirts.

And she said, "No whinin', Kane. Act like a man."

His uncle picked him up. "We're carryin' you a long way off —to Manton. You're not alone, boy."

Kane was tugged from his reverie by Uncle Wes's timid grasp on his sleeve. "Just take you a few minutes," he was saying.

"Sure." Kane slipped over the yellow leather seat and followed him through the gate. Across the sloping lawn he saw the old brown-shingled house, its long L-shaped porch still cluttered with his aunt's potted plants, lined, in their colored silver-foil wrappers, across the top of the railing.

Three cats romped on the grass. A mangy fox terrier slept on the steps. Two puppies nipped at one another, rolling on the porch. And beneath the old, creaking glider, Kane knew—even before he saw the cardboard box—there would be an ailing squirrel or a crippled bird. Mady Barrett thought all organizations (except the Presbyterian Church and the Daughters of the Confederacy) were a waste of time, and refused to join the Humane Society. But people had always brought her wounded chipmunks, mangled strays and deserted fledglings. Kane's first memory of the house was Aunt

Mady standing on that porch, clucking over a ball of fur, and feeding it with an eye-dropper.

He saw his aunt. She backed against the screen door, pushing it open, and leaning on the arm of a green wicker rocker, then on her cane, she managed to seat herself. She was the same, Kane decided as their eyes met, still playing Victoria Regina in modem dress. Cool dignity. Noble brow. Severe, iron-gray coiffure. Long, crooked fingers. Transparent skin. Fine, blue veins in her cheeks. Now she held her hand out, palm up, and Kane took it. "How are you, Aunt Mady?"

"My arthritis is worse. And you?"

"Great."

Uncle Wes stepped beside her chair and touched her shoulder. "Cy insisted Kane stay with him. He's got plenty of room, dear."

Aunt Mady smiled with one corner of her mouth. "I see you're a hero."

"He got a real welcome home, Mady."

"I've been readin' you've gone and got yourself a Christian conscience, Kane."

Not today, Kane thought. You don't bait me today. "I've got to run, Aunt Mady. I'll be back as soon as I pick up Laurie."

Judge Barrett was uncomfortable. "Fine. We'll be ready for dinner when you are."

Back in the car, Kane relaxed. He pulled away from the curb and turned toward Laurie's. No change, he thought. The old witch is cold, polite and ready to knife you.

He hated the woman, not with the fire of new anger, but with the determination born of long, smoldering resentment, with the thoroughness born of a child's meditations. It was Aunt Mady who had discovered the examination notes scribbled on his cuffs. And Aunt Mady who had berated his uncle for allowing him to go to "the Papist church." It was Aunt Mady who had found him and Cy in the attic of the old house, drinking wine. And Aunt Mady whom he had overheard telling his uncle, "He can fool you, Wes, but I see the corrosive streak in him." And it was Aunt Mady, tortured by the racking pain in her limbs, who had told him at sixteen, "You're like your father, Kane. Good-lookin'. Conceited. Loud-mouthed. And evil."

At Laurie's back door, he tried the latch, found it open and stepped into the kitchen. Viola Eden, still wearing her band uniform trousers under her wrapper, turned, gasping at the sight of him. Before she could speak, Kane caught her in his arms and kissed her on both cheeks. "Shh! Where's my girl?"

"Been waitin' out front since I got back from the airport. Had her poor little heart broken."

"What's wrong?"

"Better let her tell you. You know Laurie. Just needs to be buttered-up some."

He looked down at her. "Okay. And you sure did have that band playing pretty out there. Sounded great."

She pressed his hand in both of hers. "You really gave 'em a speech, Kane. Oh, you did fine!" Releasing him, she said, "It's good to have you home again."

He held her at arm's length. "If you keep getting younger and prettier, I'm going to drop Laurie and marry you. We'll have to late-date and talk it over. Here's a sexy one to hold you." He kissed her full on the mouth and walked out of the warm, familiar little room, leaving her flustered, happy and laughing.

Through the screen door, he saw Laurie. In the fading light, her auburn hair blowing gently about her shoulders, she sat on the porch rail, facing the street. He watched her unguarded moment; and he marveled at the inability of his memory to hold the image of her over their time apart. He had remembered the full underlip, the violet eyes, the smile, the not-quite-straight nose. But the whole of her, the harmony of coloring, the expression, the calm loveliness of her, he had been unable to recall. Now he opened the door and she saw him at once and stood there, waiting for him to come to her.

"Hi!" Kane said.

"Hello, darling," she whispered, still watching him.

"Come here."

She obeyed. And in that moment he knew why his memory had failed him. There was no way to capture the softness, the firmness, the fragrance, the taste of her. They sat side by side, and Kane held her chin in his right hand and kissed her again. "Now you better start talking fast," he said. "Why weren't you out there waiting for me?"

Resting against him, holding his hand to her side, she told him how she had been shunted away, and so, left the ceremonies. "But I've got you all to myself now. Luke Biddle can go hang."

He kissed her again. "Nothing's changed, has it?"

Her fingers explored his face, tracing the firm line of his jaw. "With us? Never."

"I mean this town. Still Old Man Biddle's private preserve. If you want a new wing for the library or you just want your girl waiting for you at the airport, you've still got to get his permission."

"I don't need his permission for this," she said, burrowing closer to him, bringing his lips to hers. "Heard you on the radio," she whispered, still clinging to him, feeling his breath now on the crown of her head. "You were awful good."

"You shouldn't have left, Laurie."

"And I heard that little girl sayin' you had lipstick all over you, too! Oh, darlin', the whole town saw it or heard about it . . ."

Gently, he held her away with his free arm. "More of Biddle's . . ." His voice dropped. "Why did you let him do it? Dammit, Laurie."

"Who're you 'dammit-in'?' " she said softly, and found his lips again.

"You've got to stand up to people. You can't let yourself be pushed around." Annoyed, he reached into his pocket for a package of cigarettes, and fumbled with them. Laurie took them, lit one for him, one for herself, and leaned against him. "Since when did you start smoking?"

She inhaled, pressed her lips against his, and forced the smoke into his mouth. Then, laughing as he choked on it, she said, "It was the only safe vice I could manage while you were away. It's the fault of my libido," she explained, (pronouncing it lee-bye-do). "Didn't realize it 'til I got into your psychology book. But I must have taken up smokin' to work-off my frustration!"

She didn't sound like the Laurie he remembered, Kane thought. But that Laurie was younger and time had changed them both. He had trained in five states, had lived in England and France, had known a different world. All that lay between them. And four years of college and two of law school lay between them as well. Before the first flush of reunion was an hour behind, he found himself trying to bridge the gap of their separation, identifying names and places she did not know and struggling to recall the people and events they had once shared, but were now hers alone. There was so much he had planned to tell her, so many questions he wanted to ask. But they all seemed used-up so quickly. In time they were sitting silently, rocking on the glider, barely touching, not yet sure of one another, not yet completely comfortable with one another, talking in brief rushes, exhausting the subject, and trying again to find common ground.

"Funny, isn't it?" he said. "I've thought about this for so long. And now that we're together, I'm tongue-tied."

"Me, too."

"Brought you some presents," he said. "A tablecloth—a big one from Brussels. And some Dresden china and some earrings from France."

"Thank you, darlin'. With all you had to do, you found time for that! And I've got some things for you, too. Old Lawyer Thompson died and I bought his office furniture. Bookcases, desks, chairs, typewriter . . ."

"But, honey, I don't even have a place . . ."

She put a finger to his mouth. "You just hush and let me finish. You know that new buildin' Cy's daddy built a block from The Square? Well, there's a corner office."

"I'm sure it's beautiful, Laurie, but isn't it a little rich for my blood?" Smiling, he stroked her cheek. "For a guy just getting started, I'll need something cheaper and around some other lawyers."

"I've already paid the first month's rent," she said, slipping away, her lower lip pouting.

"Cy'll let us out of it," Kane said, patting her knee. "You're a doll to have done it, darling, but . . ."

She moved his hand away. "I thought you'd be pleased. The furniture's all moved in. I even took the money I had left—more than five hundred dollars—and started a joint account for us."

"But I wrote you that I didn't want you to put your money . . . oh, hell, Laurie, I know you were trying to please me. And I appreciate it, but after all. . ."

"Never mind," she said, a choked-down sob in her voice. "I'll change the account. I'll sell the furniture. You can pick your own office."

"Laurie, darling . . ."

"That's okay."

He smiled. "Now it's like old times. I'm beginning to recognize my girl again." He lifted her chin. "Like the good old days. You're being martyred, aren't you, baby? I'm acting like a dog and you're suffering."

She nodded vigorously, and wiped a knuckle at the corner of her eyes, although there were no tears. "I was afraid of you for a minute, when you were growlin' at me. You're still my fella. You haven't really changed at all."

When they were driving toward Judge Barrett's home later, Kane tugged Laurie's hand and she moved across to him. "We'll take a look at the office," he said. "Maybe it'll work out."

Pressing her head against his shoulder, she said, "Are you goin' to be mad at me for givin' you another little gift?"

He smiled down at her. "What now?"

"They're second-hand, but the judge says that doesn't make any difference." She searched his face for some indication of his mood. "I bought you a law library. Two hundred volumes."

He stopped the car in traffic; and while horns blew and pedestrians stared, he kissed her.

At midnight, high above the town, on a canted granite boulder in the shadow of Tower Rock, they lay in one another's arms, whispering through touching lips.

"How about all those women whose names are on your cast?" Laurie said. Then, solemnly, "Kane O'Connor, were you faithful to me?"

"I'll cross my heart."

"No, don't. I don't want to know."

She turned her neck, and his mouth swept down across her throat; and she felt the brief tick of pain as he nipped her earlobe. "I love you," she said. "I've missed you, missed you." She held his face in her hands and kissed his eyes and lips and chin.

"How's your libido?" he asked.

"That the way you pronounce it?"

"Mmm-huh."

"I'm afraid it's tellin' me to forget I'm supposed to be a good girl."

"Fine!"

She laughed softly and held him closer. Suddenly pulling away, she said, "She does bird calls at Kiwanis and Rotary meetin's."

"Who?"

"Miss Manton Mills."

"You can't do bird calls," he mumbled in her ear.

She shivered. "Nope."

"But you're a better kisser . . . the best and most willing kisser in this town!"

The two lovers, long hungry for one another, whispered and kissed in the darkness.

4

APPOINTMENTS
January 15, 1946

Morning: Courtroom.
12:00: Luncheon, Board of Directors, Red Cross.
1:30: Greet visiting Legionnaires.
2:30: Mr. L. B. Boord (Accident Liability).
3:30: Mrs. Mark Woodmire (Divorce).
7:00: Preside, Jaycees.
8:30: Conference at Judge Barrett's.

Kane re-read Laurie's uneven scrawl and underlined the final entry. The evening's meeting at his uncle's home could mark the culmination of all his preparations and the beginning of a career in politics; and his mind dwelt on it as he filled the margins of his appointment sheet with doodles of five-pointed stars, mustaches and B-24 silhouettes.

From across the desk came the constant drone of his client's voice, but Kane was hardly aware of it. ". . . but you've got to make sure I keep my children, Mr. O'Connor."

Kane bit the eraser on his pencil, removed the rubber from his tongue, and leaning back, studied the woman. Though she was a little overdressed—the sparkling veil on her shell of a hat, the large earrings—though she was a little over conscious of herself—the too-fine line of her eyebrows, the too-careful arrangement of her skirt over her knees—she was, he decided, a handsome woman. The lush body held regally in the deep leather chair, the grace of her tapered fingers as she spoke in her curious hoarse voice, the deep-seated green eyes that looked at you boldly, the chignon of fire-red hair that crowned a delicate, yet sensual face, the way she moved—all those things denied the apparent brittleness of her manner, the cool, nearly-detached way in which she spoke of her personal life.

This was her third visit; and she was repeating her story again, reviewing all the details, as if she were confiding in a psychiatrist, Kane thought.

"Mark's changed, Mr. O'Connor. When we first got married..."

"Have you done as I suggested?" Kane asked, sitting up and resting his elbows on the desk. "Did you talk over your differences with your husband?"

"It's so difficult to talk to him. He works all day. Then, after dinner, when most people go out or have friends over, or even sit and read or listen to the radio, he's out half the night at a meeting." Her voice broke in resignation. "And he spends his weekends hunting or fishing. I hardly see him anymore . . ."

Kane looked at his watch. Four-forty. And he had to pick up Laurie, find some time to talk to Cy before the night's conference. So much could hinge on that. He'd give her another ten minutes he decided, and then, somehow, get rid of her.

"When we got married, Mark walked right into an assistant's job with the union, and I worked in a day nursery. Wonderful, honestly! I figured we were only starting and there was so much ahead of us . . ."

Then the first child had come. And the second. And always moving. Small, sagging places near the company homes, removed by circumstances from the companionship she sought. "You know what I mean—no chance to be with my kind of people. That's nothing against the mill workers. It's just that . . . what could I talk to them about? Then there's a stigma attached to you if you're with the union. The better people act like you're a Red or something."

Kane cut her off. "Mrs. Woodmire, you've got to have other grounds for divorce. As long as your husband is supporting you, and isn't abusing you, there's no way . . ."

"I just don't know what I'm going to do, Mr. O'Connor."

Kane stood. He realized that she had no intention of getting a divorce. He had her catalogued: a bored, lonely woman, married too young, with children too soon, to a man without time for her.

"Mrs. Woodmire, there's nothing I can do until you talk to Mr. Woodmire." He walked around the desk. "Perhaps we can arrange a two-year separation. The only grounds . . ."

She slipped easily out of her chair and faced him. "It's as if we were separated now."

He walked toward the door. "Well, we'll do what we can," he assured her, turning the knob.

In the doorway, Melba put her gloved hand on his arm; and he smelled the whisky and cloves on her breath. "I want you to know how much I appreciate your help."

"That's all right," Kane said, steering her through the outer office and into the hall.

As Melba glided off toward the waiting elevator, Cy Woodward passed her and caught Kane at the door of his office. "Man, who's that piece of plunder?"

"Wife of the organizer out at The Mills."

"What's her trouble?"

Kane shrugged. "Probably just needs to get laid."

"If you're recommendin' therapy," Cy said, "remember your ole buddy!"

'Come on in, you lecher, we've got to rehearse our strategy for tonight."

Cy followed Kane into the inner office and dropped into the one comfortable chair. "Where's Laurie?"

Glancing at his watch, Kane said, "Right now she's probably cussing me. I was supposed to pick her up ten minutes ago. She's been searching a deed for me."

"So let this ride until later. Laurie's been working for you for peanuts, but you don't have to treat her like hired help."

"This won't take long."

Cy frowned. "Kane, why the hell don't you marry the girl?"

"Give me time."

"I'll be your best man."

"What makes you think I'd want a woman-chaser for a best man?"

"It's a good way to bribe me to keep my lip buttoned about our little adventures in Charlotte and Atlanta. Laurie'd skin you if she knew our monthly business trips for the bank were really parties to get re-charged!"

Kane made a face. "Why're you so damned anxious to get me married?"

"I don't give a hoot about you. But Laurie's been ready to hunt the preacher since you got home."

"Well, don't let on to her, but she's got some waiting to do. I'm not set. If I make it in the election, maybe then. . .

"For your sake, Kane, you've got to realize what you're up against. Bev Crater's been District Solicitor for three terms, and he's the County Democratic Executive Committee's boy. You're just twenty-seven. You're a Catholic. You've never held an office. You've been home only six months. Most of the folks remember you when you were just a kid, callin' square dances in The Park."

"And they'll vote for somebody they know."

"They'll vote for somebody they know Luke Biddle's committee wants them to vote for."

"You don't think I can win!" Kane accused him.

"I don't want you plannin' on it."

"Uncle Wes says I've got a chance."

"Uncle Wes is anglin' for the next congressional nomination. He can't afford to buck Luke Biddle any more than you can." Kane straightened the picture frame in which his Distinguished Service Cross medal and citation were mounted. "He's going to have Biddle there tonight."

"As county chairman, he's not stickin' his neck out for you any more than your Uncle Wes will. You can make book on that."

"That's okay with me."

"What's the point?"

"I want Biddle to leave there tonight convinced that if I decide to file for the primary I've got a good chance to get a big vote, maybe not big enough to win, but big enough to split the party . .

"So you figure he'll stay out of the primary?" Cy considered that. "Maybe. But how do you give him the idea?"

"We show him I've got money, reputation and people behind first cousin of half the voters, and if Biddle is for Bev Crater—and you can bet your tail he is—you haven't got a prayer."

"You could have the Chase National Bank behind you and be first cousin of half the voters, and if Bittle is for Bev Carter—and you can bet your tail he is—you haven't got a prayer."

"Shut up and listen!" Kane said. "I know the facts of life as well as you do. One: The Democratic nomination is equal to election. Two: There are more Democratic voters in this county than in the rest of the district combined. Three: Whatever Biddle and his precinct men decide, that's it. So, our job is to show them that plenty of voters will want me; and plenty of them'll resent any meddling in the primary; and that I've got the money and ability to get people to the polls."

"So you think you can fool Luke Biddle?" Cy asked incredulously.

"Hell, I'm not trying to fool him. I only want him to realize we're not just a bunch of kids."

"I hope you're right."

"You're damned tootin' I'm right."

"Okay. You get my vote. And the fellas I promised to get there'll be there."

"You've got to carry the ball for me tonight. Talk like we can't lose, like it's a sure thing."

Cy put two sticks of gum in his mouth and chewed noisily. "Kane, do you want me to tell you a bunch of hogwash? Or do you want me to tell you what I really think, so we know where we stand?"

Kane lit another cigarette. "I want you to tell me the truth. But everybody likes to be on the winning side. And if we don't talk that way, some of the guys who'll be at Uncle Wes's tonight will scare off, and we won't make our point with Biddle." At his desk, Kane riffled through a stack of bills and letters. "I want to read something to you. Damn! Laurie never puts anything in the right place." He began to look through his files. "Letter I got from a buddy of mine—Matt Fallon. You know. I've told you about him. Met him overseas. Christ! She's got it filed under the m's!"

Glancing at the letter, he sat on the edge of his desk. "Now, granted Matt doesn't know anything about Manton or small town politics. But he worked on the *Daily Times* in Gainesville, Georgia and covered Washington for an Atlanta paper before going into the service. And he's a political reporter for Universal Broadcasting now. So he knows the score. Let's see. . .He says: '. . . go to it, Kane. You pack the gear. I expected you to get your hand in the public till sooner or later.'" Kane laughed. "Now, here's what I was looking for: The illusion of political strength begets political strength. Any damned fool knows that. The situation you describe is made to order for you. . . .'" Kane dropped the letter on his desk. "Well, Cy? Does that make sense or doesn't it?"

"I know from nothin'. I've seen your friend Fallon on a couple of television panels and he's a bright fella. But Manton's a long, long way from Washington. What Fallon thinks is interestin', and what our buddies who are cornin' tonight think, that's important. But what Luke Biddle thinks—that's everything."

"Your friend Tod Sands can't make it tonight," Kane said. "Going down to the capital to push some advertising project. But all the others are firm."

"Oren call you? Promised me he would."

"Yeah. He'll play up the veterans' angle. As VFW Commander, he's got a lock on at least a thousand votes."

"What makes you think they'll vote with him?"

"Dammit, Cy, Crater's just another old coot they've known around town since they were kids. I'm a guy who fought a war with them."

"How about Hugh Lester?"

"He'll be there. He's not overloaded with brains, but he's a nice guy and he's got the Young Democrats in his pocket. And Ray Burnham . . ."

"Think he can help with the county?"

Kane dropped ashes on the carpet and rubbed the spot with his foot. "I don't know. Can he?"

"Might. He's in feed, fertilizer and farm equipment. Has lots of friends around."

"What does he want?"

"He's honest, Kane."

"I'm honest, too. But I want something."

"He doesn't want anythin' the District Solicitor could give him."

"All right. Then we're real sincere."

Cy laughed. "That's your department. Now, come on, let's get out of here and pick up Laurie."

"You're not very excited about this. Are you, you old tub?"

"Nothin' to get excited about yet. We'll see."

That evening at nine o'clock, Kane and Laurie arrived at Judge Barrett's home. They were a half an hour late. But Kane had planned it that way. He wanted to give his uncle and Cy time to get everyone seated, to steer the discussion to the issue of his candidacy, to praise his merits unfettered by his presence.

In the foyer, Laurie kissed him lightly, then had to struggle as he held her. Finally she pulled away, biting his ear savagely.

"You're a maniac," she whispered. Taking his coat, she walked down the hall to leave it in Aunt Mady's sitting room.

Kane listened to Judge Barrett's deep, booming voice: "Hugh and I were makin' a list of Kane's advantages as a candidate. Would you go over them, Hugh?"

The Young Democrats' leader read off the notes Kane had prepared that afternoon. "Air Corps war hero . . ."

"That won't hurt with the veterans' vote." Cy's voice. "Active as President of the Junior Chamber, Organizer of the Manton Gymkhana, Commander of the Legion, director of the Red Cross, director of the Young Democrats . . ."

Kane glanced into the damp, musty, well-remembered room. His uncle was seated behind the black walnut table, fingering the conch shell they had brought back from Myrde Beach twenty years before. And Luke Biddle, his face blotched in colored shadow from the mosaic lampshade, slouched in the lyre-backed rocker. Cy was across the room on the piano bench, leaning against the old upright where Kane had taken lessons until Viola Eden had given up on him. The others sat uncomfortably on the needlepoint divan that still bore the stain of glue Kane had spilled there when he was only twelve. He stepped inside, making his entrance.

Judge Barrett motioned him to a seat. "Gentlemen, you all know my nephew, of course."

Kane crossed the room to shake hands with Luke Biddle. "No, don't get up," he told the squat, heavy-set little man. "I'll sit here with you, sir. After all, I used to work for you, cleanin' looms durin' the summer. I'm practically one of your boys."

Biddle smiled warmly, arching a shaggy gray eyebrow. "These folks been talkin' all this time 'bout what a good politician you're supposed to be. I reckon you convinced me in one sentence!"

There was an uncertain moment when everyone seemed to wait for a cue to a proper reaction. Kane gave it to them by laughing, and the others joined him. "Sure I'm politickin'," he said, slurring his words in the manner of Biddle's speech. "No use makin' out this is all news to me."

"I think we might summarize just what we can do as individuals," Judge Barrett suggested. "How about you, Oren?"

The young man in the rust corduroy jacket pushed his hands deep into the pockets of his green slacks. "Fellas, I figure it's time for the returnin' vets to take part in their government; and we couldn't pick a better man than Kane to start off with."

"Thanks, Oren," Kane said. "But I don't expect folks to vote for me because I happened to win a medal. Hope I'm not one of these characters who's a professional veteran, tradin' on the few years he's given to his country."

"What about you, Cy?" the judge said.

"Well, I can't speak for the bank. But, *I'm* prepared to help financially if Kane decides to run; and, of course, my business friends believe that with his record and ability and popularity, he's sure to win."

"How do you feel, Hugh?" the judge asked, nodding to a ruddy-faced youngster who had gotten up and walked to the yellow-brick fireplace.

Hugh Lester knocked his pipe into the heel of his hand and tossed the ash into the fire. "We never take a stand in the Young Democrats until election. We feel it's a mistake to get into the primary." He watched Luke Biddle, and spoke softly, but directly to The Old Man. "Of course, 90 per cent of our people would be for Kane," he continued, remembering what Cy had told him. "But if a political organization is goin' to be effective, it can't risk splittin' its membership. Right, Mr. Biddle?"

Biddle nodded. "I'd go along with that last statement."

Aunt Mady limped in, supporting herself on two canes. Laurie followed her. The men all stood. "Please don't," the old woman told them. "Just gettin' some refreshments for you in the kitchen." Passing Kane, she said, loud enough to be heard around the room, "So you're out for big game now, Kane. You're goin' to try to fool the whole district!"

He could have killed her without a stain on his conscience. Instead, he put his arms around her, kissed her cheek, and smiling, he said, "I can fool anyone but you, Aunt Mady."

Even his aunt laughed as she walked with Laurie through the dining room, into the kitchen beyond.

When they were all seated again, Cy hammered at Luke Biddle once more. "If we're goin' to get young people to join the party, fellas, we've got to show them elections aren't just a formality of votin'-in the same old faces. Am I right, Mr. Biddle?"

"Mmm," Luke Biddle said. "Like to see young people interested."

Judge Barrett smiled at what he interpreted as encouragement. "What have you got to say, Ray?"

Ray Burnham pulled at the pencil stuck in his boot top. "Well, the most important way to keep the party strong is to have good men in office."

"Exactly," Kane said. "I'm sure that's what Mr. Biddle and the other members of the committee keep in mind. Isn't it, sir?"

Biddle started to put his short legs up on the marble coffee table, and thought better of it. "We try to keep that in mind along with other practical considerations."

"Well, you have any advice for the boys, Luke?" Judge Barrett asked.

"It's been an interestin' and instructive evenin'," Biddle said, smiling wryly. "And I've learned some things." He paused, as if in serious meditation. "First, you fellas feel there's a need for good government. You believe that new blood is needed in the party, that the veterans' vote is important and that civic responsibility is generally a virtue." Seeing their serious, intent faces, he laughed. "Now I'm not makin' fun, boys. I know you're all here out of good motives. And I get the point!" He stood up. "When are you goin' to announce, O'Connor?"

Kane was taken by surprise by Biddle's frankness. "Why . . . I haven't decided definitely if I will, sir."

Later, when the others were drinking their coffee, Luke Biddle asked for his hat and coat. Kane went to the sitting room for them, tripping over one of Aunt Mady's stray cats on the way.

Before opening the door, he heard Laurie inside. Her voice was low, bitter. ". . . it was a cruel thing to do, Aunt Mady!"

"That's the way it is with the truth."

"It's not the truth. There's somethin' in Kane that makes him want more from life. And he'll get it."

"Of course. I've seen him set out to get things for the past twenty years nearly. And whether it was a baseball glove or a place on the debatin' team, he's schemed and lied . . ."

"Kane's no schemer. He's no liar!" She flung the words passionately. Outside the door, Kane's throat tightened as he heard himself defended. "But you'll see. He *will* be somebody, and he *will* get ahead . . . and partly because you've told him all his life he'd end up in the gutter."

"It's in his blood."

"Don't say that again!" Kane listened to the tapping of Aunt Mady's stick on the hearth, then heard Laurie again. "Oh, sometimes he's weak. But I know his weaknesses. And I love him." There was a pause, then Aunt Mady's voice, breaking slightly. "You're a good girl, Laurie. He doesn't deserve you."

Kane scuffed his shoe against the bottom of the door and opened it. Aunt Mady was sitting before the iron grate of the fireplace, stroking a tawny puppy in her lap. Laurie stood at the mantel. "They're getting ready to leave now," Kane said, going over to the pile of coats on the settee. "I'm looking for Luke Biddle's things."

Aunt Mady pointed her stick to the black coat and gray hat on the needlepoint chair. He picked them up and left the room. Neither of the women had spoken to him.

Luke Biddle was waiting at the front door. Kane helped him into his coat. "Thanks so much for cornin', sir," he said in approximation of Biddle's soft drawl.

"My pleasure, son." He smoothed his bristling eyebrows. "I imagine you'll announce soon?"

"Well . . . maybe, if you have a spare evenin', you'd let me come by to talk it over with you, sir."

"You don't need my advice," Biddle said, winding the scarf around his short, wrinkled neck. "You've already decided there's no need of learnin' to shave on another man's beard. And that's all right. You may nick yourself a few times"—he chuckled—"or even cut your throat. But you end up learnin' right good." He patted Kane's back. "You're a smart young fella. When the election's over, then you come talk to me."

"Thanks a lot, Mr. Biddle."

"Don't thank me," Biddle said, his lips pursed. "I'm not figurin' on helpin' you a damn bit!" He opened the door. "But I'm not figurin' on helpin' anyone else, either."

When Kane entered the living room, Cy motioned him aside. "Man, you really put it on for him—even talkin' like him!" He grinned. "How you doin', Kane, you old coot?"

"Fine as wine, smooth as cake."

"Then let me have the ole handshake!"

5

CLOSETED IN the mahogany-and-plush office of Luke Biddle on a cold March afternoon, the Democratic Executive Committee heard Beverly Crater's demands for support. Listened —but had no opinion. Weighed—but made no decision. Concurred —but voiced no judgment. Disagreed—but stated no arguments.

The Old Man hadn't spoken yet. Bemused, he sat in his swivel armchair.

"What do you know about O'Connor?" Beverly Crater asked the faceless committeemen. "Who're you scared of? Wes Barrett? Why he hasn't taken a dump in twenty years without askin' Luke's okay! You worried about Cy Woodward? He's a damn' fool kid with too much money whose father gave me a five-hundred dollar donation this afternoon! And what about O'Connor?" Crater made a hasty inventory of the members present. "You afraid of a Catholic nobody who won't get fifty Baptist votes in the whole damn district?" For emphasis he pounded his fist on Luke Biddle's desk.

The Old Man didn't look up. "You worried, Bev?"

"Hell, no!"

"Then how come you're so excited?"

"Because this thing was all settled months ago; and now you're goin' back on your word," Crater said angrily. Then, goaded by the logic of his arguments, "I don't give a pea-turkey what you told O'Connor or how lightly you take his chances."

The committeemen, amazed at Crater's ballooning anger, were now prepared for his deflation. They watched Luke Biddle move around his desk and glare up at the tall, craggy-faced District Solicitor. "Are you all through now, Bev?"

Crater nodded. "I had to put it on the table, Luke," he said apologetically.

"Sit down, Bev."

Crater sat.

"Save your oratory for the campaign," Biddle said softly. "I don't care for people poundin' my desk and makin' speeches. Let's just talk business without the arm wavin'." It was a slap on the wrist. Crater had expected a walloping.

"There's no need of alienatin' a bunch of young folks who are good Democrats," Biddle said. "They know we've got no call to be in the primary; and if they get sore enough, they'll be votin' Independent or even Republican when we need them most."

Crater backtracked. "That sounds reasonable enough, Luke. But where does that leave me?"

"I'm not worried about your winnin', Bev. We're goin' to stay out until we see just how strong O'Connor shapes up. He's no slouch. Boy's got spunk, knows how to talk and could charm a snake off a tree. He'll make us a good man in time. But he's in too much of a hurry. We'll have to learn him you don't get nowhere without talkin' it over with those that been workin' for the party before he was housebroken. He'll find out you don't *get* without you doin' some *giviri* first."

"Sure. When did he ever do a day's work for the party?" Crater asked. "He's not entitled, by glory."

"I'm still talkin', Bev."

"Sorry, Luke."

"For the time bein', we'll take care of the money end on the quiet. And that doesn't mean tellin' your wives about it!" Biddle returned to his seat. "Later, if we find it's necessary, we'll go to work down in the precincts." He looked around the room at the members of the committee—the representatives of the Democratic voters. "Anyone think we oughta jump in before we know how things shape up?"

No one thought so.

Across town in Cy's cluttered living room, Kane lay on the maroon carpet, sketching ideas for campaign posters on lined legal paper. Cy, his flabby stomach riding over his pajama belt, sat on the gray sectional sofa.

"How much we got in the kitty?" Kane asked his campaign manager.

"Besides the dough you got on a note with the bank, there's my one thousand, five hundred from my dad . . ."

"Brother that teed me off!" Kane looked up from the ELECT O'CONNOR poster. "Why in hell did he have to give Crater dough, too?"

"Plenty of merchants in town'll do the same, Kane. It's good business to have insurance no matter which way the vote goes. If we're really up against it, I think dad'll come through with another five hundred."

"How much you figure it'll take?"

Cy examined his toe. "About eight thousand. That'll cover posters, radio time, newspapers, transportation on primary day, plus handouts for the precinct workers."

Frowning at the sketch before him, Kane said, "I've already borrowed from the bank up to my eyeballs. You think we'll raise the rest?"

"We've got Chief Sawyer out workin', and he'll do all right. He and Bev don't get along. Went 'round and 'round over Bev's habit of callin' on the state police every time he gets a chance. And I got dad to call Joe King—won't hurt to have a city commissioner goin' around with a tin cup."

"How about your pal, Tod Sands? Is he working on the Armenian who runs the auction place?"

"Probably. Tod's gettin' a charge out of your runnin' without Biddle's blessin', but he's mighty busy right now. That labor trouble at The Mills. This guy Woodmire's pushin' for a union election. It looks like he might get it, so the Chamber's got Tod sweet-talkin' around the plant." Cy started out to find his scissors.

"What's the Secretary of the Chamber of Commerce sticking his nose in that for?" Kane called after him.

"The directors turned him loose to help Biddle beat the union crowd. If they organize here, we'll have a time gettin' any more industry to come in."

"Biddle doesn't *want* any other industry in here . . . make him compete for labor." Kane picked up a sheet of clean paper and marked a border around it. "Sands is a queer choice for a job like that."

Cy returned to the sofa and began to trim his toenails. "You don't like Tod, do you?"

"I haven't made up my mind. Worked with him on the Gymkhana a couple of months ago. Pretty sharp, but I never could tell if he was laughing with me or at me."

"He's a cynical joker, all right. But he's smart. No matter if it's politics or a committee sponsorin' a folk dance festival, you try to get Tod in on it. The other guys usually have the dough and position. Tod's got the brains and imagination."

"If he's that good, I can stand him," Kane said laughing. Then, seriously, "Cy, you think we can lick Crater?"

"Hey, you're the guy with all the rah-rah and confidence. What do you think?"

"I'm asking you."

Sensing his friend's need for reassurance, Cy's round face crinkled in a smile. "Sure, we'll wallop hell out of him."

Tod Sands stood before the redwood facade of the Manton Auction Galleries. He held his small, smooth hand cupped against the display window, cutting the glare. Inside he saw George Amon wedged into one of the theater-type seats before the auctioneer's platform. Tod tapped on the window and pointed toward the shuttered door. Amon motioned for him to come in.

"How's it going, George?"

The hefty auctioneer started to pull his bulk from the seat, then gave up. "Getting ready for a slow season. Afraid it'll be like last year with too many penny ante Charlestonians and a bunch of old ladies from St. Pete. And my asthma's bothering me again." Tod sat beside him, dwarfed in the shadow of the panting man. "You know, George, there's not a jewelry or gift or furniture store in town that doesn't think he's losing a lot of trade to you. They've been pressuring me to get a petition down to the capital to outlaw auction galleries in the state."

"Believe me, I appreciate what you're doing," Amon said. "Those merchants should have my headaches."

"Well," Tod said, the thin line of his lips hardly moving as he talked, "I always do whatever I can for you, George."

More small talk. Casual mention of the campaign. And Kane O'Connor—"a good man, liberal."

Then the inevitable: "How much is it going to cost me?" And George Amon's five-hundred dollar cash contribution.

Tod took the money. Fifty went into what his wife June called "The Sands' Fund." The remainder would be turned over to Cy Woodward. Tod promised himself to talk the boys into laying off George when the horse show came up.

41

Chief Sawyer reached into the pocket of his uniform for his list. He checked it. Six-hundred and forty dollars so far, and two more places to go.

After twelve years of it, the taxi owners didn't have to be sold. There was no mention of parking privileges, no hint of a crackdown on liquor peddling, no joking about rigid safety inspections. If an underling came by, they would put up a flat fifty dollars; and if the chief made the call himself, they knew it would cost them twenty for each car.

The short, florid-faced policeman entered the Blue Tag Cab Company's office. He took off his cap, scratching his bald head. "Nick," he said, "Wes Barrett's nephew, Kane O'Connor, is runnin' for District Solicitor in the primary . . ."

City Commissioner Joe King passed the hot rolls across the table. "You're puttin' out a good feed these days, Hal. There's not a Lion here who hasn't mentioned how much better the food is."

The hotel manager turned his head for a moment to allow Joe to reseat his teeth without embarrassment. "Sure makes us feel good to know the changes have been noticed."

"Of course they're noticed," Joe told him, loosening his size forty-two belt. "We were settin' in a commissioners' meetin' the other morning'; and we all agreed it's a credit to the town to have a first class hotel like this." Joe lifted a forkful of green peas after mixing them with his potatoes. "That reminds me, Hal, there's been some talk about a room tax. Think that would hurt you any?"

"Why, hell, it'd hurt the whole town! Tourists won't come in here when none of the surroundin' towns have . . ."

Joe listened. That's all for today, he thought. I'll let him think about it for awhile. The next day, Joe knew, he'd say nothing about any room tax. He'd just ask a favor. And then he'd deliver the check to the Woodward boy.

Kane folded his arms on his office desk and rested his head. He slept fitfully, despite the sounds of traffic by his open window, fatigue blotting out his thoughts, then teasing him into half-consciousness with worry over the slow progress of his campaign.

Another all-night meeting. And more fruitless argument.

Cy: "Can't get the courthouse for a speech until two weeks before the primary. And we've got to get another thousand bucks somewhere."

Uncle Wesley: "Luke Biddle's not as disinterested as you think. Bev Crater's spendin' money like he's not worried about it. Still, with the congressional nomination cornin' up in another year, / just can't afford to raise a fuss with Luke. . .

Hugh Lester: "Crater's passed the word to the VFW board that we can put the slot machines back in. Kane, he didn't hurt himself at all with most of the boys."

Ray Burnham: "You've got to watch your language when you're talkin' to folks out in the county. There are lots of good people out there that don't hold with swearin'!"

Tod Sands: "He's right, Kane. You get in a small group of five or six and you figure you've got to be one of the boys, figure you've got to describe everything from a Chinese sunset to an inside straight with a four-letter word! And, ferchrisakes, nobody expects you to change your way of speaking. When you're around some yokels, you're always trying to talk as mush-mouthed as they do. Hell, be yourself. Nobody minds that you can speak English. And knock off the platitudes in your speeches. You're not running for president of the senior class!"

Only one bright spot in the evening: Matt Fallon, too profane to be sober, had phoned from New York to announce his elevation to status of television commentator. And then, after listening to a recital of Kane's problems, Matt had said, "Stop crying, loverboy. My heart bleeds for you! You're young and a hero and a spellbinder and not too ugly or too stupid, and your opposition is bound to have made some mistakes in office. If you can't parlay that into a political upset, you don't deserve to win!"

Laurie saw Kane sleeping at his desk. Bending over him, she kissed his cheek. "Morning', darlin'."

He brushed back the black tangle of his hair and yawned.

"Didn't hear you come in. Where've you been?"

"I waited for Lily. She's upset somethin' terrible. In all the time she's worked for us, I've never seen her this way. She wants to talk with you."

"What's she done?" he asked, walking to the water cooler.

"It's her daughter."

Kane lifted the paper cup to his mouth and gargled. "Have her come in, honey."

Lily sniffled through her story. Her seventeen-year-old daughter, pregnant and unmarried, had gone to Lucinda Nelson's to be "fixed-up." The old Negro woman bit her lip. "I'm so 'shamed, Mr. Kane. I found out and went down there to see Cora Mae last night; and she's sick unta death. I want you should get the law on that Lucinda."

"We better get Cora Mae to the hospital first."

They drove to the Blue Heaven section of Manton, and Lily pointed out an unpainted box-shaped house down a mud road. They left the car and picked their way through the rutted street.

A Negro man watched from his porch as the two white folks stood before Lucinda Nelson's door. The fat old Negress, a huge breast escaping from under the armhole in her soiled print dress, answered the knock. Laurie, Kane and Lily walked in.

The smell of a generation of cooked pork hung in the room. A radio was blaring. "Y'all jes' have a seat there." Lucinda pointed to a green velveteen sofa.

"I tole you I'd get the law onto you!" Lily said. "Mr. Kane's gonna lock you up!"

"What for? What I done?"

"Laurie, you two get the girl ready." When they had gone, Kane turned off the radio. "You know that what you've done is against the law?"

"Lawsakes, sir. I jes' tryin' to he'p that pore chile."

"Don't you realize you've committed an abortion?" Kane said angrily.

Lucinda Nelson knelt before the fireplace. With the hem of her apron, she wiped the spittle from a tarnished brass andiron. "I he'p as good as I know," she grumbled.

"Turn around here and look at me when I talk to you," Kane said, glowering at her. "Why you may have ruined that girl, damn you!"

"No need you cussin' me, sir. That girl done ruined when she come here. An' I ain't took no money 'ceptin' for some medicine and room rent. They's plenty folks knows me, knows I tries to do good. I midwifes for Holiness Star of Bethel Church. You go ask the pastor if ever I charges anybody to midwife for 'em."

"You been arrested before?"

"I never been in jail, sir."

"You been arrested, dammit?"

"Sheriff stop me one time for transportin'."

"And how did you get out of that?"

"It was my first time; and Mister Beverly Crater, he let me off. But I never toted another bottle of liquor since, so he'p me God!"

Laurie called from the doorway. "Ready, Kane."

Lucinda Nelson's neighbors saw the tall white man carry the blanket-wrapped girl in his arms. Saw Lily get into the back seat beside her. Saw the white girl fetch the scuffed cardboard suitcase. Then watched them drive away.

The next evening Judge Barrett, Ray Burnham, Hugh Lester and Tod Sands—"Kane's Brain Trust" Cy dubbed them—met again in the paper-littered living room.

Kane showed them his ideas for new posters: O'CONNOR'S THE MAN FOR THE JOB. . .O'CONNOR'S A MAN YOU CAN TRUST . . .O'CONNOR, A LEADER WITH VISION.

Cy stood at the leather-padded bar mixing drinks. "What do you think, Tod?"

Working at a portable typewriter on the coffee table, Tod glanced at the sketches Kane held up for them. "They stink," he said, and turned back to his typing.

"Well, that's a helluva reaction!" Kane snapped. "Just what's wrong with them?"

Tod didn't smile. Patiently, as if talking to an errant schoolboy, he said, "No guts, Kane! Use some imagination, some shmaltz." "All right, dammit, if you think you can do better . . ."

"Wait a minute," Judge Barrett said. "Let's save the fire for the campaign."

"No," Kane insisted. He stared at the unruffled Tod. "If he thinks he can do it better, I want him to do it!"

Reaching under his papers, Tod pulled out three sheets. "They're a lot of hockey," he said, "and that's what makes them good for the purpose."

Kane crossed the room to examine the sketches. "Gentlemen," he said, laughing, "the winnah and new champeen, Tod Sands!"

In the following weeks, telephone poles, store windows, trees, billboards, taxis and buses carried Tod's posters.

The first showed a newspaper picture of Kane, his arm in a sling, getting off the Army plane in New York. Across the top were the words: HE SERVED YOU BEFORE, HELP HIM DO IT AGAIN.

The second poster featured Kane, in flight gear, his hand on the holster of his .45. THE FIGHTIN' BOMBARDIER appeared above the picture, and below it, PUT A MAN IN A MAN'S JOB.

Slanted across the third was a mock headline from the local paper: KANE O'CONNOR WINS HERO'S REWARD. In bold letters on top of the sheet were the words: WIN WITH O'CONNOR.

Kane appeared at the Farmers' Federation picnic, at the Junior Welfare Club's skit night, before the Humane Society. He spoke at every stop along the chicken-a-la-king circuit, in all the counties of the district. He met every precinct registrar. He managed to be quoted at least three times a week in *The Manton Argus.* He spoke to the PTA and to the Women's Club, in the social hall of the First Baptist Church and in the main courtroom of the Manton County Courthouse.

But although people were polite, though they applauded his fifteen-minute luncheon club speech on "Good Government" and laughed at his tax collector joke, though they listened quietly to his thirty-minute auditorium address on "My Pledge—Your Protection," though they gathered in small groups for his five-minute courthouse-steps talk on "Public Safety," Kane was not satisfied. The enthusiasm he had foreseen, the contributions he had expected, the gathering strength for which he had hoped, the signs of victory he had assumed would come, were all absent. And he was worried.

A week before the election, "Kane's Brain Trust," with only Judge Barrett absent, held another strategy session. It was one o'clock in the morning and the men sat with their shoes off and made their final plans.

"We've got to save the rest of the dough for the riffraff vote," Cy said. "It comes to one thing: a hundred bucks has to buy a hundred votes."

Ray Burnham leaned forward in his chair. "I'm against any vote buying. It's immoral and the decent people in the community . . ."

"Grow up, Ray," Tod said, annoyed. "If the decent people in the community gave a damn, they'd get out and vote. They don't vote *for* anything. When they do vote, it's *against* something. The rest of the time you couldn't blast them out of their stores or offices long enough to check a ballot. Every bohunk, loafer, riffraff—whatever you want to call them—is going to be out for his buck or his drink on Primary Day. You can be damned sure Bev Crater's not going to let one pass by!"

Cy nodded. "He's right, Ray. It's not a pretty thing, but he's right. The riffraff votes—and the riffraff elects."

"I won't have a thing to do with it," Ray insisted.

"Okay," Cy said. "You keep the taxis runnin' to pick up the voters. There's nothin' wrong with that, is there?"

Ray ignored him. "It's all wrong."

"Listen," Kane said. "Both of you are right. We can't hold out on the riffraff vote because Crater's going to be working them. On the other hand, that's where he's strongest."

"What's right is right and what's wrong is wrong," Ray observed sagely.

"Sure. I know," Kane said. "But why can't we get out the vote a buck won't buy?"

Tod opened his second pack of cigarettes. "I'll tell you why, Kane. Because the good old middle-class homemaker and businessman and doctor and lawyer and clerk won't come out full force unless there's an issue that affects them personally—like state liquor stores or city limits' extension or a bond issue, or maybe something that's dramatized like embezzlement or graft. What's your issue?"

"Good government!" Hugh Lester answered.

Tod laughed. "Yep, Kane O'Connor's for good government and America and Motherhood. Kane O'Connor believes The Good Ole Southland's the sole repository of the nation's 'old values' and remaining virgins and God-fearing native stock! A helluvalot of people are going to break their necks to get to the polls to support him!"

Laurie, carrying a covered tray of sandwiches, came in the front door and hurried through the room. "Sorry I'm so late," she said. "I'll get some coffee."

Kane went into the kitchen with her while the others resumed the argument. He held her silently for a moment. "Missed you. Where've you been this late?"

"Cora Mae died tonight. I was with Lily."

"Sorry. Wish I could do something to help."

"Maybe when you win this election you'll get Lucinda Nelson out of town."

"When I win!" he said sarcastically. "Lady, the way things look, I haven't got the chance of the proverbial snowball in hell!" Laurie put a pot of water on the stove to boil. "You'll win, darlin'."

"How?" He began to count-off on his fingers. "Luke Biddle's done a gentlemanly job of cutting my throat. Crater's taking some of the vote I counted on . . ."

"Oh, Kane," she said, putting her hands on his shoulders, "if everyone only knew you as I do, if they only knew how good and thoughtful and . . ."

He took a sandwich from beneath the napkin on the tray. "It's just a front I put up especially for you." He winked at her and motioned her to silence while he munched the chicken sandwich. "This is good. My strength's coming back. Let's go someplace and neck."

She patted his cheek. "I suppose it was a front when you went down to that awful woman's house and carried that poor girl out of there in your arms?"

The idea pierced his brain and ricocheted there. Kane stood for a moment, dazzled by it, amazed by it, thinking it out. It was an answer to the question he had posed only a few minutes before: *"Why can't we get the vote a buck won't buy?"* He picked Laurie up off her feet and swung her around. Then, before she could speak, he was into the living room. "Fellas," he announced, "sit back and listen. Kane's going to tell you how to win this election."

"You can't get away with shootin' Bev," Cy said.

"I'll do better. You remember I told you boys about Cora Mae, the Negro kid? Well, everybody in this town's going to know what happened to her. If Bev Crater would have jailed the Nelson woman, Cora Mae wouldn't have died tonight!"

"You can't do that!" Laurie told him, coming into the room.

"Niggers are always gettin' themselves in trouble," Ray said.

"Lily's gone through enough without bein' shamed before her friends, the whole town," Laurie said.

"But, darling . . ."

"Hold it," Tod said. "We've got something . . ."

"You'd be using her," Laurie said, interrupting again. "You'd be tryin' to buy votes with that poor old thing's misery!"

Kane dropped to the sofa. "Okay. Okay." He sighed. "Laurie's right, I guess."

"Of course she's right," Tod said. He got up, and like a strutting bantam paced the floor. "You won't mention her name. Let the public identify themselves with her. Let the public picture her as a pure, white, Protestant, native American!"

Kane grabbed Tod, swinging an arm around his shoulders. "I'm beginning to like you, you damned Yankee. I'm beginning to like you!"

Tod's voice cut through the hubbub that swept the room. "Like I always say, 'hard work's a poor substitute for a good angle!'"

By Primary Day few people in the district had not heard the story. No one knew who the girl was or who her mother was or where she had lived. They heard only "that's something I'll never forget . . . the shivering child, racked by the torments of hell, lay in my arms, another victim of the abortion racket. And as I carried her from that hovel, the words of the abortionist came back to me. She had admitted being arrested. But she'd told me, 'Beverly Crater let me go!' No, friends, she didn't say why he had seen fit to turn his back on the law, to forget his sacred trust. And, in the spirit of fairness, I surely don't mean to suggest that there was any financial consideration, any other connection between this woman and the administrator of your law . . ."

The Manton Argus had printed the first story: O'CONNOR ALLEGES ABORTION RACKET; and papers throughout the district had followed with O'CONNOR PROMISES COMPLETE INVESTIGATION...CRATER DEMANDS NAMES, PLACES, DATES...O'CONNOR DERIDES CRATER DENIAL...

In Luke Biddle's office, Beverly Crater and the Democratic Executive Committee listened to The Old Man.

"Whatever cash you need, you'll have. Get every car you can round up runnin'. O'Connor's men will be workin' for the church crowd and the country club bunch and the likes. So, we've got to get more than our share of the bums. Understand?"

"That lyin' no-good!" Beverly Crater said. "He won't answer me. He's made up this stupid. . ,"

Biddle glared at him. "Why don't you shut up, Bev?" Then, softly, to the others: "Let's get to work now."

Primary Day.

A washroom in the Manton Fire Department, a few steps from the voting booths: "Gingerale or water?" the O'Connor man asked his friend. Then, pouring the bourbon, "This boy O'Connor's okay, Sam. He's good folks."

A country house in another part of the district: "You got eighteen people in your family that can vote, J. D.," another O'Connor partisan said. "You got to help us get 'em to the polls." He pulled twenty dollars from his pocket. "It's goin' to cost you for gas and oil and stuff. This'll help out."

The hallway of a colonial mansion in Sunset Hills: "Hurry, Annie. We've got to get to the polls before closin'."

"I'm comin', dear. This is one election no respectable person should miss."

"That's the way I feel. Thank God for men like Kane O'Connor!"

That night Kane wired Matt Fallon: "You were right. We've got it made."

And Matt's answering telegram said: "God help the taxpayers. Loverboy's on his way!"

So it was that ten months after his return to Manton, the "Fightin' Bombardier Hero" who had "served them before" won by a landslide.

6

NEVER BEFORE had Kane known the joy and satisfaction f prestige, influence, authority and ten-thousand dollars a year.

If he was not as skilled a solicitor as the district had ever known, he was surely the hardest working. If he was not as learned in the law as his predecessor, he was far more popular. If he squandered time on inexpert investigation and finally turned to the state for aid, he was still as accessible as the humblest justice of the peace. If he was relentless in the cross-examination he loved so well, he was equally as compassionate in the privacy of his office.

He worked with the devotion of a monk, arriving on the scene within the hour in which he was notified, procuring evidence from local authorities, interviewing witnesses, seeking indictments, following his uncle from county to county to try current cases, preparing for the next term of court, handling routine postponements. And often, tumbling into bed at night, tired with the bone-weary fatigue of a warrior, he marveled that he was actually being paid for a labor so exciting, so rewarding; and he thought with zest of the next day, anxious to meet what it would bring, devout in his mission.

September: Kane wanted time "to learn the job, get comfortable in office." Laurie agreed, after fruitless, tearful argument, to set their wedding for the following June. Kane closed his office, confining his private practice to the Manton Bank's legal work.

October: His initial haphazard dabbling in the stock market, with Cy as his mentor, netted him a new Pontiac convertible. Although he still owed the bank five-thousand dollars borrowed for campaign expenses, he bought a tract in Skyline Hills, five wooded acres where he planned to build a home.

November: He was so busy trying cases during the criminal term, so involved in meetings and dinners and speaking engagements, that he and Laurie were alone together only on

Saturdays and Sundays. And even then a phoned report from a sheriff or police chief or a bulletin flashed over Kane's radio-equipped convertible, would send him scurrying away. Laurie often showed him pictures of rooms she had clipped from women's magazines, but to Kane they were too small, too ordinary, too modem or too plain. "I want something more . . . more traditional . . . stately . . . a place where, when people step inside, they realize that everything belongs there—the furniture and carpets and paintings and us."

December: Kane tried his first murder case and, within a week, he had enthralled the jury, produced sensational evidence, angered the old defense attorney to the point of red-faced fury, agreed to the defendant's change of plea, and been called "brilliant" by a *Manton Argus* editorial. Meanwhile, his growing fascination with stocks and bonds prompted heavy speculation. First the car was mortgaged. Then the five acres in Skyline Hills were sold. Finally, Cy bailed him out with a ten-thousand dollar loan from the bank. Kane emerged wiser, but intent on recovering his losses.

January: On the first day of 1947, Kane was named "Young Man of the Year" by the state's selection committee. Laurie sat beside him when the governor presented the award to the "citizen who proved it takes a fighting young fellow with dedication and courage to shake things up every once-in-awhile." Laurie reached for Kane's hand beneath the table. And he whispered, "This is just the beginning. We're only starting."

February: Kane came to Laurie, shamefaced, to admit that he had withdrawn nine-hundred dollars from their joint account— and lost it. With boyish logic he brought a "peace offering." It was an expensive locket-watch. The enclosed card read: "It's time for you to forgive me."

March: Kane won convictions in the cases of a hit and run driver, a rustler, two prostitutes and a mercy-killer. He also made two thousand dollars in the commodities market and lost it within the month on a real estate venture.

It was in April that Laurie's mother became ill. The doctors agreed on the diagnosis—cancer. "Six months, maybe a year," they had told Laurie.

Laurie and Cy had planned a surprise birthday party for Kane that evening; and saying nothing, she managed to get through the night of too much food, too much liquor and too much high-spirited talk. Only when the last guests had gone tipsily home and Cy was in bed, and Kane was drying the dishes she washed in his kitchen, did she tell him.

She watched the expression of pain and distress spread across Kane's face, seeing that he was struck—as she had been—with helplessness and despair.

He dropped the dish towel on the sink and, meditating, leaned against a cabinet, shaking his head. "We've got to do something for her. We can't just wait . . ."

"Darlin', we won't be able to get married in June as we planned." Laurie caught her breath, forced herself to hold back the tears, to concentrate on scraping a plate of baked beans and cigarette ashes. "We'll have to put it off. Mother's cornin' home from the hospital. I can't leave her now."

Though she was certain he would tell her it made no difference that her mother could live with them, she had told herself she was allowing him to make the choice. And yet, she knew she was really giving him no choice at all, only the illusion of choice. Not fair? She had been fair too long, she had decided. She was twenty-three. And time was robbing her of him. Now, watching Kane as he pulled absently at a rumpled tablecloth, she waited for his reassurance. "Well, darlin'?"

He tried to frame his reply, knowing what he should be prepared to say. But he told himself that nursing a sick woman was no way to start a marriage, that he was heavily in debt to the bank and to Cy personally, that another six months or so might give him a chance to recoup. "We can't think of ourselves," he said at last. "We've got to think about your mother, what's best for her."

He looked out the window above the sink to avoid the sadness, the incredulity at his self-sacrifice that he thought he read in her eyes. "We'd better wait. You owe her all your time."

One evening in November, at Cy's home, Tod Sands sat astride a dining-room chair while Kane and Cy finished dinner. "But you can't tell Luke Biddle to go to hell!"

Kane put another teaspoonful of sugar in his coffee. "I'm doing it. Biddle wants me to threaten Woodmire," Kane said. "That's a good way to have the N.L.R.B. hang a federal offense around my neck."

"The Old Man's hopping mad," Tod said, and fanned the smoke away. "Woodmire's pulled some dirty angles. Two weeks ago he passed out union buttons at a meeting, told the men Biddle couldn't stop them from wearing them in the plant. . . ."

"He's right," Kane said.

"Let me finish! After fifty or more showed up wearing them, Woodmire tells them they'd better get the union in, or Biddle will fire them all after the voting!"

Kane dusted ashes in his saucer. "Smart boy, Woodmire."

"Yeah," Cy said, laughing, "and he's got a sexy wife!"

Tod waved them to silence. "Luke didn't think it was so damned funny. But it's nothing compared to the general production slowdown that's costing the plant a fortune."

"I feel for poverty-stricken Luke," Cy said.

"Give the guy credit," Tod said. "After all, he's doing better by his people than anybody else around here—as good as the union can do for them."

Kane poured another cup of coffee. "Save that for your pitch out at the mills."

Ignoring him, Tod said, "What topped it off was what happened yesterday. The Old Man's been getting too many cancellations of orders lately, and one of his boys told him that some of the hotheads around the plant have been writing to the mill's accounts, warning them Manton Mills won't be able to make fall deliveries because a big strike is in the offing. Well, when the kid left Luke's office, the word got around. Last night someone beat hell out of him. He's in the hospital."

"What do you expect me to do—put a bodyguard on every informer on Biddle's payroll?" Kane shredded a piece of roll in his hand and tossed the crumbs in his cup. "If he's got troubles, let him take them to the N.L.R.B."

"He's tried that. The government can't do anything without proof." Tod scratched the gray bristle of his head with a matchstick. "Biddle wants you to put it straight to Woodmire. Tell him that if there's any more rough stuff, you're going to lock him up for inciting to riot or disturbing the peace or assault—anything."

"Tell him yourself," Kane said, pushing back from the table and dusting his palms. "Or better still, let Biddle tell him. That's not my battle out there. I don't give a damn if they unionize or not."

"I don't care myself, Kane," Tod said patiently, reaching for his coffee. "The Chamber's put me on this and I'm doing what I'm told. Biddle wants *you* to see Woodmire because you've kept out of this wrangle—and because everybody in town knows you got your job despite Luke. Woodmire'll know you mean business. Do this favor for The Old Man and he'll be indebted to you."

"You expect me to forget what Biddle did to me? He broke his back trying to lick me."

"Yes," Tod said, pushing his cup aside. "Biddle's forgotten it. He bore no grudges. Put you on the board of his youth center, put you up for membership in his country club, invited you to speak at the dedication of his ball park . . ."

"His. . .his. . .his. . .! It's Manton's youth center, Manton's country club, Manton's ball park."

"Come off it, Kane. Don't be a five-alarm jerk. They're his, Luke Biddle's. His money built them. Just like his money built damned near everything else in this town. If he throws his weight around, he's damned well bought and paid for the privilege!"

Kane slapped the table with his open palm. "Are you bought and paid for, too?"

Tod stared him down. "I'm willing to forget you said that."

"Hey, cut it out!" Cy said, coming around to stand between them. "Kane, you didn't mean that."

Releasing a deep breath, Kane shook his head. "No, I didn't." He held out his hand. "I apologize."

The thin, taut line of Tod's mouth slowly relaxed. Nodding, he took Kane's hand and grasped it firmly. "Let it pass, Kane. You're cocky right now, but damnitahell, don't you ever intend to go on to something else? Well, you can kiss it off if you try to ignore The Old Man."

"Now we're talking!" Kane scraped the tablecloth with his knife, raking crumbs into a triangle. "I was waiting for you to make an offer!"

Tod took a light from Kane's cigarette. "Well, stay right with The Old Man and when the time comes . . ."

"Got to be more definite than that."

"You expect to get it in writing?"

"No. But I didn't get a definite word from Biddle once before, and I try to profit by my mistakes."

"What do you want?"

"My uncle vacates his seat to run for Congress in next year's elections. A year from now I want to run for Superior Court judge."

"Come down to earth, Kane. My name's Sands. And this is November 19, 1947. I remember the day you got back to town— that's been a little over two years. What's your hurry?"

"If this is as important as you say, the price is cheap."

"It's promised," Tod said, "to Bev Crater."

"Tell Biddle to break his promise."

"Ferchrisakes, Kane, it took your uncle twenty years to get that job. You can't expect . . ."

"That's it. That's what I want."

"He can't cut Crater out."

"Then just go back with my original suggestion, Tod. Tell him to go to hell!"

Kane stopped his car in front of Mark Woodmire's white frame bungalow and sat there in the darkness, reflecting on his triumph.

An hour before, Luke Biddle had told him, "You're a natural politician, my boy. You've got the rare talent of hiding your dagger beneath your coat!" Then he had promised him the Superior Court judgeship. "Now, you start lookin' out for me with the same devotion you give to lookin' out for O'Connor," he said, laughing. "Let's see how you take of this little errand."

"This little errand." Kane didn't even like the sound of the words, implying as they did a relationship between master and servant. Well, this is no errand for Biddle, he told himself. It's an errand for Kane.

He had no intention of delivering a warning to Woodmire. From what the man's wife had told him, from what he had learned of his local activities, from what he had read in the report Biddle had drawn on him, Kane had pieced together a picture of Mark Woodmire. And that picture made it clear he would not be intimidated easily. He was obviously clever, ruthless and totally committed to his job. And he was nobody's fool.

Flipping his cigarette away, Kane opened the car door and stepped out. He proposed to be polite to Woodmire, and direct. He proposed to ask his co-operation, not to demand it. He proposed to make it clear that as District Solicitor he had no interest in the outcome of the union voting, and that as an individual he'd like to see Biddle humbled. All Kane wanted was the assurance that there would be an end to violence. That would be enough to satisfy Luke Biddle.

As he swung down the toy-littered path and walked toward the house, there was only one uncertainty that bothered him: Woodmire might reject him, might push Biddle to the wall during the final week before the voting. Then Biddle would expect Kane to jail the organizer on a charge that would stick. And that in turn would mean a protest from the national union, a planeload of Yankee lawyers, pressure from Washington and from the governor. And worst of all, it would put an anti-labor label on Kane's own record. Well, he thought, as he knocked on the door, I'll worry about all that if it happens. Meanwhile, O'Connor, turn on the charm!

Melba Woodmire, looking like a disheveled housewife and not the polished matron she had appeared in his office, answered his knock. Surprised, she said, "Why hello, Mr. O'Connor!" and smoothed the wisps of hair from her forehead.

"Hello. Your husband in?"

Reaching behind her, she took off her apron and adjusted the twisted belt on her faded blue housecoat. "He's at a meeting right now."

"When do you expect him back?"

"Soon, I guess. If you'd like to come in and wait . . ."

Kane smiled—his shy, friendly smile. There was invitation in Melba Woodmire's throaty voice. Not coquettish. Not suggestive. Sexy—it was the only word he could find for it. "All right," he said. "If you don't mind."

She took his hat as he stepped into the Chinese-decorated living room. "Please sit down. I'll be right back. Have to finish with the children."

Kane helped himself to a cigarette from the cloisonne box on the teakwood coffee table, found that the silver lighter didn't work, fumbled through his pockets for the matches he had left in his car, and finally dropped the cigarette into the box again. Surprised by the opulence of the small room, he strode across the Chinese rug to examine a carved bookcase. Behind him, from another room, he heard Melba reading to her children:

". . .and Pinky the Monkey wanted, more than anything else in all the world, to be free of the zoo. . ."

Kane picked up a book that saddled the arm of an ebony, high-backed chair. It was a biography of Jefferson; and as he flipped through it, he saw underlined passages and notes on the margins. Turning to the inside cover, he read: *Marcus Paul Woodmire, Aycock Dormitory, University of North Carolina, Chapel Hill.* He smiled. Luke Biddle had called Woodmire "a crazy radical from one of them New York Red colleges."

"Say good night to Mr. O'Connor." Kane turned to see Melba and her two children standing across the room. The baby looked at him, giggled, and hid her head against her mother's legs. The older child, about seven, rubbed her tongue in the gap of her teeth. "They talk you to death when you're alone with them," Melba said. "But just try to show them off . . ." Shaking her finger at them, she took their hands and led them from the room.

Within a few minutes she was back. She had put on makeup, tied a green ribbon in her fire-red hair, and changed to a neat, green print dress. That was all. And yet, Kane found the change in her startling. The green eyes seemed even larger, the high cheekbones more pronounced, the lips softer, fuller. And the ribbon, tied so simply to a pony tail, was a contradiction that only underlined the difference in her. Like the dress—simple, modest, with high neck and long sleeves. And yet, it emphasized subtly all the contours of her remarkable body.

She was still blotting her lips. "Something wrong?" she asked, examining herself in the ornate mirror that hung behind Kane's chair.

"No. You're . . . you look very . . . nice. I was just thinking — you've got two beautiful kids. It's easy to tell they're yours."

She smiled. And there was no artifice in the smile now. "It's wonderful how they grow up and start being real little people; knowing how to get something out of you." She saw Kane grinning at her, and sat in a chair in front of his. "I guess I baby them too much, but . . ." Her voice resumed the brittle quality he remembered from sessions in his office—"I hardly see anyone all day. They get to be like friends, too." She stopped abruptly. "Couldn't I get you something to drink?"

"Thanks. I'd like it."

"I don't know what we have. I think Mark says it's bourbon. That all right?"

Kane nodded, recalling the liquor on her breath when she came to his office. "Sure, with water, please."

He tore the seal and opened the bottle while Melba went for ice cubes and water. It was nine o'clock. He decided to leave by nine-thirty if Woodmire didn't return before then.

"Some men don't like women who take a drink," Melba said, handing him a glass.

"I'm the kind of a man who likes women. Period!"

"Then I'll let you in on a secret," she said, pouring the jiggers with practiced skill. "I like men who like women."

By ten o'clock, Kane's glass had been filled three times; and she had more than kept pace with him. He admired the room; and she, mimicking the accents of Manton Mills's workers, told him how their committee had reacted to it: "Shor purty, looks like in the movies, mam!" He mentioned his wartime duty in Europe; and she, drinking her bourbon straight, with ginger ale chasers, recalled the month she'd spent with her parents in Paris and Venice and Athens: "Kane—I'm going to call you 'Kane'—*they* know how to live!" He complimented her on her perfume, wrongly identifying it as the same she had worn in his office; and she, kneeling on the sofa beside him, bending over him, said, "This is a different scent. Can't you tell?"

I just wonder, he thought, as she slipped down beside him, whether I'm imagining things, or if she's amusing herself. He tried to put the thought out of his mind, even when she, filling his glass, again reached across him and let her arm rest for an instant on his leg. Must be careful, he thought. And yet, he couldn't resist the temptation of finding out just what she intended. When she handed him his glass again, he took the red hank of her pony tail between his fingers, felt of it. "I like your hair this way," he said, and let his hand slip casually to the down at the back of her neck.

She was watching him, her eyes holding his gaze. Then she put her hand over his and pressed it. "Got a crick there," she said, closing her eyes, leaning back. "Rub it a minute."

He worked his fingers and the heel of his hand across the muscles of her neck, massaging the pliant flesh, moving down to her shoulders. And he watched her as she leaned back, smiling, making soft animal sounds, her eyes closed. And still, he thought, still, it could be perfectly innocent. Impelled by reason, he took his hand away, and stood. "I've got to go now. I'll get in touch with your husband tomorrow."

"But it's so early!" She reached for his hand. "Don't go. He'll be back."

"I really should. There's work. . . His voice trailed off as she came up to him.

"It's such a treat for me, having someone to talk to," she told him. "Let's have one more, and I'll send you on your way." Her smile was pleasant, her gaze open, frank. Stupid to read things into her guilelessness, he decided. So she brushed against me. So she asked me to rub a crick in her neck. He felt sorry for her. She was a pretty decent woman, just lonely. "Okay. Last one," he told her, sinking into an armchair.

She poured. "You know how long it's been since I sat down like a human being and talked to someone?"

Kane shook his head.

"Guess."

"No idea."

"Haven't been out of this house for a party or a dance or a . . ." She turned up her glass. "You dance?"

He nodded. "Had a terrific band at the country club last Saturday night."

Melba turned on the radio, flipping the dial until she found some music. "Dance with me?" she asked, holding her arms out to him.

"I don't feel much like dancing."

She put down her glass, and stood before him. "Mark never takes me out to dance anymore. Please?" she said, kicking off her shoes.

The plea in her soft, throaty voice, the scent of her leaning toward him, the natural animalism of her body overcame his doubts. That husband of hers must be a louse and some kind of an idiot, Kane thought. He didn't feel drunk. But now, on his feet, he swayed and steadied himself. "Hot in here."

They danced.

"I wish it was a tango." Melba closed her eyes. "I like to tango," she whispered as they turned, and Kane spun with her.

"You're a good dancer, Mrs. Woodmire," he said. And thought: If we were a hundred miles from here, I'd have made a pass at you already, and you'd have probably swatted me. He chuckled at the idea; and then she rested her cheek against his.

"Melba," she said. "My name's Melba."

Kane danced well. It was something he did effortlessly, instinctively. Aunt Mady had told him, "It's my sister in you, Kane. She was all beauty and grace. And then she married that father of yours. . . ."

He touched Melba's back lightly, and she glided away from him in the break. Then the pressure in his fingers called her back, and they dipped together. He felt the full length of the woman and her mouth touched his chin very lightly and her eyes held his for an instant and then he felt her breath close to his ear, and felt her fingers tighten on his shoulder. Granted, it was sign language, Kane thought. But now I understand every word. And to hell with this. It's asking for trouble.

The music stopped. Kane shook himself from the desire that seemed to hem him in. "I'm leaving now," he said. "Will you get my hat, please?"

"Wait. It won't be long now."

He went past her into the room where he had seen her take his hat. He found it on the double bed. As he turned to leave, she stepped before him. "Please," she said huskily.

The telephone on the night table rang. Still holding Kane's arm, she answered. "Hello?" A voice on the other end, Melba nodding, then: "All right. I'll see you later." She hung up. "Mark," she said flatly. "He's going coon hunting with some of his cronies. Won't be home."

"Well," Kane said, and had to clear his throat, ". . . well, it's late."

She put her arms around him. And fitted herself against him. And let her fingernails bite into his shoulders. And turned off the light.

The living-room door slammed. "Melba? Where the devil are my huntin' boots? Told you to leave 'em in the car. Melba?"

Kane, his mind in chaos, fear constricting his throat, flung himself from the bed. "Quick! My God, get out there," he whispered frantically to Melba.

The next brief instant was a surrealistic painting, framed forever in Kane's mind.

The tinny click of the light switch . . . and the sudden, heartless glare. Mark Woodmire in the doorway, a baffled gorilla with green-and-black plaid shirt sleeves rolled-up, long, hairy arms hanging limply at his sides. Then his grunt of surprise and animal pain. Kane—standing outside himself—seeing his phantom-image on quivering knees beside the bed with the lemon-yellow spread . . . blinking . . . blinking . . . feeling dumbly for his shoes . . . blinking and unable to do otherwise. And fluffs of dust-lint beneath the bed, like wisps of gray cotton candy . . . and a knotty bed slat angled there against a child's lost purple bedroom slipper. And the scent of Melba's perfume. She was sitting up, pulling her rumpled dress over the pink curve of her thigh. And nausea for the phantom-Kane who fumbled with the laces of a shoe that needed a new heel. And Mark Woodmire's tan whipcord hunting trousers with the blue ink stain . . . like a Rorschach test. The horn blowing outside—*shaveanda-haircut*—its strident blare exaggerated in the frozen silence of the room. And the click-click-click as Melba snapped the front of her dress, and then the yammer of the horn again, resolving itself with *two-bits*. And someone's adenoidal breathing. And the incongruity of Woodmire's glossy black dress shoes and the polished grain on the stock of his .22 rifle. And the insinuating squeak of the bedsprings. And Melba cracking her knuckles, and a screen door slapping dully down the street, and the kneeling-Kane, hearing his heart thump painfully against his ribs . . . and a frantic roach, revealed by the sudden light, scurrying to safety beneath the red and yellow throw rug. And Mark Woodmire clearing his throat. . . . All this in the passing of a moment.

Kane's voice came from deep within him. "I . . . I . . ." He had no idea of what he was trying to say. But he felt he must speak, must release some of the pressure stifled in his chest. "I know . . . what you think . . .he managed, grabbing his coat from the foot of the bed.

Woodmire, moving toward, him, tore the coat from his grasp. "No!" he said, and the single word sounded like a stifled sob.

Confused, lost in a labyrinth of fear, Kane tugged at his coat. "Listen," he said, and caught his breath, "nothing . . ."

"Shut up, damn you!" Woodmire blocked the doorway again. "You finished?" he asked, staring at Melba, communicating in phrase and look all his anger and shame and revulsion. "I asked you a question, Melba dear," he said sarcastically. "Don't you answer your husband when he talks to you?"

Her hands were about her throat, and she was trembling. As if she hadn't heard, she opened the drawer of the night table and took out her comb.

"Answer me!" Woodmire shouted, his voice breaking. "Answer me, you no-good, whoring tramp!"

As Melba slammed the drawer, a photograph of her gleeful younger child fell face down on the table. She glanced at Kane who stood at the foot of the bed, fingering his tie, his eyes fixed on her husband. "What do you want me to answer you?" she whispered.

Woodmire was gasping for air, as if he were suffocating. "I asked you . . . if you . . . were all finished."

Shivering, she started to speak, couldn't, and nodded.

"Say it, goddamn you!"

"Finished, Mark."

"No!" Kane said, finding his voice at last. "Nothing happened. We were . . . were just . . ." He shrugged. There was no explaining, he knew. What could he plead? Ignorance? Hardly. Naiveté? Impossible. Lust? Yes. And only that. "I'm sorry," he said lamely "But nothing happened. Honest to God!"

"Nothing?" Woodmire repeated shrilly. "Nothing? Rolling together like pigs in a sty? Tumbling on my bed! Caught with your dress up!" He chewed on his lip. "Oh you slob," he said painfully, advancing on Melba. "You filthy slob! I suspected somethin' in Gastonia with that greasy plant superintendent. But I believed you. Believed you!"

"I swear to God, Mark. I never even saw that man when you weren't around. On my children, I swear it!"

"Don't mention them, you pig!"

Kane, sweating profusely, took his coat from the floor where it had fallen and began to back toward the door.

Woodmire saw him and, swinging his rifle to his hip, blocked Kane's path. "I'm not through with you," he said. "I knew Biddle would be sending someone to see me, but I hadn't figured on you, O'Connor."

"Will you listen a minute?"

"You're the District Solicitor," Woodmire said, ignoring him. "You know the law, you bastard. Don't I have a right to protect my home, my family?" He waved him toward the bed. "Sit down!" Kane backed away. He knew that he was going to die, that his future promised the span of a few minutes. He saw Aunt Mady's face. She said nothing, only nodded in satisfaction. Like his father, she would be thinking, like his no-good father. Kane wrenched himself back to reality. "Put that gun down," he said, forcing strength into his voice. "Be sane, Woodmire." He dared a step forward. "I'm wrong. And my apology won't help, I know. But. . . at least it didn't go any further than . . . than a few kisses . . ."

"And whose fault was that?" Woodmire still held the rifle before him. "I'm tellin' you to stay put."

Kane's mind was churning. He dared not take another step. Beyond the door was freedom and his path was blocked. "It wasn't . . . wasn't intended to . . . We had a few drinks. It's bad enough. Don't make it worse."

"I could kill you, O'Connor," Woodmire said. "I could kill you," he repeated. Then he rested the butt of the rifle on the floor, and heard Kane's involuntary sigh. "But I can't afford the luxury. Now you and your crowd get in my way and I'll prefer charges against you for molestin' my wife." The last two words were said like a curse, and Woodmire glanced at Melba, and turned back to Kane. "I'll ruin you, O'Connor! May God strike me dead if I don't mean that!"

Kane got his shoes on, not bothering to tie the laces.

"And you!" Woodmire spat the words at Melba. "You're finished, too."

Kane backed through the doorway, catching a last glimpse of Melba as she wiped her beaded forehead with the top of the spread.

"Remind me to give you two bucks," Woodmire called to Kane. Then, raising his voice, shouting, "You can get a better piece in any joint in town!"

Kane felt his way through the dark living room. Behind him he heard Melba crying. "Stop it, Mark. Please . . . please . . . leave me alone . . ."

7

KANE UNLOCKED his front door. *Dear God, what am I going to do?*

He moved through the maze of the darkened living room and threw his hat on the sofa. *". . . if you and your crowd get in my way I'll ruin you . . ."* He meant it!

Cy's deep-throated snore greeted him as he went to his friend's room. *Got to talk to somebody!*

Sitting on the edge of his bed, he tossed his jacket across the room. It missed the chair and fell to the carpet. *Fool. I was such a fool. Like a kid with hot pants. And for what?*

His shoes thumped to the floor and he dropped his socks on them. Standing, he unzipped his trousers and let them fall, kicking them aside. *If Biddle finds out what happened, he'll renege on his promise. Judge Kane O'Connor! It was right in my hand . . . only a few hours ago.*

Pulling his undershirt over his head, he smelled sweat and Melba's perfume. His features contorted as he heaved it at his jacket and he stepped out of his shorts. *And Woodmire . . . What happens to me if Biddle provokes him? Six days to wait. Six days until the voting.*

Nude, he walked down the hall to the living room. Reaching over the bar, he felt the outline of the bourbon bottle. The liquor gurgled in the glass, and he gulped it down. *Everything's going wrong. The drop in the market. Now this—a misstep that can cost me years—or everything!*

He poured another drink. *Think! Think!* he commanded his anguished mind. Then, drowning in his own despair, he lay down on the sofa.

Cy found him there in the morning.

After a shower and breakfast, they sat at the kitchen counter drinking coffee, and Kane told Cy everything. "What am I going to do?" he said, putting his cup down and sliding his stool back. "If there's any more trouble at the mill, I'll have to keep my promise to Biddle. And if I do that, Woodmire'll ruin me."

"I wouldn't worry about that. No man wants to tell the world that another guy's been in his bed," Cy said as he clipped his bow-tie onto his collar.

"You don't know him!" Kane stood and paced nervously. "He's capable of anything."

"Well, you'll have to keep Biddle quiet, that's all. If anything does happen, you'll have to refuse . . ."

"He's been mad as the devil," Kane said, breaking in. "And it looks like he's going to lose the union election. One more thing. Just one more thing!"

"Take it easy. It's not the end of the world."

"Come off it, Cy!" Kane said, his voice strident in the small room. "I held the judgeship right here." His fingers closed as if he held the office in his hand. "Superior Court Judge. Just the start!"

"I think your best bet is to have Tod tell Biddle you've kept your part of the bargain: you've seen Woodmire and warned him."

"But suppose . . ."

"Hellfire, Kane, there's no use supposin'. Now go on and call Tod."

Kane sighed, lifted the phone and dialed the Chamber of Commerce office. "I guess you're right."

"Maybe you oughta come right out with the truth to Tod. He may have better advice for you."

"Got to be damned careful who I tell anything. Can't take a chance of this getting out." The phone on the other end began to ring, and Kane held his hand over the mouthpiece. "Besides, nobody helps you if there's nothing in it for him."

The plump face rippled with laughter. "That's so? Well, what's in it for me?"

"Hell, Cy, you old pogue, you're different."

Laurie sat on the green porch rocker listening to Kane, her eyes unable to disguise the hurt.

He stood beside her, looking across the lawn to the street, avoiding her gaze. "So she asked me to dance. And a few minutes later, he came in and started to raise the roof." He flopped down on the glider. "These next six days are going to be sheer hell. I don't know what to do!"

"You can start by tellin' the truth," Laurie said quietly.

"I am telling the truth!" he blazed at her.

"Kane?"

"Yes?"

"If you love me enough to want me to believe a lie rather than be hurt, why don't you love me enough to tell me the truth?"

He leaned over her and put his hands on the arms of her chair. "Darling, I've told you everything that counts."

"Everything, Kane?"

"Well what the devil do you want? A blow-by-blow description?"

"The truth—that's all," she said, finding her voice after a moment's struggle.

He slapped his hands to his sides. "All right. We had a few drinks. And we danced. Then . . ." He looked despairingly at her and read torment in her face. "Laurie, darling, why go into . . ."

"Please, I want to know."

Kane pounded his fist into the palm of his hand, rubbed a knuckle over his nose, scratched his temples. "She kissed me," he said finally. "And there was some smootching-around. Oh, to hell with it! Forget it."

"I'm going to try, Kane," she said weakly. "But it's hard to understand. The first time some woman . . . some married bitch. . ."

"Laurie! What kind of language is that?"

"That shocks you? You can casually commit adultery—but that shocks you?"

"Now you get quiet; and don't let me hear you use that kind of . . ."

"You're surprised that I can use a word like that?" She had been speaking softly, sitting back in her chair. Now she stood, glaring at him. "Bitch! Bitch!" she said, raising her voice, unable to still her anger any longer. "That's what she is!"

Amazed by her intensity, Kane leaned back, his jaw hanging slack. Then, laughing suddenly, he pulled her down to him, held her while she struggled to avoid his mouth. "Honey, you're a hellcat, an adorable hellcat." When she gave up trying to escape him, he kissed her. But there was no response. She pushed him away and stood, deliberately wiping the back of her hand over her lips.

"I guess that's supposed to make it all right," she said. "Everybody in this town's goin' to be whisperin', feelin' sorry for me and thinkin' what a lady-killin' devil Kane O'Connor is, and I'm supposed to get kissed and forget about it!"

Her mouth was quivering, her eyes flashing, and Kane subsided on the glider, restraining a smile. "What do you want?"

"Now *you* hush and listen to *me*. Like I said, the first time this *bitch*"—and she chewed the word, emphasizing it—"gives you a chance, you crawl into bed with her! Despite your religion. Despite me. Despite everything."

Kane leaned forward, his face hidden in his hands. "Laurie, I'm a man," he said patiently. "And I don't care who the guy is, when it's thrown in his face, he's not likely to turn his back on it. I got all hot and bothered. I didn't think about anything else—not that she was married, not anything." He looked up at her and saw that he wasn't denting her resolve.

"That doesn't make sense," Laurie said. "Men don't have all the urges, you know. That *bitch* has her share of them. And I've got mine! How do you like that? I've got mine! But when you were away for years I didn't crawl off in a comer with somebody and get myself pawed. I don't hold myself so cheap. I don't expect you to be without those cravin's, Kane. But I expect you to respect me enough to overcome them."

"You're a woman, Laurie. With a woman it's different. My God, I'm human. A man needs . . ."

"I don't want to hear anythin' else, Kane. I wish I could tell you to go to the devil. I wish I had enough sense to tell you to marry me now or find yourself another girl. But I can't. I love you anyway. And there's nothin' I can do about that."

He went to her and pulling her to her feet, made her sit beside him on the glider. "Darling, my darling," he said, kissing the tears on her cheeks. "I haven't even thought about losing the nomination or the chance Woodmire might prefer charges." He kissed her eyes, put his face in her neck, rested his head on her breast. "All I've thought about is what it might do to you and me."

Tod was waiting for him at the District Solicitor's office. Even before he spoke, Kane knew there would be no six days of waiting.

"The Old Man wants you to put Woodmire in the cooler."
Tod turned his back and looked out the window. "Had another man
clobbered last night."

"But he can't blame that on Woodmire! I was with him last
night. It's undoubtedly some of the roughnecks at the plant."

"I'm just telling you what he wants you to do, Kane." Tod
walked back to the desk. "You made the deal."

Kane knew that he had to refuse, but he could not surrender
his prize so easily. One more thing to try, he thought. "Will you
meet me here in an hour? I want you to go out with me and help
me talk him out of it."

"Won't do any good," Tod predicted.

"You've got to help me reason with him."

Tod picked up his hat from the desk. "Okay. I'll go. But I'm
telling you . . ." He didn't finish the sentence. Waving, he left the
office.

Kane walked down the corridor to Judge Barrett's chambers.

There his uncle listened to his story, grunting with distaste.
"When you're in politics, my boy," he said, frowning, "you've got
to watch yourself all the time."

Kane put his hands on the desk and leaned across it. "I don't
need a sermon now, Uncle Wes. I need your help."

Tipping back in his chair, Wesley Barrett nodded. He
recognized the anguish, the uncertainty and fear in his nephew's
face. "What do you want me to do, Kane?"

"Call Biddle. Tell him that, even if Woodmire were picked
up, he couldn't be held without bail. Tell him if we do it, we'll
have half the county on our necks. Tell him there's no proof
Woodmire had anything to do with the men who've been hurt. Tell
him anything!"

His uncle pulled at his wing collar. "That's all true. Why
don't you tell Luke?"

Kane dropped his hands to his sides in a gesture of
helplessness. "If I refuse, Biddle's sure to get me cut out of the
nomination. Maybe, comin' from you . . ."

"You're not actin' like yourself, boy. Sit down there. And
let's look at this thing straight." The judge waited while Kane
slouched in the seat across from him. "Before you got yourself into
that unfortunate situation last night, you knew you might have to
jail Woodmire. Am I right?"

"Yes, but . . ."

"No buts! You knew Luke might demand that as his part of the bargain. The law hasn't changed since last night, Kane. Only your situation has changed. It would have been just as illegal to lock up Woodmire before he caught you with his wife as it is right now. Still, you were apparently willing to do it, or to promise Luke you'd do it."

"I know the law, dammit!" Kane said, sitting up. "Are you on my side or not?"

"I'm tryin' to show you how Luke's goin' to look at it."

"He doesn't know about last night."

The judge frowned. "Quietly, Kane. Quietly." He wagged a finger across the desk. "Luke'll know sooner or later. And the truth is, my boy, that you made a promise to him that you couldn't possibly keep."

"Uncle Wes, you don't have to point out that I'm wrong, that I've been wrong all along. But now that I'm in it, I've got to get out."

Judge Barrett removed the white carnation from his lapel and placed it in a glass of water. "Let me think it out for a few hours."

"I can't wait. Biddle wants to see me. I want you to talk to him first. If I talk to him and he gets wind of what happened last night, he'll figure I'm just trying to cover myself."

"Aren't you?"

"I've admitted that," Kane said, scratching his nails over the back of a leather chair.

The judge took his black robe from a wall closet. "Did you ever think, Kane, that Luke might resent my interference, that he might find out about what happened between you and Woodmire from someone else and then be furious with you for doing it, and at me for concealing it? Did you ever think that my meddlin' could cost me a nomination I've been workin' for most of my life?" He slipped his robe on and began to button it. "I can't do it."

Kane followed him across the room. "You won't even try?"

"I can't."

"I've come to you for help!"

"Then take my advice, Kane. I'm not a great man or a wise one. I'm not even a particularly good judge, just about average, I suppose. And I've been as greedy as the next fella when it came to bein' rewarded for work by gettin' a chance as State Senator or

Solicitor or Judge. But, Kane, one thing I am, and that's an honest man. When I go into that courtroom, even when you're there pleadin' cases before me, I'm my own man. You know you get no favors, and as many reprimands as the defense. And Luke Biddle gets no favors. I'll compromise with campaign tactics and I'll run around makin' appearances or such for political advantage. But I won't use my office for that purpose."

"Uncle Wes . . ."

"Hold on until I finish, boy! In this case, the law tells you what you must do. Don't disregard the law. Do what you've taken an oath to do. And if that means Luke Biddle or anybody else is displeased, then, by dum, damn 'em!"

"Of course. I never considered doing anything but the legal thing. But, Uncle Wes, you can still help me salvage this chance. You could if you wanted to. I've seen you have your way with Biddle before."

The judge started for the paneled door. "Recess is over. Last case in civil term. I've got to go."

"Uncle Wes, are you refusing me?" Kane demanded, holding the door closed.

His uncle turned to him. "Kane, in politics a man has to look out for himself." Then he walked out to dispense justice in his courtroom.

8

KANE AND TOD drove to Luke Biddle's French provincial home in Sunset Hills. They found The Old Man in his acre-wide backyard, digging in his tulip beds. He stood as they approached. "Well, is he in the jug yet?"

Although Kane explained the law, pleaded, cajoled, Luke Biddle was unmoved. "I've made up my mind," he said, squatting among his bulbs. "Now you have him picked up on an assault charge. If that won't stick, book him for somethin' that will. I'm tired of havin' my boys smacked around. I want him held, one way or another, until the votin' is over Monday."

"Tempers get short at times," Kane said, stepping over the flowerbed to look down on Biddle. "It's a reputable union. They wouldn't stand for strong-arm methods. For your own good, you can't go off the deep end." He looked to Tod, begging his support.

"Maybe Kane's right," Tod said. He was leaning against a tree, and left the shade to stand beside Kane. "You don't want to get yourself in trouble with the federal government. Why not wait and see what happens?"

"Wait? You want me to wait while this union greaser takes my plant away from me?" Luke threw his trowel to the ground. "You want me to sit on my tail and take orders from a bunch of gangsters who think they know my business—the business I started and built—better than I do?" He grasped Kane's elbow. "Now you go on along and pick him up."

There was, Kane knew, only one thing for him to do. A formal charge against him by Woodmire would do more permanent harm than disinheritance by Luke Biddle. He pulled his arm away. "I'm not going to do it. There are laws in this country; and when you try to be bigger than the law, you're looking for trouble."

"Well, it's damned strange how moral you got recently," Biddle said, stepping closer to him, looking up into his face. "I might have listened to your advice, O'Connor. I might have let you talk me into some legal maneuver. But I know better. You're mighty righteous all of a sudden!" His gnarled hand waved before Kane's face. "Got that way since last night when Woodmire caught you diddlin' his wife!"

Kane felt winded, dazed, as if he'd been struck a blow to his mid-section. "That's a lie," he managed to say.

"You can crap your uncle, O'Connor, but don't try to crap me!"

His uncle! For an instant, Kane had trouble believing it. Then Uncle Wes *had* called Biddle. But he had called to put himself in the clear, to report to The Old Man so there could be no doubt of his loyalty. "Don't you ever repeat that," Kane said, making an attempt to be unperturbed. "If you do, I'll sue you for . . ."

"I don't repeat dirty stories," Biddle said. "You can sleep with the hogs for all I care. But I'm glad I know you for what you are . . . a self-seekin', sharp-talkin' liar and cheat!"

"All you know about me is that I'm the one guy you've run across who won't take your orders and kiss your ass!"

The Old Man stood there, his face scarlet with anger. "When I finish with you, you won't be able to get two votes for constable, you scum. Now get the hell off my place. Get off!"

For the first time in his memory, Kane heard Luke Biddle shout. He walked past Tod, back to the car, his shirt and underclothes clinging to him, drenched with sweat. Taking off his coat, he laid it across the back of the seat. Well, it's over, he thought. Despite his loss, he was relieved.

Meanwhile, Luke Biddle instructed Tod. "You heard me, son. You get two of my people . . ."

"Now where am I going to get anybody like that?"

"Out at the plant. I'll tell you . . ."

"You're asking for trouble."

"I want to end all the trouble." He was still breathing hard, and he sat down in the shade on the grass, and brushed his face with his sleeves. "You get these boys. And have 'em get Woodmire alone somewheres. And be sure he gets a good workin'-over. Did you see the kid I've got in the hospital? Well, I want Woodmire to look like that. And then let him go. But tell him the next time any of my boys gets smacked around, he's goin' to pay for it in hide."

"Ferchrisakes! You can't get away with. . ."

Biddle interrupted. "I don't give a hoot. If I can't get the police to do somethin' about lockin' him up, I'll get it taken care of myself. Now don't argue. You pick up the boys."

Tod spoke calmly, knowing exactly what he was going to say, as if it had been engraved in his mind long before. "I owe you my job, but you've been paid back. I've written your fake ads for you and pressured your workers out there, and handed-out your booze and cash down at the capital. I've lied for you and kept my mouth shut for you. Well, I'm not above that kind of thing. But I'm not hiring out as a hatchetman!"

Biddle stared at him, unbelieving. "You ungrateful, stupid..." But Tod was already gone.

On the ride back to town, Tod spoke first. "You didn't tell me you'd been playin' around with Woodmire's wife."

"It's not as bad as he made it sound," Kane said, giving Tod his version of what had happened.

When Kane had finished the tale, Tod said, "A broad in heat hasn't got a conscience."

Kane laughed unconvincingly. "My Uncle Wes really reamed me. I told him about it in confidence, and I couldn't have been gone five minutes when he reported every word to Biddle."

"What did you expect?" Tod asked. "He's one of Biddle's people. He needs him." He yawned and stretched his short arms over his head. "But I give him credit for having spunk enough to work on your campaign, although he did cover himself by keeping Biddle informed on everything we did—except the abortion business. And that nearly ruined him with The Old Man, only your uncle wasn't there that night."

Kane had slowed the car and was staring at Tod, glancing at the roadway, and turning back. "I don't believe it!"

"Hell, I thought you knew. Being naive doesn't suit you, Kane."

They drove on, neither talking, while Kane fumed over his uncle's duplicity. Then, forcing himself to think of his more immediate problem, he said, "You think Biddle will lay off Woodmire now?"

"He tried to get me to have him worked-over by some of the toughs at The Mills." Tod drummed his fingers against the dashboard. "I've got a feeling I'll be looking for a job soon, but I told him to get himself another boy."

"Good thing you refused," Kane said. "He won't go through with it on his own."

"Like hell he won't. When he's mad—and he has to be pretty damn mad to yell and cuss—he'd cut Orphan Annie's throat. Providing, that is, he could get someone else to hold the knife!"

"I've got to warn Woodmire. If anything happens to him, he'll figure I'm responsible." Lifting one hand from the steering wheel, Kane bit nervously at his thumbnail. "Tod, I swear, if I ever get out of this . . ."

"What about Uncle Tod? All of a sudden I'm in it with you."

Four hours later, at nightfall, no one had yet contacted Mark Woodmire. Kane had called the union hall and Woodmire's home, and had followed-up the other leads unsuccessfully. Cy was busy on the telephone in the outer office. Tod had gone out to The Mills to look. Chief Sawyer had police cars cruising the streets. Kane was frantic when Tod, at eight o'clock, finally called in.

"I saw him. Caught him at the union hall," Tod said. "He's been out of town."

"Did you tell him I want to talk to him?"

"Yeah."

"What did he say?"

"What he *meant* was 'no.' What he *said* doesn't make any difference. You'd have to be a contortionist to manage it."

"Did you tell him what Biddle's up to?"

"He didn't give me a chance. Made that crack about you, brushed past me and took off in his car."

"How can I find him?"

"He's got to go home sometime."

Kane hung up, and started out of the office. "Say a prayer for me," he told Cy. "I'm going to talk to Woodmire, and I've got a feeling I'm going to need all the help I can get."

Mark Woodmire drove home. There were six more days before the election, and he believed he might win it. There had been a long phone conversation with union headquarters that afternoon. Again he'd been cautioned about his methods. "A helluvalot you know," he had told them. "You oughta spend a few weeks dealin' with Luke Biddle."

He pulled up in front of his house. Weary after his long trip, he relaxed behind the wheel and looked at the house, hating it. His train of thought led to Kane O'Connor, and a gnawing pain of frustration and hatred gripped him. *What are you goin' to do?* he asked himself. Tell the world you're practically a cuckold, not man enough to keep your wife in line? Last night she had made many promises, and he had heard her sobbing far into the night while he lay on the living-room sofa. And in the morning, he had put her on a train for Baltimore and driven his children to stay with his parents in Rock Hill. I've made it tough on Melba, he thought. Leavin' her alone—never takin' her anyplace. And damn little money. He opened the door of the car and stepped out, resolved to get the voting over with, and then possibly get sent north or even to California. Slamming the door, he started up the walk, moving a tricycle out of his way, and immediately thinking about his children. If he could only rid his mind of that first moment when he'd turned the lights on, he thought . . . and Melba on the bed . . . and O'Connor . . .

As he passed the shrubbery and stepped up on his porch, he heard a footfall behind him, and in the same instant, his arm was yanked from behind and twisted painfully behind his back. "Take it easy, Woodmire. We jes wanna talk some." Mark Woodmire started to turn. "Uh-uh! Let's slip on 'round the back where it's quiet."

As they approached the driveway, Woodmire stepped aside nimbly. Grabbing his assailant's hand, he twisted, and threw him to the ground, falling on him, jamming his knee into his stomach, clapping his hand over the scrawny throat. Then he looked at the man's face for the first time. It was small, nearly feminine, clown-white in the moonlight, and it was a vaguely familiar face . . . around The Mills, somewhere around The Mills, he thought, and tightened his grip around the man's neck. "Who sent you, you bastard?" he said, shaking him.

Someone was running toward them. Woodmire got up and, kicking his victim in the groin, he turned to meet the second man. Already a tall, hefty shadow was on top of him. He felt the breath go out of him as a fist smashed into his chest. He went down to his knees, caught a glimpse of a boy's face, kinky blond hair . . . and then a shoe flashing . . .

When Woodmire regained consciousness, both men were standing over him. White Face was bent over, holding himself. "Planted one in the family jewels," he said, straightening up.

"You okay?" Kinky Hair asked his friend.

"Reckon so."

Woodmire opened his eyes carefully. Garbage cans. Chicken-wire playpen. Garage. He had been moved—the backyard. He shut his eyes again as Kinky Hair leaned over him.

"He's breathin', ain't he?" White Face said, and prodded Mark with his toe.

"Yeah. C'mon, let's get outta here."

"He don't look bad off," White Face said.

"Bad enough."

"Supposed to mark him up."

"Hell with it. I don't hold with hittin' a man, he's out on you," Kinky Hair said.

"Supposed to," White Face said uncertainly.

"Well—get him on his feet."

Woodmire was pulled to a sitting position. Then, his legs under him, he sprung erect and swung his fist. Kinky Hair grunted, grabbing his stomach, and Mark smashed the flat edge of his open hand across the Adam's apple. He saw the man go down, gurgling, coughing. Then he felt the weight of the second man on his back. Woodmire stumbled forward, carrying White Face. Got to get to the drive, to the street, to light, he thought, tugging all the while at the arms that yanked his chin back, choking him. He reached the gravel driveway and turned around the corner of the house.

Kinky Hair had gotten to his feet and now loomed before him. As White Face pulled from the rear, pinning Woodmire's arms, Kinky Hair stuffed a soiled handkerchief in Woodmire's mouth, and began to pommel him, flailing away in short, rhythmic strokes. No one spoke. It was a ghastly shadow play, a pantomime broken only by grunts and smothered moans and the sharp intake of breath and the shuffling of shoes in gravel. In time Woodmire ceased to struggle and went limp, conscious only of his own warm blood against his face and the relentless, timed regularity of the pounding knuckles against his ribs and stomach.

He heard, as if from far away, the squeal of tires rounding a corner. And saw, flashing momentarily, the white glare of headlights and the grind of gnashed gears . . . then the car was gone.

"Too many cars passin'," White Face said, and let Woodmire crumple to the gravel. "We better shag outta here."

From the moment he had seen Woodmire's car at the curb before the blacked-out house, Kane knew that he was too late. When he turned the corner and the twin fingers of light probed the darkness, revealing for a suspended second the whole stark scene, his first impulse had been flight. Get to a phone. Call the police. Call an ambulance. But when Woodmire's body fell to the white gravel and twitched there, something impelled Kane to go to him. He had coasted down the street, stopped silently, and now, stealthily, he moved around the far side of Woodmire's house. There, their grotesque shadows looming against the shingled facing of the garage, were two men, standing over the twitching body of Mark Woodmire.

Kane crouched at the corner of the house. Got to see them, he told himself. Identify them. He moved softly across the grass, holding close to the wall, seeking concealment in the shrubbery. He was within ten yards of them now. There was a little man with a girl's face—a face Kane recalled, somehow, under a baseball cap. And beside him, legs akimbo, was a tall sandy-haired young man. Through his legs, Kane could see Woodmire, prostrate, his blood staining splotches of gravel, his hands working convulsively, his head coming up, slowly, wavering.

"Jes you set here a spell 'til we get gone. Or you'll get more," the blond youngster was saying. Then, turning to the little man with the girl's face, he said, "Get me my handkerchief outta his mouth. He won't yell fer awhile."

"But he ain't out," the little man said.

Kane, flattened against the house, could see Woodmire trying to rise, finally managing to support his weight on his hands. Then the little one with the girl's face, the one that belonged under a baseball cap, bent down, pushed back Woodmire's bleeding chin, and kicked him in the pit of the stomach. "He's out now."

Fury seized Kane. Fury at the brutality he had seen, fury at the pitiful odds. Fury at Luke Biddle. The little man kicked Woodmire again. "You goons! You filthy goons!" Kane shouted. He was charging toward them.

The youngster saw him. "Christ! It's O'Connor," he shouted. "Take off!" And he ran. The smaller man followed, but Kane tackled him. The man wriggled away, got to his feet briefly, and Kane was up, turning him around. Kane smashed his fist into the chalk-white face. The man went down, lunging for Kane, pulling him to the earth. They rolled there. At last Kane came up on top, pommeling his foe, battering his head against the crunchy gravel.

"Paul! Paul!" the white-faced man yelled. And a moment later Kane heard returning footsteps, and felt a hand clawing at his shoulder. He glanced up to see the blond boy holding an automatic, pointing it, as if he were afraid it might go off.

"I'll use it! Swear I will."

"Put that gun down, you idiot. You want to end up in the gas chamber for Luke Biddle?" Beneath Kane, the little man was struggling for breath, unable to move. A few feet away, Kane could see Woodmire lying on his side, retching. Sucking for breath, Kane stood.

The boy lowered the weapon, and Kane pounced on him in that same moment. "I know you. I know you both," he yelled. He jabbed his fist into the boy's midsection, smashed his other hand into the muscled side. The automatic lay in the gravel, and Kane kicked it away and simultaneously caught a blow in the face, and then another that staggered him. He tasted his own blood and stood there weaving, shaking his head, trying to focus on the bigger man.

"Why don'tcha butt-out. This ain't no skin off'n your butt," his opponent said. "Didn't want no trouble with you."

"You got trouble," Kane said, moving in on him. His rage was gone now. He was no longer thinking of Woodmire. It was the sheer joy of battle that consumed him. And as his opponent, he saw Luke Biddle in a younger, stronger body. He threw his fist into the blond boy's jaw, and took one to his own ribs. And then, working inside the taller man's arms, he feinted a jab to the body, and brought over a straight, short blow that smashed the big man's nose. Blood ran. And Kane hit him again, felt him buckle, and struck him twice more as he fell to the ground.

Kane turned then, seeking out the little man. Too late, he saw him, saw his hand raised, saw the blue glint of the automatic again, and then it crashed against his skull.

Minutes later, Kane stirred. The yard was silent. He lay there on his back, feeling one great throb in his head where the steel butt of the pistol had cut a gash. Then he heard a moan. He got to his feet, weaving, stumbling across the yard to Woodmire's crumpled body.

"Woodmire? Woodmire?" Kane took off his coat and placed it beneath the battered head. "Woodmire?" he called, shaking him gently.

The eyes opened, filmy, dull. The lips moved, working wordlessly. Then, in a faint whisper, Mark Woodmire cursed. "You! Oh, Jesus God . . ."

9

THE NURSE opened the blinds and let the morning light filter into the hospital room. "Just a few minutes," she told Kane. "I'll wait outside."

Standing by the bed, Kane leaned over, his own bruised face bent down to the bandage-swathed head on the pillow. "Woodmire? You hear me?"

"I hear you," Mark Woodmire said, still groggy with anesthetic.

"Anything I can do for you?"

"Get outta here."

"I tried to warn you. Tod Sands got in touch with you for me . . ."

"All right," he rasped and cleared his throat. "I owe you somethin'. Now get outta my sight, damn you!"

Reporters were waiting for him when Kane left the room. Pleased, he saw that Matt Fallon, who had accused him of pulling a hoax on the phone that morning, and who had laughingly sworn "I won't be party to making a national figure out of you, Lover-boy," had come through for him. He had dispatched a cameraman from a network affiliate a hundred miles from Manton who now stood ready to record the story of Kane's battle with hoodlums.

"Nobody goes in there except the doctor or nurses," Kane cautioned the policeman stationed outside the door.

"What's his condition?" one of the newsmen asked.

"Hold it!" the television man said. The camera began to whirr. "Okay. Ask your question again, buddy."

And when he did, Kane, his voice heavy with regret, replied, "He's in bad shape. But he'll be all right. Suffering from concussion, some bad bruises."

The Manton Argus man wedged his way through the reporters who had arrived from all over the state to cover the story. "Were you badly hurt, Kane?"

"Few bruises and a gash and this shiner," he said, pointing to his swollen eye and bandaged forehead. "But you should have seen the other guys," he told them, laughing. A flashbulb went off. The photographers had Kane repeat the pose.

"How did you happen to be there when it happened?" one of the reporters asked.

"I had a tip that something like that might come off. I had several people, including the Chief of Police, searching for Woodmire so we could give him protection. We didn't have any luck. On a hunch, I went by his house and blundered right into it."

"Have any idea who the toughs were?"

"I'm not at liberty to give out any details right now, boys." Smiling, he rubbed his knuckles. "You can say I'm looking for one man with a broken nose!"

"What action do you intend to take, Mr. O'Connor?"

Hemmed in against the cream-and-brown wall of the corridor, Kane held up his hands. "I can tell you this, men. As long as I'm solicitor in this district, we're not going to have this kind of lawlessness. I'm not interested in the union election. But the workers have a right to organize if they want to, and this attempt to terrorize them is un-American. No one is bigger than the law here. I'm going to get to the bottom of this."

Late that afternoon, Kane found Tod in his partitioned office at the Chamber of Commerce. "You're fortune's child, Kane. Last night you were neck-deep in manure; and you come up this morning smelling like a rose!" Laughing, he said, "I caught your performance on a newscast from Charlotte a little while ago. You really looked the part of the battered but valiant protector of the law. 'No one is bigger than the law here. I'm going to get to the bottom of this!' Brother!"

Kane sat on the folding chair across from him. "I meant it. I'm going to get Luke Biddle. I recognized those toughs—that husky blond boy who drives the recreation bus for The Mills, and the guy they call 'Breezy' who used to pitch for Manton High. Now tie that to Biddle telling you to see that Woodmire got a beating. All you have to do is testify to that . . ."

"Why should I?" Tod got out of his chair. "What's in it for Uncle Tod?"

"Jeezuz! It's your duty."

"Leave Jesus out of it," Tod snapped. "Don't give me any of that duty business, Kane. You stand to do all right if I testify. That's your payoff. Meanwhile, I sit around waiting for my two-weeks' notice. What's my payoff?"

Kane knew there was no subterfuge with Tod. He would give it to you straight—even if you didn't like it. "Hell, buddy, I expect to get the judgeship out of it, but . . ."

Tod sat on the table. "I thought you had more on the ball, Kane. You don't have to settle for that any longer. If I tell what I know, you can do a lot better than Superior Court Judge."

As soon as he got back to his office, Kane called Luke Biddle. "I want to talk to you. Come down here."

"If you've got anythin' to say to me, you can come out here," Biddle answered.

"You be in my office in an hour or I'll have a police car pick you up and bring you here." Kane hung up.

While he waited, he sat at his desk, thinking over his earlier conversation with Tod. He was excited, no longer nervous or confused, no longer counseled by anxiety. He had a plan. There were some things about it he didn't like. But the goal! If everything turned out as Tod predicted, if Biddle acted as they expected him to . . .

When The Old Man arrived, Kane let him stand, waiting. Finally, after occupying himself with the dead file on his desk, he said, "You can sit down, Biddle."

"What do you want, O'Connor?"

"I want some advice." Kane grinned, enjoying the chance to toy with the fierce political lion, relishing the hatred he saw in the smoldering eyes.

"Get to the point."

"If you had a choice," he said judiciously, solemnly tapping his fingertips together, "and you had a man in his declining years, a man with a business and a name in the community, and you had to decide whether to indict him for..."

"Lay it on the line!" Biddle cut in. "I'm not here to listen to your . . ."

"Shut up!" Kane said, his manner changing abruptly. He slapped his palm on the desk. "You'll listen. You don't have any other choice!" Seeing Biddle grumble and subside, Kane had the satisfaction of knowing that the strange weavings of chance had reversed their positions. Now he could command and Biddle would obey. "As I was saying," he went on, speaking softly again, "would you indict this hypothetical character for conspiracy to commit an assault? Or would you be harder on him and make it conspiracy to commit an assault with a deadly weapon?" He watched Biddle chew nervously at his upper lip. "Or would you make sure he got a good term in prison—and make it conspiracy to commit murder?"

"You can't prove a dam' thing," Biddle said, but his tone of voice gave him away. He sounded uncertain. "Don't think you can threaten me, O'Connor."

"Oh, but I'm not threatening you," Kane said, as if he were amazed by the accusation. His voice hardened. "I know you tried to get me to lock Woodmire up, illegally. And I know I refused to flout the law, even tried to get a Superior Court Judge to convince you of that. Then you told Tod Sands to hire some thugs for you and he refused." Kane saw the color rise in Biddle's face.

"Then I met your boys personally." He dabbed at his swollen eye, fingered the bandage on his forehead. "And though I understand they're both 'on a trip out of town,' I think they could be found." Kane stood. "So, I'm reminding you that though you can control the jaypees and you can pick the sheriff and you can put the judges in your debt, you can't tell a jury what to think!"

Biddle wiped away the saliva that ran down the weathered grooves on either side of his mouth. "All right," he said, recognizing defeat. "You want the nomination for Superior Court Judge. You can have it."

"Are you trying to bribe me?" Kane asked innocently.

"Don't push me, O'Connor. Every man has his price!"

"Right. But you underestimate your man, Biddle. And you underestimate his price." He leaned across the desk to watch The Old Man's face as he delivered the thunderbolt. "I'm going to be the next congressman from this district!"

Biddle stared at him, disbelieving; then, realizing that he meant what he said, "I knew you were a louse, but I didn't think you'd go this far. Your uncle's waited a long time for that job. He's earned it."

"How?" Kane asked bitterly. "By doing your errands for you? By being your stool pigeon? By outlasting the other slobs who couldn't wait out your generosity?" He walked around the desk.

"You heard me. That's what I want. And I'm not asking any favors from you, not taking any bribes from you. I'm just being decent enough to give you fair warning. I'm going to run. And if you try to do anything—and I mean anything at all—to stop me, I'll make you curse the day!"

"You're no good, O'Connor. You're rotten."

Kane stood there, looking down at him. "I'm not interested in your opinion of me, Biddle. I'm not facing an indictment. I haven't tried to ride roughshod over the law. I haven't had a man beaten senseless!"

Biddle pushed himself out of his chair. "I'll have to think about it. Come out to my place tonight, and we'll . . ."

"If you have anything to say to me, you come here. At eight o'clock. Because by that time I'll decide just where my investigation goes from here."

When Luke Biddle came through the office doorway that evening, he was followed by Judge Barrett.

Kane's stomach went hollow. He busied himself at his desk, opening drawers, searching for old papers. He was trying to think, to decide what to say. He hadn't counted on his uncle's appearance. When he looked up at last, his Uncle Wesley was watching him.

"I brought the judge with me because, when I told him, he couldn't believe it," Biddle said.

The judge walked across the room to stand by his nephew. He put his hand on Kane's shoulder. "That's right. I don't believe it. I know you too well, boy."

Kane rolled his chair back. "I've made up my mind."

"Then change it," his uncle said softly.

"Why?" Kane swiveled his chair, turning his back to his uncle. "Biddle was ready to wreck me when I refused to muzzle Woodmire for him. He did his damndest to beat me when I ran for this job."

"We're not talkin' about Luke now," the judge said, his voice calm, but determined. "We're talkin' about you and me."

Kane had heard the tone, the inflection before. He thought of the many times his uncle had saved him from a birching by Aunt Mady, had defended him, had sat with him in his room and reasoned with him. He sounded that way now. Patient. Gentle.

"You're usin' your position to extort the nomination—*my* nomination," the judge insisted.

Kane drummed a pencil against the green blotter on his desk. "I suppose it's a damned crime when I use my position for myself, but it's only fair and right that I use it for you!"

"You're forgettin' I helped you get this job," his uncle said, hovering over him.

"Oh no I'm not. You were helping me with one hand and scratching Biddle's back with the other. But you both got fooled in the end, because I won in spite of you." He threw the pencil down. "And yesterday you couldn't wait for me to get out of your chambers so you could report to him, so you could blab what I'd told you in confidence, as my uncle, my friend!"

"I thought I was doin' the right thing, Kane," the judge said lamely. "I thought it best . . ."

"Sure. You thought it best for you," Kane said fiercely. This was Biddle's last play, he reasoned. Well, he told himself, he's not going to pull a fast one on me. Looking up, he met his uncle's gaze.

"I'm not askin' you for anything," the judge said. "But I expect you to be at least as thoughtful of me as I've been of you. And that covers a long, long time."

"What do you want me to do? Get down on my knees and thank you?"

"I don't want any return for anything, Kane," the judge said, walking around to look at him, then bending over him. "But you can't forget what I've done for you over the years."

"I know. I know that, Uncle Wes . . ."

"If it wasn't for Wes you wouldn't be sittin' in that chair now, O'Connor," Biddle said.

Kane got up and stalked across the room. Luke Biddle offered a better target than his uncle. "Listen, damn you," he said, glaring at Biddle. "You're the one who's in trouble around here. Not me. Remember that!"

Judge Barrett shook his head at Biddle, frowning, warning him to be silent. "I'm waitin' for your answer, boy," he said, quietly determined.

Kane felt sorry for his uncle. He toyed with alternatives. He could be generous, perhaps, put him in his debt. The judgeship was his for the asking . . . there'd be another chance at Congress. It would mean waiting. And yet, it was clear enough that his uncle had betrayed him to Biddle . . . and more than once. And besides, with something to go to the people with, he could win a seat in Congress. Easily! There was so much within his grasp.

Biddle broke in on his thoughts. "All right, O'Connor. I'll guarantee you the nomination for Congress when Wes retires. And that's the only way you'll ever get it. You'd never beat him in a primary!"

Kane lashed back at him with the malice he could not bring himself to use against his uncle. "You think not? Well, run him then! I haven't asked you not to. I'm willing to take my chances. You're the one who's afraid to run against me. I don't need you, Biddle. I'm on the right side; and the voters will know it. I'll run against a candidate who takes his orders from you—a man who's been indicted for conspiracy to commit murder!"

Judge Barrett crossed the room to his nephew again. He had been sure of himself. Now he was uneasy. He put his hands on Kane's arms. "I want those two years to round out my career. I won't run again, boy. Two years from then you can have it!" Unable to read the reaction in Kane's eyes, he clutched at his sleeve. "You're still so young," he insisted. Then, painfully, "I'm sixty-five."

Kane pulled away. "I'm not interested in waiting. You want to run? Go ahead. I'm not stopping you. I don't give a damn if I get the nomination by default or if I get it by running for it."

Wesley Barrett saw his dreams slipping away. "You'll have those years as judge," he argued desperately. "It'll give you the seasonin' you need. You'll be better prepared." As Kane walked back to his desk, his uncle followed him. "You're just a beginner in politics. You're not ready for Congress. You're a youngster with very little practice and a fluke election behind you." He tried to control himself, but his mouth trembled as he continued. "Please, Kane, this is the only thing I've ever asked you to do for me. . ."

"Don't beg, dammit! Don't beg!"

The judge stopped in mid-sentence. He caught his breath, drew the shreds of his dignity back around himself. "I'm not beggin'," he said, forcing the words to disguise the turmoil of his mind. "I'm merely askin' you to . . ."

Kane turned on him savagely. "I asked you to do something for me just yesterday—and you weren't interested. You could have prevented all this from happening. Because of you a man was nearly killed and I got mauled and two stupid kids are fugitives and the whole country is aware of little Manton! You know what you told me?" He watched his uncle, in his clothes of another era, the high collar, the striped tie, the morning coat, the wilted flower. He saw him sigh, breathing heavily. "You told me that in politics a man has to look out for himself! Well, I'm just following your advice!"

Kane tore open the Universal Broadcasting System envelope, already certain that the letter would be from Matt Fallon. Inside was a raggedly-torn clipping from *Time* of December 31, 1948; and although Kane had saved a drawer full of them, he glanced over the article again:

GIANTKILLER

Handsome, wavy-haired Kane O'Connor, thirty, the new wonder-boy of southern politics, packed his suitcase and his old Air Corps footlocker this week. He was off to conquer Washington. . .there was little doubt that O'Connor has lived up to his billing as "Fightin' Bombardier," and his reputation as "Giantkiller."

A hero of the air war in Europe, he returned to his home town of Manton, North Carolina, to practice law. (For news of his wartime exploit, see *Time*, January 7, 1945.) Within eight months, he was bucking the entrenched political machine in a fight for the District Solicitor's post. . .he exposed an abortion racket alleged to be flourishing under the eyes of the incumbent.

Despite three political strikes against him—Catholic, anti-organization and age twenty-seven—the young crusader won by a landslide. He took office fourteen months after his triumphant return to civil life.

Though lesser men might have settled down to comfortable obscurity, O'Connor continued his giantkilling ways, compiling a brilliant record as Solicitor.

When O'Connor had been District Solicitor for little more than a year, Marcus Paul Woodmire, a labor organizer at Manton's huge textile mills, was dragged from his home and severely beaten. . . . O'Connor took on the armed thugs with his bare fists. . . .

The thugs were never identified, but Woodmire's successor was given police protection, guards patroled union meetings and the N.L.R.B.-supervised voting was held on schedule. The union won.

Political soothsayers had long since chosen O'Connor's uncle—Judge Wesley Barrett—for the Democratic nomination to Congress. But now the young giantkiller overshadowed the white-maned jurist.

It was O'Connor who was unopposed in last May's Democratic primary. In the general election, he polled the highest plurality in the district's history. Though others have traveled the distance from military acclaim to political recognition even faster, few could match either his DSC or the magnitude of his victory.

Said Giantkiller O'Connor on the eve of his trip to the nation's capital: "Being in Congress is no different from any other position of public trust. You decide what's right and what's wrong. And then, without fear of work or responsibility, or pressure or personalities, you stick to what's right. I've always tried to do that. I intend to do so in Washington; and I think I'll manage it."

No one in Manton who knew him—least of all the slain Goliaths he left behind—would disagree.

A short typed note was clipped beneath the article: *Loverboy, I've got mixed emotions—happy for you, you Giantkiller, and in sympathy with the voters who love you so! Will see you in D.C. on my return from Near East, Honorable Loverboy. My God! On The Hill, they'll call you, "The Gentleman from North Carolina!"—Matt.*

BOOK TWO

10

KANE STOOD beneath the freshly-painted black-and-white sign that hung beside the entrance to his office in the Old House Office Building. Hitching his briefcase under his arm, he fumbled for his key.

Tod Sands opened the door.

"Didn't think you'd still be here," the freshman congressman told his aide. "Why the hell don't you go on home?"

Picking up a stack of letters from the mailing table, Tod carried them into the inner office. "Wanted to get these ready for your signature," he called over his shoulder. "I'm on my way now."

Kane followed him, dropping his things on a chair. "You do more work around here than I do."

Tod shaped the pile of correspondence into a neat bundle on the desk. "Where've you been all day?"

"Sat with folded arms like a good boy and listened as usual," Kane said. He slipped into his swivel chair and rested his feet on the rim of a wire trash basket. "Then I voted to pay a claim against the government—two hundred and fifty bucks each to three survivors of a ship torpedoed seven years ago. And, while one of my senior colleagues was reading a Winchell column into the record, I stepped out for a drink with a congressman from South Carolina who raises goats and has a similar personality."

"For this you get the taxpayers' hard-earned money?" Tod laughed as he left the room to get his coat.

"I'm bored stiff," Kane said, raising his voice so Tod could hear him. "You know what it reminds me of?"

"Go on. I'm listening."

"It's like getting your second looie's bars, and making your first visit to the Officers' Club. Custom says you've got all the privileges—but watch yourself! Don't raise your voice. Don't argue with a superior. Don't discuss taboo subjects. Don't fail to speak first to your seniors."

Back in the doorway, Tod made a clucking sound with his tongue and wagged his head in mock sympathy. "Buck up, man! After all, you can put your congressional frank on your congressional letters, have your congressional back rubbed by the congressional masseur, fill your congressional gut at the congressional restaurant, have your congressional locks snipped at the congressional barbershop. . . ."

"Yeah, I know. I'm a member of the greatest legislative body on the face of the earth."

Tod twirled his hat on a lifted finger. "Why don't you get away from it all? Come on home with me. I'll call June and have her put some more gin in the martinis."

Kane pulled the stack of letters across the desk. "Thanks. But I'm going to sign these and shave. And then, I've got to make that box supper at the rally tonight—fried chicken, hard-boiled eggs and oratory. Congressman Reade is going to introduce me to the right people."

"I'm impressed." Tod, laughing, started out and then turned in the doorway. "I'm going back to my hideaway in Alexandria, give my kids their baths, get June playfully tight, and make up dirty limericks about congressmen!"

When the outer door closed, Kane glanced through the letters in his incoming basket, recognized the Manton Bank's envelope, and ripped it open, already prepared for another reminder about the eighteen-thousand dollars he owed—an accumulation of bad investments and campaign expenses. A note from Cy was appended to the statement: ". . . the worth of your stocks, held as collateral, has dropped during the past few months. We think you should reduce the principal to bring the collateral in line with your required margin." And below it, Cy's friendly scrawl: "A thousand bucks would help stall the board, buddy."

Kane wrote in pencil on the bottom of the statement: *I'm on my uppers now. Can't raise a hundred bucks, much less a thousand. I'll take care of it as soon as possible. Please explain to your dad.*

To the empty room, he mumbled, "I'm in a bind . . . on top of all that, I owe Cy. . . ." Grunting, he turned to the stack of neatly typed letters on his desk. They were form messages addressed to each of the registrars in his district. All were the same except for a single personal reference in the last line. Nearly two years before another election, Kane thought, smiling, and Tod's already remembering the home folks.

Having the little bantam with him had been a good bargain. The post was the answer to "What's in it for Uncle Tod?" But in every way it had been an advantageous arrangement. Though Tod was listed as administrative aide, he acted as public relations expert, adviser, expediter, speech researcher, office manager and guide.

Tod's experience in lobbying bills through the state legislature was helpful, too. He was a wily mentor. "Go through the *Congressional Directory,* Kane. Study it. Check the men who run the committees. Be damned sure you know and recognize The Big Five—The Speaker, The Majority Leader and the chairmen of Appropriations, Rules, and Ways and Means. It's important, chum. I'd hate to see you wind up on the Merchant Marine and Fisheries Committee!"

Later, seated in the bar at The Ambassador, watching the door, Kane waited for Shepherd Reade.

His patron, he mused, was another result of Tod's wisdom. Kane recalled how he had argued, "I don't need that cadaver," and how Tod had shown him that Reade had precious seniority, that he was chairman of the important Government Administration Committee, a member of the powerful Ways and Means Committee, a man to be cultivated.

The Alabaman, a sincere plodder who had moved up the echelons of seniority for eighteen years, who had set out to make himself a specialist on administration, was now considered an expert by his colleagues. Both seniors and juniors in Congress, advisers in the White House, and Cabinet officers conferred with him on administrative problems. He was respected; and his influence on legislation, though generally unsung, was considerable.

Reade liked to talk; and Kane became a good listener. In a short time he had picked up scattered bits of information about Shepherd Reade:

He owned three Oldsmobile agencies. He was among a minority of congressmen who were not lawyers. He made his permanent home in Washington and spent long, hot summers in the district he represented. He donated his salary to the support of a non-sectarian home for the aged. His father and grandfather had been congressmen. During his second term, he had broken the jaw of a newspaperman who had called him a liar. He believed that Negro blood differed from white blood, but that the Negro should not be denied political rights because of this inferiority.

He was thoughtful, dependable, opinionated, honest, patient, sincere, wealthy, sixty-nine, a quoter of maxims, childless, tired, conservative, courteous and generous. Kane decided that he liked him. And besides, in time, Tod's counsel had proved itself. It was Shepherd Reade who had proposed Kane's name to the Ways and Means Committee's majority and secured his appointment on Reade's own Government Administration Committee as well as the Special Committee for Military Planning.

At last, Kane saw the Lincolnesque figure threading his way through the tables. Standing, Kane shook hands with the senior congressman. "Good evening, sir. We have time for a drink before we leave for the rally?"

The fine white brows went up, the dark patches under the faded eyes wrinkled. "I think so. Bourbon and water with . . ."

"A twist of lemon," Kane volunteered.

Reade smiled. "Yes. Twist of lemon."

They ordered. Then, settling in his chair, Reade said, "This place makes me feel old, always full of young people havin' a good time."

"Used to come here myself, sir," Kane said. "I was stationed at Bolling for a few weeks before going overseas. We'd make this liberty headquarters." He laughed. "Used to sit at this same table, trying to get up enough courage to talk to a stray government girl. Washington's changed a lot since then." Their drinks came and Kane held up his glass in an unspoken toast. He was hoping for good news; but he wanted the older man to bring it up himself. "You must be mighty busy, Mr. Reade."

"I have my hands full." He sipped his drink. "Responsibilities multiply when you've been here as long as I have. Then, too, I had opposition in the last election—first time in ten years. I've got lots of fences to mend before the next one. But you're the one who must be busy. You been makin' out all right?"

"Just following your advice, sir, keeping my mouth shut and my ears open." Kane turned the glass in his hand, wiping off the frost. "Afraid I'll be bothering you for advice for a long time."

Reade pulled at the shriveled lobe of his ear. He liked the youngster. Had a good record behind him and, by gosh, he was one young buck who didn't pretend to know all the answers, who knew how to talk, but hadn't forgotten how to listen. "Be glad to help you son," he said. "No use you makin' the same mistakes I made when I got here."

Kane was nearly sure of his footing now. "I'm a little worried, Mr. Reade." He took another step, slowly. "You know the Special Committee on Military Planning will have its sub-committee assignments this week; and I've been hoping desperately I'll get on Installations and Equipment."

"The chairman is a close friend of mine," Reade said. "And we had a talk about you."

Kane looked surprised. "The chairman? You did, sir?"

Reade finished his drink. It was good to find a youngster who was polite, who had some respect. "Why don't we drop the formality? Never mind the 'sir' and the 'Mr. Reade,' " he said magnanimously. "You call me 'Shep.' All right?"

"Thanks. Thank you, sir! You were saying you spoke to the chairman about me?"

"Told him you'd be a natural. Frankly, my opinion usually carries some little weight. So, though it's not yet official, I feel it's a sure thing. That will give you two important seats, Kane. It's a good start for you."

11

KANE HAD MET twenty people by the time he and Shepherd Reade had elbowed their way through the crowd at the armory door, picked up their name tags and found seats in the vast, bunting-draped hall.

"I've got to see some people. I'll be down to eat with you later," Shep said, leaving him at their table.

The speeches got underway, and the upperclassmen began to tear the Republicans apart. "The Party of Privilege, the Party of the Wealthy Few," the keynoter called them. And the partisan audience applauded and cheered. Kane, uncomfortable on the slatted folding chair, leaned back, canting it on its rear legs, and searched the crowd around him for a familiar face. He half-heard the speaker's injunction to "look back, my friends, to the Hoover Administration. Look back to the time when the American people, saddled with the G. O. P.—the Grumbling Old Party—(laughter) were without hope, without sustenance and without leadership!"

Stamping feet. "Give 'em hell, Tom!" they yelled. "Let 'em have it!"

"Tell the faithful what they want to hear, Thomas!" It was a woman's voice, from the press table beside Kane's; and he tilted his chair back still further, turning his neck for a glimpse of the striking girl in a shimmering champagne-colored dress who sat there, her finely-molded chin resting on her thumb. A second later, Kane's chair collapsed and Kane, amid the clatter, was on his back at her feet.

There was good-natured laughter around him, heads craning in his direction. Stunned for the moment, Kane ignored the proffered hands, got to his knees and found himself looking into the incredibly-lashed, deep blue eyes of the girl at the press table.

The speaker bellowed on. "The mission of our party is to remain the party of the people. . . ." The audience, no longer diverted by the spectacle of a prone freshman congressman, roared its approval.

The girl was restraining a smile. Her long, slender fingers brushed the silky bangs on her forehead as she bent toward Kane. Then, shaking with silent laughter, she offered him her hand. "I'm sorry," she whispered, grinning impudently, biting her lips. "But you were so funny. Hurt?"

Mute for the moment, Kane shook his head, and getting to his feet, lifted the chair, silently cursing his clumsiness. His chair refused to open. He tugged at it, upended it, looked for a hidden latch, examined it impatiently and unsuccessfully, certain all the while that a thousand pair of eyes were staring at him. In his confusion and embarrassment, he had ignored the five empty chairs at his table. Now, sliding the broken one out of the way, he slipped into a seat next to the press table, brushed himself off as well as he could, summoned enough courage to look surreptitiously around him, saw that he had been forgotten, and relaxed at last.

"The destiny of America must not be entrusted to those who refuse to look forward. Our Democratic party has made a covenant with the people. We shall not fail them; and they will not fail us!"

"Hurray!" It was the girl again, now only an arm's length away. She began to applaud; and a thousand loyal Democrats took her cue. Kane stole a glance at her. She was leaning back, arching her throat, laughing, her diamond earrings and the coronet on the honey-blonde hair sparkling in the dim light. Her confederates at the press table were laughing with her.

Kane hadn't seen her before. He was certain of that. It would have been impossible to have forgotten her.

"If they expect to find us weak and divided," the speaker roared, "they will be sadly disappointed. We cannot advance America's interests or solve America's problems unless we are firmly united in this great Democratic party!"

The crowd shouted its agreement; and Kane, on a sudden impulse, spoke to the girl. "I haven't seen you in a long time," he said, hoping that her reply might remind him of some inexplicably forgotten meeting.

"You've never seen me at all, Mr. O'Connor," she said, and smiled again. Her teeth, he noticed, were like all the rest of her— well cared for, bright, perfect.

He said, "Then how do you know my name?"

She motioned him to silence as the speaker pounded the rostrum and cried, "Let us dedicate ourselves anew to the task ahead . . ."

Pretending to be intent on his words, Kane looked to the front, but concentrated on seeing the girl in his mind's eye. She had a cool, distant beauty, the idealized kind of beauty you saw on the covers of fashion magazines or in the ads for Cadillacs and Lincolns. And yet, her laugh, her soft voice were so warm and unaffected, her gaze so open, so direct, that the whole effect was that of— He couldn't summon the word to describe it.

The keynoter raised his hands in supplication. "Grant us the faith, the will and the knowledge to bring continued prosperity and peace to the common people of America!"

The audience stood and applauded the stirring sentiments, the end of oratory and the arrival of the box suppers. When Kane looked for the girl, he saw her surrounded by the occupants of the press table. And when the circle broke, it was Shepherd Reade who emerged with her. His arm about her shoulders, he guided her to Kane. "Dany says she's met you, Kane."

"Well, practically. I read his name tag, and then tried to pick him up," she said.

"But only because I threw myself at your feet," Kane said.

"Impossible. There wouldn't have been room there," Shep said. "Too many ahead of you."

Kane took her hand. "Hello, Dany." Her grasp was firm and strong; he had expected it to be delicate.

"I wish Lucy and Mel would show up," Shep said. "Kane ought to meet them."

Dany nodded. "They're the influential part of the family— my brother and sister-in-law," she explained, identifying them for Kane. "We were on our way to a party; and Lucy insisted we stop over for a few minutes." She glanced at her tiny diamond wristwatch. "That was two hours ago. And I haven't seen them since they left me at the press table. Probably waylaid by some politician."

"You're going to have dinner with us," Kane said. "Aren't you?"

She looked at him steadily. "Yes, thank you. I'll have dinner with you."

"My dear, you're far too radiant, too elegantly attired tonight to settle for cold fried chicken and hard-boiled eggs," Shep said, and pulled out a chair for her. "But havin' you with us will make it a banquet."

Despite the echoing clatter in the cavernous hall, Dany and Shepherd talked. About the Brider Syndicate. (Her brother was apparently Brider's son-in-law and editor of *The Washington Express.*) About the admission of Hawaii into the Union. (She had been brought up there, and favored statehood. He was disturbed by the large non-white population and its susceptibility to communism.) About federal aid to education. (She believed it would equalize educational opportunity. He saw it as a prelude to an invasion of states' rights.) About Faulkner. (She insisted on his genius. He lumped him with Caldwell and accused them both of slandering the South.) About a minimum wage and the forty-hour week, the alliance of conservative Republicans and southern Democrats, TV A, Sidney Lanier's poetry, poltergeists, Menotti's opera, *The Medium,* the Egyptian domestication of cats, and the merits of the Lightning Class in sailing.

Although Kane was tempted to speak, perhaps to share the girl's viewpoint as her ally against Shep, Kane entered the conversation only when he was asked a specific question, and then he answered in generalities, unwilling to chance a blunder that might reveal his ignorance of matters they discussed so glibly. He did not always agree with either of them, but he learned something of Dany and confirmed his opinion of Shep as he listened.

Shep was positive about everything. His ideas were all developed and formulated; and he reeled-off his beliefs in concise and cogent phrases. He spoke in absolutes. He no longer had any questions about anything. And he was vain. He preened himself on his erudition. This Kane had not detected before, and he noted it, put it down as a telling flaw in Shepherd Reade's character.

Dany revealed something of herself, too. It seemed to Kane that the poetry and novels she had read, the philosophy she had studied, the music she had heard, were all personal experiences to her, part of her savoring of life. And she had an empathy for ordinary people, for people whose lives hers—obviously isolated, wealthy and secure—never touched. She listened intently. She admitted it frankly when she had no answer. She had an incisive, sometimes malicious sense of humor. Watching her now, as she inclined her head toward Shep, a puzzled look crimping her brow, Kane was drawn to her. He wanted to be alone with her, wanted to hear her talk, wanted to ask her questions, wanted to make love to her. The thought brought with it a physical reaction; and he felt a nervous twinge in his chest, a sensation akin to pain.

". . . so the First Lady went down to Woody's and bought herself a girdle, Kane!"

He looked up, jarred from his reverie. "What?"

Dany was laughing at him. "You haven't heard a word, have you?"

"I heard you . . . but it didn't make sense."

"It was an attempt to awaken you," Shep said, getting up. "I must leave. Mrs. Reade'll raise sand if she knows I've spent the evening in such dazzling company." He passed his wrinkled fingers over Dany's bare back. "I leave you in good hands, my dear."

As Shep moved away, Dany said, "He's sweet, despite his blind spots." She paused, smiling. "But he's at that age where he can't resist a friendly pat on a girl's fanny."

Kane laughed. "That's another privilege of seniority," he said, walking around the table to sit beside her. "Shep's been great to me."

"He likes you. And he's a good man to have like you."

Kane leaned closer to her, and with a sudden movement that surprised her, took her hands. "Come on. Let's get out of here."

She canted her head, started to answer and then was silent a moment. "I'm waiting for my sister-in-law and my brother. We're long overdue at a party."

"Damn the party. It's a beautiful mild night outside. We'll go someplace where we can walk and it's quiet and you can tell me the story of your life."

"Did it work the last time you said that to a girl?"

Kane had never said it. He had heard it—in a Cary Grant picture two days before. Nodding, he said, "Yes. It worked."

"I'd better go then. I don't want to ruin your average."

Kane held her fur stole. For an instant, when her hair touched his chin, and her body brushed his, he had a nearly overpowering desire to hold her in his arms. "Mmm, you smell good!"

Dany turned and took his arm. Her lips were pursed, her eyes alight with amusement.

Hours later they walked hand-in-hand around the circling path below the gleaming colonnade of the Jefferson Memorial, then across the expanse of granite steps above the waters of the Tidal Basin. They sat there, in the lee of a bulwark, speaking softly, the great rotunda glistening white behind them, the distant lights of passing cars probing the far shore, and beyond, the sleek shaft of the Washington Monument, glowing in the night. The April breeze, brisk now, nudged the budding limbs of cherry trees as their living shadows shivered on the water.

Dany had taken off her coronet and earrings. She leaned forward, speaking earnestly. "Aren't most people ordinary, no matter what their job? No matter if they're saleswomen or senators? Good, maybe, and honest and loyal—but ordinary." She clasped her palms tightly and rested her chin on her knuckles. "Take the bulk of the men at the rally tonight, politicians all, but how many of them are ever adamantly for or against anything? There's no flame in their dreary, dull-gray souls. I can name the passionate liberals in Congress on this hand," she said, holding it up before her. "And there's no such thing as a passionate conservative. Why do all the zealots have to be either reactionaries or radicals? Why can't a man be zealous without choosing one of those distant poles? He can be!"

Kane was lounging on the steps, listening carefully. "And you think that's all a man needs?" He smiled. "You've never been a congressional freshman."

"I don't mean that's all a man needs, but . . ." She paused, biting her lips, concentrating. "Read your history if you want to know what makes great leaders. Of course, great events helped make them. But they all had a—a sense of destiny, and tremendous self-assurance and a real hunger for fame and power!" She watched the stem expression on his face, and laughing softly, she leaned against the bulwark, nuzzling her cheek against her stole and stroking the fur.

"It's getting a little cold," Kane said. "Want to get in under a roof?"

"No. I love it when it's like this."

"All right. Go on with what you were saying."

"No. Not another word. I talk too much. I'm going to listen for a change. You tell me some more about Kane O'Connor."

He was leaning back, propping himself on his elbows, looking up at the languid clouds that scudded in silhouette against the moon. "You've heard enough about me—everything from the coal mines to Congress. There's nothing left to tell." He sat up again, and bent toward her. "Come on, talk to me, Dany."

"I'm all talked out."

Kane wanted to talk about Congress, about the unnumbered restraints he faced, about the routine, the stagnation. He wanted her to tell him he wasn't another mediocrity—or need not be. But her mood had changed, and reluctantly, trying to please her, he went along. "Tell me about you."

"I've been rattling off my qualifications like an applicant in a matrimonial agency. You should have all the details by now."

He edged closer to her. "Well, you have a fantastic appetite."

She laughed, closing her eyes. "Two little hot dogs and a bowl of chili. That's all."

"And fried chicken and boiled eggs at the rally and coffee and pie at the Hot Shoppe."

"I'm an expensive date. What else do you know about me?"

"You got your degree at USC in political science."

"UCLA. And a Master's . . ."

Her eyes were still closed and Kane got up and sat beside her, raising her head so that it leaned against his shoulder. She hadn't opened her eyes. "And you've tried too many jobs—from naturalization teacher to swimming instructor to a fashion model at Gar-finkels . . ."

"Did. Three months. I liked the girls, and it was fun. But too strict. Felt like I was back in finishing school!"

"If you'd have had to work to eat, honey, you'd have stuck to something. Isn't there anything you've ever really wanted to do?"

She raised her head and looked up at him. "If I'd ever lived anyplace besides the non-voting Islands or the District, I'd be sitting right there with you in the House. And I'd make some noise. I'd get things done! Now don't pursue that any further," she said, putting her head on his shoulder again.

"You—a Congresswoman?"

"You're darned right. And a good one!" She opened one eye and glared at him as if she dared him to disagree. "Now go on with my vital statistics before you get me into an argument and I poke you."

Laughing, Kane said, "Let's see. . . . Well, there's one obvious thing, suggested by your dad's sugar plantation and a highbrow school in Switzerland and all the diamonds and this mink."

"The jewelry's borrowed from Lucy. And the stole's not mink. It's squirrel."

"All right, borrowed and squirrel. But you're undoubtedly loaded with the long green."

"I had ten thousand dollars insurance—all of which is gone. And I live on an allowance from my dad—all of which is spent before the check comes in."

He turned his head, inhaling the fragrance of her hair, aware of her warmth against his side. "I don't know anything else. Only. . . only that you're the most . . . the most . . ." He fumbled for the right word.

"Well?"

"Miss Payne, I'd say you're some girl!"

She sat up, laughing. "And Mr. O'Connor, I'd say that's some compliment," she said. Then her expression changed abruptly and she wasn't smiling any longer. "It's not *Miss* Payne. It's *Mrs.* Payne."

He had experienced the same sensation before. When his instructor in pre-flight had done an outside loop without warning him. When the light switch clicked on and Mark Woodmire stood, baffled, in the doorway. "Why didn't you... you could have told me," he said, realizing in that instant that their meeting meant so much to him.

"My husband's dead, Kane."

A surge of relief flowed through him. "Oh! I'm glad. I mean, I'm sorry. . .What I want to say is that I'm sorry he's dead, but I'm glad . . .You know what I mean."

She nodded. "I know. Now it's awfully late. Three in the morning." Standing, she held out her hand to him. "Come, take me home." They crossed the steps and walked back toward the parking area. Out to the front, a train whistled across the railroad bridge that spanned the Potomac. And Dany's heels clacked against the pavement in sharp counterpoint to the night noises of the insects. The amber gleam of an anchor light lolled out in the Basin, an aircraft beacon whipped against the sky, and headlights curved toward them from the highway, then swerved away toward Virginia.

"I like Washington best at this time of night," Kane said, if only to break the silence while his mind smoldered with other thoughts.

Without preamble, Dany began to speak softly as they followed the sidewalk to his parked car; and Kane wrenched himself from his musings as she told him about her marriage. "Martin and I were in school together. Looking back on it, I can't really understand how two people so completely different could..."

Her voice trailed off and she paused a moment, glancing up at Kane. "We decided to get married—or rather I made the mistake of deciding for him. And his parents were stunned. And my dad was furious. My brother Mel flew out to give me away. And we lived on what Mel sent me. Martin and I quickly learned to detest one another."

She sighed audibly; and Kane looked at her, but couldn't read her expression. "The Navy called him. And we both made promises we'd make a go of things. And then he went to sea. In a few months he wrote, asking for a divorce. I wasn't a very good Catholic then, I guess. Still, I couldn't do that. Being married was a terrible mistake. But I just couldn't. . . . So I refused. And then I didn't hear . . . until his ship was hit off Okinawa by a Japanese suicide plane. That was the end of it."

Kane didn't know what he was expected to say, and so, was silent. When they reached his car, he opened the door for her. "You must be hungry again," he said, smiling. "Maybe I oughta buy you breakfast."

"I think I'm going to like you, Kane."

The door hung between them and he bent down to her face, framed in the open window. "Why?"

"I don't know why exactly."

"Can't you give me a 'for instance?'"

"For instance—you've got a nice smile. And you're ambitious. And you know when to talk and when to keep quiet. And because . . . because I know you can do things. You can be somebody." She touched his hand that lay on the door panel, and looked up at him. "One more 'for instance': You haven't even tried to kiss me yet."

"Don't be misled. I've considered it."

"I've considered letting you."

"What did you decide?"

"That it would be the friendly thing to do." She kissed him lightly on the lips.

Kane stood there a moment, throttling an impulse to drag her out, to hold her hard against him, to kiss her properly. She's right, he told himself. I *can* do things, be somebody. It was as if she had known him always, and knowing him, had sensed his ravening appetite, his unquenchable thirst for turmoil and action and reward. He slammed the door, walked around the car and slipped under the wheel, conscious of Dany's eyes on him.

What was it he mused, that he felt surging deep within him now, stirring like new life, swelling and buoyant, expectant, exultant? If greatness came because you were certain, had always been certain in the solemn secret moments of self-knowledge, that you *would* be somebody—*a sense of destiny,* Dany had called it— if it came because you were searching ceaselessly for *something, someone* to single you out from the crowd, then for him it was inevitable.

"I feel so . . . so agitated," he said to her.

She turned to him, her features obscured in the darkness. "What is it?" she asked.

He had no answer. And then, laughing, he said, "Lust!" And knew that he lied.

12

IT WAS DUSK on an April afternoon, nearly four weeks later. And Kane, as he had done on at least fifteen other occasions, pressed the UP button and waited for the self-service elevator that would whisk him to Dany's apartment.

Mirrored in the glass mail chute, he examined himself. He buttoned all three buttons on his new brown single-breasted suit and tugged at the satin-print tie, loosening the knot. His face was sore from the day's second shave, and he smoothed it, rubbing away the talcum that had caked in the corner of one eye. His upper lip was perspiring. Reaching for his pocket handkerchief, he checked himself and dug into his trousers to find another.

As the elevator whined upward, Kane noticed the dulled shine on his new wingtip shoes; and he polished first one toe, then the other, across the back of his trouser legs. Going to catch it, he thought. I'm late.

Dany, already in her wrap, answered his ring. "Kane, do you know what time it is?"

"Sorry."

Backing him out of the doorway into the hall again, she closed the door behind her. "Being on time is an attribute in this town. Nobody else ever is."

"Am I ever going to see the inside of your apartment?" Kane asked.

"Of course," she said, taking his hand. "Any time you like—providing the door is propped open, we're chaperoned and you're handcuffed."

As he had so often during the past weeks, Kane felt unable to cope with her. She was so sure of herself, so much the mistress of any situation. Tonight she wore a cocktail dress, a cloud of blue; and her graceful, tanned shoulders were bare. "You're frigid," Kane said, "but mighty damned pretty."

She led him down the hallway. "And you're wearing a new suit. I like it."

He was pleased that she had noticed.

"Please, Kane. Only one button closed—the center one." She unfastened the other two.

In the elevator, she held him away from her, like a fussy mother inspecting her son before a party. "You've done pretty well, Congressman O'Connor. We'll do something about that tie, and we'll be ready to go."

"What's wrong with it?"

"Too Christmas tie-ish."

"I like it," he growled.

"You may know something about politics, dear, but you know nothing about clothes. The tie is too conspicuous."

"Well, that's just too damned bad!" He had expected praise, had chosen the suit and tie and shoes with special care. Now, as usual, she was making him feel his inadequacy. "Why the hell do you go out with me? You're always picking me apart!"

She leaned against the polished oak wall of the elevator, smiling tolerantly. "You want me to be kittenish and adoring?" Pushing out her lower lip in an exaggeration of his, she walked across to him, chucked his chin as if he were a sulking child and put her face against his. "I can't simper and pose, Kane. I'm not sweet. I'm a brat." She pinched his cheek and brushed her lips lightly there. "So stop scowling and make the best of it."

They walked through the narrow marble vestibule. You'll come down off your high horse, Kane was thinking. He had admired women before, had desired them, enjoyed their companionship, respected them. But in Dany he had found, for the first time, a woman he considered his equal. And still, she made him feel like Samson, shorn of his locks.

Kane drove down F Street, and Dany motioned him to stop before a men's shop. "I'll run in for your tie. Just circle the block."

"Dammit, Dany!"

She was already out of the car. He watched her walk away, taking each step as if there were a regal carpet beneath her feet. Horns behind him sounded, and he put the car in gear and nosed into the traffic.

He turned right and skidded over the streetcar tracks. Pondering the past weeks, he realized that he had sought Dany out. Even when Laurie had come to Washington for a week-end, despite the guilt he felt, he had taken her to her hotel early one

evening, feigning work, and had eaten a midnight dinner with
Dany. There was some quality, some color that distinguished Dany
from anyone he had ever known. And though he had begun to
know her, to understand her, their every meeting was another
revelation. It happened when she was introspective, when she
didn't talk for a long while, listening instead to him, or when she
was accommodating her mood to his. It happened when she
suddenly remembered the names of characters in a Dostoevsky
novel, or argued with him, quoting Aristotle, after he'd made a
passing remark about women in politics. It happened when they
had browsed in a bookshop for a birthday gift for her brother, and
she had finally selected a handsomely bound copy of Maimonides'
Guide to the Perplexed, a book she had apparently read and
understood. Or when he called for her one Saturday evening, and
she insisted on going to confession before they had dinner. Or
when she had taken him to a revival of *Peer Gynt,* and they had sat
around with several of the actors later, and she had talked about
Ibsen as a scholar might.

He remembered the evening they'd spent at Tod's home in
Alexandria. Dany had volunteered the men for kitchen police. She
had been a girl-on-a-date, interested in June's maid problem,
admiring the two sleeping children, intrigued by the small town
girl's dining-room drapes. And later, talking politics, she had
argued like a ward heeler. Kane laughed to himself as he recalled
Tod, standing tipsily in the doorway as they left, and telling Dany:
"You're the only gal I know who's got the shape of Venus, the
wiles of Mata Hari, the mind of Eleanor Roosevelt and the
inhibitions of Lucrezia Borgia. Woman, I adore you!"

At the Congressional Club reception, she had been charming
and alert, holding his arm, introducing him and being introduced.
At the embassy party she had whispered names to Kane as
nameless faces appeared, had reminded him what legislation most
concerned a particular Cabinet member. While Kane worked
nights on his pork-barrel bill for a mountain highway, she had
charted the states and districts the proposed road would pass
through. "It doesn't pay to lone-wolf all the time," she had said.
"Cut some of the boys in if it will help you. You'll get yours."

Kane summed it up in his mind. She's cool, smart, beautiful,
ambitious. Why should I complain? I've got nothing to offer.

Dany was waiting for him when he completed the circuit of the block. He pulled up to the curb, jumped out, ignoring the yammering horns, and held the door for her.

"Loverboy!" It was a remembered greeting, a remembered voice. And it came from behind them on the street. Kane turned and saw Matt Fallon, his square, freckled face sticking out of the window of an airport limousine. Matt flung the door open and sprinted to the sidewalk. "I've been trying to call you, Kane," he said, pumping his hand. "You ole sonovabitch, it's good to see you again." Then, noticing Dany for the first time, "Pardon me!"

After the introduction, Kane pounded Matt's shoulder. "Brother! It's been years. . . . First time I've seen that homely puss in the flesh since the day I came back from overseas and you treated me to my initial civilian hangover." To Dany he said, "A few phone calls and wires and letters from this character, but he couldn't find time to see me, not until he figured I was a congressman and important enough to rub shoulders with a high-priced TV commentator!"

"Kane, I've followed your career with foreboding—from hero's welcome to your first election to your sterling defense of the working man to your campaign victory and your recent immortalization by *Time*—and I knew, sooner or later, you'd show up right here!"

"Ten minutes after we met I threatened to poke him," Kane said. "You can understand why, Dany."

The limousine honked and Matt yelled to the driver. "With you in a minute." Then, turning to Dany, "I was a sergeant with *Yank* and Kane was a lieutenant-hero; and he charmed me into making him famous."

"Then Kane hasn't changed," Dany said.

"Frightening, isn't it?" Matt said. "Everybody loves Kane. Only a miracle'll keep him out of the White House."

"I'll make you my press secretary," Kane said.

"If I don't get a sponsor soon, I'll take you up on it. Say, have you caught my show? Started from Frisco last week. On sustaining right now. Friday nights."

"I saw it; and I'm impressed," Kane said. "I even dropped you a note and got a reply from your secretary telling me you were still out of town."

"Haven't been back to New York yet. Returned from Cairo through New Delhi and Frisco, got in here late this afternoon. Called your office, but didn't get an answer. And now I'm off again." He yelled at the driver. "All right. Hold it a minute!"

"I've seen you often on *Meet the Press* and *Face the Nation* and some other panels," Dany said. "And you're the rare bird who dares to have an opinion. I'm for you."

Matt winked at her. "That's probably why I'm still looking for a sponsor."

"We're gonna miss the plane, mister!" the driver of the limousine called. "I can't wait no longer."

"Coming!" Matt yelled, taking Dany's hand.

"You're not going anywhere," Kane insisted. "This is a reunion, dammit."

"We've got a lot of kibitzing to do, but it'll have to wait. Ought to be back in a few weeks."

"Stay overnight. You can sleep at my place."

"Can't. Got my show tomorrow night. And I'm off to London Monday."

They said a hurried good-by.

Kane watched Matt Fallon step into the limousine and wave to them. "We've had some times together," Kane told Dany.

"He has what it takes. He'll do all right."

Kane held the door for her and got behind the wheel again. She showed him her package as he turned down Fourteenth Street. "Did you notice the neat, simple, good-looking tie your friend Fallon was wearing? Well, I've got one something like it for you."

They stopped for a light; and Kane frowned at her. "I like what I'm wearing. And I'm damned well going to keep it on!"

Dany, pulling her knees up and resting against the car door, said, "Don't be grumpy, dear. Your tattered ego is showing."

As they passed the Bureau of Engraving, crossed the bridge over the Potomac and joined the traffic near the Pentagon, neither spoke. Kane kept his eyes straight ahead, determined that at least in this thing, he wasn't going to give in.

"You ought to see more of Matt Fallon," Dany said finally. "I think I like him already. And someone in his position can be a big help to you."

Kane nodded, maneuvering the car into the center lane to make the turn-off on the Shirley Highway. Matt Fallon. . . . From the start, Kane thought, we've understood one another. In his mind's eye Kane could see that hospital solarium on that dreary day, see himself on the rubdown table with the nurse's aide, a blue-eyed, flat-chested English girl with lovely skin.

"Which one of you is the hero?" The question came from a six-foot-four shadow in the doorway, and Kane, startled, pushed the girl away and peered across the room, finally making out the sergeant's uniform, the red mop of hair, the burly shoulders.

"Who the hell are you?" Kane said.

"Name's Fallon. Sergeant Fallon, Lieutenant. They sent me here to interview the hero." He grinned as the girl fled past him, out of the room. "And I suppose you're the hero."

Kane didn't like the way he said "lieutenant." It was nearly a sneer—but not quite. "Anyone ever tell you about knocking on doors, Sergeant?"

"It's not a private room. . . He shrugged. "We enlisted men haven't had the advantages of a genteel upbringing, Lieutenant."

"You think you're a pretty smart guy, don't you, Sergeant?"

"Begging the Lieutenant's pardon, sir," Matt said with unctuous politeness.

"*I'm* supposed to be asking *you* questions."

"Well, I'm not answering any. Get the hell out of here!"

"Listen, Lieutenant," Matt said, smiling. "I've got three months to do before I get home for awhile. I'd like to stay out of trouble. . ."

"You're too damned fresh to stay out of trouble, Sergeant."

"Yes, sir. That's my problem, Lieutenant. I don't know when to keep my mouth shut and I'm used to the privileges and courtesies accorded the Fourth Estate. You might say I'm still having difficulty adjusting to military life."

"I'm no chaplain," Kane said. "Now, beat it!"

Matt started for the door, and turned back. "Lieutenant, I'm a pretty good judge of human nature. So, I'm about to risk getting locked up by asking you one simple question."

"Don't tempt fate," Kane said, pulling on his bathrobe.

"Lieutenant, my question is: How would you like a slug of His Majesty's best scotch?"

Kane grinned. He couldn't help himself. He had to admire the man's nerve and good-natured impudence. "You know bringing that in here's a court-martial offense?"

"Lieutenant," Fallon said, taking out a flask, "there's lots of things you can get court-martialed for doing in a hospital—if you get caught."

Laughing, Kane said, "Sit down, Sergeant. What do you want to know? About my citation?"

"That's what I've got to write about," Matt said, pouring a drink. "But what I'd like to know is how the hell, shut off in this place, watched by doctors and nurses and orderlies, completely without privacy, you manage to get a broad in the hay?"

Kane downed the drink. "If it wasn't contrary to the articles of war, I'd bust you in the head with this cast!"

"By God, I'll bet you would! Have another shot, Lieutenant. I think I've blundered into a man after my own heart; and I'm anxious to take down the story of your life from your first infant squawl to that damned fool stunt that got you the DFC."

When Matt finally got around to asking questions, he concentrated on only two—probing, pushing Kane to recall, then enlarge upon, his feelings and motives. "How did you feel when it was going on? I mean, what were you thinking about?"

"Sergeant, when you've still got a load of gas and an engine's on fire, and you're not sure how to fly the damned crate, and there's a guy groaning behind you, you just feel scared. . . . And I didn't have time to think about anything but getting that baby on the ground."

"If you were scared, why did you do it? You could have jumped."

"I don't know why."

"Did the guy who was hurt owe you dough? Were you worried about his family?"

"No. I didn't think about him at all after that first minute or two."

"Then, why?"

"I . . . I guess . . . maybe because it was up to me. I never really thought about that part of it until just this minute . . . But we'd just dumped a load of incendiaries on a half-a-million people, without even thinking about where the stuff was going or what it would do . . . And I'd pushed that button. And then, ten minutes later, there's only one life at stake . . . and suddenly, it's important. Maybe, in the back of my mind...Christ! I don't know why I did it. It just happened."

Matt had written the story, a story that translated Kane's impulsive heroism into an act of penance, a story that—as a routine Air Corps release—had rated two inches and an eighteen-point head, but under Matt's byline, was picked up by wire services and newspapers all over the world and was the subject of editorials and sermons.

Later, when Kane was on recuperative leave, he spent three days in Paris with Matt. There was a flight in a cargo plane that netted them a case of some general's scotch, a party with a Swiss war correspondent that ended when Kane tried to prove he could swim the Seine in his underwear, a meeting with two women when Matt organized and led a community sing in a Montmarte night club, and a fight with two humorless French husbands and their enraged relatives.

Back in London, for two weeks they roomed together in Matt's flat, talking far into the night about politics and government, history, economics and journalism, about the war and their ambitions and ideas and errors. And in the early hours of the mornings they would roam the streets, searching for an open shop where they could buy rolls and buns to eat with the stolen GI coffee they would brew in their rooms.

"Kane! Look where you're going," Dany said. "And turn off at the next exit. Now smile. You've given me enough of the silent treatment. Come on, give me the boyish grin that warms the voters' hearts!"

He gave up trying to discipline her. "How far do we have to go to this hunting place?"

"It's not a 'hunting place.' It's called 'Hunting Acres'; and it's a beautiful old plantation on the river. Now, since Lucy's bought it, it's a rendezvous for the great and near-great who come to pay homage to Lucy, eat her caviar and pheasant and cultivate the magic power of the Brider Empire."

"Your sister-in-law sounds like a moron."

"Oh, no, she isn't. Mel has the title of editor of *The Washington Express*, but it's Lucy who really runs her daddy's newspaper. She's a bright gal."

"I'm not going to like this place."

"You will. You like excitement and there's plenty of that. More deals are hatched at Hunting Acres than in the House cloakroom."

"And how do I fit into this crew?"

"You don't—yet. But you will. Because I want you. And Lucy, for all her posturing, is a model sister-in-law who'd rather get me with an eligible male than have the Duke and Duchess of Windsor as week-end guests." Dany fingered the back of Kane's neck. "Poor Lucy's been working on both projects without much success."

"Sounds like a bunch of stuffed shirts to me," Kane said, feeling her cool, strong fingers stroking beneath his ear.

"I'm not taking you out there to find fault with them, Kane. You're going to meet them and make friends of them. It's so much easier to get things done in this town if you have allies. Sometimes it's a newspaperman who trades favors—you leak something to him and he gives you coverage when you need it. Sometimes it's a man with connections in the Cabinet or with congressional leaders who can reach them when you can't. Sometimes it's a lobbyist who can get you organizational support from a veterans' group or a trade association. Or maybe it's a man who just likes to know a congressman on a first-name basis, and is willing to pay for the privilege when campaign time rolls around." Suddenly she clasped her fingers over her mouth. "Sorry. I promised myself I wouldn't make speeches at you tonight."

"Couldn't we just find a nice place to park? And you could teach me all the mysteries of politics and I could teach you all the mysteries of love!"

"Politics is more fun," she said, smiling.

"Honey, somebody's been giving you bum dope! How much further?"

"Pull over a minute," she said. "We're nearly there."

He stopped the car on the shoulder.

Dany slid over on the leather seat, closer to him. Then, loosening his bright satin tie, she pulled it over his tousled hair, threw it into the back of the car and slipped a new tie under his collar. It was beige, with a neat, dark-brown panel in the center. Tying a small, triangular knot, she dimpled the fabric at the top and smoothed it on his shirt front.

"You know how to do everything, don't you?" Kane asked, his face just a breath away from hers. He put his hands on her smooth shoulders, drawing her to him, closing his eyes. His lips met her cheek. When he opened his eyes, she winked at him and retreated to her side of the seat. Kane slammed the car into first, grinding the gears, and sped down the road.

"Right around the next curve," Dany said.

They passed through a white brick gateway. On a knoll five hundred yards away, Kane saw a stately colonial mansion, its windows gleaming in the darkening night. Before him was the winding drive, and on either side, the graceful elms, the manicured lawns and boxwood-bordered walks of Hunting Acres. It was Kane's vision of good taste and privilege and security. It bore the stamp and label of success. It certified the pedigree.

"Well?" Dany said.

"It's all right."

As they skirted a serpentine hedge, she pointed to a lily pond beyond it. "I used to come here to visit when I was a child. Used to pull a tiny boat around that pond."

"Were you a pretty little girl?"

She gave no indication that she had heard him. Talking softly, as if recalling the incident to herself, she said, "My mother died while I was visiting here. She'd never really liked the Islands, and dad brought her back to the States to be buried. . . And I remember that there was a lot of whispering going on, but no one told me. And then, my dad arrived. I hadn't seen him in two or three months. And he came into my room—the one on the corner there, on the left, on the second floor. And he hadn't shaved. And when he saw I was awake, he came over and sat on my bed. You know what he asked me? He asked me if I loved him." She turned to look at Kane. "Wasn't that an odd thing to ask? We'd been apart so often that I felt strange with him. And I told him, 'of course, I love you.' And he asked me why. For a time, I couldn't think. And then, I remembered that one day, years before, when he had taken me right over here, near this spot, and we'd sailed my boat in the pond—and I lost the string. And he took off his shoes and waded in after it." She smiled, shaking her head at the memory. "So all I could think to say was 'I love you because you went after my sailboat.' And he kissed me, scratching my face with his beard, and he left the room. And I felt so sorry for him . . ."

Kane waited for her to continue. But apparently that was the end of the story, or at least all she chose to tell. There was something so wistful about her at such times. A street or a home or an odor, a book or a song would evoke memories for her, and she would confide them to him; never it seemed, finishing the story.

They parked behind the house, and Kane caught a glimpse of the formal garden and the folded cabana awnings and the outline of a swimming pool. Beyond was a white carriage house and the stables, and the surrounding woods. And still further he could see the glistening coil of the Potomac. It was all there. Ever since he could remember, this world—Dany's world—had been for him the ultimate and the unattainable.

13

MOMENTS LATER, as they stepped up on the mansion's columned veranda, Dany whispered, "Remember, Congressman O'Connor, the first rule in politics is to always be at your best."

Lucy Field greeted them at the base of the curving stairway in the foyer. She was a plump, full-breasted, plain-faced woman in her fifties. "Dana, dear! I see you've finally brought your congressman." She put on the horn-rimmed spectacles that dangled from her neck, and tok stock of Kane. Then, pushing the glasses up to rest over the blue-gray hair on her high forehead, she held out her hand. "So glad you could come, Mr. O'Connor."

"Thank you, Mrs. Field. 'Dany's congressman' has been anxious to meet Dany's family."

Lucy laughed. When Dany and Kane finally moved on, Lucy said, "We're going to be friends, Kane. From now on we won't have to be polite to one another." To Dany she said, "See if you can find Mel, Dana. I want him to meet Kane."

Dany moved beside him, piloting him through the sea of people who jammed the spacious rooms. "I don't know how you do it," she said, "but you charmed her all right."

"I was expecting a younger, slinkier type—a mistress of intrigue. She looks more like somebody's grandma who lives in a beauty parlor." He turned his attention to the room—the paneled bar managed by a trio of white-jacketed Negroes, the full-length glass doors that closed off the area from the gardens outside, the lavish buffet spread on lace-covered tables. "There must be a helluvalot of dough in the newspaper business," he told Dany.

They stopped before a bald, mustached man who was fishing for the cherry atthe bottom of his old fashioned. "Mr. O'Connor, Mr. Harris," Dany said. Then she cued Kane. "The congressman was telling me this evening that he's a faithful reader of your column."

Kane recalled the name. Harris, distributed by the Brider Syndicate, was anti-New Deal, anti-British, anti-union, anti-communist. "The Spokesman of Reaction," the liberal press had dubbed him. "Never miss that column," Kane said. "Sometimes we get so close to what goes on here that we lose perspective. I find it helps to get your viewpoint."

Randolph Harris, whose daily diatribe was written by a well-instructed underling, acknowledged the tribute. He nodded and showed his gold-edged front teeth. "Mentioned you on my radio show last night," he said, filtering his words through his magnificent nose.

"The first one I've missed in a long while," Kane said. "But I was with Dany. And she's a Fibber McGee fan." He felt her fingernails dig into hi palm, and grinned malevolently at her. "About your show . . ."

"I noted that you got two choice assignments," Harris said, and took a deep breath. "Reade's Government Administration Committee, I think it was. And some new special committee." Another gasp for air. "What have you people got on the roster?"

"Why don't you two get together for lunch one day and talk about it?" Dany suggested.

"That's an idea," Kane said. "I might be able to give you a story."

"And you'd be able to get some of Mr. Harris' ideas," Dany ad fibbed.

"I'll do that," Harris said. "I'll ring you at your office."

Finally managing to get away, Dany pinched Kane's arm. "I owe you something for that Fibber McGee crack."

"Aw, to hell with Harris," Kane said, lowering his voice. "He's a prize jerk. By his standards Calvin Coolidge was a dangerous radical."

"Sure he writes garbage, Kane. But around four million readers eat it up every day."

As they moved about the room, pausing at one group after another to meet people, listening to a baseless rumor, adjudging a pointless argument, Kane was amazed by the crudities, the rudeness and the banality of most of the conversation that swirled about them.

They talked of literature: "Darling, all of his novels are about himself. He examines all his motives for being a homo. Really, he reminds me of one of those fakirs who spends his life contemplating his navel."

They talked of travel: "But the Germans, sweetie, the Germans are my kind of people. The West Germans, I mean. Of course Hitler was horribly brutal, but what could the people do when that little group of Nazis had all the machine guns? And after all, the Jews were taking over everything. And if we'd have just let him alone, Hitler would have gotten rid of the Russians for us. But the German people . . . well, they're really so much like us. I mean clean, industrious, efficient, decent roads and decent plumbing. You can have the French, my dear, with their *pissoirs* and their Reds, and the British with their mutton and their superiority complex. . ."

They talked of their friends: "I swear I saw him in Jamaica. And he was with a girl as black as a pimp's heart. Of course, he's on another kick. This time he's in love with niggers. Not so long ago he was a Townsendite, then a vegetarian, a Willkie Republican, and a booster of Esperanto. A few years back he took instruction for awhile in the Catholic Church. Then, having discovered Ingersoll and Payne, he became an atheist. It's the scientific process. Every action has an opposite and equal reaction. . ."

They talked of taxes, the government, psychiatry, philosophy. And they spoke in intellectual abstrations, profound and positive, as if they could take the place of the complex, uncertain realities of living. Their voices were imposing, self-satisfied, heavy with authority. It seemed to Kane that they had all moved through life on a deluxe train, knowing only their fellow passengers, seeing only a blurred vision of the passing landscape.

"Let's get a drink," he whispered to Dany.

"In a minute we can escape."

A slim, hawkfaced young woman with an incipient mustache who had been a combat correspondent in Europe, was wading through the Rhine at the moment after having hidden in the hedgerows of Normandy and crawled from the trap at Bastogne. . .and this freckled-faced youngster smiled at me and told me . . ."

They were always freckled-faced, Kane thought. And they always smiled and they always talked. The woman reminded him of all the lecturers with homey voices and pat phrases who put war in neat little tintypes that showed that all American fighting men are fearless, without doubts and would not wish to be elsewhere.

". . . so the padre, a jolly, red-faced Irishman . . ."

Kane took Dany's arm and tugged her away from the gathering. "They're always jolly," he muttered. "And invariably redfaced and positively Irish. What kind of a story would she have with a serious, plain Italian priest or even a dull, sallow-complexioned Protestant chaplain?"

"Hush!"

"I don't know if I can stomach any food right now, but I'll try. And I damned well need a drink after the tour you've had me on."

She took his hand. "They're pretty awful, aren't they?"

"I had an urge to swat that dumb bastard who loves the Germans. God, if these are the socialites, the influential—"

"You've just been listening to those who always come early to get tight faster, the ones whose money alone gets them in. They keep Lucy's charities going." They walked across the room. "I used to jump for the bait when I heard that kind of talk, and make speeches about fascists and the American Way. But I gave it up. They're all talkers, not doers. And they won't give you any argument. They just act hurt and tell you how many of their friends are Jews and how fond they are of Negro spirituals and how they didn't really mean it the way it sounded." She smiled at Kane. "I'll get us some food. You get the drinks. And I'll introduce you to some people you'll like. Okay?"

She left him in the center of the room under the great crystal chandelier, and he watched her move away, around the ornate furniture, to the buffet. Kane got their drinks at the bar and dodged through the crowded room to meet her at the buffet table.

"How come you loaded your plate and only gave me a few slivers?" he said.

"I didn't bring you here to eat."

"I'm hungry now, dammit." He turned, bumping into a plump, rosy-cheeked man with merry eyes and shiny, white false teeth. "Sorry!" he said. "But this girl of mine won't feed me. You look like a man who enjoys good food. Am I supposed to go hungry while she gorges herself?"

The stranger chewed, swallowed and licked his fingers. "Hell, no. You leave him be, Dany."

"Name's O'Connor," Kane said, extending his hand. "And I'm glad to find an ally."

Caleb Lawton introduced himself and Dany's description of him was immediately recalled: "He's in oil, chemicals, insurance, cattle and California real estate. His dough could pay off the national debt."

"I suppose I ought to know you," the corpulent millionaire said.

"I'm just a farm boy they've sent up here to vote," Kane said. "By the way, I've been doing some checking on the low supports on cattle. Tell me, from one farm boy to another, how does it affect you out in California?"

Lawton told him.

When Kane and Dany excused themselves, Caleb Lawton crossed the room to talk to Lucy. "That O'Connor's a sharp kid," he told her. "He's as interested in cattle as I am in your French perfume, but I'll be damned if he doesn't sound like he knows what he's talking about!"

"There's Monsignor Halderman," Dany nodded toward the former Holy Cross quarterback. "He's the best-looking and most literate man in the place; on top of which, he works miracles. Even got me going to Mass again." She led Kane across the room and introduced him.

"O'Connor!" the handsome cleric said. "Good to see a young Irishman in Congress." Then, taking Dany's hand, "especially one who's obviously got the kind of blarney and charm that can merit so beautiful a lady."

"It's a pleasure to know you," Kane said. "But I'm having difficulty convincing her that I have either the blarney or the charm."

"If the monsignor says it, I bow to divine knowledge."

"I wish you could have helped me settle an argument yesterday," Kane confided to the priest. "Several of us were talking in the House restaurant about the question of relations with Spain. I tried to make them see that working with Franco is surely to our best interests."

"And they brought up the persecution of Protestants," the priest said. "Isn't that natural enough? I should hope that, since we expect tolerance, we should be tolerant. But only one cardinal is responsible for the situation in Spain. It surely doesn't represent the feelings of the Pope."

"Exactly! In one breath they say we're taking dictation from Rome. In the next, they raise the devil because the Pope doesn't dictate to the Spanish Cardinal."

"I can understand the Protestant position," the priest said. "We must not be so sensitive to criticism that we ignore their honest anger. If the situation were reversed, we would probably be a great deal more voluble."

"Say, who's on whose side?" Kane shook his head. "To tell you the truth, I was trying to make a good impression with you. I thought you'd surely agree with me. But, frankly, I didn't have any success arguing with my friends because I find, deep down, I have my own doubts."

"And most American Catholics are embarrassed or upset about it," Dany said.

"Often, when we attempt to persuade others, we may only be trying to convince ourselves." The priest grasped Kane's arm. "You interest me, Mr. O'Connor. It's always rare for a man to disclose his motives—as you just did. There's a conspicuous shortage of honest men; and you appear to be one."

A few minutes later, as they left the priest, an awkwardly tall man with thinning gray hair and a face like tanned leather intercepted them. "Lucy sent me looking for you, Dany." He kissed her forehead. "First, I want to meet Mr. O'Connor and then I want to play big brother long enough to give you what-for about not writing home."

Dany put her fingers to his lips, and introduced her brother to Kane. Mel Field took Kane's extended hand. "A little advice, Kane. Don't let her start managing you."

"How do you stop her?"

"Clout her one," Mel said and slapped Dany smartly on the rear.

"You're getting to be an old girdle-thumper!" Putting her arm about his waist, she said, "And you're supposed to be the most prominent editor in town."

"The truth is that I'm a bridge-playing legman who works on his father-in-law's paper."

"A bridge player!" Kane said. "Any damned fool can be an editor. But a bridge player, that's something else. We'll have to team up."

"Great. If I play with Lucy any longer, we'll end up in the divorce notices. How about making it Wednesday night?"

They made the date; and Mel hurried off to greet another guest. "That brother of yours seems like a nice guy," Kane said.

"You're doing all right, O'Connor." Dany took his arm possessively. "You notice I'm not introducing you to any other women. They're all looking covetously at me, too."

"A helluvalot you care!"

"C'mon, I want you to meet Nate Starbecker. He's Hunting Acres' court jester." She led him toward a carved divan opposite the bar where a wizened man who needed a haircut was stretched out reading *The Chicago Tribune.*

Starbecker held out his limp hand. "Pardon my not rising, but I'm feeling like hell."

"You're always feeling like hell," Dany said. "You'll outlive me." '

"Dany tells me you're the court jester," Kane said. "Say something funny, Mr. Starbecker."

The grizzled old dwarf swung his legs off the divan, and looked up at Kane. "Well, I'll be damned! Young man, you can make history in Congress—a character who doesn't hesitate to say what's on his mind."

"It's just his bad manners," Dany said, amused.

"No. He's obviously not a hypocrite," Starbecker insisted.

"You want me to go away so you can talk about me?" Kane said.

"You stay right here, Mr. O'Connor. You're the first person I've seen all night who interests me."

"Don't you like these people?"

"Of course. Only thing wrong with them is that they believe the editorials they read in *The Express.* Otherwise, they're charming, friendly, moneyed, harmlessly-bigoted, bridge-playing reactionaries. I'm fond of them."

"I've got fifty dollars to invest," Dany said. "You have a good tip for me?"

"Columbia Railroads. They're due for a stock split," Nate Starbecker told her matter-of-factly.

Dany kissed his forehead. "Nate's responsible for my whole fall wardrobe," she told Kane. "I was overdrawn on my allowance and he made me buy Purmincar Engineering when it was way down. I talked Mel out of a loan and made six-hundred dollars in three weeks."

"Don't explain *why* I'm responsible," Starbecker said. "At my age, it's flattering to think that maybe we exchanged favors!"

She patted his cheek. "Three days after I bought, the RFC came through with a huge loan, and up went the stock."

"It'll go up again—and soon, I hope," Starbecker said. "They've got a semi-automatic rifle with a sixteen-round clip that will make the Garand obsolete. Of course, trying to get research funds is a monster task. But, if we can get the money to develop it further, you'll see another jump in the stock."

"Maybe you don't realize it, Nate, but you're talking to a member of the Special House Committee on Military Planning," Dany said.

"How do you think I keep my job, dear?" Starbecker said. "I realize it."

"Tell him how much you know about guns, Kane."

"I'm too modest," he said, sitting down beside Starbecker and tugging Dany's hand to make her join him. "Apparently the important thing about this weapon is that—if it's any good—it could increase small unit firepower." He put his arm around Dany's waist. "That's one of the things the committee is discussing, the best way to keep manpower down and still improve the effectiveness of the men who do the actual fighting."

Dany took Kane's hand away from her waist and held it. "You see, Nate? I told you he's brilliant. He's already convinced me the services ought to buy your gun."

"Well, it's not quite at that stage," Starbecker said. "What we're aiming for is a Defense Department research contract so we can continue to work on it."

"Might be a good thing," Kane conceded.

"You'll be able to appreciate what this weapon can do, Mr. O'Connor. Most important, it requires little machining. Tolerances are such that many parts can be stamped-out. Also has a terrific rate of fire. High muzzle velocity. Increased range..."

"You sound like an expert yourself."

Starbecker pulled a corncob pipe from his jacket pocket and began to tamp tobacco into the bowl. "No, I'm what is called a 'special interest lobbyist.' I represent the company."

"I've got a feeling you're good at it," Kane said. Although the conversation revolved around the new weapon and Kane contributed a few questions, his mind was still on the stock market and the promising railroad stock.

Drawing futilely on his pipe, Starbecker held another match to it. "I'd like to see you get interested in this rifle, Mr. O'Connor. With your background you could do the country a great service by introducing it."

Kane laughed. "I'm more interested right now in collecting pennies and buying some of that Columbia Railroad stock." He was thinking of his debts and the gentle, but growing pressure from the Manton Bank.

Dany was teasing Starbecker. "I'll be honest with you. If you'll guarantee the investment, Kane and I will buy."

"Since we're being so frank," Kane told them, "I've got to admit I already owe nearly all of my next two years' pay."

Starbecker gave up with the pipe and put it back in his pocket. "I've got an idea, Mr. O'Connor. Perhaps we can work something out where you could advise me on the Purmincar weapon; and I could do something for you." He didn't give Kane a chance to answer. "I have a suite at the Mayflower. Please drop by for a drink Monday night."

In the early hours of morning, Dany and Kane drove toward Washington.

"Are you going up to see Nate?"

"What kind of a fool do you think I am? I can't take a chance of accepting dough from him."

Dany watched his face in the glow of the dashboard lights. "He's not offering you a bribe."

"Nobody gives you something for nothing."

"*Something* to him may be *nothing* to you."

"That's gibberish."

"Somebody once defined politics as the science of how who gets what when and why." She slid across the seat, closer to him. "What can you lose? Go up to see him Monday."

"We'll see."

She rested her cheek against his sleeve. "I'm growing fond of you, Congressman O'Connor. You did very well tonight."

"I'm not doing so well with you."

Her eyes closed. "You're doing better all the time."

They drove in silence, each thinking about the evening. "They're quite a bunch," Kane said at last. "Money. Power. Fame." He blinked his lights at an oncoming car. "That's the way to be!"

Dany yawned and burrowed her face into his shoulder. "Everything comes with time . . . and maybe, just maybe, now's the time."

14

DANY, WEARING only her pajama jacket, sat propped against the pillows on her rumpled bed, Sunday morning's *Washington Express* spread across the easel of her bare legs. Turning to the society page, she glanced down the column headed, *Fascinating Folks.*

Aloud she read: "Congressman Kane O'Connor, Air Corps hero and one of the capital's most eligible bachelors, and Dana Payne, Washington socialite, were among the guests at a party given at Hunting Acres, the Virginia estate of Mr. and Mrs. Melvin Field . . ."

The phone rang and, reaching for it, Dany leaned over the cream-and-gold night table. "Hello."

"Good morning!" It was Kane.

Squinting at the porcelain clock on her vanity, she said, "It's good afternoon."

"You know what I've been doing all night?"

She yawned and let the newspaper slide to the hyacinth-blue carpet. "No. Tell me what you've been doing all night."

"I've been thinking. This weapon we talked about with Starbecker—the whole idea is terrific. Could save a fortune when you think of the cost of the intricately-machined rifle we're using now. Besides, it could mean a great manpower saving by increasing fire power."

"Kane, I don't know what you're talking about. All that technical talk confuses me."

"I've come up with an idea. Come on over."

"Thanks, but no thanks!" She slipped down in the bed and stretched expansively. "I've already got an idea of what kind of an idea you have."

"You'll be safe. I'm absolutely de-sexed this morning."

"That's quite a metamorphosis." She arched one long, supple leg, flexing it toward the ceiling. "What's your big scheme?"

"That's something we'll talk over when you get here. I'll have Tod pick you up."

She kicked away the covers. "What time?"

"Half an hour. I'll fix sandwiches."

She unbuttoned the cerise silk jacket. "And coffee."

"Coffee, too."

"Okay. 'Bye." She cradled the phone, her mind dallying with Kane. "He's enamoured of my intellect," she told the room; and, wriggling like a sun-lazy kitten, rubbing her smooth back against the silken sheet, purring with pleasure at the itch relieved, she finally slithered out of bed. As she padded across the carpet, she assumed the chin-up, casually haughty expression of the fashion model. "You may still look like you're twenty-one," she whispered to herself; and let her pajama top fall to her feet. Then, kicking it in the air, she caught it in her hand. "But, Dany, my dear, you're going to be twenty-six soon. And you'd better get yourself a man!"

As they drove across town, Dany told Tod about the evening at Hunting Acres.

"So our boy was in his glory."

She turned the rear-view mirror to check her makeup. "He was impressed, all right."

Tod got into the wrong lane and had to wait while a streetcar unloaded. "Kane's really in love with the trappings of success."

"And who isn't?" Taking her comb from her purse, she smoothed her hair, pulling one blonde wave toward her eyes. "The difference with Kane is that he means to have it."

"Probably true. But he's always in a hurry."

"Tod, dear, when you're in a hurry to get success, it just means you're ambitious."

He took a cigarette from his crushed pack and pushed in the lighter. "Well, you've got to be ready to take advantage of a break. But you're a fool if you outreach your luck and your ability. It's one of the dangers of trying too hard to be a success—you risk ending up a *schlemiel.* "

"Do I have to recite the American success story to you? You want me to list the men who've climbed mountains or made millions on nerve and drive and initiative?"

"Dany, sure . . ." Pausing, he lit his cigarette. "Sure you can climb mountains or make millions. But, if you're not lucky and you're not prepared, you chance breaking your damned fool neck or losing your hat and butt! You argue just like Kane. I'm saying one thing, and you're talking about what you want to talk about."

She leaned back, smiling, resting her head against the seat. "I'll have to tell him you said that."

Trying to make his point, Tod hesitated. "It's like his apartment. There's an example for you! You been up there?"

"Uh-uh. I talk like a *femme fatale,* I suppose. But I'm afraid I'm not accomplished enough to handle him at close quarters." As they turned a corner and she rocked toward Tod, she said, "I've got a feeling his path is strewn with broken hearts and lost virtue. Right?"

"I assume he's not a virgin, if that's what you mean."

She tried to picture Kane's girl, but there was only the photograph with the maudlin inscription she had seen in his office, and the chance remarks June Sands had passed. ("Laurie's a sweet girl. For one reason or another, they've put off getting married. They're really an odd pair in a way. But I guess Laurie's good for him. God knows she adores him.") Of course, Dany thought, any man wants to be adored, wants some woman to put herself at his feet. But Kane needs more than that, she reasoned. Much more. He's on his way up; and he needs a woman to help him.

"You know damned well what I mean, Tod Sands. I mean, is he taken, spoken for?"

"Don't pump me," Tod said.

"Okay," she said, patting his arm. "So you won't squeal." She took the cigarette from his hand and puffed thoughtfully. "You were saying something about Kane's apartment."

"Forgot what I was . . ." He frowned, concentrating. "Oh, yeah," he said and retrieved his cigarette. "The point I was getting at is that he couldn't wait to find a place he could afford. He had to have something that, in his opinion, reflects success. It's one of these monuments of glass and chrome and marble."

"Bet it's got a high-speed elevator, piloted by a boy dressed up like a British admiral."

"You've got it. The living room's about the size of a two-Cadillac garage. And he sits up there and looks out of his glass wall window on the tenth floor like he's on top of the world." Tod shrugged. "But he had to have it. He owes his right arm, but he had to have it."

Amused at Tod's concern, she said, "Well, the first time he doesn't pay his rent, they'll toss him out."

"Like hell! He'd mortgage his soul first. He's in love with his bathroom. Maroon and pink with piped-in ice water and music, all the necessary and usual equipment and a convenient magazine rack!"

Kane circled the black wrought-iron table in his living room while Dany and Tod sat there drinking coffee and eating ham sandwiches. "As far as I'm concerned, the fee is just gravy. I'd get behind this thing if there wasn't a dime in it." Plunging his hands into his pockets, he paced the narrow room. "It could mean revamping the whole concept of small-unit organization. It could be the answer to the whole infantry manpower problem."

"All you know about this thing is what this guy Starbecker told you," Tod said. "I'd feel better about it if you talked it over with Shepherd Reade."

"What for? I'm sick of listening to his platitudinous speeches." Then, mimicking Reade's deep-voiced drawl, 'To do business, you must *mean* business. Compromise, my boy—that's the cement that holds the House together. . . . Patience wins more arguments than rhetoric. . . .' Nuts!" Kane slapped the glass-topped table. "Dammit, I wasn't sent up here to let somebody else do my thinking. I wasn't sent up here to spend two years being an apprentice."

"I just don't want you to go off half-cocked, chum," Tod said.

"Shepherd's in a position to give you a hand," Dany said. "No harm in talking to him."

"Okay. Okay. I'll get ahold of him in the morning." He smiled at them and sighed. "You've got to understand this is a chance for me to get out of this rut. A chance to make myself heard."

"I'd like to see you make yourself solvent first," Tod said, dousing his cigarette in the saucer before him. "What's the price on your services and what's the gimmick for getting you paid?"

Kane helped himself to a bite of Dany's sandwich and, sitting down between them, outlined his plan. When he had finished, he asked, "What do you think I ought to get for it?"

"Five thousand," Tod suggested.

"No." Dany went into the blue-tiled kitchen alcove and turned on the coffeepot. "It's worth more. Seventy-five hundred, anyway."

"You think Starbecker will go along?" Kane asked.

"I think so," she said, returning to the table for her cup. "It's ideal for him. You're a member of the Special Committee on Military Planning. It's perfectly natural for you to take an interest in getting the D. O. D. to finance the research."

Tod tilted his chair back. "She's right."

"Hope I'm not sticking my neck out."

"You're not," Dany insisted. "The whole thing's absolutely legal. What's more, as Nate said, you'll be doing a real service for the country." She looked to Tod for confirmation.

"I think you're covered," he said.

The phone rang and Dany picked it up, listened, and held it out to Kane. "Long distance."

Puzzled, he sat astride the iron chair in the dining area and took the receiver, prepared to hear Laurie's voice and already worrying about how to talk to her with Dany present. But the operator channeled the call through the Universal Broadcasting System's switchboard, and Kane heard her announce, "Your call, Mr. Fallon."

"Where the devil have you been?" Kane asked in answer to Matt's greeting.

"Busy. Just back from London."

"Thought you were coming here to spend some time with me." Dany motioned to him and he held his hand over the phone, explaining to her, "It's Matt Fallon." Then, to Matt, "What've you been doing? Chasing English tail?"

He heard Matt's hoarse laugh. "No luck. My favorite procurer's a congressman now! All of which brings me to the point, buddy. I got the scoop you're a member of this new Special Committee on the military. Right?"

"Yeah. I'm working on the Installations and Equipment subcommittee. We're going to survey overseas bases. I'm not a big-shot like you, Matt. It's the only way I'll ever get another free trip across the briney."

"A con-man like you?" Matt said. "Listen, seriously, I've got a nut to crack. The network's doing a series of shows on U. S. occupation troops. I'm handling it. Germany next month and Italy later, then North Africa. The Far East is slated for early fall. We've run into the usual snarl—everybody in the Pentagon thinks it's the greatest idea since electricity, but nobody will authorize co-operation. Can you help me?"

"What do you want me to do?"

"How the hell do I know? You mean you've been in Babylon on the Potomac all this time, and you don't know the angles yet?"

"Guess I could call the public information people over there or maybe talk to the legislative liaison officer. Write me the details and I'll do my damndest."

"Great. Thanks, Kane. And how's the chippie-chasing?"

"I'm giving it up for Lent, but when you come down to see me, I'll take off a few nights and give up rhubarb and collard greens instead!"

"I'm coming to D. C. on the first of the month, so get something lined up for me. And meanwhile, call me collect when you squeeze an okay out of the Pentagon."

When Kane had hung up, Dany said, "He can help us. He has a big audience."

"Why didn't you tip him on this Purmincar business?" Tod said. "Maybe you could con him into a little air time."

"Matt Fallon's never been conned into anything." Kane walked across the room and dropped into the green leather armchair. "But I'm going to do something for him, and he's not the kind that has to be reminded. It's a helluva note, but the only time I get the feeling I'm more than a congressional digit is when somebody's looking for a favor." For a moment he was lost in his own musings. "The thing I like about Starbecker's rifle is that I'll have something I can get ahold of. I'm so damned tired of sitting there listening like all the other peasants. I want people to know I'm around."

Late the next afternoon, Nate Starbecker reclined on the settee in his Mayflower Hotel suite sipping milk. His business had been transacted and he listened while Kane talked about Hunting Acres.

"They've arrived," he said, putting his martini glass on the mantel. "They've got the world by the tail."

Starbecker pounded a pillow behind his head. "I know. They move in a technicolored universe without rainy days, nursing their impaired digestions and their blind prejudices, shaking their heads over the state of the country and pledging themselves to protect their vested interests."

Kane helped himself to another martini. "I thought they were your friends. I don't even pretend to like a lot of them. I just envy them their security."

"They are my friends. But I can still see them for what they are. Their dishonesty stems from merely lying to themselves about their motives. And that's the acid test of integrity. I think a scoundrel who admits he's a scoundrel and out for what he can get is to be trusted far more than a banker who tries to convince himself and anyone who'll listen that he's in banking to do good for mankind." He sipped his milk, pursed his dry, blue lips and dropped an ice cube into the glass. "They talk about what's good for the country, my friends at Hunting Acres. They mean what's good for themselves."

Kane sat opposite Starbecker, holding his drink on the arm of his chair, swirling the olive about. "You're a helluva one to talk, Nate. Are you any different?"

"One thing in particular I like about you. You say what's on your mind. Now, about me: I've been here twenty years; and I'll admit to having obtained favors for my clients. But at least 90 per cent of the time I was acting as an honest broker, selling an idea."

"And the other 10 per cent? Don't tell me you haven't greased some palms to pull off a deal for some private good."

Starbecker sat up, swinging his short legs off the settee. "Do you think I'm greasing your palm now?" he asked, watching for Kane's reaction.

"No. And I'll tell you why." He finished his drink, ordering his thoughts as he put the empty glass on the carpet beside his chair. "Because something important is going to come of this, something that will help the country. It's not a favor I'm doing for you, so don't get the idea that it is. I'm doing it because I'm convinced it needs to be done. As for the money . . ." He shrugged. "You won't feel that it's anything but right that your client pays you for services rendered; so what's wrong with my being paid for the extra time and effort I put out?"

"I've always believed that government's no place for a sensitive man," Starbecker said, leaning forward, stroking his chin. His glance stripped away the curtain between thoughts and words. Then, laughing, "I won't bother to puzzle out your logic, my friend. But I might tell you that over the years I've done damned little paying. The overwhelming majority of officeholders, despite their small salaries and high obligations, ignore the temptations, as great as they are."

"Because of timidity or ethics?" Kane stood, dropping the discussion. "I've got work to do. Having dinner with Shepherd Reade. I told him a little about the weapon this morning. He's interested; and I think he'll help me steer this thing."

Starbecker shook hands with him. "You'll need all the help you can get. You're taking on a tough customer when you start swinging at the Department of Defense."

"I'm not afraid of them," Kane said. "If they withhold the development money, they're jeopardizing the nation's safety."

"That's our argument, and we're stuck with it."

"It's a good one." Kane opened the door. "Now you get that letter off to me in the next couple of days. I'll do the rest."

Within a week, Tod brought a letter to Kane's office.

PURMINCAR ENGINEERING CORPORATION
Washington Office

The Honorable Kane O'Connor
Old House Office Building
Washington, D. C.

Dear Mr. O'Connor,

Our representative, Mr. Nathan Starbecker, has informed us of your interest in our experimental model semi-automatic rifle. It is gratifying to know that you appreciate the potential worth of this new weapon. We feel that with additional development and research, it can well mark a significant milestone in increasing the firepower and effectiveness of our fighting units.

To present the weapon to the American people who, we feel, are entitled to know the full story, we are most anxious to have a booklet prepared which will tell, in simple language, the great advantages of increased firepower.

We understand that you have been drafting an article, "Firepower Is the Answer," for future publication. It occurs to us that such an article would be an ideal feature for the booklet Mr. Starbecker discussed with you. We would, therefore, be pleased if you would undertake to prepare this pamphlet for us.

Since this work will require the employment of a special staff for a period of weeks as well as a considerable outlay for transportation, communications and research, we wish to help defray at least a portion of this expense. We are advised by our public relations department that the usual fee is $7,500. If you are agreeable, please advise us.

In any case, we thank you for your interest. We truly believe that any aid you are prepared to give in getting the facts before Congress and before the nation will be a great service to America's security and strength.

Very truly yours,
N. B. Purcy,
President

Kane finished reading the letter and handed it to Tod.

"I've read it."

"What do you think?"

"We've got it made, chum. We've got it made in the shade."

Drumming his pencil on the desk, Kane said, "As soon as that check comes in, I want you to buy me two-hundred and fifty shares of Columbia Railroads. Send the stock certificates to Cy as additional collateral for the dough I owe them."

Tod made a note on his pad. "Now what about the pamphlet?"

"I knocked out some stuff for the main article. Dany's going to polish it for me. It'll run maybe eight or ten pages."

"And how are you going to fill the rest of it?"

Kane held his hands out and shrugged. "The company will get you some information and you can call the D. O. D. and tell them I want some World War II pictures and casualty figures." He winked. "You can do it."

"For the thousand bucks I'm getting out of it," Tod told him, "I'd sell my old lady to a harem!"

"You can't put a price tag on what I'm getting out of it," Kane said. "I'm getting my start."

15

LONG ENMESHED in the tangled coils of routine, Kane now seized his chance to be free and hurled himself with furious energy into the task of preparing for battle.

Instinct dictated his tactics. First, there was no appeal in the weapon alone, so he must improve it, strengthen it by alloying it with the harder, purer issues of manpower, efficiency and economy. Second, a lone freshman congressman could not hope to succeed unless he attacked the men who were nominally to blame for neglect of the weapon. Provoked to defend themselves, these men would lend him the prestige he did not have. Third, he must strike hard and fast, leaving his foes unprepared, too dazed for anything but feeble counterattack.

But Kane's friends counseled otherwise. They wanted no battle and foresaw none. They insisted that his purpose should be to present an idea to Congress, and in doing so, to present himself as a calm, reasoned, thorough young man with imagination and a willingness to work; a young man who knew how to use political channels, who knew how to speak, who had mastered his subject, who was constructive; a young man who had the essentials for success in Washington.

In the end, though he was not completely convinced, he reluctantly agreed to follow the painstaking course they devised. In doing so, he traded one routine for another. And though he gave up the tactics of battle, he never relinquished his belief in its eventuality. In the long, weary weeks when he and his clerks prowled the Library of Congress, seeking precedents, when, hoping for allies, he cornered his colleagues in cloakroom or barber shop, when, hungry for information, he kept himself awake on benezedrine and coffee, and studied technical reports on small arms, when, bleary-eyed, exhausted, he faced friends and sought, then denied their advice, he insisted that his introduction of the radically-new weapon would provoke a furor which would reverberate in the halls of Congress and across the land. Hungry for recognition, he fed on his daydreams.

It was at Shepherd Reade's home in Georgetown that Kane slaved over the construction of his maiden speech. In the early hours of evening, Reade, Tod and Kane sat at a bridge table and, fortified by notes, data, a dictionary and thesaurus, rewrote a single paragraph over and again, striving for what Reade called "an old man's notion of legal perfection."

"But, Shep, all I want to say here is that funds are available in normal procurement channels." Kane scratched the stubble on his chin. "What's wrong with that?"

In deep thought, Reade waved him to silence and sat there, sucking in his gaunt cheeks. Then: "It would be prudent, first off, to check your figures with the Chairman of the Military Affairs Committee—a considerate, politic gesture. And you'd have your statement substantiated or perhaps modified."

"Okay. I'll put a question mark by that," Tod said.

Later, at midnight, with Reade's fragile, kind, ever-hovering wife above them insisting they try fruit, then cookies, then fudge, tempting them with sandwiches, urging them to finish for the night at every lull in their conversation, Kane continued to read from his projected speech.

"It's amazing to me that . . . ("No thank you, Mrs. Reade, but I'm not much for hot chocolate.") . . . It's amazing to me that a Senate committee which last year dealt with the military manpower problem, refused to hear testimony . . ."

"Now hold on there!" Shepherd Reade, eyes tearing, weary, took the sheet of paper. ("Another half hour, my dear, and we'll call it a night.") He reread Kane's words. "You can't say that. It amounts to a criticism of the Upper House. It's a breach of order."

The line finally emerged: "Unfortunately, until the present time, no agency of Congress has considered—"

Kane read another paragraph: "Restrained by a wasteful, hidebound bureaucracy, a bureaucracy lacking in vision, the Department of Defense is ignoring one of the great problems of American security."

"Oh, my boy, my boy!" Shep rubbed a knuckle around the violet patches beneath his eyes. "What do you hope to gain by that kind of statement? You're talkin' about *our* party, *our* administration, *our* Department of Defense. The opposition keeps tellin' the country that this administration is wasteful, inefficient and lackin' in vision; and you're offerin' them more ammunition!" Yawning, he patted his gnarled hand on Kane's fist. "Let's work that over."

The passage was changed: "I know that this administration is anxious to implement long-range plans which will improve the efficiency and readiness of our forces..."

"But, Kane," Tod said, rereading it again, "that's not what you want to get across. It doesn't *say* anything!" ("No, really, Mrs. Reade. I don't care for hot milk.") He pushed the glass aside. "It doesn't sound like Kane. I figure he's got to call the shots as he really sees them."

He was halted as Shep held up one hand like a traffic policeman. "Tod, both parties have some mavericks in Congress. And they get their names in the papers, even manage to get re-elected with regularity by using the party label they often ignore in practice." ("Honey, I promise. Just a few more minutes.") He sighed. "Kane, I don't say you have to always stick with the party, surely not when it's against your principles. But my boy, if we went off every which way, with every shade of opinion splinterin' this way and that, we'd never accomplish anythin'. Every so often one of these independent fellas will do somethin' outstanding, worthwhile. But over the years, the mavericks aren't the ones who get the business of Congress done. It's the fellas who've learned that to *get* along, you've got to *go* along."

"But can't we at least . . ." Kane blinked his eyes and leaned back in his chair, not bothering to complete his thought. "Better hit it again tomorrow."

"We've got plenty of time yet," Shep said as they parted. "Let's do it slowly, gentlemen. Properly, judiciously. Most of the time a gentle nudge works better than brass knuckles."

Kane and Tod walked down the steps to the street. "I don't know," Kane said. "I've still got the feeling we ought to sail into them, slug it out. All this detail and haggling over phrases . . ."

Tod tipped his hat back on his head. "Reade's an old lady, Kane, but he does know the ropes; and it's probably good sense not to look for a fight out of your weight class."

Kane jogged his shoulder against Tod's. "Why not? We've done it before, buddy."

"Yeah, but this isn't Luke Biddle you're sparring with. This is the whole damned U. S. Army!"

As his deadline approached, Kane's pace became even more grueling. He attended committee meetings, managed to make roll calls in the House, took off a day to push through Matt Fallon's request for help, studied the photographs and charts Tod had prepared for the booklet on firepower, conferred with an ordnance officer who had tested Purmincar's weapon and favored its development, arranged for a display of a working model of the revolutionary rifle, met with Shepherd Reade to work over the final polishing of his speech, dictated letters to his constituents, met delegations in his office, spoke to an Air Force Association meeting.

It was never earlier than two in the morning when he would finally stumble to bed, exhausted. And yet, the excitement, the anticipation, the promise of his impending debut stimulated him, acting as a tonic after the sluggish days of inactivity.

It was a Saturday morning when he realized that he had forgotten a date with Dany the night before. He called her. "I'm sorry," he said ruefully. "I just plain forgot."

"Did you just plain forget to call me all week?"

"I've been so busy . . ."

"I've been busy, too. You were in such a hurry for me to rehash that article for your booklet; and I worked like mad to get it ready—three days ago! You didn't even have the courtesy to pick it up!"

"Okay. I'm a rat. But I've been running around in circles, Dany. I meant to pick up that article, told Tod I was going to. And about last night, I got involved with Shep Reade and our date didn't cross my mind."

"I'm not used to being forgotten that easily."

"I'll make it up to you. I do remember that we're supposed to play tennis at Lucy and Mel's this afternoon. I'll pick you up in an hour; we can go someplace for lunch . . ."

"Don't bother!" She hung up.

Kane drove to Hunting Acres. Lucy Field, looking like a plump, bespectacled pigeon in riding clothes, greeted him at the door.

"My sister-in-law's girlishly furious with you," she said, taking his arm. "She told me that if you called, she's not here, and if you came, not to tell you she's in the gym." Comfortably happy in her duplicity, Lucy led him to the gymnasium door and, ponderously, wandered off.

Kane's knock was answered by a Negro maid. He belittled her prediction that "Miss Dany'll have a fit." But she stood her ground, smiling, pleasant, agreeable, firm and immovable. He offered promises of his own good behavior, assurances of sanctuary from Dany's wrath, excuses for her disappearance and a three-dollar bribe. She suddenly remembered duties elsewhere, and was gone.

Only Dany's towel-wrapped head protruded from the steam cabinet. She saw Kane. "Go away!"

As he approached her with a towel, he said, "I'm here to wipe your brow."

"I don't want you to wipe my brow. That's what the maid's for."

"I'm more tender than the maid," he said, and dabbed at her face as she twisted her head back and forth, trying without success to avoid the towel.

"Get out of here or I'll let out a yell that'll bring the house down!"

"Go ahead."

She opened her mouth, glaring at Kane still. He smiled back pleasantly. "All right. I warned you!" She uttered only one shrill note before he had cupped his hand over her mouth.

"You scream, honey, and I'll open this cabinet and give you something to scream about!" he said, releasing her.

"I dare you," she said with venom. "I just dare you!"

He flipped one outside latch and steam began to escape from the seams. "I always take dares."

"Damn you! When I get out of here I'll brain you with a chair."

"Come on, do it now," he said, laughing at her, and snapped the latch shut. Pulling a rubdown table across the tiled room, he got onto it, stretched out on his stomach, and leaned toward Dany, his face only inches from hers. "Now, as I was saying when you hung up on me, 'I'm sorry.'"

She frowned. He frowned. She glared at him. He glared back.
She exhaled, making a noise with her lips. He imitated the sound.
She turned her head away. He moved up on his elbows and
confronted her still.

"You're not funny," she said.

"You're the most amusing girl I know."

"You're hateful!"

"You're lovable!"

"I can't stand the sight of you!"

"I'd rather look at you than be President!"

A smile stole down from her eyes and twitched the corner of
her lips. "You're a dog, Kane O'Connor."

"You're a bitch, Dany Payne."

She smiled grudgingly as her anger subsided, and she turned
her face up to be wiped. He leaned closer and brushed the towel
gently over her damp forehead, smoothing the graceful arch of her
brows, patting her high cheekbones, dabbing at her chin. She
closed her eyes. "Oh, Kane," she said.

He leaned forward, accepting her invitation to be kissed. But
instead of yielding lips, he felt her teeth bite into his chin and he
cried out in pain. When she released him, he rubbed the tooth
marks. "You asked for it," he muttered. "I'm going to . . ."

"Hurt?" she asked. And she sounded as if she was really
concerned. "Now *I'm* sorry. That makes us even. And if you'll
agree to two things, we'll be friends again."

"Name them."

"First, I want you to come to early Mass at St. Matt's with me
tomorrow."

"Make it twelve o'clock Mass and I'll take you to lunch
afterwards."

"Agreed. Now the second thing—I want you to read the
article I worked on for the booklet."

He rubbed his knuckles over his chin. "Okay. Where is it?"

"Upstairs in a manila envelope with my pocketbook. Lucy or
Mel will get it for you. And by the time you're back I'll be
dressed. Now get out of here and send the maid in."

When Kane returned with Dany's manuscript, she was still in
the shower; and he sat down to wait for her, idly flipping through
the neatly typed sheets. Surprised by its bulk, he had expected no

more than a dozen pages, he began to read. He had finished the first page when she stuck her head out of the dressing room.

"No. Don't read it yet. I want to go over it with you. Have some questions to ask about things you might want to change. Put it down!" she said and closed the door.

Kane dropped the manuscript on the rubdown table and walked around the gym, waiting impatiently. Idly at first, then with concentration, he began to work with weights, flexing his arms and legs, testing them. Before the horizontal bar, he reached, jumped and raised himself easily. As he loosened up, he began to swing on the bar, his body floating through the arc, swinging higher.

Dany had returned. She stood in the doorway, silent, watching him, surprised by his agility, the perfect rhythm of his movements. Aware of her presence, Kane performed for her, lifting himself until his belt touched the bar, revolving slowly, then faster.

Never before had she been so conscious of his hard, lithe body. The snug-fitting black knit shirt showed the outlines of his broad shoulder blades; the white flannel trousers stretched taut over his flat stomach and slim hips; the pliant muscles of his arms coiled and flexed as he moved. His strong, shapely hands changed their grasp, and she saw his heavy knuckles, prominent and white, tense with leashed power. He began to swing again, his long, sturdy body held in a taut, straight line, higher, higher until he was balanced for an instant in a handstand, and then swept down to complete the circle. He dropped lightly to the floor and, keeping his back to her, sauntered toward the sidehorse, vaulted it, and stood beneath the parallel bars. Now he lifted himself, raising his legs parallel to the floor; and the corded sinews of his arms seemed to swell as he forced his legs up in a shaky handstand. He recovered as he came down, dropping to the floor, facing her. "Oh! Where'd you come from?" he asked, as if he were just discovering her presence.

She walked toward him barefoot, wearing dove-gray slacks and an electric-blue cashmere sweater. Her hair hung loose, waving about her shoulders. And she held her loafers and socks in one hand. "You're good! I didn't know you could do that."

He was breathing heavily and he flopped on a mat. "Can't do much anymore. Haven't had a chance very often since I left school." He caught his breath. "Whew! I'm winded." On his back, he smiled up at her. "You're beautiful."

She sat on the mat beside him, placed the manuscript in her lap and began putting on her socks. "You look boyish and healthy and clean-cut and uncomplicated right now."

He mopped his face with his handkerchief. "I'm feeling like I'm eighty . . . and you pick a time like this to wear a sweater like that!" He turned on his stomach and shielded his eyes. "Go on. Let me hear it. I won't look."

As Dany read, his admiration for her grew. He had asked her to polish his work. Instead she had rewritten it, expanding his ideas, broadening its scope. On her own she had researched the material he had only generalized about in his own first effort. With faultless logic she had built up a case for the weapon. The article was concise and factual, the arguments well developed, the possible objections weighed. And the style was direct and readable.

"*. . . the facts of atomic war require us to have small, compact, highly-mobile forces capable of operating independently. Such forces need weapons which increase the effectiveness of every man, which can be produced rapidly, which can be repaired simply. It is not enough to be prepared for a big war, a war of bombs and rockets and ships and airplanes. We must be prepared for any type of war the communist world chooses to force upon us. It is only reasonable to assume that with their overwhelming numerical superiority, they may choose to fight with conventional forces, that they may choose to push us into small wars, not a big one. But we must be ready in either instance . . .*"

"That's good!" Kane said. "That's damned good!" He sat up when she had finished. "There's a lot of it I could use in my speech. Better than what I have. Dany, I. . . I didn't realize . . ."

"What didn't you realize?"

He was on his knees beside her and he didn't answer. They watched one another for only an instant. And then he kissed her and her arms went around him. They lay side by side on the mat, his lips wandering over her face, lingering on her eyelids, brushing over her gently-parted mouth. His hands kneaded her shoulders, slipped down her sides, raising her sweater, caressing the firm flesh at her midriff, exploring the catch at her back, unhooking it.

His body was hard against hers, his tongue darting at her ear, along her neck. And the throb of his heart was in cadence with the frantic drumming of her pulses. She could hardly catch her breath and still she strained closer to him, her hands pulling his head to her neck again. As he moved to turn her to him, she saw her exposed breast. "No, Kane," she gasped. But he wouldn't hear her. "Please. Kane, please, please," she whispered hoarsely, trying to push him away, still gently. And then: "Kane. The door. The door!"

He cursed under his breath; and kissing her lightly, caressing her, he whispered, "Don't move, Dany," and bounded to the door. When he had locked it and turned back to her, she was standing, leaning against the sidehorse, her sweater hitched up, still revealing a firm, white belt of flesh, her hands behind her back, fastening her bra catch, her golden hair tumbled around her face. And she was smiling, trying to slow her thumping heart. "I told you that you were a dog, Kane O'Connor!"

Still breathless, he frowned at her. And then, smiling in spite of himself, he went to her. "And I told you that you were a bitch, Dany Payne!" For a second he recalled Laurie's use of the word and laughed. "Okay. You win this time."

Dany laughed with him. "Now let's get to work."

"I'm too frustrated for work. My hormones are banging their heads together," he said, brushing the hair from her forehead. "But I think that's one helluva good article. It'll hit the Department of Defense right between the eyes. We'll get that fight going. You wait and see."

She smoothed the shirt over his shoulders, pulled it down over his back, feeling the supple muscles there, and stuffed his shirttail in. "I'm beginning to ken you, Kane. It's because you want a brawl that you're so certain there'll be one."

He took her hands and drew her outside. "You've done a terrific job for me, Dany."

"Then promise me something."

"Promised."

"Don't cut me off again. Let me be part of things."

He kissed her nose. "You are," he said. "And we're going places, Dany. Really going places."

16

KANE AWAKENED, his mouth dry, his eyes sleep-swollen. Sirens shrieked below his window and then their melancholy voices wailed off into the dawn. He lay there on the edge of consciousness and contemplated the fragmented scenes and images of his dream.

The high-vaulted chamber of the House of Representatives . . .crowded, packed galleries intent, aroused. . . . The Press, with thoughtful faces and busy pencils, leaning forward as one to grasp the full import and meaning. Kane taking his seat. . . a moment of stunned, respectful silence and then applause that dinned the Speaker's rapping gavel into helpless quiet. . .

The wind slapped the blinds against Kane's bedroom window; and he awakened. "Today," he mumbled to the dark room, and laughed at his dream. And still, with overwhelming certitude, he knew that his vision was a miracle of prophecy, that he and fame were linked, fated, inevitable.

When he arose in the House Chamber that afternoon during a lull in a foreign aid debate, a Speaker Pro-Tempore recognized him. Fewer than a hundred congressmen were sprinkled over the banked tiers of seats. Eight bored faces glanced down from the press section. A delegation of high school children surrounded Dany and Tod in the gallery. This was the scene Kane faced as he began his maiden speech.

"Our historic duty to provide for the defense of this nation is more than a matter of appropriating funds. It is a solemn obligation to maintain an efficient.

The high school listeners passed the teacher's comments down their solemn ranks; and Kane thought he could read their lips. *"Article 1, Section 8."*

". . . this House has initiated legislation that helped raise this nation from a struggling federation of states to the world's greatest power. Our efforts turn now to retaining the way of life we have won by work and war and sacrifice."

A representative from California probed diligently in his ear. Kane watched him examine his findings.

". . . what then, is the paramount issue to anyone who studies our military posture?"

Kane let the question hang, remained silent while three congressmen strolled in from one of the lobbies, a janitor wiped spilled ink from the floor, the Sergeant-at-Arms and the presiding officer conferred and a former legislator chatted amiably with the Minority Whip. No one seemed to notice Kane's prolonged silence, and he launched into the tenth page of his text. "Manpower, gentlemen!" And he raised his voice. "And its most effective employment!"

The high school students began to straggle out of the gallery; and a woman with a big, red hat sat down behind Dany and Tod. A platoon of tourists then arrived by squads.

"There is not a man here who is not vitally interested, vitally concerned . . ." Kane said. For twenty minutes he tried every oratorical trick he knew. He spoke softly, but no one strained to hear him. He sought out the gaze of a few men whose attention he seemed to command, but their eyes soon wandered. He mentioned the names of other legislators, but arrested their notice only briefly. He departed from his text to tell a joke about a congressman and a faithless constituent, but there was only scattered laughter at the punch line, and for ten minutes thereafter the joke was retold to those who had started to listen too late.

"Let us examine some figures now," Kane said. "In the year World War II ended . . ."

Below him a tin of aspirin was passed hand-to-hand down one row of Republicans, across the aisle, along another tier of seats until it reached a suffering Democrat who then acknowledged the manifestation of bipartisanship by a wave and a courtly bow to his benefactor among the opposition.

One of the page boys brought Kane a note from Shepherd Reade: *Please yield briefly to Shoat, Oregon. His Governor is present, but must leave.*

Kane relinquished the floor while he was thanked profusely by his colleague and the distinguished guest was introduced. Standing again, uncertain of where he had left off, Kane fumbled through his papers. The buzz of conversation increased and he had to request the floor from the Speaker Pro-Tempore before the House could be gaveled back to order.

"And so, I commend to your attention this answer to our military problem . . ." Kane plodded on. But there was no heart left in him. The muted talk on the rostrum, the intermittent traffic to the cloakrooms, the vast emptiness of the chamber, the few, good gray faces that appeared to be listening—all seemed an affront to him, a betrayal. He felt like an actor in a bad play, mouthing lines to a restless audience that only wanted to be free to go home. And when he sat down again and was greeted with an enthusiastic motion for adjournment, his throat was constricted, his chest tight, his stomach queasy, hollow. He knew the physical pain of intolerable frustration.

Shepherd Reade congratulated him: "Well done, son. Made a fine impression. Good platform manner, too!" He put his arm around Kane's shoulder. "Be sure to check the transcript carefully and weed out your joke and a few loose constructions before it goes into the record."

Dany and Tod were waiting for him outside the chamber. "It was a fine speech, Kane," Dany said, grasping his hand.

"Yeah."

"Really." Her eyes gave her away. "Well, the papers'll pick it up. After all, you haven't had time to get a reaction."

Kane looked soberly at Tod. "Well?"

"Well, what?"

"What do you think?"

"I think you 'shoulda stood in bed,' but, hell, chum, I don't know."

"I felt like . . . like I was all alone, like a priest mumbling in Latin to a bunch of restless savages."

"There's still the booklet," Dany said.

"Yeah, there's that."

Tod said, "Just have to wait and see. Could catch fire all of a sudden. Stranger things have happened."

The passing of a week brought no reaction from the Pentagon, no questions from the press, no passionate converts to the cause of firepower, no supporters of efficiency to Kane's camp.

The miracle weapon was a dead issue; and the attempt to breathe life into it had failed. In Matt Fallon's Carlton House suite, with Matt, his date, Tod and June Sands, and Dany, Kane held the wake—a late-night vigil over the semi-automatic, gas-operated, rotating magazine-fed, lever-actioned corpse of Purmincar's rifle.

"This is what we've got to show for all our work," Kane said, and waved a handful of clippings at his listeners who were seated on hotel-brown sofas on either side of him. "This from Randolph Harris . . ."

"That boob!" Matt Fallon slipped his hefty arm around his date's fragile shoulders. "Isn't he a boob, Windy?"

The girl, Dany's friend from her modeling days at Garfinkel's, was very petite, very pretty, very gay and just a little bit drunk. "Politics has—have?—I mean it's always fasc'nated me."

"Me, too, honey," Matt said with his tight-lipped smile. He had come to Washington to enjoy himself; and for him there was humor and fun to be had in the aftermath of what Kane considered a tragedy. Matt Fallon had few of the formal requirements for success as a commentator. His knowledge of history was sketchy. He had a faulty memory. He had read too little, knew it and could find little time to read more. He was unconventional in his personal life. He was impatient with painstaking research and routine. But he had two characteristics that gave him a chance at success: a healthy disrespect for most people and institutions, and an insatiable, wide-ranging, easily-aroused, perceptive curiosity. "It looks like you're going to insist on reading that tripe," he said to Kane. "So get it over with."

Kane was mumbling over the first two paragraphs of the Harris column. "He says, 'The Administration isn't interested in an American weapon. They're too busy playing patty-cake with the Limeys who, as usual, have their own plans on how to spend our money. For years our military program has been hatched and directed from 10 Downing Street.'"

"Well, he's a horse's ass," Tod said. "But the Brider Syndicate edit was good, I thought. And, after all, that's a helluvalot of papers."

"Mel told me they only used it in the smaller towns," Dany said. "Nothing in Chicago or New York or Philly."

"I've got it here somewhere," Kane said.

"Tod, honey, our baby-sitter's going to have a fit if we don't get home." June Sands, a big, raw-boned, gentle brunette who had given up high heels, a career as a department store demonstrator and an independent spirit for her husband, started to rise and was firmly tugged back.

"Here it is," Kane said, and read: "'A few brass hats in Washington have their own little empire. It's time a man with backbone stood up and insisted that the American people get the full story.'"

Matt had coaxed Windy's head to his shoulder and now his meaty, freckled hand cradled it there. "I recall seeing a column or something in *The Register* in New York. Did you get ahold of that?"

"The ethics business, Kane," Dany said, and getting up, helped him sort the clippings to find it.

"It was a blast," Tod said. "You probably deep-sixed it along with the *New York Times'* article."

"It's awfully late, Tod," June said.

"Let's stay up all night," Windy said, rousing. "Let's drink coffee and play charades."

Dany found the clipping and read it. "'Is it ethical for a member of Congress to accept funds from a private enterprise, particularly when the congressman is sitting on an influential committee? Does Mr. O'Connor, in preparing a booklet for the Purmincar Company, lay himself open to criticism when he accepts money, no matter for what purpose, from a corporation that stands to benefit from his actions?'"

Kane ground out a cigarette on the sole of his shoe, looked for an ash tray, tossed the butt, and missed. "You see, they ignored the real issue entirely and went off on their own petty, unjustified tangent."

"Like hell they did," Matt said and stroked Windy's milk-white arm. "It's the only newsworthy item, from a newspaperman's viewpoint—and I don't include your brother's reactionary rag, Dany dear—that's worth any space at all. How much did they pay you for writing that stuff? And, incidentally, it was smoothly done."

"Too little to talk about," Kane said.

"How about 'bottichelli?'" Windy said. "Tha's a won'erful word game."

"They tell me you picked up quite a fee, Kane," Matt said.

"Did they tell you that . . .?" Tod began.

"We've got to go now," June said, interrupting.

"In a minute," Todd said and leaned toward Matt. "Did they tell you that when the second half of the fee came in my high-minded boss refused it, sent it back because . . ."

"Because it wasn't the job I promised to do. It didn't work out. I need money," Kane said. "But not bad enough to take it that way."

Dany sat on the arm of the sofa. "Kane did the right thing, the honest thing."

"We shouldn'ta lef' the club. Loved that band. Never min' the politics. Let's play somethin'," Windy said.

"We'll play—later," Matt told her and squeezed her delicate arm.

"Matt, tell me, what did I do wrong? Why couldn't we reach anybody?" Kane bent over the table and mixed another bourbon and water. "That's what I don't understand."

Dany said, "Kane, we've been over this a hundred and one times."

"We didn't dramatize the thing," Tod said. "We're agreed on that."

"Matt?" Kane said.

"Well, Tod's hit the main point. Hell, Kane, accept it. People will forgive a lot—practically anything—but dullness. And that speech was dull, dull, dull. You didn't have an issue in the first place. All right, we ought to have more firepower per man per unit. Everybody agrees, even the Army. But they intend to do it their way; and even you will concede they know a little more about weapons than you do."

"It's the military mind, Matt," Kane said. "They're never receptive to new ideas. They're still using a machine gun developed in 1914."

"Right!" Tod said. "We should have crawled some individuals. We should have questioned the testimony they've been giving before the Senate. We could have proved that the Army's spending a fortune to develop something on their own, from scratch." He turned to June. "Baby, will you please sit still a minute? I'm coming! Just hold your horses."

"So what?" Matt said. "If you wanted to criticize the Army, you should have baldly done just that. Instead, you beat the drum for some commercial outfit."

"Matt's right." Dany smoothed the lap of her dress and took a light from Kane's cigarette. "If you'd have made direct charges on the floor, the least that would have happened is that the Military Affairs Committee would have had some brass on the carpet."

"Kane couldn't make any charges. He couldn't even talk straight-honest-to-God English. Shep Reade was calling the shots," Tod said.

"I got an idea," Windy said. "Let's sing songs."

"You know why Reade was calling the shots?" Kane stuffed the clippings in his pocket. "Whose idea was that?" he asked, nodding to Tod. "Who insisted that . . ."

"We both thought," Dany said, "that you ought to get his advice."

"What's the use of hashing it all over, Kane?" Matt said. He stood and stretched, yawning. "It's finished. You didn't accomplish anything. But you got some experience. As somebody's said, 'Wisdom comes from disillusionment.' And— aside from a few articles like that bit on congressional ethics, you didn't get hurt. Now you nice people go home."

"No!" Windy said. "Too early. Let's. . ."

"Lets you relax. I'll let you hang around awhile before I ferry you to your quarters. But these older folks have got to go."

When Tod and June and Dany had said their good-bys and stepped out into the corridor, Kane shook hands with Matt. "Enjoyed the evening, old buddy. When are we getting together again?"

"Maybe I'll get back once more before I'm off to the Orient. They know you at the Pentagon, pal. Our series on the occupation forces is set. We'll start shooting in about six weeks, probably work in Japan in September."

"I'm going out there, too," Kane said. "Start in Hawaii on a sub-committee tour of bases with four other congressmen. Then to Guam, the Philippines and Japan. No dates yet. Probably depends on adjournment."

"I'll write to you. Maybe I can handle it so we'll be in Japan the same time you are. No reason why I can't work it out. We'd have a ball."

"Matt, about this fiasco I've been through . . ."

"Take my advice, Kane. There are certain hidden laws that govern politics. They've been made by time and tradition and selfish men. But, somehow, they seem to work, and for the best. So don't fight 'em. Join 'em. And even when it hurts, stay honest!" He glanced over his shoulder to the sofa where Windy, her shoes off, her tiny feet wriggling in the air, was singing *"Give me lan', lotsa lan' . . . da-da-da-da-da-da-da . . . don' fence me in . . ."*

"Now get out of here, Kane," Matt said. "I've got a feeling your old pal's going to score tonight!"

Down the hall, they all waited silently before the elevator.

"You know what our real mistake was?" Kane asked suddenly. "We didn't do what I knew we had to do all along. Remember how we won that first campaign, Tod? We woke people up, didn't we? We didn't mince around. We slugged. And that's what we should have done this time."

"Yeah," Tod said.

"I hate to face the baby-sitter," June said.

Dany held Kane's arm and leaned against him. "You're right. I know it now."

"Well, if nothing else, I've learned. I've learned that no matter how right you are—and we were right—it means nothing if you don't get people behind you. And I've learned that I'm *me*. I'm not Shep Reade and I'm not a sit-on-your-butt-and-behave-till-you-get-seniority-congressman. I'm *me*! And I'm going to act like me. When the time comes I'm going to fight the only way I know how. In Manton we didn't have Shep Reade and we didn't follow anybody's book of political etiquette and we didn't kiss anybody's rear. That's the way it's going to be with me from now on."

From that moment of avowal, his life was to turn on that promise, a promise made in the flush of anger and frustration and despair.

17

JUNE CAME and with it a gradual diminishing of Kane's pang of disappointment, a resumption of dull routine, daily involvement in committee meetings, the happy release oplanning his congressional tour, a social round of ever-increasing tempo with Dany.

And still, since he worked in the shadow of men of renown and played in the shadow of men of wealth, since he moved always on the fringe of national events and on the dizzying edge of public notice, he was persistent, undeterred in the fervor of his intent to "do things, be somebody."

One afternoon, tired after a day-long session of the Government Administration Committee, Kane returned to his office to find a constituent waiting.

Joe King, the pink, smooth, pudgy city commissioner who had helped raise funds in both of his campaigns, greeted Kane. "Good to see you. Damned if I realized you fellows actually did any work."

They disposed of the initial pleasantries as Kane led him to his inner office. Then, while King talked, Kane examined an unopened letter he found on his desk. It had the Manton Bank seal on the upper left-hand corner. They're on my back again, he thought.

"I'm behind you a hundred per cent on what you're doin' here," King said, swallowing an incipient belch and patting his protruding belly as it growled ominously. "Read how you gve the Army the works. Editorial in *The Argus*. But you can't neglect the things that keep the folks at home satisfied," King droned on. "Right now I'm counsel for State Salvage; and we're havin' a helluva time gettin' anybody in Washington to release some surplus property. There's an omnibus bill, but it's settin' in committee. I need your help, Kane."

"I'll check it for you, Joe. How long will you be in town?"

"Until I find out why these bureaucrats up here are keepin' the heavy equipment under wraps."

Kane agreed to call him at the Shoreham as soon as he could investigate the situation.

Tod ushered Joe King out and, with a significant raising of eyebrows, handed Kane another letter. It was a note on Mayflower Hotel stationery; and a check was clipped to it. *"You're a gentleman, sir. But our agreement was dear. You produced the pamphlet as ordered. Check returned with thanks."* Nate Starbecker's signature was scrawled at the end.

It was with a sense of relief, of reprieve that Kane put the note and check aside and opened the bank's letter—from Cy.

". . . the State Examiners are not satisfied with the status of your loan. It remains unreduced; and, in addition, we are holding two notes from you for unpaid interest. The collateral you forwarded recently still leaves the margin requirement below our agreed amount. If you can't send us at least eight thousand dollars, I suggest we sell enough collateral to bring the principal down. The Columbia Railroad shares, on recent quotation, have increased in worth. It might be best to take your profit now. The Examiners require our action in the next ten days; so it is important that you give this matter your immediate attention."

For a moment, Kane toyed with the Purmincar check that had come back to him. But, actually, he had promised a thousand dollars to Dany and a thousand to Tod as reimbursement for their work. He owed that to them. And the remaining seventeen-hundred and fifty dollars would be too little to satisfy the bank. The railroad shares—if they continued to go up—were his chance of regaining solvency. He did not want to sell them.

His helplessness, his inability to be free of the dunning, his fear that the future promised no solution—these things gnawed at him. And he vowed that somehow he would pay off his obligations and would never be in debt again.

He noticed the blue envelope on his desk, and knew that it was another letter from Laurie. Opening it, he read: *"My darling, I'm so tired of the separation, so sick of the endless waiting. . . ."* Kane tossed it aside without finishing it. "Same business," he muttered. "As if I didn't have enough on my mind!"

Meanwhile, Tod walked with Joe King down the corridor from the office. "Tod, see to it for me, will you?" Joe said. "Don't let Kane give me the brush-off on this."

"You know what I always say, Joe: 'What's in it for Uncle Tod?' "

"Well. . ." uneasily. Then: "I won't forget you come Christmas."

"My birthday's tomorrow."

Joe King jingled the coins in his pocket. "How many birthdays you had this year?" Then, watching the fixed smile on Tod's face, "Okay. It'll be a happy birthday."

A few days after his first visit, Joe King returned to the office in response to Tod's summons.

"Everything depends on the omnibus bill," Kane told him.

King wanted to know what the chances were. "We've got enough foreign orders right now to put us in the dough, but we've got to get our hands on the stuff."

"I think the bill will pass," Kane said. "But it's going to take a lot of pushing. There's one segment of Congress that thinks the gear should be junked to keep it off the market. Another group wants it kept in mothballs. We'll have to fight it out on the floor, if it ever gets reported-out."

King slouched in his seat, scratched at a gravy stain on his sleeve. "I'm not interested in the armament stuff. I'm talkin' about construction machinery—bulldozers, cranes, earth-movers. It's all in a depot not eighty miles from Manton."

Kane had rehearsed his strategy. He was determined to see it through. But first, he reasoned, he had to make King realize that everything depended on his own actions. "You see," he said, rapping his knuckles against the desk, "it's all on one bill. Of course, if we could get the construction gear on a separate bill . . ."

"That's the thing to do!" King hunched over, his heavy jowls drooping like hound's ears. "To the devil with fightin' the battle for ever'body else. We want the construction equipment released."

"It's an awfully delicate maneuver, Joe," Kane said tentatively. "Of course, it'll take time and persuasion and . . ."

"There's a heap at stake, Kane. It's 'bout time for you to be thinkin' of the Senate in another few years, you know. It'll help to have influential friends down home. This is a big outfit; and we're countin' on you." He lowered his voice. "Tell you the God's truth, Kane. this is the biggest thing I've ever come on. Means a lot to me."

Means a huge fee and a nice hunk of the profits, Kane thought. "Joe," he said, "I'll tell you frankly. I'm just a freshman."King sat up, his eyes narrowing. "What do you mean?"

"Nothing illegal, of course. But it's easier to sell an idea if you can get the boys away for a week end. Have some entertainment for them, maybe a few gifts for the wives." Kane relaxed in his chair, slapping his hands against his knees and sighing. "That's not my kind of pool, Joe. And I don't want any part of it." He shrugged. "But that's the only way you'll manage to get this through."

King pinched his pudgy double chin. "How much, Kane?"

He scratched his head now, as if deliberating. "I'd say two thousand ought to do it."

King smiled, nodding. "Sure, Kane. That sounds all right." Kane sensed that King had been prepared to pay more and reluctantly told himself that it was too late to change the figure.

"Now that that's out of the way, Joe, there's something you could do for me."

King thought: The nerve of the guy! He said: 'Of course, anythin' I can . . .'"

"Well, I'm a little strapped at present. Could you lend me five thousand dollars? Say for ninety days?" Before King could answer, Kane said, "Now if you can't manage it, why that's perfectly okay. Understand now, it won't make a bit of difference as far as the salvage thing goes. That's my duty to a constituent and, besides, the gear is wasted, rusting away where it is. The government ought to realize something from it."

"Sure, Kane. Sure, I understand."

A week later the *Congressional Record* reported: *Congressman Kane O'Connor: While equipment lies rusting and rotting, while the money of the American taxpayer is wasted, the web of bureaucracy spins tighter . . .*

Within a month, with Shepherd Reade's help, a special rider was tacked on an appropriations bill. And late in August, two days before the House voted itself a holiday, efficiency triumphed over bureaucracy. The bill was passed.

On the night before his return to Manton for the recess, Kane and Dany stood before her door.

"I'm going to miss you, Kane. Two weeks at home, and then you'll be going overseas."

"Why not break tradition and let me come in for awhile?"

"I'm a firm believer in tradition."

"Please?" He put his hands on her shoulders.

She leaned against him, her cheek brushing against the grain of his face. "What will the neighbors think?"

He tilted her chin. "To hell with the neighbors."

"Good-by, Kane." She kissed him. He held her closer, stroking the warm smoothness of her back. Her hand pressed gently, firmly against his chest, pushing him away. Then she stepped inside and closed him out.

Late on the night of his homecoming, Kane and Laurie drove to Tower Rock. She had been quiet, depressed during the evening; and he had taken her there—the scene of youthful rendezvous — hoping to break her mood, dreading the inevitable confrontation.

They sat on a giant granite slab covered with moss as thick and soft as a bed, and looked over the rhododendron-starred slopes of the mountain, into the moon-swathed valley below, hearing only the wind and the sound of their voices.

"Darlin', I've waited," Laurie said. "I've agreed to anythin' that would make it easier and simpler for you."

He tried to kiss her, but she moved away. "I know you're tired of waiting, honey," he said, putting his arm around her shoulders. "But being moody like this isn't like my sweet gal."

She stood up and moved to the guardrail before the precipice. "Stop tryin' to humor me, Kane!" The wind blew her hair behind her and she held to it with one hand. "I'm sick and tired of bein' the good, sweet girl back home. I'm sick to death of feelin' like a ghoul, waitin' for my mother to die!"

Never before had Kane analyzed his reluctance to marry. His life, as he lived it now, was satisfying. He didn't feel the need for fireside and nursery. The shackles of domesticity were not inviting. He knew that Laurie was loyal, pretty, honest, kind, devoted—the things one assumed a wife should be. And he hadn't considered giving her up. He knew that he would marry her—one day. And he knew, too, that whenever that day came, she'd be waiting. "It won't be much longer, Laurie." He went to her and took her hands. She was so wretchedly unhappy, so defenseless, so lovely with the swimming eyes and trembling lips. But why, oh why, Kane thought, does she have to whine?

"When you first came back," Laurie said, "it was 'as soon as the office is set.' Then it was 'as soon as the campaign is over.' And then you wanted to 'learn your job.' And now. . ." She drew her hands away. "What's it goin' to be next time, Kane?"

"Laurie, it was your idea that we should wait when your mother . . ." He looked out into the darkness again. "I thought that's what you wanted. At least you told me that's what you wanted. It wasn't my idea. Now, as soon as I get back, you go into a sulk and start blaming me!" He had a point; and knowing that it was weak at its core, he continued to belabor it. "I took you at your word. I went off to Washington, living in a tiny apartment, trying to save enough to get free of my obligations so you wouldn't be burdened with them."

In five minutes he restated his innocence and her responsibility with such force and injured pride that he all but convinced himself, and she was retreating.

"Kane, I know it was my idea at first."

"You think I'm making something up? Ask Cy how I'm sweating to pay off the bank." He saw that she was crying softly; and he put his hand lightly on her shoulder and turned her to him. "You're still a baby," he said, and taking the carefully-folded handkerchief from his breast pocket, he held it to her nose and commanded, "blow!"

She dried her eyes, still sniffling. "I'm no baby. I'm twenty-four and gettin' older by the minute."

"Poor thing," Kane said in mock sympathy, "I can see you now at fifty, waiting coyly in the marriage bed."

They laughed. "When you're here it's different," Laurie said. "But when you're not, I—Kane, I'm so lonely." She kissed him.

During his stay in Manton, Kane was with Laurie constantly. Together they took long rides through the mountains, resting their horses beside trout streams, picnicking there. They climbed the peak of Samson's Ridge; and Kane told her that it was a foothill compared to the Rockies. They danced in the mile-high air of the Sky Casino. They attended the Community Theater's production of *John Loves Mary*. They ate savory, spit-turned barbecue and potatoes baked in the coals of a campfire. They spent time with Cy and their married friends. These were happy, proud evenings for Laurie; and they were dull, weary ones for Kane.

Those were evenings of watching home movies of faded honeymoons at the beach (with Cy convulsing the viewers with an off-screen commentary). Evenings of admiring wrinkled infants, having them thrust in his arms and worrying lest they foul him. Evenings of planned stunts and ice cream, cake and punch, of women in one comer chattering about their gynecologists, reducing exercises, obstetrical experiences and domestic help, and the men in another comer, snickering over dirty jokes about Frenchmen (told in a modified Italian dialect), speculating on the next president of Rotary, trading the jovial insults of civic-club fellowship and modestly admitting their unfailing business acumen.

Kane saw his Aunt Mady and Uncle Wesley only once.

He had left the small Catholic church with Laurie after attending Mass. They walked down the street together to his car and he thought of the many times he had taken those same steps from his church to wait for his aunt and uncle as they left their services. Then he saw them. The judge was holding Aunt Mady's elbow, helping her down the steps. Kane left Laurie, walked over and offered his arm.

"I don't want your help," the crippled old woman told him. "Now get out of here before I use my stick on you!" His uncle, head down, had not spoken. Kane shrugged and turned away.

During the second week of September, two days before his scheduled flight abroad, Kane said his good-bys, left Laurie and Cy and the serenity of Manton and flew back to Dany and Washington and the MATS plane that would take him to the Orient.

18

FROM HIGH above Kyoto, at the window of his room in the Hotel Miyako, Kane watched the setting sun, the prism of its rays reflecting a mosaic of rose and amber and magenta and blue. Below him were the crimson columns of the *Heian* shrine, glistening in the twilight like a lone island of order amid the swooping waves of gray tile and thatch. And lying beyond was the exquisitely graceful garden of the *Ninnaji,* a sward of green, of rock-bound ponds and bridges and artificial hills and arbors and pagodas. And still further, seeming to swallow the sinking sun itself, he thought he could see the tinted-glass surface of Lake Biwa.

"Right purty, huh, cousin?" Congressman Stewart Denton, wearing only a broad-brimmed Stetson, a limp towel and handsomely-tooled western boots, stood at Kane's elbow and scratched himself. "In a way it makes me think of sundown around Rocky Branch with Catseye Lake off in the distance."

"Stu," Kane said, "for a Congressman, you've got some amazingly original thoughts!"

Stewart Denton laughed. "You know what I mean. Sure, - home's a lot different. You don't get this hemmed-in feelin' and things aren't scaled down like here. But the colors and all . . . the sky . . . the water . . ." He dropped his long, gawky frame on the unmade bed and stretched. "Of the five of us on this subcommittee, Ward Roberts and you are bachelors, havin' a hoedown, and the other two geezers love bein' made over by the Brass, and I'm a sick dogie, all tuckered out. Ole cowboy like me's been runnin' around too much, too far from his own range."

The "Ole Cowboy" was twenty-five. He had been forced to wait three months before being seated, since he was only twenty-four when elected to Congress. And in the preceding years he had managed to graduate with honors from Montrief Christian College, work four months playing a guitar, singing and announcing in a small town radio station, marry the boss's gay, pretty daughter, make a recording of "The Lord Sure Is Waitin' For Me," (Gospeline Records—1,000,000 copies), become what *Downbeat* called "the nation's top country singer," announce for Congress and strum and sing his way to a run-off victory over a man who had not been defeated in ten years.

Kane padded across the thick-ribbed matting on the floor and found his shoes under the American-style bureau. "Get moving, you 'Ole Cowboy.' Matt Fallon ought to be in from Osaka by now. You and I and Ward have to get down to the bar to meet him before the two senior old maids on this subcommittee decide we ought to work on reports tonight. Let's go. Matt's taking us to the *House of Heavenly Reward!*"

"I'm a married man, Cousin Kane. And I'm mindful of my responsibility to the United States. And I've got a good upbringin'. And if you think I'm gonna go catin' around some geisha house with you and your television friend . . ." He sat up in bed and tugged his boots off. ". . . you're durn right!"

Kane said, "I promise you'll come out as pure as when you go in." He slipped into his jacket and loaded his pockets with loose change and cigarettes and keys. "Now, move! I'll see if Ward's back from the pool yet. Meet you down below."

Kane knocked at the door of the adjoining suite and was invited in. Congressman Ward Roberts was combing his thick, black hair in front of a full-length mirror, then smoothing his gray temples with his handsomely-manicured fingers. "Good evening, Kane," he said, and his manner was nearly shy as he motioned him to a seat. "Couldn't resist having a swim when I got back from the museum. I wish you'd have come with me."

"The chairman handed me a brief this afternoon. I'm supposed to visit Atami Field at Yokohama day after tomorrow, and I've been working on it." Kane reached for a cigarette, but before he could take it from his crumpled pack, Ward snapped open a silver case, offered it, and held a light for him.

"Sorry you had to miss the museum," Ward said, and began to polish his tie clasp with a blitz cloth. "You liked the gardens we saw this morning. Well, the pictures in the museum can be compared to those gardens. Beauty is there all right, all around you, but it's concealed. You discover it for yourself, and in the discovery is what's been called the tryst between artist and beholder."

There followed an appraisal of Japanese art which was incisive, informed, appreciative and fifteen minutes long. Ward Roberts, his soft, musical voice rolling on, his short, slim body turning first to the mirror as he knotted his tie, then to Kane, talked about the idealistic and impressionistic and romantic and realistic styles in Japanese art. He explained mood—"the painting of what one feels, not only what one sees." He dwelt on life-motion and the quality of brush strokes, and then talked about spacing and the preservation of tradition—none of which interested Kane, much of which impressed him, and all of which could be found, though Kane did not know it, in volume II, page 444A of the *Encyclopaedia Britannica.*

Ward Roberts was carrying volumes II and III on his tour so that he might keep up his avowed intention of completing the entire encyclopaedia by June of 1956. He had read a Marquand novel where the hero had the worthwhile intention of doing the same thing; and Ward had decided—though he had left the book unfinished in an Altoona hotel—that it was a good idea.

Kane listened; and when Ward, at last, paused briefly, Kane said, "I see what you mean." And didn't.

Ward Roberts was born in Carbondale, Pennsylvania in the shadow of the railroad shops, not ten miles from Kane's birthplace in the anthracite fields. There Ward's short, slim, frail body and soft voice had forced him to do battle. At fifteen—because he looked twelve and had the appearance of a waif—he was earning forty dollars a week as pick-up man for a butter-and-eggs numbers' game. At seventeen, because he told the registrar how he'd ridden a freight to Philadelphia, because his milky-fleshed body was evidence of the sacrifice he had made to get there—he was admitted to the University of Pennsylvania and given a self-help job. At twenty-two he was in law school, booking risqué movies into fraternity houses to earn his tuition.

When he graduated, he promised himself he would repent his delinquencies by being scrupulously honest. And, in fact, considering the nature of his practice, he was as honest as was feasible. For the next fifteen years he had been a successful trial lawyer; and he had done so by playing the part of the perennial juvenile, appearing to jurors, judges and opponents as an inexperienced, naive and frightened youngster, gentle with witnesses, deferential to opposing counsel and apparently frightened by the majesty of the court. Since he was thirteen, Ward had been using his handicap of physical frailty and youth. And now, serving his first term in Congress, he was still using it.

"Spent the afternoon with our intelligence people," Ward said. "Nearly missed the museum, but it was something I had to do, sort of an informal survey I'm making for some friends of mine in the American Patriots. You've heard of the organization, haven't you?"

Kane had a vague recollection of a militantly patriotic group that had polled his views on communism, fascism, racial-mixing and the United Nations. "Yes. Don't know much about the outfit, though."

"In my part of the country it's gaining strength every day," Ward said. "Money behind it. They really came through for me during my campaign. Well, I'm writing some articles for the newsletter, *Truth*. We're concerned about anti-American feeling and communist influence in the countries, like Japan, that are living off our charity. . . ."

Kane started to dust his ashes on the matting, but in deference to Ward's immaculate habits, caught them in his hand. "Sounds interesting," he said, cutting into what promised to be a long speech. "But we'd better talk about it some other time. Matt'll be four drinks ahead of us."

Ward tried on a glen plaid sports coat, examined himself in the mirror, tried a camel's hair jacket instead, liked it and announced that he was ready. He opened the door and held it for Kane. "It's a great thing, you and Stu and I being on the same two committees. We'll make a good team. And I want to talk to you both—particularly you, Kane—about the American Patriots."

The rickshaws clacked down the cobbled street, their runners striding smoothly through the night. The roadway was alive with pedestrians and street vendors and honking taxis; and the jogging Japanese cursed as they were stopped by traffic. Up ahead a black-uniformed policeman was berating a truck driver, emphasizing his abuse with a rain of blows on the man's head. And, crowding around the rickshaws, little boys held out their hands and cried, "Chew gum? Chew gum?"

Kane turned to Matt Fallon who rode beside him. "Got any?" Matt tossed a stick of spearmint and Kane threw a handful of yen notes, laughing as the boys scattered, diving for the money.

A few yards behind, Stu and Ward rode abreast. Warm with rice wine, happy with their freedom in Kyoto, they sang, "Oh, my darlin', oh, my darlin', oh, my darlin' Clementine. You are lost and gone forever . . ."

Again the rickshaws halted. "Just a honey cart," Matt explained as they watched a man dip excrement from a sidewalk well and load his rickety wagon. Across the street stood a pastry shop and the good warm smells of hot pies and bread mingled with the foul odors of the road.

"Hey, Cousin Matt," Stu called. "Where in blue blazes is this joint? Ward here keeps plyin' me with spirits, so I already broke one resolution tonight. I wanna be sober enough to hold to the other one!"

"Just a little way now," Matt shouted back as the runners turned down a canopied alley.

"I'm depending on you, Matt," Kane said. "After the buildup I've been giving you, my friends expect to find women."

"Don't think I don't appreciate the honor of pimping for a congressional tour."

"This junket's really surprised me," Kane said. "I thought it was going to be a joy ride, but we've seen a lot; and we'll take back ideas for consolidating facilities . . ."

"Borax!" Matt said, smiling. "Newsmen and Congressmen who come out here see what they want us to see."

"No, honestly, Matt, maybe we've been wined and dined and buttered-up along the way, but we've seen everything we've asked to see."

"I'll bet you fifty bucks there's something in Yokosuka you won't see. I conned one of the Navy medical officers into telling me about it. It's too strong for TV. The FCC would cut me off the air if I used it. But, Loverboy, I'd like to look the place over."

"Well what the devil is it?"

"Fifty bucks says even your congressional pull can't get us inside. Okay?"

Kane hesitated briefly, then: "It's a bet. No matter what it is, I'll get to see it. Now what is it?"

"You get rid of your buddies in Yokohama tomorrow, and we'll ride over to Yokosuka to the naval base. You can try to use your influence on the Navy. Now don't ask me anything else. Just wait until tomorrow."

Behind them Stu was singing again. "Lay me dowoon, lay me dowoon. I'm a pore weary sinnuh . . ."

". . . poor weary sinner," Ward echoed, off-key.

The rickshaws stopped and Ward insisted on paying the runners. Matt knocked on the shutters, calling out in Japanese. A small bowlegged woman, bowing and smiling, opened the door and let them in. "Ah! Fallon-san!"

"Ah! Mama-san!" Matt said and pinched her cheek.

They entered and climbed to the top of the stairs where the woman left them in a dim, lantern-lighted hallway and plodded off to gather her girls.

Matt led them to the doorway of a raised, rice paper-walled room. He sat on the single step leading to it. "Take off your shoes."

"Always keep my boots on in a joint," Stu roared. "Don't wanna take a chance of catchin' athletes' foot!"

No one got the joke. In stockinged-feet they entered the mat-covered chamber. The teak-beamed ceiling slanted down to either wall; colored lanterns hung from the center. The men smelled lush incense and saw it burning on a stand in a far corner. A doorway, draped in transparent silk, was centered in each of four walls. The fifth wall in the pentagon-shaped chamber was one large sliding *fusuma* with black-and-white landscape paintings of snow-dusted mountains and gnarled trees. In the center of the floor was an ebony serving table, inlaid with mother-of-pearl and held two feet above the plaited mats by carved dragons' legs.

"It's like a stage set out of *Madame Butterfly,*" Ward said, and taking a silver flask from his jacket, passed it to the others.

Matt seated himself on a red silk cushion by the table. The congressmen sat on either side of him. "Just relax. The lovelies will be here shortly."

Four Japanese girls stepped into the room. One rushed to Matt. "Papa-san! Gahd-Bress-Amureeka," she recited proudly, recalling her instruction when Matt had visited Kyoto alone weeks before.

Matt rewarded her with a proprietary slap on her obi-encased bottom. "Kaniko," he said, "meet your benevolent protectors from the Great White Father in Washington."

She bowed. The other girls, dressed in print kimonos, brocade obis about their waists, stood silently by the half-open *fusuma.* Matt's pupil called to them, saying each name as the owner smiled and dipped in a deep bow.

Kane stood. "We'll never remember those." He tapped a finger on his forehead. "If I had water, I'd christen them for my buddies." His voice became ecclesiastical. "Each according to the dictates of his own conscience," he intoned. "I'd sprinkle one for myself, since I'm the only practicing fish-eater here. And I'd immerse one for you, Stu, you cowboy Baptist. And you birds," he said, glancing at Matt and Ward, "are going to hell anyway so it won't make any difference." Laughter. "Since we've got no equipment," Kane said, "I'll just distribute the wealth without benefit of clergy." He pointed to an oval-faced girl with large eyes and long, long lashes. "You look like Stu's type." He took her hand and brought her to Stu Denton. "Stu, meet Almond Eyes." The girl bowed again and backed out the open doorway.

"Whatheheck did I do?" Stu asked.

"She just went out to get your wine cup and start chow," Matt explained as Kaniko, too, backed toward the *fusuma.*

"Let's see." Kane rubbed his chin and waved away the flask as Ward offered it again. "Ward, I've got to find something special for you, something young and innocent looking." He walked around the remaining two geishas as if he were examining cattle at an auction. "We have on my left, Passion Flower." He pointed to a slim, childlike girl whose rich jet hair was wound high around her head. "And on my right, this vision of oriental loveliness, this porcelain doll, this daughter of Nippon, Angel Face." The girl took his arm and Kane laughed. "That leaves Passion Flower, Ward, my friend; and she looks delicate enough to handle you."

Ward hoisted himself to his feet and reached for the geisha's hand, but she padded away. Almond Eyes and Kaniko returned. They bowed and brought hot rice wine and thimble cups to the table; then they poured for their men, bowed once more and crossed the room.

"Hey, don't run off, Almond Eyes honey!" Stu said. But the two geishas sat on the mats and began to play their mandolin like instruments as Passion Flower and Angel Face entered carrying trays. They placed a copper charcoal burner on the table, melted butter and began to heat razor-thin slices of beef.

Wine was poured and the men drank. They toasted one another and their return to the States. They toasted the Democratic party and, out of deference to Stu, the Republicans. They toasted Almond Eyes and Passion Flower and Angel Face and Kaniko. Stu's geisha sang a plaintive, tinkling song; and they toasted her song and her voice and the *shamisen* and *koto* accompaniment. Kane danced a polka with Angel Face while the others sang, "Roll out the barrel. We'll have a barrel of fun. . . ." And when Kane tripped on the girl's kimono and fell, breathless and laughing to the floor, they toasted him. They toasted Pennsylvania and The Golden West and the Universal Broadcasting Company and Woofies, Matt's newly-won breakfast food sponsor.

"Let's keep things rolling," Ward said, waving his hands and standing before the girls. "Hold everything, you slant-eyed maidens. We're going to have some American music for my colleagues. Come on, Stu. Grab one of these mandolins while I direct the girls' chorus!"

Stu, moving with the deliberate dignity of the mildly drunk, lumbered across to the giggling group. "Cousin, if you think I'm soused enough to play one of these oriental git-fiddles, you're outta your head."

While Ward and Stu drilled their charges, Kane and Matt drank the oily wine and lied about the women they'd had and swore eternal friendship and assured one another that it couldn't be true "what they say about oriental broads."

"*Sukiyaki's* on!" Matt called.

"With you in a minute," Ward said. "First you've got to listen to my singing-swinging Nips. Stu can't play Puccini, so we're going to be a little lowbrow." He raised his hand and as Stu plunked at the accompaniment, he conducted his quartet.

"Goo-buy, Ma-Ma. I oaf to Yokohoma for ray why and broo, contree and yoo . . . Unaccustomed to the harsh vowels, unable to pronounce some of the letters, the girls stumbled over the words, contorting their mouths into grotesque shapes. Their faces were serious, intent as they watched Ward, standing before them, mimicking their pronunciation.

When they had finished, Stu and Ward pounded one another and then the floor, laughing until tears came. Kane stood before Kaniko. He kissed both her cheeks and when she went to stand beside Matt, waiting for him to stroke his praise, Kane passed down the fine, bestowing his congratulations on the other singers.

The men washed their hands and faces with a steaming towel that was passed around. Then they made inexpert attempts to use their chopsticks. Only Matt, who held the bowl under his chin and scooped the crisp meat and vegetables into his mouth, succeeded. Kane and Angel Face sat cross-legged, facing one another and shared his bowl. Ward sat like a sport-coated Buddha, and Passion Flower fed him. Stu lay on his back, his head in Almond Eyes' lap and she dipped the meat in the raw egg cup, then dropped the food into his mouth, waited while he chewed, and offered more hot wine.

When the dinner was removed, the geishas served bean cakes and tea. And the men took off their jackets and their ties, poured more wine and stretched out on the colored cushions while the geishas entertained. They did pantomimes: "Japanese Girl See GI," Kaniko explained. "Fat Man Take Bath." And later, while the other girls played their instruments, Passion Flower danced and the men, though drunk, were charmed into silence, a silence interrupted only by Ward's cold-sober declamation on the intricate beauty of the movements and his discovery that the fan represented the sun at one point, a cup of poison at another, and his insistence on telling Matt that "it's like a tryst between dancer and beholder. And we're all beholders."

Soon only Matt Fallon and Kaniko remained in the room. Stu had played the three-stringed *shamisen,* and while the others hummed like an asthmatic organ, sang his campaign song: "Let me work for you. Send me off to Congress." (Adapted from the old hymn, "I'll Have My Reward When I See My Maker."— Gospeline Records, 943,000 copies.) Then, holding stubbornly to his virtue, he had fallen asleep and was carried by Kane and Matt to a pallet in a tiny, darkened room. Almond Eyes sat beside him now, rubbing his temples with her long, straight lingers.

Ward, although he entered into the gaiety, although he drank and danced and sang and laughed with apparent abandon, was always curiously alert, his eyes following the others, his smile a service of the lips—cool, controlled, indulgent, self-possessed. In time he had displayed his hairy chest to Passion Flower and followed her, with lewd announcements to the others, into the chamber beyond.

And Kane, fired with rice wine, had torn Angel Face's *obi* from her waist, lifted her in his arms and carried her, protesting, through another portal. The waddling madam, hearing the screams of the girl, had rushed in to quiet Kane. In her confused babble she explained that Angel Face was a dancing geisha and no more. And when he roared at her, she took the quaking girl away and promised to bring him another.

Matt, his back padded with a multicolored mound of pillows, sat upright in a comer. Kaniko's *shamisen* played a strange oriental counterpoint as he sang. From this huge pile of man—freckled, pug-faced, dimpled, homely—came a startling, incongruous voice. In a tipsy, haunting tenor he sang, "I dream of Jeannie with the light brown hair, borne like a vapor . . ."

Kane lay on a silken pallet of blue, staring at the bamboo-webbed ceiling. His hands cupped over his nose and mouth, he smelled his stale breath and wished for his toothbrush. "Damn ole bag," he said aloud. "Damn ole moth-eaten bag!"

And he heard Matt: ". . . many were the wild notes her merry voice . . ."

A phantom creature, wrapped in sapphire knelt beside Kane. He looked at her calm, finely-etched face and felt her strong fingers as they unbuttoned his shirt. Her hands, cool and soft and caressing, undressed him; and he lay nude on the pad. "You'll do, baby. You'll do," he muttered.

But she was gone. Returning, she brought a bowl and held it to his lips. He sipped. It was cold and faintly sweet; and he washed the vile taste away. She bathed him. A soft sponge brushed his face; and when he tried to grab the girl's hand, she looked at him with patient eyes, and drew away. "I can wait, you tease. Ole Uncle Kane's got what it takes," he said groggily. And relaxed and was drowsy.

". . her smiles have vanished and her sweet songs flown . . ." Kane half-heard Matt's voice. The girl sprinkled Kane with talcum. And with a fluff of feather she dusted his neck and his straight, hard shoulders. He felt the wisp glide over the rounded muscle of his forearm, felt it slip across the breadth of his molded chest and flick down the smooth lines of his sides. Now she spread the talc over the cup of his ankles, across his knees, against his long, muscled thighs. Kane groaned and reached for her, and again she pulled away. Her cool hands kneaded him and rubbed him, brushed softly against the flat, quivering stomach, artfully along his hips. Again she was gone.

". . . flitting like the dreams that have cheered us . . ."

Kane watched, his cheek pressed against the silken pad, as the geisha undressed behind a ricepaper-paneled screen. He saw her silhouette, each practiced, graceful movement as her clothing slipped away. "All part of the game," he mumbled. "Buncha bull." Then she stood above him and he saw the amber ivory of her body. Closer. Upon him. He put his hands about her tiny waist. And she lay her head on his chest. And he smelled the exciting fragrance of her.

At once the madam stood over them, lifted both edges of the pallet and tied them together. Kane and the geisha were imprisoned in the carnal caisson. Neither could move. He found himself fondled by the deepest sinews of the silent girl; and in his glorious inebriation he knew nothing else. Drugged in exotic ecstasy, he slept.

Kane opened his eyes and looked through the wisps of the girl's hair and saw Matt Fallon, red-eyed, drunk and laughing, standing over him.

"Damn yer hide! I'm tired carryin' on b'myself. Ever'body's gone t'bed but me."

"Go sleep, Matt," Kane told him thickly. "Get your broad and go sleep and let me be."

"Hellyousay! Let's get outta here! Tired this place and damn' posturin' women. C'mon, Kane. C'mon with yer ole buddy."

"Go away!"

"Nobody tells me t'shove off! I'm bored, you ole mick O'Connor. Wan' com'any. C'mon!"

"I'm not leavin' this, you stupe. Beat it!"

"Have it yer way. We'll take her 'long." Matt put his great hands on the gathering of the pallet, strained, grunted and lifted it and Kane and the girl across his shoulders. "Okay, friendo! I'll tote you through Kyoto while y'get yer rocks off," he roared and stumbled across the dim room to the chamber outside. The girl screamed. And Kane cursed. And Matt howled with coarse laughter. And the madam rushed in, chattering and pleading.

"Put me down, you goon!" Kane yelled.

"You m'buddy?"

"I'll kill you, Fallon, you ape!"

"That's 'gainst reg'lations for congressmen t'kill cit'zens." Matt rocked with his mirth and spun around and around with the precarious parcel still on his shoulders.

"All right. Okay. I'm gettin' sick," Kane pleaded.

Finally, still laughing like an unfettered maniac, Matt lowered the two frantic bundlers; and the madam untied them. Matt sprawled in the comer on his pillows and laughed until he choked while Kane, sitting on the table, dressed. "You shoulda got a look at the dame's puss when I picked you up!" Matt crowed.

"I hate your guts!" Kane said. And then he looked at Matt who was still shaking, sputtering, trembling with laughter. And Kane laughed, too. "Get me a drink, you crazy red-headed boob. I'm dizzy."

Two pitchers of *sake* were poured empty as they sat in the center of the room and swore mighty oaths; and were meticulously polite; and chased off the madam who tried to quiet them. They agreed in their intoxication that Stu and Ward must be carried into the streets. And then, with tender solicitude, rejected the idea since their friends were drunk and had to sleep it off.

They confided in one another.

"This series we're doin's gonna make me," Matt said. "Good time slot. Sponsor. New kinda joum'lism. TV with point-a-view."

"Who he'ped you with it, buddy?"

"You. You fixed it, Kane, you sweet dream of a pol'tician. You did it."

"I been he'pin *you*, Matt. Time *you* he'ped ole Kane."

Matt held up his right hand. "Swear I'll do it. Watcha wan', friendo? You wan' me t'sen' ya case Woofies? Wan' me t'get ya press pass? Or a Un'versal TV set? Watcha wan'?"

Kane squinted at him, waved a finger in his face, opened his mouth and forgot what he intended to say. "Don' know yet. But. . . one these days. He slapped his hands together. "Maybe I'll run fer Senate."

Matt shook his head in drunken compassion. "Ya not big nuff, pal. Can' run fer anythin' less ya got frien's who'll han' you nom'nation and give out with cash t'run campaign. Gotta have frien's."

"I got frien's."

"I don' like yer frien's—'cept Tod. Straight-shooter. And Dany, oh, I'm hot fer that woman! Got style." He glared at Kane. "But don' like her brother's rag and don' like Madman Brider and his synd'cate and don' like you hangin' 'round 'em, pal."

"That's a stinkin' att'tude, Matt. Why don' ya like 'em?"

"'Cause Mel Field's dad-in-law don' care 'bout truth. To him, truth is shiny word he uses on mas'heads of his papers. Just wantsa sell his rags to poor slobs who wanna know who was in bed with who las' night—whom!" he corrected himself.

"Ya say so, s'okay by me." Kane tried unsuccessfully to snap his fingers. "But Dany . . . she's a doll, huh? Keeps me at arm's . . . er . . . keeps me—she's cold, Matt," he said sadly. "Banked fires. But she's livin' doll."

"Wish she'd kep' ya 'way from Brider crowd, though," Matt said. "Don' need 'em. You wanna be Senator, y'need people. People gotta love ya and y'gotta love 'em back. Don' matter 'bout crummy pol'ticians. Long run, y'can trus' people. Surprise hell outta ya sometimes; an' don' vote way they're tol', way they're s'pposed to. Fool ever'body and vote fer what they think's right!"

"Then I'll be right, dammit!" Kane sat up, shifting another pillow behind him. "Wha'ever people wan', I'll do fer 'em. Wha'ever they think's right, I'll think's right. Hellfire, Matt, I'm a'ways on side of poor slobs."

"Sorry, buddy," Matt said dolefully, pouring another drink. "But ya gotta un'erstand poor slobs t'be on poor slobs' side. You don' un'erstand poor slobs."

As Matt spoke, Kane wagged his head from side to side. The fabric of his memory was being unwoven. He saw himself as a skinny child of seven, lying awake in his sagging bed in a miner's cottage, and in the darkness hearing his parents across the room and flinching from his father's oaths as he cursed his mother's "stinkin' high and mighty family." He remembered a winter's dawn, cold, gray-blue in first light, when he was carried to a neighbor's shack, and he lay in a strange bed, knowing with the unfathomable knowledge of childhood that his mother was dead. And he could recall, too, the night after her funeral when he had stumbled, crying, through the rutted street, sick with grief and fear, while his father—drunk and snarling—fought two policemen and was carried off to jail . . . and the lights from the police car had blinded Kane . . . and there was a crowd . . . and a thick, big-busted woman named Morski who smelled of babies had lifted him up and carried him home with her.

All these things unraveled in the passing of a second as Kane sat there. "So I don' un'erstand poor slobs! Like hell I don'!" Now, grasping for words, nearly inarticulate with drunken self-pity, Kane tried to explain to Matt.

"I been a poor slob!" he insisted, shaking his fist at his friend. "Jes don' know!" Memory tugged at him again. "Was in third grade. Eight years ole. An' we were gonna have program. Was bes' speaker in class, too! The bes'. An' they gave me mos' importan' thing t'say. Was a poem." He waved his hand before him as if to brush away the webs that skeined before his eyes. "An' teacher . . . name was Miss Bessie, I remember . . . Miss Bessie . . . I don' know what else—but usta call her that. Was eight then," he reminded Matt. "Miss Bessie wan'ed me t'be dressed up fer my part like other kids, an' I didn't have fine clothes. Livin' with my pa alone. An' my mother dead, an' buried on a hill . . . on a black hill, no higher than a smokestack."

"Poor kid. Poor li'l kid," Matt said.

Kane was entranced now. And he mumbled on as Matt leaned across to hear him. "On day of program I came t'school . . . an' Miss Bessie brought out a shirt an' pants she'd borrowed from preacher's wife . . . and pants were knickers . . . blue serge . . . blue serge knickers with li'l brass buckles on 'em. An' she tole me I could wear 'em!"

"Good fer Miss Bessie!" Matt said. "Good fer tha' teacher."

Kane nodded. "I never put 'em on. Never."

"Why?" Matt demanded. "Why?"

Kane hiccoughed. "Jes before we were s'pposed to dress, one kid turned up with nits in his hair "

"Wha's nits?"

"Nits are lice eggs, an' they started t'look 'round t'see where they came from . . . an' they made me undress in coatroom . . . an' they foun' nits an' lice all over me. I was dirty—filthy, dirty, lousy."

Matt frowned. "Poor kid."

"Wen' home," Kane said, recalling the long walk through the black, unpainted town, remembering how his father had found him sobbing on his soiled bed. "Never got t'wear those blue serge knickers with th' buckles." Kane looked at his open palm. "Never." He bit his lips, nodding. "I been poor slob. I'm through bein' poor slob. Jes you wait an' see!"

Matt studied him for a moment. "That's th' spirit, buddy. Tha's th' spirit! I was 'fraid ya were gettin' maudlin fer awhile there!" He nudged Kane. "Le's drink t'blue serge knickers an' brass buckles . . . an' poor slobs!"

An hour later, the liquor had lifted them to boisterous hilarity, heated their blood with its fire, released them to unrestrained drunkenness.

Kane pulled himself up, supporting his weight on Matt's beefy shoulders. "Gonna sing Air Corps song, Matt. An' y'gonna stan' an' join me like a genelmum."

"Off we go inta wile blue yon'er," the baritone and the tenor sang, "climbin' high inta sun. Down we dive spoutin' our flames from un'er at 'em boys, give 'er th' gun!"

They marched out of the room, picked up their shoes on the stoop, did a flanking movement and started down the steps. The madam called from behind them, screaming for her money over the sound of their voices. ". . . off with one helluva roar! We live in fame er go down in flame, boys—nothin'll stop th' Army Air Corps!"

Kane tripped, fell blindly on the stairs and lay there, momentarily dazed, but unhurt. Matt, below him, pulled open the outer door and smashed through the shutters to the street below. "Where are ya, buddy?" he yelled.

Kane, brushing himself clumsily, put on his shoes and followed Matt into the cool dawn. "I'm here," he shouted, holding up his hand. "Righ' here!"

They staggered down the alley to the comer where two glassyeyed sailors and a buck-toothed marine were being wretchedly sick. And Kane and Matt, soothingly, gaily superior, held their heads and put them on the liberty bus for Camp Fisher.

"You goin' to Yokosuka with me t'morra?" Matt asked as they waved the bus off.

Kane's numbed mind did not recall the naval base near Yokohama or the mysterious sight Matt had bet him he could not see. "Go an' where with ya, pal," he said.

Matt put his arm around him. "Are ya my buddy, Kane?"

"I'm ya buddy, ya buddy-buddy."

The two reeling comrades, clasped in the embrace of drunkenness, lurched off down the winding street.

19

IT WAS EARLY the next evening when Kane emerged from the Officers Club at Yokosuka with Matt Fallon and a lieutenant commander. A waiting driver held the door of the Officer-of-the-Day's car open for them; and the three men got in.

"Pay me," Kane said to Matt and held out his hand.

Matt counted out ten five-dollar bills. "You're impressive, Congressman O'Connor. I just didn't realize the tremendous power, influence and prestige your office commands." Then, laughing, "It's a legitimate expense for the swindle sheet."

"The Row, driver," the naval officer said, and knocked back the brim of his cap in a belated attempt to return the heel-clicking salute of the gate sentry.

"I'm taking your money, Matt," Kane said. "It's reimbursement for a terrific headache on the plane from Kyoto, a dark-brown taste in my mouth all day in Yokohama and the dough I repaid Stu and Ward when they stumbled in this morning. But I've got to admit I didn't have any trouble arranging this tour. Right, commander?"

The Officer-of-the-Day was a young man with a lumped-putty nose, a Navy Cross, an Academy ring and the belief—which his commanding officer insisted was only half true—that all United States congressmen are moral giants and mental pigmies. "Well," he said with a grin that admitted Kane to his confidence, "I doubt that we'd have suggested it, sir, but it's something we've got to live with and we're not trying to hide it."

"Soon as you told me what it was all about, Matt, I called the executive officer and got permission to visit one of the joints. It was as simple as that."

"And I had to gift a medical officer with a bottle of Chivas Regal just to get him to tell me about the area!" Matt rolled down his window and dropped his cigarette out. "I suppose there's a sane reason for having this kind of thing. But, no matter how you look at it, it's a brothel operation with the Navy's blessing; and Uncle Sam's like a procurer-in-absentia!"

The commander said, "If you really want to understand our problem, you've got to face certain facts, gentlemen. Prostitution is legal in Japan. We can, of course, put all such places out-of-bounds, and ignore the fact that the civilian population is sure to be molested. What we've chosen to do is to provide other entertainment facilities to distract the men, to encourage them to stay away from the houses for moral reasons, and to make the houses as clean as possible."

"I know you've got a problem," Matt said.

"The slogan we've been using is: 'Stay Clean Mentally, Morally, Physically and Spiritually.' But thousands of men of all the services move through this base. Some of them are going to ignore any kind of advice. We allow the places to stay open for the hell-raisers who've been at sea a long time and the virgins who want to be able to brag they've had a Jap girl. Of course, there are damned few Japs. Most of the girls are Koreans."

Kane glanced out the window as they neared the docks. "Sounds like a helluva way to have sex."

"Not very esthetic," Matt said.

"At least regulation is preferable to having things wide open. We've tried it both ways—not only here but in other places, like Cuba."

"And that makes it right?" Kane crossed his legs and tried without success to get comfortable between Matt's bulk on one side and the commander's on the other.

"I suppose nothing makes it right, sir," the commander said, with only a hint of impatience. "But it's at least practical. What we're doing is condoning the operation of a group of whorehouses; and we can't excuse it on moral grounds. On the other hand, we can't allow the men to hole-up in every out-of-bounds, filthy crib in town." Reaching into his coat, he took out a graph on yellow paper. "Here's a picture of the venereal rate. You see how at the beginning the curve climbed like crazy? Now it's way down and leveling off."

"I guess you've accomplished something," Kane said. "But it's a pretty grim setup."

"I've tried to explain, sir, that we don't like it any more than you do," the commander snapped, and immediately smiled, recalling his orders and the DSC pin Kane wore in his lapel. "You've been a fighting man, sir," he said, moderating the heat of his reply. "And, after all, our first concern has to be our mission. We're here to maintain an effective military organization, and a good relationship with the country. If a youngster's man enough to fight for his country, we try to steer him the right way, make provisions for his lapses and expect him to act like a man."

"I agree with you, commander," Matt said.

Kane nudged Matt with his elbow and winked, then went back to his diversion of baiting the officer. "Bet your chaplains are screaming."

"We're on their side. But how are you going to change human nature?" The commander leaned toward the driver. "Take it easy, son. People in the street."

"Have you ever been to one of these places?" Kane asked the driver.

"Only once, sir. I got me a real deal now."

"What kind of a deal?"

The driver hesitated and caught the commander's glance. "Sir?"

"It's okay," the commander said, and blotted his perspiring face with his handkerchief.

"Well, Your Honor, I got me a Jap broad. Got me a apartment for liberty. Good chow. I ain't in no hurry to go home. Not for awhile anyway."

Kane laughed. "Living like an admiral, huh?"

"Pretty good, Your Honor. I give her four bucks American a week; and she pays the rent, cleans the place, does my laundry, cooks chow and acts like a nympho!"

"My boy, the Navy ought to use your testimonial for recruiting," Matt said and whistled the first few measures of "Anchors Aweigh."

The driver and Kane laughed with him. The commander said, "We've managed to run the world's finest Navy, and our men don't join to play house in the Orient!"

Matt and Kane exchanged solemn glances. The driver bent in studied concentration over the wheel. And, in the silence, they turned into a cobbled street, passed a section of docks where a transport was unloading and two destroyers were tied up, turned again into a narrow alleyway—The Row. It was lined with two-story graystone buildings; and shore patrolmen and military police stood guard before every door.

"Take your choice," the commander said.

"Over there'll be all right," Kane said.

They stopped before a set of wide concrete steps. At the top, before barred double doors, stood two ancient square-jawed stone lions guarding the blue-and-gold sign: UNITED STATES NAVY PROPHYLACTIC STATION NUMBER ONE

They left the car. Inside, in the glaring, sterile hallway, amid the mingled odors of disinfectant and stale smoke and oiled flooring and creosote, two shore patrolmen snapped to attention. "At ease," the commander said. "One of you come with us. We're going to look around."

"How does this thing work?" Kane said.

The commander introduced Kane as a congressman and the sentry, frozen in the self-inflicted attitude of "attention," stumbled over the explanation. "Well, sir, each man comes in . . . and, er, uh . . . leaves his liberty card here. And er uh . . . before he can get it back and leave, er uh, he's got to show a slip from the corps-man in the er uh clap-shack that says he's had a er uh pro."

Kane counted the slips in the exit box. There were sixty-three. "This about average?"

"Just about, sir."

"Considering how many servicemen pass through this port," the commander said, "you can see things are pretty slack."

Matt said, "You've got to admit it sounds efficient."

Kane walked toward the stairs at the end of the hallway. "Brother! What a place for romance!"

"It gets worse. Take this ladder topside," the commander said as they reached the treadwom stairs and passed a poster that proclaimed: "The Man With Brains Is The Man Who Abstains!" On the second floor, on either side of the whitewashed corridor, there were lines of servicemen. Some of the men leaned against the walls. Others sat on the splintered floor, playing blackjack with matchsticks.

The SP shouted, "Attention!" Everyone straggled up and stood against the wall.

"As you were," the commander said, and the men immediately forgot the intruders.

Kane, Matt and the commander stopped at one group where a humpbacked Korean woman stood arguing with her next patron. "One 'merican money," she insisted.

"Like hell!" a fat airman told her. "You think you got a virgin in there?"

"Ver' good. Young gir'. *Sheba-Sheba,*" the toothless crone argued.

"I don't give a damn if she's got four boobs. I ain't payin' more'n half a buck. Fifty cents."

"One 'merican money. Last price," the woman pleaded.

A sailor at the end of the line yelled, "Go on, buster, that's what she's been gettin'. Give it to her, buzzboy."

"I don't need no advice from you, swabbie. Everytime you guys come in town you send the price up! Fifty cents. No more," he told the woman and offered her the equivalent in yen notes. She held out her hand for the dirty bills.

At the next door a marine came out laughing. "Gonna try again," he announced, walking to the end of the line. "Been so long that I spent my dough before I got my pants hung up good." Then he saw the commander and flattened himself against the wall at attention until the party had passed him.

Down the hall an argument was raging. They heard the whine of a cursing woman and saw a group of men around the doorway. The SP cleared the way, calling, "Gangway! Gangway!" The commander pushed by the clutter that jammed the hall.

A Korean woman, thick-lipped, pig-eyed, jaundiced, broke through to him. "He take money. He kill me." She jerked the commander's arm and Kane and Matt followed them into a squalid chamber. There was a single window high on one wall. In the corner stood a pot. The brown-stained bureau with its taped mirror now held a pea coat and a cracked porcelain mug. Beside the sloping iron bed, a nude, bald, tattooed sailor was standing at rigid attention.

"Well, what's happened here?" the commander asked.

"She's a cheatin' sonov . . . She cheated me, sir."

"No! No!" the woman protested.

"Shut up!" the commander said, scowling at her.

"I was the first one in line because she was promising a new girl," the sailor said. "Then I got in here, undressed and started to climb in the sack. When I saw the broad, I slammed this old bitch in the teeth and took my money back."

For the first time, Kane noticed the small form hidden beneath the bedcovers. Matt walked over and pulled the blanket away. The girl, no more than thirteen, cowered there, naked and crying. She did not sob; but tears streaked the pasty red rouge on her hollow cheeks. And her teeth made tiny white marks below her painted lower lip. Her head was covered with a faded blue towel. Now she reached for it and held it across her tiny child's breasts.

"Money! Money!" the old woman wailed.

"Take her down below," the commander told the SP who stood with a group of onlookers in the doorway. "Throw her out. Hold the little kid. I'll be down in a few minutes."

While the SP pulled the screaming woman from the room, the commander picked up the sailor's uniform and tossed it at the naked man. "You take the kid down. And get the hell out of here. A man your age oughta be an example!"

"Sorry I bashed her, sir, but when I saw this little kid. . . . I got one 'bout her age at home."

Down below again, Kane and Matt were guided to the treatment room where a Navy corpsman presided. A long, pony-size trough ran the full length of one wall. White, black, smooth, pimpled, fat, lean and hairy backsides were lined up before it. A dozen pairs of green, olive drab, blue and bell-bottom trousers hung around twelve pairs of ankles. "You in charge here?" Kane asked the medic.

The corpsman, a spectacled, hollow-faced youngster, yawned, and looked open-eyed at the commander. The officer nodded and the corpsman said, "Yes, sir, I'm in charge. Got the worst watch — eight to twelve. Seems nobody wants sex till after dinner; and everybody who hasn't had some by midnight is tired of lookin'."

"How does this thing work?" Matt said.

The corpsman regarded him suspiciously, awaited the commander's nod and got a crisp, "Tell him!"

He recited his standard speech for the Officer of the Day: "Well, they come down and ask me for a slip so they can get out without takin' the pro. And I tell 'em hell no. And they call me a swabjockey or a chancre mechanic. And they step over to the wall and take care of themselves—except for the shy ones that use that." He pointed to a sheet-screened area. "Then they toss their soap out and deposit their towel. I give 'em a quick check to be sure there's no fudgin'. Then I sign the slip so they can get their liberty cards back. End of the watch we total up my slips and the expended pro packs and . . ."

"Okay. Okay," the commander said. To Matt: "Answers your question, doesn't it?" To the corpsman: "Get this place sprayed. It stinks."

"Sir, there's nothin'll take this smell away."

"Spray it!" the commander ordered.

"Aye, aye, sir!"

Outside at the entry desk, Kane saw the little girl from upstairs. She sat on a backless gray bench, her feet not quite touching the floor. A green marine raincoat was around her shoulders and a swarthy sergeant knelt beside her, wetting his handkerchief with his tongue, then wiping the caked paint from her face.

The bald sailor was arguing with the SP. "Look, fella, we want our cards back. We ain't been with no women and we ain't goin' to no pro shack."

"Sorry, friend," the SP told him. "I got my orders."

The sailor spotted the commander. "Sir, how about gettin' us our cards back? Me and my buddy wanna take the kid outta here and get her some chow and find somebody to take her in."

"Give them their liberty cards," the commander said wearily.

"Thanks, sir. Thought we might find a place for her in the galley at the Red Cross Club. We got a decent Korean cookie over there."

"Okay. Go ahead."

The marine carried the child in his arms. The sailor took their cards and headed for the door. "Here," Kane said, handing him a ten-dollar bill. "She can't go around in your friend's coat."

"Well," the commander said, "You gentlemen satisfied? Have you seen enough?"

"Yeah," Matt said.

"I've seen plenty," Kane said.

"These are really good men, sir," the commander said, holding Kane's gaze. "On duty they're well disciplined, well trained. But they are *men.* Just because you see what . . . well, what you see here, don't think . . ." He paused. "They're men."

"Sure," Kane said. "I understand."

Kane and Matt refused the commander's offer of a ride and walked off down the street. "Well?" Matt said.

"Sickening."

They walked into the street to avoid a cluster of men coming out of another house. "The commander was right. It's pretty awful, but you can't change human nature."

"Those men—like animals."

"Come off it, Kane. I realize you've had no commerce with the opposite sex for nearly eighteen hours and, therefore, have a right to be self-righteous, but after all. . ."

"Like animals," Kane repeated.

"At least they're generally healthy animals. And they're not pulling Jap civilians off into the bush. Hell, all the services are forced to do this kind of thing in one form or another."

"Maybe so. Maybe so."

Matt whistled. "But can you imagine the hell that'd be raised if the mommas back home got wind of this? Man, if I could only get away with it!"

Matt's jocular observation remained in Kane's mind. It was there back in Yokohama later that night when the five-man delegation posed for photographs. It remained with him when he saw Matt off on the train the next morning. It was on the edge of his thoughts the following afternoon at the bazaar when, without the expected haggling, he bought jade earrings for Dany, an *obi* and kimono for Laurie, a cloisonne cigarette box for Lucy and Mel, a porcelain vase for June and Tod, a musical cigarette lighter for Cy. He could not forget it during his inspection of Atami Field. It plagued him still on the plane trip to Honolulu while Ward sat beside him, talking endlessly about the American Patriots and Stu was up front, singing hymns with the crew and the other congressmen dozed or played cards. But Kane said nothing to his colleagues.

Then, on the morning of their departure, on the last leg of their journey back to the States, because he was appalled by what he had seen in the brothel, because he was sickened by the crudity, the ugliness of man's basic animalism, because he believed that the end could not be justified by the means, and possibly (though Kane would have denied it with sincere protestations) because he knew it would get his name in the papers, he called Tod in Washington, instructed him to contact Dany and Mel Field, and to arrange a press conference on his return.

"Can you imagine the hell that'll be raised if the mommas back home get wind of this?" he asked Tod on the phone. And then answered his own question. "Plenty. And I'm going to be the one that tells them."

20

SO IT WAS that in October of 1949, upon his return from Japan, Kane made his sensational charges of immorality in the armed forces.

In the hectic days that followed, both Houses of Congress approved military and foreign aid bills totaling $7,123,990,000 and adjourned *sine die* after the longest peacetime session in twenty-seven years; the Atomic Energy Commission was accused of mismanagement; Evangelist Isadore Schlossburg, "The Hebrew Who Knows Jesus," slashed his wrists for love of a Nashville matron and was buried in Beth Israel-Shalom Cemetery by an estranged wife who had his insurance and a sense of humor; Russia cast her thirty-ninth veto in the Security Council; the airlift to Berlin was suspended; and Oklahoma's Drys triumphed in a special liquor election.

But Kane crowded these lesser events out of the headlines. (Except in Oklahoma where, at a bootlegger's celebration, a tipsy state senator joyfully disrobed in the lobby of a Tulsa hotel.) For a time, Kane O'Connor was nearly as well known and as easily recognized as the highly-publicized mammaries of Hollywood's newest discovery.

Kane had learned a valuable lesson in the Purmincar affair; and this time he did not repeat his mistakes of sober appraisal, detailed research and well-reasoned, but dull speeches. In his first press conference he launched his attack and he continued to push it against feeble opposition.

Some members of his delegation privately cursed him, but publicly admitted they had not seen the depravity in question. His colleagues in the House damned him for ignoring the authority of the subcommittee chairman; but publicly they voiced concern. No one was willing to defend immorality.

The Secretary of the Navy issued one statement: "Less than 5 per cent of transient and permanent personnel made use of the supervised area. Every facility of the command—recreation, information, guidance and religious—was used to persuade over 95 per cent to abstain. For the small minority it was necessary to make provisions to guard the men's health and protect the civilian population."

But that was hardly a defense. And Kane, sought after for radio and television appearances, pressed for interviews, invited to speak on convention programs, did not pause to consider it.

When he addressed churchmen, he told them, "There is a breakdown in morality among our young men. What our churches have taught them, the armed services are destroying in a few months."

To women's organizations, he said, "The American home is an edifice erected by mothers to make future generations decent and strong. But, my friends, the foundations of that home are being worn away."

Businessmen were enlightened by Kane's reminder that "We cannot allow our ever-increasing burden of taxation to perpetuate frivolous, socialistic ideas at home and immoral dens abroad."

Medical meetings heard Kane's reminder that, "You, the custodians of America's health, are expected to believe that venereal disease can be wiped out by encouraging exposure!"

The Overseas Press Club heard Kane declaim that "Freedom of the press must be observed, whether it's in this country or overseas. A correspondent traveling with us in Japan had to bribe a naval officer to get information. When I heard of this willful affront to a member of the Press, I insisted that he accompany me."

A Forty-and-Eight banquet was told, "I wish I might have come here without the title of congressman. I wish I might have been able to sit down with you, as one veteran to another, and talk horse sense. We're not mollycoddles who can't have a party or use a few choice GI phrases, but as men who have risked their lives for this great nation, we have insight into what happens when a bunch of kids are thrown into."

To the glum, silent convention of the Navy League, Kane said, "It's a rare occurrence when a buzzboy gets the chance to talk, unrestrained, to a bunch of navy men." (A few half-smiles.) "It's even rarer when, after giving a snow-job to organizations of dogfaces and gyrenes, a fella dares face a bunch of fighting sailors who know snow when they're asked to shovel it!" (A few chuckles and a quickening of interest.) "The rarest thing of all is to find a politician who dares suggest that motherhood, after all, is slightly more sacred than the United States Navy!" (Hearty laughter.) Kane then belabored the Army, Marine Corps and Air Force for operating "similar pleasure palaces but not having the courage and honesty to admit it" as the Navy had done.

Within a month of his return, Ward Roberts and Stu Denton were the only members of the Special Committee on Military Planning who were talking to him. He had been interviewed on *Meet The Press;* Matt Fallon, visiting him on a week end, had told him, "in the interest of truth, Loverboy, you're an unmitigated fraud." Then, in the interest of his own Trendex Rating, Matt had invited him to appear before his television audience.

Dorothy Kilgallen commented on Kane's trip to New York with Dany. His name was mentioned, with paeans of praise, in *Time*'s letters column; and *Newsweek*'s Periscope had predicted future prominence for him. The Loew's Capitol and Warner's theaters both ran newsreel shots, and Kane went to both showings twice. Shepherd Reade and the Majority Leader, Abel Garren, had seen him in the House restaurant and invited him to their table. Frank Farrell's column, in a double-edged paragraph, had called him, "The Billy Sunday of Politics." Twenty-one resolutions had been passed—one by the American Veterans' Organization which paused in its four-day orgy in Los Angeles to condemn immorality in the services.

Through it all, Dany and Tod worked with Kane, planning strategy as if they were directing a military campaign. Kane commanded — an aggressive, cocky, impatient field marshal. Tod was his perceptive, tireless chief of staff, running the routine operation of the office. Dany was his imaginative, subtle-minded G-2, gathering information, co-ordinating it and relating it to their battle plan.

At every lull in the action they pressed the silent enemy, hoping for a counterattack that never came. They demanded a report from all services on similar existing facilities. They challenged the Navy to refute their facts. They phoned advance tips to columnists. They tested their plans by leaking them through the Brider Syndicate. They combed newspapers and magazines for editorial comment and gleefully fed them back in press releases. Though the enemy retaliated feebly or not at all, Kane would not let the battle fade, but kept it alive by probing action, by daily assaults and by constant harassment.

The three often worked all night in Kane's apartment, with Dany finally falling asleep on the sofa and Kane and Tod sharing Kane's bed. She would awaken them with coffee in the morning and force them back to work until another speech was finished and she and Tod might drive Kane to the airport for another foray against immorality.

One cold morning early in November, while the three stood in the North Concourse of the National Airport terminal awaiting his plane, Kane took Dany aside. "You've been pushing yourself too hard. We haven't been having any fun lately. But I want you to know I appreciate it. I'll do better by you when I get back."

She kept shaking her head while he spoke. "Kane, by now you ought to know me and you don't. If any thanks are due, I owe them to you. You're getting a little big for your britches and your mouth could stand a good soaping, but I've never had so much fun in my life. I've never felt so alive."

Smiling, he grasped her hands. "You're pretty special," he said and led her back to where Tod was sitting on the short metal ledge before the windows, watching the field. "I *am* accomplishing something, Dany."

"No you're not, not really. If someone wants to think so, and apparently they do, that's all right. But we're not going to fool ourselves."

"Chum," Tod said, "we have a realist with us. I figure we're about through. Last week or so we've been beating a dead dog."

"All we've accomplished," Dany said, "is to get people to know who you are, to identify you with something damned near everyone must agree with you on. This is preparation. It'll make it easier for you to accomplish something when the right something comes along. And it will. Just give us time."

"Listen, I'm the one who goes out and talks to the people. I'm the one they're flocking to hear! And I know better. People are behind me."

"Of course," Dany said. "You're news right now."

"And nobody's given you an argument, Kane. Sooner or later people tire of a one-sided gripe."

No longer listening, Kane said, "It seems to me that the least I can do with this girl is put her on the payroll."

"Sure. You tell me where the dough is coming from."

"I don't need a salary," Dany said.

"Okay," Kane said as they walked down the steps toward the waiting plane. "Dany's going to be our dollar-a-year woman. We'll make it official. List her on the staff." He laughed and brushed his knuckles over her chin. "She throws cold water on me, like you, Tod, but the girl's got possibilities." Then, putting his arms around Dany on one side, Tod on the other, he said, "I'm on my way—and you characters are with me!"

Although the slugging match of O'Connor versus the Navy was spurred on by Kane's speeches, editorial comment, a spate of sermons and constant exposure on television and radio, six weeks after the first furious round the tussle began to disintegrate into a few mild clinches, a low blow or two and glancing punches that were all but unnoticed. Finally, though the last bell never sounded and no judges turned in their verdicts, the bout went into the record books as a contested victory for Kane. No one bothered to note whether or not The Row in Yokosuka was still doing business.

The thrill of the fast-paced weeks gave way to monotony and boredom. Although Congress would not reconvene until January, although he craved a rest and felt guilty for neglecting Laurie, Dany and Tod held Kane in Washington.

Dany forced him to work on his mountain highway bill to have it ready for presentation to the next session. Shepherd Reade was back in Alabama, meeting the challenge of an opponent who had already announced for his seat. And it was only with the aid of Mel and Lucy Field that Kane found an influential co-sponsor for the road measure.

Tod, prodding Kane with warnings that "we've got another election coming up next year," insisted that they work on a mound of neglected correspondence, send an open letter to the districts' newspapers as a report on his first session in Congress, record a five-minute radio address boosting Manton's Community Chest, and write forty-three condolence letters to his constituents.

Kane felt like a high school athlete who, having tasted briefly of glory, was now back in the classroom, trying—with a host of other students—to puzzle-out the intricacies of plane geometry and worrying if, after all, he might not make the team next season.

By mid-December he had finished his work; and though Dany tried to persuade him to remain and Tod encouraged him to go to Manton for political reasons, it was a tearful phone call from Laurie that prompted him to return home.

21

ON HIS FIRST evening in Manton, carrying an extravagant bouquet for Viola Eden, Kane arrived at Laurie's home, rang the bell and walked into the sprawling old living room.

Laurie called his name; and he turned, seeing her as she stepped from behind the door. She wore the kimono and *obi* he had bought for her in Japan. Her auburn hair was rolled high on her head and the tiny souvenir parasol from the only gin sling she'd ever tasted dangled over one ear. Her cheeks were two round pats of rouge. Her eyes were slanted crookedly with a blunt eyebrow pencil. She came mincing toward him, her palms together beneath her chin, like Yum Yum in Manton High's production of *The Mikado*.

"How do you say 'hello and I've missed you and I love you' in Japanese?"

Strangely moved by her little girl's game of make-believe, Kane took her in his arms. "Like this," he said and kissed her.

Later, they sat with her mother before the fireplace and Kane talked of Washington. He tried to tell them of the excitement, the enchantment of the capital, of his committee assignments, of the daily give-and-take of legislative action, of his battle with the Navy, of the wide green lawns and shaded drives of Hunting Acres.

But when he mentioned "boondoggling" or "logrolling" or "pork barrel," Laurie face was uncomprehending. When he was reliving the stirring days of press releases, television kinescopes and newspaper streamers, she kept asking him for definitions. A mention of Lucy Field's parties, with political savants, millionaires and press lords in attendance, drew only one simple question: "What did Mrs. Field wear, darlin'?"

Kane was annoyed. She seemed so provincial, so naive, so limited. And at midnight, when he pleaded weariness, and started to leave, Laurie held onto his arm, watching his face for a moment, recognizing his displeasure and sensing the reason for it.

"Darlin', I know I'm not up on all the things I oughta know about. But I . . . .I mean, about what you're doin' and how everythin' works." She was so painfully serious, so pathetically childish in her attempt at Japanese clothes and make-up, that he knew a moment of utter sadness, as if for no reason at all he might weep. "Oh, hell, Laurie," he said gruffly, "if you knew it all, I wouldn't have the fun of telling you things."

"I'm goin' to learn, Kane. I'm goin' to learn all about how you write up bills and . . . and the names of things . . . and all."

"Sure you are."

"I want to be able to help you," she whispered.

"You've always helped me."

"Not since you went away I haven't."

He put his arms around her, held her face against his chest, rubbed his chin in her hair and felt her shivering. "You go on to bed; and stop imagining things."

Leaning back, she looked up at him, her face distorted by smeared rouge and eyebrow pencil. "Do you still love me, Kane?"

He tried to laugh and couldn't. "You ought to know by now!"

"I love you," Laurie said. Then, smiling, dabbing at the comers of her eyes with her knuckles, "That's all that matters then. That's all I need. That's enough."

But Kane, as he finally escaped into the cold night, and faced himself, was no longer certain that it was enough. Depressed, absorbed in his thoughts, he had walked two blocks before he remembered that he had left his car in Laurie's driveway.

Kane devoted his days to strengthening his political position. He took part in laying the cornerstone for a new wing on the local YMCA as Luke Biddle, unconcealed hatred in his eyes, helped him hold the trowel. He promised the tourist bureau that his bill for the scenic highway would pass the next session. He spoke, in a single week, to Lions, Rotarians, Kiwanians, Optimists, B'nai Brith, Knights of Columbus and Soroptimists—and since their meetings were all held in the same dreary hotel ballroom, he had five lunches of congealed salad, chicken a la king, cold lima beans, candied yams and peach cobbler; and he endured two dinners of congealed salad, sliver of roast beef, cold gravied rice, succotash and cherry cobbler.

He hunted with politicos in the national park. Through Laurie, he became friends with the Catholic priest, a scholarly man with incisive wit, a quiet manner and a bottle of madeira which, doled out in drams, lasted through an even half-dozen afternoon bull sessions. Once he slipped off to Charlotte for what Cy called, "a quick swim in iniquity." But otherwise, he gave his time to Laurie.

And she, afraid that Kane's new life threatened to erect a partition between them, brought home books from the library and attempted to learn more about the government of which Kane, she believed, was so important a part. She was diligent. She referred to the index of her texts. She looked up words in her Webster's. She borrowed a dictionary of American slang and dutifully searched the section on politics until she found: *Filibuster: Continuous usurpation of the floor by a single person or persons in order to prevent action on certain legislation.* Then, to be sure, she looked up *usurpation.* And later, *Caucus. Hopper. Gerrymander. Boondoggle. Logrolling. Rider.*

Alone with him, she would introduce politics into their conversation. "It's amazin'," she told him one evening, "how one committee chairman can pigeonhole an important bill simply by not reportin' it to the floor." And, ignoring his answer, "Kane, it seems to me that the Rules Committee is certainly the most powerful. And, by the way, have you put your highway bill in the hopper yet?"

And Kane kissed her and praised her and feigned amazement at her knowledge.

Christmas night Laurie and Kane joined Cy and his chattering date for the Union Welfare Club's annual Olde Merrie England Dance.

It was held in the Tudor splendor of Manton's colonial-French provincial-Swedish modern country club; and it featured sour eggnog, boughs of Woolworth holly, Commissioner Joe King's wife (who year after year managed to simper drunkenly and unkissed beneath clusters of mistletoe), and a four-piece pick-up band that painfully heeded the committee's injunction to play Guy Lombardo arrangements. There was also a buffet of Olde English roast beef, Olde English potato salad, Olde English slaw, cold Olde English muffins and Olde English southern fried chicken.

Surrounded by his friends and constituents, Kane found little time for the party. He was besieged by men offering advice and seeking favors and gently reminding him of his duties as their representative.

There was the mortician's son who took Kane's arm and led him to the linen-covered table that served as a bar. "I remember when all the Republicans went to one funeral home and all the Democrats went to another." (General agreement from his listeners and one anecdote about a misplaced corpse.) "Feelin' was that high! But nowadays it don't seem party means a hoop-er-a-holler. Seems like you fellas just try to beat one another givin' handouts to foreigners. Hated to see how you been votin' on some of this foreign aid, Kane. With our textile people sufferin' the way they are, Republicans and Democrats fall over theirselves helpin' the Nips flood the market with cheap cotton goods. I swan, Kane, I'm for you on your stand against the joints the services are runnin' over there, but we're goin' to get hurt a lot worse by Nip cotton goods than by Nip poontang."

Hugh Lester, Kane's old campaign aide, called him aside. "Tell you the truth, Kane, I don't have any idea the way you been votin' on most things, but I sure hated to see you down as against a raise in veterans' pensions. And then, you didn't do a thing when they decided to close the Rocky Ford post office. Kane, you got to keep in mind the folks that sent you up there. . .

Kane started to dance with Laurie, was cut on, and then led off by another constituent. "Appreciate the way you've been answerin' my letters, Kane. And you sure went down the line on the housing bill. But, buddy, seems to me the most important thing these days is cuttin' income taxes. You take a fella in my bracket..."

It's a long, long way—and yet, not really far at all, Kane reflected—between Hunting Acres and the Manton Country Club.

Later, when he had taken Laurie home and stood beside her at the door, his overcoat collar turned up against the blowing snow outside, she clung to him. "Darlin', I've known all along that mother was goin' to give us the deed to this house for a Christmas present. And . . .I know you don't like it sometimes when I do things and don't ask you, but I got Arthur Miffler to draw some plans for renovatin'. He's not really an architect but he's got good ideas for enclosin' the porch and combinin' the livin' room and dinin' room. . . ." She looked up at him, searching his face, hoping desperately that she could make him commit himself. "Darlin', stay a few more minutes, huh? And look at them with me."

"It's awfully late," he said. "I've got that plane to catch in the morning."

"You're angry because I didn't ask you."

"I didn't say that." He was talking too loud and he checked himself. "It's fine. But we don't want to rush and do things without considering . . . well . . ." He fumbled for an explanation and finally found one. ". . . considering where we'll be living and how much we can afford . . . and about your mother."

"We thought you'd be so pleased," she said softly. And she was crying.

"Oh, dammit, don't start bawling on me!" He sighed and took her in his arms. "I'm sorry. I'm sorry. Of course I'm pleased." Tenderly he tilted her chin but she averted her face to conceal her tearless cheeks, hating herself for pretending, and yet justifying it as her only weapon. "Tell you what," Kane said as she managed a bitter sob against his chest, "you send me those plans, honey. And I'll go over them when I've got plenty of time. And I'll get some estimates of costs and whatever else you do with plans."

When he left her she was smiling, apparently happy again. And as he drove back to Cy's, he told himself: *You're a heel and a louse. She's such a kid and sweet and unselfish and never tries to push you really.*

It was after two in the morning when he got home. He found Cy still up in the living room, his dinner jacket, shoes and tie draped over the furniture and across the carpet. "What're you doing up?"

"Just got in," Cy said. "Dropped my date off when I saw there was nothin' doin' and she was just goin' to bruise my ear drums with that infernal yackety-yack. Then, comin' back through town,

I nearly ran over Mrs. Biddle. Poor dame was stinko, looped. I took her home. The Old Man was out lookin' for her, I guess. And you shoulda seen his face when he thanked me, all choked up, could hardly talk." Cy motioned toward the bar. "Let's have a nightcap. I won't have a chance to talk at you for awhile after tonight."

Kane poured bourbon and water for himself and a scotch on the rocks for Cy. "What are you going to talk at me about?"

"You've got to get yourself straightened out," Cy said as he removed the studs from his shirt. "I don't like the sound of all this financial maneuverin' you've been doin'. Why don't you sell your stocks and pay off part of your indebtedness?"

Kane brought Cy his drink. "I'd still owe the bank a lot of dough, Cy. And if I lose the stocks, how will I ever get even?"

"Send somethin' out of your salary every month."

"You know how long that would take me? Besides the bank, I still owe you three thousand."

Cy deposited his cuff links in an ash tray. "About that three thousand, I want you to forget it."

"But I can't let you do that!" Kane said, suddenly adamant. "It's only money."

"Yeah, I know." He dropped his dinner jacket on the sofa and sat down. "Money can't buy happiness—confederate money, that is."

"I'll give you the notes tomorrow," Cy said, and rolling his socks in a ball, tossed them through the doorway into the hall. "We'll wipe it clean."

"No. I won't take it," Kane said.

"That's the way it's goin' to be. It's a weddin' present. Now you get together with Laurie and make plans to get married before she's a wrinkled old hag!"

Kane's brows knitted and turning his glass in his hand, he sat on the sofa. "Listen, buddy. I been meaning to say something to you. . . . I wish you wouldn't keep riding me about getting married—particularly in front of Laurie."

Cy finished his drink and put it on the carpet beside his chair. "Why the devil don't you get married? Give me an answer and I'll let it lay."

"I'm not ready. That's all."

"How many years you think this can go on with you in Washington and Laurie here?"

"It'll work out," Kane said. He dropped back on the sofa, stretching out, his glass on the floor. "I don't know, Cy. But . . . well, I look at some of our friends around here. They're all preoccupied with their babies and their installment plans and their mortgages and buying insurance. And the women—like Ellie Martin—she was a good-looking girl, full of the devil, fun to be around. And I saw her tonight with her rear end as big as a Mack truck, all puffy, and all she could talk about was that some Jewish guy, sponsored by Biddle, wants in the club. Ellie Martin, who used to party with me and you and Joe Schwartz! You'd have thought this guy Greenberg, alias Green, was trying to gain admittance to her personal heaven."

"What's that got to do with you and Laurie?" Cy said, unzipping his trousers. "You think that if Laurie gets married she's gonna automatically get fat and dumpy and bigoted?"

"It's not that." Kane sat up and started to take off his shirt. "It's . . . well, like Ray Burnham's wife. Man, she's holy as hell, a real religious nut these days. Give her a chance and she'll Jesus-you and God-you to death!"

"So you think that's how Laurie'll turn out." Cy pulled his suspenders off, dropped his trousers and tossed them into the hall. "You're a first class, all-American jerk, Kane. If you're not goin' to marry the girl, tell her so. But don't go on tyin' her up so nobody else can look at her. She'll be twenty-five in a couple of months and you can't go on and on, year after year, puttin' her off with one half-assed excuse after another, even if she still keeps takin' it without a murmur! Serve you right if somebody came along and snatched her away from you!"

"You're griped at me, aren't you?" Kane asked, aware of Cy's seriousness for the first time.

"Nope," Cy said, leaning in the doorway. "I'm not griped. But two things would make me like you better. One—-get yourself on keel financially. And two—get yourself married or get yourself disentangled." Without awaiting a reply, he walked off to his bedroom.

Kane sat there, finishing his drink, thinking. All right, he mused. I have no reasons. But things'll work out.

In Washington the idea of eventual marriage had been somewhere in the back of his mind, filed away for the future. In Manton, confronted with Laurie and the not-too-subtle questions of her mother, and the good-natured prodding of his friends, he was being forced to consider it an urgent matter. And he knew that the arguments he had given Cy were only barely relevant, only vaguely related to Laurie. Then why was he hesitating? Viola Eden had baffled the doctors, but she was wasting away. And then there'd be no backing down. So why not get married now? Because . . . although he could easily imagine Laurie as his wife, he could hardly imagine her in Washington. Because . . . there was no hurry now. Because, there was Dany.

Kane went to his bedroom, packed the red-and-gold silk robe and matching pajamas and slippers that Laurie had given him for Christmas, got his things in order for the morning, and put his papers in his new dispatch case. That was Dany's gift. It was fitted with writing stand, pencils, memo pad and a photograph of Dany. Inside, too, was a leather bound copy of *The Prophet.* Kane thumbed through it idly and for the first time saw the quotation from the book that she had copied on the flyleaf: *"I, of your longings, have built a tower in the sky."*

Cy came into the room. "Remind me to give you those personal notes before you leave in the mornin'."

Kane looked at his fat, faithful and loyal friend and he wanted to say something that might tell him how he felt about him. "You crazy sonovabitch," he began. "You're not going to . . ."

"How you doin', Kane, you ole coot?" Cy said.

"Fine as wine. Smooth as cake."

"Then let me have the ole handshake!"

Kane said, "Thanks, Cy."

"Aw, shut up and go to sleep!"

22

SHEPHERD READE, seated beneath his photograph in the Occidental Restaurant, looked across the table at Kane and Dany. "Religious discussions are always fruitless," he said nervously. "Let's talk about somethin' else."

Dany, determined to change the subject herself, pressed her knee against Kane's leg, warning him. "What plans do you have for the committee, Shep?"

The gaunt old man, sensing her discomfort and sharing it, told her. "We've got our work cut out for us."

"One more thing about Catholics, since you brought it up, Shep," Kane said. "People usually inherit their religion along with their bank accounts and the shape of their noses, but they don't necessarily inherit their politics. And it's for goddamn sure . . ."

"Kane!"

"Sorry, Dany. It's for sure Catholics don't vote the way the priest tells them any more than Jews do what the rabbi likes or Protestants follow orders from their preachers."

Shep finished the last piece of his broiled chicken, his rising cheekbones wrinkling the pouches beneath his eyes as he chewed. "I didn't mean to imply that."

Dany glared at Kane and turned her attention to Shep. "What were you saying about plans for this session?"

"It's a new project altogether."

"The work's been so dull," Kane grumbled, pushing his plate away. "Here it is February; and we've wasted a month studying accounting procedures . . ."

"Kane's impatient with detail," Dany said.

"Yes, with detail and with me and with the routine that makes up 75 percent of a Congressman's duties," Shep said sourly, drumming his fingers on the table.

"What's troubling you, son?" he asked gently. "Has your little jaunt in the headlines gotten you off balance? Ask yourself what it did to improve the armed forces, what it did to improve the country."

"Why we did plenty! We made the . . ."

"Kane!" Dany said, grasping his hand. "Listen for a change."

"Now don't bother to defend yourself, Kane. We're friends and I'm not goin' to judge your actions," Shep said. "But my point is simply that, in the long run, if improvin' the country is the test, you accomplished a great deal less with that than you've accomplished by the work you've done with my committee. In time what we've learned will grow into a bill that'll save millions of dollars over the years."

Kane stirred his coffee and, commanded by Dany's stem gaze, forced himself to avoid further argument. "What I really mean is that I don't think a committee ought to bother with problems any civil service hireling can handle."

Shep smiled. "Our government's a ponderous creature, Kane. We move slowly. But we've done exactly what a congressional committee is supposed to do. We've found abuses—in this case with administrative procedures—and now we've got somethin' on which to base corrective legislation."

Reaching for the jeweled cigarette case he had given Dany for Christmas, Kane borrowed a cigarette. "Okay. Okay. So what's the new project you're ready to start on?"

"The administrative organization of governmental loyalty boards," Shep said. "We're startin' by studyin' a classic case. At war's end, people holdin' jobs in emergency wartime agencies were switched from the defunct groups to other departments where they were screened for peacetime employment."

"What has this got to do with loyalty boards?" Dany said.

"From the action taken on these cases, we want to develop government-wide procedures for future use. That will assure employees protection against unwarranted dismissal and enable us to tighten existin' regulations so we can dismiss undesirables."

"What happened to those screened initially?" Kane said.

"There was a recommendation against permanent mployment in over two hundred cases."

Kane shredded his cigarette, piling the tobacco before him on the tablecloth. "What was wrong with them?"

"Some were incompetent. Some were drunks, perverts, dope addicts, blabbermouths. Some were Communists." Shep rubbed his bald spot and examined the palm of his hand. "After a final investigation, nearly half of them were dismissed."

"What about the others?" Dany said.

"A large group resigned or dropped out. Where there was no conclusive evidence on some, additional F.B.I. checks were ordered and they were rescreened. Those remaining were put back to work."

"Where's all your information coming from?" Dany asked.

"Oh, it's a matter of record," Shep said. "The report was compiled three years ago by all of the executive departments."

"Then some of the people who were suspected, then cleared, are still at work?" Kane asked.

"Yes. And, of course, without prejudice. You'll have to read the report or listen to testimony to get the full picture. But, generally, some of them were the victims of circumstance or spite or their relationship with other people was shown to be tenuous—that sort of thing."

A tall, shapely redhead who reminded Kane of Melba Woodmire passed the table. Kane turned in his seat, watching the woman move toward the rear of the restaurant.

"Are you listening to what Shep's saying?" Dany said icily.

"Sure," Kane said. "We find out what procedures were used in the past and come up with standards for the future. Right?"

Before she could reply, Shep stood. "I've got an appointment at the Statler in twenty minutes. It's another good friend of mine who'll warn me that the folks at home are tired of my spendin' all my time on national affairs." He pursed his lips. "You know, that's how I nearly lost the last election—my opponent accused me of workin' for everythin' but my own district."

After dropping Shep, Kane turned his car down Sixteenth Street, toward his apartment. Dany, who had not spoken since they left the restaurant, said, "Take me home."

"I'm sorry."

"Why carry a chip on your shoulder? Shep's worried about the next election. He made a casual remark that he appeals for the Catholic vote in his district through the priest, and you had to pop off."

"Now, listen, Dany, I can sleep even when I eat a good steak on Friday night, but it gives me a royal pain when someone who ought to know better. . ."

"He didn't mean anything by it."

"I wouldn't give a damn if it came from an idiot. But with someone like Shep it's different. People listen to him. Vote for him. And all the time he's as bigoted as any holy-roller who thinks all Jews are alternately Reds and international bankers and the Catholic hierarchy has a private line to the White House! I'm not the kind of guy who sits still and lets someone sound off like that. And anyone that knows better and listens to it and says nothing is no better than the character who spouts the bilge!"

He stopped for a traffic signal. The reflection of the red light bathed her face.

"Kane, what's the matter? Ever since you came back from Manton . . . no, even before, when the Navy thing died a natural death, you've been . . ."

"Bored," he said. "Bored and disgusted and . . ."

"Snapping at everyone around you," she said, interrupting him. The light changed and they pulled away into the flow of traffic. "And you've been impatient and griping and sarcastic and resentful over your committee work. That's what I don't understand, Kane. I've seen you work day and night over your speech on the Purmincar weapon, and the times you hardly slept when you came back from Japan!"

"That was different. Of course I don't mind work—not when I see something happening as a result. But to sit in committee and hear a bunch of self-styled administrative experts testify, to labor over petty details of housekeeping, to listen to the stupid wrangling over the use of an adjective in a report! I thought I was through with that, but I'm still treated like a recruit in basic training."

Dany snapped down the lock on her car door and leaned against it. "I think you've done remarkably well. Your second session is just starting, Kane. Look how much you've learned already."

He sped through the caution light at an intersection and turned the car down a side street. "Dany, before long I'll have to start campaigning all over again. And, aside from a few weeks there when I amounted to something, when I was doing things, I'm still just another nobody whose usefulness is confined to voting like a good Democrat and helping somebody's kid brother get an appointment or somebody's nephew get a job, of trying to get my district thirty-seven miles of federal roads, by writing a bill, coercing a co-sponsor, promising to support another porkbarrel, hoping that—among five thousand other measures—it gets through committee, and praying that it'll someday survive and be passed. Despite everything I've tried to do, I'm still a nobody." He didn't believe it, but he wanted her to tell him otherwise.

She didn't. "It's all experience. It all adds up finally. It's something you've got to have."

"How are you going to get experience by shuffling papers for Shep Reade? The only way you get any place in this town is by outliving or outlasting the other guys. Sooner or later you wind up with enough seniority to get yourself a committee. And then, when someone has to listen to you, when you can get legislation through because you have influence and power, you're so dried up you don't have anything to say. You play statesman like Shep Reade and waste months proving that it's stupid to have misfits with government jobs and you frame a bill that says so in forty sections and fifty 'whereas' clauses!"

Dany relented. "I know you, Kane O'Connor. What you want is for me to tell you that you're really a big man, that people recognize you on the street, that you've had your name in the columns and you don't have to worry about re-election and you've gotten a reputation as some kind of an orator, and you're building a reputation as a moderate who isn't afraid to vote with the liberals on some issues and the conservatives on others." Watching him, she went on, "I recognize your mood. You average a sulk to the half-week now. And I'm not going to tell you what you want to hear!"

He stopped the car before his apartment. "Okay. Don't tell me. Just help me dream up my speech for the convention in Miami."

"If you want to work, Kane, let's go to your office."

"I've got my notes upstairs in the apartment."

"I don't want to work there, Kane."

"Why not?"

She didn't reply, though she had an answer. She contemplated the truth: she had been nearly overpowered by his ardor before. And she had made up her mind that he would not have her cheaply. Cheaply won, she could be cheaply put aside. And that would mean losing him to the girl in Manton, a foe represented by the regular arrival of blue envelopes in Kane's office, a foe she considered a hangover in Kane's past. The advantage, Dany believed, was hers again. Given time, she decided, the unequal contest would be a victory for her.

Kane had gotten out of the car and was holding the door open for her. "I told you," she said, "if you want me to help with your speech, we'll work at your office."

He scowled at her. "Grow up. You won't get raped!"

I can handle him, she thought, and followed him inside.

It was midnight when Kane finally leaned back on the sofa, his feet on the coffee table, and Dany sat on the leather ottoman facing him, reading from his proposed speech.

"Go over that last paragraph again, will you?"

She glanced over the erratic shorthand on the pad. "The future of our nation," she read, "depends on these things I have talked about tonight. But it is not enough to pay lip service to democracy, to be willing to fight for freedom, to understand the origins of liberty. We must *live* democracy." She puzzled over the next phrase, then began haltingly, "We must strengthen freedom. We must perpetuate liberty."

"Stinks!" Kane said.

"It's not much. But it won't hurt anybody's feelings."

"Doesn't mean a thing. I'm the warm-up attraction on the roster, just before the main speaker. I'm talking to a bunch of characters who're celebrating being away from their wives for a few days. Some of them'll be half-crocked, wishing I'd shut up so they can get the main event over with and take out some waitress they've lined up. I've got to wake them up! Got to give them something their imagination'll feed on.

"Why don't you mention your brawl with the Navy?"

He pushed himself up. "Hell, no. Let it lay. Trouble with the speech as it is, as Tod would say, is that it's got no . . . well, guts."

She turned to a clean page in her notebook as he stalked across the room. "Got any other ideas, Kane? It's late. I'm going shopping with Lucy in the morning; and you've got a committee meeting."

"I'm going to skip it. Just the start of that loyalty board stuff."

"Wait a minute! What about that? Use something on the work of congressmen, the committee meetings, sessions, research on legislation, duties to constituents . . ."

He stood in the center of the room, rapping his knuckles against his teeth. "Who the hell's interested?"

Dany drew great swooping eagles with tiny heads on the notepaper. "How about what Shep said? You know, finding procedures to assure people against unfair dismissal and making it easier to get rid of undesirables?"

"That sounds damned exciting," he said sarcastically. "The only people who are . . ."

"Hold it!" Dany snapped her fingers, trying to concentrate on the nucleus of the idea that now split and multiplied in her mind. "That business Shep talked about this evening! That's what we need. Then you won't just spout about democracy and freedom and liberty. You can use this illustration of the importance of protecting them! It's double-edged. Protection of the individual and protection of the government . . ."

"Before you get too wound up, remember the report is old hat. It came out three years ago."

"I didn't know about it and you didn't. I'll bet few people do."

He nodded thoughtfully. "You're right there."

Pleased with the idea, Dany was intent on selling it. "You know when people are willing to defend their rights? When they're threatened with losing them."

The possibilities of the subject began to spur Kane's mind. He recognized the logic in Dany's argument. "Who said that line about 'Eternal vigilance is the price of liberty'?"

"That's not the exact quote, but Curran said it, I think. Why?"

"That's the angle to hit it from." He walked about the room, starting to ad lib: "Even in peacetime there are dangers in our midst, people who seek to undermine our liberty, usurp our freedom and destroy our democracy!" He was happy with it now. "Dany, how do you manage to be so pretty and so smart at the same time?"

She was yawning. "I couldn't even answer that question right now. I'm too tired. Couldn't we work tomorrow night? You've got a week yet."

They left the apartment. "The first thing I've got to do tomorrow," Kane said, "is get ahold of that 1946 report on security screening. I'll have Tod pick it up from Shep's secretary."

She was basking in the praise he had given her, positive he would come to know how much he needed her. She hadn't heard him, had only been conscious of his speaking. "Tired?" she asked.

But Kane didn't reply. His mind, too, was employed elsewhere. "You know," he told her as they walked through the ornate lobby, "I might just have something!"

BOOK THREE

23

KANE SLAMMED his apartment door. "You've been nagging at me for one thing or another all night, Dany," he said, taking off his dripping trench coat. "Dammit, I'm me! And I'm not going to change into some kind of pseudo-intellectual pansy like some of your friends, or become as inhumanly polite as Ward Roberts. So lay off. Stop bitching at me. I don't want to hear anymore."

"That's your trouble," Dany said. "You're so wrapped up in yourself that no one can possibly find fault with you." She carried her drenched coat to the bathroom to hang it up.

"I don't mind criticism," Kane called after her. "But how many times do you have to repeat the same business?" He heard the sweeping rain battering at a kitchen shade and went into the alcove to shut the window. After putting a pot of coffee on the small range, he walked back to the living room.

Dany was standing before the mirror that topped the false fireplace. Laurie's picture smiled from the mantel; and Dany admitted that the girl was pretty—without real beauty, she thought— but pretty. As she combed the water sparklets from her hair, Kane stepped behind her, putting his hands on her waist, and looking at their reflection in the mirror. "You're even more beautiful when you get angry with me," he said. It was his gesture of conciliation.

She took his hands away. "Let's get back to the speech." With theatrical indifference, she reached for her notes in her purse, pulled a straight-backed chair from the desk to a place before the sofa and sat down in proper secretarial pose.

"Did you talk to Lucy about the speech?" Kane tossed his new sports jacket on one end of the divan and, opening his collar, pulled his tie away.

"She said it sounded all right from what I could remember of it, but she thinks you should tie it in a little stronger on how it affects the individual. What did Mel say?"

"Not very encouraging. Told me he had all the information in his files, offered some clippings from his morgue. They ran some stuff on it a couple of years ago."

"Well, it's hard to get an opinion out of him."

Her voice was cold, formal. She knew that, with little justification, she had been unduly critical of Kane; and she was angry with herself for her behavior. For it was more than fury that burned in her throat. More than frustration. It was jealousy, too, and she felt powerless to fight it.

Late that afternoon, while waiting for Kane to dress, she had prowled around the living room emptying ash trays and straightening papers. That's when she had found, open on the breakfast room table, a set of blueprints and a rendering of a house. It had been labeled: *Proposed Residence, Mr. and Mrs. Kane O'Connor*. And, apparently, Kane had received it in the mail and had neglected to put it aside. She had said nothing to him. But all through the long evening at Hunting Acres, the knowledge of it and of what it meant, throbbed in her mind.

"As bright as Mel is about most things, I trust Lucy's opinion, maybe because I want to think she's right," Kane was saying. "Dany? You listening?"

"Mmm-huh," said Dany who had not heard a word.

Kane stretched out on the divan, pillowing his head with his jacket. "We've got to make this important to the individual. It's Tod's old theme: 'What's in it for uncle?'" He locked his hands behind his neck.

"People get interested if something's going to make them richer or poorer or put them in danger or give them safety. Those are the only issues they give a hang about."

She smiled wryly. "That sounds like contempt for the common man."

"Why do you think the average Joe doesn't get excited about tariff legislation?"

She sat watching him, her chin in her hand, wondering how he could ignore how she felt. Tonight, as every other time they went to Hunting Acres, she had found herself half-listening to the conversation, glancing over the room to find Kane's back, struggling to keep her mind on the cards when she heard his hearty laugh. "I don't know," she said. "I'll be your straight man. Why don't they get excited about tariffs?"

"Because they haven't been shown that a tariff reduction on an English bicycle would knock down the price of Junior's Christmas. Or, if you happen to work for a bike manufacturer, it could cut the hell out of your salary in time."

Dany tried to concentrate on what he was saying, but her thoughts kept tearing her away, nagging her with the fear that he had already made up his mind, that he was going to marry the girl from Manton.

Kane kicked off his shoes and, turning on his side, pointed his finger at her. "When you talk to the public, you've got to tie your subject to what they want, what they value, what they're afraid of."

She sat up in her chair and glanced at the picture of Laurie. *How can he throw himself away on her?* she thought. Then, rousing herself from the reverie, "Kane, do you want to finish writing your speech, or do you just want to deliver one to me?"

"Okay. I'll get the coffee and we'll get to work."

Kane had his own method of writing a speech. He walked around the room, waving his outline and talking in long bursts of rhetoric. When he thought he had made his point, he would look to Dany for her reaction. She would nod her "yes" or shake her head. Then she would read back his rambling construction, his dangling participles, his prepositional endings. And they would pare and edit and rephrase. The reworked version would be read again and then he would begin on another tack.

As she watched him, wandering about the room, his collar open, his free hand fingering his tie, she knew he needed her. She could help him, could grow with him. What tied him to the girl in Manton?

". . . and so, the time of decision has come. We must protect America," Kane began. "No. No. That's not right. Change it." He made another turn around the room, stood thinking for a moment before the rain-streaked glass wall. "This way: The blue chips are down. We must protect our children, our homes, our heritage . . ."

It was two in the morning before Dany was able to read back the final paragraph: "Tonight I hold the key which will unlock those carefully barred doors, bare this guarded secret and expose those who would destroy us from within. Who will dare deny it? Who will turn his head from treachery? I am but one voice among a multitude. I am, like you, another veteran who has shed blood for his country, who has faced death that this nation might live. But this I pledge you, my friends: I have never turned from a fight, never flinched before a battle. God willing, I shall not fail you now."

He dropped to the easy chair. "I like it! If we get the breaks, we'll make papers all over the country!" Yawning, blinking at Dany, he said, "We've done it together, Dany. Thanks."

"I'll get my coat now. I'm ready to go."

"You still mad at me? And if so, for what this time?"

"I don't think it makes any difference to you how I feel." She wanted to say, bluntly, *Are you going to marry her?*

"Come on, Dany. I give up. You can keep on trying to improve me if you want."

"I haven't tried to improve you," she said, and knew that, like all women, she had tried, and like most women, she had largely failed.

"Get my coat, please."

"Let's make up first."

"There's nothing to make up," she said and started to go for her coat.

Kane grabbed her hand. "I hereby issue a blanket apology. For the chair I didn't pull out for Lucy tonight, for missing Mass again and . . . for the two cuss words you caught me at . . . no, for one. When I called that guy a bastard, it was justified." Laughing, he lifted her hand to his lips while she glared at him. "What more can I do? You know we're going to end up liking one another again. Why postpone it?"

"That's the way it always ends, Kane," she said, pulling her hand away. "No matter what you do, you think your apology makes everything all right again."

He slid over the arm of the chair and took her arm. "I'll listen to all complaints right now. Go ahead."

"Please. It's late."

Kane put his arms around her, his broad palms at her back. She stood stiffly. "Did I tell you that you were the most beautiful, the most brilliant, the most charming woman at Hunting Acres tonight?"

"I didn't know you noticed."

"I've always told everybody that you're the loveliest . . ." Her anger flared. She spoke, caution and pride forgotten, the pressure of her thoughts forcing her words to the surface. "Have you told Laurie? She probably wouldn't like it!"

Kane was shocked for the moment, and covered his surprise by drawing her closer. It was the first time Dany had ever mentioned Laurie by name. "You're jealous!"

"Like hell I am! But if you think you're going to chase me around the furniture while you moon over that maiden on the mantel . . ."

"Truce!" He dropped his hands from her waist. He had known that sooner or later he'd have to face this moment, but he wasn't prepared for it, and without thinking, he tried to tease Dany away from a subject that he had avoided so long. Reaching into his pocket for his handkerchief, he waved it as a white banner before her. "I give up! But at last you're admitting you've got a crush on me!"

Dany, raging, grabbed the handkerchief and threw it to the floor. "Don't flatter yourself. You're already weak from patting your own back. Go build your damned dream house with your corn-fed dream girl."

Kane glanced at the breakfast room table and remembered in an instant that, after another prodding by Laurie, he had at last opened the plans and looked at them. And then, he'd left them there —for Dany to see. "So that's what you've been so burned up about all evening! Don't let it bother you, Dany. It's a house I own in Manton . . . and I was thinking about renovating it so I could resell it at a profit . . . and . . ."

"You're a double-damned liar! And save your explanations. You don't owe me any!"

His arms tightened around her again and he hugged her to him roughly. "Dany, cut it out. That fool architect put Mr. and Mrs. on the thing out of habit."

She turned her head and strained against his arms. "It's clear enough what you want, Kane. And you're welcome to it. You see that girl's counterpart all over this town. She'll fit in fine! She'll be just like a hundred other women who married young men with ambition and then stopped growing, stopped living!" The words had been damned up, held back by the looming structure of propriety. Now they tumbled out, flooding her reason. "Twenty years after the wedding, hubby is a congressman or a senator or a cabinet member. He's still learning, still going someplace. And the wife hasn't read a book or had an original thought since the orange blossoms wilted. She's just baggage, just a bad habit her husband can't easily break. That's what you want; and as far as I'm concerned, you can go right ahead!"

Even as Kane heard her he knew she was phrasing the elusive thoughts that had not become coherent in his mind. He remembered Laurie trying to catch up to him, studying his books, discovering that George Eliot was a woman. He remembered her asking about Lucy's dress. He remembered her ignorance about what he was doing, her inability to understand the language of politics. And he knew that there was truth in what Dany said, that somewhere along the way he had outgrown Laurie. But then, he reasoned, other things matter . . .

He was really arguing with himself, but he defended Laurie. She was good and honest and loyal. "Goddammit," he swore, "if you want to act like a jackass, go ahead. There's one thing about Laurie. She's a woman. She acts like a woman. She makes you feel like a man. She doesn't argue and pick and nag and gripe and tell you how to tie your bow tie and how to blow your nose. She cries when she's sad and she fusses when she's mad and she lets you know you're the boss. She's more woman that you'll ever be!" He followed Dany as she backed away from him. "Oh, you've got the equipment. You look like a woman and the few times I've been able to get close enough to you, you felt like a woman. You dress like a woman. You smell like a woman. But I'll be damned if you act like a woman!"

Dany slapped him, as hard as she could, across the mouth. "You expect me to mush all over you and pet you and tell you you're wonderful and weep prettily to make you feel manly? To hell with you, Kane O'Connor!"

He laughed at her. "It hurts," he said, rubbing his mouth, stalking her. "Kiss it and make it better." She stepped back. "Kiss it, I said!"

"I'm not afraid of you, Kane!" But she was, and she turned to go for her coat.

He reached for her. "Come here!"

She struggled, pushing at his shoulders. But he pinned her to the wall with his body, held her face with his hands and kissed her. She tried to turn her head, but couldn't. She felt his warmth and strength against her, saw the anger and excitement in his eyes. Pulling her arms free, she scratched his face; and he grabbed her hands and held them with one of his behind her back. Dany clenched her teeth as he kissed her. Her breasts ached with his weight, and his beard, rubbing against her chin, hurt her, too.

Kane, excited by the pursuit, by her unrestrained fury and the sure strength in her hands, by the male triumph of knowing that her protests were only an affirmation of her jealousy, thought no more about Laurie. That could wait.

Dany considered her mistake now. She had tried to take Kane from the other woman, but had denied herself the use of her strongest weapon. Relaxing, she let him kiss her; and she put her arms around him, running her hands across his shoulders.

He stepped back. She was standing against the wall now, watching him. There was a smug smile on Kane's face. He wet his lips. "I want some more."

"Don't touch me!"

As he reached for her, she hit him with her clenched fist and saw the ugly red imprint on his cheek and felt the tingling numbness in her hand.

He was smiling still, smoothing his cheek with his fingers, watching her, moving toward her. "I'm going to paddle your fanny for that!" He lunged at her, picking her up in his arms as if she were weightless.

"Put me down!" She pulled his hair; and he roared with laughter. She scratched his face; and he bit her wrist until she cried with pain. She struggled to be free of him; but he held her fast. She was crying now, her face flushed with tears. "Stop it! Stop it! You're crazy!"

Kane carried her to his bedroom. He had neglected to close the window and the wind lashed gusts of rain across the bed. There was a spreading puddle on the floor.

"Put me down, damn you!"

"Sure!" He threw her onto the bed and as she attempted to sit up, he forced his weight against her. She lay pinioned there as he kissed her again. His lips were at her neck; and she felt his kisses at her ear and the rain's cool embrace across her forehead.

His mouth, insistent, moved down her neck to her shoulder. His hands searched and fumbled. "No!" she screamed. But his mouth pressed against hers, stilling the word in her throat. He tugged at her dress again and she pulled away, hearing the gliding whush of the zipper. She tore at his shirt, ripping it, hearing the rattle of a button on the floor. "Damn you! Damn you!" She got her hands free again and beat at his head, his back. The rain gathered strength now, and splattered through the window, bathing them. Wet and furious and aroused, she fought him while her judgment wrestled with her passion.

Kane was breathing heavily, nuzzling her ear. "Dany, darling. Dany, darling," he kept repeating. And she realized he had never called her that before. Then he kissed her, writhing as she seared his back with her clawing nails. "Beautiful, beautiful," he said. "Love you. Why don't you let me love you?"

The words, nearly incoherent with frenzy, reassured her as she groped for reason. "I want you, Dany. I want you so," he said feverishly. And this she translated into an acknowledgment of his love and his need for her.

He kissed her mouth; and she tangled her fingers in his hair, held him, drinking him in until, gasping, he freed himself. They were drenched. The wind-scattered rain dripped from his shoulders, ran down her face.

"The window," she said breathlessly. "The window."

"Not this time, you don't," he said. And burying his face against the rising rhythm of her breast, he gasped, "To hell with the window!"

24

DAYLIGHT CREPT softly into the room.

Dany awakened and for a moment, in the dim, early light, she was lost. Then her arm touched Kane's. She arched her back and ran her toes down the fuzz on his muscled leg. He still slept.

Getting up, careful not to awaken him, she went to the bathroom. There, before his mirror, she ran her fingers along the scratches on her shoulder and smoothed the hair from her face. Then, humming softly, she showered and dried herself with his huge, rough white towel.

In the darkened living room she opened the blinds, allowing the sun to filter in. The pleated light threw bands of shadow over her nude body; and standing there, she examined herself, pressing her palm against the flushed bruise Kane had left on her side, holding her hands beneath her full-parted breasts, breathing deeply so that even the gentle roundness of her stomach appeared flat. I'm beautiful, she thought, pushing her hair straight back, admiring the golden sweep of it against the smooth tan of her shoulders.

Kane was still asleep; and she got back into his bed, pulling the sheet aside so she might look at him. He was disarmed now, his lower lip pouting, his beard bristling black on his jawline, barely showing on his cheeks. One clenched fist lay on the island of curly hair on his chest. He stirred and she was afraid that she had awakened him. But he pulled his legs up in fetal position. Resting her head against the backboard of the bed, she smiled when his knee cracked and she drowsed, remembering his words, treasuring them. When she glanced at him again, his eyes were open, watching her.

"Good morning."

"Morning." Kane batted his eyes, and his hands stretched above him as he flexed his body and began to laugh softly, then louder.

"You always wake up in such a good mood?"

Through his laughter, he told her, "No. Just thinking of you—last night!"

"What's funny?" she asked, on the defensive.

"Dany, darling, you should hear yourself!" He shook the bed with laughter. "The things you say when you're making love!" She flushed. "Don't tell me. But call me 'darling' again. It sounds so possessive."

"All right, *'darling,'* you're a fantastic cusser."

She slipped down beside him, her body touching his, and she held his face in her hands, rocking it gently. "I'm pretty ungrateful. You told me you loved me and I cussed you. But I don't remember a word."

"You're a helluva one to complain about *my* language." He rolled over on his back, laughing again.

Dany pulled herself over his leg and rested her face against his. "Tell me again. Do you love me?" It was the question ten times ten billion women have asked, the justification for everything, the magic incantation that changed the base metal of "lust" to the pure gold of "love," the salve for conscience, the balm for fear, the deed to possession.

As he lay there, his hair awry, his eyes glinting, his hands lightly on her back, her belief in him, her belief in their sameness, in their joint destiny, was strong and compelling. The very roughness and crudeness that she despised in him, fascinated her. He wanted fame, power, wealth, excitement. He hated weakness. He feared obscurity. She shared his desires, joined him in his hatred and his fear. This was love, she told herself. And since she had surrendered something, the one thing she might have withheld, since loving someone is a happiness second to being loved, she asked him again. "Well, do you? Do you love me?"

"What do you think?"

"I know what *I* think," she said and nipped his ear. "I want to hear it, though."

"I love you." And how many times had Kane said those words? He could not have recalled the number with prodigious effort and a deliberate probing of his memory. For a man is by nature the invader; and he can make love to a woman, whisper the hot breath of lies in her ears, find satisfaction and never know his mistress' name. "I do love you, Dany," Kane repeated. And at that moment, although he would have preferred silence, an understanding and not an exposition, he knew that this morning was different from all the others, that what had happened between them in the fury of anger and passion was a beginning and not an end, that this woman was wiser and stronger than anyone he had ever known, and that she had given herself to him—not only her body, but her wisdom and her strength.

She kissed him lightly. "And I love you, Kane. Oh, my dear, my darling, I mean it. I mean it. And what else is there to say?"

The doorbell jangled, far away. It rang again. The lovers awakened simultaneously, sitting up in bed, clutching the sheets. They felt like stagehands caught by the rising curtain.

Kane, remembering the earlier awakening, tossed the covers off, revealing her, and grinning, ran his hand down her bare thigh as he swung his feet to the floor. The bell was persistent, but ignoring it, he bent over her and kissed her. "You're some woman!" he said as he started out of the room.

"Put something on!"

The bell rang once more. Kane reached into the closet for the robe Laurie had given him for Christmas, and dragging it after him, hurried to the front door. When he opened it, Matt Fallon was standing there.

"Hell, man, I thought you'd already gone out."

"It's Sunday! I forgot you were coming this morning."

"It's not morning, friend. It's one o'clock and you promised to buy me lunch."

Kane was trying to organize his thoughts. What to do about Dany? Should he ask Matt to come back? Meet him later? Well, he decided, Matt's a big boy. "Sit down and read the Bible or something. I'll get cleaned up."

When he returned to the bedroom, Dany, in her slip, was standing at the window, tilting the blind, watching the sun drink at the shiny-wet pavement far below. "Who was it?"

"Matt Fallon."

"Get rid of him?"

"He's in the living room."

"Kane!"

"He won't ask any questions."

"I haven't even got a dress to wear! It's soaked."

"I owe you a dress. And you owe me a shirt," he said kicking at the tattered one on the floor. "Here. Put my robe on."

"I can't go out there like that!"

"Now stop the whispering and be sweet and get some coffee on."

"But Matt's in the front room!"

"It's no use being silly about it, Dany. You want to hide in the closet? We won't say anything and Matt won't ask any questions."

Dismally, she sat down on the bed. "He'll think I'm a tramp." Kane took her in his arms. "He won't think anything; and *I* think you're wonderful."

She put on the robe grudgingly; and he rolled up the sleeves for her. "I think I hate you," she said without conviction, looking beautiful and forlorn in the oversized robe.

"No you don't hate me. You've just never really loved anyone before . . . and it takes time to get used to."

"And I suppose you have!"

"Over and over and over again!" he said, and laughing, walked into the bathroom to shave. "Ask Matt to come in here while I get dressed."

She girded herself for her entrance into the living room. "Good afternoon, Matt."

He turned, surprised at the sound of her voice. "Oh! I didn't know . . ."

"I'm going to make a pot of coffee. You want to keep Kane company while he dresses?" She tried her best to sound unconcerned. "This is the second time I've tried to make coffee. I got here a half-hour ago to help him finish his speech. He was still asleep and when I went to put some coffee on, I spilled the pot over my dress . . ."

Matt's incongruous dimples pulled in, but he managed to restrain a smile.

"Let's face it," Dany said. "I can't lie very well without preparation!"

"Got a cigarette?"

She pointed to the box on the coffee table. "I've been here all night."

Matt drew the first puff. "Good thing," he said as he went to join Kane. "It sure rained like mad early this morning."

Dany took Laurie's picture from the mantel and put it in the desk drawer.

Matt sat on the edge of the tub while Kane shaved. "Dany's dying of embarrassment," Kane told him.

"You're doing damned well for yourself, friend."

"She's quite a girl."

"I'll bet!"

"Really knows politics. And people in government and the Washington angles . . ."

"Uh-huh!"

"All right you stinker!"

Matt laughed. "What did you want to talk to me about that's so important?"

Kane edged the razor over his upper lip. "Got a speech coming up Wednesday. It's going to shake things up. I want you to cover it."

"What's the subject?"

"Subversives in government."

Matt reached over and dusted his ashes into the commode. "What's the angle? It's surely not news any longer."

"It is to a lot of people," Kane insisted.

"Not if they can read. How about the Grace trial? Justice Department pinned him. And that character in the OSS that was nailed by one of those recanting Commies? And all the stir when he testified against Grace?" Matt leaned against the glass door of the shower stall. "You're a latecomer on this pitch, buddy. When you were still in college Martin Dies was sticking pins in voodoo dolls."

"I'm talking about subversives who are working right now, in all the departments. And nothing's being done about it."

"You mean as far as we know."

Kane washed his razor under the hot water. "I mean nothing's being done as far as anyone knows."

"The F.B.I. keeps an eye on them."

"Then why don't they lock them up?"

"Got to have evidence to convict them."

"I've got evidence."

Matt was wary of Kane's enthusiasm. He recalled the Purmincar campaign and the pointless squabble with the Navy. "Then why don't you give it to the F.B.I.?"

Kane hadn't expected an argument. "I think I can do more good by getting the word out myself."

"Since you're so hot to do something, you might get some enabling legislation through Congress to make the F.B.I.'s work easier."

Kane had his argument now. Matt had given it to him. "What do you have in mind?"

"Get a legalized wire-tap bill through covering suspected treason cases. Make the Communist party register for what it is— an agent of a foreign government. Have the Constitution amended so the Fifth Amendment is not applicable in cases involving treason. Those things will help the Justice Department get to them."

As he began to brush his teeth, Kane stopped, his mouth full of foam. "That's exactly what I plan on doing. But first we've got to rout them out in the open."

"Nope. Don't kid yourself. J. Edgar Hoover's got a file on every subversive in town. His people know where they are and who they are. But he's got to get evidence that'll stand up in court. The right legislation'll do the job."

"Nobody's going to push any bills through until the people scream for it," Kane argued. "I'm going to wake them up. Then I'll get to work on the proper bills."

"You cleared your information with the authorities?"

"Of course," Kane lied.

"And you have specific data? Names?"

"Plenty of them," Kane said, patting on shaving lotion.

"In government now? Or during our wartime shot-gun marriage to Russia?"

Kane wasn't sure about that. "Now," he said.

"Give me numbers," Matt said.

Considering the meagre facts he'd garnered from Shep's conversation and the three-year-old report he had read, Kane wondered what would convince Matt. "I can tell you that it's an amazing number."

"Where'd you get the beat?"

Kane smacked his face with talcum. "I've got to protect my source of information."

"Friend, you're learning!"

Back in the bedroom, Kane pulled on his shoes. "I want you to help me get this thing across, Matt. It's important."

Matt grunted, and his freckled lips pulled back in a smile of tolerant amusement. "Important for whom? Congressman Kane O'Connor?"

"No, dammit. Important for the country."

"Where are you speaking?"

"Miami. It's a convention audience. Big crowd. But the radio and TV coverage is for the principal speaker—some tycoon who follows me. I want you to have my part of it filmed for your Friday show."

"No can do. Too much dough involved."

"You can swing it."

"Why don't you just tip the AP, UP, INS?"

"I have."

"You're sure you've got this down pat, that it's not just another one of your big deals?"

"In black and white."

"I can't get it filmed, Kane. But I'll tell you what we'll do." He thought a moment. "My guess is it won't get much reaction. But if it should, you appear on my show and repeat the important dope next Friday."

Kane shook hands with him, and in the same motion pulled himself to his feet. "Thanks, buddy. You don't realize it now, but *I'm* really doing *you* a favor!"

25

THE MIAMI audience was aroused.

Kane sensed it. His eyes flicked across the front row and he saw his listeners staring at him. He glanced down the columns of serious, intent faces along the center aisle, down either side of the great auditorium. He looked into the balcony where the mass seemed to lean forward as one. He heard not a cough, not a creaking chair, not a whisper of conversation.

"I call it treason!" he said, cutting the air with the blade of his hand. "Sitting in Washington tonight are men and women known to the Secretaries of the various departments as members of the Communist conspiracy!"

Now he stepped from the podium, purposely leaving the public address microphone. He wanted the conventioneers to strain for his words, to follow his movement across the platform, to wait eagerly for his next sentence. "Treason," he said softly; and then, louder, riveting their attention, "Treason!"

He heard a murmur, saw heads turn to their neighbors. Knotting his fists, shaking them before him, he said, "These traitors in our midst are planning the actions of our State Department! They are influencing the decisions of our Treasury Department! They are handling the codes and war plans in the Department of Defense! They hire and fire in our civil service! They stand before the test tubes in our top-secret laboratories!"

And then he crossed the platform again, his eyes sweeping over the upturned faces that moved as he moved. Deliberately, glorying in the drama of the moment, he shook his head as if, for a moment, he was speechless in dismay. "There are traitors at large," he said at last, and his arms stretched out to encompass the audience. "And these traitors are shaping the policies, the plans, the very destiny of our country!"

The morning after his address, Kane O'Connor was news again.

Matt Fallon, drinking tomato juice with tabasco at his desk, checked the wire service reports that were laid out before him: "Congressman Kane O'Connor (Dem. N.C.) told an audience in Miami last night . . ."

Mrs. Lucas Biddle, taking a bottle of gin from its hiding place in her linen closet, poured herself an after-breakfast drink and settled down to listen to *The Other Life of Nancy Hill* as it unfolded on Manton's **WWMG**. Then a news bulletin: "Congressman Kane O'Connor last night told a convention audience in Miami, Florida that known Communists are shaping the destiny of this country."

A newsboy, still sleepy-eyed and cold, rushed from a stand on Market Street in San Francisco and cut the ropes that bound the package thrown from the Brider truck: O'CONNOR SLASHES AT GOVERNMENT COMMIES.

A Cabinet member—late of the blast furnaces of Pittsburgh —sipped his orange juice in the Wardman Park coffee shop. He unfolded his *Washington Post:* O'CONNOR ACCUSES ADMINISTRATION OF HARBORING REDS

The earnest, casual, confidential man on the TV screen in Fort Worth put aside the tin of youth-giving pills: "Congressman Kane O'Connor charged last night that, with the knowledge of members of the Cabinet, Communists are infiltrating the government. . . ."

The fickle brood returned.

When Eastern Airlines' three-thirty flight landed at National Airport in Washington, the press was waiting. Newsreel and TV cameramen eased Kane toward their microphones. Reporters jabbered questions which were parried with a promise of a press conference at Kane's office. Flashbulbs glowed as photographers ordered him from one position to another. Kane posed with clenched fist, with pointing finger, with a second vice-president of the American Patriots who gave him a certificate attesting to honorary membership, and with a throng of apparently militant women. (Members of the Eddie Joy Fan Club, conveniently on hand to await the arrival of their crooner-idol.)

Tod carried Kane's suitcase to the car in the congressional parking lot. Dany was waiting there; and Kane slipped in beside her.

She kissed him. "You've really done it this time!"

"You should have been there! When I sat down they cheered and applauded for what seemed like ten minutes. Over a hundred people waited in line just to shake my hand!"

Tod turned the car out to the Mount Vernon Highway. "I can think of people right here in D. C. who'd stand in line to wring your neck!"

Dany entwined her fingers with Kane's. "Shep's been calling for hours."

"What's his trouble?"

"He's furious. Wants to see you."

Kane had anticipated Shep's anger. "He's probably sore because I made something out of an issue he was too damned dull to recognize. I'll calm him down. In a week he'll have forgotten about it."

"And so will everyone else," she said. "Unless you can keep it alive."

"Oh, no. Not this time. This is big, honey. It's bigger than either of us thought."

"All you've got to do is find some way of keeping it big," Tod said as they turned off to Highway 1.

Dany and Tod had discussed a plan all morning. Now she broached it to Kane. "Instead of crawling to Shep with apologies, you've got to make him give you a subcommittee—now, while you're in a position to ask for it."

He looked at her, amazed. "Now? With the old boy fuming? Hell, he'd have a stroke!"

The drawbridge was up and they waited while the river traffic passed. "Listen to me," Dany said. "All this interest is only going to last until the newspapers and the public have something else to talk about. This is too important to die. We've stumbled on it, Kane, but it can be the very thing that gives you a chance to contribute something. With this, darling, you can do more for the security of the country than another fleet of ships or another ten divisions, more than Shep has done since he's been in Washington. You can force a clean-up of the whole rotten mess. You've got to keep it alive!"

He was looking at her face, his own expression reflecting the intentness, the seriousness in hers. "I know what you mean, Dany. But a subcommittee . . ."

She grasped his arm. "Kane, you can't lone-wolf it. A subcommittee gives you prestige and power. It lends dignity. It makes you a part of Congress, not just an individual. Without it, this will fizzle. And you can't let it. It's not nebulous like that damned rifle. It's not a cheap sensation like the Japan business."

"But, honey, why should Shep give me a subcommittee?"

"Just among us three," Tod said, leering, "you ought to understand some political trading."

Kane was thinking of what he could do with authority. "But Shep would never agree!"

"I've got faith in you," Tod said. The drawbridge went down and the car moved on. "I saw you handle Luke Biddle." When Tod stopped on New Jersey Avenue to let Kane and Dany out, reporters clustered around the door.

"Later this afternoon," was Kane's only answer to their questions. They followed him inside, up the stairs, through the corridor.

Kane opened the door to the front office, saw Tod's secretary talking on the phone, hanging up, picking up the receiver again.

"Working hard, Hattie?" He winked at her; and she waved and answered another ring.

Dany stopped the newsmen at the door to Kane's private office. "There'll be an interview at five o'clock," she promised.

When Kane stepped inside, he found Shepherd Reade waiting for him. The cadaverous old man was looking out of the window. "Hi, Shep!"

"I want an explanation from you!"

"What's wrong?"

"You know what's wrong. Damn it to hell, you've taken confidential information I gave you and you've blown it into a phony issue," Shep said angrily.

"You're wrong," Kane said.

"Don't tell me *I'm* wrong!"

"You said yourself the information was three years old." The gaunt face contorted, the sunken eyes bulging, cheeks sucked in like a death's head. "That's another thing. You'd think from the papers that you'd discovered America."

"I don't write the papers, Shep." Kane sat down in the swivel chair behind his desk, then got up and deferentially offered it to Shep.

"I expect you to straighten this business out, Kane." Shep slammed his hand on the leather back of the chair and slumped into it. "Today!"

"What do you want me to do?" Kane said calmly, and pulled up another chair. "You don't expect me to lie to the press, do you?"

"Every allegation you made is an outright lie or a mangled exaggeration!"

"Take it easy, Shep. You'll get no argument out of me. We can work this thing out. I've always listened to your advice—and regretted it when I didn't follow it. Why, if I hadn't gotten that information from you, I wouldn't have used it. I've always known that you, above all people in this town, are reliable; that when you say a thing, a man can count on it. Now let's talk reasonably. Tell me what's bothering you."

"First of all," Shep said, still agitated, undeterred by Kane's attempt at flattery, "you neglected to say that the people who are still employed in government work were all screened by the F. B. I."

"I wanted to be fair, Shep. I made that clear. I made a point of it."

"Like hell you did!"

"That's what I said. I'll repeat it on the House floor, to the newspapers, to anybody else."

"And what about this business of the Secretaries bein' aware of Communists in their departments. Who told you that?"

"You did."

"That's a lie! I've been sweatin' out a meetin' in the Speaker's office all mornin' where a lot of folks wanted to know the source of that bit of information. Don't you try to saddle me with it!"

"You said the Secretaries furnished the statistics for the report."

Shep wiped the perspiration from the top of his head. "You're twistin' what I said. I told you the Secretaries reported on how the screenin' worked, that's all. When their reports were compiled, one group survived the screenin's. And that's all there is to it!"

"Isn't that enough? There's a group which may be loaded with Communists and fellow-travelers and security risks and pansies. Doesn't that bother you?"

"It's not true! And I'm not goin' to listen to any more of your evasive reasonin'!"

Kane leaned across the desk. "Shep, honestly, do you think there are *no* Communists in Washington?" His voice was tinged with sarcasm, but his demeanor was polite, serious.

"I'm not sayin' that."

"All right."

"Does that give you license to go around makin' false charges against the Administration, against your own party? Does that give you the right to twist innocent facts?"

Kane walked around and sat on the edge of the desk, nodding grimly, apparently acknowledging his error. "Shep, believe me, I've been sick about this thing all day. I didn't dream it would be all over the papers. You're my friend. You know I couldn't violate your confidence."

"I want an answer."

"I'm just as anxious to straighten this out as you are. Maybe I made an error in judgment. I didn't intend to. You're angry because you think I've hurt the party. Well, I'm sorry. I didn't realize how it would be misinterpreted. I promise I'll say nothing more about the Secretaries being aware of it. But you've agreed there are Reds in Washington. I think I've helped smoke them out."

"That's no way to go about it."

"Shep, you've told me yourself that the job of Congress is to get information and then pass legislation. That's all I want to do."

"Then you're on the wrong track."

"All right." Kane dropped his hands to his sides. "I'm not a hundred per cent right." He spoke carefully, his tone conciliatory. "I'll get this whole mess cleared up. I'll make it plain to the papers —and on the floor tomorrow—that our committee, under your leadership, has been disturbed about the problem for some time, and that the Administration has been co-operative . . ."

"Never mind the Administration. You clean up your own mess." He patted the arm of his chair, punctuating his words. "And from now on . . . you remember that I'll speak for the committee as regards the Administration or anythin' else. By damn, I've got my hands full at home right now, gettin' ready for the election. I can't afford to have things upset here. What I need is some time off to do some campaignin'," he said wearily. "Or maybe a minor miracle or two . . ."

Kane chose that moment for attack. "Shep, I want a subcommittee."

"Ridiculous! For what possible reason?"

"Well, for one thing, to get you your 'miracle,' and for another, to do what you tell me is the job of Congress. Let me have a small group—maybe just four other members. We'll make plans for legislation on this Communist issue. When we finish, we'll present the information to the full committee. And you'll announce how we can get rid of the Red threat."

"You're too junior, Kane."

"There are others just as junior."

Shep rested his elbows on the arms of the chair and stroked his chin with a mottled hand. "There's no need for it. There's just no need."

"It'll do a lot to quiet the papers."

The argument continued for an hour; and still Kane's bid for a subcommittee was unresolved. Shep stiffened, refused, argued, wavered, questioned, weighed his decision. "Kane, there's a great deal to be considered."

From his dispatch case, Kane took a stack of clippings. "Here's a dozen editorials or more—and these were written in a hurry to make a deadline. You can imagine what we'll see this afternoon. All of these say one thing 'Let's get to the bottom of this!'"

Shep hesitated. "It's true somethin's got to be done; but the first thing is for you to clear up your statements of last night."

"I'll do that. But the question will still be there. You and I and everybody else in this town can be sure of that. There are Communists here and the public wants to know what we're going to do about it."

"Perhaps . . ." Shep pondered alternatives.

Kane pressed him. "You'll be the first man in Washington with enough guts to actually do something! As chairman of the Committee on Government Administration, you appoint a planning group to lay the groundwork for legislation. And, Shep, let's be honest. If you don't, some other committee chairman with a tenuous relationship to the thing is going to do it himself."

Shep rubbed his coarse cheek. "Everybody's pretty angry with you, Kane."

"Who votes, Shep?" Kane demanded, getting up and walking around Shep's chair. "Who votes? The people back home? Or some of the deadheads on The Hill who're crying for my scalp?"

"You spoke as a member of my committee. In a sense, I'm responsible."

"If you appoint a subcommittee, it'll show you're on your toes." He stood behind him, gripping his shoulder. "It'll put me on the spot, too. I'll have to put up or shut up."

"You'd have to work quietly. No ballyhoo. Small budget."

Kane was tensed for victory. "Right. You'll be able to release a preliminary report yourself just before the primary. That won't hurt you at home, Shep."

"I'll think it over."

But Kane pushed his advantage. "Now's the time for action. Now. You take a stand now. Act now. It'll be firm action by an experienced, respected member of Congress." He faced Shep who, perplexed, started off across the room. "It's the answer!"

"Are you going to clear up the discrepancies?"

Kane took his hand. "On our friendship, I promise."

"Well, then, I'm goin' to go along with you. I'll give a statement to the papers in the mornin'." He walked to the door, then came back and held Kane's arm. "I'm dependin' on you. You've got good stuff in you. I don't want you goin' off half-cocked again."

When Shep had gone, Kane buzzed for Dany.

She came in and stood beside his desk. "Well?"

"Get Matt on the phone for me, honey."

She frowned. "What happened with Shep?"

He was playing at ignoring her question. "And there'll be no press conference this afternoon. Tell them I'll have something to say tomorrow night on Matt's show. They won't like it, but Matt's my friend . . ."

"Kane!" she said ominously.

He laughed. "And get hold of a good clipping service. We're going to have plenty of work for them."

"Darling, please!"

"Sit down, my girl. The chairman of the Special Subcommittee of the Committee on Government Administration would have a word with you!"

The next afternoon Dany and Kane flew to New York. That night he appeared on Matt Fallon's program.

FALLON: "Can you straighten out this question of whether or not the F.B.I. cleared the government workers you referred to in Miami?"

O'CONNOR: "I said that there were some people who appear to me to range from card-holding Communists to downright security risks. Now all this confusion and argument concerns whether or not this particular group was cleared. That's the only area of disagreement. No one has denied the essential truth that there are Communists at work in Washington."

FALLON: "Do you have any comment on Congressman Shepherd Reade's announcement that you'll head a subcommittee?"

O'CONNOR: "I'm going to rout out the facts. I'm going to stop this infiltration of government by members of the Communist conspiracy. The great danger to our country, Matt, is defeat from within, the gradual erosion of the foundations of democracy. I haven't forgotten an oath I took as a fighting man to protect and defend this nation from all enemies, and the oath I took when I became a Member of Congress. . . ."

The plane flew through the night toward Washington.

"You've done it, darling," Dany said.

"You mean *we've* done it. You gave me the idea."

"You made something out of it."

"And you had sense enough to make me push Shep." He squeezed her hand. "We're a helluva team, darling."

Dany decided to consolidate her gains. "Kane, you know we're not really being fair . . . to Laurie, I mean."

"I know."

"You've got to tell her."

He thought miserably of having to face Laurie, knowing that she loved him, knowing that she had waited so long. "There was a time when I could have been happy with her," he said, speaking only to convince himself. "But it's just like you put it, Dany. She could never keep up now. There's so much I've got to do; and Laurie would be . . ." He searched for the words. "Well, she just wouldn't fit in . . ."

"You've got to tell her."

"Yes." In the quiet that followed, he watched the glow of the engines sparking in the black night outside the window. "I've got that speech in Manton next week. I'll tell her then."

Dany rested her head on his shoulder. Comforted by the drone of the motors, by the smooth fabric against her cheek and by her victory, she slept

26

ON THE MONDAY following his return from New York, Kane sat in the House restaurant sipping coffee, his face hidden in the folds of a newspaper. The eager colleagues who stopped by his table to introduce themselves, to congratulate him, to inquire about his plans, to offer their help, waited fruitlessly for an invitation to join him in his crusade or at his table. He answered politely and briefly, remembered their names for almost a minute, waited impatiently for them to go, and sought refuge behind his newspaper again.

Though his eyes were fastened on the front page picture of himself, Kane's mind was preoccupied with matters of more personal importance. Saturday night he would speak in Manton. He would see Laurie; and somehow he had to tell her that he could not marry her. Despite the tenderness he felt for her, he knew that there was no alternative. It was Dany he wanted and needed now.

"May I join you, Kane?"

He looked up, startled. Ward Roberts was standing above him, smiling, one hand already pulling out a chair. Since their trip to Japan, Kane had been with him at committee meetings and a few times at Hunting Acres; and Ward had somehow contrived to sit beside him or play bridge as his partner or ask for a ride or invite him to a college operetta. There was something so sincere, so naively worshipful in his deference to Kane, that Kane was both pleased and embarrassed. "Sure, Ward. Have a seat."

Ward couldn't have been more appreciative if he had been offered a throne. "I know you're busy," he said. "And I've hesitated to impose on our friendship, but I decided that I'd have to talk with you. You see, I happen to be squarely behind you on this Communist issue; and I don't want to see you licked before you start."

"I'm not going to be licked," Kane said carefully.

Ward glanced around the restaurant, making sure that he would not be overheard. Satisfied, he inched his chair closer and crossed his legs, revealing the dazzling gloss of his elevator shoes. "In a way, I'm afraid I'm violating a confidence in telling you this, but the stakes are too high, what you want to do is too important, to see it jeopardized. I've admired you for a long time. I'm not a fair-weather friend hoping to grab a ride on the bandwagon. You have brains and fortitude and drive. You're the kind of man who gets things done, the kind of man I like to work with, who can teach me."

"Now wait a minute," Kane said, amused by Ward's earnestness and a little uncomfortable at being extolled. "What are you getting at?"

Ward tapped his slim, perfectly manicured fingers on the table. "Shepherd Reade intends to tie you up in your subcommittee. He's going to pack the group with Stu Denton, two other decent but not-too-bright gentlemen, and one first-class troublemaker. You'll operate on the contingency fund with a counsel and a clerk. Your budget's going to be pennies."

"I don't think Shep has any intention . . ."

After approximately twenty minutes and two thousand well-chosen words, Ward convinced Kane that his information was correct. Without sufficient funds to hire an investigative staff and harassed by at least one ultra-conservative watchdog, the group would be ineffectual. Shepherd Reade, despite what he had told Kane, had been astute enough to see that such a subcommittee could do no harm, would by its existence reflect credit on the man who appointed it, and would successfully disguise the shelving of the whole issue and thus protect the Administration.

"You're practical, Kane," Ward told him. "So you know that I have more than one reason for giving you this information. I've told you before about my connections with the American Patriots. We've been fighting the Reds and radicals for a long time." He withdrew a flat, alligator wallet from his breast pocket and flexed it in both hands. "Being on your subcommittee—and with you running it it'll be an important one—would put me in a good position before election."

Kane watched him, wondering what was coming out of the wallet. He knew Ward Roberts was a shrewd and willing worker, and though he was annoyed by Ward's long-winded discourses and his nearly-painfully courteous manner, he reflected that he might prove valuable. "What can I do for you?" Kane said, knowing the answer.

The wallet lay on the table. Ward was absently twisting his cat's-eye ring, smiling shyly. "If you get me assigned to your subcommittee," he said, as if he had suddenly gained the courage to plunge ahead and commit himself, "you'll have a strong supporter, someone who'll help you whip the others into line." He opened the wallet and took out a certified check. "I've arranged to get this thousand dollars from the American Patriots, just as I arranged to have them give you honorary membership when your plane came in from Miami. And no strings. They just want to help with your work."

Kane was amazed. "Thanks! We've been getting hundreds of letters and wires, donations of ten, twenty-five, fifty dollars. But a thousand!"

"Money's not the big problem. All you need is enough to get under way. And if Reade won't give it to you, there are hundreds of individuals and organizations in the country that will. We could raise fifty thousand dollars in a single evening at Hunting Acres. I promise you that. And it's perfectly legal for you to build up a personal staff. Done all the time." He reached across the table to light Kane's cigarette. "You have a tremendous thing. If you handle it right, the next time appropriations come up the people will demand that you get all you need."

Kane beat the edge of the check on the table. "You've been giving this a lot of thought, haven't you?"

"I'm as new as you are in Congress, Kane; and I'm not nearly so knowledgeable, but I always try to think things out. And I have this situation figured. Money we can raise, but we've got to keep Reade from packing the subcommittee. At least get one good man on it, one you know is loyal."

Kane was thinking ahead, laying out his plan of action. If Shep was ready to deceive him, it was only fair to trade deception. Ward would let Shep know that he was opposed to Kane's ideas.

Kane would object to one member of the subcommittee and finally agree to compromise on Ward's appointment. . . . "You meet me at my apartment this evening, Ward. I want to talk to some friends of mine."

"Shouldn't you see Reade right away?"

Kane stood. "I'll see you tonight. Tomorrow's time enough to see Shep."

The first session of the new subcommittee was scheduled for nine-thirty on Friday morning in the only free room Kane could find—an oblong, poorly-lighted cell, formerly used for storage, in the Old House Office Building.

By nine o'clock, Kane arranged his papers before him on the committee-room table. Removing the chair at the foot, he placed two on either side and set the high-backed armchair at the head for himself.

Dany arrived, sniffed at the aroma of stale smoke, dust and steam heat, and struggled unsuccessfully to open the single window. "I hope you graduate to a decent meeting room."

"We will. This is temporary." He put paper and pencils before each place while she arranged the name cards. Republicans Brantley and Denton were to be seated on the left, Democrats Pugh and Roberts on the right.

"You're going to have trouble with Pugh, Kane. He's been in Congress before—for two terms—lost his seat and is back again. All his seniority is down the drain and he's going to resent you."

"Ward's briefed me on him; and I can handle the guy. I conned Shep into putting Ward on just to balance Pugh." Kane stacked his notes. "Ward's already talked to Brantley and Stu Denton. They'll go along with me."

"I don't care for Roberts," Dany said, opening the door and bracing it with a paperweight. "And I don't even know why except that there's something . . . well, sinister's nearly the word, only—you know the Charles Addams' cartoons? The little kids who cut the tails off cats and that sort of thing? Roberts strikes me like that for some reason."

Kane laughed. "That's just his way. He's so damned sincere it seems too good to be true. But he's going to be useful."

"All right. You can have him."

"He put us wise to Shep's plans. The idea of getting Lucy and Mel to help us raise enough money to get started properly is his. And he's not being sinister about what he wants out of it. He was frank and aboveboard. He wanted on the subcommittee and said so."

She kissed his forehead and then rubbed the lipstick away with her fingers. "Okay. You've got yourself a doting slave for your entourage. I won't argue with you."

"There'll be plenty trying to ride my coat-tails, Dany. Nobody's fooling me."

"Well, it's time you were educated about intrigue in high places." She picked up her purse. "Got to run. I'm modeling a gown in a charity fashion show this morning; and then I'm having lunch with Lucy to make plans for the masquerade party where we'll raise some money. . . . "

"Why the masquerade baloney? Seems damned silly to me."

"Because you've got good legs and I want to see you in a costume that'll show them off!" She patted his cheek. "And, incidentally, because we want to make it a social event, something that our well-heeled guests won't want to miss."

"All right. You're the brains in this outfit."

"I'll be back to take you to the airport by three."

When she had gone, Kane tried to put his trip out of his mind, tried to stop thinking of Laurie. He looked over his notes on each of the committeemen. Tod had gotten the biographical information together for him; and Kane studied the facts on their backgrounds and interests.

Luther Brantley was the first to arrive. Though Kane's contemporary in politics, the Iowan was fifty-seven. His rumpled, hard-finished suit looked as if it had just come out of the mail-order box; and his breast pocket was stuffed with fat, green cigars.

Kane shook hands with him. "Good to have you, Luther. With us, party lines don't make a doggone (Tod's notes said Brantley was a church elder) bit of difference."

Brantley extracted one of his cigars and bit off the tip. "Afraid I'm not going to be much help to you, Kane. I'm giving nearly all my time to the Agriculture Committee. But I don't see any question of partisanship here. We're all for doing something to stop the Communists."

Casually glancing at his notes (Owns 1000-acre farm—experiments in organic farming—wife—six kids.) Kane said, "Do you have anything in print on your ideas for organic farming? I was thinking I'd like to send out some information on it to my farm constituents."

During the next fifteen minutes, while a clerk came in, stood uncomfortably by the window, tried and failed to open it, fiddled with the broken handle on the steam radiator and finally walked out to stand in the corridor, Luther Brantley kept Kane busy with an enlightening discourse on the merits of the two-wheeled rubber-tired manure spreader over the four-wheeled wagon. It seemed that drag-chain conveyors and upper beaters and rotating spiral fins worked best and gave uniform spread when the manure was thoroughly rotted. Furthermore, tests with solid and liquid manures as well as chemical fertilizers proved something or other. Brantley was explaining his patented invention (all proceeds to Four-H Clubs of America) which successfully rotted manure by a fermentation process, when Milton Pugh walked in.

"Right over here, Mr. Pugh," Kane said, pointing to a seat. "See you're here right on the dot."

"This is my third term," Pugh reminded him. "I make it a practice to always be on time." It wasn't the only thing that distinguished him from his colleagues. Milton Pugh also wore the only beard in Congress. It was close-cropped, nearly white and came to a severe point at the chin. He pulled out his rimless glasses, wiping them on his handkerchief, and rested the bifocals on his beaked nose. His deep-socketed eyes appeared to bulge forward. With the beak and beard and magnified orbs, he looked like a grumpy silver owl.

"Luther here was telling me about his invention . . ."

"Hmmm," Milton Pugh grunted; and zipping open his briefcase, he removed a file and began to flick through it, licking his thumb as he turned the pages. He had just come from Shepherd Reade's office; and he was riled. "I've forgotten more about government than this kid O'Connor will ever know," he had told Reade. And Reade had replied, "I'm doin' two things to hold O'Connor in line. I'm keepin' the budget to a minimum; and puttin' you in there to watch him."

Since Pugh was flattered, since he was a loyal supporter of the Administration, since he was promised aid in his next campaign, and since he still owed Shepherd Reade fourteen-hundred dollars, he agreed to take the post.

"Mighty glad you're with us," Kane was saying. "I'm depending on you to guide us, what with all your experience and knowhow."

"That so?" Milton Pugh said. And in his mind, which was as neatly ordered as his precisely-trimmed beard, as perfectly catalogued as his vitamin-stocked medicine chest, he filed his first observation on Kane: *A liar, but a smart liar.* He dipped into his briefcase again, brought out another file labeled "James Blodgett Portermaul." In perfectly-formed letters, he made a note to "discuss JBP's relations with Congress." (James Blodgett Portermaul, Milton Pugh's grandfather, was a colonel in the Union Army, a Greek scholar, one of the three best oboe players in America in his time, an unsuccessful candidate for Vice-President, an Undersecretary of State, and the subject of a biography Milton Pugh intended to write when his research was complete. It was to be his second book. The first, published by a co-operative publisher, had been a biography of Alexander Hamilton. It had an excellent library sale, fine reviews in scholarly journals, one printing of 2000 copies, and cost Milton Pugh the fourteen-hundred dollars he still owed Shepherd Reade.)

"Mr. O'Connor," Luther Brantley said, "I'm of the opinion that the time will come when Congress will be forced to act on the manure-chemical fertilizer controversy."

"I hardly think so," Milton Pugh said, surprising them both by speaking. "But I've studied your paper on the subject carefully; and it was well done. I have no doubt but that if man consumed great quantities of bone meal, dates, figs and sunflower seeds, ate only unrefined sugar and flour and organic vegetables and stayed away from meat, he would prolong his life span. It's probably also true that he'd be better off without the stimulation of coffee, whiskey, cigarettes and women. But I fail to see the advantages in survival under those conditions."

For a moment, the first and last moment in their relationship, Kane was fond of Milton Pugh. Then Stu Denton arrived.

"Mornin' ever-body," he said, with the same genuine, good-natured smile that millions of Americans had seen on phonograph albums.

Luther Brantley nodded pleasantly. Milton Pugh eyed him, took a thesis on Civil War decorations from his briefcase, and began to read.

"How's it going, Stu?" Kane said.

Stu opened his collar, yanked his tie down and took his seat beside Brantley. "Man, I'm gettin' in foul shape. Ole cowboy's winded. And gettin' fat, too."

"We'll have to work out in the gym together," Kane said.

"Let's do that. Betty Jo's been givin' me the word lately. Says I gotta lose some weight or sleep on the floor. I'm so heavy I weigh down my side of the bed. Says it's like sleepin' uphill."

Milton Pugh glanced at Stu, puzzled over his tall, gawky, slender frame, frowned over the lack of avoirdupois, recalled Stu's remarks and decided that the whole matter wasn't worth his concern.

Ward Roberts came bustling in. "Sorry I'm late, gentlemen. Just overslept. Stayed up half the night reading. Got interested in an article on the Communist party—*Encyclopaedia Britannica,* Volume VI, page 137—and then I went on to read about the International. I never realized the complexity of the organization, the absolute control from Moscow . . ."

"Can we get started?" Milton Pugh said, speaking over Ward.

"Oh, I am sorry, sir. I didn't mean to delay things," Ward said.

Finally, when the clerk had returned, Kane sat at the head of the table and looked on either side at his subcommittee. To his right the Democrats, owl-like Milton Pugh and shrewd Ward Roberts. To his left, the Republicans, homespun Luther Brantley and guileless Stu Denton. Kane saw them as a single instrument which he might wield. "Gentlemen," he began, "we're all in this fight together. Our responsibility to the country transcends any loyalty to party."

Eight hours later, as he read those same words from the text of his press release to the afternoon papers, he was aboard a plane, flying to Manton, propelled toward a final confrontation with Laurie.

27

MANTON WELCOMED its warrior home that evening.

Opening his campaign for renomination before a cheering crowd in the County Courthouse, Kane revealed that "traitors abound in our government," warned that "the fight against subversion has only begun," swore that "our liberties will be safeguarded," pledged that he would "eradicate the scourge of communism."

When he had finally posed for the last picture, answered the last question and shaken the last hand, he reluctantly left his admirers for a task less dramatic, but more formidable than the one he had dedicated himself to perform.

He sat beside Laurie on her front porch glider—scene of so many partings and reunions, of arguments and tender reconciliations—aware of her voice but not hearing her, cornered by his own decision and knowing he could no longer postpone the inevitable break. There was no need to balance her against Dany. The scales had been tipped long before. He hesitated only because he lacked the courage.

And Laurie, knowing that his letters had become shorter, less frequent, that he had not even commented on the house plans she had sent him, that he no longer confided in her, hesitated over her own decision, a decision conceived in desperation, to insist on their marriage and to insist that it be soon. That meant an ultimatum; and there were dangers in threatening Kane. And yet, she realized, it was the only thing left for her to do.

"Darlin', I was so excited." She leaned back and her hair fell against his cheek. "I counted the times they stopped you with applause." Holding up both hands before his face, acting like the delighted, naive young girl she believed he wanted her to be, she said. "Ten times!"

Kane had tried all evening to find something, anything that would justify an argument, but he couldn't. Wouldn't it be better, easier for her, he thought, if I just wrote her a letter?

"Kane, we'll be married right here in Manton. I've decided." He frowned. Hadn't she always made decisions and wept when he balked at them? And hadn't he always given in? No, Kane answered himself.

"The way everyone feels about you, they wouldn't stand still for a Washington weddin'. And mother'll be able to be there. She's awful weak, but we could manage it. And there won't be any problem with her. It's her idea that Lily stay with her while I'm away"

Her idea! Yes, and her idea to give us the house and foist those blueprints on me. But, he thought, ashamed of his reflections on the kindly, dying woman, it was only natural for a mother. . . .

"Laurie," he said, "I don't think we should plan . . ."

She had expected him to say that, but her throat tightened, and she had to force herself to go on. "'Course we got to plan. It was a fool idea of mine that we should wait. Nothin' could make mother more happy . . ."

Happier, he thought, correcting her mentally and knowing some painful pleasure in being able to find fault with her.

". . . than for us to get married, I'm not leavin' it to you any longer," she said, holding his arm, pressing against him, and feeling no response. "I've decided no man's goin' to give up his freedom unless the right girl hog-ties him!" Laurie laughed, but it didn't come out right; and she was suddenly aware that it sounded nervous, nearly hysterical. And still, she plunged on. "'Bout time you knew I'm the right girl . . ."

If they had argued or fought—anything, Kane mused. Here she is, the same Laurie, so good and decent. And she hasn't changed, just waited and put up with it. But, he reasoned, I have changed. And that's the trouble. She's stayed the same. And I've grown. He held her arms. "Laurie, honey, sometimes plans don't work out."

But she wouldn't be stopped. "All these years of waitin' for you I've put off the plannin', not darin' to. All the time you were in school, when I knew we had to wait. And when you were overseas . . . and I had nightmares, Kane. Did I ever tell you?" she asked plaintively. "Not that you were killed, but that you'd never come back to Manton—to me. And then, when you were gettin' started in practice . . . "

"Laurie!" he had to tell her now. "I don't want you to talk about a wedding and all the . . ."

She recognized the impatience in his voice, but she was impelled to go on, to settle it once and for all. "You hush!" she said. "Men would always rather go off to a justice of the peace or somethin'." She looked up at him, forcing a smile. "But I'm not goin' to let you talk me out of a weddin'—a real weddin'. I want three bridesmaids." Suddenly she pulled away, her face rapt with the vision. "No! I want four! And I want a white satin gown with a sweetheart neckline . . . and a train." She caught her breath. "A train that'll billow for yards . . ."

Kane saw the tears in her eyes. "Please, honey, listen to me!" Even as he spoke he fumbled for his next phrase, not knowing how to say it, how to appeal to her. "I don't want you to . . . well, when you get married you've got to be sure."

She put her hands around his neck, locking them. "I'm sure, sweetheart. Oh, Kane, I've been sure ever since I can remember." Tenderly he took her hands away. "Laurie, I want you to understand . . ." His features were contorted by frustration, by pity for her. "Sometimes people marry and they find that. . . "

He saw that her expression had changed, saw doubt and defeat creep into her eyes, slacken her jaw, make her lips quiver.

"What's wrong, darlin'?" she asked, knowing the answer. And then, hopelessly, "What have I done? Tell me, Kane, what's wrong with me?"

"Nothing . . . nothing . . . If only she had done something, something he might have flogged her with, something that would have given him an excuse. He licked his dry lips. "We've grown apart these past few years. And I don't think we'd be . . . Laurie, I'm not ready to get married . . . and . . . and . . . " He seized on the thought that had come unexpected to his mind. "And, well, I realize I've been unfair in asking you to wait. I can't ask you to wait any longer. There's no reason why you should."

"Kane!" She agonized over his name, recognizing the truth, but still not willing to give in to it. Her mind, reacting to the shock, forwarded the message to the nerve centers that made her frail and human.

He coughed nervously, averting his face. "Laurie, I didn't want to hurt you."

"Hurt me?" she asked, as if not comprehending. Perspiration dotted her forehead. Her hands were suddenly damp, cold. She moved away where he wouldn't touch her.

Kane stood. "It's not your fault. And I honestly don't think it's mine." Digging his nails into his palms, he stole a glance at her. "You'd hate Washington. The things that mean so much to me now would be boring and tiresome to you . . . ."

As she listened, a knot of pain swelled in her throat. She put her fingers there to soothe it away. Later, she knew, she'd think of the things she should have said, what she should have told him. But now she was living her nightmare. And like a nightmare, everything was distorted, out of place, her mind unable to put them right. Though Kane's mouth moved and he was talking, she really could not hear his words. She wanted to shout, to beat her fists against his chest, to curse him for what he had done, for what he had taken without return, but she could not speak. Like the terror of a nightmare, like the immobile moment of awakening, she willed herself to act, but her voice, her limbs refused. She could think only of the years she had waited for this to happen, of the structure of hopes she had built—all with Kane as the keystone.

He tried desperately to find a way to comfort her. "Can't you see, Laurie? It's best we realize it now and not be unhappy later." He looked down at her. She's such a child, he thought.

A shiver trembled through her. "Please. Please, Kane. Go away."

He had planned to say more, though he knew she understood; and he felt impelled to explain. "It's not fair to you to try to hold this thing together. We've just . . . we've just. . ." he quoted Dany, "outgrown one another."

"Go away," Laurie repeated dully.

But he didn't want to leave now. It was unfinished. It was over too soon. He had expected anger and recriminations. He had expected her to cry. Laurie always cried when she wanted something of him. He tried to bolster himself with that thought, but it was too weak to support him. He would have felt better about it if he could have at least defended himself by listing her failures, her inadequacies. But she offered no battle, gave him no opportunity to retaliate.

"I'm sorry, Laurie." For a moment he watched her, her face resting against the plastic cushion of the glider. Then he walked away, leaving her alone. Thank God it's over, he told himself. I wouldn't go through that again for a seat in the Senate!

He listened to his own footfalls. Down the stairs. Across the sidewalk, moving away, leaving her alone in the darkness. It was done. He was free of her.

28

THE MASQUERADE at Hunting Acres was conceived by Ward Roberts, planned by Dany and presided over by Lucy. But it was Kane's party.

Periwigged, fitted sleekly in knee-britches and stockings, his rugged face eager and laughing over his frilled jabot, his strong hands gesturing above the lace at his cuffs, his gold brocade coat tight across his shoulders, Kane was a youthful, handsome and historically inaccurate James Madison.

Dany, a slim, blonde Dolly Madison, stood at the bar in an elegant full-skirted blue silk gown, one hand fingering the embroidery on her elbow sleeve, the other holding a martini. She watched Kane moving among the guests in the ballroom as if he were the host, shaking hands vigorously with a Senator he despised and admiring the old man's purple toga, patting a dowager's withered cheek and swearing she was a perfect Jezebel, complimenting the Baroness von Schtort (nee Barbara Marie McClung of Houston) on her bedraggled wig and balsawood lyre and guessing correctly that she was supposed to be Harpo Marx.

Dany's gaze followed him as he passed through the room. Smiling. Bowing. Praising. Confiding. Congratulating. Advising. Then she intercepted him. "Any charm left for me?" she asked.

Before she could duck away, Kane leaned over, bit her ear and whispered, "Dolly, if I wasn't such a handsome dog in this outfit you talked me into, and if you weren't so be-girdled and be-skirted and be-stayed and stuff, I'd grab you right now and take you out in the bushes!"

"Jimmy Madison! And you the Father of the Constitution!"

The crimson-uniformed hussars on the bandstand began to play "Smoke Gets in Your Eyes" and Kane held out his arms for Dany. They danced across the floor, gliding, turning, as Kane released her, then enfolded her in his arms. And they swept around the outer edge of the room, free of the other dancers, Dany's face turned up to his, her lips soundlessly pronouncing "love you."

Lucy, a plump Marie Antoinette in horn-rimmed glasses, called to them. Tilting her farthingale, she pushed her way toward them. "We're here to raise money. Let's get to work and stop mooning at one another," she said fondly.

"Where's Mel?" Kane said. "Want to give him hell. He postponed the picture story on me for two weeks; and I could have used it in Sunday's paper."

"Mel's tending a sick horse in the stables," Lucy said. "He doesn't know Kane O'Connor's alive. Now I've got some people I want you to meet, Kane. Buckmasters. Malcal Motors."

They went to the bar where Lucy introduced them to Carolyn and Mike Buckmaster. Carolyn, who nearly thirty years before had reigned as debutante of the year before eloping with a mechanic in New Hyde Park, Long Island, was a petite, beautiful Queen Elizabeth. The muscular, silver-haired Essex at her side was that same mechanic, inventor of a turbine engine, and recently the winner in a proxy battle for control of Malcal Motors. Obviously uncomfortable in the motley political crowd, he fidgeted in his doublet as Carolyn entwined her slender fingers in his thick, blunt ones.

"So you're the famous Kane O'Connor," Carolyn said.

"Fame's a relative thing," Kane said. "When I'm standing beside a famous beauty and a famous industrialist, I don't amount to much."

"Thank you, Mr. O'Connor. I'll be forty-seven the day after tomorrow and I'm a grandmother and this costume is too damned heavy for my weary legs. So a little flattery goes a long way."

While the masqueraders pressed around them and Carolyn finished two old fashioneds, Kane, prodded by Dany, told them of his plans for fighting subversion.

"Get out your checkbook, Mike," Lucy said. "This is deductible."

Mike Buckmaster released himself from Carolyn's grip, felt for a handkerchief in the pocketless costume and finally wiped his perspiring neck with the palm of his hand. "I'm burning up. Carolyn, hon, how do you stand that gear you're wearing?"

"I can't much longer," Carolyn said, patting his hairy knuckles. "I've got to get out of this thing before I smother."

"All right, sweetheart," Mike said. Then, to Kane: "I agree with you that us people who have the most to lose ought to be the first to fight the Reds. If you're not just another con man dreaming up an issue to get votes, we want to help. We'll make a contribution now. Six months from now, if you've proved yourself, we'll double it."

"Say five thousand now," Lucy said.

"Say twenty-five hundred," Mike Buckmaster said.

"Mike, you're not getting out of here for that kind of money," Lucy said.

"Let's see how it works out," Carolyn said. "In a few months we'll talk about it again. . . ."

"That sounds fair enough," Dany said.

"Wait a minute," Kane said, speaking directly to Mike, but loud enough to dent the encircling wall of conversation. "I haven't got the price of a new suit in the bank, but I've got my brains and sweat and guts to give. And I'm going to give that if I don't get ten cents from anyone. So don't haggle about this thing. Your money will make the job easier. But it won't get the job done. For fifteen minutes I've been talking about the security of our country, and your concern is over how you can arrange to pay for it . . . a little down and a little when the spirit moves you. Well, if you want to help, okay. If you don't, say so. But don't bargain with me like I'm raising dough for a charity or I'm a poor relative putting a touch on you. I'd rather have five bucks from a foreman in one of your Malcal plants, knowing he believes in me, than five thousand from you, knowing your attitude. I don't want that kind of help."

"You're bluffing, Mr. O'Connor," Carolyn said, smiling. "The wise man takes help where he can get it; and I don't think you're a fool. Twenty-five hundred dollars is a lot of money, even to a congressman. That's not the value I put on what you say you want to do, but it's an investment we're prepared to make on the basis of a few minutes of conversation with you. If conditions are what you say they are, and you actually do what you say you'll do, we'll give more than our share. But we don't know anything about you, Mr. O'Connor. We're against communism; and you are. But that's hardly enough. We just don't want to be taken, that's all. So don't try to high-pressure an old hand."

Kane looked at her sternly as he spoke. "Mrs. Buckmaster, we've got to raise a hundred thousand dollars tonight. Your share is five thousand. Yes or no?"

Carolyn shrugged; and her eyes revealed a hint of admiration. "Mike, if you believe this tough customer, go ahead and give it to him. And if you don't, darling, don't give him a sou," she said, facing Kane again.

"What do you believe, Mrs. Buckmaster?" Kane asked.

"Okay," Mike said, winking at his wife as if they shared a private joke. "I'll send you a check in the next week or so, Mr. Connor."

"It's O'Connor," Kane said. Then, to Carolyn, "Thanks. Queen Elizabeth was a pretty shrewd gal, too."

The orchestra was playing "Moonglow." Carolyn Buckmaster listened for a moment as if she had not heard Kane. Then she stepped into her husband's outstretched arms, pressing against him. "Queen Elizabeth was also a bastard," she said sweetly. "I like you, Mr. O'Connor. But I'm not sure I trust you."

As they danced away, Mike pumping Carolyn's arm, Lucy said, "You handled them perfectly."

Dany said, "You were rude."

"People with big money are used to being fawned over," Kane said. "And a guy like Buckmaster respects you when you talk up. If I'd have taken that twenty-five hundred and kissed his tail, he'd have figured me for a pennyante politician, pleasant and well-mannered and nauseatingly humble. Now he'll remember me, Dany girl; he'll think of me as that tough s. o. b. O'Connor who had gall enough to tell him where he could shove his dough. I don't give a damn if he likes me. He respects me. And so does his old lady. And that's going to pay off. You'll see."

They talked with Caleb Lawton as they made the rounds of the room. Lawton, dressed like a Spanish grandee, listened while Kane explained that it would take money to rout the Communists out of Washington, that investigators and clerks and contacts and witnesses and travel were expensive, that the subcommittee was being forced to work on a paltry budget.

Lawton was not worried about Communists. "Give a guy three squares a day, a place to flop, a job and a chance to work himself up, he won't be playing footsy with the commies," he had told his son-in-law. And the son-in-law, then still a junior in college, had quoted Marx and talked about protecting the working man and patiently explained how simple it would be to change the world for the better. Five years later, Caleb's son-in-law winced when Caleb told the story at least once a month at board meetings. For now the young Field Operations Manager for Lawton Petroleum was making $100,000 a year, driving a Mercedes-Benz, cursing the union for demanding a five-day week with double time on Saturdays, and advising his father-in-law to "let the pogues walk out. We'll let the rigs sit, by God!"

Though Caleb Lawton wasn't disturbed about Reds, he did like Kane. He saw him as a realist who could understand the need for the oil depletion allowance, who had supported a bill to restrict Argentine beef. And one day soon the Tidelands Bill would get before the House. "I've got a friend at home who's quite upset about the communist business," he told Kane. "I want you to fly out to San Diego to meet him. Meanwhile, I'll send you my check for ten thousand dollars."

Lucy, Dany and Kane moved on to the dining room. There a great fringed canopy of purple and gold hung from the ceiling. Below it was a circular table. Arranged on its silk and linen cloth was a sumptuous pattern of delicacies. The centerpiece was apparently a regal Indian peacock whose head, crowned in green and white, surveyed one end of the table, and whose incredible plumage reached to the other end. (Only Lucy and her caterer— sworn to secrecy—knew that a humble turkey was masquerading beneath the magnificent feathered costume.) On every side were massive trays of chicken Riga and succulent, rare tenderloin of beef, checkerboards of black and red caviar, a glacier of crushed ice covered with Persian melon and *prosciutto*. There were platters of pungent cheeses. And mounds of steaming rolls and a festive bowl of salad *forestiere*. There were silver boats of exotic sauces: Piquante, Beamaise, Troubadore. And around the rim of the great board an electric train tugged gondola cars of black and green and almond-stuffed olives, pickled and sour onions, mushrooms, artichokes and endives.

On one side of the table two uniformed chefs in black hats presided over a battery of gleaming chafing dishes of Homard Neubourg and curried shrimp. Across from them a wizened buccaneer, Nate Starbecker, stood at the controls of the laden train, sending it racing precariously around the curves and beneath the peacock-feather tunnel he had fashioned. "Isn't this the damndest thing you ever saw?" Nate said to Dany. "Lucy, you must have gotten this idea from a cartoon in the *Daily Worker*."

"Go to hell, Nate," Lucy said.

Kane laughed. "Had a buddy when I was a kid—Joe Schwartz —killed in the war. Haven't seen this much chow in one place since Joe's *bar mitzvah!*"

While they heaped their plates and ate, they talked of the demise of Purmincar; and Nate managed to mention the subsidy he sought for his new client. Kane told him of his need for funds to fight subversion.

"Something can be worked out," Nate assured him. "I'm associated with an operator now who's got more gelt than Lucy's dad has prejudices!"

Lucy stroked Nate's brow. "I'll have more to say to you about that later. I want Kane to meet Dottie Wilkerson."

"Take him, but this creature stays with me," Nate said, putting an arm about Dany's waist. "She's going to race over to the bar and get the old man a B and B, and I'm going to sip it quietly and let her tell me what she sees in Kane, America's first political pin-up boy!"

Lucy was already leading Kane toward Washington's foremost hostess, Dorothy Wilkerson. The name most seen in *The Express'* "Fascinating Folks" column, the undisputed champion of a marathon of reception lines, the madame chairman of everything, Dorothy was dressed as Salome. "I think you're better looking than your pictures, Mr. O'Connor," she said. Balancing the silver tray on which was affixed a hairy mannequin's head, she handed it to her husband and extended her hand to Kane.

"My God!" Kane blurted, staring at the gory replica of John the Baptist. Then, recovering, he took Dorothy's hand. "I've heard and read so much about you, but you exceed all my expectations," he said, and felt Lucy's sharp nails dig into his back.

Aaron Wilkerson, a short, pot-bellied Samson with leather wrist bracelets and watery eyes, was holding the tray at arm's length, his face pained, as if he could detect an odor. "Christ," he mumbled. "Christ . . ." The nervous ghost-creature who in society page photographs was always caught listening to his fabulous wife, listened to Dottie tell Kane how glad she was that something would finally be done about stamping out subversion. "You must let me give a little affair for you," she insisted. "And I'm going to see that you get a nice little donation for the cause. Mmmm, Aaron?"

"Christ!" Aaron Wilkerson said.

Ward Roberts stood in the entrance of the adjoining den, his arm about the broad, slumped shoulders of a tall, heavy-set young man. He waved to Kane. Excusing himself, Kane worked his way through the crowded room.

The two men who waited for Kane were a study in contrast. Ward was immaculate. From the curl of his shoulder-length wig, across the well-tailored back of his green brocaded coat, his silk stockings, the silver buckles on his shoes, he was Louis XIV. *(Encyclopaedia Britannica,* volume VII, *Dress.* Plate V.) His slim, short body bent forward as he offered Kane a hand, and in his soft, musical voice introduced him to Norman Keller.

The rumpled young man wore an ill-fitting tuxedo with ashes on the lapels. His massive shoulders were hunched over and with one ape-like arm holding the door, his free hand gripped Kane's firmly. "I've been wanting to meet you," he said in a deep, strong voice, looking with dark, heavily-lashed eyes directly at Kane. And Kane, studying the hockey-puck scar on Keller's temple, the hard line of his jaw, the heavy eyebrows, thought he looked like a worn-out old fighter with a young man's clear eyes.

It was only when Kane stepped inside and stood before the fireplace, and Ward followed him, that Norman Keller moved. Supporting himself first on the door, then on the back of a chair, he swung his crippled legs painfully, but with no indication of pain on his face. Then, retrieving his canes in the long, uncomfortable silence, he slipped into a deep leather chair and looked up at them, smiling faintly at Kane's look of compassion. "Polio," Keller said flatly.

During the next half-hour, as they sat in the paneled den— designed by Lucy to resemble a saddle room—Kane learned about Norman Keller.

Ward enumerated the statistics: Age, thirty-four. Phi Beta Kappa. *Yale Law Review.* Graduated magna cum laude. Supreme Court clerk. Five years of private practice, primarily criminal cases. Special assistant to the Department of Justice. No political affiliation.

"I knew I'd heard your name before," Kane said. Removing his wig, he dropped it on the mantle and ran his fingers through his damp hair. "You're the fellow who defended some kid for murdering his high school teacher. Court appointed. And you won on a self-defense plea!" Smiling, he leaned toward Keller. "Tremendous case. How'd you ever get the jury to believe that?"

Keller's deep-set, intent eyes had not left Kane's face. "Because I believed it. And if you're certain enough, with no reservations and doubts, you're ahead of the average juryman—a man who's afraid of making a mistake, who doesn't know what he ought to believe. He's not sure. So he'll believe in a man who is."

Kane tried to turn the conversation into other channels, but Norman Keller talked on about his one publicized case, reliving that highpoint in his youthful career. "Winchell wrote 'there's a new Liebowitz in the making,' " Keller said, smiling grimly, nodding his head. "And a year later I couldn't walk from a witness stand to a jury box."

"When did you get back to Washington?" Kane asked, hoping that Keller's reminiscences were over.

"I left Warm Springs and came back to D. C. three years ago," Keller said, his head cocked to one side as if he were listening for the sound of his own voice. "And you're the first man I've seen who's had the nerve to bring this issue of Reds in the government out into the light of day. Frankly, I'm doing all right where I am, but I'm willing to give it up to go with you."

"Why?" Kane said, restraining a smile at the young man's intensity. It seemed that his simplest words were not spoken, but delivered.

"Because I think you can do the job," Keller said without hesitation. "I've studied your voting record. Liberal on housing, public works and education. Moderate on labor restraint, taxes and immigration. Conservative on federal controls, the budget and civil rights. . . ." He paused, running the flat of one finger over the bridge of his nose, thinking. "You don't fit into the mold of the radicals who usually speak out against the Reds. You're not a Negro-baiter or a Jew-hater or an isolationist or a hair-brained idealist or a brain truster. You've been in Congress long enough to gain experience and a short enough time to be without enemies — or nearly so. You're a war hero. You're the kind of man most of this country can identify with and will rally to."

Kane was pleased by Keller's evaluation of him, amused by his oratorical manner, and impressed by his record, intrigued by the incongruity of his demeanor and his appearance. "So you think the people will rally to me."

"Yes. And that's the most important part of the job. Someone has to get the people off their complacent duffs. Somebody has to make the people demand an end to Red infiltration. Somebody has to . . . to scare them, by damn . . . before the commies destroy us!" Keller's fists were clenched before his face, and he shook them, beating the air angrily, as he slumped back in his chair. "And then, when the people are ready—when you've made them ready, Mr. O'Connor—they must have the spectacle of public exposure of the traitors who are intent on destroying us. You're the man," Keller said, pointing at Kane, emphasizing each word with his finger. "You're the man who can make the American people wake up."

"I know about my qualifications," Kane said, smiling broadly. "But we were starting to talk about *your* qualifications."

Keller had his finger wedged beneath his collar, trying to soften the starch where the shirt rubbed his neck. "My best qualification is that I can do the job you must have done, Mr. O'Connor. And I can do it better than anyone else I know."

"Norman's dad is a good friend of mine, Kane," Ward said. "He's responsible for the American Patriots' donation."

"Don't get the wrong idea from that," Keller said, thumping his thick-knuckled fist against the arm of his chair. "I'm not entirely in sympathy with the American Patriots. They get involved in too many side issues and associate themselves with rabble-rousers too often. I could have had the job of general secretary for them. But I worked for them before; and my father doesn't agree with my ideas." He gave a humorless chuckle. "He's a fine man, a generous man, my father; but he's a compromiser. I don't compromise," Keller said. "I believe what I believe."

"Well, what do you say, Kane?" Ward said.

"Incidentally, what my father contributes has nothing to do with my working for you," Keller said. "I want the job on my own merits."

"I think we may be able to find something for you," Kane said, deliberating.

"I'm not interested in just any position on your staff," Keller said, blinking nervously. "I'm interested in the chief counsel's job. Nothing else."

Kane settled himself in an odd chair made of barrel staves. The guy's got brass—and guts—he conceded. And we think in the same general direction.

Peering intently at Kane, Keller ran his hand across his high forehead, down over his broad, flat nose, to his square chin. He seemed to be straining, trying to reach a decision. "You need me, Mr. O'Connor," he said at last. "I started fighting Reds the day I got out of college when I became legal counsel for the American Patriots—and in those days it was really tough. The Communists were posing as our allies. Since that time, I've had experience in trying subversives; I've got contacts in nearly every government agency; I know my law. I've worked . . ." He caught his breath, nodding at his legs as if they belonged to another body. "Before this," he said, "I worked as an investigator. I know how to handle a staff. I'm capable in a courtroom. I already have information that will be valuable to you. . . ."

Nate Starbecker had been standing in the doorway, listening. "If you're that good, why waste your time with Kane?" Laughing, he walked to the sofa and flopped down, folding a saddle blanket into shape beneath his head. "You could make a fortune in private practice."

"This isn't just a job!" Keller said, turning on him. "This is a chance for me to do something for my country." He was quietly positive.

Nate grinned. "I'm too mellow tonight to quote Sam Johnson. But, patriotism—the sins that have been commited in thy name!"

"Do you have to debunk everything?" Kane said, annoyed. He considered asking Nate to leave, but decided that his presence might prove valuable. It would give him a logical excuse for postponing a decision on Keller. He wasn't sure about the man. There was something about him—his intensity, or maybe you'd call it dedication—but whatever it was, Kane thought, it attracted and yet repelled him.

"Forgive me," Nate said. "I'm not in my cups. I'm just looking for amusement." He lifted his pirate's eye patch, then snapped it back in place. "Go ahead. I'll only keep one eye on you."

"Tell Kane what you were telling me about the Justice Department, Norman," Ward said.

Keller bent forward and, grasping one knee in an outsized hand, lifted it to cross his legs. Then, slowly, shifting his weight in the chair, he turned toward Kane again. "It's just that I'm sick of conditions there. We're stymied. I know of Reds working in sensitive spots; but I can't do a thing about it. We're tied down."

Kane was immediately interested. "Who's tying you down?"

"Not *who,* but *what.* The laws of evidence, the Constitution itself, existing statutes. It's damned near impossible to get a conviction while the commies hide behind the laws of the government they're trying to destroy." He sighed. "Those laws have a place in a court of law, but a congressional committee doesn't have to be plagued by them."

Seeing Dany in the doorway, Nate beckoned to her, patting the seat beside him. "Come in, dear. You're missing an interesting and instructive conversation. A young radical here who is opposed to the Constitution."

Keller glared at Nate. Lifting his crossed leg, clicking his braces, one hand grasping the arm of his chair, he hoisted himself to his feet and supported himself on a single cane. He was the only man to rise. "How do you do?" he mumbled, acknowledging Ward's introduction of Dany.

Nate slipped over to make room for her. "In other words, Keller, you assume a man doesn't need the protection of the law when he arrives in a congressional hearing room?" He clucked his tongue.

Keller had crossed behind a mahogany desk. He continued to stand there, holding himself erect, his legs hidden, leaving him apparently whole. He knew Nate was playing with him, goading him. "This isn't any laughing matter," he said, surveying his audience. Nate and Dany were watching him. Kane was waiting for him to continue. Ward stood against the bookshelves, his eyes on Kane. "I've fought Communists before," Keller said. "And let me tell you, you can't fight them according to the rules. Suppose I know a man is a subversive." He paused, shaking his head. "I still can't touch him! And do you know why? Because it's no crime to belong to the Communist party. Because wire-tap evidence is inadmissable. Because guilt-by-association isn't proof that will stand up in court." Keller lifted a fist and shook it at the room in a gesture of frustration. For a moment his penetrating gaze searched the reaction in each listener's face. "I must show, without use of the damaging evidence, that he actually committed a subversive or treasonous act; and I must prove my allegations beyond any shadow of doubt." Nodding, he lowered his voice, turning to each one in the room, directing himself to them in turn, as if they were jurymen, as if they were still undecided. "But before a committee hearing, it's a different story. You can make your own rules of procedure. You can use all the facts that come to hand. . . ."

"That's a nice dramatic little speech," Nate said sarcastically. "But my young friend, did it ever occur to you that those laws were made for our protection, to prevent abuses against individual freedom through due process?"

"I think I know as much about due process as you do, Mr. Starbecker," Keller said, his head angled again, his eyes glaring. "And the only way we're going to protect that right and all the other rights we Americans have is to get rid of the Communists in this country. They're out to destroy us," he said bitterly. "And the only way to beat them is for us to be totally committed, committed so deeply that there are no pros and cons to weigh. Our purpose is either all-important or it's worthless." Speaking softly, emphasizing each word with ominous deliberation, he said, "anything else confuses the issue. Anything else saps the power of our commitment and strengthens theirs."

Nate grunted. "Nietzche's maxim, my friend, is worth consideration. He said that everything absolute belongs to pathology."

Dany slapped Nate's knee. "Stop parading your erudition, you old fraud. Listen for a change."

Keller glanced at Dany. His face softened and he smiled shyly. "I'd better listen for awhile, too. I ran away with myself."

Kane had found in Norman Keller's arguments the justification for his plans. He got out of his chair and stood across the desk from Norman. "You're right. First we'll alert the whole country, wake them up, prepare them for what's to come. And then we'll smoke the bastards out, show them up for what they are." Turning to Nate, he said, "Sure a few people might get hurt. But in the long run we'll chase the skunks out of government. And the whole country will be behind us . . ."

Nate broke in, laughing. "Ah, a crusade! Frank Keller's son will be its prophet . . . a new epiphany with Kane O'Connor emerging as a God!"

Dany and Kane sat in his apartment later that night. He was stretched out on the sofa; and she sat beside him, bent over the coffee table, tabulating the evening's pledges.

"That's one hundred and nine thousand dollars!"

Kane turned her to him. "Now we'll set the whole country on its ear."

"What do you think Shep's going to say?"

"I don't really give a damn. We don't need him any longer. The dough is in. And the subcommittee's behind me. Stu Denton gets one man on the investigating staff. Old farmer Brantley's too busy with manure spreaders and fertilizer to get interested. Pugh'll be hog-tied. Ward gets Keller in as chief counsel . . ."

"Oh, was Roberts responsible for Keller?"

"What difference does it make? Hell, Dany, getting Keller's a real break. He does a little too much orating, but he's got the goods. He's a fighter. He's smart. Has all the procedures, the statistics at his fingertips."

"He hates being crippled," Dany said.

"Who the hell wouldn't," Kane said, leaning back, cradling his head in his hands. "Keller's just what I need. You know how I hate to fool with details."

She smiled at him, smoothing his hair. "Something about him . . . like some jungle beast . . . you know, a lion, alone in his den, or do lions have lairs? Well, that's what Norman Keller makes me think of. That huge head held to one side and the tremendous shoulders slumped forward . . . staring with those burning eyes . . . like he was alone and wounded . . ."

Kane reached for her face and kissed her. "You are the damndest gal! Now don't worry about Keller or anybody else. You be my woman. You worry about me. And I'll run the show."

29

FOR A MONTH the nation cocked its ear, listening to the explosive rumblings from Washington. Every day for thirty days the press reported, editorialized and speculated on Kane's mounting charges of subversion in the Department of State.

The initial target had been selected by Chief Counsel Norman Keller who convinced Kane of the proposed victim's vulnerability. Then, impatient, unwilling to let the public furor cool during the preliminary investigation, Kane launched a constant barrage of accusations, a daily onslaught against the nameless traitors who he believed were directing American foreign policy, a continuing attack that named no names, offered no proofs, provided no dates, avoided specific references and still suggested that treachery was rampant in the State Department and that Kane O'Connor— undeterred by the immensity of the task—would protect America.

It was a frantic, hectic period. For three weeks Kane missed every roll call in the House. Days blended one into the other. He lost track of dates. Only Dany's insistence forced him to his meals. He was consumed by the enterprise.

He exulted in the pace, in the whirl of excitement that followed his every pronouncement, in the columnists and commentators who quoted his words, in the all-night sessions with his expanding staff, in the secret meetings with informers, in the mounds of mailbags stacked before his office door, in the constant jangle of his telephones, in the two clerks who spent all their time clipping newspaper features, pictures and editorials, in the piles of unanswered telegrams that pledged support, begged for speaking dates, offered information, in the cartons of gifts that littered his apartment, in the eyes of tourists who saw him in the House passageways or on the street, in the admitted vanity of watching himself on TV , in seeing himself caricatured by Herblock as a bad boy throwing mud at the State Department building while a

Russian oaf urged him on. All this, Kane was convinced, meant recognition—promised fame and security.

In less than a month he became a national figure. AU this without a single hearing, a single traitor revealed, a single investigation completed. *The New York Times* called it "mass hysteria." And London's *Daily Express* said "it is strictly an American phenomenon." *France Soir* described it as "an indication of the sickness of the American mind."

But Norman Keller, sitting in conference with Kane, Dany, Tod and Ward, had a different theory. "There's nothing so remarkable about this public support. I knew it would happen," he said, rolling his chair back from the desk in Kane's office.

"I felt it would, too, Norm," Kane said. "But not so quickly. After all, Americans are usually so easy-going, slow to anger . . ."

"That's a myth, Kane," Norman said. He spoke softly, earnestly, almost as if he were talking to himself in an empty room. "This country isn't calm. It's often violent in its reactions, easily stirred, and sentimental."

Tod balled up a sheet of paper and tossed it at the trashbasket, missed, and got up to retrieve it. "Let's skip the philosophy and get down to some practical things."

"I haven't finished," Keller said without raising his voice. "And this is important. We should all understand just what has happened."

"There's never been anything like this," Ward said.

"Of course there has," Dany said. "But Kane knows that public interest wanes in time."

"This is different, Dany," Norman said. He had hooked one cane over the edge of the desk. The other one he rolled before him between the palms of his hands. "In the past all this excitement and passion has been directed from a dozen different directions, for or against trivial things. There are always a bunch of assorted idiots that join the Ku-Klux or wear shirts of one hue or another and make it their business to hate something. And there are others who are devoted to someone with half-baked ideas like Father Coughlin—someone the rest of the country immediately rejects. Or they get behind a bird like Huey Long while most of the country laughs at him. Or they get together to vote against Al Smith . . . or to win fantastic old age benefits . . . or shut down immigration . . .

or bring back prohibition . . . or get a new trial for Mooney . . . or defend the Scotsboro boys."

Norman dropped his cane on the desk and leaned back in his chair, talking above the others, at some distant point over their heads, across the room. "The whole country's never been scared about the same thing at the same time, and wanted the same thing at the same time; and stood behind the same ideal at the same time. And so the force of these little groups has been dissipated. Now it's different. Everybody can focus on this. You can be a banker in Milwaukee or a sharecropper in Georgia and still be afraid the Reds will take over the government. For the first time, all this natural American tendency to organize, to become excited, to adopt a new idea, won't be concerned with trivia, but will have the power of a single will. That's why all this has happened. And that's why it's going to grow."

Tod yawned. "Fm no big thinker like you, chum," he said to Norman. "But if there's anything Fve figured out about the public it's that they can't be figured. Anybody who's spent a few years in politics knows that, no matter how you plan, no matter what all the signs seem to say, the people consistently fool you. They don't do what they're expected to do."

In the weeks that followed, the pace of work increased. Kane, Dany, Tod, Ward and Norman examined the trickles of information that investigation revealed to them.

Keller—intense, exacting, hard-working—dominated the sessions. He cited law, quoted precedents, suggested strategy, assigned duties. "Now if you'll look at the 1927 Supreme Court decision involving the Tea Pot Dome investigation," he told them, "you'll find affirmed the right of Congress to investigate for the purpose of framing legislation." To prove a point, he argued: "Let's examine the case of Kilboum vs Thompson. . . ." Or: "In the first congressional investigation in 1792, Congress probed to find whether or not the Executive branch of government—in this case the Army— had mishandled a situation leading to the massacre of our troops."

Tod interrupted. "Listen, Keller, all these damned meetings start off with you declaiming and end up as bull sessions. For once, let's get down to work. Then, if you want to quote law and comment on how famous you're all going to be, well okay. But let me get a few things said, and then let me get out of here." He stared down Norman's glare. "I'm interested in some orderly process around here. I want the staff expanded to do the job properly. I want a legislative aide appointed, Kane, so I can stop doing that job and get back to running the office. I want to know when this investigation kicks off the hearings. And how many witnesses you're going to call. I want you people to start signing vouchers for the transportation and meals and that sort of thing we're paying out. .

Kane sided with Tod; and day by day, as the stream of data deluged them, new people were hired to bolster the ranks and volunteer helpers, sighting the banners of the crusaders, offered their aid. A skilled lawyer, an open-handed financial backer, a public relations man—these were a few of the willing reservists in the Army of Salvation.

The lawyer, a brilliant but arrogant old man who had spent his life on the fringes of government, felt his advice would guide the erring nation's destiny. Tod gave him the title of Special Assistant and put him to work answering the unceasing flood of mail. Late into the night the lights burned in Kane's offices. And the old man, dictaphone in hand, sorting clerks on either side, mailbags stacked before him, would write warm, brief letters to the thousands from every part of the country who had rallied to Kane's cause.

The millionaire, sincerely concerned that traitors were at large, saw his utilities-eamed dollars creating a gigantic dragnet. Tod made him Special Advisor, gave him a congressional license plate which allowed him parking privileges in New York City, presented him with engraved calling cards indicating his special position, and turned him loose at an NAM convention where he raised fifty-thousand dollars in forty-five minutes.

The dedicated public relations man, who concealed his experience as an organizer for the German-American Bund, believed his plans would enroll the country's support in the holy war. Tod tried him at preparing literature for Kane's forthcoming campaign, at investigating inquiries for public appearances, at correlating information for press releases. But the man was haughty, officious and had a furious temper. Norman Keller objected to him as "a nut, anti-Semite, anti-Catholic, a Fascist and a fool." For once, Tod agreed with Norman. He advised the volunteer his help was no longer required. The public relations expert objected. Tod insisted. The big man cursed him. Tod stood on a chair and broke an umbrella over the man's head. Within the week, *Christian America* branded Kane's committee, "A Jew-Catholic Plot to Conceal The Real Traitors."

And there were other volunteers, too, some moved by patriotism, some by malice, some by honest concern:

A troubled dock worker who arranged to meet Norman in New York and provided a detailed report on the communist leadership that dominated his union.

And there was a telephone call at Kane's apartment. A man's voice: "There's a Red cell operating in the Interior Department. They hold their meetings in a boarding house on East Capitol. . . ."

And once, a student from Maryland University was waiting for Kane when he arrived in the lobby of his apartment house. "There's a literature professor at College Park, and advisor to the Voice of America," the trench-coated young man told Kane, "who tells his classes that communism offers greater rewards for artists than democracy. And he put *Das Kapital* on his collateral reading list.

A retired police detective came to Kane's office, refused to talk to anyone else and gave Kane the names and addresses of four State Department civil service workers who were on the mailing list of *The Daily Worker*.

Letters, too, surged across Kane's desk:

. . . I was formerly a member of the Communist party, but broke away at the time of the Hitler-Stalin pact. Now I am greatly disturbed at finding several of the men I once knew as Communists in responsible, policy-making positions in Washington. I'm prepared to give any information. . .

A woman wrote: I'm a native-born American citizen, working for the State Department. Last month a foreigner was transferred to my section and put over me. I think it's part of the communist plot to get foreigners running everything. . . .

Meanwhile in the old State Department Building in Foggy Bottom, Undersecretary of State Richard Southgate, formerly the majority leader of the House, led the task force for the opposition. The aging, frog-voiced warrior stomped through the corridors late at night, checking on his subordinates, suggesting new tactics, calling for coffee and cigars.

He marshaled security officers and clerks, lawyers and statisticians and drove them relentlessly. He checked files, reviewed reports, questioned harassed employees who had survived Keller's preliminary inquiries. But there were no specific charges, no lists of names, no times and dates and places. So Southgate proceeded on hints gleaned from the vague remarks of Kane's investigators and the inflated reports Kane himself fed to the daily papers. The Department, Southgate told the Secretary, had to fight back. But he wasn't quite sure what they were fighting.

Milton Pugh, Kane's ever-present opposition on the subcommittee, attempted to delay the opening of the hearings and obstruct Kane's plans by objecting to Keller's staff. But Ward Roberts was loyal to Kane; Stewart Denton was convinced that the group had accomplished much, and Luther Brantley rarely attended a meeting. So, despite Pugh's rancor and his outspoken objections to method and purpose, he was overridden.

Shepherd Reade, badgered by Abel Garren, the Majority Leader of the House, tried to quiet Kane, threatening to cut him off from patronage unless the State Department hearings were held in closed session. Kane, conscious of Shep's new role as subservient mediator, conscious of his own position of dealing indirectly with the White House, posed a counter-threat: If no patronage came to him he would expose the attempt to stop the investigation.

Kane slept fitfully these nights, waking suddenly to jot down a note on the pad beside his bed, stalking his apartment in search of cigarettes while he phrased aloud a speech he was to make, calling Dany to the phone in the early morning to discuss an idea. And he dreamed of the opening hearing as a club fighter dreams of the opening bell in Madison Square Garden.

30

THE CAUCUS ROOM of the Old House Office Building reverberated . . .

With the stampede of spectators, rushing for seats: "Whatta ya mean no more room? I been waitin' since seven o'clock."

With the shouted questions of reporters: "Kane, can you give us a line on today's witnesses?" . . . "Any comment on those people picketing the State Department?"

With the invasion of television cameras and technicians: "Awright, cut that damned reflector. You wanna roast me?"

With the cries of newsreel men: "You fellas at the press table, hunker down a minute, huh? I'm tryin' to pan this crowd. . . ."

With the angry threats of uniformed policemen, mediating the photographer-newsreel-television-radio battle for position: "Gentlemen, you have your assigned spots; and we expect your cooperation."

With the protest of a forty-man delegation of American Patriots: "Either you let us bring our signs in, or we go to Congressman Roberts. . . ."

While the clamor was at its height, Kane stood, glanced at Stu Denton, Luther Brantley and Norman Keller on his left, and Ward Roberts and Milton Pugh on his right, and banged his gavel on the mahogany table.

"Hold it!" a television engineer called. "We've got a minute and ten seconds before we go network."

Cameras flashed in front of Kane; he shielded his eyes. "No more pictures!"

"Just one more. Hit the gavel again, Kane."

Policemen came forward to herd the photographers back to their table; one man tripped over a cable and swore; the American Patriots' delegation, disgruntled, stacked their "Save America

From the Reds" placards at the back of the room and marched in a body to their reserved seats; and Kane rapped his gavel again.

"Not yet. I'll give you the signal," the engineer said, and readjusted his head phones.

Matt Fallon, at the press table, whispered to the *Los Angeles Mirror* correspondent: "Who the hell does Kane think is running this deal—O'Connor or the networks?"

"Gentlemen," Kane said, striking the table once more. "Gentlemen, this hearing is not going to start until there's order."

"I see the American Patriots are on hand for the kill," the *Newsweek* man said to Matt.

"I caught part of the rally they staged at Uline Arena last night. Before it was over, they were damned near in a frenzy . . . like the morning after the Reichstag fire!" Matt said, and waved to Dany who sat across the room behind the empty witness table.

"Kane'll give them what they came for," the AP man said, "a combination of starchamber and sideshow."

"The kind of copy we've all been pounding out on it, the kind that seems to whip up rallies and picketing in Foggy Bottom and delegations of American Patriots, is no credit. If this is a sideshow, we're the barkers."

"Steady, Matt," the CBS reporter said, "That sort of talk can get you investigated—or a Pulitzer."

"Gentlemen," Kane said, raising his voice above the rumble of conversation, the coughs and squeaking chairs. "Gentlemen, we're going to have order. . . ." Kane saw Shepherd Reade, Richard Southgate, and Winfield Parcher, the Minority Leader, enter together and move down the side aisle toward the committee table. Immediately, he was on his guard, welcoming them cautiously, exchanging greetings, and waiting for them to take seats.

The *Boston Herald's* correspondent leaned across the table toward Matt. "What do you make of that—Shep and Southgate making a grand entrance with the Republican bossman?"

"Only thing I'm sure of right now is that I'm going to stay and watch."

A late arrival rushed into the chamber. A strikingly handsome man in his fifties, he strode rapidly toward the committee table, ignoring the ripple of conversation, the turning heads that followed him. After shaking hands with Kane, he bent over to whisper to

Norman Keller, nodded, ran his hand through the shock of wavy, silver-gray hair that was brushed straight back from his high forehead, and nervously stroked his smooth, lean cheek. Then, alone, he took a seat before the microphone at the witness table.

The delegation from the American Patriots stood and began to applaud. The witness glanced at them, smiled with the corner of his mouth, and turned his back.

Kane rapped the gavel again. "Please take your seats," he said patiently.

"Disgusting!" Milton Pugh said, and his voice carried to the press table where his observation was recorded on note pads. "Tomorrow he'll have the Speaker in here, hawking balloons and popcorn!"

"Ten seconds," the engineer called. "Take it!"

Again Kane raised his gavel. And the hot lights went on above the committeemen. And policemen on every side of the great room held up their hands, gesturing for quiet. And the photographers readied their cameras. And the newsmen lapsed into silence. And the millions in the viewing audience stood by, anxious to watch and appraise Kane O'Connor as he opened the first hearing of the Special Subcommittee of the Committee on Government Administration.

"The purpose of this investigation is to show the extent of communist infiltration into the State Department," Kane said, addressing himself to the nearest camera. "American Communists are agents of a foreign power; and yet, they have grown so bold that they are responsible for a shocking series of international decisions which have endangered this nation and given aid and comfort to Soviet Russia!"

"Mr. Chairman!" Milton Pugh took his recognition for granted, and began to speak. "It may be true that the purpose of the chairman of this committee is to show the extent of communist infiltration into the State Department. But the chairman does not speak for me; and I doubt that he speaks for anyone in the Congress of the United States who believes that conclusions should be reached *after* the facts are revealed and not before. We have not made up our minds beforehand that the accused is guilty; and I resent the implication by the Chair that we have."

A murmur of agreement and dissent arose from the spectators, and at the press table, there was hasty note-taking and some chuckles. "Matt, your buddy just caught one in the solar plexus," the *Herald Tribune* man said.

For a moment, Kane paused, thinking desperately of some rejoinder; but he could not organize his thoughts. "I will not use this investigation for personal vituperation, nor will I indulge in semantics. Time is too short. Treachery is too evident. We'll now call the first witness, an American who has returned from the enemy camp, and has come here to help us preserve our democracy."

Boyce D. Reardon, a confessed former Communist, was called and sworn.

Norman Keller, with infinite attention to detail, probed Reardon's background for a full hour. Then, by repeating questions he had asked the witness in private, began to build Kane's case against the Department of State.

Impatient with the slow pace, Kane whispered to Norman, "Get on with it. Get to the point."

Norman frowned. "And you say, Mr. Reardon, that during the period you were employed by the State Department you were acquainted with Communist party members who also worked there?"

"I remember six," Reardon said.

"Did they have access to secret material in the files which was vital to the security of the United States?"

Reardon dipped a pipe into a leather pouch and tamped the tobacco. "Arnold Turpin handled top secret material. I'm sure of that."

"Now about Turpin," Norman began, "was he . . ."

"In your opinion," Kane said, interrupting, "didn't these members of the communist conspiracy influence the decision of the State Department? Weren't they responsible for the surrender to Stalin, for the betrayal of Chiang Kai-shek and four-hundred million Chinese?"

Milton Pugh pulled his microphone closer. "Opinions have no probity in a court of law."

"This is no court," Kane said coolly. "We're trying to get the benefit of the witness's experience. Answer my question please, Mr. Reardon."

Aware of the hovering television camera, Reardon puffed speculatively at his pipe. "Wherever Communists operate, they try to do what is best for the Soviet Union."

"And you were one of them," Luther Brantley said, as if the words had escaped him without his willing it.

Reardon stared straight ahead, and softly, he said, "I make no secret of the fact that I was a fool. I'm trying to atone for my mistakes by being here today. However, Mr. Brantley, if a man isn't to be allowed to rehabilitate himself, we will be unable to reclaim many who might leave the Party and make amends. I *volunteered* to come here."

There was a wave of applause from the American Patriots representatives that washed back over the rows of spectators. Kane gaveled for silence. "We're appreciative, Mr. Reardon," he said. "Now, if we can proceed, will you resume the questioning, Mr. Keller?"

"Nice recovery," the *Pittsburgh Press* reporter whispered to Matt Fallon. But Matt was watching Shepherd Reade and Richard Southgate and the Minority Leader, wondering about their presence at the hearing.

"One moment," Milton Pugh said. "Reardon, you mentioned six people who you say are Communists who worked with you in the State Department. Will you give us those names?"

Norman Keller said, "I have them, sir."

Half-rising, Pugh held out a gnarled hand. "May I see them, Mr. Counsel?" When Norman passed the list to him, Pugh subsided again, scratching at his beard. "When did you leave the Communist party, Mr. Reardon?"

"In 1946 when I became convinced that the Communists plotted revolution in this country."

"I see," Milton Pugh said, his mouth curled in distaste. "You suddenly saw the light! You suddenly found out that Stalin and his gang of cut-throats, who had been giving you orders for years . . ."

Kane slammed his gavel on the table, quieting Pugh and the undertone of protest from the spectators. "The witness is not on trial here! This is no inquisition; and I don't intend to see abuse against . . ."

"All right, Mr. Chairman, I know that the idea of an inquisition is frightfully appalling to you," Pugh said. "Now, Mr. Reardon, I have examined this list of yours. I also have here a memorandum prepared by the State Department which shows that Turpin was discharged on security grounds three years ago. Tell me, the five other names, are they presently employed by the Department?"

Reardon was sitting erect now, kneading his fingers. Hesitating, he said, "I don't know."

"We are trying to establish . . ."

"Mr. Keller, I don't care what you're trying to establish. I'm going to establish the fact that these people are not employed by the State Department at present. Now, are they, or are they not? I presume you know, Mr. Keller."

"No, they're not, sir. However, we're trying to establish . . ."

Kane sensed the immediate surge of interest from spectators and the press; and, aware that Milton Pugh's question had to be answered, he tried to regain control. "Mr. Pugh, you will have an opportunity to . . ."

Pugh's rasping voice prevailed over Kane's. "I presume we're here to get the truth of this matter; and before Mr. Keller spends another hour and . . ." He looked at his pocket watch, shaking his head. "Another hour and eighteen minutes *establishing* that he intends to *establish* a method of *establishing* something or other, I want to *establish* only one thing. A renegade Communist has testified that during the war, when Russia was our ally, six Communists, none of whom are now employed . . ."

Norman, his face flushed, his lips trembling, broke in. "If I can explain what we are trying to get at . . ."

"You'll explain when I finish," Pugh shouted. "And I have some questions yet—about the credibility of this witness. I'd like to know how much he's being paid for this performance and how much he usually gets for his self-flagellation routine from lecture bureaus and magazines . . ."

A covey of reporters perched on the edge of their chairs, ready to leave for the telephones. "Ain't we got fun?" the *Washington Star* reporter said. "How's Kane going to shut that sweet old bastard up?"

"By calling a recess," Matt said.

And Kane stood at that moment and announced: "The subcommittee will recess for one hour."

As the chamber slowly emptied, Matt worked his way forward into the phalanx of newsmen around Kane.

"No questions. No statements," Kane was saying. "Please, boys, I'm terribly busy."

"Got a minute for me?" Matt asked as the reporters drifted away.

"Matt, buddy, see me at my place . . . around six. Meanwhile, take Dany for lunch, huh? She's supposed to meet me in my office." Without awaiting an answer, he sat down beside Norman Keller. "We screwed up, Norm. Pugh was waiting for us, and in front of the whole damned world, we screwed up!"

"We'll have to talk to Reardon before the recess is over," Norman said. "If I could have explained my approach . . ."

"Dismiss Reardon," Kane said. Off to his right he saw Shepherd Reade and Richard Southgate talking to Milton Pugh. And a few feet away, the Minority Leader was arguing with Stu Denton, nodding, ticking off some points on his fingers.

"Kane, if we're going to develop our case, we've got to have Reardon on the stand."

"Do as I say, Norm! I don't know what's going on, but those bastards are hatching something; and if we call Reardon back, which is what they expect, they'll get away with it."

The Minority Leader had called Luther Brantley to his side, and together they herded Stu Denton off to lunch. Ward Roberts joined Kane and Norman. "Ready to eat?"

"You go ahead, Ward. We've got some work to do. And something's going on with Pugh and Shep and Southgate . . . and their friend on the opposition and Brantley are in on it, maybe even Stu. See what you can find out."

"Sure, Kane."

"And Norm, you call Ledbetter to the stand. He'll do fine. We've got to even the score this afternoon, and then some. Pugh rode all over me this morning. By God, if it takes a tyrant in the Chair to run things, they're going to damned well get one!"

Kane kept his word. He was grim when the afternoon session opened, his manner cold, his voice firm, his words unequivocal.

"These hearings are not going to be turned into a circus despite the efforts of some to do so." He looked directly at Shepherd Reade, seated with Richard Southgate and the Minority Leader on the front row, and was surprised to see that Majority Leader Abel Garren had joined them. "I will not allow these hearings to be cheapened by insidious, politically-inspired attacks against witnesses or members of this committee. Decorum in this chamber and at this table will be in keeping with the high purpose of this investigation and the dignity of the Congress of the United States!"

Norman Keller announced that Boyce Reardon, "who, against his doctor's orders, got out of a sick bed to be here today," had become ill and asked to be excused. "He will, of course, testify at a later date."

"Kane doesn't look surprised," Matt told the correspondent beside him. Noting the animated conversation going on between Shepherd Reade and Richard Southgate, he wrote on his pad: *R. and S. upset over development. Something's up.*

Norman A. Ledbetter, an educational consultant for the State Department, was called and sworn. A fair, blond-headed man in his early forties, he remained slumped in his chair as he answered Norman Keller's preliminary questions, speaking slowly and easily, apparently sure of himself.

When he had denied any affiliation or sympathy with the Communist party, Kane took over. In two hours of exhausting, driving examination, Kane flayed the witness with questions about his past. Although Ledbetter was soon erect and pounding the table, although he wrangled over the meaning of certain acts and insisted on qualifying his statements, he was forced to admit that Kane's information, in substance, was correct. Twice Milton Pugh tried to interrupt, and both times Kane refused to recognize him.

"In review, sir," Kane said, pointing a pencil at the witness, "you have admitted that you taught at a summer session in Moscow in 1938, that you wrote the forward for a book entitled, *The Russian Future,* that you were a member of a Communist-front organization, The American League for Peace and Democracy, that in speeches before left wing groups you have praised technical education in Russia as superior to that in this country, that you have personally recommended an entire bibliography of books on communism to be placed in American overseas libraries, that you have advocated that the armed services teach courses in communist ideology. Do you wish to reconsider, Mr. Ledbetter? Do you wish to deny any of these facts?"

"I don't deny them. I say . . ." He paused while his counsel leaned over his shoulder. "I say that my reasons are perfecdy valid. For instance, how can we live in a world with Communists without attempting to understand what they believe as it conflicts with what we believe? Mr. Chairman, every item on your list can be answered easily enough; and not one of them in any way reflects on my loyalty to this country."

"That's a matter of opinion, Mr. Ledbetter. But, let's get on. You say you are not in sympathy with the Communist party. Why, then, are you quoted in a recent issue of this law review"—Kane held up the copy—"as being opposed to the legal abolition of that party?"

"If you'd take the trouble to read it in full, I said it would complicate the problem by driving Communists underground. Besides, the number of them in this country is infinitesimal compared to our population."

"True," Kane said. "But only 60,000 took over Russia. I believe these hearings will show that Communist influence— because it exists in strategic spots—is far greater than their number indicates. But let's pass to other things. Tell me, do you believe in God?"

"I don't see that's any concern of yours."

"You affirmed your oath. Do you object to stating your convictions?"

Ledbetter deliberated a moment, sitting forward, tapping his fingers on the table. "I don't believe I was called here to testify on my religious beliefs."

Milton Pugh came to life. "Did you subpoena him to examine him on specific facts and actions? Or did you call him to find out what goes on in his mind?"

Kane kept his eyes fixed on the witness as he spoke to Pugh. "You have not been recognized, sir. You will have your opportunity to examine the witness. Meanwhile, you will observe the rules of procedure. Now, Mr. Ledbetter, since you object, I won't press you on that. Tell me, do you believe in public ownership of the means of production?"

"What has that got to do . . ."

"Will you answer?" Kane said sternly, "or are you going to hedge again?"

"I believe in public ownership. Do you believe in T.V.A., Mr. Chairman?"

"My beliefs are not at issue here. What you believe, as a man with access to the nation's secrets—is at issue. Now, tell me, do you believe in a planned economy?"

Ledbetter toyed with his briefcase, leaning back as his counsel whispered in his ear. "The question's so broad . . . Since there are obvious flaws in the profit system and since the methods of distribution . . ." He paused, shaking his head. "All right. I believe in a planned economy."

With relish, Kane leaned back in his chair. "Is it not true that the Communists do not believe in God? Is it not true that the Communists believe in public ownership of the means of production, in a planned economy, in the abolition of the profit system? And don't the Communists object to being taken off the ballot, despite your assertion that they would do better underground? Since you obviously share the un-American principles of the Communists, it is . . ."

Ledbetter slammed his fist against the table. "If you're trying to make a Communist out of me, you're being ridiculous. I happen to be a Socialist, Mr. Chairman; and I challenge you to produce any other group in this country more antagonistic to communism! Furthermore, I assume you've read the Constitution and the Bill of Rights. There's nothing in either that requires me to believe in any particular kind of economy or in any God. My loyalty is to this country and its Constitution; and any changes I would like to see made to help it prosper would be made by constitutional means."

"Mr. Ledbetter, we have no time for speeches."

"The Chairman finds time for speeches," Milton Pugh said, managing the sentence before the gavel struck.

"Mr. Ledbetter," Kane said, ignoring Pugh, "didn't you help finance a committee for the defense of Earl Browder when he was in prison?"

"He was sentenced to four years plus a big fine for some passport violation," Ledbetter said. "They were out to get him because he was a Communist, not because . . ."

"Answer my question! Did you help defend Earl Browder?"

"Yes!" Ledbetter shouted.

"Yes . . . yes . . . yes. . . . In the end, that has to be your answer, Mr. Ledbetter. You try to evade, to cover up, but time and again, you are forced to answer, 'Yes.'"

Kane kept at the witness for another hour; and when he finished, he pointed to Norman Ledbetter as "a man whose beliefs —foreign to this country—are shared by many in the State Department, a man who has sided with Communists time and again, a man who shelters himself with the cloak of socialism, as many Communists do, and denies God and denies the fundamental principles that built America!"

When Ward Roberts had asked a question and Stu Denton and Luther Brantley had passed, Kane finally recognized Milton Pugh. "To list the offenses committed today would . . ."

Kane cut in. "Are you going to make a speech or ask questions of the witness?"

"I am going to let the witness go home, and rest and prepare for the task of redeeming his reputation after the assortment of meaningless assertions made against him today. But, before we adjourn, I move that this committee go into executive session."

Unprepared, Kane stammered, "I think it's late . . , too late for that."

"I have made a motion, Mr. Chairman."

Kane turned uncertainly to the other committeemen. "All those in favor of the motion . . ."

The lights above dimmed out as the television coverage ended. Matt left his seat and joined Dany at the rear of the room. "What gives?"

"I haven't the slightest idea," Dany said.

"I've got an idea what Shepherd Reade and Southgate and company were doing all afternoon . . ."

Luther Brantley, Milton Pugh and Stu Denton voted for the executive session. Kane nodded to Ward; and the vote was unanimous.

While the caucus room was being cleared, Ward Roberts leaned over Kane's shoulder, whispering, "They're going to try to close the hearings, put it under wraps."

"We'll stop that in a hurry," Kane said. "You and Stu and I will . . ."

"Better talk to Stu. They've been working on him."

Kane left the committee table, walking toward the door at the end of the chamber; and then, as if it were an afterthought, called to Stu Denton who joined him. "What's up, buddy?" Kane said. "I know somebody's been giving you a hard time. Did you tell them to go to hell?"

Stu, his hands thrust in his pockets, glanced back over his shoulder to where Luther Brantley and Milton Pugh were watching him. "I'm in a box," he told Kane. "The ole cowboy owes a favor; and they came to collect it. Besides, there's a conservation project for my state in the hopper. Well, Kane, they put it to me straight. . . and I've got to go along."

For a moment, Kane hesitated. He had been outmaneuvered. If he lost Stu, all of his future plans would come up against a preordained three-to-two vote; so he could not afford to antagonize him. It was better to lose his vote this one time than to lose it completely. "I know what you're up against, but they're really blackmailing you, Stu. They're making you sell your vote."

"You know I'm with you, Kane. If they were trying to dissolve the subcommittee, stop the investigation, anythin' like that, I'd buck." Grasping the back of a chair, leaning his gawky frame against it, he shook his head. "I can't see that closing the hearings'll hurt any, except to get those damned hot lights off of us and get the spectators, like those loco American Patriots delegates to hell out . . ."

Because there was no other way, because he had to salvage Stu's support, Kane put his hand on his friend's shoulder. "I understand, buddy. Do what you have to do."

Ten minutes later, when Kane convened the executive session, he ignored Milton Pugh's bid for recognition, and told his subcommittee: "I think today's been an important experience for the American people. We've made our point. From now on, I'd like to have unanimous consent from you gentlemen to close the hearings so we can get on with this serious . . ."

And that evening, talking to Matt Fallon, Kane said, "Here's a beat for you. I talked the subcommittee into closing the hearings. There's too much at stake to allow it to disintegrate into a public trial!"

Matt shook his hand. "Kane, I was beginning to give up on you. That ruthless examination you ran today, the backbiting between you and Pugh, the high-handed manner you have with witnesses. But, by damn, there's some hope for you when you realize it wasn't good. Loverboy, you've redeemed yourself!"

And Dany said, "Isn't he a helluva fella?" Laughing, she took Kane's arm. "Sometimes he even surprises me."

The closed hearings began.

And as the days passed a routine developed. Hearsay would filter out of the chamber; a promising rumor would circulate during the luncheon recesses; and each afternoon Chairman Kane O'Connor would emerge to brief newspapermen and broadcasters and to pose for television and newsreel cameramen. Within a week the nation was waiting avidly for its newspapers and radio reports, impatient for new accusations, new victims and new sensations.

Kane sat in his office early one morning, trying to concentrate on the reports in the papers and studying the notes his secretaries had made on favorable editorial comment: *It appears that those who denied O'Connor's charges will now have to defend themselves with less bombast and more facts."*

Tod came in. "Got a check from Michael Buckmaster for five thousand and another from Aaron Wilkerson for three thousand."

Kane put his newspaper aside. "Sit down, buddy. Let's talk."

"What's the problem?"

"I got a terrific tip from Ward Roberts this morning. He picked up some dope from Brantley's legislative aide that a smart guy should invest in com futures."

"Well, why don't you?"

"Because I'm broke as usual. And the bank's on my tail again."

Holding the two checks up, Tod said, "You've got this."

"That's what Ward says." Kane knew what he wanted to do, but uncertain, he needed Tod's approval. "Of course, I could borrow the money from the account and pay it back."

Tod scratched the gray bristle of his hair. "For the time being, we're depositing all contributions to a special account. Then, later, we can set it up properly in some sort of trust fund."

Kane played with the idea. He had explained too many of the large donors that the additional funds would not be used for accountable purposes. "It's like intelligence work," he had told them. "There are expenses you can't itemize." *What difference would it make?* he thought now. According to Ward it was a sure thing to triple his money. Tod could handle the transaction. . . . "Well, what do you think?" he said.

Tod stood. "Hell, chum, you don't need my opinion on whether it's legal. But if you want to know what I'd do, I guess I'd take a flyer."

Kane was thinking of the promise of insured speculation. It would mean freedom from the eternal heckling of the Manton Bank, independence from the strict bounds of his congressional salary, an opportunity to make some real money. In another year or so, he'd be ready to get married. He would need a home, servants. He would need to entertain. And he wanted the best for Dany. That evening he had first met her, when they sat and talked beside the Jefferson Memorial, she had made him dare to dream. Now, with luck and work and time . . .

He made his decision. "Draw ten thousand for me, Tod. It's too good a chance to miss. Oh, and this is just between us, huh? Don't mention it to Dany."

By the tenth day of the hearings, the country hummed and seethed with outraged denials, countercharges, alarm and amazement.

Milton Pugh, who had spent the evening before conferring with Shepherd Reade and Abel Garren, listened to another witness. The man on the stand was Joseph Croft, a legal assistant in the State Department.

(Excerpts from Hearings before a Special Subcommittee of the Committee on Government Administration.)

MR. KELLER: Mr. Croft, do you know Joseph Tarleton is a member of the Communist party?

THE CHAIRMAN: Before you answer that, I want to be absolutely fair. It is already established, through testimony we heard yesterday, that you attended Communist party meetings with Tarleton, and you recommended his employment in the Interior Department.

MR. PUGH: Since we're being absolutely fair, I want the record to show that no such thing has been established. We heard testimony from one witness to that effect. Until this moment no attempt has been made to procure evidence in support of or denial of that testimony.

THE CHAIRMAN: Can we have your answer, Mr. Croft?

MR. CROFT: I never attended any meetings of any kind with Tarle-ton. At the time I wrote that letter, I didn't know he was a Communist.

MR. DENTON: Do you want us to believe you were his roommate, knew him over a period of eight years and still did not know his political beliefs?

MR. CROFT: I didn't know he was a Communist.

THE CHAIRMAN: Mr. Croft, if this country should get into a war with Russia, would you be willing to take up arms for this country against Russia?

MR. CROFT: If this country were invaded . . .

THE CHAIRMAN: I didn't ask you that.

MR. CROFT: I am an American citizen.

MR. PUGH: Come now, sir. I know you have the right to refuse to answer, and I consider the question an insult. However, I advise you to reply.

MR. BRANTLEY: How can anyone refuse to answer that question?

THE CHAIRMAN: Are you going to answer or not?

MR. CROFT: (After conferring with counsel) I would fight for this country in any war at any time in any place against any enemy. Is that a satisfactory answer, Mr. Chairman?

THE CHAIRMAN: It is, if it's true.

When Kane faced newsmen that afternoon, he reported: "A trusted employee of the State Department admitted that he attempted to get a known Communist into the Interior Department..."

On the investigation's eighteenth day, Herman Simon, clerk in the State Department, testified before the subcommittee.

(Excerpts from Hearings before a Special Subcommittee of the Committee on Government Administration.)

THE CHAIRMAN: Mr. Simon, didn't you fight for the Communists in Spain?

MR. SIMON: I was a member of the Abraham Lincoln Brigade. I fought for the Loyalists and against the Fascists in Spain.

THE CHAIRMAN: Didn't the Soviet Union support the Loyalists?

MR. SIMON: There are probably some Communists who like the New York Yankees, as I do. That doesn't mean that."

THE CHAIRMAN: I suggest you answer my questions seriously. You're not here to entertain, but to explain. You're in serious trouble, sir, and the sooner you realize it, the better."

When the witness was dismissed, Kane remained in the committeeroom to talk to Luther Brantley, hoping to feel him out on the speculation in com futures. But Stu Denton and Ward Roberts joined the conversation and Milton Pugh stood beside them checking his notes with a stenographer. Brantley evaded Kane's inquiries and turned the conversation to the problem of price supports.

So it was Norman Keller who was first to leave the hearings. The waiting newsmen stopped him at the door. "How did it go today? What kind of witness was Simon?"

Norman stopped, his head at its characteristic slant. "Well, we're not through with him yet. We've been able to prove he was in the Abraham Lincoln Brigade in Spain; and that put him on the communist team."

"Hold it a minute. Let's get something on film," a C.B.S. man said, and began to motion his cameraman in alongside the N.B.C., U.B.S., and newsreel equipment.

Norman dropped his briefcase on a hall bench and backed away where he could prop himself against the wall. Then, putting his canes aside, he steadied himself by gripping the arm of the bench. "This all right?" he asked, his voice hoarse.

"We'll ask the questions off-camera," the Telenews man said. Norman forced his shoulders back and cleared his throat. "I'm set."

The door of the committeeroom opened and Kane came out. "Don't you boys ever go home?" he said, laughing. "Somebody ought to set up a bar out here."

By now the newsmen and photographers were crowding around him. "Kane, Mr. Keller says you're not through with Simon. Do you think his background is damning enough or his job important enough to warrant all this stir?" one of them asked.

Kane winked at Norman. "Norm, you've got the job specification on Simon, haven't you?"

Norman nodded and, bending for his briefcase, found that he could not reach it. He picked up his canes, swung his legs before him and moved around the bench.

"Hey, let me do that, buddy," Kane said, crossing to him quickly.

"I've got it," Norman said evenly, and took the papers from his file.

"Same routine?" Kane asked the cameramen as he thumbed through the papers. "If I keep doing this kind of thing, I'm going to get a makeup man or find somebody that can tell which is my better profile."

Laughter from the Press.

"Stand-by," one of the cameramen said.

"Hold it," Kane said. "I want Norm in here with me. He's the workhorse of this outfit—investigator, law expert, chief counsel. And a real tough examiner." Pointing to the *Herald Tribune* reporter, Kane said, "If Norm was as tough as your paper says he is, he'd be beating the witnesses with a cane!"

Laughter from the Press.

"Come on, Norm. Over here," Kane said.

Norman turned away. "Got to meet somebody," he said. He zipped his briefcase, pushed it under his arm, lifted his canes, hunched his shoulders and moved off down the hall. Behind him he heard someone say, "Stand by, Kane. . ."

When Kane arrived in the committeeroom the next morning, Norman Keller and Milton Pugh were glaring at one another across a table. Both spoke at the same time, Pugh's shrill voice raised above the cold, deep insistence of Keller's. And when the canny, dour old man, red-faced and perspiring, stopped for a breath, it was Norman who spoke on calmly, coolly.

"Whatever methods we use against these people are justified," he said, shifting his weight on his arms, grasping the edge of the table with his meaty hands. "The rules were made for Americans, not for communist traitors!"

Squinting angrily with his magnified eyes, Pugh, like a bearded owl, glared at Keller. "And who's going to play God? Who's going to single out the good Americans who rate the rights guaranteed them by the Constitution?" He waved one thin, hard hand across the table, then slammed it on Norman's briefcase. "I suppose you're going to make that decision, Keller. Or is Mr. O'Connor? Or am I? What the hell gives us the right?"

"We're a judicial body in a sense," Kane said, joining them.

"Judicial!" Pugh's laugh was a hoarse croak. "You're supposed to be a lawyer, O'Connor. And so is your henchman. Do I have to remind you that the purpose of a judicial body is to learn the truth? What you're doing is setting out to prove what you already believe is the truth!"

"Don't get emotional, Mr. Pugh," Norman said.

"Don't raise your voice to me," Pugh said. "I don't like you Keller. And I don't trust you. You're too damned shrewd to be honest."

"Now cool off," Kane said. "No point in blowing your top." Then, putting a hand on Pugh's shoulder, he said, "After all, Milt, look what we're accomplishing."

Pugh shook Kane's hand away, glowering up at him. "I'm looking, O'Connor. And I'm sick." He picked up a folder labeled "Biog. Notes, JPB," and carefully put his biographical material on James Blodgett Portermaul into a dispatch case. "I've got more important things to do than to listen to your convenient, over-simplified, ends-justifies-the-means philosophy," he said, and turned his back on them, moving to his chair at the end of the table.

"He's dangerous," Norm whispered to Kane. "He uses the same arguments that were used to smear Martin Dies!"

When the session opened, Charles Hobart, a former employee of the State Department, dismissed by its security board, was called. He refused to co-operate under questioning.

(Excerpts from Hearings before a Special Subcommittee of the Committee on Government Administration.)

MR. KELLER: I ask you again, Mr. Hobart, are you a member of the Communist party?

MR. HOBART: I plead the Fifth Amendment and refuse to answer on grounds that it might tend to incriminate me.

MR. KELLER: Do you advocate the violent overthrow of this country's established government?

MR. HOBART: I refuse to answer that question on the grounds . . .

MR. PUGH: Do you have the nerve to claim the rights of citizenship, and still refuse to tell this committee whether or not you'd like to see this country overthrown by revolution?

THE CHAIRMAN: I see no point in continuing with this communist traitor.

MR. HOBART: You have no right . . .

THE CHAIRMAN: The witness will be removed.

(Session recessed. Resumed 2:45 **P.M.** *Mr. James B. Eastoy called and sworn.)*

MR. KELLER: Please state your name, address and current occupation.

MR. EASTOY: I decline to answer.

MR. BRANTLEY: Are we going to go through this all over again? THE CHAIRMAN: The witness is directed to answer or be prepared to be charged with contempt.

MR. PUGH: Are you pleading the Fifth Amendment?

MR. EASTOY: I plead the Sixth Amendment. An American citizen was insulted here earlier today because he chose to plead the Fifth Amendment. Since you find that part of the Constitution odious, I claim the Sixth. It says, "In all criminal prosecutions . . ."

THE CHAIRMAN: This is no criminal prosecution.

MR. BRANTLEY: Not yet.

MR. EASTOY: "In all criminal prosecutions, the accused shall enjoy the right to speedy and public trial by an impartial jury of the state and district wherein the crime . . ."

THE CHAIRMAN: You will be in order.

MR. EASTOY: ". . . to be informed of the nature and cause of the accusation, to be confronted with witnesses against him, to have compulsory process for obtaining witnesses in his favor. . . ."

THE CHAIRMAN: You are not going to use the Congress of the United States for a harangue, Mr. Eastoy. You are not going to make a mockery of the Constitution by hiding behind it when you're sworn to destroy it. Remove the witness.

There was no mention of the State Department's dismissal of Hobart and Eastoy when Kane told newsmen of their appearance, no indication that these were old cases, that the security section of the State Department had removed them from their posts more than a year before. For Kane believed that to explain those things would be to mitigate their seriousness. "We dug out two more employees of the State Department," he told reporters, "who are Fifth Amendment Communists."

But the big story for the day came from Milton Pugh. He issued his statement without consulting anyone. He had held his rage within. It had incubated. Now he expelled it:

"These hearings are a great fraud perpetrated upon the American people in the name of justice and security. And the press, starved for sensations, has aided and abetted this travesty by distorting, oversimplifying and doctoring the truth. If the purpose of the subcommittee is to be realized, the Chairman will agree to announcements only by the majority. He will not discuss hearings 286 until the evidence is in. He will make no speeches unless authorized by the majority. But the purpose of the Chairman is not to investigate communist influences in this country. His purpose is simply to provide headlines for Mr. O'Connor. This is the most shameful display of deceit and demogoguery I have witnessed in all my years of public life."

Recriminations flew. Kane recognized Pugh as the check-rein Shepherd Reade had forced on him, and he attributed Pugh's statement to personal jealousy. He answered by accusing him of "trying to discredit the investigation so the truth won't come out about the Administration's failure to provide for the security of the nation." He protested that "a definite pattern of communist infiltration has emerged." He released the verbatim report of the Hobart and Eastoy hearings. "Some people may be fooled by deception and lies," Kane told a televised press conference on Matt Fallon's program. "Some may be intimidated by the threat of smear and slander. I will not be! I'm going to chase the traitors like Hobart and Eastoy out of Washington no matter who gets hurt!"

31

SHEPHERD READE stood in the center of Kane's living room lecturing. "You're tellin' the whole country the Administration is allowin' Communists to run our affairs!"

"The whole country is drawing its own conclusions," Kane said, reaching for a handful of cherries from the bowl on the coffee table.

"Can't you realize that by makin' allegations of the kind you've made you're even affectin' foreign policy?" Shep paced the length of the room. "If you keep this up, our allies are goin' to believe our diplomatic service is riddled with Communists. You're playin' with a dangerous . . ."

Kane stopped him. "I'm not playing," he said sternly. "The greatest danger is communism. . ."

"Nobody's arguin' that with you. But do it sanely!"

"I'm tired of hearing that crud. Who cared about Communists in government until I stirred it up?" Kane pulled his tie off and flung it on the sofa. "If we're going to get rid of the rats, it's going to take one helluva fire to smoke them out."

Shep nodded wearily. "And you want to burn down the barn to get the rats out."

While Kane and Shep argued, Dany and Norman waited in the bedroom where Kane had sent them prior to Shep's arrival. Dany stood leaning over the bed, the evening paper spread before her. Norman sat hunched in the only chair, watching her.

"We're getting some awfully good press despite our friend Pugh's blast," Dany said.

"That dried-up old fud didn't hurt us at all," Norman said. "And he put himself in the soup by defending something that's indefensible."

Dany folded the paper and put it on the night table. "Of course, Hobart and Eastoy were already fired by State, haven't worked there in . . ."

"Now you're getting into subtleties, Dany. And people aren't interested in subtleties. They need simple statements of black and white, right and wrong."

She walked around the bed and sat on the end, facing Norman. "But nothing's really that way, is it? No blacks and whites in the world, mostly grays."

He reached into his jacket for his pipe, dipped it into a pigskin pouch and settled back in the chair, his eyes fixed on her face. "Dany, our job's education. We're going to teach by examples. It's not enough to say it's so. We're going to show them day after day that it's so."

"For a minute there, you sounded almost like Kane."

"Me? Like Kane?" He shook his head. "Hardly, Dany. Hardly. Kane has drive, but. . . well . . ." His voice dropped and his words faded away as if he had started to evaluate Kane and then changed his mind. "He's got drive, all right."

Dany walked to the door and, pressing her ear against it, tried to catch the overtones of the conversation in the living room. "Kane's got to be careful. Shep's a powerful man. He can still make plenty of trouble."

"Don't worry about Kane, Dany. He's fortune's child. You know Herodotus?"

"No, but I know Kane."

"Old Herodotus said that fortune commands men, and not men fortune."

"He didn't know what he was talking about."

"I think he did," Norman said. "Look at Kane objectively. The plums always fall in his lap. He's one of those people who has good things happen to him effortlessly. He couldn't stop it if he tried."

For a moment Dany did not reply. There was no anger in Norman's words; but something else, something that had passed over his face as he spoke. Norman himself, she knew, had the breeding, the wealth, the education, the intellect Kane lacked. "You can prove anything you want to prove with a quotation," she said. "Kane is proof that men command . . . what was it, fortune? Because without any of the things that fortune provides, he's been strong enough to fight his way up." Smiling, she said, "Your friend Herodotus was an ass."

Norman laughed. "Maybe you and I ought to switch jobs."

"Well, it's about time!"

"What?"

"Until just now I'd never heard you laugh."

His lips quivered, and rubbing the hockey-puck scar on his temple, he half covered his face. Then he looked up at her, forcing a smile. "I'm not usually very comfortable being alone with a woman."

"Thank you."

In the silence they could hear the argument raging beyond the bedroom door. Dany listened intently. Norman, clicking the stem of his pipe along his teeth, watched her.

Kane walked to the trash basket and dumped the ash tray full of cherry pits. Shep followed him, trying to speak reasonably, holding his impatience in check. "I'm not a lawyer, Kane. But you are; and you know proper procedure."

"We're not in a courtroom. I tried to explain that to your boy Pugh."

"I've watched you. I've read over some of the hearings; and you're consistently unfair to the witness. Making assumptions from the chair without any basis in fact, and then handing out exaggerated announcements to the papers."

Kane walked back to the coffee table, took another handful of cherries and sat on the sofa. "You don't really believe that, Shep, not if you read the record on Hobart and Eastoy."

"All right, I agree with you on those two cases. But, after all, they're no longer in the government. . . "

"You sound like Pugh now, Shep. And I don't like Pugh."

"I'll tell you frankly, Kane. I don't care if you like him or not. I happen to agree with him."

Kane turned on Shep, relishing the power he held. "All right, Shep. I've listened to you. Now I'm tired of listening. You don't like the way I'm doing things? Well, that's tough because I'm fighting to destroy the greatest threat this country's ever faced . . ."

"I'm aware of the threat, Kane."

"Sure you are. Because I made you aware."

"I'll even grant that. What I'm askin' you for is a sane, honest, fair investigation."

But Kane was not listening. He plunged on, over Shep's soft voice. "You don't like it because I'm using brass knuckles. Well, don't expect me to act like a little Lord Fauntleroy. You're the kind that won't fight because gentlemen don't, the kind that won't take short cuts because it's against the rules. You're too damned honorable. There's no juice in you. I'm ready to hit the Reds with everything I've got; and all you can muster is refined indignation!"

Shep had argued for an hour. He was hoarse now, choked with anger, hating the calm, insistent freshman who had risen to dominate him. He spoke quietly. "I gave you that subcommittee; and God forgive me for that stupidity. But remember I can still take it away from you!"

Kane laughed at him.

"I'm warnin' you. And this is the last time," Shep said grimly. "If you keep on with this noisy display, you'll have reason to regret it! I know a little more about Kane O'Connor than the papers know, a lot more than you'd like to have spread around. You think I don't know how to fight? Don't put me to the test!"

"Are you making a threat?" Kane said belligerently. But already he felt a tight knot of worry drawing taut in his chest.

"I'm not speakin' for myself alone. I spent last night in a conference with Abel Garren and some party leaders. The House has rules, you know, traditions that have grown up for over a hundred years—and we're agreed that those rules serve a purpose. We're not goin' to see you destroy them."

Kane glared at him. "You don't scare me, Shep. You don't scare me because the people are on my side—the right side— and I'm too strong for you and your cronies."

Shep picked up his hat and walked out of the room, closing the door quietly behind him.

Dany, followed by Norman, emerged from the bedroom. "Well?" she said.

"You heard it."

She sat beside him on the sofa. "You think he'll make trouble? He can, you know. He's not alone. He was sent to talk to you." She took Kane's hand, grasping it tightly in both of hers. "Don't get too cocky, darling. You're still a babe in Congress. The old pros can rip you apart."

Kane was taunted by Shep's threat, by his cryptic reference to things the papers didn't know. "What can he do?" he asked uncertainly. Then, his pride goading him, he said, "If he starts something, I'll let him have it for trying to wreck the hearings."

Norman stood leaning against the back of the sofa. "Let's get on with what I was telling you when Reade showed up. I'm in a hurry. I think we're on to the biggest thing yet. Fellow called, asked to be met in a French restaurant over on Connecticut. I went over. He was an Army officer, thin, milky looking kid. Nervous. Anyway, he's attached to the National Experimental Center in New York. He's here on leave."

"All right, Norm, get to the point," Kane said.

"He says the whole Center is full of Reds, that there are scientists there who worked on the A-bomb who are really Communists, that the whole section developing a new missile is run by a commie."

Kane stood. "Where is this guy?"

"He's due at Ward's office about now," Norman said.

"Ward's office? What's wrong with my office? And why the hell didn't I know before now?"

"Ward wanted to relieve you of the details. Thought we'd come to you with it when we had something concrete."

"You let me worry about what details I want to be relieved of!" Kane had already pulled on a jacket and was putting on his tie. "Let's go."

"I'm coming," Dany said.

"Then come on!" As he held the door, waiting for Norman to swing past him, Kane said, "In the future, when something as big as this could be crops up, you make damned sure I know about it. First. Not after Ward. Not after anybody. First. Understand?"

"Lower your voice, Kane!" Dany said, and grasped Norman's arm. "Shep's got you upset, and you're taking it out on Norm."

"That's all right," Norman said, his face a placid mask. "I'll remember to check with you, Kane."

"To hell with Shep," Kane said, slamming the door. "I'm not afraid of him." He put an arm around Norman's shoulders and took Dany's hand. "If he takes me on, he takes on all of us. He takes on the whole country. Right?"

"Right!" Dany said, smiling up at him, relieved that his anger had passed.

"Right," Norman said. "You're right, Kane."

For two more weeks, attended by an orgy of publicity, the State Department hearings wore on.

They were still closed to public scrutiny. The country learned, through Chairman Kane O'Connor, how subversion was being exposed. His indictment of the Department was so devastating many believed the fight was a conscientious effort to clean house in Washington.

The day after the investigation closed, the State Department issued a rebuttal, voiced by Richard Southgate. It was Southgate the Undersecretary who spoke. But it was Southgate the elder statesman who commanded nationwide attention and respect. His condemnation of the inquiry was a concise record of events that purported to examine each case and reveal a distortion of truth. "There can be no doubt," he said, "that the picture presented the public was considerably doctored. Mistakes have been made which are acknowledged by the Department. However, by making charges against the innocent as well as the guilty, the O'Connor subcommittee has done a grave injustice to the guiltless and has aided the cause of traitors."

The anti-O'Connor faction seized on the denial. Southgate, a national figure with strong political backing and a brilliant record, was an important voice. What had appeared to be an uncontested triumph for Kane now became a debate.

The accused State Department employees were forgotten. The fight was now O'Connor versus Southgate. Although Kane was criticized in editorials, maligned in speeches, the conflict won him new friends, too.

Millions had followed the daily headlines during the inquiry. Few had read the long text of the rebuttal. There were those who could not understand the "cover-up for those Communists." And others who felt that "with all the argument, there's bound to be something to it."

Kane's supporters stood on firm ground: The aim of international communism is world revolution. There are Communists in Washington. It is imperative that they be removed.

But his followers did less to strengthen him than his enemies.

His foes' views were often too erudite, too couched in legalistic terms to be readily accepted by an aroused public. They took the form of scholarly discussions of the Alien and Sedition Acts of John Adams' Administration and suspension of *habeas corpus* during the Civil War, the actions of A. Mitchell Palmer after World War I, the activities of Martin Dies.

Motivated by rage, other anti-O'Connorites condemned congressional investigations, not Kane's use of them. They blasted the "Red hunt," rarely considering the possible presence of Communists.

In describing their dragon, they pictured him out of proportion, crediting him with strength he did not possess. Unwittingly, they increased his influence.

But Kane was stung by Southgate's statement, furious at the detailed argument which, point-by-point, attempted to destroy the public image of Kane and the public acceptance of the investigation's success.

While radio and television, newspapers and magazines aired the battle, he took counsel with his staff and friends. Some suggested a diversion, a new inquiry to turn attention elsewhere. Some urged him to remain in Washington during the recess, despite the coming primaries, to reopen the investigation while Congress was scattered and involved in campaigning. All warned him of Southgate's position and prestige. Cautioned by reason, driven by anger, it was anger that prevailed.

The House chamber was crowded, swathed in confusion. Papers littered the floor. The public address system echoed with the monotonous voice of the clerk calling the roll. Page boys carried documents through the clutter. The legislators had been working feverishly to complete their business so that they might be off to the hustings.

"The Chair recognizes Congressman Kane O'Connor."

Kane took his place in the well of the House and waited for silence. The Speaker rapped his gavel. A few men wandered off to the cloakrooms. Several returned to their seats. As the stir subsided, Kane began to speak. "Gentlemen of the House, we stand in peril in the world today because there are individuals high in government circles who are intent upon reducing this mighty nation to serfdom at Russia's feet! In all recorded history there is no counterpart for such infamous, evil and immense treachery!"

He watched his colleagues put papers aside and turn their attention to him. Above him, the galleries were still. "One of these men—Undersecretary of State Richard Southgate—has again revealed himself before the nation for what he is!"

Kane allowed the shocked murmur to fade, disregarding the few who whispered to their neighbors. "Either by stupidity or design," Kane said, "Southgate is guilty of deeds that amount to no less than treason against the United States!"

There was a scramble in the press gallery as one wave of reporters rushed out to flash word of the attack to their papers.

"Mr. Speaker!" Shepherd Reade was attempting to get the floor. "Mr. Speaker, will the congressman yield?"

"I will not yield!" Kane called out. "I intend to tell this House and the country what I know about a man who poses as a devoted. . ."

"Mr. Speaker!" Milton Pugh was on his feet, waving his hand. "I rise to a point of personal privilege."

"I intend to finish my remarks," Kane shouted.

The Speaker called for order. "Mr. O'Connor has the floor."

Kane smiled, nodding pleasantly to Reade and Pugh as they took their seats. Then, ignoring the muted conversations going on around him, he addressed himself to the galleries. "Do I shock you by what I've said? Then be assured that I searched my conscience a long time, and knew that I must speak out, because the security of our nation comes first, before any personalities. Because—in these dangerous times—there can be no sanctuary for traitors or fools." Kane pounded the lectern rhythmically as he spoke, looking around the chamber. "I will make no blanket indictment as Mr. Southgate has done. I will be specific about his treachery. First, let's examine his handling of Lend-Lease, an operation which allowed Russia to strengthen its army and navy and air force with American money and American materials and American blood!. . ."

Kane watched as Shepherd Reade walked to the rear of the room and spoke to Abel Garren. The Majority Whip then joined them as Kane went on with his attack. . .

". . . who made it possible for Russia to increase her arsenal so that in some future day we may have our own ships and guns firing at us?"

In the press gallery there was a constant flurry of excitement as reporters, hastily alerted, rushed to their seats or out to the telephones, speculating on the effect of Kane's speech and the way it would be answered.

"Now let us examine his failure to keep subversives out of the State Department," Kane said. A page boy put a note before him and he paused to read it. It was from Stu Denton: *You're hurting yourself. Sit down.* Kane glanced at his friend and shook his head. He began again. "Southgate attacked my investigation with good reason." He raised his voice. "He did so because I showed that the Department has been honeycombed with men who played Stalin's tune and made America dance to it!"

The Speaker was leaning on his elbows, his chin supported by his thumbs, his hands covering his face. He was amazed at the charges against the revered former member of the House. He contemplated the animated conversation going on around Shepherd Reade in the rear of the chamber.

"Can you imagine a situation where a loyal American citizen would not proudly proclaim his loyalty?" Kane sighed audibly and held out his hands before him. "Southgate has told this country that I am a liar. My friends, I swear before Almighty God that I sat in a room within sight of this building, only a week ago, and had State Department employees refuse to assure a congressional committee of their devotion and patriotism."

Kane lowered his voice. "Either Richard Southgate is a liar, or I am. Either Richard Southgate is blind, or I am. Either Richard Southgate is a dupe or a traitor, or I am!" He saw the Majority Leader moving across the room, whispering to small groups. On his left, the Minority Whip and Shepherd Reade were talking to others. Then, as Kane spoke on, a few men at a time began to leave their seats.

"Decision after decision has been made where American interests were made subservient to the interests of the communist conspiracy for world domination!"

Two Democrats in front of Kane stood and walked past him. Milton Pugh strolled up the aisle. Luther Brantley.

Kane tried to hold them by addressing himself directly to section after section. Meanwhile, the Republicans, amused by the interparty fratricide, settled back to listen. Upset, Kane lashed the men who were leaving. "If you have doubts about the adherents the Reds have in high places, you have only to watch the frantic efforts being made by Southgate and his cohorts to stop me from telling the American people of the conspiracy to enslave us!"

Below him two GOP men slipped from their seats and walked out. Six more Democrats followed them.

"Do you think it was simply an accident of fate that China was sold down the river?"

A whole row of Republicans filed out. As Kane's charges against Southgate mounted, from both sides of the aisle, slowly, silently, the chamber began to empty. He watched the congressmen escape to the cloakrooms. Finally, fewer than fifty remained. Stewart Denton was still there. Shepherd Reade. Ward Roberts. The others were dotted among the maze of empty seats.

Shepherd Reade's eyes were upon him; and Kane read the scorn in them, saw the old man's mouth curl in disgust. The Speaker leaned back in his chair. Stewart Denton tapped his fists together before him. Ward Roberts picked at the end of his tie.

It was a cold and desolate chamber. And Kane felt the sharp slap of the silent rebuke. He had been struck with the weapon of ridicule, had been all but silenced by the refusal to hear him. He tried now to raise his voice to the galleries, but when he looked there he imagined he saw pity on the blank faces of his listeners. That old nameless fear and insecurity that had assailed him before burned through his senses. Although he continued to speak, his mind was tortured. Finally, defiant, he finished his remarks. "I see many of my colleagues have left us. All right. They need not listen today. But this nation is listening. The people who sent them to sit in this Congress are listening. And, in the American tradition, the owners of these empty seats will answer to the people!"

When Kane had taken his seat, the Chamber filled again. Shepherd Reade was recognized. Courtly, deliberate, he replied in a calm voice. "Richard Southgate needs no defense from me. My colleagues on both sides of the aisle have illustrated their respect for this great man and their contempt for calumny." He rubbed a bony hand across his pinched face. "It is obvious to all by now that the world is divided into two parts. One part is populated by the despicable traitors and saboteurs who serve Stalin. The other part houses saints and patriots who serve the Gentleman from North Carolina."

The bitter sarcasm battered at Kane; and he wanted to leave, but would not be driven out. Conscious of the eyes upon him, he forced himself to appear at ease, unconcerned, unruffled, but sweat dampened his back and his face was flushed with suppressed fury as he tried to get Ward Roberts' attention or Stu Denton's . . . someone who could rise to defend him, to silence Reade.

"The self-anointed Emperor of Slander and Smear is sure he can satisfy the citizens of his realm; for they—like their Emperor —prefer a simple, bold lie to a complex and boring revelation of the truth. And so he substitutes malice for objectivity, slander for evidence. . . ."

Kane saw Ward Roberts watching him, and in the same instant, caught Stu Denton's sober expression. Staring at Ward, trying to shut out the snickers from his other colleagues, ignoring the slim smile of the Speaker, Kane's eyes ordered Ward to act.

Reade was brandishing a fist at Kane. "The Gentleman from North Carolina has invoked the attention of the voters of America to this chamber today. I welcome that. And I trust that his constituents will take note of his behavior, will recognize his personal crusade for the mockery it is. . . ."

"Mr. Speaker!" Ward Roberts was on his feet. "Mr. Speaker, I move that the words of the Gentleman from Alabama be . . ."

"Mr. Speaker," Shepherd Reade said softly, his voice on the public address system drowning out Roberts, "I will save the Gentleman from Pennsylvania the embarrassment of having to defend something he knows in his heart is not worth defense; and I will save the Speaker the trouble of having my remarks read and ordering me to take my seat. I am fully aware of the rules of this House against attacking a member; and I assure the Gentleman from Pennsylvania, and the Gentleman from North Carolina, if he is interested, that—for the first time in my career—I have consciously, purposely done violence to those rules. This great House has withstood demogoguery before. And the culprits have passed away and their words and works have been forgotten. And yet, by its very nature this House still stands. It has the means and will to protect itself; and it will use those means and exert that wiU . . ."

"Mr. Speaker!" Ward Roberts waved his arm, shouting for recognition. "The Speaker is ignoring . . ."

Shepherd Reade was undeterred. "The lying tongue is like a fire that consumes everything around it, and then, in the end, must consume itself!"

32

ON THAT EVENING, Shepherd Reade, conferring with the Speaker, the Majority Leader and a White House assistant, was called to the telephone to discuss his campaign plans with aides in Alabama. "Stay out of this Red business, Shep," they told him. "The radio and the television and the papers got you raisin' hell with O'Connor; and this is a foul time to get yourself on record apologizin' for the commies. We got enough to do down here without makin' folks wonder 'bout stuff like that!"

On that evening, Ward Roberts, dining with Norman Keller, confided, "Norm, Kane hurt himself today. And in doing so, he hurt us, the committee, the whole fight against communism. The thing that worries me is that—in the public mind—there is no committee or staff or chief counsel fighting the Reds. An individual is too easily attacked, Norm. And Kane is vulnerable. He's too intemperate, too anxious to borrow trouble. If you're to do the job I know you can do—and, after all, you're the one indispensable man in the outfit—we can't have it look like a one-man show. You've got to see to that, Norm. And I'll help you."

On that evening, Tod Sands wiped the frost from his martini glass, swirled the olive, meditating, and sat down beside his wife, one hand patting her thigh. "Yep, June, baby, the ring around O'Connor grows wider. At first there was only Cy and Tod and then Dany. Good old boot-licking-not-too-bright-sweet Cy and dependable, shrewdie Tod who respects The Boss and allows for his failings, and beautiful-sharp-honest Dany who loves the guy from up so close she's never seen a full view of him. But now the lion-hunters and the politicians and the money boys have joined the circle. And we've got Ward Roberts, who'd cut the testicles off his grandfather if they were negotiable . . . and Norm Keller, a fanatic if I've ever seen one, who doesn't much like anybody with legs and is psychopathic on Kane's current fling with communism." He belched. "Save your money, baby doll. The Sands' Fund is all that stands between us and social security."

On that evening, Dany adjusted the scoop-necked blouse on her shoulders, satisfied that the sapphire color complimented the blue of her eyes, dabbed a touch of perfume on each ear lobe and between her breasts, and went into her tiny kitchen. Kane and Matt Fallon were due for dinner; and she rushed to get ready for them. She seasoned the steak, placed it on the stove, and put the salad ingredients on the drainboard of the sink so Kane could make his special salad. As she was arranging a bowl of flowers on the dining table, she heard Kane knock and, without waiting, enter the living room.

"I don't give a damn if Jesus H. Christ says I've done something wrong . . ."

Matt Fallon interrupted him. "I just want to know the truth. I talked to Reade and, according to him, they've got plenty on you if they decide to use it."

Dany stopped the argument. "No politics on an empty stomach. Come on in the kitchen where I can watch you. Matt, you bartend."

Matt told her she was beautiful.

Kane, giving her a slap on the rear, advised Matt that "at least there's one thing we can agree on." Pausing to sip the cocktail Matt offered him, he went to work on the salad. Matt pulled a chair away from the table and sat, his long legs stretching across the narrow room.

Dany turned the spatula under the French fries. "Wait till you taste Kane's salad. It's a masterpiece."

"I didn't know he had any domestic abilities."

Kane cut two tomatoes into eighths and dropped them into a salad bowl. "It's a secret Greek recipe," he said. "Passed down to me from my boss in the restaurant where I washed dishes when I was in law school."

"Nice to know you're an expert at dishwashing," Dany said, trying to keep the conversation light.

Kane shredded the lettuce atop the tomatoes and dropped in raw onion rings. "Matt's been trafficking with the enemy. He spent the past couple of hours in Reade's office."

"You've got to admit, Loverboy, that it's possible they've got a case against you. I'm not saying it's legitimate."

"That's decent of you, Matt." Kane mixed a heavy sprinkling of salt into the salad. "You louse!"

Dany, inspecting the steak beneath the broiler, said, "Remember we're not going to talk politics."

Matt picked the olive from his glass. "Reade's too smart to start something when he can't make a good showing."

"You, too!" Dany warned him. "Talk about anything else. Talk about how you won the war."

Kane, dampening the salad with olive oil, added a cap of vinegar, sprinkled oregano over the top and began to toss the mixture. "You heard her," he told Matt, laughing. "I've just got one more thing to say and I'll shut up. I'm going to get Shep."

"Forget the melodrama, Kane."

"I am, Matt. I'm going to fry that bastard for what he said today and for the implied threat he made."

"Don't snow yourself." Matt poured another drink. "The next time you step out of line, you're going to get clobbered. Why do you think they've been going to the trouble of checking up on you?"

Dany brought the salad bowl to the table. "Please! No more."

"All right." Matt got up, holding Dany's chair as she sat.

They had only finished the shrimp cocktail when the conversation was back to its preordained place. Dany gave up. She was used to withdrawing when the two men got together. Their recent meetings had been limited to twice in Kane's apartment, a few dinners, a party at Hunting Acres and a celebrity-spangled dance at the Pierre in New York. Matt—serious, frank, critical, always forcing Kane to defend himself—would offer his advice: moderation. Kane respected him and enjoyed his company. He would listen, then do as he pleased.

"I wish you could understand, Matt," Kane said, "that all Shep's interested in is blasting me and collecting some free publicity. If there's anything that makes me sick it's a two-faced, headline-happy idiot!"

Matt grinned and heaped potatoes on his plate. "I don't make any secret of my distaste for the way you've been handling yourself lately. I read the transcript of your attack on Southgate this afternoon. And it wasn't only poor politics. It was pretty damned disgusting."

"Now I'm going to hear all that bull from you!" Kane tapped his fork against his plate. "You're not impressed with facts either."

Dany interrupted to head off the rupture she feared. "Matt's just saying . . ."

"I know what he's saying! He doesn't know what the hell he's talking about, but he's talking . . ."

Matt reached for the broccoli. "You threw some words around today—'traitor,' 'dupe,' 'liar'—that showed bad taste, poor judgment and a disregard of history that's appalling."

"What do you want me to do? You think I ought to keep quiet when . . ."

"It's not what I want you to do. It's what I know you'd better damned well stop doing! You opened your jaw today; and Shep Reade, with the good, gray Speaker temporarily deaf, neatly put his foot into it!"

"One thing at a time," Kane said angrily. "What's gotten you so hot and bothered? What I said on the floor? Or what Shep told you in his office?"

"Reade's got plenty of information on your financial manipulations."

"It's all part of the same thing." Kane dropped his silverware. "Dammit, they're trying to smear me, that's all!"

"Well don't act so outraged. What the hell were you trying to do to Southgate but smear him?"

"Smear? Goddamn it, I . . ."

"You're not going to wish away the facts, Kane. For a change, you might try facing up to them!"

"It's not the material they've got that could hurt me. It's the interpretation they put on it." Kane pushed his food aside unfinished. He was still shaken from his experience in the House, still seething with hatred for Reade, for the Speaker.

Matt turned in his chair. "What about the Purmincar deal?"

"They've got nothing there," Dany said. "It's all been in the papers."

"I prepared a booklet. I got paid for work I did," Kane said. "I even returned the fee to the company; and they sent it back, assuring me it was common practice to pay for services. I can prove that!"

"Damned good salad," Matt said, helping himself again. "What about Dany and Tod buying Purmincar stock? Reade says he knows that for a fact."

"So what? They're free to buy anything they want if they've got the money to pay for it."

"They got part of the Purmincar fee, didn't they?"

"Sure. They worked on the pamphlet. They were entitled to get paid." He shook his head gravely. "I thought you believed in me, Matt."

Matt buttered a roll. Studying Kane for a moment, he said, "I don't know what gave you that idea." Then, laughing suddenly, "What about Reade's information that you borrowed dough from the counsel of some salvage concern?"

Dany went to the stove for coffee.

"What about it?" Kane said. He was surprised, wondering where Shep had gotten his facts.

"Don't you deny it?"

"There's nothing to deny."

"What the hell's wrong with you, Kane? If what Reade says is true, money was given to you by the representative of an organization that profited from your help. You mean you don't see anything wrong in that?"

"Be sensible, Matt. Do you think there's a congressman or senator in this town who doesn't go to bat for his constituents? Ask Shep who helped me get that bill through for that salvage firm. He did! Ask him what he would do if an influential man came to him, wanting to get a reasonable bill passed."

"That's different," Matt said. "There's no money involved. In this case, you admit that you accepted . . ."

Kane broke in on him angrily. "I've accepted nothing! Joe King's an old friend. He campaigned for me. I didn't care about the company he represented. I asked him to do me a personal favor."

"But the way it looks . . ."

"The way it looks!" Kane stalked across the room. "The way it looks! Is it fair to look at anything but facts? That's what a court does. It examines facts. It doesn't *suppose* anything. It doesn't take anything for granted. It doesn't convict someone on the basis of suppositions and innuendo and circumstantial evidence..."

Dany, poised by the sink, was alarmed at Kane's ranting. "Matt's just trying to help."

Kane put his hand on Matt's shoulder. "Sorry I blew up. It just hurts when I hear the way they've misinterpreted everything."

Matt smiled. "I wish I could have recorded that last speech, Kane. Then you could play it back to yourself before your next investigation."

"Just what do you mean by that?" Kane was on the offensive again.

"Nothing . . . nothing. Oh, Kane, how your mind works! How illogical your logic!" Matt took his coffee cup from Dany. "As of today, my friend, you've bulled your way into a vendetta with Shepherd Reade and some other powerful characters like Abel Garren, the Czar of the Majority. If Reade lives up to his promise, during the next session, the least he and his friends will do is to needle you regularly on the floor, enough to take some of the play away . . ."

"Like hell! They won't dare. I'll take care of that."

"Oh? How are you going to manage it?" Matt said, smiling.

"Never mind." Kane smacked his hands together. "Shep and all the boys who give him orders are anxious to stop Kane O'Connor, and how they stop me just doesn't matter. But they're not dealing with one of the average congressional peasants. And, believe me, Matt, they're going to find that out!"

Later, when Matt had gone, Kane sat in a deep chair, his eyes on the drama on the television screen, but his mind darting elsewhere. Dany sat on the floor, resting her head against his knees. "I didn't like the way Matt talked," she said. "He usually kids you. But tonight, most of the time, he was dead serious."

"He was just pumping me, Dany. Reade expected Matt to come to me, hoping I'd scare off. Don't worry about Matt. He's sitting next to the biggest story in the country every day in the week. He knows when he's well off; and if he rides me it's only to kid himself into believing that he's really impartial."

Taking his hand, Dany held it against her cheek. "I guess . . . I hope so . . ."

He turned her to him. "You'll help me. Won't you?"

"Of course. How?"

"I've got to get Shep Reade."

"You have enough troubles without taking on more."

He tugged at the skein of hair on her neck. "Don't you see, Dany? The first time I do something they don't like, they'll start a diversion by trying to smear me. And next session Shep might force a full committee vote to dissolve my subcommittee, or stop appropriations on the floor."

She saw the logic there. "You can't fight everybody," she cautioned him. "Today was just a warning, just an illustration of what they can do if you push them."

"You know why those peons walked out today, why Shep slandered me, why the Speaker let him get away with it? Because they were afraid to buck the big boys, afraid they'd get their patronage clipped, afraid they'd get no dough from the party war chest, afraid no presidential crony would shake hands with them on the platform in their district, afraid they'd get no kind words from the White House. Well, dammit, I can get to them the same way. They're all going to be afraid of *me* before this little deal is over. I'm going to whip Shep. I'm going down to his district; and I'm going to beat him."

"Kane, Shep's entrenched. He's an important man here and at home. He has an open door to the White House. You're riding a popularity wave with the public. But the public doesn't run politics. The public doesn't decide elections."

"Oh yes they do. I didn't need the politicians to win any election I've ever entered. If the people are mad enough, if they've got something to vote *against*, they'll vote. And Shep's been worried a long time about this election. He's not as secure as you think."

Dany knew that Kane needed her, just as he always had. He hadn't gone to Ward Roberts or to Norm, or even to Tod. He'd asked only her. Smiling up at him, smoothing his face with her fingers, she said, "All right. I'm with you, darling."

He bent to kiss her. "You're a bright girl, Dany. You're the one I can depend on."

"Is that the only nice thing you can think of to say to me?"

"Well," he said, winking at her, "you're awfully good in bed!" Reaching for her, he made her sit beside him and kissed her again, his lips lingering on hers, then passing over her throat.

Gently she pushed him away. "Kane, please darling—"

"Are you going to be coy with me?" he whispered in her ear.

Dany stood and he started to rise, but she held his shoulders. "Darling, you know I love you. God, how I love you! But it's wrong, what we've been doing."

"Dany, if we love one another . . ."

"Please, let me finish. I've tried to say it before. And then you were close and touching me. Kane, it is wrong."

He was frowning, shaking his head, his arms folded across his chest. "Jesus, Dany, you're no silly kid . . ."

"No, I'm not. I'm a woman, so I don't have a silly kid's excuses. I've been to confession three times since. . . . Since the first time you made love to me. And I've confessed and I've told the priest I had a firm intention not to do it again. And I've been granted absolution. And then I haven't been able to help myself."

"Dany, it's no sin, not when we're in love."

"It is, Kane. I love you, but you'll have to let me show it some other way . . . by helping you in whatever you want to do, by giving you the trust and the warmth . . . all die things I've never given anyone else."

Kane sat there silently, looking at her. "All right," he said at last. "If that's what you want."

"It's not what either of us wants. It's what we've got to accept."

They looked at one another, searching the expression in one another's eyes. And Kane's mouth twitched. He laughed. "What's funny?" Dany said.

He came to her, put his hands lightly about her waist and kissed both her eyes, then held her at arm's length. "Shep's in for a bad time. If there's anything that'll make a man mean, it's a lack of loving. . ."

33

KANE WANTED no pitched battle with the Administration. He needed time to court allies and enlist mercenaries, time to snipe at his enemies one by one, time to demoralize them with the weapon of fear. He was determined to prove, in terms they would understand, that he could not be abused and vilified with impunity. He resolved to make them see that to fight him in the decisive battle—at the polls—was to welcome disaster. Then, he believed, they would be forced to seek a truce. Obsessed with the desire for retribution, he left Washington with his strategy determined and set out to direct the skirmishes which would insure its success.

Sitting in the living room of Cy's home in Manton, the two old friends made plans again.

Six years had passed since Kane had returned from the war to begin his quest.

Four years before it was here they had plotted his bid for the District Solicitorship.

Two years had gone by since the decision to fight his uncle for the congressional nomination had been made in the same room.

"After this one," Kane was saying, "we're going after the Senate."

Cy, grown plumper, sat on the sofa, his shirt flung aside. "Let's win this one first."

Kane mixed Cy's bourbon and water and handed it to him. "I don't think there's anything at all to worry about. I've licked Bev Crater before."

"Don't underestimate Bev. He's got your Uncle Wes on his side. And Luke Biddle. That'll give him a good block of votes."

"I'm not worried," Kane said. But he could not turn his mind from his uncle. Only that afternoon Kane had driven by the Barrett home, seeing the familiar potted plants on the porch, two cats walking the railing, hearing the yap of his aunt's mongrels playing on the lawn. His uncle was sitting in a rocker, so much older it seemed, stooped, his white hair awry, a newspaper blowing at his feet. For a moment Kane had resolved to stop his car, to walk across that yard, to confront his Uncle Wes, to offer to forget their differences, to promise to support him for the congressional seat when Kane ran for the Senate. He applied the brakes. The car slowed, stopped. On the porch his uncle looked up, straining it seemed to see. Then Aunt Mady hobbled through the doorway, banging the screendoor. His uncle had stood, walked to the steps and looked out toward the street. He had recognized Kane's car, turned his back, and gone into the house. Kane had driven on.

"Uncle Wes doesn't like Bev any better than I do. It's Aunt Mady who's probably made him announce he's backing Bev. And Luke Biddle's been pressuring him, I bet. It's just not like Uncle Wes to hold a grudge, Cy. But he's never even spoken to me since we fell out. Or sent me a Christmas card. . . . Nothing."

"After all, Kane, you did him in; and you had your eyes open when you did it."

"He would have done the same to me under those conditions. He was with Biddle all the time. He . . ."

"All right. Let's drop it. Nobody stays in politics without makin' some enemies. You just happened to make one in the family. Now back to Crater. He's hittin' your attendance record. He's pointin' up those accusations made against you in the House. How're you goin' to answer him?"

Kane mixed his own drink, swishing the ice cubes around the glass, still thinking of his uncle. "Huh?"

"I said how will you answer Bev?"

"I'm not going to answer him."

"How can we just ignore . . ."

"We'll label the character. He's taking the same position the Reds are taking: Smear O'Connor. I don't think he's going to get a lot of votes while he's mouthing the commie line."

"Knock it off!" Cy laughed. "Bev's no more a Red than the Pope!"

"I'm not calling him a Red. Plenty of people aren't Communists but do the Communists' work for them. That's all I'm going to have to say about him."

Cy took his shoes off. "I'm not sold on your scootin' around the country helpin' somebody else get elected. Your first job's to win at home."

Kane chewed a sliver of ice. "You and Tod have everything in perfect shape here. Hell, I'd win if I never showed up for the primary."

"Well, I'll admit it hasn't been tough. We've got all the money we need for a change. Fact is, we spent nearly as much on the barbecue as we had for the whole campaign last time. And Joe King's salvage outfit picked up the whole tab."

"Be sure your books don't show that!" Kane grinned. "We'll have that report to make later."

"How're you doin' it? Open-handed for our campaign here—cleaned up every penny you owed us at the bank. And Tod said he has up to ten thousand to spend on the Alabama campaign. Where's it cornin' from? You about to expose commies in the Mint?"

"I've told you about Caleb Lawton, buddy. Caleb and some of his friends have more dough than the Federal Reserve. I flew to California just before I came back here. And the trip netted sixty thousand! They don't give a damn how it's spent. It's their way of getting their licks in against communism."

Cy lifted his feet. "Sit over there, will you? I wanna stretch out."

Kane walked across the room. "Some of that money's working for me here. Some of it's going to deep-six Shep Reade in Alabama. Five thousand goes to Pennsylvania to help a friend, Ward Roberts. I'm sending two thousand on the quiet to the Republican who's running against a wily bastard, Milt Pugh, in the general election. Then, I'm contributing to five campaigns here in the state. And I'm helping Stu Denton, too. Wherever it will get rid of a louse or elect a good man, that's where I'm putting it."

"About that kind of politics," Cy said, "I know from nothin'. I can see why you'd help here in the state. They'll help you when you're out for the senatorial nomination. But goin' to Alabama and Pennsylvania and all—that doesn't make sense."

"You'll see." Kane got up to fill his glass again. "It's got to be obvious that I'm responsible for their winning. That's why I've been making speeches for them. That's why I want the communist issue to be the centerpoint of their campaigns."

Cy pulled his undershirt over his head. "Is it workin' out that way?"

"Everywhere except where I need it most, in Alabama. We've got a character there who's running on white supremacy and against FEPC. He's willing to take my dough all right, but aside from my one speech there, my fight against the commies is being ignored."

"Is he the one Tod calls 'The Pig'?"

Kane nodded. "That's the one."

"He said the guy's got a chance to whip Reade."

Kane sat down again and sipped from his drink. "That's just it. The jerk figures he's going to take it. He's not sure he needs me. That's why I've got Tod in Renfrow. He's doing publicity for next week's speech up there."

"It'll work out."

"Hope so." Kane put his half-finished drink on the floor beside his chair. "If I bring this off, I can write my own ticket. There'll be nothing I can't have."

"Kane?"

"Yeah?"

"I wasn't goin' to mention it . . . but, it's been gratin' on me. Why couldn't you get down here for Mrs. Eden's funeral? Laurie never said anythin' about it, but I figure it was a rotten thing for you to do."

"I'm sorry about that, Cy. But, honestly, I couldn't get away when you called." Kane had salved his conscience with that excuse at the time. But he knew that the real reason was that he could not bring himself to face Laurie. "I couldn't help myself," he said.

"Okay. I think you could have made it. But there's no need to fuss about it."

"When did Laurie leave?"

"I took her to the train two weeks ago."

"Why did she decide on New York?"

"I don't know. I tried to get her to stay, offered her a good job, but she wouldn't. Guess she wanted to go someplace where she could be swallowed up for awhile. She's got no kin up there."

Kane stuffed his socks inside his shoes. "Next time I'm in New York, I'll look her up."

"Best if you wouldn't. I've gotten a couple of letters from her, talked to her on the phone on her birthday. She's gettin' along okay now. Just leave her be, Kane."

Kane looked at Cy quizzically. "Guess you're right," he said. It seemed that he could hear Laurie's choked voice . . . and the squeak of the porch glider. He shrugged. "Well, let's hit the sack. Have to be in Philly tomorrow, then to Ward Roberts' district for a speech."

Cy swung his legs off the sofa. "You're gettin' to be an awful important guy!" He picked up his shirt and joined Kane. "You'll get so damned big one of these days you won't even remember your hick buddy."

Kane laughed, grabbing Cy's arm. "How you doin', you old tub?"

"Fine as wine, smooth as cake."

"Then let me have the ole handshake!"

The four-story Stonewall Jackson Hotel was the tallest building in Renfrew, Alabama. It was also the oldest. For a century the county's luncheon clubs had met in the ballroom which had never seen a dance; and traveling salesmen and cotton brokers had endured its antique plumbing, its lazy open-cage elevator and its sweltering accommodations.

Raymond Hyder stood at the clerk's desk. Taking off his straw hat, he wiped the sweatband with a damp handkerchief. "Mr. O'Connor get in yet?"

"Registered about an hour ago, Ray."

Shepherd Reade's opponent took off his linen jacket, laying it on the counter. "You need some fans in here." He ran his thumbs under his green galluses, pulling his shirt at the armpits where it clung to him. "How about ringin' the room for me?"

"Sure. Come on around."

Upstairs Tod talked through the doorway while Kane bathed. "Hated to call you, but we've got to do something. I would have bet 'The Pig' couldn't lose at first. Then Reade opened up on him the other day and practically crucified him."

Kane stood up in the tub and reached for a towel. "Does Shep really have anything on him? Or is it just a lot of noise?"

"Hell, I don't know. My guess is that 'The Pig's no worse than a lot of operators in the housing racket, just taking advantage of the angles. He swears he's been framed. But the papers have

311

been full of it. Owning all these car agencies in the area and being a big space buyer hasn't hurt Reade on his press coverage."

There was no bath mat. Kane dropped another towel on the floor and stepped out of the tub. "As I get it, it cuts down to this: Shep says Hyder's been making a fortune by selling sub-standard homes to GIs. He's getting high loans on the joints, building them for a song and cheating the government and the veterans."

"Right. And like I say, Reade's been quoting chapter and verse. First mentioned it in a speech, then came out with a full-page ad in both dailies."

"Sounds bad." Kane left the closetlike bathroom, a towel wrapped around his waist. "Well, what's Hyder doing about it?"

"Not enough," Tod said. "The guy just hasn't got any push. He's a dull tool."

"Can't understand why Shep's been worried about him." Kane tracked across the worn, floral-patterned carpet.

"Because the old boy got careless about keeping the home folks happy. He involved himself in national affairs without giving much time to his own district. And worse, he's open to reaming on this FEPC business. He hasn't been for it; but he's done nothing to fight it. He also made the mistake of supporting federal aid to education—which 'The Pig' considers an assault on states' rights. If this thing hadn't come up, we'd have walked away with the voting."

"We would have to get a lemon!"

"Actually, Hyder's a pretty nice slob when you get to know him." The phone rang and Tod answered it. "Sure. Come on up, Ray."

Kane stood in front of the dresser, combing his hair. It was thinning a bit in the center; and he moved the heavy tuft in front over the sparse spot. "That our candidate?"

"That's him." Tod sat on the glass-topped desk, banging the Gideon Bible against his hand. "He means well, Kane. He's a God-fearing, radical-hating, overstuffed country boy with a prosperous insurance and realty business and a healthy, apple-cheeked family. He's worked his way up from school board to city council to mayor to state assembly. Now his idea of immortality is to be a congressman."

Kane sprinkled talcum under his arms and across his chest. "So you think he's up the creek?"

Tod threw up his hands. "I don't know. But I've got a feeling Norman Thomas would have a better chance to win an election in Maine."

"Well we damned well have to do something."

Ray Hyder knocked and Tod invited him in. Kane, standing a head taller than Hyder, walked across the room to offer his hand to the perspiring, ruddy-faced candidate.

"Time I met you," Hyder said. "Sure am obliged for your help."

"I hear we've got troubles, Ray."

"I hope you don't believe none of this. Ever'thin' I done is absolutely legal. Absolutely! I been runnin' a clean campaign, real clean! I'd never stoop to tactics like that."

"Sit down, Ray. We've got some talking to do."

Hyder sat in a rocker beside the window. "Thought I had him licked. And now this. I swan, it's not like Mr. Reade to do somethin' like this. Why I been buyin' my cars from him for years; and he bought the first fire insurance policy I ever sold."

Drawing on the trousers that Dany had bought for him, Kane watched his protege. Tod's name for him was apt enough, but all-in-all he wasn't as bad as Kane had feared. "What are you going to do about it?" Kane asked.

Hyder frowned. "I been doin' well, real well. The voters know I got business experience and worked for them right here at home and was brought up on a farm. They know I'd act for their best interests . . ."

Sitting on the bed, Kane pulled his socks on. "All right, Ray. I know all that. What are you doing to lick Reade?"

"I'm denyin' it. I'm runnin' ads denyin' what he said about me."

Kane stepped into his shoes. "And?"

"I'm goin' to release my income tax returns. All my returns."

"You want my help, Ray?"

Hyder patted his high forehead with his handkerchief. "Of course. Sure I want your help."

"Then I'm going to start helping you right now. I'm going to tell you what Shep Reade's done—and what you're going to have to do to beat him. He's taken one word—honesty—and he's shown the voters that he stands for that word and that you don't!"

"But that's not true."

"That's not what matters! It's what the voter thinks that matters. You've got to have an issue; and you've got to be on the right side."

"Only issues 'round here," Hyder said, "are the nigger question, farm supports, employment, taxes. Mr. Reade's got his votin' record to prove where he stands. And where he's weak—like he is on federal aid to the schools—I been bringin' it to the public. Been tellin' folks that soon's you let the radicals in Washington get control, they'll be lettin' niggers in the white schools. Niggers!"

"Tod, hand me my shirt, will you?" Kane turned back to Ray Hyder. "All right. There you're on the right track. But he's fighting with heavy artillery and you're throwing mud clods! We've got to hit back hard. We've got to take two issues: Negroes and communism; and we've got to show that you stand for white supremacy and democracy and that he stands for mingling of the races, that you fight the Communists and that he helps them."

"I'm followin' you on the nigger question," Hyder said, "but there ain't many folks 'round here much interested in the communist thing. I been tryin' to tell Tod that. Been tryin' to right along."

"Wake up, ferchrisakes! The two go together perfecdy." Kane tucked in his shirttails. "Don't you know the Communists preach that it's right for black and white to marry? Don't you know they're in favor of putting darkies in the legislature? Don't you know they want to take everybody's land away and split it up with shares for the colored people?" He cinched his belt tighter. "Don't tell me your folks aren't interested in stopping communism!"

Tod was stretched out on the bed. He never ceased being amazed at Kane. He'd been trying himself to convince Hyder that the communist issue had to be in the forefront of the campaign. But he had been unsuccessful. Now he listened while Kane worked his magic on Ray Hyder.

"Ray, I don't know how I can stick with you on this thing. I just can't risk losing with you." Kane had no intention of withdrawing his help. Defeating Shepherd Reade was his overriding concern, his obsession. He shook his head, sighed and walked to the window. Let him worry a little, Kane thought as he looked out over the sterile, shabby town below, at the jagged lines of melting asphalt on the baked street, at the "Woodmen of the

World" sign above the McClellan's store. Turning back to Hyder, he said, "I'll put it to you straight, Ray. Either you go along with me and do it my way, or I pack up and let you screw yourself out of this primary."

Hyder pinched his chin, ruminating. "All right," he said finally. "But you've got to be careful to stay in the background. Folks 'round here don't cotton much to outsiders runnin' their politics. No sirree, bob!"

Kane crossed to him. "Okay, let's get to work. First thing tomorrow, Ray, I want you to rent a vacant store. Right on the main drag if you can. Get phones and desks and typewriters. Have the front decorated with placards. Get a big sign up." He thought for a moment. "And find us about four rooms in a motor court or a decent hotel."

Ray Hyder noted the requirements on the back of an envelope he drew from the jacket that lay across his expansive lap. "This'll take money."

"Don't worry about that," Kane said impatiently. "Tod, call Dany. Tell her to fly down here. Have Norm put the staff to work digging up anything they can. And tell him to stand by to come down if we need him. Get hold of Cy. I want him to take his vacation now. This is his kind of situation. He can think the way these people think."

"You figure we can lick the odds, Kane? We've only got a month," Tod said.

"It's not going to be easy," Kane said. "But the harder it is, the more it means. This is the big one. We can't lose here. Remember that, Ray. One way or another, it can be done."

Tod grinned. "And you figure you're just the guy to do it!"

34

TWO DAYS later the task force was assembled. Dany and Cy were due to arrive within an hour of one another in Mobile. Kane drove over alone to meet them.

Cy's plane landed first. Puffing and disheveled, he tramped down the ramp. "I don't know what the devil I can do for you here," he said.

"There's plenty for you to do."

"You know I'm supposed to have a job?"

"Hell, Cy, you've got to admit the bank'll get along better with you away. Since you stopped writing duns to me, there's nothing for you to do there anyhow."

"I've got to get back there sometime," Cy said. "You might have forgotten, but there's a little campaign going on there, too." Kane laughed. "I'm going to be in Washington two or three days a week. I'll make all my dates in Manton. Don't worry about that." Kane briefed Cy on the status of the Reade-Hyder campaign while they waited in the air terminal for Dany's plane. When the public address system announced the arrival of her flight, Kane and Cy moved up to the railing. Kane pointed her out as she stepped from the ramp—cool and lovely in a white suit. She saw him and waved.

"Brother!" Cy said.

"Wait till you get to know her, boy. She's got brains, too."

Before the ride to Renfrow was over, Cy was ready to agree. "Kane's done doggone well for himself," he told Tod later.

They held their first conference in one of the cottages Ray Hyder had found for them in a tourist court. The low-ceilinged room was a hot box, designed by the owner, a man with an affinity for plywood and battleship gray paint. The new smell of damp plaster and cement, the old smells of beer and sweat were oppressive.

Cy sat in his undershirt, astride a chair. Dany, in gray slacks and red jersey, lay on a blue cotton throw rug, her pencil and pad before her. Tod was, as usual, draped across the bed, welcoming the full blast of the electric fans.

Kane roved about, talking above the whirring blades, pausing briefly to ask Ray Hyder a question, to give instructions to Tod, to ask Dany's advice, to get a suggestion from Cy. Finally, content that he had covered everything, he sat on an ottoman facing Hyder. "Okay, now you characters bat it around awhile."

The phone rang. Tod answered it, grunted and held the receiver out to Dany. "It's long distance. D. C. The twentieth century Torquemada, your friend and Kane's, Norman Keller."

"How many times a day does he call you?" Kane said, winking at Tod. "I think the guy's got a case on her."

Dany waved him to silence, listened to Norman's report, motioned for her pencil and pad and began to write. "Let's have the name again. Dates. Thanks, Norm. You're a gem. Don't know what we'd do without you. We'll see you next week."

"What's next week?" Kane said when she had hung up.

"Norm's working up the personal data on Shep; and he's coming down to make use of the local records, check real estate dealings, property holdings. He can give us a hand for the final push."

"Okay," Kane said. "I hope he digs up something we can use." "He'd dig up his dead mother if he thought she'd ever read *The Daily Worker,"* Tod said.

Dany laughed. Tapping her notepad, she said, "How's this for digging? The first concrete thing we've come up with. Norm got a tip from Mel and Lucy and followed it up. It's on Shep's appointments. It seems he's got a colored boy as an alternate on his list for West Point."

Hyder, surrounded by the hustle and energy of Kane's staff, was buoyed by their enthusiasm. He was starting to believe in his chances again. "I'll bet no one 'round here's heard about that! I don't have nothin' against niggers, but sendin' them to West Point, well that's somethin' else. Somethin' else entirely."

"What's the background on it?" Tod said.

Dany flipped through her notes. "He's second alternate. From Tuskegee. Shep makes his appointments on the basis of competitive exams."

"This is a break," Kane said.

"You've got to hand it to Shep," Dany said. "It's a square thing to do."

"All right, he's a good Christian," Kane said. "But coming from Alabama, he's a lousy politician."

"Folks are goin' to be mighty resentful," Hyder said.

"Well, let us handle it, Ray," Kane said. "You got any other thoughts right now, Cy?"

"Far as I can tell, Mr. Hyder isn't organized properly. We need precinct workers, watchers, haulers. . .

It was four in the morning before they left to go to sleep. Kane got into his pajamas, waited until it was quiet outside, and crossed the hall to Dany's room. He tried the door. It was locked.

No group ever dedicated itself more energetically to aid the voters in exercising their franchise.

They had their difficulties. The press was unsympathetic. The electorate was unconcerned. The candidate was colorless. But they also had advantages. Their own funds were practically unlimited. They had the political acumen to attack the enemy. The opposition was caught unprepared for the vigor of their efforts.

Kane was forced to return to Washington regularly and twice answered Ward Roberts' urgent summons for help in Pennsylvania. Meanwhile he managed to satisfy Cy by weekly campaign tours of his own district.

Throughout his absences the work went forward. Dany, Tod, Norman and Cy operated on their own. He trusted their judgment and ability. Although he might prune and revise and polish when he returned to Renfrew, he never countermanded their proposals.

Despite the strain of travel, despite the unequal fight, he was happy in the excitement, in the goal to be attained, in the hope for victory.

The schedule was followed.

The First Week:

The campaign headquarters at the county seat was crowded with volunteer workers. Dany, enlisting the aid of Ray Hyder's pretty young wife, initiated a door-to-door committee. Tod's new posters—PROTECT OUR WAY OF LIFE. ELECT RAY HYDER—were mounted on poles and billboards across the district. Cy, through the local campaign manager, prepared the mailing and phone lists that would be needed.

Ray Hyder, speaking from Norman Keller's script at the County Courthouse in Brewster, shed his coat and stood in homey shirt and suspenders before the electorate. "We must enlist in the battle against communism. Congressman Kane O'Connor, a great American, has started to build this dike to hold back the traitorous tide. If you vote for my opponent, you will send to Washington a man who is anxious to tear down what has already been done."

Tod criticized the speech. "Don't give Hyder fancy words and similes, Keller. It's not Kane you're writing for. You can't make him sound brilliant—but you can damned well make him sound like himself!"

"When I need your advice," Norman told him, "I'll write you a letter, asking for it."

"Drop dead!" Tod said.

Dany stopped the argument by asking Norman to buy her a cold drink. On the way down the dusty street they stopped to look in a pet shop window; and Dany admired a parakeet. That evening the bird, in a handsome gilt cage, was delivered to Dany's room. There was no card with the gift; and when she tried to thank Norman for it, he was embarrassed. "Just a bird, Dany. You don't have to act like it's such a big thing."

"It is a big thing. You know, I've never had a pet before. My mother was allergic to animal fur. One time I found a kitten and brought him home and hid him in my bed . . . but they found him, and my father made me keep him in a bam, a long way from the house. But when I went back, he'd run away. Until now, I've never had a pet, Norm." She kissed his forehead.

Norman reddened. "Come on," he said gruffly, "we've got too much work to do around here to spend our time with small talk."

The Press across the country took a second look at the minor southern campaign. They billed it as a contest between Reade and O'Connor. "There can be no doubt," Ed Patterson, the political columnist and commentator, said on his radio program, "that the

primary election in Alabama is a test of whether or not
O'Connor—the publicity-hungry demagogue—is strong enough to
defeat one of the few men in Congress who has had the courage to
oppose him."

Kane rapped back in an interview in Washington and again in
a radio address in Manton. "Patterson fools no one except his
sponsors. He is paid to report. Instead he lies and smears. I urge
every good American to keep that in mind when he has occasion to
make a purchase. A dollar to Patterson's sponsor is a dollar
contributed toward his campaign of slander, a campaign first
conceived and launched by the Communist party." At week's end,
Patterson's sponsors, Marbleton Paint Products, received six
thousand letters, 40 per cent of which backed Kane's stand.

Matt Fallon phoned Kane. "Do you have any idea what
you've suggested? You're asking the public to boycott Patterson's
sponsors because the guy doesn't agree with you."

"What do you expect me to do, turn the other cheek?"

"Answer him if you want, Kane, but a boycott . . ."

"I'm telling the public not to support that bastard. Is it any
different than his telling the voters not to support me?"

"Christ! There's your logic again!"

"Is the guy a friend of yours?"

"No. But you are, Kane, and I don't like what you're doing to
him or yourself. Nobody with a shred of decency is going to
respect you for tampering with a man's right to say..."

Kane broke in on him. "Matt, I'm through with Patterson.
Nobody ever heard of him until he started in on me. I've had my
say."

The Second Week:

In a major address, quoted by all the press services, Kane
spoke in Shepherd Reade's hometown. First he read an editorial
from *The New Masses* which damned Kane O'Connor. Then he
read from the *Congressional Record,* quoting a few lines from
Shepherd Reade's attack. Operating on the sure ground that one
and one always makes two, he advised his listeners of the
conspiracy to bring communism painlessly to America. And he
told them his version of what communism meant to Alabama.

Meanwhile, Cy planned Primary Day strategy, talked with
Hyder's supporters, handed out money. And Norman and Dany

prepared circulars and a special bulletin while Tod helped Kane with his final radio address.

Ed Patterson, smarting under Kane's reply to his radio attack, again dared challenge him. "O'Connor has attempted to silence me as he is attempting to silence Shepherd Reade. If he is successful in either case, the time will come when no man will dare to criticize him. No one denies that O'Connor has attacked communism, a vicious menace to our country. But no right-thinking man is willing to have him destroy American justice and fair play in the process. That communism should be fought wherever and whenever it threatens us, we have no doubt. But it should be met with our methods, not theirs, and it should be met by our constituted agencies that are trained, skilled and able to do it effectively."

"I need not answer Patterson," Kane said in an interview. "The American people will answer him, for they are tired of the pussy-footing do-gooders who are more concerned with getting rid of O'Connor than they are with getting rid of the communist traitors."

That week end Cy and Tod flew back to Manton for a meeting with the County Executive Committee. Dany, Kane and Norman accepted Ray Hyder's invitation to dinner on Sunday.

The Hyder home revealed the hand of Ray's petite, pretty wife. As clean as his freshly-scrubbed eight-year-old daughter, as handsome as his three sons, it was set among old ivy-clad oaks on a sloping green lawn, a newly-constructed Georgian home with large rooms and high windows, a winding stairway that swept from the foyer to the upstairs area, a playroom where eight games—from hopscotch to shuffleboard—were laid out on the tile floor, a den where all the bookshelves were filled with porcelain knickknacks, record albums, Ray's stamp collection and an assortment of musical instruments.

It was to the den that they adjourned when they finished dinner. "We never eat that way 'cept when we get company from the North," Ray Hyder said. "But Martha says Yankees'd be disappointed if we didn't feed fried chicken and stuff."

"These two are Yankees," Kane said, nodding at Dany and Norman. "I'm a corn bread, buttermilk and fatback man myself."

"I swan, you talk more like you're from up North," Ray said. "Don't mind the mess in here," Martha Hyder said, pouring their coffee from a silver pot into the bone china demi-tasse cups.

"I figured me and the kids had to have some place to wallow when we left the old house and moved in here," Ray said.

"So this is the only room we use," Martha said, explaining the worn armrests covered with linen antimacassars, the old rug which had been gnawed fringeless when the Hyder's sleepy-eyed old collie was a pup, the painted white spinet piano with the scuffs of countless skates around its base, the green leather chair, rump-sprung from Ray's bulk.

"Don't know why I should wanna go to Washington," Ray said, gulping his coffee and leaning back in his chair to loosen his belt. "Set comfortable now, but I had to do plenty of scratchin' and shufflin' for a long time . . . till the war . . . and seems as things just been breakin' right for us since then."

"You in the war?" Kane asked.

"Daddy had the draft board," the oldest son said.

"I been ruptured twice," Ray Hyder said.

"Ray!" Martha said.

"I mean I been. . . . hemia-ed twice."

"You get hurt in the war?" the oldest son said to Norman.

"No."

Dany put down her coffee cup. "Who plays all these . . ."

"Mr. O'Connor got a medal in the war," Ray Hyder said. "A hero. Real hero. Right, Kane?"

Smiling, Kane said, "They had one left over and I happened to be around when they were giving them out."

"Why that's a story!" Martha said. "I read it in *Colliers* or maybe the *Journal.* He saved this boy's life and flew this airplane that was burnin' up . . ."

"Man!" one of the boys said, crossing to sit on the arm of Kane's chair. "Man alive! How'd you do it with it burnin' and all?"

"I'm not going to listen to any gory war stories," Dany said. "I want to know who plays all these musical instruments."

"All of us," Ray said. "We try to keep the Lord's Day sorta special; and we set together and talk and play some music and all."

The Hyder family played. Ray was at the piano, Martha on a violin, the oldest son with an accordion, another on a guitar, the youngest son on a clarinet and the daughter banging unconcernedly on a toy drum. "This next one was written by a fella in Congress," Ray said; and patting his foot in time, he led the others in *"The Lord Sure Is Waitin' for Me,"* Stewart Denton's greatest success.

"How about you, Mr. O'Connor," one of the boys said. "You play?"

"All my music's in my feet," Kane said. "I can dance a little, but my only attempt at the piano nearly gave my teacher a nervous breakdown." In that instant he could see Viola Eden's face and he had a taut feeling in the pit of his stomach. "Couldn't learn."

"Mr. Keller?"

Norman had been sitting morosely, his mind concerned with a speech he was trying to write, something that would sound reasonable with Ray Hyder's limited vocabulary. "Pardon me, Mrs. Hyder?"

"You play an instrument?"

"The piano. Used to . . . but not for some time." He patted his legs. "Can't use the pedals."

"Heckfire, Norm," Ray said, already off the piano bench, "I can't hardly use the keys; now you get on over here and play some for us."

Dany saw Norman's hesitancy and sensed that he wanted to play, but was afraid to try. "Let's go, Norm. I'll sit with you."

The Hyder family besieged him; and when Dany went expectantly to the piano, Norman pushed himself up and swung across the room to sit beside her. From the first moment he ran his fingers expertly over the keys, testing his hands, testing his reach, Dany knew that—at one time—Norman Keller had played well.

"Go on," Ray said.

Working his hands above the keyboard, his shaggy head bent over, Norman hesitated a moment, then began to play.

"Chopin," Martha said.

"Nocturne in E-Flat," Norman mumbled.

"We've got that record," the youngest son said.

But Norman was not listening. His face was intent, his eyes narrowed as if he were trying to remember each note. And then, as memory returned, he relaxed, his heavy body moving gracefully, his curved, strong fingers sure, deft. "Can't use the pedals," he said again.

When he finished, Kane led the applause. "You're good, Norm! I'm a dope when it comes to the long-hair stuff, but I can tell you're good." Standing, he stretched. "That dinner nearly did me in. One of you boys want to go over to the playroom with me? I saw a parallel bar there I'd like to try out."

Dany frowned at him. "It's a little warm for that, Kane. Let's listen to Norm . . ."

"Oh, we got two big fans in there," the oldest boy said. "You know anything about. . .I mean, sir, you worked on bars much?"

Kane laughed. "Lately, mostly cocktail bars. But, when I was young and in shape, I was on some pretty fair gym teams."

The three boys had clustered around him. "We'll be back," the oldest boy told his mother. "I've got the trampoline down pretty good. But I can't get my hands right on the bar."

"You stink. I'm better'n you," the youngest said.

Kane put his arms around their shoulders and led them, chattering, from the room. "Come on, men. Let's see how good you are."

When they were gone, Ray Hyder's little daughter came up beside Norman, slipped under his arm and sat beside him on the piano bench. "Play some more," she said.

"Know any Gershwin?" Martha Hyder said.

Norman nodded, smiling faintly; and with intense concentration, he began to play *"The Rhapsody in Blue,"* modulating to *"Love Walked Right In"* and *"I've Got Rhythm," "Summertime," "It Ain't Necessarily So,"* and back to the *"Rhapsody"* again.

Dany watched him as he finished, his head bent, his eyes closed, glistening sweat on the scar on his temple.

"Lordie-Moses," Ray Hyder said. "Me stompin' chords at that piano and you able to play it like a pro all along!"

Later, when they had been sitting quietly, talking about the campaign, and Hyder's daughter lay in her chosen spot in Norman's lap, Kane returned with the boys.

"He's great!" one of them said. "And he showed me what my trouble was—all in the grip." Picking up one of Norman's canes, the youngster demonstrated for his father. "See? I was holdin' it backwards all along."

"Time for us to go," Dany said, and taking the cane from the boy, she put it beside Norman's chair. "It's been a wonderful evening. Wonderful food and company and music." Putting her hand lightly on Norman's shoulder, she said, "I even discovered what a remarkable fellow this is."

The little girl in Norman's lap awakened. "I'm gonna pray for you," she told Norman. "I'm gonna pray God to help you walk."

The Third Week:

"Facts for the Voter," a two-page handbill of uncertain origin appeared throughout the district. A hundred thousand copies were placed in screendoors, left in rural mailboxes, circulated at rallies, posted on bulletin boards, dropped in barber shops and doctors' offices.

The front page of the five-column sheet featured a photograph. It was captioned, *Reade's Choice For West Point.* The cut was an enlarged snapshot of a gangling, smiling Negro boy standing before a decrepid shanty, his arms about a mongrel dog.

One story in the tabloid featured quotations praising Kane O'Connor. Beside it was a thumbnail biography titled, "American Hero." A brief article was devoted to Ray Hyder and his family. Still another explained the issues involved in the Fair Employment Practices controversy. Below it was a short editor's note, asking why Shepherd Reade had not fought the proposal.

A Negro professor at an Alabama school spoke out against the tactics of the campaign: "We deplore the use of the race issue in this election. We have problems, but they cannot be solved by hot heads and bigoted minds. Mr. Shepherd Reade has always been a considerate friend of Negroes, despite his conservative position. Although we have not always agreed with him, we believe he has tried to serve the best interests of the Negro voters as well as the white."

"That's the opening," Norman Keller said when he read the statement. "That's the wedge we need." Although Dany objected, Kane, Cy and Tod agreed to Norman's plan for "settling this Negro question once and for all."

"It's rotten," Dany insisted. "Low and dirty politics."

"It's also successful politics," Tod said. "It's the kind that wins campaigns."

"Try to get this through your head, Dany," Norman said. "Our winning—that's all that counts."

Kane laughed at her objections. "You're as silly as that damned parakeet of yours. You can be sure Shep would do the same thing if he had the brains to think of it."

So, on Kane's instructions, Dany bought space in the local dailies. The advertisement Tod wrote was headed: **THE NEGRO'S CHAMPION.** It quoted "pertinent excerpts" from the educator's statement: "Mr. Shepherd Reade has always been a considerate friend of Negroes. We believe he has tried to serve the best interests of the Negro voters. . . ."

"Fine," Norman said when he read the advertisement. "Now, next Monday we administer the *coup de grace!*"

On Friday of that week, Matt Fallon wired Kane: "Important you catch my show tonight."

That evening, Kane watched Milton Pugh turn aside Matt's questions and take over the program: "Kane O'Connor's no Democrat. He's a political hermit, a one-man show, a chairman of a committee of public safety! I know that he sent thousands of dollars to my Republican opponent to use against me next November. At the same time, he's politicking against Shepherd Reade; and he has his staff—at least two of whom are paid by the taxpayers— working full time in Alabama."

Kane wired Matt: *Sorry I can't help your ratings. Too busy to demand equal time. Dany loves you. Tod likes your sense of humor. I forgive you.*

But to reporters, Kane said: "Pugh's a scared old man. He knows the voters are out to get him; and he's trying to divert attention from his own situation. He may wrap the comforting blanket of Party around his shoulders and accuse me of not being loyal to political big-shots. I make no secret of the fact that I'm an American first. My first loyalty, above party, above politics, is to this country."

That week end Kane, Cy and Tod flew to Manton for the dedication of the new wing of Biddle Memorial Hospital; and Kane gained a personal triumph when he read the Sunday morning papers. The makers of Marbleton Paint Products counted the letters that arrived after the Patterson-O'Connor clash. They reasoned that those who sided with Ed Patterson would not increase their purchases of Marbleton Simplcoat, and that the people who were vehemently against him would take their business elsewhere.

Insisting that the controversy had no bearing on their decision, they announced that Patterson's contract would not be renewed.

The Final Week:

On Monday twenty thousand postal cards were mailed to box-holders and those on the campaign list. The cards read: *Stop O'Connor's Communist Hunt! Vote for Shepherd Reade, a friend of the Negro Race.* The card was signed by the American Association for Advancement of Colored People.

Few noticed the discrepancy in the name of the sponsoring organization, and assumed the card had come from the NAACP. All saw the New York postmark on the front.

At two in the morning, the day after the voting, Dany and Norman waited for a call from Kane, Cy and Tod in Manton.

"I'm nearly sorry it's over," Dany said. "I've had fun working. I've lost four pounds I needed to get rid of. And I've got my parakeet to take home."

"I wouldn't have missed it, Dany. Even with all the chaos, I felt relaxed, not all tensed up." He shifted in his chair and cleared his throat, but he couldn't bring himself to say any more. "You've done a good job," he told her at last. "Maybe, if you like, on our next investigation—and I want it to be the big one, the National Experimental Center—we could work together. I mean, if you want to."

Dany started to pat his hand, but something in his expression, his mood, warned her that the gesture might be misunderstood. Since the start of the Alabama campaign, their relationship had been taking a turn she had not anticipated; and she found herself constanly on guard, careful not to bruise his ego or notice his legs or encourage affection, and at the same time, testing her words before she uttered them, her gestures before she made them, to be certain he would not read into them a meaning she did not intend.

Over the weeks when they had been together so much, he had lost his sullenness with her, gradually becoming comfortable in her presence, inviting her confidence, asking favors with the manner of a man making concessions. He had invited her to listen to records in his room, and had sulked whenever she begged off. He had expounded his political philosophy at dinner, holding her at the table with the dirty dishes and the congealing food long after the others had left, growing petulant if her attention wandered. He had expected her to go with him to every new movie that came to Renfrew, and had hardly spoken to her the day she had gone swimming with Tod instead.

And Tod had said, "If I thought that guy was capable of love, I'd say he's got a thing for you, Dany." And Dany, knowing it was true, had laughed and denied it.

Because Norm had been cheated by life, because he had no friends, because Tod was caustic and Kane insensitive to him, because there was something so defenseless, something so nearly childlike in his response to her slightest consideration, in his attempt to make her his friend, Dany felt drawn to him. And yet, now, as she sat across from him, and he lifted one knee to cross his legs, and she turned her eyes away from the milky, cold white-stick limbs, she wondered, what is it I feel? And forcing herself to be honest, ashamed at her self-knowledge, she named it: Pity. And she said, "Working with you's been half the fun, Norm."

The phone rang. Kane reported that he had trounced Beverly Crater by over eighteen thousand votes, that all five of his home state candidates had won easy victories, that both Ward Roberts and Stu Denton appeared certain of endorsements in forthcoming primaries.

Dany held back her own excitement, waiting for him to finish. Then she announced: "Shep's conceded! With only four precincts unreported, we're ahead by seventeen thousand votes!"

Ray Hyder, the insurance and realty salesman from Renfrew, Alabama, the champion of white supremacy, the foe of communism, the builder of veterans' homes but above all, the friend of Kane O'Connor, had unseated Shepherd Reade, Elder of the House of Representatives.

Kane's enemies were shaken by his triumph. The friendly press gloated: GIANTKILLER DOES IT AGAIN!

35

BUTTRESSED BY his campaign successes, Kane returned to Washington. His appetite for excitement, his lust for the caress of fame, his passion for the stimulation of intrigue, were now insatiable.

He found new allies in Congress.

Many were amazed by the magnitude of his victories. They accepted them as a sign of public support. Uncommitted before, they became O'Connor partisans. Others, genuinely concerned about the communist menace, saw Kane as a leader who could dramatize the danger to the country. In the past they had merely accepted him. Now they began to court his favor. Even the core of his congressional opposition grew more cautious. Though they despised his actions, distrusted his motives and belittled his influence, privately they recognized his strength. A few who had attacked him previously became neutrals. Though opposed to his tactics against Shepherd Reade, they were wary of becoming victims themselves.

And there were also the political moths who, though afraid of the flame, were attracted by its brightness.

There was little change in the tenor of the press. His supporters analyzed election results and editorialized on "O'Connor's mandate from the people." The opposition compared him to Hitler.

Though spurred by restlessness, anxious to push his advantage and continue his assault, Kane divined the watch-and-wait intention of the Administration. Despite Ward Roberts' insistence and Norman Keller's arguments, he sided with Dany and Tod and withheld his plan to investigate the National Experimental Center. Reasoning that an attack against a government agency might bring Executive pressure that could cripple the subcommittee, he decided to merely fortify his position until the new Congress was organized in January.

With as many as fifty speaking invitations on his desk each morning, Kane had no trouble commanding attention. His audiences waited avidly for new sensations. And he did not disappoint them. Without striking at the government itself, he pecked at targets across the nation—newspapers, fraternal groups, co-operatives, labor organizations, youth clubs. He held no hearings, but reported the unassimilated information that came unsolicited in the mails from volunteer informers, from unidentified voices over the telephone. Over television and radio, at civic banquets and political rallies and union meetings, he appeared before an ever-increasing audience. His revelations continued to rate black headlines and long editorials; he managed to please the uninformed and fearful and to puzzle and intrigue millions more.

By September Norman Keller had prepared the groundwork for an investigation of the universities. Kane promised to "determine the extent to which Reds have infiltrated our institutions of learning."

He routed out a professor who had once been a member of the American-Soviet Society.

He exposed a student association as a direct adjunct of the Young Communist League.

He published a bibliography of communist-tainted textbooks in current use.

He discovered an influx of foreign students with bolshevist ideas.

He revealed that Earl Browder had once debated at a forum sponsored by an eastern university.

He found that courses were being taught on the origins of the Russian revolution, on the history of contemporary Russia, on the rise of the communist movement which glorified the achievements of the Soviet Union, while courses in American history suggested that it was economics that primarily influenced the founders of the United States.

After the hearings were suspended, Kane advised Congress that many colleges "are maintaining sanctuaries for leftists and fellow-travelers who use their positions to poison the minds of their students."

Before the November elections Kane diverted his energies toward aiding Ward Roberts' campaign. He spoke throughout the

Pennsylvania district; and drew on his mounting anti-communist funds to bolster Ward's chances in the last uneasy days before the voting. Kane's appeal was evident on Election Day. Contrary to the predictions of political pundits, Ward gained a close victory. At the same time Kane defeated his Republican opponent by over a hundred thousand votes; Ray Hyder was unopposed in Alabama.

Despite Kane's attacks, Milton Pugh was returned to the House. And Stewart Denton, without active O'Connor support, won handily. Still, Kane's followers claimed the Pennsylvania success as further proof of O'Connor's invincibility.

In December Shepherd Reade, beaten and bitter, made his last lame duck address. Disclaiming personal bias, he asked the House for an investigation "into fraudulent tactics used in the campaign against me." He spoke of the principles of democracy, the importance of due process of law, the danger of taking short cuts to national security.

Then, his voice breaking, he ended his valedictory. "Gentlemen, I commend to you these words of Abraham Lincoln: 'Our reliance is in the love of liberty which God has planted in us. Our defense is in the spirit which prized liberty as the heritage of all men, in all lands everywhere.'"

The worn, emaciated old man paused. Unashamed, he wiped tears from his sunken eyes. Then, mastering himself, his voice firm again, he continued. "'Destroy this spirit, and you have planted the seeds of despotism at your own doors. Familiarize yourselves with the chains of bondage and you prepare your own limbs to wear them. Accustomed to trample on the rights of others, you have lost the genius of your own independence, and become fit subjects for the first cunning tyrant who rises against you!'"

Soon after the new Congress was sworn and Kane had introduced his protege, Ray Hyder, to his colleagues, committee assignments were arranged. Aware of the national concern with the communist threat, cognizant of O'Connor's far-ranging support, hopeful that he would turn his attention away from government agencies, the Administration sent down the word. Kane was continued by the leadership as chairman of the Special Subcommittee of the Committee on Government Administration.

A month later his two hundred and fifty thousand dollar budget was approved.

To Kane these victories meant that he was finally secure. The enemies he had left battered along the way, the muffled but persistent sniping of the opposition, the silent, vengeful hatred of the leaders of his party, the uneasy truce with the Administration, the concern of victims still unnamed, the untested allies—all these Kane discounted or ignored or chose to forget. With masterful self-delusion he turned his back on them and went in search of greater glory.

"I want to know why the hell we can't get started with the National Experimental Center!" Kane paced the floor of his living room, circling the sofa on which Norman Keller and Ward Roberts were sitting. "Dany, I thought when you and Norm got back, you'd give us the go-ahead. It's been hanging fire for months now." Dany put her coffee cup on the mantle. "Let's let it hang a little longer."

"No!" Norman turned to her. "Don't fight me on this!"

"I'm not fighting you," she said gently. "I've thought about it objectively, Norm, and it's not right for Kane now. We're not ready."

"I'll buy that," Tod said.

"Well, I don't," Norman said, glaring at him. Then looking at Dany again, shaking his head, he said, "You agreed it looked bad. You told me that!"

"What about it, Dany?" Kane said. He was amused by the wounded look in Norman's eyes, his doleful expression. He's been fawning over her for months, Kane mused. And now she's disagreed with him and he's feeling sorry for himself and betrayed. "Can't you make up your mind?"

"I've had time to think, Kane. It does look bad, but we haven't any substantial proof that it's as bad as it looks. Norm has had five men there for six weeks now; and they've put together only a flimsy . . ."

"You saw their reports!" Norman said. "My God in heaven, woman, do we need signed confessions?" Clenching his fist, he drove it into the open palm of his hand in a gesture of frustration. "Can't you understand?" he asked the others. "Are you blind? Every day counts. If one of these characters at the N.E.C. walks off with just what's in his head, it'll be a disaster for us. Our whole plan for massive retaliation depends on what's turned out at this place."

Kane pushed his hands deep into his pockets and stood before them, rocking back on his heels. "Well?" he said to Dany.

"Maybe it's true, Kane. But how do we know it's true?"

"It's in the personnel records!" Norman said angrily.

"And they're really incriminating, believe me," Ward said. "Names of all the people they've had before their screening board, instances where they've disregarded all the facts and cleared pinkos and fellow-travelers . . ."

"Ward, you don't know any more about it than I do," Kane said impatiently. "Go on, Norm. How do we prove what's in the personnel records?"

"By getting hold of them," Dany said. "But we can't subpoena them. We've got to depend on our informant; and he can't get his hands on them until his superior checks out on leave. So we have to wait at least that long."

"We've waited long enough," Norman said, his eyes moving from Dany to Kane, watching their faces intently. "We don't really need the records. We get a man on the stand. We show he's had undeniable communist connections. We show he's working on top secret projects. It stands to reason he shouldn't be any place near a security installation. And what more do we need?"

"But, Norm, that's not the way to do it," Dany said, walking across the room to stand before him. "It's time we settled down to actually proving something that can't be refuted. When we use something that isn't documented—and we've done it time and again—it challenges the validity of things we can prove. And here, if what you say about the personnel files is true, we can prove everything. So let's wait until we can get hold of them."

"We've got to protect that installation," Ward said.

"I'm for protecting Kane right now," Dany said.

"If Kane was interested in protecting himself, he wouldn't have taken on this job," Ward said. "He's not afraid to do what he knows is right."

"Don't talk about me as if I were somewhere else! I'm right here; and I can talk for myself. I'm not afraid of anyone or anything. But I'm damned well going to know where we're going before you people take me there." He was disturbed at the conflict between Dany and Ward, between Tod and Ward, between Tod and Norman. He was annoyed by Norman's fervent, zealous approach to the most fundamental problem, at Ward's habit of studying files and reports even before they had crossed his desk. He glanced at Tod. "Well, what do you think, buddy?"

"I'm not dedicated like you people," Tod said. "I'm concerned with politics—at least that's what I was hired for." He walked to the window, stretched and turned back toward the others. "I know enough about political etiquette to be wary of busting somebody in the mouth ten minutes after you've agreed to let bygones be bygones. The Administration gave you your subcommittee, gave you your budget . . ."

"They had no other choice," Kane said.

"Look, chum, you asked me a question. You want an answer, button up and listen!"

Kane smiled, feeling a comfortable sensation of respect and affection for Tod. "Go ahead. I'm listening."

"I think you're absolutely right, Kane," Ward said. "The Administration had no other choice."

"No, you're absolutely wrong, Kane," Tod said, his thin lips half-open in a smile as he exchanged glances with Dany. "They did have a choice. They had the choice of giving it to you or fighting. They were smart enough to bide their time; and you ought to be smart enough to wait them out. Only two things could make them fight. One: a big . . ."

"Don't you think . . ." Norman interrupted.

"Shut up!" Tod said, and continued. "One: a big mistake on your part that gives them a good chance to whop hell out of you. Two: You force them to the wall so they have to take you on."

Dany said, "If you start in on a government agency again, unless you've really got the proof—and we haven't yet—you're asking for a fight."

Kane pulled a chair from the dinette and sat astride it. "I thrive on fights."

"Okay," Tod said. "But the smart politician chooses his time and his opponent—as you did with Shep Reade. You knocked him off at a time when he was already in trouble back home. A year earlier or next year might have been the wrong time. You're in the big leagues now, Kane. You're going to be knocking heads with the President if you get careless. You got where you are because you're a smart political operator; so don't start talking and acting like a dumb politician."

"Politicians! Politicians!" Norman said, his voice rasping, rising in anger. "There's more at stake here. The very future of our country!"

"Crap!" Tod said. "Can the theatrics, Keller. The country won't be sold out tomorrow if you don't expose the N.E.C."

"You want us to turn our backs on communist infiltration into the very heart of our defense, just to protect our own skins?" Norman said. "I know you don't really mean that."

"The hell I don't!" Tod said.

Dany crossed the room to stand beside Kane. "Until we have the personnel records, I'm for leaving it strictly alone."

"We can't sit and do nothing," Kane said.

"I agree with Kane," Ward said.

"Naturally," Tod said.

"All right!" Kane said, scowling at them. "Let's knock off the family war. The question is, where do we stand on N.E.C? If not now, when's the earliest we can go at it?"

"As far as I'm concerned," Norman said, "we're ready now. We could begin hearings in . . . let's say . . . two weeks, maybe three."

"Not the kind of hearings we need," Dany said.

"This is urgent. We can't wait." Norman's face was flushed as he spoke, and his voice trembled. For the first time, Dany was turning against him, questioning his judgment, and every word she uttered he took as a personal affront. "Please, Kane, listen to me," he said. "The politicians be damned! The President be damned! You can't let traitors destroy this country. You can't sit here and talk about politics and who will make whom angry!"

Kane studied Norman, watching the quiver of his lips, the tension in his hands as he closed his fists, opened them, closed them, waiting for an answer. "Then you're for immediate hearings, Norm. And Ward is. And you two," he said, nodding at Dany and Tod, "are against moving now."

"I don't vote," Dany said. "This is your staff, Kane. Make your own decision. But make it realistically, knowing what you're letting yourself in for."

Kane's impulse was to start the hearings. But in weighing the issue, he discounted Ward's opinion because Ward rarely disagreed with him; and he discounted Dany's caution because he felt she was moved primarily by concern for him, disregarding the practical need to move on, to continue to stir the country. On the other hand, Norman was so positive, so intent on his course. . . . And Norman, more than anyone else, was acquainted with every aspect of the N.E.C. investigation. He should know what he was talking about. A good man, Kane thought, devoted, loyal, but a little too fanatic to be practical. It was Tod's judgment that Kane valued above the others, for Tod could divorce himself from emotional considerations. Tod spoke frankly, without deference, without trying to please him, interested only in the realities.

"Well," Kane said at last, standing, leaving Dany by his chair and striding across to Ward and Norman, ". . . well, I think we'll just wait this out, see which way the ball bounces when we get those."

"You can't!" Norman edged forward as if he would get up, then subsided to the sofa again. "Not if you believe in what we're trying to do, Kane."

"I can, Norm," Kane said. "And, for the time being, I'm going to."

"Kane, I believe in you," Norman said softly. "I think you know that. I know this thing couldn't have gotten off the ground without you. You can reach the people. You've got energy and drive. . . ." Holding Kane's gaze, Norman spoke only to him. "But all your energy and drive and charm aren't enough, Kane. You've got to have conviction." Tapping one cane in a measured beat against the floor, he said, "We're right! And if we're going to succeed, if you're going to succeed, you've got to have honest and complete devotion to the cause. This cause, this movement, this..." He sought the words, his mouth open, his eyes closed, ". . . this rallying of the people, is more important than any individual. Even you aren't bigger than that!"

Kane shook his head slowly, and yawned. "I've decided that we're going to wait, Norm. When you get the loyalty files we're after, we'll go ahead. That's final."

"I won't let you put it off!"

Frowning, Kane turned back to Norman, standing over him. "You won't what?"

"Norman means . . ." Ward began.

"Hasn't he got a mouth?" Kane asked. "Well, what *do* you mean, Norm?"

Norman looked straight ahead, as if he were seeing through Kane's belt buckle. "You made me your chief counsel. My opinion should mean something to you."

"I must have heard wrong," Kane said evenly. "I didn't know that's what you said."

Norman, feeling like a child who has been spanked before his friends, stole a glance at Dany. She was looking at him, pity in her eyes, he thought. Anger pushed him to speak when he knew he must not. "Kane, if you ignore the situation at N.E.C., you're telling the whole country you're a fraud, that you're afraid of the Administration."

"Can't you open your mouth without making a speech?" Tod said. "Don't worry so damned much about the country. It's conceivable that it'll manage to keep going."

"I'm not talking to you, Sands," Norman said, his voice heavy with emotion. "If I was . . . oh, God, if I could get out of this chair and stand, I'd break you in half!"

Tod didn't even look up. "Yeah, I know. If you hadn't had a tough break, you'd have been a hero in the war. You'd have been a great criminal lawyer. You'd have been sitting in Kane's chair. Like hell you would! Plenty of other guys got the same shake you got, but they don't go through life sniveling about it, using it as a crutch and an excuse. You're what you are, Keller. And what's wrong with you is all above the waist!"

Dany had been trying to silence Tod by pulling at his arm, but he had talked on. "That was an awful thing to say. It was . . ."

"Cruel," Tod said. "Okay, I'm an insensitive bastard!"

"Shut the hell up, all of you!" Kane shouted, then, lower, "Damned if you're not always at one another's throats." The others grew silent, watching him. "Now let's get this straight. I don't want any more of this backbiting. I'm sick of it. And I don't want any more questioning of my decisions when I make them. Without me, there's nothing. And don't you forget that! If I sound immodest, that's too damned bad. But don't question my motives; and don't tell me I'm afraid of anybody. And don't try to stampede me into something." Kane stared at Norman as he spoke; and when Norman's eyes finally dropped and his hands were fidgeting with his canes, Kane said, "And don't you ever call me a fraud again, Norm. When you really think I am, there'll be only one thing for you to do . . . and you know what that is."

Norman caught his breath; and the others in the room heard it. Looking up at Kane again, he said, "I thought you wanted me to speak my mind, Kane. And I don't think what I said rated the answer it got."

Kane laughed, forcing it to ease the taut atmosphere. "You're a big boy, Norm. You can take care of yourself. Tod reams me out, too, but I manage to live with it," he said, winking at Tod who stared back without visible reaction. Kane reached over and patted Norman's shoulder. "Forget it if I hurt your feelings, buddy. Let's get back to business. Problem is, we take a chance of letting interest dry up if we don't move on to something else. Now how long will it be before we can get those files you need from the N.E.C.?"

"Our Army officer, the one who started this whole business, should get them in about six weeks. As soon as he does, we'll make copies, then return the originals to him for the files," Dany said. "That right, Norm?"

Norman, biting his lips, nodded.

Ward was smoothing his cuticles with a fingernail. "We might sustain interest by making a fight for those classified files, Kane. It's the Presidential blackout that makes files inaccessible. We could demand them, make it clear that they're trying to hide something. Fact is, I'm going to be speaking in Philly next week. Thought I'd hit that point. The Executive branch is trying to handcuff us. What do you think, Norm?"

"I think I'll handle it myself," Kane said before Norman could answer.

"I've been toying with another idea," Ward said. "Norm thinks it has possibilities. Suppose we investigate foreign aid programs. We could find out if there are any Reds in our setup in Europe . . . or in South America, let's say. You know the sort of thing."

While Ward pointed out the plan's virtues, Kane considered it. It would expand his activities, would give him an important inquiry until the N.E.C. hearings could be held. "How many people do you think we'd need to make a tour like that?" Kane said. "Don't think I could take off too long right now."

"Well, it would be best if you could go," Ward said tentatively. "But we need you here to do the things no one else can do. After all, you're the symbol of this whole anti-communist movement." Ward smoothed the graying hair at his temples. "I'd rather be here to help you any way I can, but . . . well, if it makes it simpler for you, I could go myself, make a preliminary investigation, and then send a team to get the facts together."

"Tod?" Kane said.

"No opinion. But if it's between South America and Europe, I'd say South America. Too damned many congressional junkets to Europe to get any attention for one more."

"That's true," Ward said.

"Yeah," Tod said.

While the others debated the idea, Dany mulled it over. Conviction—that was the word Norman had used. Devotion to the cause. Well, she thought, she had no conviction about it, no devotion to it. Perhaps Kane had convinced himself that he believed, but she wasn't even sure about that. She was certain only that it all couldn't last forever. Somehow she had to convince Kane to turn to other things; and as long as Ward Roberts was at his elbow, full of clumsy flattery, as long as Norman Keller spurred him on, it would be impossible to make Kane see that the time for flash-and-noise was past, that he must be more careful about his attacks, more skillful in his contacts with the Administration and the House leadership, more dignified in his approach. He had made his name, had gotten attention, had become a man to be feared. Now, she believed, he had to become solid and respected. He could afford to be generous, could afford to be fair and meticulous and patient.

She sat on the arm of Kane's chair. "I like the idea. Why not send Ward down there with Norm? It has lots of advantages . . ."

It was settled. The trip was arranged. And, at Dany's suggestion, Kane decided to ask Cy to accompany Roberts and Keller on their mission. "He'll get a big kick out of it," Kane said. "We'll hand old Cy a fancy title like 'Financial Advisor' on foreign aid. Watch out, senoritas!"

It was Kane's way of paying his old friend for his campaign services. But Dany was thinking of something else. Cy was sane and loyal. With Ward leaving Kane's immediate control, with Norm as unstable as he appeared to be at times, it would be well to have someone along on whom Kane could depend.

When the others had gone, Kane lay on the carpet before the false fireplace, watching the electric glow of the artificial logs, groaning with pleasure as Dany, seated beside him, rubbed his back. "Damned shame it's not real," he mumbled. "But one of these days I'm going to have one ten feet across . . . and a den with walnut paneling. . . . Going to build it for you."

"Why are you going to build it for me?"

"'Cause you're a helluva back-rubber-scratcher. Why else?"

"We could do it now, Kane. Maybe not ten feet across and maybe not walnut, but something."

"We will, Dany. Promise." He reached behind his back, indicating his shoulder blade. "Scratch there."

"Darling, there are only two things I want," she said, reaching beneath his shirt, pulling her nails over his shoulders and back. "I want to marry you . . ."

"Might as well. You treat me like I'm your husband already . . . in every way but one!"

"How do I treat you?"

He reached for her hand and moved it across his back again. "Well, I bend over some silly doll at a party and catch you looking at me like a wife. . . . And you expect me to remember not only your birthday, but the anniversary of the first time we ate lichee nuts . . . and went swimming and . . ."

She bent over him and bit his neck. "And that makes me a shrew, huh?"

"I'm also supposed to remember that you don't like gladiolas and you don't like me to say words a Boy Scout mustn't and you think I ought to go to Mass, and I shouldn't wear green socks with blue suits, and I ought to introduce the woman to the man and not vice versa, and only boors crack their knuckles, and I shouldn't overtip, and I shouldn't undertip . . ."

She put her hand over his mouth, and tugged him over on his back. "And you love me anyway?"

"Kinda hard sometimes, but I do," he said, smiling up at her.

"Then I'll let you do all those things you say I don't like . . . except for bending over women and ogling them. You just do one thing for me."

"A bargain."

"Darling, I'm not discounting all you've done on this communist issue, but I think it's time you started thinking of something else to turn your energies to." He started to speak, but she kissed him. Then, drawing back, a finger to his lips, she went on. "I've thought about it before, darling. But tonight, when Norm started talking about conviction, you were pretty rough on him; and what Tod said was inexcusable."

"Well, Tod talks sometimes when he ought to be listening. But he was right as usual, you know. Norm suffers too much. And even before he got sick he drifted from job to job . . . looking for something to do with himself. He wears blinders—can't see left or right, just straight ahead. That's why I got so impatient with him and sounded off. Hell, I don't mind his thinking he's smarter than I am. But I want him to know who the boss is; and I want him to learn to live with it."

"Kane, what he said about conviction . . . How do you feel, really feel about it? Do you believe——the way Norm does, as strongly as he does—that what we've been doing is as important as . . ."

"Of course!" Propping his elbows behind him, he started to rise, and then lay there, thinking. Until that moment no one had ever asked him that question; and he had never asked it of himself. Though his mind was working at an answer, it was not searching or probing for the truth of the matter. He thought best while he was talking, as when he was preparing a speech and he would ramble on until he stumbled on the right phrase, the pleasing idea upon which he could build his oratory. So, at that moment, while Dany waited for his answer, he began to talk. "Do I believe every word I've uttered over all these months? Do you, Dany? Does anyone believe every single thing he has said over a period of time? Of course not. Maybe Norm Keller tells himself he does. But he lies, then. Do I believe every man who's been before our subcommittee is a Red spy? No, I don't. Some of them are just plain damned fools. Some of them are dupes. Some are misfits who flirted with the Reds and then didn't have the guts to go through with it. Do I think they got what they deserved? You bet I do! We don't need half-safe employees in the government."

"But we've gotten people frantic about it, Kane, as if the danger was the greatest the country's ever known, as if . . . Well, take Norm tonight—he feels this N.E.C. thing is so urgent . .

"Well, I don't think the Reds are ready to take over. But if we don't do something to stop their infiltration, we'll wake up one day and find that they've moved in . . . not tomorrow . . . or not next year . . . but one of these days. And you can't get the public to worry about something that could possibly happen ten or fifteen years from now. There's got to be a sense of urgency or they put off worrying about it, no matter what it is."

"When Norm used the word 'conviction,' I had to admit to myself that I'm not satisfied we've accomplished anything . . . except that the country's aware of the Reds for maybe the first time."

"That's our accomplishment! How can you possibly question—"

"Hush! Don't defend yourself. Not with me. The point I'm making is that . . . well, darling, countless people have risen briefly on a single issue in Congress. Then they've been forgotten or discredited or passed over by events. It's even happened to you, hasn't it? That's why I know it's time for you to turn to other things. Your name ought to be on legislation. You're assured of an audience; and you ought to be using this valuable time to talk about foreign affairs, social security, education, labor, housing, unemployment, trade, finance . . . everything. To ride on the single track of this communism issue is just . . . it's not good. You keep getting closer and closer and closer to the very end of the line."

"Sure, you're right, honey. I want to move on to other things. I'm not kidding myself. But not just yet. When we've licked this communist thing, we'll turn to something else."

He reached for her, pulling her down beside him. "I'm tired of talking. Let's not yack about politics now that we're finally alone. It's so damned seldom we can be alone."

"Kane?"

"Yes?" he said, and turning toward her, nibbled at her ear.

"Let's decide on a definite date when we'll be married."

"I already have." He kissed her eyes, her mouth. "Next year. Next year I'll run for the Senate. And we'll travel around the state together. And I'll show my wife off to the voters."

She closed her eyes, arching her neck so he might kiss her there. Dany was smart, tempered by experience: she wanted to believe him. "Promise me you'll try to get interested in other things . . . and talk about other things. You're on Matt's show next month. You could start then. Show people you've got good ideas, that you have something worth hearing about aside from . . ."

He kissed her, shutting off her words. "Come on, I want to show you something."

"Where?" she whispered.

"In my room."

"All you'll let me see in your room is the ceiling!"

"Please, darling! I'm in love with you. I'm a normal, healthy man; and I want you . . ." His hands slipped down the curve of her hips and his tongue was at her ear again. "I've been good, haven't I? I haven't forced myself on you, have I? Don't tell me you don't want me, too, darling. I can hear you. I can feel you."

"No." Feebly, she tried to push him away. "I've sworn, Kane. I've promised . . . it's wrong." She held him closer. "I do love you, damn you," she admitted, brushing her lips down his face, seeking his mouth.

"Just tonight, Dany. Please!"

She followed him as he tugged at her hand. In his bedroom he released her, crossed to the bed and threw the spread back. She turned on the light and saw herself—hair and dress disarrayed— staring at the mirror on Kane's bathroom door. "No darling," she said. "Please, no." She left the room. Behind her she heard Kane's oath, the click of the light switch, his heavy footsteps.

"You know what you're doing to me?" he said, grabbing her arm and turning her roughly to him.

"No more than I'm doing to myself," she said softly.

He took her in his arms, put her head against his chest and smoothed his hand over her hair. "You win, Dany. You win." Then he held her at arm's length. "Now, you damned tease, keep away from me," he said smiling. "Get in there and fix me something to eat, and we'll sit on opposite sides of the room and talk about something safe, like politics."

"We can talk about us," Dany said, caressing the back of his neck.

He took her hand away. "Hell, no. And stop jazzing up my erogenous zones! We'll talk about the career of Kane O'Connor— and our mission to South America . . . and the best way to be a member of the Senate . . . and how you're going to make a statesman of me . . ."

36

ONE EVENING in March, after seeing his team of investigators off to South America, Kane faced a battery of reporters on Matt Fallon's television program.

He went armed with Dany's notes, to assume a new posture. And, in his opening remarks, using statistics Tod had gathered, he insisted that "Red power isn't in subversion alone. It's in their success and the example of that success. True, it is success accomplished by slave labor and mass murder and a wanton disregard for human rights. But we are only fooling ourselves if we don't give them credit for what they've done in around thirty years. Subversion is the immediate threat to us; and that's why I've been concentrating on revealing it wherever it pollutes our national life. But the communist example to the undeveloped, uncommitted nations of the world is also a great threat. Our investigating group that has flown just today to South America is going there for the purpose of seeing just what we can do to strengthen our neighbors against communism. In time, our hand of friendship should go out in the same spirit to all the world. You and I know that this country of ours is the best hope of man, but we must prove it to those nations who are not yet convinced. . .

"We must turn to correcting the causes of unemployment, increasing opportunities in education, improving our hospital and scientific facilities. And then we can show, by example, that our way of life is far superior to that of Russia. And when we do that we will have destroyed communism abroad as thoroughly as we intend to destroy it where it has infected our country."

The newsmen on the panel, surprised by the subdued tenor of Kane's words, readied their questions. It was a new O'Connor, a more moderate O'Connor who faced the reporters before the television audience. But the more familiar O'Connor, the angry O'Connor made better copy. So, all but ignoring his initial statement, the newsmen succeeded in forcing Kane to defend his record. They quoted his opponents, took note of a growing undercurrent of public opposition, prodded him with inquiries about his future plans, questioned his figures. They insisted on discussing the abortive State Department hearings, Richard Southgate, the Reade campaign, the investigation of colleges, the verbal broadsides against newspapers, co-operatives and labor groups, the pending investigation of the National Experimental Center, the purpose of the mission to South America.

When the program was over, Kane left the studio with Matt. "Brother that was one rough crew!"

"It's going to get rougher, Kane. I got the opening pitch tonight; and so did they. It was a not too subtle way of telling the Administration you're going to be a good boy. But you're going to have to keep plugging at it for a long time, friend. When you first started picking at the Reds in Washington, nearly everybody was on the outside looking in. But you've spread out since then and you've hit more people, more important figures. And they're all standing by, hoping to get a knife in one day."

Kane laughed at him. "I'm not apologizing for what I've done; and I'm making no promises on the future. My record's good enough to suit me."

"I go along with you just so far. The Communist party is controlled by Moscow and wants to overthrow the United States government; therefore, any individual Reds who've worked their way into labor and education and government are a threat. But you've actually uncovered nothing the F.B.I. and most informed people didn't already know. You've only dramatized it. And I suppose there's some value in that."

Kane held up his hands. "You get no more argument out of me. Your buddies on the panel have me groggy already," he said, smacking Matt's arm. "I'm your guest tonight. Are you going to entertain me on the swindle sheet?"

The elevator stopped on the street floor and they stepped out. "Definitely," Matt said. "You're a below-the-belt politician, an opportunist and something of a demagogue, but you're also a good news source and an asset around the broads. Like to go to a club? Or do you want some female company?"

"That I could use."

"You ever been to Della's?"

"What's Della's?"

Matt shoved the revolving door and pushed Kane ahead of him. On the street he explained, "Della's is a good place to gab, have a drink, play cards, get some sophisticated loving. It's a high-class callhouse on West End Avenue."

"Lead the way!"

"Are you alive?"

Kane heard the silken voice and hazily remembered. The pale gray walls. . . . the gold and burgundy brocade draperies. . . . the Chippendale furniture. . . . the tapestry-covered piano. . . . Matt Fallon's tenor rendition of "Ivan Skavinsky Skivar." And the girl . . . petite with green eyes like Melba Woodmire's . . . and brown hair. . . . Smart, too.

"I've brought something for you."

The purring voice again. His eyes opened. Morning light was filtering through the blinds. The girl—now unexpectedly in a flesh-colored negligee—stood over him. "I'm not hung-over," he said groggily.

"Not much! Drink this anyway." She handed him a beer mug brimming with red liquid. "It's Worchestershire and tomato juice and some of Della's special remedy."

He tasted it. "Not bad." *What the hell's her name,* he wondered, and recalled it at once: *Lenore.* "Did I make a real ass of myself? I'm blank after I ordered champagne. . . . And there was a guy there pouring red wine down somebody's ample bosom . . ."

She laughed in her cat's voice. "You were very good, Kane. Maybe a little immodest—you made a speech on how important you are. But then you finished your bottle of champagne and politely passed out."

He wiped the seeds from his eyes. "You think I'm important?" he asked, putting the mug on the nightstand.

"You get your picture in the paper."

He nodded solemnly. "That's true."

"You've got drag."

Kane held two of his fingers down, counting off her list. "And what else?"

Lenore smiled. "Let's see." She pulled at her ear lobe. "You're looked up to by a lot of people. And you spend money like you haven't had it very long . . ."

"Well, that's a pretty good evaluation."

A laugh rippled out. "Sure is. That makes you just as important as Della! She gets her picture in the paper. She's got drag and money. And there are plenty of people who think a lot of her!"

Kane grinned. "Honey, I want you to borrow a dictionary and look up the difference between fame and notoriety."

She sat on the bed beside him. "I'm no dummy. I know the difference; and I think 'notorious' fits you better than it fits Della. For one thing, there are lots of people afraid of you and I can't think of a soul who's scared of Della."

He slapped her thigh and glared at her, feigning anger. "Now who's afraid of me?" he asked, enjoying himself.

She thought for a moment. "I suppose the Communists are afraid of you." Tapping her fingernail against her teeth, she paused. "But I don't know why. They oughta love you. You put them on the map. Until you came along, I thought they were all little guys from C.C.N.Y. with big heads and glasses and too much hair."

Laughing, Kane slipped out of the bed. "How the hell did I get up here?"

"Matt Fallon carried you. You were promising not to investigate him for singing Russian songs."

"I must have really been polluted."

"Oh, how you can put it away! But you're not a mean drunk, Kane. You're a funny, sort of sweet and cute kind of drunk."

"Lenore," Kane said, working his toes into the thick carpet, "that's the nicest thing anyone ever said to me! And since I'm starting to feel a little rocky, I appreciate your cheering words."

She watched him as he yawned, stretching his arms over his head and then scratching himself. "Get your things off and take a shower. You'll feel better. Wake you up."

"Matt still here?"

"Having breakfast with Della."

Kane stripped to his shorts and walked toward the bathroom —a rectangular chamber as large as his living room and done in maroon and black tile with gold-plated hardware. "Brother! This place makes me feel like I'm on the declining end of an orgy. What I need is an eye-opener."

"No drinks served here until afternoon. When Della makes a rule, she sticks to it. So, use the razor and toothbrush in there. They'll make you feel just as good."

"Yours?"

"Razor's mine. Toothbrush is compliments of the house."

"Come talk to me."

Lenore stood in the doorway while he lathered with soap and scraped at his rough black beard. "This is one of the fringe benefits of my work," she said as he watched her in the mirror. "Never know what celebrity'll be using my razor."

"Surprise you when you saw me walk in last night?" he said.

"A little. We don't get a lot of bachelors around here."

He grinned. "I mean . . . you know. You've heard about me, I suppose."

She eyed him, aware of his vanity, and decided to deflate him. "Sure I'd heard about you." Stepping inside, she perched on the maroon commode seat, hugging her knees. "Least I've heard your name mentioned around here, I guess around fifty times. They call you everything from anti-intellectual to an un-mustached Hitler. And I've got to admit I've agreed. I always agree with a guest, no matter what he says. When they've said you're egotistical, ruthless, arrogant, irresponsible, reckless . . ."

Kane grinned, taking up the chant. ". . . unprincipled, evil, indecent, demagogic, despicable . . ."

She stopped him with a wave of her hand. "But, personally, I think I like you."

He washed the razor and put it back in the cabinet. "Do you like me well enough to take a shower with me?"

"I've had my shower this morning."

"C'mon," he insisted, dropping his shorts.

"Well . . ." She stood before him, looking up, watching his eyes as she slipped her negligee off her shoulders, and let it fall. "Well . . . 'cleanliness is next to godliness!'"

He cowered against the mottled tile wall while she adjusted the water. The first flush of the shower was cold, and she laughed as he jerked away and grabbed at the faucets. "This stall is big enough for a cavalry regiment!" he said, and caught the washcloth she threw at him. Then warm water drenched them; and she stood on tiptoe before him, her small, tilted breasts pressing into his abdomen. His chin rested lightly on the transparent cap she pulled over her hair. Reaching behind her, soaping her hips, he raised his voice over the splatter of water. "You're a strange one, a little bit . . . a bright gal."

She giggled deep in her throat. "And you want to know why I work here."

"I wasn't going to ask you that at all."

"Everyone does sooner or later." She took the soap from him. "Why do you do what you're doing?"

"I enjoy it," he said. "And don't get off on me. I'm wary of the way you draw parallels."

She soaped his back, then worked her fingers over the muscles of his neck and shoulders. "I enjoy my work, too," she said. "And I've money in the bank and a decent place to live . . ."

"This is a helluva place to live . . ."

"I can't understand a fellow like you," she said, spreading soap over the hair on his chest and playing with the sculptured waves and swirls of lather. "You fill a girl with food and compliments, buy her gifts, let her tease you and browbeat you— and just on the chance she'll break her heart and give you fifteen minutes use of her body, if you can pry the girdle off."

"The chase!" Kane said, smiling. "That's part of it. The chase."

"Then why're you here?"

"Well . . ." Kane cringed as she pushed him under the full blast of the shower.

"You came because you're tired of the chase," she said. "You want someone to play with you without being coy and sacrificial."

"Sex is sex."

"Uh-huh. Two kinds—good and better. But it's best when it's friendly and gay and you've got a sense of humor. It's the chase that makes it sordid and ugly and a problem of hygiene!"

Laughing, Kane reached for her. But she slipped away. "Okay," he said. "That makes it fine for me. But what about you."

She was behind him, scrubbing his shoulders, and he felt her wet body slither against his soapy back. "You think I'm not better off than plenty of the girls I went to school with? If they're going to get out at all, sooner or later they've got to fight off somebody. But I don't have to slap some drunk or get pawed by some overstuffed pig who smells bad. Those kind don't get in here. Most of my old girl friends go to bed with a fellow, too. But they do it for a meal or a week end in Connecticut!"

"And how about the girls who don't?"

"They're content to eat chicken salad sandwiches for lunch and wear collars and Stern's jewelry with their basic black dresses. They're willing to live with their roommates and their virginity. And that's all right." She slapped the washcloth against his thigh. "I'm not built for abstinence."

"Ow!" Kane winced from the smart slap and as he started to turn, she held him from behind, her fingernails sliding rhythmically down his sides, her knees pressing beneath the backs of his, her breasts just barely touching him. He caught his breath. "You know what you're doing to me?"

She giggled. "Sure, I do!" She wouldn't let him turn around. "It's part of what I'm saying. I like my job and I'm good at it." She pinched his rear; and he grabbed her and bit her shoulder while she shrieked. Then, breaking away, she backed across the stall and raised one foot to fend him off. "I'll bet I like it as much as you do," she said. "Only I'm the one who gets paid!"

Laughing with her, he ran the cloth over her stomach. "But where does it all get you?"

"Where does anything get you? You live and things change and something always turns up. How do you know what your kick's going to get you?"

He gave her the soap, raising his leg, bending his knee so she could reach his thigh. "I'm going up," he said, blowing water from his face. "I'm on my way up."

She stopped and looked at him, mischief hiding in the comers of her wide mouth. "Wow! Am I taking a shower with a future President of the U. S. A.?"

"Nobody with a name like mine will ever be President," he said, amused. "But there are other things—like who's going to decide who the President's going to be, and what he's going to do."

Lenore draped the soapy cloth over his shoulder. "You better finish up," she said, sliding back the glass door and stepping out. "I've got to write home to mother and tell her I've just bathed with an important man."

Kane finished his shower and dried himself. When he returned to the bedroom he found Lenore dressed. "Let's stretch out for awhile."

"My day off. I'm going to buy a silly hat and get my hair done and go to the bank . . . and send off some microfilm to Russia." She winked. "Want me to get someone else for you?"

"I want *you*, " he said.

She buckled the wide leather belt over her slim skirt and fluffed the balloon sleeves of her blouse. "I know you do. I've been telling you how good I am, and you're intrigued."

"You're a screwball. That's the damndest thing I ever heard a girl brag about."

"Bye, Kane. I'll see you again, maybe."

"You'll see me again, definitely." As he sat on the bed and picked up his socks, he said, "What do I owe you?"

"Nothing. See Della when you leave."

"I'd like you to have something."

"Why?"

"You've been nice to me. You took care of me when I goofed out. You know all my secrets."

She walked to the door and opened it. Smiling, she said, "All I know about you is that you've got a sense of humor and you snore." She stepped out. He rushed after her as she started down the steps to the floor below.

"When will I see you again?" Kane called.

"Give me a ring!" She waved, leaving him standing nude in the hallway.

37

THE VIPs walked past the blue-clad Marine sentries who stood at attention before the United States Embassy in Rio de Janeiro.

Ward Roberts grasped Norman Keller's arm. "How do you like being treated like royalty, Norm?"

Norman stopped, balancing himself on his canes, breathing hard. Perspiration was beaded over his face; and slowly, holding both canes in one hand, he took out his breast pocket handkerchief and patted it over his mouth and neck. "They're afraid of us," he said, nodding toward the Ambassador who had walked on with Cy and waited at the massive paneled door. "All this smooth talk and dinner party stuff—trying to cover up something."

"Can we give you a hand there?" the Ambassador called to them.

Norman shook his head. "Thanks. No."

"You gentlemen go on in," Ward said, waving them on. "We'll be right along." When Cy and the Ambassador had entered the building, Ward said, "We don't want them to be afraid of us, Norm. Remember that. Kane gets some kind of cheap thrill out of being feared; and he's paying for it by piling up enemies. I don't want to be feared. I want to be liked." He smiled, the same modest, shy smile that had convinced juries that he was still young, inept and needed their help. "They've all heard about Kane down here— the Foreign Service people and the banana-country press. So, the State Department boys are on their guard, suspicious, hardly likely to confide in us. And the newspapers are ready to pounce—both the papers here and the Left-wing rags in the States. Well, we're not going to give them what they expect, Norm."

They reached the steps, Norman swinging his body from side to side, his face flushed, his jaw sagging with exertion. He had insisted on walking from the plane, standing for an hour to pose for pictures, moving unassisted from hotel to car to embassy; and he was near exhaustion. "Let me get my breath." Again he mopped his face with the handkerchief. "Ward, I'm here to find Reds in the foreign aid program; and, by God, if they're here, I intend to speak out. Kane won't have Dany standing over my shoulder seeing that I don't open my mouth. That's why she hung around me all the time. I've tried to figure why she gave me all the soft soap, made over me, listened to me like there were pearls dropping from my lips—well, that's why, to spy!" He licked his lips. "And there won't be that illiterate bastard Sands to edit what I want to say. And Kane won't be here to take the analysis I've sweated over and then, without even time to digest it, vomit it at the first reporter he sees." Norman swung forward again. "No, Ward, I'm going to open up my mouth for a change."

"Sure," Ward said, following him. "But you've got to keep in mind that Kane's soft-pedaling these days. You saw how he shoved the N.E.C. investigation aside. I showed you the transcript of that Fallon TV show your dad mailed me. Well, we're not going to sit by and let this die, not after you've given your strength and brain to it. As long as I've got breath, Norm, you can be sure I'm in the fight beside you. It's just the approach I'm speaking of."

Norman nodded, indicating that he understood, and looked ahead at the granite steps that appeared to loom before them. "I happen to agree with you, Ward. Kane's using us, using anti-communism, giving not a damn for you or for me or for destroying subversion. If Dany has her way, we've got maybe another six or eight months before Kane drops the whole investigation and finds something else less controversial and more respectable. Well, I've got a few weeks out from under his thumb; and I'm going to use them."

"We won't let it be dropped, Norm," Ward said, grasping his elbow as he neared the steps. "The one blow I've made against communism is getting you in as chief counsel. Together we'll keep this going. But try it my way, Norm. No bombast, eh? And be pleasant, interested in everything and everybody, anxious to learn. But every day we'll hit them with an eye-opener. If Kane wants to forget the movement, he can. But the American people aren't going to forget. You and I, Norm, we'll see to that."

"All right. I'll go along with you," Norman said. "We'll see." The vein in his temple was taut, throbbing. He swung one foot up and hoisted himself over the first step while Ward helped him.

"This reception . . . do the reporters need interpreters or do they speak English?"

"Probably speak English. Wish I could talk Spanish. That'd go over big."

Norman hoisted himself to the door. For a moment he looked at Ward, evaluating him, vaguely annoyed by his perfectly starched collar, the faint aroma of his shaving lotion, his crispness, his ease—wondering what went on in Ward's mind. "This is Brazil," Norman said. "That encyclopaedia you haul around must have told you they speak Portuguese here."

As Ward opened the door, he frowned, and reached for the typewritten card in his pocket, glancing at it surreptitiously: *Brazil: Larger than U.S. Indep. decl. September 7, 1822 near Sao Paulo. Constit. modeled on U.S., adopted 1891. Stay off Vargas. With us in both wars. Coffee!!! Biggest customers.* "Sure," he said to Norman. "Portuguese. That's what I meant."

Inside, the assembled journalists met Congressman Ward Roberts, Counsel Norman Keller and Financial Advisor Cy Woodward, representatives of the United States. The formal reception room—deep-carpeted, heavily-draped, elegandy-appointed, furnished in traditional dignity—was crowded.

Ward was surrounded by an editor from *O Globo,* correspondents from *O Estado de Sao Paulo, The New York Times* and a Reuters' man who took notes in shorthand. "We're down here to learn," Ward said, swirling the cherry in his drink. "Brazil has always been a great friend of the United States. This country fought at our side in two wars. We're Brazil's biggest customer. Why the Brazilian constitution is modeled after ours, I believe. That right?" he asked the *O Globo* man.

"Correct, sir."

"Let's see," Ward said, glancing at the beamed ceiling, trying to recall his next bit of information. "I've always been sort of an amateur student of Latin American history, but I'm not much on dates. Wasn't it 1891 when you adopted your constitution?"

The reporter from Sao Paulo smiled. "Yes. You have a fine memory, sir."

Ward shrugged modestly. "I always get that date mixed up with the date you declared your independence . . . right outside of Sao Paulo. But that was September of 1822, I think."

"You shame me, sir," the *O Globo* editor said. "The exact date even I did not recall."

The New York Times correspondent jingled the change in his pocket, watching Ward closely. "What do you expect to accomplish on your tour?"

"We want to be certain our agencies down here are giving all the aid they can to our friends in Latin America, and that there's no subversive element interfering with that purpose."

"Do you believe it is possible to make a thorough investigation in such a short time?" the man from Reuters said.

Ward smiled, held up a finger while he chewed at the slice of orange in his old fashioned and smacked his lips. "Fruit down here is something wonderful," he said, drying his hands on a napkin, folding it, and putting it on the mahogany table at his side. "To answer your question, I've got my assistants to help me. Mr. Keller is an expert on communism. Woodward's my financial wizard. And, of course, we have our investigating team. We're not trying to indict anybody; and we don't intend to make a lot of accusations or ruin any reputations . . ."

The New York Times reporter broke in. "Would you say that's a departure from the normal practice of the O'Connor subcommittee?"

"I can't speak for the activities of the subcommittee. Mr. O'Connor is the chairman. It's his job to run the group, not mine." Ward signaled a waiter, handed him his empty glass, thanked him, and turned back to the reporters. "I can only tell you what I intend to do here."

"Then you intend to act differently?" the Reuters man said. "You don't approve of the methods used by Mr. O'Connor?"

Ward grinned and patted the correspondent's shoulder. "You fellows are trying to pin me to the wall, aren't you?" he said in good humor. "Well, I think it's fair to say that . . . well, every individual has different ways of attaining the same end. I've always been one to stay in the background, helping wherever I can. It's my nature, I guess, to be a little cautious. Other people have a different temperament. They're more—let's say, direct."

"Then you think Mr. O'Connor isn't cautious, that he's. . . " *The Times* man began.

"Whoa! Don't go putting words in my mouth." Ward rubbed his forehead, frowning, as if he were stumped for an answer. "You can say this: If there's subversion in our aid program, I'll find out about it from the people who are qualified to tell me. But I do hope that we can report to Congress that our Foreign Service personnel here reflect credit on the American people."

Norman Keller was presiding over another conference before the room-high curtained windows. Sitting in a chair, he looked tired, bleary-eyed as he answered questions.

The correspondent of *The Chicago Tribune* said, "As I understand it, Mr. Keller, you're convinced that Communists have infiltrated the government of the United States. Do you think they've gotten into the Foreign Service as well? Do you expect to find evidence of it on your tour down here? And if so, what steps do you intend to take?"

"One question at a time," Norman said, scowling. "Yes, I think they've infiltrated the government of the United States, but slowly, in time, we'll rout them out. One of the most important scientific establishments in the country is now under investigation, for example. Now, what was your second question? Oh, about the Foreign Service. All I can say is that it will surprise me if the Communists haven't at least tried it. As for what we'll do if we find them, you can be sure they'll be exposed."

The Associated Press representative approached Cy who stood before the bar, talking with some embassy personnel. "Don't believe I met you," he said, offering his hand. "You're on the investigating team, aren't you?"

Cy introduced himself. "I'm along to help wherever I can," he said uncertainly. "Heckfire, it's all new to me. This is the first time I've been out of the country."

"You formed any impressions of South America yet, Mr. Woodward?"

"Just call me, Cy. At home folks don't call me Mr. Woodward unless they're strangers tryin' to borrow money." He sipped from his bourbon and water. "Only impressions I've gotten are that folks have been real nice, real co-operative."

The AP man puffed on his pipe. "Understand you investigated the Industrial and Economic Service yesterday. You give them a clean biff?"

"They must have about four or five hundred employees. You can hardly investigate that many folks in one office in a few hours. Best thing I got out of it was just talkin' with people, havin' them take me into their confidence about things goin' on at home that seem to be troublin' them. . . ."

"Any of them tell you that the publicity given the O'Connor subcommittee hasn't been good down here?"

"Look," Cy said, "you're goin' to print stuff I say, aren't you?"

"If it's news."

"Well, Kane O'Connor's my buddy. You can print that. And I'm not doin' or saying anythin' that could hurt or embarrass him. Okay?"

The AP man shook hands with him again. "Okay!"

Within the hour—in clear view of reporters and photographers from seven countries—Cy lay on the sidewalk before the American Embassy with a bullet in his shoulder; Ward's head was bleeding from the impact when he dived for cover and struck an iron fence rail; and Norman sprawled, shaken but unhurt, in the street while a Marine sentry beat a would-be assassin unconscious with his rifle butt.

Kane's mission to South America forced him off page one. He could not compete for the headlines with a trio of heroes.

The American press converged on Rio de Janeiro, and then followed Ward, Norman and Cy across the continent, to banquets and conferences, to hotel suites and television studios, to receptions, public speeches, church services and sightseeing tours. Every thought, statement and move of Kane's minions was detailed and dutifully reported to the anxious American public. The attack had been unprovoked; the South American press had only praise for Ward's "obvious knowledge of and love for our people and our history"; and the assailant had been easily identified as a known communist agitator. So, day by day, newspapers in the United States, both Republican and Democratic, liberal and conservative, pro-O'Connor and anti-O'Connor, celebrated the group with attention normally accorded only to visiting royalty, victorious athletes and political conventions.

There were news stories: Ward's statement upon being released after a night in the hospital: "Our Lord said, 'Forgive them, Father, for they know not what they do.' How can I say less? It is a tragedy for all the world that this poor boy who was ordered to murder us is but one of countless thousands who have been enslaved by communist leaders. . . And Ward's comment when he presented a check as a contribution toward his attacker's legal defense fund: "In our country every man is entitled to a defense; every man is presumed innocent until proven guilty. There, as here, it is democracy's answer . . ." Ward on his plans: "Of course we'll continue our mission. To have the Communists scare us off is unthinkable."

There were photographs: Ward leaving the hospital with Cy, Ward shaking hands with the Marine sentry, Ward, Cy and Norman at a press conference, Ward, one hand raised beside his bandaged head, as he boarded a plane for Buenos Aires. . ."

There were cartoons: Ward, with blood-soaked rag about his forehead, Cy, arm in sling, Norman, on canes, walking arm-in-arm as "The Spirit of '76." Ward extending a hand of friendship while an armed puppet, manipulated by Stalin's clenched fist, prepared to fire on him. Ward, Norman and Cy in battle dress, standing bravely by the barricades—"The First to Fight."

Speaking before a veterans' meeting in Norfolk, Kane tried to divert attention from his assistants. With Tod's approval, and against Dany's advice, he felt compelled to make new charges against the Administration: "The Executive branch is attempting to stop our investigation of the highly secret National Experimental Center. A Presidential directive, aimed at making government files inaccessible to me, has made my task immeasurably more difficult. . ."

That same evening a filmed "Report to The People," was flown from Lima. Sponsored by the American Patriots, the program was aired simultaneously by two television networks. Sitting in his hotel room, Ward chatted with Norman and Cy: "We all want to thank the thousands of friends who have written and cabled us wishing us a speedy recovery. Now, I know you folks at home are anxious to learn just what we've accomplished thus far. I'd say we've learned, at first hand, what happens when communist agents are able to roam free. They become bold—bold enough to order the execution of representatives of the greatest, most powerful nation on earth. We can't allow this to happen in the United States."

"True," Norman said. "I'm more certain than ever that we must continue to uncover and expose Communists who have wormed their way into all our institutions . . ."

Cy entered the conversation only once: "Everyone's really been real nice to us, real co-operative. Let's see. . . . Oh, and Congressman O'Connor phoned me right after this happened. He's keepin' in touch, and I know he's goin' right ahead and finish the job he started."

Kane answered questions at a press conference in Miami: "I sent the mission down there to gather information. There's no investigation going on. I'll make the decision on whether or not one is needed when I've examined the facts after my staff returns. I'm not giving a clean bill to the Foreign Service. If the Communists have infiltrated there, the American people are going to know about it."

The next day in La Paz, Ward granted an exclusive interview to a reporter from *La Razon:* "My future plans? I intend to devote myself to the task of destroying the last vestige of communist infiltration in my country. I can't, of course, speak for the subcommittee. But I assure you that I, personally, will give all the time, energy and funds at my disposal to see the job accomplished."

Kane was furious as Ward continued his usurpation of the spotlight, for he saw himself and his work subordinated for the first time to the name and activities of an underling.

Kane cabled Ward to call him at once.

When the overseas operator rang his office, he grabbed the phone from Dany. "Listen, you . . ."

But it was Cy's voice that answered him. "Kane, I'm cornin' home. I've had enough."

"Where's Ward?"

"Left this morning for Quito, before your cable came. I have a reservation on a plane leaving Caracas tomorrow."

"Where can I reach him?"

"Try the embassy, I guess."

"Cy, what's the guy up to?"

Cy's voice was troubled, serious. "He's been traipsin' around like he was makin' campaign speeches for home consumption. Hell, gettin' shot at was the best thing ever happened to him. You been readin' the papers, I guess."

"You bet I have!"

"Well, everyplace we go there's a photographers' car and a reporters' car and delegations with flowers and microphones and TV and all. He doesn't have to do anythin'. He just fell into it." Dany was on the other phone. "Cy ought to go to Quito and tell Roberts . . ."

"I can't do anythin', Dany."

"Try, will you, Cy?" Kane said. "Tell him you talked to me, that I said he's to refuse to make any statements. He's got six more days according to his itinerary, and I don't want him sounding off or giving any interviews."

"Kane, he's a fourflusher for my money, goin' around with five yards of bandage around the quarter-size scab on his forehead. But, givin' the devil his due, he's got everybody eatin' outta his hand. And he hasn't said anythin' bad about you . . ."

"He's insinuated enough. Damned headline-happy idiot! You go to Quito, Cy. And tell him to keep quiet, absolutely quiet. I'm still the chairman of this subcommittee; and he'd better not forget it. You tell him I said that!"

"Okay, I'll do it. But it's gonna take somethin' special to get him home on time. Talks like he's goin' to stay another week. Edward R. Murrow's due down here for a TV thing he's plannin' for South America. And, from what I hear, some of Norman's friends . . . or maybe it's Ward's friends . . . anyway, they're tryin' to line up an appearance for Ward."

"That'll never happen," Kane said. After he hung up, he discussed the problem again with Dany and Tod, as he had every day during the past ten.

Dany sat behind the desk. "You've got to recall them. Roberts is the kind that can parlay something like this—an accident— into a big deal."

Kane paced the office. "I sent them over, Dany. If I recall them without reason, I'll look like a jackass."

"You're not looking too good now," Tod said as he slipped into the armchair by the desk.

Frowning, Kane shrugged off the remark. "All this stuff in the papers will blow over. That's not what worries me. It's this grandstanding by Ward. Those subtle remarks, those suggestions that he'd do things differently. All over the papers! Every day!"

"It's going to take a long time for this to be forgotten," Dany said, handing him a folded copy of that evening's paper.

He read it: *Frankly, we've been surprised, by the statesmanlike conduct of Congressman Ward Roberts and the mission he heads. His gesture of supporting the right of his attacker to a fair trial is not only good international relations, it is a good omen. Perhaps his views will be given new weight in the O'Connor subcommittee, and there will be a more zealous adherence to the principle of fair play which Mr. Roberts has stated so eloquently and Mr. O'Connor has heretofore ignored. . . .*

Kane threw the paper on the desk. "You're the one who talked me into sending them over in the first place!" he said, glaring at her. "Talk about other things, you told me. Well, he's done pretty damned well at the same old stand."

"Lay off," Tod said. "What's to do? Are you going to recall him or aren't you?"

Pulling at a pack of matches, Kane tore the back into small pieces. "Have to have a legitimate reason."

"I'd like to figure out a legitimate reason for dumping him from the subcommittee," Dany said.

"He's just taken advantage of the situation to get himself known." Kane tossed the torn cardboard into the wastepaper container. "Well, from now on, I'll watch him. For the moment, I've got to get him back here without making myself look stupid."

The discussion wore on through the evening, through a late dinner at Tod's, through a midnight session; and finally, a tactic emerged. It was tailored to a double requirement: Get the mission back home and turn the attention of the public to something else. It was really an elaboration of Kane's standard device. Attack. Always attack.

At a press conference the next day, Kane announced that the foreign aid inquiry in South America would be suspended until he could visit the scene personally, since new developments required immediate action on a more important investigation of the National Experimental Center. There, Kane said, "Communists are draining away our secrets and our strength; and everything points to alarming espionage, to a spy ring that may reach into every scientific laboratory in the nation."

He told reporters, too, that he had summoned home subcommittee member Ward Roberts and Chief Counsel Norman Keller so the full staff could begin work.

Ward had one last taste of glory. When his plane landed at the MATS terminal in Washington, he was met by a thousand cheering partisans bearing placards that welcomed him home. The rally had been organized by the American Patriots; and although Kane was not invited, he managed to be the first up the ramp when Ward— his head still swathed in bandages—stepped out.

Then, as cameras recorded the event for posterity, Kane embraced his friend and posed with his arms about Ward and Norman, while Cy—his wounded shoulder unseen beneath his jacket—stood by, smiling.

It was Kane who led Ward to the microphones, and Kane who introduced him to the crowd. "My good friends have returned to help me as I prepare to launch the most important investigation . . ."

Ten minutes later, Kane was still speaking. "The National Experimental Center is a prime target of the communist conspiracy."

After twenty minutes, when the crowd had cheered often and lustily and had been photographed in the act, when Kane had exhausted his subject and much of his audience, he presented Ward to the rally.

But the life was gone out of the celebration by then. The placards rested on the ground. The banners drooped. The confetti lay in flattened coils across the runway. Ward spoke to an audience that had stood too long in the hot sun, heard too much oratory and was starting to dwindle. "The time has come to decide who are our friends and who are not, who are influenced by Communists and who are not, who tolerate them and who do not."

A few feet away, Norman Keller, seated on a folding chair, half-listened to Ward, instead watched the restless crowd. He reached up and tugged at Cy's sleeve. "How long have you known Kane?"

"Forever," Cy said.

"In some ways he's a remarkable man. Never known anyone quite as daring, as astute politically."

"No flies on Kane," Cy said.

"God! What that man couldn't have, what he couldn't be!"

"Better hush," Cy said. "Some of Ward's friends are givin' us the evil eye . . ."

"No matter," Norman said wearily. "No one's listening; and if anyone is, they'll forget all about it tomorrow."

As Norman predicted, as Kane anticipated, the South American trip was soon forgotten. A new and electrifying manhunt was on.

38

JOSIAH MARTINGALE, Director of the National Experimental Center, stood at his office window. Resting his hands on the sill, he looked out at the steel-fenced enclosure before the administration building. His two visitors, an hour late, were being passed by the guards.

Since Kane O'Connor's prediction of espionage, sabotage and subversion, a great flare of publicity had swept over the laboratories. Norman Keller and his staff had invaded Martingale's domain six months before, causing a brief flurry of discontent and excitement. But since his recent return from South America, Norman and his inquisitors had wrought chaos.

The Director had received two resignations from heads of departments, was besieged by reporters and photographers, was plagued by long-distance conversations with Washington. Now, while he fought against release of personnel records, while he denied charges against his workers and his security board, while a climate of fear enveloped his staff, Martingale watched the orderly operation of the Center disintegrate.

He was normally a gray, ghostlike, submissive man too absorbed in his own life to concern himself with the political life of his country. Democracy, to his scientist's mind, meant freedom to explore the unknown, to theorize, to speculate, to question, to discard the unproved equation, to devise another, and finally to learn the Truth. Totalitarianism meant the antithesis. It meant that man's laws could influence the laws of science. It meant that Lysenko could deny Mendel. It meant sterility of thought. If Martingale had a political philosophy, then this was it.

Now, certain that his colleagues were about to be pilloried without proof, convinced that men were being condemned for what they had once believed, seeing others denied the right to change their minds, he rebelled. He saw O'Connor's aides, not as protectors of democracy, but as forerunners of totalitarianism. And he lost his submissiveness. For the first time in his life he was ready to do battle.

The intercom announced Congressman Ward Roberts and Mr. Norman Keller. Josiah Martingale pressed the buzzer at his desk, unlocking the office door; and Ward and Norman entered. "I thought you said three o'clock," Martingale said to Norman. "I've been waiting . . ."

"I'm pretty busy myself," Norman said, easing himself into a chair beside the desk and putting his canes atop the scientific journals on a magazine table.

"My name's Ward Roberts, sir," Ward said, offering his hand.

"Oh, sorry," Norman said. "Thought . . ."

"How do you do," Martingale said. He had never heard of Ward Roberts and was unimpressed. He shook hands limply, and motioned Ward to a seat.

"I'm terribly sorry we're late," Ward said. "I hope you'll forgive us. To keep anyone waiting is bad enough, but a man with your responsibilities—well, it's inexcusable."

Martingale went behind the desk, perched his gawky frame on a high stool beside his drafting board, and faced his visitors. "You sounded upset on the telephone," he said to Norman.

"That's because I'm not getting the co-operation you promised."

"I'm doing everything I can legally do."

"I see you are," Norman said sarcastically. "I've seen the letter you sent out to all employees. I don't like it. Congressman Roberts doesn't like it. And I can assure you Congressman O'Connor isn't going to like it either."

"Just a moment there, Norm," Ward said. "I can't really blame Dr. Martingale for sending out that letter. It's his job, as director of the Center, to inform the employees of their rights." His voice was soft, warm, in contrast to Norman's truculence. "Now, Dr. Martingale, my only exception to the memorandum you sent out is that it seems to say that we're interlopers, people sent here to interfere with the highly important work that's going on. That's simply not so, sir. This is a government installation. We're part of that government; and we're here to ascertain specific facts. We need your help and guidance. Won't you give it to us?"

Martingale studied him in silence. Turning to Norman again, he said, "I do my job as I see fit. That memorandum was written to inform the people here of their constitutional rights. I consider that they should know."

"That's not the problem," Norman said, cutting in. He pulled a copy of the letter from his briefcase. "You say here that they are not to discuss classified information with any investigators."

Martingale nodded. "That's in keeping with security regulations, Mr. Keller."

Ward smiled. "Of course, sir. But you know we're not interested in finding out how to make bombs or how to go to the moon. We just want access to records concerning current and past employees. That doesn't seem too much to ask."

"That information is also classified," Martingale said.

Norman picked up a copy of the *Bulletin of the Atomic Scientists* and began to fan himself. "It's amazing how security conscious everyone gets when we show up." Glancing back at the memorandum in his lap, he said, "You say here, 'every effort will be made to protect you from unwarranted attack.' That's a cut at this subcommittee, and an invitation to your employees to refuse to testify."

Martingale said, "I don't see anything wrong with that."

"You don't?" Norman said. "We're down here to clean this place up; and you co-operate by putting out that kind of advice to the very people who are under suspicion."

"At the moment, Mr. Keller, no one who works here is under suspicion."

Ward said, "Sir, I want you to know that you personally have absolutely nothing to worry about. We're convinced of your loyalty."

"Well, that's gratifying," Martingale said.

Ward wasn't sure if the man was being sarcastic or was genuinely pleased. "The point is, Dr. Martingale, you must understand how it looks when you refuse to co-operate with us. It makes it appear that you're trying to hide something. It reflects on your own good name."

"I've been all through this before," Norman said. "I just wanted you to hear it yourself, Ward."

"Sir, I do wish you would reconsider," Ward said.

"I have not made the decision regarding the classified files. I have orders to deny them to you or to anyone else," Martingale said, standing. "I admit, of course, that it is the decision I would have made if it had been left to my discretion."

Norman reached for his canes, bending over painfully to retrieve them. "You've been suspiciously unconcerned about the subversives you have working here. Maybe we haven't checked your own record carefully enough. And maybe we will when Washington hears about your attitude!"

Standing, Martingale spoke with deliberate coolness. "I don't care who hears about it. I am not running these laboratories to please some witch-hunting congressional committee. We have more important things to do!" He walked around the desk to face Norman. "I've spent far too much time listening to your insolence, and I'll have no more of it. We're working on priority projects . . ."

Norman interrupted. "And if we don't find the Reds in this place, all your work will end up in Russian hands."

"We're just as concerned as you are, Mr. Keller."

Ward walked up beside Martingale. "It doesn't sound that way —not to hear you talk about 'witch-hunting,' not after seeing your letter advising your employees against co-operation with a congressional committee. To tell you the truth, Dr. Martingale, I take a dim view of your attitude."

Martingale was angry, but calm. "I'm satisfied that the F.B.I. can protect security at this installation. They've done all right to date. We've had some bad risks employed here; and they have been removed—without unnecessary noise and commotion either." Staring at Norman again, he said, "We may still have a few questionable people. When we have facts and not supposition, when we have valid evidence and not hearsay, we'll get rid of them, too."

Norman's face was flushed. His voice trembled as he spoke. "All right. If that's the way you want to do business!" He pushed himself to his feet, rested on his canes, and nearly fell as he dropped one and waited in frustrated silence while Martingale and Ward reached for it, and Martingale finally handed it to him. "When I get through with you," Norman said, "you'll remember this day!"

Martingale, lashed by the threat, raised his voice. "You guardians of American security," he said sarcastically, "have done the Russians more good in these past three weeks than any full-fledged spy could have done!"

"That's quite enough," Ward said. "I'm a United States Congressman, and I don't have to listen . . ."

Martingale talked over him. "Two of my top men—whose only mistake is that they thought differently ten years ago from the way they and the rest of the country think now—have chosen to resign rather than submit to your inquisition. And how much time do you think we're losing every day while my people are answering your endless questions—questions that they've already answered satisfactorily before a security board?"

Norman had turned his back, and was swinging himself across the floor toward the entrance. "Come on, Ward!"

Standing there, Martingale let them reach the door, try it, and find it locked. They turned back to him, and he said, "I'll open that door for you. But I have one thing more to ask you. How do you think we can work sanely when my people are afraid that something they say today may be rooted out of context and used against them tomorrow, when suspicion is spread among colleagues because one of your investigators tells one of them that the other has given them information, when men can not even talk to a friend without becoming suspect themselves?"

"Open this door!" Ward said.

Martingale strolled back around his desk, found the buzzer, and released the lock.

Norman, breathing hard, stood aside as Ward pushed the door ajar. "I'm not forgetting a word you said, Martingale. I promise you that!"

"You're a fool," Ward told Martingale.

Josiah Martingale, winner of the Nobel Prize, fellow of the American Scientific Society, Member of the Legion of Honor, author of *Nuclear Physics,* consultant to two Presidents, expert on guided missiles, folded his arms and watched the "guardians of America's security" retreat.

It was two weeks later.

Kane, guiding Dany through the serpentine reception line in the Congressional Club in Washington, glanced around the long, Victorian room, looking for Matt Fallon.

A group of chattering old women gossiped around the punch bowl; and Kane identified them correctly as wives of former congressmen and senators who still held to the thin strand of fame accorded them by their husbands' past eminence. Beyond the buffet table, he saw Nate Starbecker accepting a crystal plate of hors d'oeuvres from a handsome woman who wore two earrings dangling from a single lobe.

On the far side of the room, the scarlet-and-gold uniformed Marine band, veterans of White House receptions, diplomatic teas, congressional parties and military balls, played a waltz. No one danced.

Kane introduced Dany to an Associate Justice of the Supreme Court as they moved down the line, but he still watched the entrance and searched the crowd, hoping to see Matt before Dany did. As they approached the end of the handshaking ritual, and Dany spoke with the Majority Leader's wife, Kane saw Matt enter, look around uncertainly and wind through the room to a far corner. As they left the reception line, Kane tried desperately to think of some way of seeing Matt alone briefly.

A retired federal judge intercepted them, and thankfully, before Dany could extricate herself from the roving judicial hands, Kane said, "Pardon me, please. Something important." Ignoring Dany's steel-eyed, protesting glare, he hurried across to Matt.

They shook hands. "The least you could have done was to meet me some place where they serve a man a drink," Matt said. "This mausoleum! Tradition be damned!"

"Later," Kane said. Glancing behind to be sure Dany was not yet in sight, he said, "Matt, don't mention anything about the last couple of times I saw you in New York. Dany thinks I was in Manton, and . . ."

"And you don't want her to know you've got a commercial plaything in New York."

Kane frowned. "Watch it! Not so loud." He felt guilty about sneaking away to see Lenore; and the guilt had not diminished after the second or third or fourth lie to Dany. And yet, he had assured himself, it wasn't really cheating on Dany. After all, he was a male and human. But women didn't understand. Even undemanding Laurie, Kane remembered, had given him a bad time after that session with Melba Woodmire. It wasn't hurting Dany— not really. And Kane had convinced himself that it wasn't for sex alone that he had continued to see Lenore. It was an escape from his public life, a refuge that Dany no longer afforded him. Dany never let him forget his work, never ceased trying to convince him of one thing or another. Dany was so much a part of everything he did, everything he hoped to do. . . . And Lenore made him laugh at himself. Lenore poked fun at him and kept a scrapbook of anti-O'Connor clippings and bought him fur-lined undershorts and was wantonly, shamelessly, happily good in bed. The last time he had seen her, he had told her about the geisha in Kyoto; and within the hour, she was re-enacting the episode, culminating it in hilarity when she approached him with a feather duster and an over-sized box of foot powder. . . .

"What the hell are you daydreaming about?" Matt was saying.

"Oh! Nothing . . . business."

"Well, listen to what I'm saying, Kane. You don't know when you're well off. Lenore's a fun girl, one of the few honest women alive and a firm advocate of the whore's code—"Satisfaction Guaranteed"—but she's a whore, Kane. An expensive whore, but anybody's whore. And she's not fit to wash Dany's feet. You're being a horse's . . ."

"Kane, the next time you leave me in the middle of the floor to be pawed, I'm going to brain you," Dany said, coming up behind them.

Matt took her hands, and kissed them. "You're beautiful, even more beautiful than usual."

"So are you," she said, and kissed Matt's thick, freckled paw. She sat in a deep, upholstered chair, arranging the folds of her gold-and-white evening gown. "Sit down, my gallant friend," she said to Matt. "We'll ignore Kane; and you can tell me about your private investigation of the N.E.C."

"Let's find some place quiet where I can buy a drink, or better, Kane can buy us both drinks."

"We'll leave soon," Kane said. "Dany insisted I had to put in an appearance here."

Ward Roberts joined them. "I've got something hot," he told Kane. Then, recognizing Matt, he offered him his hand. "It's a pleasure to meet you, Mr. Fallon. I'm a real fan of yours, never miss your show."

Matt pushed himself to his feet and shook hands. "You're Ward Roberts, right? Didn't recognize you without your head bandaged!"

Ward laughed. "That's the only time anyone ever took a picture of me."

"Hell, I wanted to put a camera on you for a half-hour when you got back from South America; and you turned me down."

"You didn't ask me . . ." Ward said, puzzled. "When did you ask me?"

Matt looked at Kane, reading the discomfort in his expression. "Well, I asked a friend of yours to arrange it, and he said it couldn't be done. You were too busy."

"But no one ever said a word to me. Listen, any time, any time at all, if you like, I'll be glad to come . . ."

"What's up?" Kane asked.

"Can't understand it," Ward muttered. Then, aware of Kane's impatience, he said, "Norman called me this evening."

"Why didn't he call me?" Kane said. "I thought I made it clear . . ."

"He tried to, Kane. But he didn't get an answer, so he called me to get in touch with you."

"So?" Kane said, obviously dissatisfied with Ward's explanation.

Watching Dany, Ward whispered, "We've got what we've been looking for. The whole works!"

"What's the whole works?" Matt said.

"Our case!" Kane said triumphantly. "Enough information to throw the book at N.E.C.!"

"This is going to be the biggest thing yet. Right, Kane?" Ward said.

"You're damned right."

"Well, I'm going to get back home," Ward said. "Norm promised to call me again later . . . if he can't get in touch with you. And since you won't be in . . . Well, pleasure meeting you, Mr. Fallon. And you let me know if I can ever . . . well, if there's anything I can do for you."

"Seems like a pretty nice guy," Matt said when Ward was gone.

"Creates the best first impression in the business," Dany said. "He's a louse and a conniver."

"Talk about connivers! Kane, friendo, you conned me when Roberts came back."

Dany began to laugh. "Kane, you didn't tell me! But I'm proud of you, darling."

Grinning sheepishly, Kane said, "Never mind Roberts. The topic for celebration tonight is N.E.C.; and we're really going to bust that place wide open now."

"I don't believe it," Matt said.

Kane pulled over a straight chair and sat astride it, soiling the elbows of his dinner jacket on the back. "You think you picked up more information in a few days there than my staff has gotten after months of work?"

"You want my advice?"

"You're going to give it to me if I want it or not. Go ahead."

"Call your idiots off."

"Suppose you run your TV show and let me run my committee."

"I was only there for a few days," Matt said. "But I talked to the people who work there—the big names and the pencil-pushers. I sat down with Martingale—a topnotcher. And from where I sit, your pronouncements of espionage and the antics of that Keller character have already hurt the Center beyond measure."

Kane stood, pushing his chair aside. "Matt, you're all wet."

"Sit down," Matt said. "I'm going to finish."

Kane walked behind Dany's chair. "Go ahead. But you're going to eat your words one day soon."

"No. You're the one who'll eat crow; and there are plenty of guys in line to help shove it down your throat until you're gagged once and for all. I've warned you about it before, Kane. You're not exactly the best loved man in Washington; and if you go ahead with this thing, defying common sense and reality, there'll be a line from Constitution Avenue to the Hill loaded with volunteers anxious to shoot you down . . ."

Kane cut in. "And when I prove I'm right, that the Center's riddled with espionage, there'll be another line—from Bangor to Seattle—loaded with volunteers anxious to get rid of the timid, spineless bastards who are trying to cover up the stench at the N.E.C.!"

"Keep your voice down, Kane," Dany said.

"When are you going to wake up to what's going on in this country, Kane?" Matt said, shaking his head, emphasizing his words. "People are afraid. They think the country is overrun with

Red spies, that anyone who criticizes the government is a traitor, that anyone who criticizes you is either a Red or an idiot, that it's dangerous to join any group or express any opinion because they may incriminate themselves."

"Well," Kane said, "that vigilant attitude's a lot better than closing their eyes and making believe there's no danger from saboteurs and traitors."

Matt grunted. "Kane, don't feed me those platitudes. Every time you open your mouth, they automatically come out. You can't really believe all that pap!"

"When I get through with the N.E.C. . . ." Kane began.

"Kane, the most you'll prove is what anyone there is ready to admit. But when you talk about espionage, about secrets being bandied around, about a direct line to Moscow . . .

"You want me to pull out of there?" Kane said. "I can't. I'm right, Matt. I've been right all along; and this is going to vindicate me—even in your clouded eyes."

"Isn't it frightening to be always so certain that you're right?" Matt said.

Troubled by Matt's vehemence, trusting his wisdom and judgment, Dany was unwilling to risk a possible fiasco. "Kane, Matt's your friend. At least promise that you'll be careful, that you'll be reasonable, that you'll go over Norman's reports item by item. You know he tends to tell you what he thinks you want to hear, so examine them carefully, very carefully. And make him answer your questions. If you're wrong—and there's a chance that Matt is right, and . . ."

"Hold up, Dany," Kane said, smiling. Dropping his hands to his sides, he walked around the chair and stood between them. "I wasn't going to say anything yet, but just to show you how wrong you are, here's a piece of news for you: Norm's gotten hold of the personnel records without getting them through channels. And all the facts are there. No wonder the Administration didn't want us to have them. Norm says we've got enough dope to hang some people."

Matt was perplexed. "You mean you got that material illegally, that you raided classified files?"

Kane laughed. "I mean we got it, and we can prove that the N.E.C. security board has been clearing commies who are working on top secret projects."

Dany was relieved. "Are you certain, Kane?"

At that moment, Stewart Denton joined them. After the introductions, he asked, "Can I talk out, Kane? Or should the ole cowboy be rude and whisper in your ear?"

"Matt, keep your mouth shut," Kane said. "Go ahead, Stu."

"I got the poop from the Majority Leader," he said. "The White House is releasing a statement tomorrow morning expressing confidence in the N.E.C. staff and refusing to release the personnel records to the subcommittee."

Laughing, Kane leaned over Matt. "Forget to keep your mouth shut, my boy. Say you got it from an 'undisclosed but usually reliable source.'" Putting his arm around Dany's shoulders, he said, "The President's going to look damned stupid refusing to give us records we already have; and he's going to look worse when we expose the people he's got such confidence in!"

39

THE HEARINGS on the National Experimental Center began in Washington, in the marble-columned second-floor caucus room of the Old House Office Building.

The sessions were closed. But each day Kane painted his own version of the proceedings on the canvas of the public mind. As the sessions continued, new faces were sketched in. A few brush strokes of color were added. Details were illumined. And, finally, Kane's creation, a frightening picture, emerged.

Curiosity, fear and anxiety did their work. Men everywhere argued—in private clubs and church socials, in poolrooms and campus bull sessions, in Ciro's and the Officers' Club at Treasure Island, at the Moana in Honolulu and the *Boeuf Sur le Toit* in Paris.

Some were O'Connormen, measuring patriotism by the fervor of their anti-communism, by their single-minded devotion to the cause of their leader. They echoed his warnings that traitors were at large in the N.E.C., that no secret was safe from enemy eyes, that saboteurs and spies were being protected while the country stood in peril.

Some were scoffers, finding O'Connor and evil synonymous, rejecting Kane's claims, damning him on the basis of past performance. They insisted that the charges were exaggerated, that the closed hearings were designed only to prove his case. They condemned him for accepting classified information, for encouraging informers, for undermining the security system.

These two forces were the distant poles. Somewhere in between was the largest group of all—the confused, who did not know what to believe, and the inarticulate, who would not express themselves.

To N.E.C. Director Josiah Martingale, the inquiry itself was an act of sabotage and Kane's investigators were the saboteurs. Enraged by the assault on the Center, he was determined to fight. But he was unarmed. For too long he had been submerged in his work, only vaguely aware of national affairs, only interested in the events which had a direct bearing on science. He was no leader. His manner and speech and background were foreign to the public. He was blunt, pedagogical and contemptuous of those who disagreed with him. He knew little about the use of politics, publicity, pressure and the press. Armed only with conviction and energy and intellect, he set out—a gangly, awkward Don Quixote—to do battle with Kane O'Connor, the seasoned knight of anti-communism.

Although in the past he had avoided publicity, Martingale now welcomed it, appearing willingly and often. He spoke haltingly, in stilted phrases, before any group, regardless of political coloration, so long as it was anti-O'Connor. He made mistakes, alienating some conservative forces one day, unwittingly accepting communist-front support the next. He argued with congressional leaders. He took his case to the President. He countered Kane's reports with his own version of the closed hearings, denying that a single spy, saboteur or traitor had been discovered as a result of the investigation. He demanded that the inquiry be opened to public scrutiny, that he have an opportunity to testify.

Meanwhile, officialdom waited to test the current before daring the waters of dissension. And politicians counted and sorted the waves of telegrams and letters that deluged them. The hearings recessed for a week.

A year before, Kane might have plunged into combat with Martingale. Furious when the scientist first attacked him, Kane's impulse was to slash back, to answer him as he had once answered Richard Southgate. And he would have done so, but Dany lured him away on a four-day vacation, and when they returned, they had devised a more subtle tactic to deal with Josiah Martingale.

Dany and Kane had been returning to Washington after an evening at Hunting Acres when she dared him—without making plans or packing or knowing where the road might take them—to turn right on the Shirley Highway instead of left. As a joke, intending to turn around again, Kane turned right, toward Richmond. Then it became a test of which one would back down. Neither did.

During the next three days, they drove through the Smoky Mountains. Dany bought them both men's dungarees in a country store, and identical red flannel shirts. And they lived in that costume as long as they were on the road. They ate in diners with truckers—she insisted truck drivers always knew where the best food was—and they picnicked by waterfalls and waded in icy streams and hiked up mountain trails and ate com bread and drank buttermilk on the sagging porches of bearded mountaineers. And at night, sleeping in a Sears-Roebuck tent in the National Park, they talked about the future and shared single cigarettes and fell asleep in one another's arms.

"Like a honeymoon," Dany said as they drove back to Washington.

Kane, rubbing his four-day growth of beard, drew her closer to him as he turned the car down U. S. Highway 1. "But no, honey! I never thought I could sleep that close to you, and throttle all my urges."

She laughed. "It was easy, darling. I couldn't be very tempting —not in this get-up, unbathed, my hair a mess." She squeezed his hand. "It's been the most wonderful vacation I've ever had. I knew it was going to be, from the moment we called Tod that first night—and then disappeared."

"I'm ready for them now, honey," Kane said. "We're going to surprise everybody by being everything they don't think we are. Some eyes are going to be opened when we move the N.E.C. hearings to New York!"

Spectators, ending their vigil in the corridors of the Federal Building in Manhattan, were finally herded into the hearing room. Restless, eager for the heralded pageant to begin, they whispered to their neighbors and tried to stretch their legs beneath the rows of chairs before them.

Reporters clambered over television cables to find their numbered seats. Photographers argued over positions. Newsreel men complained that they were shunted aside by TV cameramen.

An announcer, adjectives at the ready, his sense of drama stimulated, described the simulcast scene:

"Those of you watching on television can see the three hundred people seated and standing around this great, oak-paneled chamber. Stationed beside each of the six massive, scroll-encrusted pillars, is a uniformed guard. And others walk the roped-off center aisle which leads to the scene of the impending action. Two stories above, sunshine filters through the dome skylight, adding to the illumination. But the blaze of TV lamps at the front of the room makes everything else appear dim, as though a stage bathed in spotlights were before us.

"There the stars and bit players are seated behind long, black tables arranged in a rough rectangle. At the head table are the members of the investigating subcommittee.

"Kane O'Connor, chairman, sits in the center. He's leaning to his right now, talking with Norman Keller, chief counsel. They're apparently discussing plans for this morning's session. To Mr. Keller's right are the Democrats, Milton Pugh, who has consistently fought the hearings, is the gentleman with the beard. Behind his chair, talking to him, is Ward Roberts of Pennsylvania.

"To Mr. O'Connor's left are the Republicans. First, Stewart Denton, famous in his own right as a recording star before he entered Congress. He is listening to the conversation on his right. Luther Brantley sits beside him reading a newspaper.

"The table to the committee's left is reserved for the staff of investigators and counsel. The table to the committee's right is used by the recorders. Directly to the front is the space reserved for witnesses. The tall, slim gentleman is Dr. Josiah Martingale, Director of the National Experimental Center, who has demanded the right to testify. He is conferring with his counsel, Jacob Krawcheck, the heavy-set, bald man beside him.

Matt Fallon, studying his notes, stood before another camera, waiting for his introduction.

"Here to give you his interpretation of the dramatic scene before us, is Matt Fallon, U.B.S. news commentator."

The red light on Matt's camera flicked on, and he dropped his notes to the floor. Hands thrust in his pockets, he leaned easily against the wall, and spoke conversationally to the vast television audience. "Sometime it's as difficult to look into the complex workings of our government as it is to look into a man's heart. But today, if you look carefully, the true stakes in this controversy may be revealed. It is more than a question of possible communist subversion in the National Experimental Center. It is a question of men and motives, of politics and power." For a moment Matt hesitated, diverted by the floor man who knelt before him, pointing at his wristwatch and signaling him to speed up his remarks. "Although he is apparently at home in the throes of controversy, although he has been at odds with the Administration before, Congressman Kane O'Connor has now, perhaps inadvertently, challenged the right of the President to withhold classified information. If he succeeds in proving his charges against the N.E.C., Mr. O'Connor will, by inference, prove that his foes have been wrong, that the President has attempted—by accident or design—to hide subversion. If he proves his charges, Kane O'Connor and his campaign against communism will be largely vindicated; and he will emerge victor over the President himself. . ."

The measured rapping of the gavel ended Matt's commentary and quieted the room.

Josiah Martingale was called and sworn; and Norman Keller began the examination of the witness, leading him through preliminary questions while cameras followed the action from closeup to closeup.

"Tell me, Dr. Martingale," Norman Keller said, "in your post . . . no, let me phrase that differently . . . since you became Director of the N.E.C., have you ever discovered subversives working at the Center?"

"I have. And they've been dealt with by proper authority."

"Just what do you mean by proper authority?"

"I mean they were reported to us by *competent* investigators of the Federal Bureau of Investigation," he said sardonically. "I mean they were given hearings before *competent* men on our screening board. I mean they were, where necessary, discharged and their cases turned over to *competent* legal personnel of the Department of Justice."

Kane leaned over to whisper to Norman who listened, then turned back to the witness. "Are we to understand that, despite the fact that the F.B.I. reported some of these people to you, you took no action after reviewing their cases?"

"It is not the function of the F.B.I. to try anyone. It is an investigative body. If they find there has been a violation of law, they move against the individual through the Attorney General. When a man has committed no overt act, but has a questionable background, we are advised so that we may give the man an opportunity to appear before us and explain. The F.B.I., Mr. Keller, is scrupulous, not only in finding criminals, but in granting to every man his rights under the law."

"Thank you for that testimonial, sir," Kane said. "We share your high regard for the F.B.I."

"Dr. Martingale," Keller said, "in your opinion, are there any subversives now working for the N.E.C.?"

Martingale relaxed his grip on the arms of his chair. He had formed his opinion of Norman Keller long before when he and Ward Roberts had invaded the laboratories. And he had expected a craftier interrogator. "If you're referring to the trumped-up charges you've made against some of our people who have already been cleared by our loyalty board . . .

"Please direct yourself to the question," Kane said softly.

"To your knowledge," Keller said, "are there any subversives now employed by you?"

"We have two men on suspension pending a review of their cases by our board. But no proved subversive is at work."

"You're positive of that?"

"Mr. Keller, we have always been able to handle our security problem."

"Of course," Keller said. "You've told us how *competent* your staff is," he said, merely a hint of sarcasm in his voice. "And it is your opinion that the N.E.C. is completely free of any communist infiltration. It is your opinion that the laboratories are manned, without exception, by loyal, trustworthy American citizens . . ."

"I'll state my opinion, if you don't mind," Martingale broke in.

There was scattered, nervous laughter among the spectators. Kane tapped his gavel patiently, and it was quiet again.

"Pardon me, sir, if I was presumptuous," Keller told Martingale with apparent concern.

Many in the television audience were disappointed. They had expected great conflict to begin at any moment. Instead they saw what appeared to be a querulous old man answering routine questions put to him by an agreeable, polite interrogator.

Martingale rubbed his long, slim fingers over his chin, phrasing his thoughts. "It is my opinion that there is no subversive activity going on at the Center now, and that, should any arise, it will be dealt with by constituted authority as it always has been."

"Thank you, Dr. Martingale," Keller said. "I hope that, at the conclusion of these hearings, when I re-read my question and your answer, we will be closer to agreement. No further questions."

Martingale was caught by surprise. "I was under the impression that there were other things . . ."

Kane smiled at him. "Thank you very much, Dr. Martingale. If none of my colleagues has any questions, you are excused."

Milton Pugh, who had been taking notes with furious concentration, tapped his bifocals against his water glass. "Mr. Chairman!"

Jacob Krawcheck stood. "Mr. Chairman, my client wants to read . . ."

"Mr. Krawcheck, counsel for the witness is not privileged to address the Chair. You may confer with your client," Kane said. Then, turning to Milton Pugh, "You have a question?"

"I have a statement," Martingale insisted, getting to his feet and waving a typewritten sheet at Kane.

"I'd like to know if the hearings of this subcommittee have obstructed your work," Pugh asked Martingale.

"If I can read my statement . . ."

"Very well," Kane said, settling back in his chair. "Go ahead, Dr. Martingale."

Martingale, still standing, still agitated, began to read. "First I want to say, without reservation, that I am . . ."

"Doctor, it's not necessary for you to stand. You may sit down if you like," Kane said.

Martingale frowned, shook his head and sat down. He cleared his throat and began again. "First I want to say, without reservation, that I am not a Communist. I have never been a Communist. In the many years I have been affiliated with the government, my loyalty has never been questioned . . ."

Kane held up his hand. "Pardon me, sir. But I assure you that you needn't present your credentials to this committee. No one has accused you of any affiliation with communism. You are not on trial here . . ."

Martingale cut him off. "I've prepared this statement, Mr. O'Connor," he said, raising his voice over Kane's. "And I intend to read it!"

Kane's opponents in the room, and in the national audience, were prepared for a display of the high-handed tactics that had been attributed to O'Connor. They waited for him to act. But he only smiled gently. "I just wanted to make it clear, sir, that this subcommittee—though it may not agree with your conclusions—

has the greatest respect for your personal integrity and admiration for your many achievements. You may, if you wish, proceed."

Conversation buzzed along the rows of reporters seated behind the witness table. Matt Fallon, among them, was puzzled as he tried to analyze Kane's strategy.

Martingale peered down at his prepared remarks, ran a finger down the page to find his place, and began again, reading slowly, deliberately, as if he were committing the words to memory. "Security is one of the major concerns of any military research establishment; and it has been scrupulously observed by the National Experimental Center. However, during the past several months not only has the work of the Center been hampered, but its morale has been destroyed. Not only has it been accused of harboring spies, but spies have been employed to rifle its classified files pertaining to security."

For a moment, Martingale stopped, placed his paper on the table and corrected a spelling error in the text. "I believe that you" —he glared directly at Kane—"have done a great disservice to the nation. And this disservice is evident not only in the injury done the proper operation of the N.E.C., but in the injury done the men and women who are employed there. They have been subjected to the unbelievable mockery of having to defend themselves against charges that have already been proved false . . .

Matt Fallon studied the faces at the committee table, searching for a clue. Kane was listening intently to Martingale's statement, holding a palm up to Stu Denton who leaned over to whisper to him. Norman Keller, apparently calm, held his elbows at his sides, and beat his knuckles together. Nervously, Matt thought. And Milton Pugh was resting back in his chair, a malicious grin pulling at the corners of his mouth, while Luther Brantley tapped a pencil against his teeth, frowning in apparent puzzlement at Martingale's words. It's like going to see a play you've seen before, Matt thought. And then you find that the plot's changed, the actors, miscast, are all playing the wrong roles. He liked the simile, and made a note to use it when he went before the cameras after the recess.

Flashbulbs went off in Martingale's face; and he stopped reading a moment to recover. "I am aware that this same know-nothing approach has been perpetrated against others in this government for some time and that not one man has been indicted as a result. I am confident that, despite the wanton appropriation of classified materials by the agents of this subcommittee, despite their disregard of existing Presidential directives, not one subversive will be found at work in the National Experimental Center. I am willing to stake my reputation and my honor on that assertion." With a gesture of contempt, he pushed his statement across the table to Kane.

Applause welled up from the rear of the room and Kane finally gaveled it into silence. The room grew still with anticipation. "Dr. Martingale, you've made some serious charges against this subcommittee," Kane said softly. "And you've staked your fine reputation on your statement that there are no subversives in the N.E.C."

Martingale spoke out, drowning Kane's words. "I can prove my statements and charges, Mr. O'Connor. You haven't and can't prove yours."

"Please, sir. I've listened patiently to what you had to say. Can't you show me the same courtesy?" His tone was that of a son, gently admonishing a senile father.

Matt Fallon scribbled on his note pad:

Impartial stranger, never having heard of Kane, seeing him for first time, would say Kane is fair, kind, patient. Perhaps Martingale would antagonize . . .

Kane was leaning forward, directing his gaze to the television cameras. "I'm sorry you feel that our procedures—as witnessed by millions on television this morning—are not orderly and fair. Now, sir, please understand that I don't think any less of your patriotism because of what you believe. What upsets me, sir, is that you are representative of a segment of our people—well-intentioned liberals, intellectuals, men who should be leaders of thought—who are so removed from what's taking place in our country that they can not or will not believe it exists. And that's our greatest danger—that men of your character and ability unwittingly aid the cause of the international communist conspiracy by shutting their eyes and their minds to our danger, and refusing to recognize the peril we face."

Martingale busied himself with a stack of papers, withdrawing a sheaf of mimeographed statements and passing them behind his chair to the newsmen.

"I have said," Kane continued, turning to the TV camera that hovered close by, "that there are subversives at work in the N.E.C. The next witness to be called is typical of the many who have testified before us. And already we've learned that the Red network exists in the N.E.C., as it extends into all elements of our national life, and that too often we all—like Dr. Martingale—are amazingly unaware of it."

The hearings were recessed for lunch.

Reporters swarmed around Kane as the session ended; and Matt elbowed his way through to Dany who waited at the door of the chamber. "Tell me what's going on," he said. "This metamorphosis of O'Connor has me snowed. He's emerging as a butterfly!"

Laughing, she took his arm. "We've got a case, Matt. A lot of people are going to be snowed when Kane is finished with the next witness."

The television floor man was calling, "Mr. Fallon!"

"Don't move, Dany," Matt said. "America's waiting for my invaluable analysis. If you wait for Kane, you'll never eat. I'll go feed the viewers their facts, and then I'll feed you a drink and a sandwich."

Across the country millions stood by impatiently, awaiting the resumption of the hearings, anxious for the arrival of the promised witness—the man whose testimony would prove the President in error, Josiah Martingale a fool and Kane a prophet, the man whose guilt would make liars of O'Connor's foes and wise men of his followers.

When the hearings reconvened, Norman Keller called Leon Hoke to the stand.

A slight, short man with thinning blond hair stood up and, prompted by Jacob Krawcheck, held up his hand to be sworn. With his free hand he unbuttoned his coat, exposing his hearing aid.

"Do you swear that the testimony you are about to give is the truth, the whole truth and nothing but the truth, so help you God?"

"I do," Hoke said, bending toward the microphone before him.

"Please state your name, address and present occupation," Keller said.

"My name is Leon Hoke. My address is 182 Sherryelin Drive,

Larendon." He caught his breath. "My occupation is Chief of Filing Section, National Experimental Center."

Josiah Martingale, who sat behind the witness, leaned toward him and spoke over his shoulder. "Don't be nervous, Leon. There's nothing to be nervous about."

Norman Keller straightened his papers before him. "Mr. Hoke, are you now or have you ever been a member of the Communist party?"

"No. Never."

"Would you say that you are—though not an active member of the party—in sympathy with the Communist movement?"

Hoke turned to Krawcheck for assistance. "I don't understand."

"Let me put it this way," Keller said painfully. "Are you a communist sympathizer?"

Hoke tugged fitfully at his hearing aid. "No, sir. No, I am not."

"Mr. Hoke, I'm going to be frank with you. We have a great deal of information about you; and I believe it would be wise for you to make a clean breast of your activities."

Milton Pugh slapped the table. "Mr. Chairman, let's not have that kind of . . .

"Mr. Chairman, I object," Krawcheck said, standing. "The implication is that . . ."

"Mr. Krawcheck, I'll remind you again that you are not privileged to address the Chair. You may confer with your client," Kane said. "Mr. Pugh, if you will give the Chair time, I assure you . . ."

"You're full of surprises today," Milton Pugh said.

The *St. Louis Post-Dispatch* correspondent whispered to Matt Fallon: "Old Whiskers is the Administration's man. If he's surprised, I don't feel so bad. I'm in good company."

"You're O'Connor's boy, Matt," the *Charlotte Observer* man said. "You surprised?"

Matt glared at him. "I'm no one's boy; and if you're not looking for a bruise, you'll lay off me."

"No offense, friend. What do you make of it?"

"I don't know," Matt said. "Somebody's paying you to find out."

"If the Administration wasn't sitting on Hoke, I'd like to get him alone someplace," the *San Francisco Examiner* reporter said.

And that might be a good idea, Matt thought. "Sorry I got touchy," he said to the *Charlotte Observer* reporter. "I owe you a drink."

At the witness table, Krawcheck was whispering to Hoke, prodding him gently to speak. And Hoke said, "I will answer all your questions, sir."

Keller looked down at his notes, shifting his weight to ease the cramping of his legs. "Mr. Hoke, isn't it true that you visited Russia at the invitation of that government?"

Hoke hesitated. Then, almost inaudibly, he said, "Yes, sir."

"Isn't it true that you won this trip to Russia as a reward for writing an article entitled *Slavery of the Masses,* an attack against life in the United States?"

"There was an essay contest. I was in college then. It's been. . ." He tapped his fingers against the arm of his chair, seemingly aware of the hostile eyes upon him, uncertain of how to explain, feeling trapped and alone. "It's been many years ago, sir. Twenty years . . ." His voice trailed off.

Keller examined the file again. "Now, Mr. Hoke, tell me, were you a member of the Young Communist League?"

"No."

Glancing at his notes, Keller said, "Mr. Hoke, isn't it true that on several occasions, in the company of a man now deceased — Theodore Belden—you attended meetings of the Young Communist League?"

"I did . . . go . . . to some meetings. But . . . but . .'" He looked to Krawcheck for counsel, and his attorney nodded, as if to reassure him. "I never joined . . . It was even before I went to Russia."

"If you didn't join, why was your name on their mailing list as late as five years ago?"

"Why, I kept getting literature. You know . . . like a company gets your name on their mailing list and automatically, for years, you get their advertising."

"Why didn't you write to them and tell them that you did not want to receive their anti-American propaganda, to take your name off their list?"

Hoke shrugged. "I just never got around to it . . . put it off."
"For nearly fifteen years?" Kane asked.
Hoke looked confused. "I didn't hear you, Mr. O'Connor."
"You continued to get inflammatory communist propaganda for fifteen years and kept putting off discontinuing it?"
"I've been getting seed catalogues for years," Luther Brantley said, "from outfits I never bought a thing from. Just never got around to stopping it. Interesting stuff sometimes . . ."
"Mr. Brantley, please let the counsel continue with the questioning. You'll have an opportunity to comment or ask questions yourself later," Kane said. Dany, sitting several rows behind Matt Fallon, winked at Kane and he smiled. "I think the question has been exhausted anyway," he said. "Mr. Keller, will you go on?"
"All right. Mr. Hoke, let's look into some of your early associations."
During the opening interrogation, Leon Hoke continued to be uneasy, on edge, exposed before the lights and cameras, the flashbulbs and microphones. Later, as Norman Keller's questions relentlessly pinpointed his past and he became aware of the magnitude of the case against him, he grew resentful. And in his confusion, he could not remember the dates and places that his inquisitor knew so well.
Matt Fallon listened as the prodding examination continued. He sensed Hoke's fear, was surprised when the man's initial nervousness gradually changed to sullen hostility. Well, Matt thought, maybe Kane's finally come up with something. . . . And maybe . . . maybe that character really sized me up, and I want Kane to be right, I'm Kane's boy. No. Not really. I've told him when I thought he was off base. But I've used him, helped him and been helped, by God, that's true! He tried to review the testimony objectively, and could find but one answer: it's all going Kane's way. Can't deny that. One damning bit of evidence after the other, all fitting together. And yet. . . . Matt's instinct vetoed his logic. Too much his way, Matt thought . . . as if everyone is reading from a script that Kane wrote, a script where everything's in black and white—characters and their motives—and no mitigation. . . . Only Kane's world is like that, Matt thought. There's got to be another side.

Matt watched Leon Hoke as he turned, stared past the angry face of Josiah Martingale, and fixed his gaze on his wife. Anna Hoke caught his glance and smiled wanly.

By the time the first afternoon recess was called, the case against Leon Hoke was emerging. And Matt Fallon, talking to Jacob Krawcheck, was searching for "the other side."

(Excerpts from Hearings before a Special Subcommittee of the Committee on Government Administration.)

Session resumed at 3:15 **P.M.,** after thirty-two minute recess.

MR. KELLER: Mr. Hoke, you've told us you're chief of the filing section. I presume that much of the material you handle is highly classified.

MR. HOKE: I can not . . . I am not qualified . . . *(witness conferred with counsel.)* I am not permitted by security regulations to discuss any details of that nature.

MR. KELLER: Well, I'm glad to see you are scrupulous about security, Mr. Hoke. This committee is very much interested in your attitude on that subject. But we'll get to that later. Right now, I want to know if, in your opinion, the N.E.C. filing section is a sensitive post.

MR. HOKE: I suppose that under certain conditions . . .

MR. KELLER: Come now, sir. I am not trying to entrap you. I want a straight answer to a straight question.

MR. HOKE: Just what do you mean by the word, *sensitive?*

MR. KELLER: I mean, would it be dangerous . . .

THE CHAIRMAN: It's obvious what counsel means. The witness will be responsive.

MR. KRAWCHECK: Mr. Chairman, my client is having some difficulty with his hearing aid.

THE CHAIRMAN: Please don't address the Chair. Let your client speak for himself.

MR. DENTON: Somebody turn up the hearing aid for the man. If he can't hear . . .

MR. KELLER: I will speak louder. I mean, Mr. Hoke, that if any enemy of the United States had access to the information coming through that room, it might jeopardize the whole future of this nation. That's what I mean.

MR. HOKE: It would be dangerous if an enemy had access to the files.

MR. BRANTLEY: Can you hear all right, now?

MR. HOKE: Yes, thank you.

MR. KELLER: Now let's move on. You lived in Cleveland before coming to New York to work for the N.E.C. Will you tell me whether or not your wife was a member of the Cleveland Alliance?

MR. HOKE: Yes. It's been some time ago.

MR. KELLER: All right. You admit then that your wife belonged to a communist front organization.

MR. KRAWCHECK: Mr. Chairman, I object to that since the witness . . .

THE CHAIRMAN: Mr. Krawcheck, you have been advised that you will not address the Chair.

MR. PUGH: Talk to your client, Mr. Krawcheck. I think your objection is valid.

THE CHAIRMAN: Mr. Pugh, the Chair will make the rulings.

MR. HOKE: *(after conferring with counsel)*: If my memory serves me, this was not a political organization.

MR. KELLER: I hope your memory serves you better in the future, Mr. Hoke. I have here the list of subversive or communist front organizations prepared by the Attorney General. The Cleveland Alliance is so designated.

MR. HOKE: There are circumstances surrounding this . . .

MR. KELLER: Of course. We will develop all that.

MR. PUGH: Let's let the witness explain if he wishes.

THE CHAIRMAN: Mr. Pugh, is it too much to ask to expect you to allow us to proceed in an orderly fashion?

MR. KELLER: May I proceed?

THE CHAIRMAN: Please.

MR. KELLER: Mr. Hoke, do you know a Byron Paul?

MR. HOKE: I do.

MR. KELLER: Are you aware that he's under indictment for perjuring himself before a grand jury, that he is a Communist, a member of the Communist party?

MR. HOKE: Yes sir, I know it.

MR. KELLER: He's written you about his troubles, hasn't he?

MR. HOKE: Not since he was indicted.

MR. KELLER: But he has written to you?

MR. HOKE: My wife got a check from him. He owed her money for organ lessons when he left. He sent it to her several months later.

MR. KELLER: Tell us about the personal message from this Communist, Mr. Hoke.

MR. HOKE: I believe the note thanked her, that's all.

MR. KELLER: Are you sure you've had no other communications? Think carefully. This is a very serious thing, Mr. Hoke.

MR. HOKE: To the best of my recollection, I don't think so.

MR. KELLER: All right, I won't press you on that. Perhaps we can get at the truth this way. Tell me, during the months of February through July of 1945, didn't Paul visit your home several times a week?

MR. HOKE: I don't remember the dates exactly, but I think so.

MR. KELLER: On these occasions, didn't this Communist discuss political subjects with you?

MR. HOKE: He was taking organ lessons from my wife. We had little time to talk.

MR. KELLER: Organ lessons? That must have been convenient. I think I should warn you, Mr. Hoke, that we have direct testimony that Byron Paul discussed politics with you and several other people in a restaurant . . .

MR. HOKE: Well, I do recall that I ran into him one evening, quite by accident.

MR. KELLER: I see. You ran into him. By accident, wasn't it? You admit then, Mr. Hoke, that you—an intelligent man employed at highly secret work—did have dinner with this Communist? Were you talking over your earlier visit to Russia?

MR. HOKE: Mr. Keller, I didn't know he was a Communist. I did think he talked like one. And I don't see anything so terrible about discussing politics with anyone. That's my personal business.

MR. KELLER: That's an interesting attitude.

THE CHAIRMAN: You want, then, to leave this subcommittee with the impression that you entertained Paul in your home, that you ate with him in a restaurant, that you listened to his communist arguments, and that you feel there's nothing wrong with any of this?

MR. HOKE: I never entertained Byron Paul. I discussed politics with him only that one time when I met him by chance. I fail to see that there's any crime in that.

MR. PUGH: There is no crime in that, Mr. Hoke, not unless someone reads something into it, or plants some suspicion . . .

THE CHAIRMAN: Mr. Pugh, you'll have your chance to ask questions when . . .

MR. PUGH: The Chair does not hesitate to philosophize, question or rebuke whenever the spirit moves him . . .

THE CHAIRMAN: I intend to have order.

MR. PUGH: Then live with the rules you set down.

THE CHAIRMAN: Go ahead, Mr. Keller.

MR. KELLER: Mr. Hoke, is it true that Byron Paul approached you to use your position to help him with plans against this country? You deny that he ever urged you to join the Communist party?

MR. HOKE: *(after conferring with counsel)*: I deny that Paul ever suggested that I betray my trust in any way.

MR. KELLER: And he never, in the heat of argument, suggested you join the Communist party?

MR. HOKE: Oh, I recall that he said . . . in a joking way, not angry or anything . . . that I had juvenile political ideas and that I could stand some education . . . that the Party could teach me something. And, he was laughing at the time, and he said that when I came to my senses—that wasn't the exact phrase, but something like it—that when I came to my senses and decided to join, I could count on him for a recommendation. It was all like a joke. I mean, like he was kidding about being a Communist himself.

MR. KELLER: Then he did ask you to join the Party?

MR. HOKE: Only the way I told you.

MR. KELLER: Thank you. Your memory is improving, Mr. Hoke. Suppose you think carefully and tell us if Byron Paul ever tried to get information from you.

MR. HOKE: I repeat that he did not. And I might say that when the time comes when we're afraid to discuss our political philosophy . . .

MR. KELLER: Let's proceed. We're wasting time.

MR. HOKE: Let me finish.

THE CHAIRMAN: Let's get on with this.

MR. ROBERTS: I see no harm in allowing the witness to complete his answers.

MR. HOKE: I say that when the time comes when we're afraid to discuss our political philosophy with anyone, it will be a sad day. As long as I hurt no one else, I can talk to whom I please.

THE CHAIRMAN: Mr. Hoke, I'm cautioning you to address the subcommittee respectfully and answer questions without making speeches. Your manner has been unco-operative. You're not doing yourself any good. Proceed, Mr. Keller.

MR. KELLER: If you don't wish to talk further about this, let's turn to another activity. Is it not a fact that, on several occasions and specifically on May 14, 1943, you passed out communist propaganda to some of your co-workers?

MR. HOKE: Mr. Keller, I've answered all these questions before a security board.

THE CHAIRMAN: Yes, and your answers have been hidden from public view until we managed to dig them out and release them. Now, you are directed to answer the questions of counsel. And, in fairness to you, I'll remind you that we have your previous replies, as given to the security board of the N.E.C.

MR. HOKE: I didn't pass out any propaganda.

MR. KELLER: I ask you this: Is it not true that at least on one occasion, when you were in contact with Byron Paul and under his influence . . .

MR. KRAWCHECK: Mr. Chairman, the question is improper.

THE CHAIRMAN: Counsel is warned again that he will not address the Chair. Restate your question, Mr. Keller.

MR. KELLER: At the time you knew Byron Paul, did you not give to other employees of the National Experimental Center booklets prepared by the National Council of American-Soviet Friendship?

MR. HOKE: *(after conferring with counsel)*: I did.

MR. KELLER: I have here the Attorney General's list showing that the National Council of American-Soviet Friendship is a communist front.

MR. HOKE: I did not know that at the time.

MR. KELLER: When Byron Paul told you to give these pamphlets out, he didn't advise you that they were for a communist cause. Is that what you mean, Mr. Hoke?

MR. PUGH: Mr. Chairman, that is patently outrageous. Counsel is not asking questions. He's making accusations, double-edged . . .

THE CHAIRMAN: Restate the question, Mr. Keller.

MR. HOKE: I understood it. No. I didn't get those pamphlets from Byron Paul.

MR. KELLER: Where did they come from? You are under oath, Mr. Hoke.

MR. HOKE: I don't remember.

MR. KELLER: All right. Here's another name that interests me since it has a direct connection with a man of your responsibilities at a sensitive post. Does the name of Nathaniel Duris mean anything to you?

MR. HOKE: He's a historian, a political scientist.

MR. KELLER: And also an expert on Soviet Russia, as you may know. Do you also know that Duris fled this country in June of 1948 and was last heard of from East Germany, where he slandered this country—as you once did—and took his place with his communist friends?

MR. HOKE: I have read it in the newspapers.

MR. KELLER: Do you know this, Mr. Hoke? Is it not a fact that on March 12, 1945, less than a month after Byron Paul started coming to your home, you extended an invitation to the infamous Dr. Duris to speak before a group of N.E.C. employees?

MR. HOKE: Yes. I asked him to be at the meeting.

MR. KELLER: Did Byron Paul suggest that he address that group?

MR. HOKE: No, of course not. I never discussed anything like that with Paul. I told you I hardly saw the man.

MR. KELLER: But you say you did ask Duris to speak. Right?

MR. HOKE: I didn't know anything about his politics. I heard—from somebody, I don't remember who—that he was a good speaker. It was for the N.E.C. current events group. We all asked him questions after he talked. Most of the fellows thought he was a Socialist.

MR. KELLER: I see. It was by accident, not by design, that you brought Duris out to speak. All the loose ends just fall in place because you're a victim of circumstances. You didn't know.

MR. HOKE: I'm telling the truth.

MR. KELLER: You want this committee to understand that you invited Duris—since shown to be a traitor to his country—to speak to a group of employees of the Center, many of whom had access to secret material, and that someone other than Byron Paul influenced you to ask him?

MR. HOKE: You're twisting what I said.

MR. KELLER: I'm repeating information you have given under oath.

MR. HOKE: You're out to smear. If you wanted the truth, you'd let me complete my answers, you'd make it clear that I've already answered all these charges before a screening board which exonerated me, you'd . . .

THE CHAIRMAN: You will be in order.

MR. KELLER: Mr. Chairman, perhaps you . . .

THE CHAIRMAN: Yes, I have a few things I want to get cleared up here. Tell me, Mr. Hoke, it has been shown by counsel that you once visited Russia upon the invitation of that government, that you wrote an anti-American paper to win that invitation, that your wife was a member of a communist front organization, that you had a Communist regularly in your home, that you held political discussions with a known Red agent who asked you to join the Party, that you passed out communist propaganda among your fellow workers, that you invited an infamous traitor to bring his message of hate and treachery to the Center's employees. It's a fact, too, that you are employed in a position where you have access to top secret material. You admit all these things, but you say that you are not a Party member. You say that you are not in sympathy with the communist cause. You indicate that there are mitigating circumstances which explain all these things. Now, will you answer this question for me? I want to know—if you were actually a Communist, would it not be wiser to pose as a non-Party member so that you could operate to greater advantage among Americans who would have no reason to distrust you?

MR. KRAWCHECK: Mr. Chairman, I object to the hypothetical line of inquiry followed by the . . .

THE CHAIRMAN: Mr. Krawcheck, I have warned you repeatedly not to address the Chair.

MR. PUGH: Mr. Chairman, you will not allow counsel to object. You will not allow me to object . . .

THE CHAIRMAN: Mr. Pugh, you will have an opportunity to examine the witness.

MR. PUGH: I notice you don't hesitate to interrupt whenever you choose.

MR. KRAWCHECK: Sir, my client has answered the questions put to him by counsel without being allowed . . .

THE CHAIRMAN: I am losing patience with you, Mr. Krawcheck.

MR. KRAWCHECK: I must insist, sir, that my client has had no chance to be heard in cross-examination to correct the implications of guilt left by the restricted range of the questioning.

THE CHAIRMAN: I am warning you for the last time. If there's another outburst from you, I will ask the members to go into executive session to determine if you are not in contempt of Congress.

MR. KRAWCHECK: I am not in contempt of Congress. But there's no doubt but that I've nothing but contempt for the methods employed by this . . .

THE CHAIRMAN: You will be in order. I am happy that the American people will not be deceived. They have watched, as a great jury on television, the proceedings here today. They will not have to depend on the Leftist press to interpret for them. I have faith in the intelligence of America. I have faith that they will not be misled by the apologists for the Communists. And though you may attempt to smear this subcommittee, smear the Congress of the United States by innuendo and abuse, the people will not be fooled.

40

KANE AND LENORE sat at the maple table in Della's homey, gingham-curtained kitchen late that night, drinking milk, eating strudel and reading the early morning papers.

They were dressed in black-and-white convict-striped pajamas with red, heart-shaped pockets—Lenore's present for him, a token in return for the diamond wristwatch he had given her weeks before.

"Bet I could get a thousand dollars for a picture of you in that outfit," she said.

Turning a page in the *Daily Mirror,* he looked for the continuation of the story on the day's hearings. "They don't need any more, honey," he said absently. "I've counted four in this one paper. And tomorrow, I pose for Ernest Hamlin Baker. *Time's* going to have me on the cover!"

"But nothing like this. Think of all the people who'd like to see you in that get-up—with a ball and chain hanging from one leg!"

He tousled her short hair. "How's the story in your paper?"

"Same thing. You're a hero." Pouting, assuming a child's expression of disappointment, she said, "Mercy! I'll have a hard time finding anything for my scrapbook."

He pulled at her underlip, drawing her face close to his while she whined a protest. "Why won't you put anything good about me in that damned scrapbook?"

"Because . . . when you don't come to see me for maybe a whole week, and you haven't called, and I catch myself missing you so much that Della gives me down-the-country for neglecting my guests . . . then I make up my mind you're mean and no good, and I browse through my scrapbook and get a real bloodthirsty thrill out of seeing where other people agree with me. Besides, you've got a swelled head anyway. You need to get taken down a peg!" She growled deep in her throat, and lunged at him, biting his ear.

"Ouch!" Kane pushed her away and rubbed at his ear. "How many ears have you bitten this week?" he said, and was instantly sorry for letting his thought reach his lips.

For only an instant her lip trembled; and then she was laughing. "Seventy-one . . . or maybe seventy-two. But yours tasted best."

He patted her hand. "We wait fifteen more minutes; and if Matt doesn't show, I'm going to sleep."

"To what?"

"You heard me."

"Hmmm . . ." She winked at him and giggled obscenely, and turned back to her paper. "Here's a picture I missed. Kane O'Connor putting Dana Payne on the plane for Washington this afternoon." She held the paper up to the light as if she were examining it closely. "She's pretty . . . admit that . . . but cold. I'll bet she's cold. I can tell by the way she holds her head."

Kane glanced at the picture. "She's pretty all right; and she's not cold; and there's nothing wrong with the way she holds her head."

"Must be something wrong with her."

"Why?" Kane said, and poured another glass of milk. "Because you're sitting here in your pajamas. . . .You sent her home and stayed here."

Kane shook his head. "I stayed because I'm speaking to the Knights of Columbus here tomorrow."

"So why didn't she stay with you?"

"Lenore, did it ever occur to you that some women might consider spending the night with a man in a hotel as being immoral, sinful . . ."

"She's cold," Lenore said flatly.

"Aw, shut up and read your newspaper," he said, smiling. "Trouble with you is you've always got sex on your mind!"

"Can you think of anything friendlier for two people to do?" He turned back to his paper. "Get me another piece of strudel, please, *friend.*" While Lenore cut the pastry and brought it to him, Kane studied an editorial in an opposition paper. "They're backtracking," he told Lenore. "Hedging their bets. Even this rag's decided that O'Connor may not be wrong after all. Nothing can stop me now." It wasn't a boast. He said it as if he were talking to himself.

Matt Fallon pushed the swinging door aside and walked into the kitchen.

"Where've you been?" Kane said. "You told me you'd meet me here at nine. What time is it, Lenore?"

She looked at her watch. "About quarter past one."

Pulling out a chair, Matt sat across from Kane. "I didn't expect to be so long. I've spent the evening with Martingale, Hoke and Krawcheck."

"They cry on your broad shoulders?"

Matt loosened his tie and unbuttoned his collar. "They told me enough to make me sick," he said sternly. "I found out just why the testimony today was so one-sided."

Kane took his cigarettes from the red-heart pocket. "Because Hoke's guilty as sin. Because I had the loyalty files they tried to keep from me."

"No, Kane . . . no, not really," Matt said, running his fingers through the red mop of his hair. He looked at Lenore. "How about getting me a drink—scotch straight—and let it take you a little while. I want to talk to Kane."

"Sure." She started out, passing the table.

Kane caught her arm. "Please, Matt, not tonight. The milk's cold. The strudel's delicious—picked it up at Steinberg's on the way over. The papers are favorable. Don't spoil it with another one of your lectures."

"You can't stand criticism, can you? You don't hesitate to blast anyone who doesn't agree with you—like Southgate or Reade or Ed Patterson or the opposition press—but you can't take it yourself."

Lenore freed herself from Kane's grasp. "There's a lot wrong with him, Matt," she said lightly, "but you can't accuse him of that. If criticism would kill, he'd have been a corpse long ago."

Kane slapped his pack of Camels on the table. "Right! God knows I'm used to getting yacked at. But not tonight. Tomorrow afternoon we'll go down to Twenty-One and relax over some drinks; and you can give me what for. But not tonight, please."

"I made up my mind to tell you something, Kane. And I'm going to."

"I'll get your drink," Lenore said, smiling. "You sound like you might use dirty words." She left the room.

Matt rested his elbows on the table and rubbed his broad palms together. "I've been making excuses for you for a long time, Kane. I saw you get in with the money crowd, saw you manipulate to get your name in print, saw you trading favors. And I said, 'The guy's ambitious. He's inexperienced, but he's got something. He'll learn.'"

"Dammit to hell, Matt! You've been over all this before."

Matt disregarded the protest and went on, determined to finish. "I saw you make this whole anti-communist campaign your personal crusade for glory. And I kept telling myself—even when I knew you were wrong—that what you were trying to do was right. I figured I was a reporter, that I was supposed to stand aside, observing." He traced his finger around the damp circle where a glass had been. "I really convinced myself that the end justified the means, that no matter what your methods, something good would come of it."

Kane drained his glass and examined it as if he were interested in every detail of its contour. "So you listened to this commie Hoke for an evening, and that old fool Martingale and their shyster lawyer, and all of a sudden you've decided I'm really a bastard."

"Not exactly." Matt slipped off his coat and hung it on the back of his chair. "I've decided you're a fake, Kane. You've deliberately misled and misrepresented and exaggerated. It's perfectly clear now. For the first time I've been able, on my own, to evaluate both sides. For the first time, I've gotten an insight into what your methods really are."

"Methods!" Kane banged his fist on the table, then grabbed his plate before it jounced to the floor. "Don't think I haven't heard that record over and over again." He glared at Matt. "Well, I'm waiting for anyone else to rout out Communists by other means. The same people who wail so righteously about my methods, who want to take a soft attitude toward traitors, have yet to expose one of the Reds by their methods."

Fallon stood, turned his back and walked to the sink. He tightened the leaking faucet. Thoughtfully, he faced Kane again. "And how many have you exposed with your methods?" He dried his hands on a dish towel as he spoke. "Method isn't important to you," he said quietly. "And you're wrong. It's simply method that distinguishes one form of government from another. If we're supposed to stand for personal liberty and fair play and tolerance, method *is* important. It's everything!"

Kane bit off a piece of strudel, gesturing for Matt to wait for his reply while he chewed. Matt's tone was too serious, too utterly devoid of humor for this to be another lecture; and Kane was deliberately slowing the conversation, trying to take it lightly. "Okay. Look at it this way . . ." He offered some strudel to Matt who waved it away. "Let's say we've got . . ." He took another bite. "This is damned good, Matt."

"Go on," Matt said impatiently. "Have your say!"

"Well, suppose we've got a big forest fire eating up the timber, threatening a whole town. And there, on the edge of it, you see a bunch of spectators too timid to do a cockeyed thing about it. Oh, they agree that the fire may be dangerous. But while they argue whether to use a hose or a bucket or a fire extinguisher, they curse the one man who's flailing away at the blaze with his coat—the only thing he has at hand. They don't like the guy's methods," he said sarcastically.

"There's no analogy," Matt said, raising his voice. "You're clever, Kane. I give you credit for that. But you're apparently not clever enough to see that only in Russia is method unimportant. If they want to raise production, they throw another thousand in a slave labor camp. They appropriate property or kill or maim or starve if necessary. If a treaty suits their purposes, promises to accomplish their goals, they sign one or break one. Honesty and integrity mean nothing. Only the end result is important. They don't care about method in Russia." He came back to the table, leaning over it, resting his hands there. "But we're supposed to care about it here!"

Kane had never seen Matt so belligerent. It disturbed him. "All right, buddy. You're entitled to your opinion; and I'm not going to fight with you about it. But, just for argument's sake, suppose everything you say is true. If there was only one choice open to you—my way of dealing with subversion or not dealing with it at all—you'd take my way. There's no middle ground. There's no other choice. So don't expect me to agree with you. I've made up my mind to get the Reds out of the country. I've made up my mind to knock heads together if necessary. I've taken abuse and slander and threats. I've had to fight for my seat. I've had to campaign. I've had to stand off every influential Left-winger and fellow-traveler in the country to do it. But it's going to be done!"

"Please!" Matt grunted, and shook his head in disbelief. "I've got a strong stomach. I can stand damned near anything. But don't give me that crap about how dedicated you are!"

Kane blazed back at him. "Who else has done it? Who else has had the nerve to take on all comers? Who else has risked as much to protect this country? By God, why shouldn't I feel dedicated?"

"Don't try to pass yourself off as a paragon of virtue, Kane. For godsake, not that! And don't try to kid me that it's your selflessness or your idealism, your devotion to democracy or your love of country that drives you. You're driven by something else, something that lets you spend a night drinking and whoring around in a geisha house in Kyoto, and then lets you go home to scream bloody murder about a few GIs doing something no worse. It's something that allows you to scream about spies getting into government files and then excuses you for doing the same damned thing!" He bent over, to within inches of Kane's face. "Do you know what it is that drives you, motivates you, plagues you?" His voice was heavy with derision. "It's fame you want, and glory. You lust after them. They're rooted in your guts!"

Kane got up, anger prodding him. "Think what you like." He crossed around the table and stood before Matt. "But spare me the dramatics in the future. Because I don't give a damn whether or not you're angry . . ."

Matt cut him off. "I'm angry all right, but not at you." He took a deep breath. "I'm angry because I've been a sucker for so long. I've recognized your rottenness before now, but I liked being close to the news, liked having an inside track, liked boosting my ratings by serving you up to the public. And I didn't have the honesty to speak out." Kane walked away, and Matt followed. "You know what Leon Hoke said tonight? He said, 'Mr. Fallon, I'm a little guy. What can a little guy do against somebody like O'Connor?'"

"That sounds corny to me. That *little guy's* been coached by more lawyers and politicians and protected by every big gun up to the President himself!" Kane picked up his cigarettes and lighted one. "Tell Lenore I've gone up."

Matt took his arm. "Wait a minute. I'm not through." Kane pulled away from him, but stood there as Matt continued. "I didn't know what to tell Hoke," he said. "But I do now. Because he's not going to be a little guy by himself against the mighty power of O'Connor. I'm going to take the trouble to be sure of my facts— something you've never bothered to do—and then, if Hoke's right, I'm going to fight you, Kane. I'm going to do whatever I can to see that Leon Hoke and all the Hokes you've ruined by delivering the Big Lie, by whipping up hysteria . . ."

"I've heard those catchwords before!"

But Matt talked over him. ". . . get a chance to be heard! They couldn't stand up to you—even if they'd had the courage. They couldn't get attention as easily as you do."

Appraising him steadily, Kane dropped his fresh cigarette into his glass and heard it hiss at the bottom. "You better stay clear of me," he said coldly.

Matt shrugged. "I don't scare easily." Picking up his coat, he walked past Kane to the door. He stopped there and looked around to find his friend of Europe and Japan and Washington staring at him. "I don't think you're as big as you've convinced yourself and a lot of others you are," he said. "I think most of the people in this country are sick of you, sick and disgusted and disillusioned."

"I'm warning you," Kane said, his voice hoarse with suppressed fury. "You look for trouble, and I'll give it to you!"

Matt smiled contemptuously. "I'll be in damned good compny."

Coming through the doorway, Lenore handed Matt his drink.

"Give it to *him,*" Matt said. "He's going to need it."

BOOK FOUR

41

COMMUNIST TROOPS swept into South Korea; and American forces, in the first agonizing weeks, rushed to stop their advance. Then, outnumbered, outgunned, they halted, stumbled, reeled back, retreated.

The Administration, converting to the needs of war, had little time for battles at home. Men, weapons, strategy, diplomacy—these were its concerns.

But Kane was not diverted. The hearings on the National Experimental Center brought him new strength; and he saw himself as the Brider Syndicate pictured him—a man of the people, bare-knuckled, courageous, battling against great odds, abused, scorned and defamed, but destined to triumph, to win the nation's gratitude and recognition. His hearings continued. And he vied with Korea for the headlines, pressing his advantage, illustrating daily that the Red danger was being laid bare by his efforts alone.

In a network television address, sponsored by the American Patriots, he told his audience, "We are faltering in Korea today because we have failed our soldiers and sailors, our airmen and marines. We can not long continue to go through the motions of fighting the Reds in the mud and heat and stench of Korea and still allow their fellow-traveling friends, their hidden saboteurs in Washington and their unwitting helpers in high places to paralyze us here at home."

The fluorescent glow shone late from the windows of the Executive Offices on Sixteenth Street. And inside, seated around the glossy table in the cool green conference room, six men—the Majority Leader and the Majority Whip of the House of Representatives, a Presidential advisor, Milton Pugh, a congressman from New York and another from Georgia—argued for hours, cursing, threatening, warning, proposing, rejecting, until all agreed to accept Kane O'Connor's challenge, to openly oppose him, and to fight him on the floor of the House.

"How?" Milton Pugh demanded, and resting his elbows on the table, jarred an empty highball glass. "By making speeches? Hell, we'll get an answering tirade on slander. I'm for doing what we should have had the guts to do a long time ago. I'm for expelling the bastard!"

The husky, bald-domed man with plans to be New York's governor one day, drummed his fingers on the arms of his chair. "Milt," he said softly, "I applaud your passion, but you're talking like a man with a paper navel! The House doesn't do that sort of thing every day; and O'Connor's no fly you can slap away. You get reckless and he'll take the swatter from you and beat you to death with it."

The shrewd veteran from Georgia had spoken rarely all evening. He sat there with eyes half-closed, underlining the figures on a pad before him, pulling at his dry underlip, listening. Now he wrote some figures on a note page and circled them. "There's simple arithmetic involved, friends. We've got 435 representatives. It would take 290 to banish O'Connor to the Carolina Hills; and that many votes'll be about as easy to come by as bourbon at a Baptist Tent Revival." He bolted his drink, and leaned back lazily in his chair. "Now let's stop frettin' 'bout what we'd *like* to do, and decide what we *can* do."

Abel Garren, the Majority Leader, reached for the pad and added some figures of his own, then scratched them out. "I'm not so sure we can't get the votes, but to get three-fourth's of the House to agree on anything'll take some doing. When it comes to O'Connor, party lines don't mean a damn. We'll get plenty of help from the other side of the aisle. . . . What we need is time to work on it."

"Time! Goddamn it, what's he got to do before we clobber him?" the Presidential advisor said. "Next week he'll be robbing the White House laundry bags, looking for caviar, borscht and vodka stains on the table linen!"

The Majority Whip, a young man whose strong convictions and quick mind had won him his position, and whose grimness and officiousness would cost him further advancement, didn't join in the laughter that followed. "I'm not in the mood for hilarity," he said. "If someone down here would have consulted a few of us poor stupes on the Hill before those security files were withheld, if someone down here would have tightened up on the Communists in this town. . . but no, we get the summons when there are chestnuts to be yanked out of the fire."

"Are you defending O'Connor?" Milton Pugh said, instantly aroused.

"Hell no! But I fail to see the humor of this situation. We're the clay pigeons who're going to get shot at. We're the guys who have to put pressure on our friends, push them to go on record one way or the other and lay themselves open to attack at home from the O'Connor-lovers or the O'Connor-haters."

At two in the morning, when cigarette and cigar butts were stacked in damp circles around coffee saucers and both bourbon and scotch bottles were empty and Abel Garren had left his seat to pace the room and yawns punctuated every argument and tempers were muffled by fatigue, it was Milton Pugh who finally offered a possible solution.

"All right, gentlemen. We can't get the three-fourths vote to expel—not right away. But we stand a good chance of getting a simple majority on a privileged resolution. Let's say we propose a special investigating committee be appointed to investigate O'Connor's activities and to report to the House if they find cause to expel him. That's watered down enough to get 218 votes, isn't it? A lot of people can live with it."

The representative from Georgia said, "I think we could count on strong support from most of the southern delegations. Most of us don't claim him as one of our own, even the Tarheel contingent."

"O'Connor's aid and comfort will come from the traditionally isolationist sections, the lunatic fringe and the honest but poor souls who have been deluded into thinking he's done something," the New Yorker said, suddenly interested. "But we can expect help from the metropolitan areas where he's had a hostile press, most of the hot house liberals, Shep Reade's friends, Dick Southgate's following—hell, we've got a good hundred and fifty, maybe more, already. Right, Abel?"

The Majority Leader walked back to the table and stood behind his chair, leaning on it. "I like the poetic justice of getting it to a special committee, discrediting him through investigation."

"Meanwhile," Milton Pugh said happily, "we'll paralyze O'Connor's subcommittee . . ."

"And we'll have time to muster the three-fourths vote we'll need if the special committee recommends expulsion. We'll have O'Connor where the hair is short!" The Majority Whip nodded thoughtfully. "And even if they don't go for booting him—and only the good Lord knows what'll happen when congressmen turn judges and strain their sacroiliacs bending over backwards—Mr. O'Connor'll come out of it smelling . . ."

". . . like a polecat with the trots," the gentleman from Georgia offered.

The Presidential advisor waited out the laughter. "Tell me what we can do here," he asked the Majority Leader. "You boys have your work cut out for you."

"Suppose I bat out the resolution," Milton Pugh said, anxious to remind them that the idea was his. "I could introduce it . . ."

"Okay, Milt," the Majority Leader said. "Go heavy on the 'Whereas' clauses, and give him hell!"

Stu Denton, highly excited, rushed into Kane's office at eleven the next morning. "Kane," he said, and stopped, panting to catch his breath. "I don't know how to tell you this . . ."

Kane laughed. "You'll manage, you ole cowboy, and by damn, you are getting old!"

Talking in brief rushes, Stu related how he had been approached in the House restaurant by another congressman from his state. "This won't be sniping, Kane," he said, still agitated. "They know what they're about; and they're confident as all get out they can pull it off."

Not moving from his chair, Kane sat there, cold anger welling in him. Like that night long before when he had fought Luke Biddle's thugs in Mark Woodmire's backyard, the anger stirred him to action; and he did not consider the danger or the odds, only the sheer joy of battle.

Within the hour he had Dany, Tod, Ward, Stu, Ray Hyder, a congressman from North Carolina, another from Illinois, a third from Maryland gathered in his office. As soon as Kane explained the reason for the meeting, the representative from North Carolina stood. "I don't belong in here," he said softly.

"What do you mean, Harmon? You afraid of those bastards?"

"No, Kane. I'm on their side."

A taut moment of silence was broken by the squeak of Kane's swivel chair as he stood. "You forget awfully fast, Harmon," he said grimly. "You forget Shep Reade and you forget . . ."

"I haven't forgotten, Kane," his colleague from North Carolina said, and walked to the door.

"You forget who helped put you in your seat, you ungrateful . . ." Dany, going to Kane's side, grasped his arm, urging him to say no more. He shook her hand away. "I bought your seat for you!"

"That's the kind of thinkin' I don't hold with, Kane. Nobody buys a congressman. I don't owe anyone anythin'—except the folks in my district who sent me here and can throw me out." He opened the door. "And, incidentally, if they have a mind to, they can help throw you out." He was gone before Kane could reply.

"He's a fool!" Ward said.

"I hope there aren't a couple of hundred like him," Tod said.

Kane slipped back in his seat and nibbled his lower lip nervously, aware of the undercurrent of tension about him. "Anybody else in the wrong room?" When there was no reply, he smiled. "Okay. Let's get to work."

Within an hour Kane's tactics were resolved. Like a company commander issuing a five-paragraph combat order, he oriented his troops and briefed them on each phase of the operation.

Enemy strength he estimated at a hundred and twenty-five votes, his own strength at a hundred and fifty.

Their mission, Kane said, was to capture the crucial one hundred and sixty votes that might go one way or another.

The time of the attack was set at once, and the line of departure was their meeting. Then Kane dictated the mission of his subordinates.

Dany was to work through Lucy and Mel Field, negating the opposition's advantage of surprise by informing all news media of the planned attack.

Ward was to get the aid of the American Patriots, arranging for petitions and wires to bombard every congressional office, and then to concentrate on the thirty votes of the Pennsylvania delegation.

Tod was to call Caleb Lawton to set up a conference with Kane so they might put pressure on California's thirty-man contingent; and Nate Starbecker was to be asked for help in arranging phone calls from industrialists to their state's representatives.

Kane and the congressmen from Illinois and Maryland were to work on New York's forty-three representatives, Illinois' twenty-five, Michigan's eighteen, Ohio's twenty-three, and the whole stronghold of midwestern states.

Pig Hyder, who admitted Alabama's eight other congressmen, as friends of Shep Reade, were lost, was assigned to work on Texas' twenty-two representatives, and the generally anti-O'Connor bloc of southern states.

When the administration details were completed, Kane dismissed his aides. "You all do your jobs, we'll knock hell out of them. Once and for all, I'm going to show them who's boss." Smiling confidently, he shook his fist at them and struck his desk. "They'll open up on the floor. And by the day after, the cloakrooms'll be littered with their political carcasses!"

The Speaker's gavel pounded again and again through the din in the House Chamber.

On the floor, conferences dispersed and high-pitched arguments ended unresolved; leaders of both parties straggled from the cloakrooms, still debating; secretaries and clerks stood in clusters along the back wall; and page boys hurried down the aisles to take their places at the foot of the rostrum.

Above the turmoil, uniformed policemen checked passes at the gallery doors; forty-two pickets, who had carried "Defend Kane—Defend America" placards before the House office buildings for two days, shoved one another aside, vying for the remaining twenty seats; and the members of the press corps— enveloped in the tension—obeyed the call for order.

Once more the gavel demanded silence. The clatter diminished to a hum. The chaplain gave the invocation. The Chamber breathed, "Amen." Congressmen, spectators and the press within the hall—and the nation beyond it—waited, expectant at the brink of conflict.

Kane's chair was his command post; and he sat there, aware that he was the true center of the room, offering no protest when the Majority Leader asked unanimous consent for consideration of a privileged resolution, and the Speaker, without objection from the floor, ordered it. For Kane was certain the resolution would be defeated—by his allies who believed in him, by others who feared his retribution, by a small group that welcomed a chance to embarrass the Administration, by men who would react to the telegrams and letters and phone calls from constituents, and by some who, though opposed to him, disapproved of the drastic action contemplated to end his career.

Confident that he could control the forces that would soon be storming around him, Kane welcomed the chance to draw his opponents into a dispute which he believed would establish— beyond doubt—his predominant position in the House and the nation.

Abel Garren, showing the strain of three hectic days of mapping his campaign, cleared his throat and, his hoarse voice barely audible, yielded to Milton Pugh. Then, as if he had expended his last shred of energy, he slumped into his own chair. He was a scarred veteran of many fights on the floor and in the caucus room, but the one before him differed from all the others. This time there would be no good-natured joking between victors and vanquished when the battle was done. This time friendships would be severed in the bitterness of debate that would not soon heal over coffee or cocktails. There were so many imponderables. . . .

No party lines were drawn here, no readily-identifiable core of opposition across the aisle, no compromises that could be made. Some of the men he had long respected and depended upon were arrayed militantly on the other side. And some who had opposed his election to leadership, and later battled him on issue after issue, were passionately committed to him on this single vote. If he were to win—and despite his half-century in politics Abel Garren still believed The Right Side always won in the end—he would have to find support in both parties, patching together a coalition of conservatives and liberals, party regulars and mavericks, civil-righters from the North and states-righters from the South. And he would need help from the Minority Leader. In the past few days he had found that men who could agree on nothing else did agree on the danger of Kane O'Connor. To rally them all . . . that was his problem.

As Milton Pugh shambled down the aisle to the dais, the Majority Leader scribbled a note: *Win, my friend, let's have a chat.*

Speaker's office whenever you say—Abel. Motioning for a page, he sent the message to Winfield Parcher, the Minority Leader.

Luther Brantley slipped into the next chair. "I've talked with every man in the North Carolina delegation, Abel; and four agreed to take the floor! The others are either afraid of O'Connor, or just don't like the idea of turning on one of their own."

The Majority Whip leaned over the table between them. "Let's throw those four, one after the other, at O'Connor; and let's do it as soon as Milt finishes. Psychologically, it'll be a real slap in the face. As for the others, the ones who won't make any promises, I'm for telling them it's either—or! They're with the President on this thing, or they're against him."

"Relax," the Majority Leader said. "They might just take you up on it. As soon as others make the break, our Tarheel friends won't feel so all alone. And we'll let one—the one he's prepared for—speak against Kane shortly. We'll save the other three for the right moment when they'll do the most good. . . ."

From ten rows behind, Kane watched the animated conversation, speculating on it, pleased that there was some apparent disagreement. He whispered to Ward Roberts. "Art Bozell owes me a favor. I want him to speak for me later in the afternoon. He can influence some Illinois fence-sitters, and probably some others."

"He'll vote with us, Kane, but he's worried about the feeling in his district. I don't think he'll risk taking the floor."

"The hell he won't!" Heads turned in his direction and Kane lowered his voice. "You tell that sonovabitch I didn't worry about my district when he needed my help on his pennyante immigration amendment last year." Ward started to reply, but Kane waved him away. "Tell him!" he said, and turned his gaze to the press gallery, searching for Dany.

She sat beside Matt Fallon. They had lunched together, and she had argued unsuccessfully, trying to mediate his break with Kane. Now, as Matt leaned over a tally sheet and entered a figure, she whispered with an attempt at nonchalance, "What's the score?"

Matt ran his fingers through his thick red hair, frowning as he added the numbers in one column. "Only a damned fool would try to predict the way this kind of thing'll go. Let's see. . . . I've got 153 probables in Kane's column, 145 against him. But that's based entirely on past performance. What we've got to watch is the uncommitted minority, 137 less the absentees."

Below them, Milton Pugh stood before the microphones, his heavily-veined hands grasping the edges of the podium, his stooped shoulders forced back, as if his mission entitled him to new stature. And as the murmur of conversation faded, he stared out at the chamber and his gaze rested unmistakably on Kane O'Connor.

Many on the floor were waiting for the exact wording of the resolution; and the reporters in the press gallery leaned forward, ready to dash up the steps to the phones with the first bulletin on the attempt to investigate the nation's most famous investigator. Aware that they were waiting, aware of the ferment, Milton Pugh savored the drama.

"Mr. Speaker, Gentlemen of the House, we are victims of a state of mind," he said. "We are afraid; and there is a terrifying weakness in fear!" The page boys were silent, listening, looking up at Pugh, who stood motionless for a moment, a clenched fist thrust before him, his lined, gray-bearded visage rapt, like an Old Testament prophet. "The cause of this fear has a seat in this House. I do not believe he should keep that seat."

Kane, apparently unconcerned, rifled through his briefcase, selected a document (a year-old transcript of the Special Committee on Military Planning), and appeared to be studying it diligently. But the page was a blur before him; his mind dwelt only on Milton Pugh's words, words delivered like the lashes of a whip, words that cut through Kane's pretense and finally forced him to raise his eyes to the podium.

"One man is dividing the American people, feeding them on a diet of lies, half-truths, innuendo and fear."

Milton Pugh did not intend to deliver an oration, but a sermon. And he spoke softly, emphasizing his words, pausing between phrases as if he wanted to be certain his listeners would not lose the significance of his message. ". . . The catechism of this man and the catechism of communism are amazingly similar. Both teach duplicity, fraud, fear and intrigue. Both teach disregard of established law. Both teach a dialectic so foreign to democratic ideals that it changes to accommodate the latest whim, the latest line of the ruling clique. . . ."

"Now what the devil does that mean?" Dany said to Matt.

He held up his hand to silence her. Unsmiling, he whispered, "Listen!"

"One man and all he stands for is a clot speeding unchecked through the veins of the nation," Pugh said. "We must dissolve it before it reaches our brain or heart!"

Get through with the com and cliches, Kane was thinking while Pugh spoke. Get through, you lowlife; and you'll get a going over. To Stu Denton who hovered over him, Kane said, "The first time he gives you an opening, you demand that his remarks be taken down. . . ."

"Shepherd Reade, an honest and good man, stood here over a year ago and warned us. We chose to ignore that warning." Pugh hesitated. Until that moment, he had not mentioned Kane by name, but as he looked out into the chamber and saw Kane ignoring him, whispering to Stu Denton, Pugh disregarded the instructions of the Majority Leader. With venom, raising his voice, he said, "Shepherd Reade met the fate of any who oppose the saintly, crusading savior of America, Kane O'Connor!"

Immediately, Stu Denton jumped to his feet. "Mr. Speaker! A personal attack against a member of this House is in violation of the rules. I move that the words of the gentleman . . ."

Milton Pugh, smiling with the satisfaction of a man who has baited a trap and seen it snare a victim instantly, broke in on him. "Doesn't the gentleman agree that the gentleman from North Carolina is saintly in his behavior? Isn't he a crusader devoted to his cause? Can I be accused of attacking him personally because I assume that he is America's savior from the Reds?"

Briefly, laughter relaxed the tension; and then the chamber snapped back as Stu Denton shouted, "Will the gentleman yield?"

"Only for a question."

"Does the gentleman intend to observe the rules, or does he intend to resort to sarcasm, to thinly-veiled insults . . ."

Milton Pugh said softly, "My answer is that I intend to observe the letter, if not the spirit of the rules!"

The Majority Leader whispered to the Whip, "Trust Milt to rock the boat." Dany asked Matt, "Why does a man like Kane have to surround himself with idiots?" And the Speaker pounded his gavel, warned both men against a colloquy, reminded Pugh that no resolution was before the House as yet, and biting his lips to avoid a smile, leaned back in his chair.

His hands folded across his chest, Milton Pugh waited for total silence. Grim-faced again, as if the exchange with Stu Denton had never taken place, he said, "Plato warned us of demogogues, too. He said, 'The People have always some champion whom they set over them and nurse into greatness. This and no other is the root from which a tyrant springs; when first he appears, he is a protector.' Gentlemen of the House, I for one recognize a tyrant; and I am not afraid to put myself in danger of a tyrant's wrath. Therefore, I introduce this resolution calling for the appointment of a select committee to investigate and determine whether expulsion proceedings should be instituted against the gentleman from North Carolina—Mr. Kane O'Connor!"

As if Pugh had given them a signal, there was a pained roar from the galleries, and a chant of "No . . . No . . . No" from the American Patriots.

The Speaker slammed his fist on the papers before him and looked sternly at the demonstrators. "Visitors will be orderly, or we will clear the galleries."

When the noise subsided, Milton Pugh began to read the resolution: "Whereas, The Constitution of the United States gives this House the authority to expel . . ."

Kane wrote a note to Ward Roberts and had it delivered. His instructions were: *Get the floor. Take Pugh apart.*

But when Milton Pugh left the rostrum and Ward was the first to call for recognition, the Speaker looked beyond him. "The Chair recognizes the gentleman from New York . . ."

For three hours the Majority Leader's chosen men held the floor, one yielding to the other, each backing the resolution, each following the well-planned routine of discussing a different phase of the charges.

"He has indulged in questionable financial dealings . . ." From the rear of the chamber, an O'Connor supporter stood. "Will the gentleman yield?" And when he was allowed a question, he asked, "Does the gentleman have access to some secret records that allows him to make such charges, or is it his intention to plant this obvious untruth in the hopes that it will be given wide circulation, and so appeal to those who believe 'where there's smoke there's fire'?"

"I will answer the gentleman from Arkansas by admitting that only the O'Connor subcommittee has access to secret records, and furthermore, that the tactic so ably described by the gentleman from Arkansas is the exclusive property of the gentleman from North Carolina!"

"Answer my question! Admit to this House that you have not one shred of evidence to support . . .

Kane called Ray Hyder to his side. "See Tod. He's in the back somewhere. I want to know what success Caleb Lawton had with the California bunch."

"Just talked to Tod," Ray said. "Mr. Lawton told him you can count on at least eight, with four against and the others refusin' to say yet."

Smiling, Kane patted Ray's arm. "We're ahead of the game," he said, and from the public address system, he heard the gentleman from New York finally yield to the gentleman from Louisiana.

"He has insisted that our government is infiltrated with Communists, but has failed to produce one. . . ."

In the Speaker's office, Abel Garren, the Majority Leader, and Winfield Parcher, the Minority Leader, relaxed in deep leather chairs and smoked the Speaker's cigars.

Winfield Parcher said, "You want something, Abel, and I damned well know what it is."

"Your help."

"You've got my vote."

"That's not the same thing," Abel Garren said.

"O'Connor's your problem."

"No, Win, O'Connor's everybody's problem."

"I'm not going to ride herd on my people, put them under the gun at home, for the President, Abel. Last time I butted into this business, I helped you close O'Connor's initial hearings by putting the bee on Stu Denton. And I did it because the State Department was looking ridiculous before the rest of the world— not that that outfit needed O'Connor's help. And I didn't hesitate in reaming O'Connor when he attacked Dick Southgate. But to your man in the White House, bipartisanship means doing everything his way. When I helped rescue his numbskulls in Foggy Bottom, I was being responsible, but when I oppose him, he tells the National Press Club his legislative program is being 'sabotaged by a Republican arsonist with a seventeenth-century mind!'"

"He was griped about the way you licked us on the foreign aid bill, Win. Don't tell me you're getting sensitive in your old age."

The Minority Leader dusted the ashes from his cigar. "It's your move, Abel. You Democrats gave birth to this bastard son. Discipline him yourself."

Inside the chamber, the gentleman from South Carolina was speaking. ". . . He has ransacked classified information—"

And he, as every other speaker before him, was challenged by one of Kane's supporters. "Does the gentleman from South Carolina believe that the Executive Branch should refuse to give Congress the facts it needs to transact its business?"

"If anyone can raid public files, disregarding the law, we'll have chaos . . ."

"Answer! Answer!" the American Patriots shouted. And five of them were escorted from the galleries by policemen.

They're all cowards, Kane thought, seething with hatred for the men who assaulted him. They wouldn't dare to stand alone, as I've done. They've gotten together, like a bunch of jackals, so they can hop me in a pack.

The gentleman from Massachusetts spoke: ". . . He has encouraged public servants to violate their oaths . . ."

And then the gentleman from Michigan: "He has engaged in campaign practices which are in violation of law and common decency. . . ."

Dany was watching Kane as he sat slumped in his seat, listening to the barrage of indictments, pulling at his ear, then suddenly sitting erect as the gentleman from Michigan yielded to the gentleman from North Carolina. He was the same man who, three days earlier, had walked out of Kane's office, the one North Carolinian the Majority Leader was ready to use.

". . . He has desecrated the privileged sanctuary of this chamber by defaming, without fear of libel, one of this country's greatest statesmen . . ."

Matt changed the figures on his tally sheet; and Dany looked at the new totals: For Kane—165, Against—168, Uncommitted—102. It was the first time the count had turned in favor of the resolution. "Why?" she asked, disturbed.

"Because I'd credited Kane with all of North Carolina's votes, and this is the crack in the solid front."

"Just because one traitor shows up, one man who has accepted Kane's favors, and now turns on him, that doesn't mean . . ."

Matt patted her hand, and laughed softly. "It just means that I'm playing with numbers again. It's my hunch. Sue me."

"That whole thing you've got there is stupid," she said angrily.

Shoving the papers aside, Matt said, "You're right. To hell with it. Kane hasn't had his say yet."

Kane was talking to Ward Roberts. "See every member of my state's delegation. Put it to them in plain English—they cut my throat in here today, make it look like my own people are running out on me, and I'll ruin them at home. I'll call every goddamned newspaper from Manteo to Murphy, and give them a rundown on their representatives! I swear to God I will!"

"Mr. Speaker!" Ray Hyder cupped his hands around his mouth and bellowed for recognition. "Mr. Speaker! Point of order . . . or point of information, I guess."

"The Chair recognizes the gentleman from Alabama," the Speaker said, and leaning forward, his elbows on his desk, his hands supporting his chin, he grinned. "But I would remind the gentleman from Alabama that I am not presiding in the Carter-Barron Amphitheatre; and I can hear him very well."

"My apologies, Mr. Speaker. Now, I don't reckon, as a freshman, I ought to sound off, but it seems to me it's time somebody get a word in edgewise on the other side of the question. All we've heard for hours now is the gentleman from one place yieldin' to the gentleman from the next place and right on down the line." His hands resting on his ample rump, Ray turned from the Speaker to his colleagues. "I figure fair's fair and there's plenty of us who believe in the gentleman from North Carolina, and want to go on record."

The hostility of debate, the angry harassment on the floor, the conferences going on in the cloakrooms, the impending reply from the O'Connor forces—all these things had expanded the strained atmosphere in the chamber. And, like combat troops who have been engaged in constant action, the legislators, seeking release, laughed easily, on any provocation. Ray Hyder had them laughing again.

The Speaker said, "The gentleman from Alabama may be assured that any member of the House who wants the floor will get it. However, I have requests to speak from thirty-nine gentlemen . . . . He looked toward the Majority Leader. "The dinner hour approaches, and unless it is the intention of the House to remain in session . . ."

Stu Denton whispered to Kane. "Might be a good time to move for postponement to a day certain, say the day after tomorrow. It would give us time to get to some of the people who still won't give us an answer."

Abel Garren stood. "Mr. Speaker, in time I will advise the House of my intentions . . ."

"He's not sure," Kane told Stu, evaluating the Majority Leader's words. "Let's hold on until we get a chance to answer. I'd like to beat them quickly, tonight," he said, smiling. "That would cut their water off!"

Ward joined them to report fourteen more votes in Kane's camp. "The way it looks," he said, "we'll need about thirty-two of the votes we still think are uncommitted . . ."

Stu said, "I'm not counting votes until I hear them answer the roll. Even some of them who are supposed to be on our side won't come out, point-blank and say so."

"Be cautious, you ole cowboy," Kane said, laughing. "But let's get the floor. Before this night's over, I'm going to shove that resolution, word by word, down the President's throat. And Milton Pugh and Abel Garren are going to get laughed off the Hill while he chokes on it!"

Art Bozell, the recalcitrant congressman from Illinois, leaned over him and whispered, "I've thought it over, Kane. I'm with you; and I'll get up and say so."

Kane stood, so the whole House would see his gesture, and he shook Art Bozell's hand. "I'm glad you don't forget favors, Al," he murmured in his ear. "You know I don't."

Matt nudged Dany. "See that? Your boy and the gentleman from Illinois? If Bozell declares for him, Kane's got an additional four or five, maybe more votes. A guy like Bozell's got influence with people on his committees, his state delegation, men who owe him favors . . ."

Dany smiled. "Okay, change your tally sheet."

"I'm through with it," Matt said. "It might predict Kane's going to beat the rap, and I couldn't stand the disappointment."

The Speaker said, "The Chair recognizes the gentleman from Pennsylvania."

Ward Roberts' soft, musical voice did not dent the stir of conversation in the chamber. His tone was so low that colleagues, straining to hear him, began to demand order. The Speaker banged his gavel. Legislators returned to their seats. Over-the-shoulder arguments broke up; and it was finally quiet.

". . . I beg you to defeat this ill-advised resolution. The gentleman from North Carolina has had a disagreement with the Executive Branch, an honest difference of opinion which many of us share. It is not right to strike at him by impugning the honor of a man who has served his country conscientiously in peace and gallantly in war . . ."

The Majority Leader sat with his head down, eyes closed, fingers smoothing his brows while Milton Pugh whispered to him. "Let's call for the 'Yeas and Nays' as soon as we can get away with it," Pugh said, scratching his beard. "We've got at least an eighteen-vote margin."

"How do you know how many votes we've got? I don't, Milt. Win Parcher's letting his people choose sides without even a nod. I don't like that at all. It louses up the picture. Sure we might pull it off without him. But why take the chance?" As he spoke, Abel Garren's gaze rested on the Minority Leader across the aisle. "Milt, this House is full of mavericks today, when what we need is a lot of responsibility and a little party discipline—from both parties. Win Parcher's a pro, God bless him . . . and sooner or later, he's going to act like one."

Ward still held the floor. "The tactics used here today are a shame and a disgrace. The conscience of this great House, its sense of fair play will not allow . . .

He's not hitting them, Kane thought angrily, helpless to urge him on. These buggers are interested in how it effects them, what the people at home think. Fair play! A lot they care about fair play!

Ray Hyder rose again to defend Kane, walking awkwardly to the public address microphones. And Kane, who had just received an offer of floor support from one of his home state congressmen, and felt sure that the others would soon fall in line, leaned back in his seat, smugly contemplating the rewards of victory.

On the platform, Ray Hyder was telling the House "a story they spin down home 'bout this big snarlin' watchdog nobody had any use for 'cause he was so doggone mean and ornery. . . . The farmer decided to poison this ole hound, poison him! And you know, they never realized what a good dog they had till they commenced to missin' him. No, sir! Soon's he was gone, they had trouble with prowlers, had varmints raidin' their chicken house."

Kane cursed soundlessly into his cupped fist. *The slob!* he thought. And still, Ray's intentions are good, probably up there for better reasons than most of them. It's just a good way to get their names in the papers. . . Attack O'Connor or go through the motions of defending him and make the front page! All except poor Ray . . . all except The Pig!

Six more men stood in turn to fight the resolution, and a report circulated in the press gallery, as one relay of reporters returned from the phones, that most of the midwestern states were nearly solid for Kane. To Kane's seat came whispered offers to speak for him, and page boys with messages that pledged support.

By ten that night, the House was still in session, and word skirmishes flared with increasing intensity between O'Connor partisans and opponents.

Some legislators nibbled sandwiches and others slipped out briefly for coffee. Dany and Matt ate cheese crackers and sipped cokes while the reporters around them left only to file reports and seek prophecies from both sides.

Rumors circulated, tipping the balance, first toward Kane, then against him.

The gentleman from California, interrupted three times by the gentleman from Mississippi's jibes at Kane, threatened to "take the gentleman outside and teach him some manners."

The Majority Leader, who had held the House in session, sat sleepy-eyed at his desk, conferring with a succession of men he had summoned.

Stu Denton, Ward Roberts, Ray Hyder and five other rabid O'Connor men roamed the cloakrooms arguing with anyone who offered argument.

Milton Pugh, the Majority Whip, congressmen from New York, Michigan, Georgia, Kansas and South Carolina rounded up the opposition.

And only Kane and Milton Pugh claimed certain knowledge of the outcome as the feverish battle moved on to its crisis.

In support of Kane, the gentleman from Ohio said, "In all history there has never been a reformer who did not have to fight off the ignorant, the beguiled, the entrenched and the envious. . ."

A fist fight started in the gallery, and while action on the floor stopped, and congressmen strained for a glimpse of the brief struggle, the combatants, still swinging at one another, were separated and carried off by policemen.

Stu Denton took his place at the podium. "Your vote today can be an affirmation of our will to rid America of its Fifth Column, or it can be an invitation to the country's traitors to continue their treachery. I've heard the gentleman from North Carolina slandered by the well-rehearsed Minority. But where were they when Kane O'Connor first discovered the Red menace? Where were they when he called witness after witness to testify and was rebuffed by civil servants who pleaded the Fifth Amendment? Where were they when he revealed infiltration of the National Experimental Center? Where were they . . ."

"Will the gentleman yield?"

Stu allowed a question, and the gentleman from Minnesota said, "If the gentleman will answer a few questions that all America is asking, I promise I shall answer the questions he poses so rhetorically. Tell me, where was the gentleman from North Carolina when his agents were rifling security files, defying a direct order of the President? Where was the gentleman from North Carolina when fantastic sums of money were received by his office and dispensed under the guise of fighting communism. . ."

"I yielded for a question," Stu Denton protested to the Speaker. "The gentleman from Minnesota is making a speech, and a scurrilous one at that . . ."

The gentleman from Minnesota, undeterred, raised his voice. "Where was the gentleman from North Carolina when reputations were dragged in the muck, when constitutional safeguards were ignored, when lies and trickery and deceit were employed in a campaign so vicious, so devoid of decency that honest men must sicken with disgust . . ."

"Mr. Speaker!" The gentleman from New Jersey waved for recognition. "I move that the words of the gentleman from

Minnesota be taken down and that he be seated, by force, if necessary!"

"I'll tell you where the gentleman from North Carolina was," the gentleman from Minnesota shouted.

"Take your seat!" some one called from the Republican ranks.

"Shame!" another congressman yelled.

"He was here!" the gentleman from Minnesota said, ignoring the gavel, the cries of outrage. "He was here in this House. And if we allow him to remain, we compound . . ."

The Speaker flailed away with his gavel, and at last the gentleman from Minnesota stopped and the angry shouts of other congressmen were halted. "The gentleman from Minnesota has done violence to the rules of the House." At the Speaker's direction, the clerk read his remarks.

"Where was the gentleman from North Carolina when his agents were rifling the security files, when fantastic sums of money . . . when reputations were dragged in the muck . . . when lies and trickery and deceit . . . He was here. He was here in this House . . ."

When the clerk had finished, the Speaker ordered the offending congressman to take his seat. But he had already left the chamber and was being congratulated by some of his colleagues in one of the cloakrooms.

Twice during the incident, Kane—his face red with fury, perspiration beaded on his forehead, damp palms clutching the sides of his chair—started to rise. And each time Ward Roberts, at his side, insisted that he remain mute. When it was over, Kane's rage still gripped him, and in the catalogue of his memory, he entered the name of the gentleman from Minnesota, and swore vengeance.

"Mr. Speaker!" The Majority Leader stood, and leaning on the table before him, began to speak. "Gentlemen, although . . ."

"Mr. Speaker! Point of order!" Stu Denton called from his seat. "I did not relinquish the floor. In the confusion during the outburst of the gentleman from Minnesota, I neglected to yield to the gentleman from Illinois . . ."

The Speaker nodded. "The gentleman did, indeed, neglect to yield, and has taken his seat. The distinguished gentleman from Maine, the Majority Leader, requested recognition. He has the floor."

"Mr. Speaker, I protest!" Stu Denton said, and turned away from Kane's angry glance.

The Speaker leaned forward. "Does the gentleman wish to have the Speaker overruled?"

Stu Denton sat down. And Kane whispered to him. "That bastard's in it with the rest of them!"

Abel Garren again started to speak. "Gentlemen, although tempers are badly frayed and the hour approaches midnight, I intend to keep the House in session until this debate is finished and the resolution is voted upon. We have to take action on other matters; and it is obvious to all, I think, that we will transact no business unless this matter is disposed of . . ."

Kane whispered to Stu Denton. "Move for postponement to a day certain. I'll show these bastards!"

"Not now, Kane. Earlier it might have worked, but now that the Majority Leader's announced he wants to stay in session, you'll be buttin' heads with him when he's got all the advantages of tradition on his side. We might not muster enough to win on a procedural point. And that would make us look bad."

"Do as I say, dammit! You gave him his chance. I've been pushed around enough. You do it, or I will!"

"Wait a few minutes. Wait until you've cooled off and can think sensibly, until we can talk to Ward and the others."

Kane stood, and the stir of conversation that welcomed him forged his determination. "Mr. Speaker, I move that action on the proposed resolution be postponed until . . ."

The Majority Leader, still on his feet, heard Kane out, whispering to the Whip beside him, "All right, my friend, you wanted it; and here we go." When Kane had stated his motion, Abel Garren told the House, "The gentleman from North Carolina is surely privileged to make such a motion, but I have pointed out . . ."

"I want a vote on my motion," Kane said, glaring at him. "And when we get it, we'll go home."

Abel Garren caught Winfield Parcher's glance, and then his shrug as he turned away, apparently unconcerned. "Is the gentleman from North Carolina afraid to have full debate on the resolution, and to have it tonight?" Garren said. "Is that why he wishes to postpone action, and with it, to postpone consideration of important legislation . . . ?"

"It is not!" Kane flared back. "The most important thing before this House, as far as I'm concerned, is the attack being made against me. I have put up with your cavalier handling of this debate; and I've watched silently while you had your bullyboys scrawl over my character like dirty-minded thugs writing on the walls of filling station washrooms, while you went about the odorous task— assigned to you by the resident of 1600 Pennsylvania Avenue— of shooting down a critic who has exposed the failures of the Administration. But I will not allow you to maneuver this House as you see fit, disregarding the rights of its members. You want to continue your organized vilification; and the vast majority of this House wants time to rest, to consider the ugly performance of your assassins, and to return at a later date to vote as they must vote, disregarding the pressures being forced on them by the leadership!"

"The sonovabitch!" the Whip whispered.

Abel Garren held his temper in check. "I ask the gentleman from North Carolina if I should resign and allow him to give this House his brand of leadership."

Kane replied, "I seek no honors. I seek no approving nod from the President in hopes of inheriting his mantle. I seek no license to attack my colleagues in this chamber, no matter what our disagreements. The gentleman from Maine, the distinguished Majority Leader, can not say the same. He may do as he likes. I seek only a vote on postponement . . ."

"Well," Matt said to Dany, "he did it. Kane's forced the issue; and somebody's going to get clobbered. He's a fool."

"How long did you expect him to keep still while they romped all over him?" Dany said, and was silenced by correspondents on either side who, taut with the excitement of the moment, strained to hear every word spoken on the floor.

It was a test of strength between the Majority Leader and Kane O'Connor. And Abel Garren knew, as he searched the faces of the members of the House, that to a man they were waiting to see what he would do. If he backed down now, agreed with Kane and so avoided the chance of defeat on a vote, he would be surrendering. On the other hand, if the vote came, and he lost it, his own prestige would be seriously undermined and the fight against O'Connor might be lost. "Mr. Speaker," he said, but his eyes were on Winfield Parcher who looked at him for a second and then dropped his gaze. "Mr. Speaker, the gentleman from North Carolina is within his rights. He wants a vote . . ."

"Will the gentleman yield?" Winfield Parcher was standing across the aisle, a grim smile pulling at the corners of his mouth.

"Gladly," Abel Garren said, and relieved, took his seat. He had known, somehow, that he could depend on Win, and listened intently now, curious to find which direction that help would take.

The Minority Leader said, "Mr. Speaker, I question the presence of a quorum . . ." And then, though it was obvious that the House was rapidly filling with the few members who had stepped out and were now, advised of the action on the floor, rushing back, the Speaker directed that the roll be called.

While the clerk tolled the names, Win Parcher crossed the aisle, and sat down beside Abel Garren. "You're too slick for anyone but me," he said with a grin. "You maneuvered him into this situation . . ."

"Like hell! Honestly, Win . . ." The Majority Leader started to protest, then shrugged. "Okay, I maneuvered him into it. Now we've got to take him."

"We, huh?" Win Parcher said. "Well, Abel, I guess we old dogs have to defend our prerogatives, but that's all I'm doing."

When the Speaker announced that a quorum was present, Abel Garren stood. "Mr. Speaker, since the gentleman from North Carolina desires that the House postpone consideration to a day certain, and my views are diametrically opposed to his, I humbly state to my colleagues of the Majority that I consider this forthcoming vote a vote of confidence or of no-confidence in my leadership. If the gentleman from North Carolina is upheld in his motion, it is my intention to resign."

There was a yell of "Blackmail!" from the rear of the chamber; and at that instant, reporters broke and ran up the steps in the press gallery, one shouting above the noise in the room, "Oh, my God!" as he fell over a row of seats. And the floor buzzed with amazement as the Majority Leader threw the full force of his great influence into the vote on procedure.

Dany said, "Kane's got to withdraw the motion, Matt!" Pained, she pulled at his arm. "He's got to get out of it gracefully, and he's got to speak for himself."

"Kane doesn't know how to take a direct slap," Matt said. "I've got ten bucks that says he'll stick to his guns rather than lose face. And ten more that says the House'll stay here all night if Abel Garren says so. He's got old Win Parcher on his side now, too."

On the floor below, the Speaker was hammering away, finally restoring order. And the Minority Leader had gotten the floor briefly. "Although the gentleman from North Carolina has raised the question of whether or not the distinguished gentleman from Maine does, in fact, speak for the Majority," he said, underfilling the issue, and facing Kane as he did so, "I am sure that I do represent the will of the Minority. And I am in agreement that, since important legislation awaits disposition and we can surely not talk sanely on anything until the matter before the House is behind us, we should continue in session until such time as we are ready to vote on the resolution."

"Kane's had it," Matt said to Dany.

She was writing a note to Kane, looking first at the paper, then at the floor, afraid it might be too late. *Darling,* she wrote, *give way on this. Not that important. And then get up there and defend yourself!*

Meanwhile, Stu Denton was giving Kane that same advice "Withdraw the motion, because if you don't, even people who'd be against the resolution, will support the Majority Leader. Please! And when you've done that, ask Garren to yield to you. He'll damned near have to do it. . . ."

"No!" Ward Roberts insisted. "We can beat them; and when we do, it'll be proof to every wavering vote in the House that we can win on the resolution. You don't want the floor. You can't speak against the resolution. They'll be interrupting you every ten seconds, asking you to yield for questions . . ."

Kane felt imprisoned by his own action; and he could see clearly enough that he might, after all, be beaten. While the Minority Leader continued to speak, Kane, his mind in turmoil, tried to think his way out of his problem. And then Dany's note arrived; and he read it, glancing up at her when he had finished. Fighting against an impulse to seek the showdown, throttling the pride that nearly overpowered his reason, he forced himself to rise when Winfield Parcher was seated. "Mr. Speaker," Kane said, and in that brief moment was tempted to plunge recklessly ahead. "Mr. Speaker. . ." An oppressive silence, the breathless awe of the hundreds around him, the steady, unblinking gaze of Abel Garren,

Milton Pugh's embittered glare—Kane was hemmed in on every side. "My political life," he said at last, "is at stake here; and I . . . I intend to save it, but I have no intention of forcing my colleagues to make a choice between . . . between . . ." He groped for the right words. ". . . between simple justice on one hand and their party duties on the other. Despite the heat of this debate, I have great respect for the Majority Leader, and I have no wish to embarrass him, no wish to lose his distinguished leadership. Therefore, I withdraw my motion . . ."

Again there was an exodus from the press gallery. Matt, without a word, handed Dany a ten-dollar bill. And the House, as if all its members were relaxing with a sigh, settled back once more.

"You've got to give him credit," Abel Garren said to Milton Pugh and the Whip. "He gets out of it practically intact. And, thank God, we didn't vote."

Milton Pugh said, "It hurt him just the same. We've got him now, by damn. We've got him!"

Kane, still speaking, looked toward the Majority Leader, without meeting his eyes. "I assume, Mr. Speaker, that the distinguished gentleman from Maine still has the floor, and I ask that he yield to me so that I may briefly state my position to the House."

"I yield to the gentleman from North Carolina," Abel Garren said, "and I request that he, in turn, yield to me when he has finished his remarks."

Dany clasped her hands together, her fingernails biting into her palms, and she prayed silently that Kane could wrest a victory from the shambles. "You'll see. You'll see," she whispered to Matt as Kane strode to the dais.

Kane put his notes before him, and in the pervasive silence, turned to survey the chamber, as if he might look into every face, as if the confrontation might bring him closer to each of his colleagues, to every visitor in the galleries. "It is a sad and strange thing, an evil thing that is happening to me here today. Those who attack me use a single weapon." He smiled ruefully. "They talk about means and methods. They say I smear these Communists. They say I lie about the grave danger they are doing here in America." He paused, moving his head slowly from side to side. "But they think it's perfectly all right for them to smear and slander and libel Kane O'Connor. It's only a sin when Kane

O'Connor exposes Communists by using methods these people do not like . . ."

Matt chewed on his eraser. He's a past master, he conceded. Looking at Dany, sensing her anxiety, he patted her hand.

"Yes, they condemn my exposure of this cancer that is eating away at America's heart. And these people who do so, unfortunately, are not the Communists alone. Instead, the Left-wing gang of the poorly-informed, the fellow-travelers, the egghead liberals—these voices join the chorus." He bowed his head, and his sigh could be heard in the quiet of the chamber. "I'm not bothered by the taunts of the Reds, but I am greatly disturbed by the willing help given to them by a few of my misguided colleagues in this House!"

Kane stepped back and again glanced over the room, seeing that all were held by his words. He recognized the friendly faces, the doubtful ones, the hostile ones. He watched the stir in the galleries. Then, turning suddenly in the silence, he smashed his fist against the podium and raised his voice. "But no one is going to be misled by this attempt to stop our investigation of the godless forces of international communism." He pointed to the spectators above him. "Least of all, my friends, will the American people be misled. I have great faith in the American people. They have expressed themselves at the polls on this issue. And they have driven from office those who were willing to silence our exposure of subversion." He tapped a pencil against his notes, and the sound was as a metronome in the silent chamber. "And they will do it again!"

He waited, wetting his lips, nodding at his listeners. "They will recognize—and I trust you will recognize—that this attack against me is of simple origin. The word has come down from the White House to muzzle O'Connor. O'Connor, you see, has not hesitated to expose the flaws of the Administration. O'Connor has gone over their heads to the people. O'Connor has not tried to protect anyone. O'Connor is only interested in getting on with this business of chasing the skunks out of the government. . . ."

Dany looked at Matt. He had stopped writing and was listening intently.

"What, you may ask, finally proved too much for them? I dared to challenge the totalitarian concept of Executive privilege. I dared to insist that, in a democracy, no one has the right to withhold information from the representatives of the people. And daring, I acted. I believe that if the President is not challenged on this issue now, the time will come when the only facts the people will get are those that the President decides they should have. The time will come when this House will have to act on the blind dictation of the President. And that time is not as far away as you think! The National Experimental Center is supported by appropriations originating in this chamber. Surely no one will deny that the Congress of the United States has a duty to appraise the functions of any agency so important to the security of the nation!" Kane's arms stretched out to his listeners and, plaintively, in a whisper, he asked, "Am I wrong?" Then, louder, "Am I wrong?"

His voice still echoing, he beat the edge of the podium with his hand. "I . . . am . . . not. Pray God I am not! Gentlemen, if you —by your action here today—agree to the proposition that the Executive Branch and its bureaucratic minions can hide any sort of treachery and corruption by simply refusing to tell the people what they are entitled to know, if you agree to that, you are presiding at the funeral of our democratic nation!"

Although his job was to understand the workings of the legislature, Matt still held to an illusion of the dignity of government. Now he heard the Presidency attacked openly, heard charges of treachery and treason hurled.

". . . So the order has come down, directing this House to act. There was a time when we would have fought against such an encroachment. There was a time—and I pray God that time will be resurrected—when every member of this body would have arisen in protest against such an Executive fiat. But this nation has been hindered for many years by a bunch of radicals hungry for power, enslaved by the doctrines of Marx, cowed by the masters of the Kremlin. These people will not be content until they reduce this House to the status of rubber stamp, until our Constitudon is a shambles and a mockery! The Kremlin's orders are being mouthed. The instructions say: Stop O'Connor at any price—at the price of your honor, at the price of your sense of justice, at the price of America's future!"

Kane lowered his voice, speaking sofdy once more, no longer angry. "My friends, there was only one life ever lived upon this earth which did not have error and failure and sin in it. There was only one soul . . . only one . . . that was completely free of pride and selfishness. And that was the life of Jesus Christ." He paused, swallowing visibly, as if he were moved by the simple truth of his own words. "I've made mistakes. I'm heir to all the weaknesses of mortals . . . anger and hatred and impatience and obstinacy. I'm not proud of those human frailties. But, gentlemen, erring though I may have been at times, I have always tried to do what I believed was right. And, if nothing else, I know and you know and the people know that I have made this nation aware of its peril. So I ask you to refuse the orders sent down to this House. I ask you to reassert the independence of Congress. I ask you to vindicate the faith and judgment of the people. I ask you to say to all America that the fight will continue. And then, God willing, I shall win it!"

A demonstration erupted in the gallery, a torrent of applause that began with the American Patriots and swept over all the spectators until it reached the floor where Kane's supporters were standing, cheering him. Amazingly, there was applause from the press gallery where Dany, her eyes wet with tears of pride and tenderness, still gripped by the drama on the floor, clapped alone. Matt smiled and handed her his handkerchief as she leaned forward and peered over the railing.

The Speaker hammered for order, and still, one lone woman dared shout, "God bless you, Kane O'Connor!"

Kane had not returned to his seat. Touching the extended hands offered to him from either side of the aisle, he walked out of the chamber, and left his fate to his friends.

"Until now, when I listened to him, and found myself half-agreeing with lots that he said, I never realized how dangerous that man is," Winfield Parcher told Abel Garren.

The Majority Leader yielded to still another gentleman from North Carolina. Within ten minutes, three representatives from Kane's home state had spoken, all declaring against him. Then, rapidly, surprising everyone in the House, the Majority Leader took the floor. "Mr. Speaker, I ask for the Yeas and Nays."

Once more reporters rushed for the phones to flash the news, and the chamber was disrupted by a demonstration in the galleries. Stu Denton rushed out, frantically searching for Kane; and in the confusion, the Speaker said, "The Yeas and Nays are ordered. The clerk will call the roll."

Again silence, broken only by the clerk's monotone, the anticipatory breath, the drone of comment after each vote was recorded. "Abbey . . ."

"No."

"Agnew . . ."

"No."

"Ahern . . . Allen . . . Amon . . . Babcock . . ."

"Ten for Kane, seven against," Matt whispered.

And Dany gripped his arm, and biting her lip, sighed. "He'll win . . . he'll win . . ."

"Cabiness . . ."

"Yes . . ."

"Caddimon . . ."

"Yes . . ."

"Chamison . . ."

"No!"

All over the chamber, legislators were keeping the count. Stu Denton rushed back to his seat in time to vote. "No!" he shouted, and then whispered to Ray Hyder, "I couldn't find him. He's wandering the halls or something."

"Dreyfus . . . Duval . . . Elrod . . . Emmans . . ."

"We're ahead by six," Milton Pugh said to the Whip.

And when the roll had reached "Vanimmon . . . Vogel . . ." the Whip whispered to the Majority Leader. "Closer than I figured."

Milton Pugh said, "All but one from North Carolina went against him!"

"Watlin . . . Weaver . . . Wilbern . . ."

But by that time, the result was obvious. And when the clerk read the names of the absentees and reported the vote, the Speaker announced, "Two hundred and twenty-eight having voted yea, 207 nay, the resolution is agreed to . . ." the tension exploded in the chamber.

"I've got to find him," Dany said to Matt as he helped her up the steps to the doors of the press gallery. "With everything against him, he came so close! He really won. He proved they'll never get the two-thirds to expel him. . . . never. . . . Help me find him! Please, Matt!"

And Matt put his arm around her, and pretended not to see the tears in her eyes. "Maybe he'd just like to be left alone for awhile, Dany."

An hour later, Kane—aware of his defeat and unwilling to face his friends and enemies in the House Chamber—stood in the muted light of Statuary Hall, dwarfed by the famous, whose likenesses stared blindly on every side. Henry Clay. Daniel Webster. John C. Calhoun. Sam Houston. Robert E. Lee. Huey P. Long.

The room was silent, and resting against the cold bronze statue of William Jennings Bryan, Kane finished his cigarette, flipped it to the floor and plodded slowly across the black and white marble, heels sounding, echoing, and rubbed the glowing tip into dust.

Why? Kane asked himself. Why has it happened to me? Walking away, through the empty passageways, past the deserted cloakrooms, his mind, dulled by defeat, still sought the reason for his troubles.

He passed no one on his way, and only oppressive quiet greeted him as he entered the House chamber and walked down the aisle to his seat. For a moment, he sat there, exhausted, and looked across the silent room, at the curving rows of committee desks, at the tiered Speaker's dais, at the void of the galleries. He was alone.

Why me? he asked himself again. And the only answer he found was that he had dared to rise above the others. Looking at the empty seats around him, he peopled them with familiar faces, thinking: I'm so far above them. And that's why they've been fighting me. They're jealous of my power, jealous because the only power they know is based on petty corruption and deceit. They're willing to come to Washington to listen, but never be heard. They're willing to vote as they're told—by pressure from Old Hands or pressure from home. They read simple speeches into *The Record.* They send home folksy newsletters. They never miss a reception and rarely miss a roll call. They're reasonably faithful to their wives and to their party. They're unknown here, but they're big men in their districts. They get re-elected.

It was a miracle, he had decided, that anything could be accomplished through them. The roof above them covered a variety of prejudices and differences, feuds and strange alliances.

There were many puny men there. Few brilliant ones. At best, they were well-meaning, but ordinary—stalwart members of a cult of mediocrity.

Blind to his own limitations, he was contemptuous of them. What qualified them to declare wars? What did these stolid men know about famine in India or currency fluctuations in England? What made them aware of the repercussions of reciprocal trade, the challenge of foreign imports? Were these plain, drab politicians statesmen who could debate on aid to Afghanistan and independence to the Philippines? Were these uninformed people farm specialists that they could vote sanely on parity prices and government granaries? What qualified these provincials to speak and act for industry and labor, agriculture and medicine and education and the arts?

These men who sat beside him, he believed, plodded on, wading through a thousand miles of papers and reports, through a hundred million words spoken on the floor. They stood by while the unwieldly, creaking, tortuously-slow machinery operated. And they thought they made the laws!

Kane had discarded that notion early in his career. He was certain that sanity prevailed, order emerged, and legislation resulted because a few strong men—ignoring the bumbling followers, ignoring the intellectual quacks—made the decisions. The action, for the most part, took place in the caucus room, in the cloakroom, at a cocktail party, in the Speaker's office, in the Majority Leader's limousine, in committee. The rest was sham, was only a trick mirror which gave the illusion of representative government. He did not know or understand the patient, even dull men who with a high sense of purpose, compromised and traded and investigated and read memoranda and listened to speeches and queried their constituents and worked with legislative aides and studied statistics. He could not accept that part for himself. He wanted to be heard and seen and consulted. Well, he hadn't done so badly, he thought. He was somebody! Who in America hadn't heard Kane O'Connor's name?

This reasoning produced no answer. It only reiterated the question: Why has this happened to me?

The lights began to go out. Kane lifted his dispatch case as if it were a great load, and trudged up the aisle and out of the darkened chamber.

42

THE DIRECTOR, sitting in the soundproof control booth in New York City, watched the wall clock. Then, cutting the air with his hand, he gave the signal that sent the image of Matt Fallon to millions of television screens.

Sitting on the edge of his studio desk, Matt faced the cameras. "Tonight we are going to spend some time with someone you know. You've read about him in your newspapers and magazines. You've seen him on television and in the newsreels. You've heard his background discussed by senators and scientists, by commentators, and by your own friends. He's not a politician, not a diplomat or a soldier or an inventor or a movie celebrity. Still, you'll recognize him at once. And in that recognition, we believe, is reflected the peril of our times."

He reached for the photograph on his desk, and the camera dollied in for a closeup of the picture. "Yes, this is Leon Hoke. A few months ago, his neighbors would have identified him as a man of thirty-seven, married, with eight-year-old twin sons. They would have known that he worked at the National Experiment Center, that his wife played the organ in the First Methodist Church, that he was active in the Rotary Club and was membership chairman of the Community Concert Association. And a few of his close friends would have known that he was paying off the mortgage on his FHA-financed home, that his salary is seventy-five hundred dollars a year and that he rarely speaks of his war service."

Camera 2 pulled back to a long shot. "Today Leon Hoke doesn't see much of his friends, is no longer active in civic work. And some of his neighbors appraise thim differently."

The director cut to the projector and to a filmed scene of a meeting hall.

"Our cameramen were on hand when the Larendon County American Patriots met two weeks ago. . . ."

On the screen, a short, jovial-looking man, crowned with a halo of gray, rapped with his gavel. "The motion calls for a petition to be circulated requesting that Leon Hoke be asked to move from this community. Is there any further discussion?"The camera caught a closeup of a waving hand, then found the speaker, a handsome man in shirtsleeves. "The way I see it, Hoke sold out this country. I'm for letting him go back to Russia since he likes it so much."

The woman beside him nodded sagely. "Maybe Hoke'll find out that in Russia they shoot people who've done less."

The screen flashed with quick shots of the approving expression of an old man, the serious face of a grammar school teacher, the thoughtful chin rubbing of a businessman, the disapproving grimace of a high school student, his hand cupped to his ear, listening.

The teacher was recognized. "Before we pass this motion, I think we should go over all the facts again. After all, this is a serious thing. A man's future's at stake here."

She was interrupted by the old man. "We're all 100 per cent behind Congressman Kane O'Connor. He's been exposing Reds long enough to recognize one when he sees him. . . ."

At that moment—two weeks after he had lost his fight in the House—Kane threw his newspaper to the floor of Dany's living room. "I let you have your way, Ward. I let you call the subcommittee meeting and preside!" He glared at Ward who sat opposite him, stiff in a straight chair. "We were going to show we're not a one-man outfit. We were going to announce an investigation on Annapolis! We were going to give the papers something else to chew on!"

Ward spoke coolly. "You don't have to shout, Kane. I tried to get them to go along with us. Then Pugh brought up the motion to suspend all hearings until action is taken on the charges against you—one way or the other." He took his handkerchief from his breast pocket, dabbed at his forehead, refolded the four points carefully, and stuffed it back. "I couldn't prevent a vote. Denton and Brantley went along with Pugh."

Kane slumped in an easy chair. "I've got a bunch of lily-livered idiots for friends."

"I did my best," Ward insisted. "You're excited now, Kane. It's my fault for suggesting you let me hold the meeting while you were speaking in Manton. But I thought the others would join me in giving you a vote of confidence. I've been on your side from the start. And if you take my advice now, you'll ride this thing out. Meanwhile, I'll talk to some of the boys on the investigating committee. I've got some friends there, Kane. I can nose around and find out just what they're doing, and when they'll be ready to bring a report to the floor."

Kane ran his hand over his beaded forehead. "All right. What else can I do?"

Ward stood. "Sorry for what's happened. I've lost plenty of sleep over it, believe me." He grasped Kane's shoulder. "I want you to know that you can count on me."

"Sure. Sorry I blew up," Kane said as he walked to the door with his friend. "When you talk to your contacts on the committee, feel around to see what charges they're going to push." When Ward had gone, Kane came back into the room. "They're out to get me," he told Dany.

She put her hands in his. "We'll lick them," she said. "Lie down on the sofa, darling. I'll get you something to drink. And we can talk it out."

He accepted a pillow, dropping it behind him and stretching out. "Come here."

As he moved to make room for her, she sat beside him. "We've got to keep our heads, darling."

"I'm going to get Pugh and Garren. They'll find out who they're butting heads with—just like Shep did!"

"Forget about them. Your only job right now is to defend yourself." Bending over him, she smoothed the hair from his forehead. "Sweetheart, the only reason for this fight against you is to get you off the back of the Administration . . ."

"You're damned right! They're furious because of what I did with the N.E.C. I made the President look like a jackass. We've got to get one thing across," he said. "We've got to show that the investigation is just a device to keep me from exposing Reds."

"No! If all they want is to silence you, let them do it. They don't expect to get the votes to expel you, Kane. No matter what the investigation committee recommends, they're too canny to believe that. All they hope to do is scare you off. And all you have to do is let them have what they want. I've been telling you, darling. We don't need it any longer. Go to them yourself. Let them know you're dropping the whole business. Then you'll be free to work without this constant pressure, this sandbagging by the papers, the threat of being unseated." She was arguing desperately, knowing all the while that she wasn't reaching him.

Kane wasn't listening to her. "We've got to do some probing on Pugh and Garren. See what we can get on them. We'll run a check on the whole Cabinet, too. And then we've got to see what we can find out about every member of that investigating committee. Norm can get started tomorrow."

"But, Kane, that's not important," she insisted. "We've got to work out the best plan to defend you, that's all. We've got to get our records in order, have to be able to answer the charges one by one." Noting his inattention, she tried to turn his face, to make him look at her. "Then, even if the committee recommends expulsion proceedings, even if the Administration won't agree to drop the whole thing, you can put your case before the country, and make a convincing defense. It's practically unheard of to unseat a member; and I believe they'll never let it get to the floor, if you'll only give them some assurances. They don't want to bring this thing to a vote. They can't afford to lose any more than you can; and tradition is all on your side. Don't force them to gamble, Kane. Let them know you're through attacking the Administration."

He sat up. "I haven't started yet!"

"Don't be so damned stubborn!"

The phone rang. Dany answered it. It was Hattie, Kane's correspondence secretary. "I've been trying to get Kane," she said, excited.

"What is it?"

"You have Matt Fallon's show on the television?"

"No."

"Turn it on."

Dany found the channel. The lines wavered, then straightened. Matt's voice boomed over the speaker, and she adjusted the volume.

Matt's face filled the screen. "The debate of the American Patriots was only one result of the charges leveled against Leon Hoke."

The scene dissolved. A kinescope recording of the N.E.C. hearings followed. Kane saw himself sitting across from the witness, heard his voice indicting the man. He nodded as his image on the screen voiced the charges: Hoke had early communist connections. His wife was a member of the Cleveland Alliance, a communist front. Byron Paul, a Red agent, visited their home and later discussed politics with Hoke. Hoke distributed literature of the National Council of American-Soviet Friendship. He invited Dr. Nathaniel Duris to speak to his co-workers. . . .

Again Matt appeared. He was standing behind his desk. "Now what is Leon Hoke's defense? Up to this moment, few people know. Up to this moment, he has had no opportunity to defend himself. The case against him appears formidable. He is a man who once visited Russia at the invitation of that government and apparently his recent activities fall into a suspicious pattern."

Matt glanced at the teleprompter. "The tragedy of this man," he continued, "is that he has not had the power to fight back. Tennyson once said:

That a lie which is half a truth is ever the blackest of lies,
That a lie which is all a lie may be met and fought with outright,
But a lie which is part truth is a harder matter to fight."

Kane took Dany's cigarette from her lips, inhaled and blew smoke toward the screen. In the next few minutes, Matt Fallon answered the charges against Leon Hoke.

First he presented Mrs. Anna Hoke, a slight, youthful-looking woman, squinting without her glasses, wearing her best dress: "The Cleveland Alliance was a piano and organ teachers' association. I moved from Cleveland three years before it became communist-dominated. . . .

An N.E.C. supervisor was interviewed as he passed through the guarded gates of the Center. Ill at ease, he punctuated his comments with a series of coughs: "Leon had Duris here all right. But that was when he was program chairman—that is, Leon was program chairman—of our current events club. Duris talked on the Far East, I remember. Sounded sort of pinko, all right. But at that time he was teaching at Columbia. Guess they didn't know he was a commie, either."

Kane was flushed, furious. He spat a piece of tobacco off his tongue, and glanced at Dany who sat on the floor before the set, intent on the screen.

Josiah Martingale spoke from his office: "Byron Paul was a student of Mrs. Hoke's. He was under surveillance at the time and there is no question but that there was little personal contact between him and Mr. Hoke. It is probable that Paul became a student of Mrs. Hoke, hoping to make contact with her husband, but there is no indication that he succeeded. Furthermore, we believe that Mr. Hoke's right to exchange political views with anyone is unchallenged. It is also most significant that, at the time of Paul's arrest, the Hokes voluntarily contributed the little information they had. The case was reviewed by our security board and Mr. Hoke was completely exonerated."

Matt was before the camera again. "Leon Hoke did distribute literature for the National Council of American-Soviet Friendship. But, at that time, the organization had on its board of directors some of the nation's most respected men and women." He held up a letterhead. "Across its stationery were written the names of generals, educators, bankers and cabinet members." A closeup of the display appeared. "It is patently unfair to judge with hindsight Leon Hoke's lack of foresight—or, for that matter, the lack of foresight of the distinguished people whose names appeared on the council's letterhead."

Dany moved to turn the set off. Kane stopped her.

Glancing at the monitor, Matt picked up the photograph of Leon Hoke. "So here is a man who—at the age of nineteen—returned from Russia, having discovered that the dream he had conjured up by his reading of Marx and Engels was fraudulent, and who recorded his change of heart in print in a series of articles for his church publication and in an open letter published by his college magazine. Here is a man who—eighteen years ago—publicly repudiated the organization that sponsored his trip. This is the man whose hearing was impaired after volunteering and serving as a medic at Bastogne, yet his patriotism is being questioned all over America."

Matt put the picture aside. "But Leon Hoke has friends, too, not only among his associates and his neighbors, but across this country. Through him, more Americans are becoming aware of the danger of Kane O'Connor. All over this nation they are beginning to protest, through their representatives, through their publications and their organizations. They are refusing to cringe before the threatening roars of a politician who has been corrupted by his own ambition, whose ruthless desire to make himself feared knows no end. They see clearly that he avoids facts—that he misrepresents, that he overemphasizes, that he decides what he wants to prove and sets out to prove it. And though they recognize the dangers of communist subversion, they know that we will not be destroyed by the Russians until we have been weakened and corrupted by the O'Connors."

Again the director switched to the projector and Matt's voice rose over the scene in the meeting hall. "There are, of course, the members of the minority who see O'Connor in a different light. The American Patriots passed their resolution against Leon Hoke. Then they stood before adjournment to sing their club song, to the tune of 'God Bless America.'"

The camera panned along the rows of singers as the piano played accompaniment:

> *Hail, American Patriots!*
> *Hail, American Way!*
> *We are ready,*
> *To stand steady*
> *And to rout out the A-D-A!*
> *Fighting Radicals!*
> *Fighting Commies!*
> *Fighting Dealers—*
> *"Fair" and "New"*
> *Hail, American Patriots!*
> *All Hail to You!*

As the scene faded, Matt smiled grimly. "Before our time, of course, there were other American patriots. They were men who believed in the importance of the individual, in his dignity, in his right to dissent, in his right to change his mind, in his right to defend himself."

The camera dollied in for a closeup of the big, freckled, pug face. "And those American patriots gave us our independence, our Constitution and our Bill of Rights. To them we owe due process of law and trial by jury. They, like many of us, were concerned with the future, concerned with the importance of the little man—of Leon Hoke. Good night and good news."

Dany switched off the set.

"The dirty, back-stabbing sonovabitch!" Kane swore.

43

KANE WAS no longer unchallenged.

His strength had been augmented by the illusion of great public support. Now that illusion began to dissipate as the investigation of his activities began. Kane's devout followers, never in the majority, but always the most vocal, opposed the investigation, seeing it as retaliation by his enemies. But millions more, who had objected to him in silence, or had dismissed him as a rabble-rouser, or had feared that to oppose him was to become an ally of Communists, or had been indifferent or had been undecided, now joined the rising chorus against him.

Hounded by newsmen, badgered by the clashing editorials all over the country, inundated by thousands of letters that either deified or vilified him, still trying to organize his staff for the fight ahead, Kane received the air time he had demanded to answer Matt Fallon's indictment.

With Tod, he went to New York for the telecast while Dany and Norman worked over the statistics and reports, the lists of unco-operative witnesses, the new changes in security regulations since Kane's campaign against Communists, the "pertinent excerpts from hearings"—all of which, they believed, would provide proof of Kane's accomplishments.

"You will notice, my friends, that many of your representatives have no time for the fight against the Communists," Kane told his audience. "They are too busy joining in the fight against O'Connor. And how do they excuse themselves? They tell you: 'O'Connor really hasn't accomplished anything.'"

Nodding, shaking his head as he bit at his lip, sighing in exasperation, Kane said, "My friends, you are my defense. Ask yourself—and answer it truthfully—whether or not you were aware of the extent of communist infiltration into our government before I brought these things to your attention. If you give the answer millions of Americans must give, you will acknowledge that, contrary to what you are being told, I have not failed you.

"I have sought nothing for myself. I have no power, no voice in the political realm. No organization bears my name. No political machine is guided by my direction. I have only wanted to make the American people aware. I have only wanted to be their tool, not to make them mine. . . ."

Kane finished his text with forty seconds time remaining. Pushing his papers aside, clasping his hands before him on the desk, speaking softly, he ad-libbed, "Let the Left-wing newspapers and commentators, the fellow-travelers and their communist friends rant and rave and lie and deceive, I have dedicated myself to this great task; and I will not be deterred."

After the program, Kane and Tod left the studio.

"I promised Cy I'd take Laurie to dinner," Tod said as they entered the elevator. "Like to come?"

"How did you get in touch with her?"

"Cy gave me her address. She's working here, lives at the Barbizon—it's a hotel for women at Sixty-third and Lexington."

"Give her my regards."

"I will."

The doors pulled back, releasing them to the crowded lobby. "See you in the morning," Kane promised, as he left Tod at the entrance. Then he walked to a phone booth and called Lenore at Della's.

Kane reached above him in the darkness and flipped the switch on the bed lamp. He looked at his wristwatch: 2 A.M. Leaning on one elbow, he bent over Lenore and tugged the blue silk sheet from her face. She still slept, on her side, her tiny hands clenched and pressed against her cheeks. "Lenore?" He moved her hands. "Lenore?"

She awakened, blinking. "Lenore is in dreamland," she whispered, closing her eyes again.

"I haven't slept at all."

She curled up again. "Try it. It's good."

He shook her gently. "How about some coffee?"

"Won't help," she murmured.

"Tea?"

Sighing, she pulled the covers aside and stepped to the carpet. "A woman's work is never done," she said resignedly. Nude, she got on her knees and felt for her slippers beneath the bed. Then slipping on her negligee, she shook her head at Kane and opened the door. "Congressman O'Connor," she said sleepily, "with all your other faults, you're also a sadist."

When she had gone, Kane got out of bed and hunted through his coat pocket for a cigarette. They're all on my back, he was thinking. They're all out to crucify me. He put the cigarette in his mouth, but couldn't find a match. He was still looking for one when Lenore returned bearing two cups of tea.

"Here. Drink it. And if you're a good boy and you promise to go to sleep, I'll read your fortune in the leaves and predict a great future, complete with heart attacks for the committee that's gunning for you and ulcers for Matt Fallon."

Kane tucked his cigarette behind his ear, took the cup and sat in a rocking chair beside the bed. "What did you think of my reply to Matt tonight?"

"O'Connor at his best—or worst—according to what side you're on," Lenore said, arranging the pillows behind her so she could sit up in the bed.

"And what side are you on?"

She winked. "Your side."

"Why?"

"Because I admire virgins."

"No, I mean really, what did you think of the show?"

She sipped her tea. "Same thing, Kane. Everybody's wrong but you. Everyone who doesn't think you're America's sweetheart, is automatically a Red or an idiot."

"There *are* Communists in high places, dammit! And anyone who tries to protect them is either an idiot, a sympathizer, or a Red himself!"

"Kane . . . Kane . . ." she said, yawning, "do you really know what the heck's the truth any longer? You've been on this jag so long, repeated it so often, that you repeat it to help yourself believe it."

"You bet I believe it!" Getting to his feet, he sloshed the tea. "Damn!" He put the cup on the night table. "You don't know what the hell you're talking about. I've *proved* that there are commies in the government, haven't I?"

"Well, anyhow, you've made so much noise about it that even I can practically see Stalin's boys goose-stepping—or whatever kind of stepping they do—down Times Square." She smiled at him, mischief glinting in her eyes as she played the familiar game of forcing him to defend himself. One night I'm going to hide reporters under the bed, she thought, giggling at the mental picture of such a scene.

Kane put his cigarette in his mouth. "Where's a match?" She took a packet from her negligee pocket and tossed it to him. "You're not kidding me," he said, drawing deeply and inhaling. "You're out to bait me. Gives you a charge, doesn't it?" He puffed again and blew a ring of smoke in her face.

She laughed at him. "You always give me a charge," she said lewdly. "The Great Man and his lovely paramour. Sure, I like it," she said impishly. "Hey, how'd you like that word, paramour?"

But Kane wouldn't be diverted. He had to talk it out, had to have reassurance. "You just don't know, as most people don't know, what I've done." He walked across the room and flipped the dead match into his cup of tea and turned to her, his face mirroring his anxiety. "My God, what do they want from me? Not a word out of that committee they appointed to frame me, not a hint in the papers, not a leak. And the N.E.C. investigation is what triggered all this!" He bit his lips, and his eyes narrowed. "Must be something we missed, something so devastating they're terrified it'll get out . . . and so they're trying to divert attention . . ."

Lenore put her cup down. "Got a smoke?"

He brought her a cigarette. "Why did the N.E.C. investigation scare them so? You're a smart girl, Lenore. Tell me. Why are they down on me all of a sudden?"

She accepted a light, holding his cupped hands after she had blown out the match. "Kane, I'm here to pleasure you, not to argue," she said, trying to draw him down beside her.

He pulled away. "You're always cracking wise. I want to hear you sound off. Come on, Lenore. Show me you've got a brain!" He had raised his voice and now, conscious of it, he spoke softly. "You're a smart girl. Tell me . . . and I won't get mad, really. Tell me, why is this N.E.C. thing so important to them?" She was sitting with her chin on her knees, watching him. "Well, jimminy, you don't have to get in a stew! All right, Kane. You want to get argued with and pay for it, it's okay with me."

"Well, go on!" he said impatiently.

"Say something, and I'll say different," Lenore said. "You want me to just make up something nasty out of my head?"

"Christ!"

She was pouting, her little girl's face looking at him pathetically. "You want me to say about Matt Fallon, like I think he's right or something?"

"Don't say anything! Just forget it. Don't say a goddamned thing!"

Lenore watched him silently while he flopped in the rocking chair, his back to her. "Kane?" she said plaintively.

"What do you want?"

"I was thinking . . . I mean, ever since Matt Fallon's television program, I've been thinking that maybe Matt's right about that fellow Hoke. And maybe the people who've been against you all along finally got fed up. . . ."

"I thought you told me you didn't see Matt's show."

"Oh! I read about it . . . in the papers . . . I was clipping for my Hate O'Connor Scrapbook . . . and I read it all. And I think Matt Fallon was absolutely right."

"You mean you don't think Hoke's guilty?" he asked incredulously.

"No, I don't," she said and, catching a glimpse of herself in the vanity mirror across the room, she reached for her lipstick and put it on.

"It's not Hoke. He's not worth their trouble. And he's too hard to defend. Lenore, suppose at the moment he's no Red. Okay, I'm not saying he is. But aren't there plenty of decent, loyal Americans who can handle his job, without our jeopardizing our security in the hope that Leon Hoke won't backslide?"

She puffed at her cigarette and leaned back against the pillows, her small face framed in blue. She was trying to remember something she had heard on the six o'clock news. Della had called her into the library . . . and the radio was on . . . and Della had asked her about going on a week-end party . . . and they'd talked about what to wear . . . and a senator . . . or maybe the governor . . . Anyway, somebody on the radio said that everybody deserved a trial, not the kind of thing Kane put on. "Even Communists deserve a trial," Lenore said. "It's not fair to do it the way you do . . . ."

"What the hell would a trial accomplish in Hoke's case? You can't prove a single act on his part. But I've branded him for what he is." He walked to her bedside. "Can't you see, Lenore? Can't everyone in this country see that we can't treat Communists like anyone else?" He sighed, as if a hopeless task lay before him. "We've got to get the Communists out or we'll lose everything." She recognized the despair in his voice, and wanted to comfort him. But she was afraid to. He wanted to defend himself; and that meant she had to keep arguing with him. Like the bandleader she knew who showed up once or twice a year with a little whip. . . . "The courts," she said, seized with inspiration. "You swear out a warrant, and bring them to court. And there's a jury and a judge. Even Communists deserve . . ."

He cut her short. "You said that! Dammit, we won't have courts or anything else if the Reds take over. Don't you realize what I'm trying to do despite all the blind fools who are fighting me?" -

Lenore paused a moment before answering. "I read something in a magazine a few weeks ago, Kane. Meant to show it to you. It's in my scrapbook now." She went to her bureau, and took the leather-bound book from beneath a drawer overflowing with lingerie. Back in bed, she turned the pages until she found what she was looking for. "I'll read it. They've got something here," she said as Kane looked at her doubtfully. "I think they're right. They're absolutely right." She began to read: ". . . Kane O'Connor has come along at a time when we have been taking our freedoms for granted, when we are not turning out to vote and we are dodging jury duty and we are ignorant about our judicial processes. O'Connor's excesses and abuses have made people realize how important these things are . . ."

"Now wait a damn minute," Kane broke in. "The people believe in me!"

She slipped out of bed and came to him. "Kane, why don't you stop it?" she said. "Why don't you quit this business now? Good grief! Congressmen do all kinds of other things without getting everybody on their backs. You can do things like . . . well, like with taxes and writing up laws and making speeches and that sort of thing. Why don't you give up this communist stuff? Why don't you quit?"

He got up and walked away from her. "You think I can end it when I *know* I'm right?" His shadow, thrown by the single light in the room, loomed black against the panel of the door. He faced her again. "I'm a symbol, Lenore. I'm a symbol." He stopped a moment, trying to express the passion of his belief. "Just like The Cross . . . like The Cross. It stands for a man who was persecuted and reviled and murdered and sold out because he spoke the truth." He saw her staring at him. "Well, it's almost the same with me." He put his hands on her shoulders. "Don't you understand? *I'm* a symbol now!"

She didn't speak. Taking his hand, she led him back to the bed. He lay down, his face pressed against her breast. She rubbed the back of his head as if to ease his mind, and she stroked his hair. "Try to sleep, Kane," she whispered.

"Can't. I can't sleep."

Later she snapped off the bed lamp and returned the room to darkness. He said something unintelligible to her. "Go to sleep, symbol," she told him gently. "Go to sleep, symbol . . . don't snore, symbol. . . ." Her tone was mocking, but also touched with compassion.

44

"KEEP YOUR shirt on!" Kane said angrily. He sat on the edge of his desk, pointing a paperknife at Cy. "I'm not asking you to do something I wouldn't do myself if you were in a jam."

"Kane, you know I'd do anything for you. But perjury? Cy tugged at his jowls. "Well, that's something else."

"Cy, can't you get it through your head? The only charges they're going to press against me are on finances. I'm not asking you to lie. Just say you don't remember."

Cy twisted in his chair, his fingers toying with the subpoena before him. "But I do remember. I'd have to be a real numbskull not to."

Kane pushed his hands into his pockets and walked to the door. Opening it, he called to Tod in the outer office. "Come in here, will you?" To Cy, he said, "You want those bastards to hang me?"

"Kane, do you realize what you're askin' me to do?"

"You're damn right I do! I'm asking you to do me a favor. And it's not going to cost you anything."

"You just don't go before a congressional committee and lie," Cy insisted. He pulled out his handkerchief and wiped his perspiring neck. "Not unless you want to get locked up!"

Kane slumped in his swivel chair. "Cy, nobody can put you in jail because you don't remember." He saw Tod come in. "Tell him what Ward said last night."

"About the subpoena?"

"Yes. And what they expect to get out of Cy."

Tod sat beside Cy, lifting his feet to rest on the wire trash-basket. "They want to prove that Kane deposited Joe King's check. They'll need your testimony to show that Kane was in financial difficulty at the time. They also want to show that Kane's money troubles cleared up as soon as he started getting support to fight communism." He looked at Kane, questioning him with raised eyebrows. "That about the crux of it?"

Kane sat upright. "That ought to be clear, Cy. They're going to try to make a direct link between my finances and the contributions. They're out to get me. Are you going to help them?"

Cy crossed his legs, slumping deeper into the chair, studying a matchstick on the carpet. "I don't know what to do," he said. "Kane, you know I'd rather lose an arm"—he patted the place where the bullet had struck him in Rio de Janeiro—"than hurt you."

Dany came in unannounced. "We've got more trouble."

Kane waved her aside. "Sit down a minute." He turned back to Cy. "I never thought you'd let me down. When I found out they were calling you, I laughed." He shook his head, frowning. "I was so sure you'd stick by me."

"I'm goin' to do everything I can," Cy said. He smacked his heavy thigh with his hand. "Kane, how did you get into this awful mess?" he asked hopelessly.

Dany was standing by the bookshelves across the room. She picked up a vase of wilted flowers and carried them across to the wastebasket. "He got into this mess by listening to his great friend Ward Roberts."

"Don't get started on that again," Kane warned her. "At least he's been trying to help. He hasn't been sitting around with his tail between his legs acting like we're already licked."

"No!" she flared back. Tod lifted his feet and let Dany throw the flowers into the trash. "He just had Tod and me and the whole staff working day and night for two weeks on a false lead, that's all." She put her hand on Cy's shoulder. "You know what his great friend told him?" She mocked the soft rhythm of Ward's voice: "'They're not interested in the financial charges. They're going to work on the Hatch Act violations and on the Communists-in-government issue.'" She looked at Kane, uncowed by his glare. "And the biggest news Roberts delivered was his terrific scoop that they're going to show you violated the espionage act by accepting classified information during the N.E.C. investigation!"

Kane's face was flushed. "Dry up, Dany!" he commanded.

But she ignored him. "So we knocked our brains out, compiling lists of witnesses, working up documents showing the number of security risks suspended during the past year, finding legal precedents for accepting information from government workers." Leaving Cy's side, she leaned over the desk to Kane. "Remember what you said when we finished? You said our statistics would make the committee look silly. You said..."

Kane was on his feet. "Listen, goddammit! If it hadn't been for Ward, we wouldn't have any idea they switched plans. He's the only reason we knew in advance that Cy would be subpoenaed."

Dany laughed. "You know what the Congressman from Pennsylvania said—-after we worked like Trojans?"

Kane remembered. Ward had told him that the committee had changed plans. They had decided to "go after you the way the government went after Capone. They couldn't make a case on his racketeering, so they jailed him for income tax evasion. They're going to concentrate on your financial deals."

Kane had been angry then. He was furious now. Dany's judgment, he felt, was twisted by her hatred for Ward. A year before Kane wouldn't have trusted him to chair a committee meeting. But Ward had proved himself in the past few weeks. While Stewart Denton was rarely available to answer his office phone, while other congressional acquaintances had made it clear that, though they would not vote against him, he could expect no help from them, Ward was always available; and Ward was the only contact that could determine what the investigating committee was doing. "Get off Ward, Dany," Kane said. "We've got a problem here with Cy."

She sat across the desk from Tod, comforted by his thin smile. "I've got some more news that. . ."

Kane cut her off. "That can wait. Now, Cy, I just want you to promise me you'll tell them you don't remember. Roberts says that they have no supporting papers on this, just rumors. If you don't recall the transactions, they can't prove a thing."

"It's perjury, Kane."

"Not if you don't confirm or deny it," Kane insisted.

Tod, as usual, thought before he spoke. "They know you borrowed from Joe, and can get the records to prove it. If Cy says he can't remember the circumstances, it's going to look like you're trying to hide the thing. That gives it more importance than it actually merits. Suppose they call Joe?"

Kane slammed a fist on the desk. "What's wrong with you people? Don't you see if I admit one thing, if they get a wedge in..."

"Tod's right," Dany said. "Cy can explain it easily enough. You and King are friends. It's not unusual for a friend to lend another money. He didn't give you anything. You paid him back. If Cy lies, it makes you look worse. Besides, the hearings are closed . . ."

"Closed? Just let them make me give an inch, and one of those characters will march out of a meeting and arrange to leak the whole thing to the papers. And they'd put a pretty picture out—giving people the idea I accepted a bribe from a lobbyist." He walked around to sit on the desk before Cy. Then, measuring him against the ruler of personal loyalty, he said, "Are you going to stick by me?"

Cy rubbed his fist into his damp palm. "I'll do everything I can. I'll think about it tonight, Kane. Honestly I will."

When Cy had gone, Kane sat in his chair again, cracking his knuckles. "Well, what were you so excited about when you came in?" he asked Dany.

"I came over as soon as I heard," she said. "They've subpoenaed the records. Statements, photostats of checks, deposit slips—everything."

"My God! I hadn't considered that," Tod said. "That puts me on the pan. My name's on all that stuff."

Kane held his face in his hands. "They're out to get me," he said again. "We've got to do something."

Tod pushed the intercom button. "Hattie, check the balance as of the last statement in both of Kane's accounts, special and personal." He looked at Dany. "They can't hurt me personally," he said, wanting to believe his logic. "Every cent I've got in my account and in June's is legitimate. I've made it in the market."

Hattie buzzed back. "Balance in personal account is $65,021. Balance in special account is $87,512."

"Thanks," Tod replied. "It's going to look bad, Kane, awfully bad."

"I know it!"

"Your salary is only . . ." Tod began.

"I know what my salary is!"

"It's going to be impossible to explain that kind of a personal balance if Cy's testimony shows you were in bad shape not too long ago—and the statements will show withdrawals from the special account that show up as deposits in your personal account, and there'll be checks drawn to your brokers . . ."

"All right!" Kane shouted. "I'm the only one who can testify about my account. Screw them! They can't *force* me to testify."

Dany spoke evenly. "Why didn't your loyal friend Roberts tell you about this?"

"Shut up! Can't you think of anything but your petty feud with Ward?"

"Kane, I made all those withdrawals," Tod said. "I purchased the stock for you. I deposited the contributions in the special account. They don't have to ask you to testify. They can call me."

"No one put any strings on the dough they let me have. All of them said to do what I wanted with it."

"And how about the five-and-ten dollar contributions?" Dany said.

He turned on her angrily. "You working for me or for that damned committee?" Then, to Tod, "They can't reconstruct every item on the special account, showing where every cent came from and where it went." But he wasn't so certain.

"If I'm allowed to say anything," Dany began.

He shrugged and, smiling at her, said, "Sorry, Dany. Go ahead."

"I think you're getting too excited about this. Don't make so much of it. The figures might embarrass you, but that's all. You've got to make the public see you're not afraid. I think you ought to call the committee and volunteer to testify."

"Are you crazy?"

"It would give you a chance, in closed sessions, to explain. It's not as bad as it looks and it's better to let them have your interpretation rather than have them make their own."

"She's got a point," Tod said.

Kane looked at them, bewildered. "Maybe she's got rocks in her head!"

Dany and Tod worked with Kane in his apartment the following night, sorting check stubs, canceled checks, deposit slips, statements and letters.

"You can't trust anybody," Kane said, slamming a ledger to the floor. "As long as I've known that bastard and all I've done for him!"

Dany bit the eraser on the stub of the pencil she held. "That's over, darling. Let's work on this."

"Supposed to be my best friend!" Kane coughed on the smoke from Tod's cigarette. "Ward says the fat slob told them everything. I was in trouble with the bank. I used Joe King's loan. I paid off my obligations . . ."

"Forget it," Tod said. "After all, Cy had a problem, too."

"Forget it?" Kane said harshly. "Your best friend stabs you?"

The phone rang. It was Cy. Kane heard him begin their traditional greeting: "How you doin', Kane, you old cuss?"

He didn't reply. He was trying to think of the right thing to say, something Cy wouldn't forget.

"Kane?"

"I'm listening."

His confederate of treehouse days seemed embarrassed. "You all right, Kane?" he finally managed.

"I know what happened today," Kane said. "You sonovabitch, you knew what it meant to me, and you deliberately . . ."

"Listen, Kane. I want to talk to you. I thought we could have dinner together. I want to help . . . anything I can do, I want to . . ."

"Drop dead!" Kane banged the receiver. While he poured a third glass of bourbon from the decanter on the dining table, he caught Dany and Tod watching him. "All he's ever wanted out of life was to be loved by everybody. My buddy Cy. I'm going to get this mess cleaned up, and the first chance I get, I'll fix his wagon. I don't know how, but I'll damned well do it!"

Again the phone buzzed. Tod and Dany looked at Kane, waiting as it rang insistently.

"You answer it," he told Dany. "I don't want to talk to him. I don't care if he calls back a hundred times."

But it was Ward Roberts who was calling. Dany held the phone out to Kane and he took it. Finally, after he had listened for two minutes without speaking, he said, "Come on over, Ward. We'll talk it out."

Before Ward arrived, Tod slipped into his jacket and gathered his papers. "I'm going," he said. "I don't relish spending an evening with Mr. Roberts. It's no secret we hate one another's guts."

Kane stood looking into the mirror over the mantel. He put his glass down, turned to Dany and Ward. "What's your plan, Ward?"

"Well, Kane, the committee majority's not anxious to have the party commit suicide," he said. "But they can't afford to come up with a complete whitewash, particularly after today's testimony and the subpoenaing of your records. They'll be susceptible to a proposition. I'm positive of it. My idea is to go to them on the quiet, tell them you're willing to drop the charges on N.E.C. permanently. That will satisfy the White House. I'll say you've had nothing to do with the handling of funds, that there's not a piece of paper with your name on it . . ."

"And hang Tod instead!" Dany said. "That's no answer. That's a good way to get yourself in deeper and to ruin one of the few people who'll stand by you."

"They're not interested in Tod. They're out to get me," Kane argued. 'He can't get hurt."

"I'm telling you," Ward said earnestly, "they'll drop the Hatch Act and Espionage Act charges. They'll drop the communist issue entirely. That's a victory for you. It vindicates you. But you've got to go at least part of the way toward a compromise."

"Are you sure it'll be all right?" Kane asked, grasping for this easy way out of his difficulties.

"Positive," Ward said. He hunched forward. "Kane, you know I always talk straight, so I don't want to say that the committee majority sent me, or even that two of the most influential members sent me, because that wouldn't be exactly true. But I can say that, in my opinion, you can't go wrong."

"That's your opinion!" Dany said. She walked over to Kane. "Don't agree to it," she insisted. "For one thing, it sounds too easy. And you'd be an awful louse to ruin Tod, even if it worked."

Kane toyed with his glass, sipping at the bourbon. "You have any better suggestion—like your advice to Cy yesterday?" he said. "We can't just sit and wait. We've got to do something. Ward's way is quiet. Nothing's going to happen to Tod. And when they announce they've dropped the other charges, we'll see that the word is plastered over every paper in the country." He was thinking as he spoke, trying to convince himself that the strategy was valid. "As Ward says, it'll mean I'm vindicated."

"It won't work," Dany said, desperate to convince him. "There's only one way to fight this. Go before the committee in executive session. Show them and the public you're not afraid to testify." She was pleading now, talking to Kane but aware of Ward behind him. "Of course they're not anxious to continue the investigation. It's nearly impossible to prove anything, and they're hurting the party every day this business goes on. Besides, they know that —even with an affirmative report—they'll never get enough votes to unseat you. Don't crawl, Kane. Explain yourself."

"I've been trying to tell you," Ward said, interrupting, "that I'm on top of the situation . . ."

Dany turned on him. "Damn you, I'm talking now. Be quiet!" Swallowing hard, she spoke to Kane again. "Let them know we've got plenty of information on Communists—in industry, in the C.I.A., in the Justice Department, things we haven't used yet. Offer to turn it over to the proper authorities. Tell them your purpose was to arouse the country. Tell them you've succeeded and now you're through with the communist issue."

Kane was listening, weighing her argument. "I don't know…"

"Let them know that you're going to fight any attempt to smear you. Let them know that Norman's dug up a few facts on two of their members—a few facts about salary kickbacks in their offices." Dany didn't know what effect she was having. But she saw Ward shaking his head. "Please, Kane, you make a concession by offering to stop your investigation. You give them something to worry about with a gentle threat. You deal with them head-on, not through an intermediary," she said, glaring at Ward. "And you give them a good reason to let the whole thing blow over. You'll be free of it. Please!"

"How can I be sure?" he said, hesitating. "I just can't go before that committee, put myself on trial. I can't! It'll make me look stupid."

"It'll make you look a lot worse to have this thing drag on," she argued.

Ward was troubled. "Kane, there's no reason to think they'll respond to your appearance as a witness. Once they get you there and under oath, they can ask you anything. There's no explaining away the finances. Remember that tip I gave you on corn futures?

They even know you invested there. You've got to show you're not responsible. There's no other way."

"I know it. I know it. I can't risk it."

Anger prodded Dany. "Do you think any sane man is going to believe you got all that money in your personal account because Tod invested for you, Tod put it there? Think! Think! The reason they started this investigation was to shut you up. The way to stop it is to let them know you're through bothering them." She held his arms. "Please, Kane," she pleaded. "You're no coward; and you're no fool. . . ."

He walked away from her. "I can't do it, Dany. I just can't. I might make all those concessions and then they'd just laugh at me. Ward's right."

She followed him across the room. "He's right," she mocked him, "and I'm wrong. As usual, I'm wrong. Like I was wrong months ago when I tried to make you turn to other things. Like I was wrong when I wanted you to drop the N.E.C. thing before it started! You're an idiot then, Kane," she said bitterly. "You're stupid. You know why you believe him?" She pointed to Ward. "Because your ego won't let you willingly lose face. When it's a question of retreating or getting the devil kicked out of you—"

"Lay off, Dany."

"You're so right there!" She stepped into the shoes she had left lying on the carpet. "I'm not going to bother you any longer. I'm not going to remind you again that if you'd done what I asked months ago, you'd have avoided all this trouble. I'm not going to ask you what's happened to all your fine friends who were patting your back and kissing your backside when you were riding high and could do them favors. I'm not going to tell you *anything* else. You can get plenty of advice from him." She nodded toward Ward and started for the door.

"Dany!"

Opening the door, she turned again to Kane who watched her, surprised at her sudden vehemence. "Go on," she told him. "Sell Tod down the river. Try to get away with it." Her voice trembled, threatening to give her away. "And when you finish ruining him, why not try stabbing me?" Fury choked her. "Listen to your good friend over there! As far as I'm concerned, both of you can go to hell!"

"Dany?" She heard her name called, and slowly awakened, propping her elbows behind her on the bed, peering into the darkness of her room, drowsily expecting to see Kane. And then the hazy shape in the doorway came into focus.

"Norm!" she said, still groggy with sleep. "How did you get in here?"

"I didn't know you were in yet. The super opened the door for me so I could wait."

"You should have called," she said. Annoyed, she raised the covers over her shoulders. "What's so pressing you had—"

"I've been trying to talk to you for days. I thought here, alone. . . . Dany, are you angry with me?"

She shook her head wearily. "Norm, go home. I'll talk to you tomorrow."

"Please, Dany, it's important. It's about Kane."

So Kane's sent an emissary already, she thought, pleased that he had reconsidered so quickly. "Wait in the living room, Norm. I'll dress."

Norman was leaning against the door jamb, staring at her, and when he spoke, he sounded as if he were out of breath. "Dany, it's all over for Kane. He's beaten!"

"Oh, no he's not. Not if he uses his head."

"Ward says the committee's going to ask for expulsion, and that they've got the votes to do it." He swung forward on his canes, approaching the bed. "There's not a chance for Kane, but Ward's going to carry on. He's promised. The work won't stop. And we can use you. We'll work together, Dany, the way we did in Alabama."

"Ward'll take over when Kane's dead and buried," she said angrily. "Ward won't see the day!"

Norman moved closer to the foot of her bed. "Kane's through," he insisted. "He's used us, used the issue, and it's caught up with him."

"Ward would like to think so! Norm, will you let me put something on?" she said impatiently.

"Dany, Kane's even fooled you. You know why he's been spending so much time in New York? Because he's got a woman there. We've had him trailed for months. And she's a tramp, nothing but a prostitute."

The sudden knowledge buffeted her for a moment. She felt ill; her heart pounded and her chest tightened with suppressed anger, anger not at Kane, but at herself, because she had driven him to it. Her pride spoke: "I don't have any claim on him. He can do whatever he pleases. It's none of my business and it's none of yours. Spying on him! It's despicable."

"I did it for you, Dany," Norman said, and moved around the bed to stand there, looking down at her.

"Go home, Norm. Please. Get out of here," she said quietly.

"Dany, everybody's going to know about Kane and this woman. You don't want to be involved. I don't want you to be. I called Matt Fallon, told him. And he wouldn't use it. But if a scandal magazine got hold of it . . ."

"Norm!" If she could have gotten out of bed, she would have struck him, but both hands gripped the sheets, shielding herself.

He sat on the edge of her bed; and she shivered, repelled, as he loomed over her, his massive shoulders hunched forward. "Dany . . ." he said. His hand went out to touch her bare shoulder.

She had that feeling of discomfort, of uncertainty of what to do that she had known before when older men stroked her arm, when a family friend had kissed her a bit too warmly. She was sickened by his damp touch on her bare skin; and yet she didn't want to make something of the gesture when, after all, it was probably innocent, and, in a way, pitiful. His hand gripped her tighter, hurting her. Easily, she tried to sit up and couldn't. And then, suddenly, those shoulders were pressing down upon her and Norman's face was against her cheek and his hand reached out again, finding her waist.

"Dany, I love you," Norman said, his voice strange, hoarse, wavering, as his hand reached her breast.

"Stop it! Take your hands away from me!" She tore herself from his fumbling grasp, rolling to the far side of the bed. And he, dumbly, impelled, reached for her again.

"You've led me on, all this time—but the idea of my touching you, that's too much, isn't it? That disgusts you. I'm a cripple and it's all reserved for Kane. You'd rather be his number-two whore than let me love you. . ." His words tumbled out, nearly hysterical, lashing at her as he sprawled over her. "It's my legs. . . I'm still a man, damn you! I'm a man . . . more man than Kane O'Connor!"

All she could remember later was her own voice telling her that she must not faint, that she must not scream. Summoning all her strength, she threw him aside, and he slid off the bed to the floor. She was up at once, rushing through the living room to the front door, opening it, standing there in her nightgown.

And by her bed, spotted in the streak of light from the hallway, Norman struggled to find his canes, and pulled himself up, straining with the exertion, grunting, until he was standing at last beside the bed. He swung through the room, toward her, past, into the outer hall. "I didn't want. . . I wouldn't hurt you, Dany, I didn't plan . . ." His voice dropped. He stood there, still not looking at her, his eyes fixed on the carpet floor. "I suppose you'll tell Kane," he muttered.

"No. I won't tell Kane," she said coldly. "And you'll tell nothing to any magazines. The day you do, I'll swear out an assault warrant against you!"

"You led me on," he said, still not looking at her.

She didn't answer.

"I'll never bother you again," he said and turned away.

Dany watched him swing one leg and then the other in his lopsided gait, slowly moving down the hall. When he was out of sight, she still heard the swush-creak as he dragged over the carpet, and then the glide of the elevator doors.

Alone, she went back inside, free at last to think of Kane . . . and what he had done to her . . . and what he was doing to himself.

45

KANE AND WARD made their plans in secret.

On Friday evening it was a secret no longer. Matt Fallon, censuring Kane's failure to testify before the investigating committee, described him as a "Fifth Amendment Congressman" and revealed that Tod Sands had been "offered as a scapegoat to save the O'Connor skin."

Kane tried to reach Ward at once. No answer. He called again on Saturday morning, but there was no reply to the insistent buzz of the phone. He went to the Old House Office Building. Ward's rooms were dark.

In a paroxysm of uncertainty, worried, without counsel, he walked down the silent corridor to his own office. In the past—whether in Manton or in Washington—there had been someone with him to bolster his courage or approve his actions or agree with his judgment or aid in his decisions. But he was alone now; and he found it difficult to choose a course of action.

Opening the door to his outer office, he saw Tod, unshaven, wearing a soiled shirt and trousers, emptying a drawer into a cardboard box on the floor. For the first time, Kane considered Tod's reaction to Matt's latest charges. Somehow, it had never occurred to him before that Tod would know. At once, it was clear that Tod knew and that Tod was leaving.

And Kane's twisted reasoning insisted that, at whatever the cost, he had to prevent Tod's defection. If Tod stood by him, Matt's blast would be refuted. "I want to talk to you, buddy," Kane said, closing the door.

Tod's expression of preoccupation did not change. He didn't look up. "I don't have anything to say to you, chum."

Kane walked to the desk. "You don't believe it. Do you, Tod?" he asked incredulously.

Tod slipped the drawer back, and pulled out another. "You think I'm a moron?"

"It was Dany." Kane moved around the desk, trying to make Tod look up at him. "She told Matt that stupid lie." He put his hand on Tod's bent shoulder. "And you believed her!" he said, apparently chagrined. He waited, but Tod offered no rebuttal. "Don't you see what happened? She was angry with me. She figured the thing that would hurt me most was to lose you. So she made it all up."

Tod grunted with disgust. Dropping a packet of letters in the box, he said, "I've seen you playing innocent before."

"I'm telling you the truth. Honest to God!"

Tod banged his fist against the bottom of the drawer, loosening the paper clips that clung to the corners. He tossed them in an ash tray. "I would have stuck by you. I really would have."

Kane tried another approach. "Of course. I've always been able to count on you, buddy. I wouldn't know how to work without you." He reached for Tod's arm, but Tod drew back and walked past him. "You can't let a misunderstanding like this break us up," Kane pleaded. "Remember how we pulled that first campaign out of the hat? Remember the first time I got angry with you because you criticized my posters . . . and I had to admit you were right? And the time Biddle had me up the creek? Tod, old buddy, we've worked together . . ."

"You're right, Kane. I've been some help to you. I've been right there when you were reaming a raft of characters. That's why I'm not complaining now that I've gotten the shaft. It's my turn. I might have known that sooner or later you'd get around to me." In the silence he lifted the heavy box to a chair and closed the lid. His voice was low and strained as he faced Kane. "Matt clobbered me with the news last night before he did his show, thought I should have the word before the rest of the world. And it wasn't Dany who tipped him. If you weren't so damned shook up and scared lately, you could see . . ."

"I've thought about it . . .thought about it all night. Didn't get an hour's sleep, Tod. Who else could it have been? Who else had anything to gain from a lie like that? At first I didn't even consider Dany, but she was boiling at me the other night and before she could cool off, she must have called Matt. She's been awfully cozy with him lately . . . even after I had it out with him . . . was in the House Gallery with him. . . . Must have been Dany. Had to be."

Tod rubbed the stubble on his chin and looked speculatively at Kane. Then, shaking his head, he walked slowly to the table, picked up the picture of his wife and children, and started to carry it back. He had not slept the night before either. He had thought and thought; had finally found the only logical answer to Kane's question. He stopped in front of Kane. "Who?" he asked, speaking softly. "Who climbed on your bandwagon for a free ride? Who tied you to his big-money friends so he could keep a ring in your nose? Who got himself elected on your sweat? Who got you Norman Keller so he could have his fingers on the inside? Who kept you on this communist hunt when you'd already sucked it dry? Who keeps making it clear, ever so subtly, that he's as dedicated as O'Connor, but more moderate? Who's playing both ends against the middle and making a jackass out of you in the bargain?"

"You're wrong!" Kane broke in. "Like Dany!" But he listened and each new accusation joined to form a black silhouette of suspicion.

Tod knew Kane's thoughts. He talked on, calmly spitting out his anger without raising his voice. "Who played Mr. Bountiful by slipping you illegal information on corn futures, and then suggesting that you could find the money to use the information? And who sold the investigating committee the idea of hitting you through your finances? And who told them that they'd get nowhere if they tried to beat you at your own game with the communist gambit? Who talked you into convicting yourself? Who's giving you a royal crucifixion because he's tired of being Assistant Messiah?"

Kane slumped in a chair. "That conniving bastard!" he said, recognizing the truth.

Tod laughed bitterly. "Conniving? Sure. But you're a helluva one to talk. You've connived since the day I met you. You've used everybody you could and I've helped you." He leaned back against the table, smiling contemptuously. "I watched you use a Negro corpse to win your first election. And I saw you use Mark Woodmire. And I know how you used your Uncle Wesley. And you followed it up by using Shep Reade. You used Laurie. You used Cy until he refused to chance going to jail for you. And you used Dany. And, nearly, but not quite, used me. Well, Honorable Kane O'Connor, you finally met your match. You've been had yourself!"

Kane heard him out. Then, frowning in disbelief, he said, "After all I've done for you, you can stand there and talk to me like that? You can accuse me of those things? Why I pulled you out of Manton. Don't forget that. And I gave you a chance to be somebody, not a seventy-bucks-a-week Chamber of Commerce ass kisser. I handed you an important position, introduced you to the biggest people. I let you sit in when great things were hatching."

Tod was unmoved. "I don't owe you a damned thing. We're even, Kane. I've already called the committee's counsel. I'm going down there and tell them everything I know. I acted under your orders. What's mine is free and clear and clean."

"Listen to me!" Kane demanded. "I've made mistakes. All right, I admit it. But it's not too late. We'll call Dany. The three of us can lick this thing," he argued desperately. "We'll work it out. We'll get that sonovabitch Roberts . . ."

"Not *we,*" Tod said, his voice still maddeningly calm. "Not *we.* No more."

Kane offered his hand. "Tod, forgodsakes, we've had arguments before. You're not going to destroy our friendship over something so ridiculous."

Tod ignored the hand. "I can understand you, Kane, even when you're crawling. Because—in my pennyante way—I've been interested in what's in it for Uncle Tod. But I've got enough decency to draw the line when it comes to knifing a friend," he said harshly. Picking up his box in both arms, he paused before the door and reached awkwardly for the handle.

Kane stepped in front of him. "Wait!"

Tod tugged at the door, pulling it open past the restraining hand, and bumping it aside with his box.

"To hell with you, then. You were nobody when I found you; and you're nobody now!" Kane yelled after him. "I don't need you. I never did."

Tod didn't reply. He was already halfway down the hall. And Kane was alone.

He knew that he must find a way out of the morass of mistakes that had entrapped him. But he needed help, someone to talk to, someone upon whom he could depend. Matt, Cy, Tod, Dany—all had deserted him. But Dany—he could handle her. He rang her phone and heard her answer. "Dany, darling, it's Kane." The receiver clicked in his ear. He dialed again. The line was busy.

Have to see that bastard Roberts first, he decided. Have to confront him. Then Dany will listen, he reasoned. He'd tell her what he'd done. He'd explain. They'd go out together and talk it over with Lucy and Mel.

When he tried Ward's number again, he got no answer. After rifling through Hattie's desk, he found Norman Keller's listing. The phone buzzed; and then a sleep-logged "Hello?"

"Is Mr. Roberts there?" Kane asked, disguising his voice.

"No," Norman Keller said. "I don't expect him until around eleven. Who's calling please?"

Kane nested the receiver on the hook.

Norman Keller yawned, as if he were unconcerned by Kane's arrival, as if his mind was not trying to contrive some way of preventing Ward Roberts from walking, unprepared, into the apartment. "Sit down, Kane. Stop stalking around."

"What time did he say he'd be here?" Kane asked.

"He said he'd call first. And he hasn't." Norman lowered himself into a drum-back chair, and carefully drew his dingy maroon flannel bathrobe over his wasted legs. "He wasn't sure he could make it. If you'd rather get some breakfast and come back. . . . Or I could have Ward call you if he shows up."

Kane walked across the white island of carpet in the center of the polished black flooring, staring obliquely at the grotesque statue—a nude black woman—that stood four feet high, dominating the far corner of the L-shaped room. "I'll wait," he said. He stood before the window, a single sheet of glass framed by bookshelves, and looked out over the street, two floors below. There was no doubt any longer, he was thinking. So many small incidents, unimportant when they had happened, now were intertwined. Dany's arguments, Tod's, Ward's actions in South America, the little favors he managed to get . . . Kane acknowledged that he had been stupid. He was determined to settle with Ward. And later, with Dany to help him, he'd pay him back—double.

Norman grunted, lifting one leg at a time to an ebony stool, and shifting his weight in his chair. He could visualize the impending scene. Ugly. "I've gotten a brief together on the members of the investigating committee. But there's nothing really important, except for the family kickbacks in salary. I'd forget it.

We'll work on another angle." Norman managed to keep talking, but he was thinking feverishly of some way to get rid of Kane. "Ward may be tied up," he ventured. "You know him. If he's got something on, he's liable to forget all about an appointment."

Kane looked contemptuously at Norman, certain that he could read his thoughts. He left the window, walked around the six identical chairs, upholstered in a nubby, teal-colored fabric, and stood before the raised hearth, his back to Norman. Tod had sized his chief counsel up, all right. Give him credit for that. Tod had seen through Norman, had known he was Ward's man all along.

"I think I'll give Ward a ring," Norman said. "If he's still at home, I could . . ."

"You're fired," Kane said, turning to face him.

For a moment, Norman did not answer. Then he said, "I'll wait until the subcommittee releases me."

"I'm the subcommittee," Kane said. "I hired you, and I'm firing you." For the first time, he raised his voice. "Today I'm getting rid of all the bastards who've been standing behind me, looking for a place to stick a knife!"

"I gave you my best," Norman said; and his words were barely audible. "For a long time I gave you everything I had . . . because, when I met you, I thought, 'there's a great man!' But I came to see you for what you are, Kane." He cleared his throat. "You've got all the tools but one—energy, drive, self-assurance, a yearning for fame. But you've never had conviction. You never believed in anything but yourself. With conviction, devotion—the kind that an Oliver Cromwell had, the kind that bums from within and ignites everyone around you—if you had that, you could have had anything!"

"Shut up! You're a goddamned fanatic."

"We were talking about you," Norman said, smiling thinly, knowing he had hurt Kane and had him on the defensive. "You've never had a rough minute. It's all been smooth and easy for you. And you haven't deserved a bit of it. What have you read? What have you studied? What do you know outside of a few sharp political tricks? What kind of a lawyer are you? What do you know about music or art or literature?" He pointed at the Utrillo that hung above the raised hearth. "Who painted that?" he taunted.

"Go straight to hell," Kane said. "I don't know who painted your goddamned picture. And I'm no piano player and I read detective stories when I can't get to sleep at night. And I've never pretended to be anything else, you stupid crum. I'm like a hundred million other guys in this country; and that's why I'm Kane O'Connor and you're a miserable, self-pitying snob. You've got everything and nothing because inside you're not even an honest-to-God human being!"

The bell rang. Both looked at the door. "Come in," Norman said.

Ward Roberts came in. "Not dressed yet?" he said. Then he saw Kane. Ward had no personal courage, but he was a realist. He knew he would have to face Kane, and it had come earlier than he had anticipated. "Didn't expect to find you here, Kane."

"You dirty bloodsucker!"

"Now, listen here . . ."

Kane strode across to him, his face reflecting his anger. "It took me a long time, you louse, but I've finally got you figured." Grabbing Ward's shirt, he held it firmly.

"Sit down, Kane, and cool off."

Kane pulled him forward, grimacing as Ward struggled. "That's some more of your advice? You lowlife sonovabitch!"

Norman yelled at them. "If you two can't act like gentlemen, get out of here."

"This is none of your goddamned business!" Kane raged. Then, to Ward, he said, "So you thought you could get away with it? You bastard, I'll ruin you."

Ward tried to pull away. "Still think you're a big man, don't you?" he said nervously.

"I'm big enough to walk over crud like you!"

Ward slapped his soft, manicured hands on Kane's wrist and tried to free himself. "I'll worry about you," he taunted, "when you're back in that hick town you came from, explaining how you got thrown out of Washington—if you're lucky enough to stay out of jail."

Holding the shirt with his left hand, Kane slapped at Ward. He ducked and the blow struck his ear. "You wouldn't be here in this town if I hadn't put you here," Kane roared. "And when I finish with you, you'll be back shystering for a living."

Norman had gotten to his feet. Now he swung himself on his canes, across the room to stand beside them. "Get out!" he shouted. "Get out of my place before I call the police, Kane."

As Kane turned to him, Ward pulled away, ripping his shirt. Panting, he backed off, behind a highbacked, thronelike chair. "I'm not worried about you, Kane. I know how you operate. Without someone to pat your back and whisper in your ear and do your dirty work and your thinking for you, you're lost!"

Kane pulled the chair aside, toppling it. He reached for Ward again, this time catching him by his lapels. His voice was shrill, harsh. "Always interested in my welfare, weren't you? Always interested in Ward Roberts! You didn't give a damn about me or about fighting Reds or about doing a decent job. I was just your ladder for climbing, somebody you could use to get what you wanted, wasn't I, you no-good slob?" He shook him violently. "A chance to get some headlines, a chance to make a reputation, to be a big operator, to have people crawling for you. That's all you ever wanted!"

Ward jerked away, tearing his coat. "You should know— that's the story of your life!"

Kane pulled viciously at Ward and smashed his fist into the glaring, frightened face.

Ward fell. His mouth was cut, bleeding. His small, furtive eyes glowered furiously at Kane, who stood, frenzied, above him. "Call the police, Norm," he yelled.

Kane looked at him; and his disgust and fury were molten. "You're not going to even give me the pleasure of fighting back, are you, you yellow bastard!" He spat on him. Then he walked out, leaving the door open behind him.

"Go on! Run!" Ward called after him. "Go back to that tramp Dany. Let that bitch get you out of this; she's been running you from the bed for long enough . . ."

He didn't finish the sentence. Norman, standing over him, had raised one cane, and supporting himself precariously on the overturned chair, he brought the cane down across Ward's shoulders. "Goddamn you!" he screamed, striking him again. "Goddamn you!" He fell, sprawling over Ward. Beyond the open door, down the hallway, he heard the elevator door open, then close. And he knew that Kane had heard him, and that Kane was going to Dany.

46

KANE PUSHED the buzzer again and heard it ring inside Dany's apartment. Again. Once more.

He was certain that she would listen to him now that he had broken with Ward. Leaning against the door, he knocked, rapping until his knuckles were sore. "Dany!" he called.

What was wrong with her? They couldn't waste time. There was the week end . . . and so much had to be done . . . and where do we start? Dany would know. And this time . . . by God, this time, he'd listen to her. Maybe Lucy and Mel— they'd help. He pushed the buzzer once more. No answer.

"Dany, I know you're in there," he shouted. "Dany, it's Kane. I want to . . . have to talk to you, Dany." This time he held his finger on the buzzer and pressed his ear to the door, listening for some sound inside that would prove that she was there.

She was only a dozen feet away, sitting on the divan in her slip, her legs pulled up under her. But she waited for him to give up, to leave. For two long days and two sleepless nights she had waited for a knock on her door—and rushed to open it to a neighbor returning soap powder, a researcher interested in her preference in automobiles, a cosmetics saleswoman who wanted her to give a party. Since then, she had kept her ear attuned to the ring of the phone, and answered it breathlessly to hear Matt's voice and Lucy's and Windy's—the model at Garfinkel's who had dated Matt so long ago. . . . And during her vigil, reliving all the time she had spent with Kane, Dany had decided that when he did call or come—as he must, she assured herself—it wouldn't be made easy for him.

"I've told you, Dany. I'm through with Roberts. I found him out. Dany!" Kane heard a door open down the hall, saw a buxom woman, her hair in curlers, staring at him, then withdrawing. He banged on the door again.

Not today, Dany was thinking. She'd yapped at his heels too long, suffered neglect, been shunted to the position of mistress, and then been supplanted as confidant by Ward Roberts, as lover by a prostitute. And it had happened so gradually. Somewhere along the way, probably that night she had given herself to him . . . yes, from then . . . she had lost control. Never again were things the same. But they would be. She'd have him. But on her terms.

Kane pushed the buzzer another time. "Dany, let me in!"

Dany's parakeet fluttered on his perch and screeched harshly, unintelligibly. Dany slipped from the divan and tiptoed on bare feet to the cage. Careful to make no sound, she unhooked the cage and carried the chattering bird to her bedroom. "Quiet, Norman," she said, and smiled, thinking of Norm Keller's reaction if he knew what she had named the squawking bird. Putting the cage on the window ledge, she went back to the bedroom doorway, and heard Kane still pounding, still calling her.

"Dany? Dany, I know you're in there. I'm not going to leave until you talk to me. Dany!"

The buzzer again. Kane was perspiring. He wiped his face with the palm of his hand. "I'm leaving, Dany! If you don't come open this door, I'm leaving!" And then, realizing that he had said the opposite only minutes before, he hesitated, forgetting all his other problems, trying to puzzle some way of explaining why he had changed his mind. But . . . explain to whom? He wondered if Dany was really out, if he was calling to an empty apartment.

And inside, waiting through the silence, listening for the knock or the buzz to begin again, Dany had doubts, not sure if Kane was still there or had gone. She moved quietly through the living room again, gliding over the carpet, until she was beside the door. It was with a sense of disappointment, a sense of loss that she decided that Kane had gone. And then she was startled by his voice once more, only inches away, on the other side of the door.

"Dany, listen. Listen to what I'm saying, darling. We've got things to do. But, first thing, we'll get a license. I'll make them open up, call a judge I know . . . and we'll get married, darling. We won't wait another day. Darling . . . darling, please!"

It took conscious physical effort for her to remain silent. She had waited so long to hear Kane say those words . . . and now they were said for the whole apartment house to hear . . . and he was on the other side of a door . . . and she must not, could not, do what she yearned to do. They'd be married, but not that way. Calm and sane and unworried, he'd ask her . . . and then . . .

"Dany? Please, Dany. I know you're in there!"

It was not pride that kept her door locked, nor anger, nor spite. It was her love for him, her desire to possess him completely, as he had always possessed her. She wanted him to acknowledge at last—not only to her, but to himself—that she was indispensable to his success and his happiness. It had been different at first, she thought. He needed her then. Well, he needed her now, and he was beginning to realize it. In calamitous succession he had estranged Matt, rebuffed Cy, driven Tod away, learned that Roberts was his enemy. Now, alone, he had come back to her. Let him worry. Let him get desperate. Let him see what she had been to him, what she had done for him. Then she'd listen. Maybe tomorrow. Maybe later.

"Dany!" Must be in there, he thought. Doorman said she was. . . No, said he thought she hadn't come down. But he wasn't certain. . . And yet, if she could hear him, why didn't she answer? Why didn't she open the door? She's angry. But not angry enough to . . . and yet, Dany had a will, a strong, stubborn will. Never anyone like her. Never a woman so strong and smart and beautiful. I love her, he told himself, and treated the thought as a new discovery, simply because he had been so involved over the past months that he had never taken the time to tell her so, never taken the time to consider it himself. "Dany! I need you, Dany. If you love me, Dany, you'll let me in."

Her hand reached for the handle. She grasped it; and then closed her eyes, clenched her teeth, as if to stiffen her resolution. I mustn't, she told herself. Mustn't.

"Dany, this time I mean it. I'm going. I'll leave. I'm going away."

You'll be back, she thought.

He pounded his fist on the door. "Are you going to let me in, Dany?"

She couldn't stand the plaintive tone of his voice, a tone that told her how afraid and worried he was, how much he needed to be reassured. She knew that to stand there another moment was to give in, to open the door and take him in her arms. Turning her back on the door, she forced herself to go to her bedroom. She lay on her canopied bed, struggling against the weakness that urged her to rush to him. Finally the pounding and the ringing and the shouting stopped.

Kane searched for some place to go, for someone to talk to.

He called Lucy and Mel. They were not in.

He called Ray Hyder. He had gone to Rock Creek Park for a picnic with his children.

He called Stewart Denton, whose wife said he was meeting someone at the Capitol.

In desperation, he called Nate Starbecker. But when Nate's voice croaked a hello, Kane wondered for the first time what he should say, and then hesitating, hung up.

He felt himself imprisoned by relentless circumstance, unable to cope with his problem, unsure of his next move. The week end lay before him. And he did not want to spend it alone. Got to relax, he told himself. Got to forget the whole damned mess. Got to get away from here.

47

KANE FLEW out of Washington at two o'clock that Saturday afternoon. By five-thirty he had rented a car at La Guardia, been refused admittance to Della's because of a private party, been warned by a policeman for double parking on West End Avenue, checked into a hotel, called Lenore, cursed her because she was booked for the night, slammed the phone on her explanation and finished half of a fifth of bourbon.

He was still alone. Sitting in the low, upholstered chair that matched the drapes in the coldly modem hotel room, he put his feet on the windowsill and gulped at a glass of whisky. His mind wandered, rambling first through the tempest of the recent past, prowling for hidden motives and meanings among his recollections and finally meandering back along the path of his memories to better times.

He thought of Laurie. As in all remembrances, her virtues took on more color, more detail, more highlights. Foibles became endearing, adding to her charm. She had been his haven. With her he had been secure. The world had not been pounding at him.

Suddenly he remembered that she was there—possibly only a few blocks away. He searched frantically through the directory, trying to recall the name of her hotel. Something for women, he remembered Tod telling him. He found it. "To Laurie," he said to the silent room, raising a toast and downing it.

He showered and shaved and brushed his teeth and, cupping his hands over his mouth, tested his breath for the odor of bourbon and brushed his teeth again and dressed. Before he left he poured another glass of whisky. "For courage," he explained to his reflection in the mirror. There was only a little more left in the bottle. Kane finished it and dropped the empty bottle into a wastebasket. Then he set out to surprise Laurie.

Too impatient to wait for his car to be brought to him, he hailed a taxi; and fifteen minutes later he was in the lobby of the

Barbizon Hotel for Women, holding a house phone, waiting to hear Laurie's voice.

"Hello?"

He recognized the soft, familiar sound of her. "Laurie, it's Kane."

For a moment she didn't reply. Her thoughts jumbled. She had watched him on television, heard him on the radio, seen his pictures. But Kane, the person, was no longer real to her. He belonged to another time. She managed to say, "How are you?"

"Come down. I'm in the lobby." Sensing the excitement in her voice, he imagined her—breathless, happy, pulling nervously at the hair around her shoulders.

"All right, Kane," she said, and hung up. Why, after all this time, after these many months? Why now, when he hadn't even sent her a sympathy card when her mother died? She called to her roommate. "Goin' down to see someone. If Cy calls, I'll be back in a few minutes."

"Anyone I know?"

"An old friend."

Down below, Kane watched the stairs and the elevator. I should have known it before, he thought. She's down-to-earth, honest. She's interested in me, not what I can do for her, not like Dany. He saw her step from the elevator. But it was not the girl he remembered. Her auburn hair was short. It gave her a pert, sleek look. She wore a black skirt and a white blouse with a gold pin at the throat. He crossed the floor to meet her and took her outstretched hand.

"Good to see you again, Kane," she said delivering the words she had decided on in the elevator.

He smiled. It was so simple, so easily done. Kane and Laurie—the years couldn't change them. "Where can we talk?"

"There's a lounge. That's as private as we're allowed to get around here."

Laurie was older somehow, he thought. She had a new poise, a new manner—or had he forgotten? He'd hurt her. He wanted to make it up to her now, to make her happy, to tell her everything she had been waiting to hear. "This won't do," he said. "Isn't there some place else? A bar? A restaurant?"

"There's a little place down the street." He looked so tired, she thought.

They entered a bamboo-thatched bar and found a booth in the rear. All the while Kane chattered, teasing her about her hair, assuring her she hadn't changed, insisting that they have dinner together. "We could go to 21. Bet you've never been there, huh? We'll go. I know—what's-his-name—Bob. I know Bob, Laurie. Or would you rather drive out somewhere? We could eat. . .haven't had a bite all day. I was in such a hurry to get here, Laurie. I've rented a car; and we can drive out on the island or something and find a place with music and dance like we used to."

"Don't you think you ought to eat something now? Maybe a sandwich . . ."

He patted her hand. "Haven't changed, have you? Don't worry about me already, darling." He ordered drinks. "I know what you'll have, Laurie. Tom Collins. Right? Just like the old days. But. . . so much has happened."

"Yes, Kane. You've done very well."

"Oh, Laurie, you can't imagine. You can't imagine what it takes out of you!" He leaned eagerly across to her and held her hand. "I've been through such hell these past few weeks. Everything's . . . not going right, you know."

She felt his damp hand grasping hers fitfully. *What's wrong with him?* she wondered. *He seems so feverish, so animated, half frightened of me.* "I've been reading the papers," she said sympathetically.

He put a cigarette in his mouth. "I've been getting some bad breaks lately, Laurie. The newspapers just blow things up. They've been waiting for me to do one thing wrong, just one thing! That's the way they are. All for you one day . . . then you do one thing, just once, that's all." He hadn't lighted his cigarette. Taking it out of his mouth, he began to shred it. "It's rough politics in Washington, Laurie. They play rough. They've been out to get me. You've got to expect that when you get to be big. But your friends? That's what hurts. That's what gets you down!" He piled the loose tobacco in a mound on the table. "You think you knew Cy? Or Tod? So did I! I was wrong about those two."

"You and Cy'll get back together, Kane. Of course you will. It's not the only time you've had an argument." She knew it wasn't true, for she'd seen Cy the day after he'd left Washington. But she wanted to soothe Kane somehow, offer him some consolation.

"No, Laurie. Don't you see how it works?" He looked at her, and recognizing the tenderness in her face, he hesitated. "No, you're too good. You couldn't even understand it. But Tod and Cy are just like all the rest of them—just like Roberts. They've used me, fed on me, like parasites, like . . . like suckers that ride along on the big fish's back." He took a long drink from his glass, finishing it. "Then, the first time there's trouble, they run out."

He's confused. He's so upset that he's not being realistic at all, she thought.

Kane built a blockhouse with the sugar lumps on the table and ordered another drink for himself and talked on, breathlessly, as he drank. "Take Tod. I made him rich. I made him somebody. I gave him authority." He searched for some way to prove it. He had to make her understand. "Did you see his picture in *Look?* You think he'd have ever gotten his picture in there if it hadn't been for me?"

"No, Kane. He wouldn't have, I'm sure." Laurie sipped at the Collins, avoiding his eyes. Everyone knew what he'd done to Tod, knew that he'd offered to sell him out. Great pity for Kane swept over her, nearly drowning her reason.

"That I could take," Kane told her bitterly, reaching for her hand again. "But Cy! You know he went and told them a lot of lies about me. Why would Cy do that? I sent him to South America, Laurie. He got on television and in the newsreels and was treated like a king down there. I looked out for him for years, was his friend when nobody else in Manton would have paid any attention to him. I was so close to him, Laurie. And still he went ahead and did that, knowing it would hurt me. I told him it would hurt me, Laurie. But he went ahead and did it. Why?" He had to convince her, had to make her see that he had been betrayed, that he was innocent. He had to make her stop being distant and cool and not like his Laurie. "I'm not licked, though. No, I'm a long way from being licked." His face took on the look of a child futilely protesting against a bigger boy's beating. "None of them are going to get away with what they've done."

He continued to spew out his bitterness. First he talked of Manton; and then he went back to Cy's betrayal; and then he snatched at a reply from her and tore at Tod again. He said he wanted to be honest with her and told her a trifle about Dany. And she listened, hardly interrupting, not questioning him. He didn't ask about her mother, about her job or her plans. He could talk of nothing but himself.

She saw and heard the shambles of the man she had known. And she knew that his reason was perverted, his logic gone. As she listened and watched him, she added up all the disconnected memories of the past; and she recognized the first slight bruises that had resulted in his total infection. She understood the depth of his weakness, though she never had before. Poor Kane, she thought. He's finally run out of people to run to.

He saw the tears flecking her lashes and accepted it as encouragement. "Darling, it's all been wrong—our being away from one another. I realize it now."

His hand gripped hers, harder. She freed herself and then, not wanting to hurt him, she patted his fist.

"It's been such a relief just to talk to you, to tell you everything the way I used to." Smiling, he examined the face he knew so well, the glistening eyes, the small ears, the angle of her nose, the place on her neck where his lips had rested so often. "You haven't forgotten, have you?"

"No, Kane. I haven't forgotten."

"We'll get married—right away. And then I'll go back there and fight them. This is what I've needed, a chance to talk it out. We can do it, can't we? Don't you think so? I need you, Laurie."

"Perhaps you do, Kane."

"You've missed me, haven't you?" He leaned across toward her, half rising to kiss her.

Laurie moved away and stood, looking down at him. There had been a time when she had thought of such a moment, of what she might say to hurt him, of what she might do to repay him for her own deep wounds. But there was no longer any appetite for revenge, no longer any bitterness in her. She extended her hand. "I must go, Kane."

He was bewildered. Standing, he moved around the table to her. "But, darling, don't you understand? I want you to marry me."

"I don't think . . ." She shook her head. "Please, Kane!" She didn't want to cry. "Good-by," she said, and hurried out.

Sheer surprise kept him standing there, alone.

For an hour he walked, moving as if bent on reaching a destination, but without a goal. His thoughts were interrupted by the impatient squawk of a trucker's horn, by a sidewalk conversation that blocked his path, by the halt of traffic while sirens sounded.

He turned up Fifth Avenue. His mind was nettled with the barbs of the day—a day of confused time and space, of unstrung hours, of Tod and Ward Roberts, of Dany . . . the airplane . . . Laurie . . . now Laurie. I didn't think she could be that way, he thought. But women will fool you. She's vengeful. She's out to pay me back. I did treat her pretty badly. . . . But that's Dany's fault! He'd done Laurie an injury, but what had he done to Dany? Why hadn't she seen him? She was in there . . . of course, she was. Or maybe not. Maybe she'd gone out. His mind raced over the places Dany might have been and then he discarded the notion. She was there. . . . It was revenge, too. Women are so petty. But why . . . why did Laurie cry?

Before Rockefeller Center he stopped in the court and stood for a moment in the shadow of the bronze statue of Atlas. He was tired, logey from the liquor, weak from lack of food. He wanted to rest, to sleep, to awaken refreshed and untroubled. He didn't remember the route he had taken. He had wandered. That strange voice on the telephone had said Laurie was out. Where could she have gone? Maybe she hadn't gotten back yet. . . . Should he have waited? Laurie believed him, though . . . he could tell . . . she had believed the truth about Cy and Tod and all the rest. Who said Laurie was dumb?

Across the street he saw the incongruous gothic of St. Patrick's rising between the concrete piles on its flanks. Goaded by a desire for familiar ground, he crossed the pavement and entered the cool, dim cathedral. He stopped beside the holy water font, and made the sign of the Cross. He was in a distant city, in a church he had never entered. The people in the pews were strangers. But here, at least, he was acquainted with his surroundings. It was as if he had been there before.

He knelt in the last row on his right, hidden behind a pillar, feeling safe, calmed by this respite from the clash of his problems. He looked around him at his neighbors. They've come to confession, he realized. It's Saturday and they've brought their problems to the priest. Problems! What bothers them in their mean, petty, unimportant lives? What have they got to fear except death? And so they hold on, sustained by the promise of an afterlife—the reward of a land of milk and honey and plenty of rent money and husbands who don't get soused on Saturday nights.

A young priest came out of the side door near the sanctuary. The ruddy-faced cleric genuflected; then, walking briskly, his head averted, not glancing at those in the pews, he moved toward the rear of the cathedral. Kane watched as he passed the confessional booths and altars at the side of the nave.

His black cassock swirling about him, the priest sighed, thinking of the long hours of drudgery ahead in the hot box. He had not looked at those awaiting him because, by now, he feared he could tell at a glance what he would hear from them. He had been thinking about his basketball team at the youth center, about the schedule, about the equipment that must be replaced. "Keep my mind on their sins and their troubles," he prayed. Reaching the last booth, near Kane, he opened the center door and was swallowed in the closet of the confessional.

A coughing, scrupulously clean old woman got up and walked to the booth, pulling aside the velvet curtain on the right of the priest's entrance. Kane's dazed and drugged mind assessed her: Probably had a mouthful of bacon yesterday before she realized it was Friday. Now she wants to be reassured she's not damned!

A younger woman, thin, sallow, walked to the booth. She drew back the curtain on the left. Kane grinned sardonically. She's caught her husband stepping out on her. Tell her, dear father, should she suffer in silence or go on relief?

He knelt there in the tinted, soft light of the great cathedral, dwarfed by its immensity and its solemn beauty, oddly soothed by the shuffling feet, the earnest faces, the hushed sliding of the curtains at the intricately carved confessional, surrounded by order and harmony, removed for a time from the shattered debris of his life. It's been a long time . . . a long, long time since I've been to confession. . . .

One compartment was vacant. Not willing it, seemingly prompted by something outside of himself, he entered, bent his knees to the kneeling bench and put his hands on the ledge. Closed off from the priest by a white linen screen, he could hear the curtain open in the opposite compartment, hear the priest shifting his weight in his chair, turning to him. Kane listened to the familiar but unintelligible Latin blessing; and in that moment he wondered if he could recall the right words.

He did. "Bless me, Father, for I have sinned. It has been . . . about two and a half years since my last confession. I received absolution, said my penance and went to Holy Communion." He paused. What should he confess? What was there to be forgiven? "Since then, I've . . . well, Father, I've been with this woman. Sleeping with her."

The priest, his elbow resting on the sill, his eyes closed, listened. "You mean you've had sexual intercourse?"

"Sure. Of course. . . . I said so."

"How long has this been going on?"

Kane recalled that first night when he had fought with Dany and carried her to his bed. "About a year, maybe a little longer . . . but not lately. . . . Decided it wasn't right . . . stopped."

"Are you going to marry her?"

"No!" Kane said with more vehemence than he intended. He fumbled for words to explain, thinking dully as he spoke. "You marry somebody, you want somebody who'll stick by you . . ."

The young priest recognized Kane's agitation. He stroked his temple with the edge of his thumb, wondering if, possibly, the man had been drinking. "Are you ready to give this one up?"

"I already have."

Slipping his hand under his cassock, the priest reached for a handkerchief and wiped the perspiration from his throat and face. "Whose idea was that?"

"What difference does that make?" Kane asked indignantly.

Patiently, the priest replied, "If you had the desire to end it, to give it up, it would appear that you have recognized your sin. If she ended it, walked out on you, perhaps you'll have another one next week."

Kane was uncomfortable, kneeling there. He didn't want to be cross-examined. "What are you pushing me for? I came in here to get forgiven," he said angrily, "not to get the third degree."

"Is that what you came in here for? Well, let me tell you something. Forgiveness isn't so free and easy." The man's anger, the way he slurred his words, his apparent anxiety—all these things troubled the priest. "Before you go out of this confessional," he said softly, "you've got to earn forgiveness by convincing me that you have a firm intention not to do this again." He paused, awaited a reply and got none. "What you've got to do is to go back to the Sacraments, do plenty of praying and show plenty of self-control."

"All right," Kane said, momentarily subdued. "I don't intend to do it again."

"Is this the only woman? Or are there others? Have there been others?"

Like all the priests I've ever known, Kane thought. Pinning you. Prodding you. Digging until they find whatever it is. "Yes . . . others."

"How many and how often?"

Kane thought now, for the first time in years, of Melba Woodmire. "Well, there were a few. . . . But, well . . . one was married."

"And how long ago was this?"

"Oh, that's been years ago," Kane assured him, and in that second knew that he was trapped.

The priest thought back over the past few moments, making sure that he sorted the right information, that he was not confused or thinking of someone else. "You confessed it at the time, didn't you?"

"Well, no," Kane admitted. "I . . . I kind of . . . forgot."

"You kind of forgot adultery? Isn't that a big thing to 'kind of forget'?"

I shouldn't have said that, Kane reasoned. It was a sin to hold back. "Father, I didn't exactly forget . . . actually, I . . ."

"You mean you withheld a confession?"

There it was! Kane prepared for the blast.

But the priest was more incredulous than angry. "You did that, and then you went to communion? You made a sacrilegious communion?"

"Let me explain," Kane said. And then he lost his thought, mumbled to himself, trying to recapture it. "Explanation . . . sure, I know . . . I can tell you . . ."

"Have you been drinking?" the priest said softly.

"I had a drink," Kane said. "I was going to explain about the communion. I'm from a small town . . . Understand, Father? Aren't many of us Catholics . . . and well, the priest knows everybody . . . and, of course, I know he wouldn't say . . ."

"You're stupid!" the priest told him. "That's the answer—
you're simply stupid. You don't even know the basic tenets of
your faith."

"I'm sorry. Been a long time ago. Don't intend to do . . . I
won't again." The heat was stifling, and Kane was having trouble
catching his breath. His head felt detached, as if he could no longer
control it. Perspiration poured down his face; and he wiped at it
with his palm. "Father, please. I'm sorry. What more do you
want?"

The priest was afraid that the man on the other side of the
linen screen was ill, or hurt, or even drunk. "All I want," the quiet
reply came from beyond the screen, "is to be sure that this time in
confession you're not worried about the same thing you worried
about last time."

"All right! All right!"

"Are you feeling well enough to go on?" the priest asked.
"You sound as if . . . perhaps you'd like to come back later,
another day."

"No! Now. I want to talk to you now."

"What else do you want to talk about?"

"I . . . I'm not . . . sure. . . . Things . . . things. I need
absolution, Father."

"Yes, you do. You need it bad. You've been living away from
the Church and the Sacraments. You've been sleeping with these
women. You've committed adultery. And you've topped it off,"
the priest emphasized, "by withholding your sins in confession,
trying to cheat God, and then making a sacrilegious communion.
You better be sure you're not holding anything back this time."

Without thinking at all, Kane replied, "I'm not."

"Don't be in such a hurry," the priest said. "Take your time.
I'm patient."

In silence, Kane thought . . . should I tell about Lenore? No.
That was included with the rest of it. "Haven't been very good
about going to Mass this year," he volunteered.

"You mean you've missed it occasionally, often or always?"

"No. I haven't been to Mass or communion . . . except to
Mass once or twice."

"Well, you've got to remedy that. Are you willing to start
now?"

"Yes."

"Good. Now, what else?"

Kane moved his knees, settling them to get more comfortable. He was oppressed with a myriad of worries, and wanted to dispose of all he could. Safely. He relaxed his body, resting his head on the sill, letting the perspiration drip, hearing it. Doing okay now, he told himself. Getting the priest on my side. Priest didn't know him, would never see his face. For the moment, Kane knew, he was blessed with wonderful anonymity. What else? What else could he tell? Outside of the women, he'd done nothing really wrong in the past few years. . . . Then the real chancre was exposed in his recollections. It had been imprisoned there in his consciousness so long, had arisen rarely but unexpectedly to plague him. Before he realized it, he was speaking, talking slowly at first, then faster as the incident became real again.

"You see . . . I wanted a . . . a job . . . wanted it so . . . And my uncle, he wanted the same . . . job." Kane stumbled as he tried to translate the incident and disguise his own position. "One man . . . the man who decided which of us would get the job . . . I made him give it to me instead of to my uncle."

"Made him?" the priest asked. "Did you use force?"

"I threatened him. I knew something on him . . . and I threatened to tell it."

"And so, you got the job."

"Yes . . . that's right. But I deserved it. Worked for it. And my uncle, he would have done the same thing. . . . It just happened that . . ." Kane's voice trailed off.

"So you used blackmail to get this job—an important job, I gather."

"Not blackmail."

"The name you give it doesn't matter."

"My uncle would have done it to me . . . refused to help me only just before the whole thing came up. Helped himself at my expense." Kane said, talking louder now, defending himself.

"That doesn't matter either," the priest said. "What matters is that you recognize that you did an evil thing, and nothing good can come from evil. If you didn't realize it, you wouldn't have brought it up, would you? It must have been bothering you."

"He was wrong, too. Wasn't he, Father?"

"I don't know. I've heard only your story."

"You don't believe me!" Kane said, accusing him. "You think I'm lying!"

"What I think isn't important. God knows if you're telling the truth or telling a lie; and God will judge you, not me. But, from what you've told me, I believe that your whole problem is pride. Pride in thinking you don't need the Church and the Sacraments. Pride in satisfying your lust without worrying about the people you may hurt. Pride in your desire to better yourself without thought of those trampled by your ambition. What made you go to such lengths, for instance, to get that job?"

"Maybe you're right. I don't know . . . I don't know."

"For a start, you can try to find out, my friend. You can go to your uncle and beg his forgiveness. You can go to your boss, the man who gave you your job, and make a clean breast of it, tell him everything, and assure him that. . ."

"You don't understand!" Kane said in exasperation.

"Won't you try?"

"I'll think about it, Father," Kane promised, and gasped for air, drawing it into his lungs in the closeness of the booth. "Now, will you grant me absolution?"

"Don't you think it would be best for you to go home and think about all this? When you come back, sober and calmer, if you can tell me honestly that you're going to show God you have the guts to make amends for your sins against Him and your fellow men, then I'll grant you absolution. But I can't excuse your failings. I can't free you of your obligation to set yourself right with the people you've hurt. I'm sorry for you. I know this is hard for you. And I'll help you . . ."

Kane was furious. He had told everything to this man. Now he was being cut off, cheated. "I want you to grant me absolution. I don't want to be put off. I've told you everything. I've promised to do better, to try."

"Come back," the priest said. "When you've had time to . . ."

"No!" Kane shouted. "After all this . . . it's not fair!" He sought for some way to retaliate, some phrase to vent his anger. "You know, you're not the only priest in New York!"

The priest held his breath, trying to control himself. He prayed earnestly that God might forgive him the surging wrath that seemed to choke him. "All right, find yourself another church and another priest. Lie to the priest! Lie to yourself! Lie to God! If that's what you want, go on! Get out and start looking . . ."

Kane thrust the curtain aside and staggered out. He was trembling, flushed and shaken. He headed for the side doorway, through which he had entered. Habit pushed his hand into the font of holy water. He looked at it, dazed. Then he shook it from his fingers and stalked out.

48

IT WAS late that night.

Kane sat on the bed in his hotel room, swirling the ice cubes in his glass of bourbon, holding the telephone receiver to his ear, listening with intolerable loneliness to the far-off sounds of laughter and music and the brittle chatter of women and a man's hoarse bellow, fading away, repeating "who called me a party-pooper? . . . who called me a party . . . who called . . And Kane imagined the scene, saw the handsome mulatto maid serving drinks, saw Della, watchful as a house mother at a sorority dance, whispering to one of her girls, saw the cream-white telephone at the other end as it lay on the ebony table in the foyer, saw people close by, ignoring it. . . . And, finally, there was Lenore's small, muffled voice saying, "Is it you again?"

"I'm waiting," Kane said.

"Please. I can't possibly leave yet. I'll come, but you've got to give me time."

"Don't be angry . . . don't Lenore," he said pleading with her.

"I'm not. Really, Kane. But you keep calling me. . . ."

"You been promis . . . promising all night . . ." His speech was thick with drunkenness and fatigue; and, hazily aware of it, he tried to pronounce his words carefully, with deliberate attention to every syllable. "Been prom-is-ing me. But you don't come. Lenore, please come. I'm by myself . . . my-self, Lenore . . . all by myself . . . feel awful . . . awful."

"Kane, believe me, as soon as I can shake loose, I'll skip the party and come over."

He belched and kicked an empty liquor bottle across the maroon carpet. "I'm sorry . . . sorry," he said, and had already forgotten why he was sorry. Rubbing the receiver over his temple, closing his eyes, rocking back and forth to the faraway music that played in Della's salon, he nearly gave in to sleep.

"Kane? Are you still there, Kane?" Lenore said anxiously.

"Mmmm. Still here. And you're still there. And if you don . . . don't come pretty damned soon, I'll . . ." He lost his thought for a moment and puzzled over it. "Give you till twelve. Don't come and I'm coming for you. I'll take my car . . . ren'ed . . . rent-ed car, Lenore. Told you, huh? Got a car. Fifteen mints . . . min-utes I can be for you . . . and I'll do it."

"No! Kane, promise me you won't drive that car."

"Yes, yes . . . I will." He could hear her protesting and it made him feel better, but he didn't answer. He was busily planning a route.

"Kane, you've got to promise me."

"All I got to do is go up Park . . . across to Fifth . . . and through Cen'ral. . . Cen-tral Park . . . and then seven . . . seven-ty-second street . . . Broadway . . . and . . . one block turn right . . . and on and on and on . . ."

"Kane, listen to me! You wait right there. Give me time. You lie down now and rest. And don't call again. Della doesn't like it."

"Lenore?"—plaintively.

"Yes, Kane?"

"Don't say 'good-by,' Lenore."

"I've got to, Kane."

"Talk some more . . ."

"Good-by. I'll see you soon."

He heard her hang up, but minutes passed and he still held the phone, looking at it. "Good-by . . . good-by," he said, and gently put it down. Getting to his feet, walking unsteadily, avoiding the table where an untouched meal stood cold, he took another bottle from the dresser, opened it and filled his glass. At the window, he gulped a long drink, gasped, and stood there, looking out at the towering mass of Manhattan. "What the hell's so beau-ti-ful in this dirty coal hole of a town?" he asked the empty room and the gaudy neon glow of adjoining rooftops and the endless "Z" of fire escapes in the hotel court and the glistening asphalt that shone like an icy lake twenty stories below. "No answer," he said groggily, and tugged at his tie with sluggish fingers, cursing the knot he could not find. "Don't feel good . . . well."

He looked at his watch again, shook it, listened to it. "Must be wrong . . . only three mints . . . min-utes since talked to Lenore." Another drink, another minute-long vigil by the window. "Four min-utes. Wrong time." He went to the phone again, heard the buzz-buzz and the welcome voice. "Wha . . . what time's it?"

"Eleven-sixteen, sir."

"You sure?"

"That's correct, sir."

"Same time I got."

"Is there anything else, sir?"

"What time . . ." He remembered hazily that she had already told him the time, and tried with intense concentration to think of something else, anything else to hold her, to make her talk to him, to help him use up the minutes. "You . . . work all night?" he asked at last, and was pleased that he had thought of a question.

"Yes, sir. Did you want to leave a call?"

"No call . . . What do you do when you work all night . . . always wondered . . . knew a boy at school . . . Fred something, worked on morning paper . . . I mean, you sleep when ever'body . . . ev-ery-bo-dy's working . . ."

"I'm sorry, sir. We're not permitted to have personal conversations with guests."

He was instantly contrite. "Sorry. Really, I am. I'm sorry. Didn't mean to be . . . personal . . . just wondered . . ." The receiver clicked as the operator rang off, but Kane still mumbled into the mouthpiece. ". . . must always eat breakfast at night and lunch for . . ." He couldn't work out the order. Putting the receiver on the bed, he went to the desk, found pen and ink, and scrawled on a telegraph blank:

Breakfast	Breakfast
Lunch	Lunch
Dinner	Dinner

He studied the two columns and began to draw intersecting lines between each meal in column one and each meal in column two. But his mind could not keep track of the combinations he rejected; and the ink ran, smearing the lines together; and he lost interest. Across the room the phone began to click. Kane listened, amused at the metallic protest, and finally he picked it up. "Okay."

"You neglected to seat the receiver on the hook, sir. Will you hang up properly now?"

"Say, what time do you eat breakfast?"

"Room service begins at six o'clock, sir. The coffee shop opens at seven."

"No! *You.* What time do *you* eat breakfast?"

Again the operator rang off. Kane shrugged and carefully seated the receiver. "Simple question . . ." He wound his wristwatch. "Eleven-twenty. Must be later. Must be. Lenore . . . where's she?" Again he put ice in his glass and poured more bourbon. "Stick to same thing, never get sick . . ."

Eleven twenty-two.

Eleven twenty-three.

"Midnight," he said. "Give her till midnight."

Thirty-seven more minutes; and each, heavy-footed, shuffling, held sixty endless seconds.

Kane searched the Manhattan directory, and compared the number of O'Connors with those in the Brooklyn directory and the Queens directory.

He recalled someone saying that, by closing your eyes, opening the Bible at random, putting your finger blindly on a passage, you would receive a message. With weary determination, he followed each step with the Gideon Bible, but could glean nothing from Mark, Jeremiah, Luke or Daniel.

He lay on his bed, eyes shut, counting to sixty. "One and . . . two and . . . three and . . ." Soon he knew when a minute had passed without glancing at his watch, but he grew tired of his prowess.

He counted the ribs in the radiator, the roses on each drape, the roses across the back of the upholstered chair, the lights in rooms he could see from his window.

He read the hotel code for New York State.

He blew sixteen perfect smoke rings on a single cigarette.

He threw matches from a line on the carpet to the wastebasket.

He threw all the coins in his pocket at the line on the carpet.

He ate four cold French fried potatoes and covered the tray with napkins.

He relived his clash with Ward Roberts, rubbing his fist, trying to remember just how it felt when it crashed into Ward's face.

He cursed himself for a fool for having thought that Ward had ever seen or talked to the committee investigating him. He cursed

Milton Pugh for his attempt to unseat him. He cursed Tod, Cy, Norman, Stu.

He thought of Dany, still not willing to believe she had really been home, had really refused to let him in. And in his drunkenness and self-pity, he sobbed.

It was eleven thirty-eight.

"Oh damn! Damnitahell! Goddamnit! Goddamnitahell! And goddamn her and goddamn Della and goddamn the whole goddamn bunch! Where's Lenore? Why doesn't Lenore come?"

There was a sound in the corridor outside. Footsteps padding by. And Kane rushed to the door. "Lenore . . ." he began, seeing in the same instant a plump, gray-haired woman already past his door.

She turned back when he spoke. "Anything wrong, sir? I'm the night floor manager. I'm going off duty now, but if there's anything . . ."

Kane, disheveled, barefooted, leaned in the doorway, shaking his head. "I thought . . . I was expecting someone . . ."

"Are you all right, sir? Can I do something for you?" She walked to him, her kind, warm voice lowered to a whisper, her eyes already looking past him, into the cluttered room. "Why don't you close your door now, and try to get some rest?"

"Hot," Kane said. "Room's hot . . . makes me feel awful . . ."

With the patient good humor of a loving wife putting a ne'er-do-well husband to bed, she took Kane's arm, and led him into the room. "Why you don't have your air-conditioner on! I'll fix that. . . and you'll brighten up all right." She turned a dial, and the unit clicked, hummed, but refused to function. As she tried it again, she saw Kane, leaning against the closed door, blinking, as if he were trying to focus on her. "Why don't you sit down, sir? I'll use your phone, if I may, and the night maintenance man will be up here in a few minutes and get this thing working. I'm terribly sorry . . ."

"All right . . . s'all right," Kane said, waving his hand before his face. He stumbled, righted himself, and reaching the chair, dropped into it.

"Maybe I ought to have the house physician come up, too," the woman said uncertainly. "He can give you something . . ."

"I'm a'right . . . all-right," he said, licking his lips, conscious of the closeness of the room for the first time.

She called the desk, and turned to Kane again. "I hope you'll feel better, sir. Good night," she said, crossing to the door.

"Don't go . . . please."

She looked at him, her head canted to one side, and Kane thought of Norman Keller and the way Norman had of doing that, and didn't like the comparison. The woman was kind, kind and sweet and gentle. "You're ver' nice," he said. "Ver-y. Wait with me 'til the man comes . . . It's only . . ." He looked at his watch. "Only eleven forty-two . . ."

Smiling, she nodded. "We're not supposed to . . . but, all right." She sat on the foot of the bed, her hands clasped in her lap, and a minute passed in which neither spoke. "You'll feel better soon," she said. "When it's so hot like this without proper ventilation . . ."

"Do you know me?" Kane said.

She nodded. "Yes, sir. Your name's on the registry."

He looked down at himself, at his wrinkled, soiled trousers with the knees still dusty from the bench in the confessional booth, his feet dirty from walking the floor. "You must think . . . I'm not very . . . I'm not what you expec'ed . . . ex-pec-ted . . ."

"Oh, no, sir, I don't think . . ."

"I'm drunk," Kane said, and waved off her protest. "Yes, I know I'm drunk . . . awful. And it makes you feel bad to see somebody's who's s'pos . . . sup-posed to be . . ." He couldn't find the word, and shrugged. "But I'm like every other . . . Just cause you're a Congressman, doesn't mean . . . mean you . . . you . . ."

"You're human, that's all," she said. "People have to let their hair down sometimes. My father, he was a wonderful person . . . but, three times a year, at New Years, Fourth of July and American Legion convention, he'd just go out and get himself . . ."

"Please!" Kane held up a restraining hand. "Don't want to be rude . . . but I want to tell you . . . cause I know you're disappointed, seeing Kane O'Connor like . . . I am. Just want you to know, people got to realize. . . . What I mean is, when I first came to Washington, I thought, God, look at me! I'm right in the middle of it. . . . Such a town, such a wonderful, wonderful place . . ." He wiped his face with his hands, and looked at the dampness on his palms. "I'm pooped. I'm so pooped. Pooped . . . pooped," he repeated, amusing himself with the sound of the word.

The woman stood, dipped a napkin in the bowl of cracked ice, and holding his head, she wiped the cool cloth over his face and blotted his forehead. "I'm going to get you a doctor, sir. You've been going at it too hard."

Kane dropped his chin on his chest as she pressed a piece of ice on the back of his neck. "Trying . . . been thinking who you remind me of . . . When I was a kid . . . my teacher. Miss Bessie, we called her. No last name. Just Miss Bessie . . . and she was good. Kind and good. Good and kind. Miss Bessie . . ."

The woman patted his shoulder. "Why don't you go over there and stretch out on the bed? And I'll make a cold compress for you." She felt sorry for him. Not because he was drunk . . . or ill. But because . . . she couldn't phrase her reason. He seems so . . . so innocent, she thought. And hurt. Someone, something has hurt him.

"You married?" Kane asked suddenly, and leaned back, taking the napkin away from her, and blotting his neck with it.

"Divorced," she said. "But I've got my children . . . and one grandchild."

"You're clean," Kane said. "You smell clean like soap, clean like . . . like baby powder. Bet you've got clean kids, huh? Bet your kids never had nits. Bet they're washed and clean . . . like soap." She tried to help him up, but he resisted her. "Please, sir, Please try to get some rest."

"What time's it?"

"Ten minutes to twelve."

"Lenore's coming soon."

"Your friend?"

"She's my friend . . . only friend that sticks is a good friend."

The woman sighed. "Well, fine. She'll take care of you, see that you rest." She started to leave, and Kane pushed himself out of his chair and darted before the door. "The maintenance man will be here any minute," she said.

"I don't wan' wait alone."

She was uneasy. His sudden movement in blocking the door had surprised her, and for the first time she was anxious to leave. Kane O'Connor was drunk and sick and disturbed, and she didn't want to be left alone with him . . . with the door closed. "Please, sir. I'm supposed to check out. If I don't, I'll get in trouble. It's a rule."

"Stay with me," Kane said. He had to keep her there . . . just another few minutes . . . just until Lenore came. He smoothed his shirt front, tucked the tail in, pushed back the hair on his forehead. "I'm all right, long as you wait. . . just 'til the man comes." He put on his bedroom slippers, watching her as he bent to retrieve them.

She rushed for the door; and again Kane threw himself in front of it. "Don't!" he shouted. "What's wrong with you? Why won't you stay?" Then, pleading, he walked toward her, his arms outstretched. "My God, I wouldn't hurt you." He tried to laugh, but couldn't. "I like you. I told you. You're kind and good. I can tell. Like Miss Bessie."

Just before Kane reached her, the woman, panicstricken, her mind churning with all the old stories she had heard and never believed, all the horror tales reported by generations of hotel employees, all the headlines in the tabloids, screamed. Dashing for the bathroom, she got inside in time to slam the door in Kane's face.

He banged his fist on the door. "Come on," he pleaded. "Wha's matter with you?"

"Please go away!"

In a daze of numbness, not understanding her rejection of him, groggy, weak, frustrated, he said, "Please. Let me in . . ."

The woman sat on the bathtub, praying that the repairman would come, praying that she wouldn't lose her job for having become involved, shuddering at the narrowness of her escape. She shut her eyes, held her hands to her ears while he shouted outside the door.

His voice trembled on the brink of tears. In his confusion he whimpered, and his eyes filled. "Dany! Please, Dany!" Leaning his body against the door, he felt the cool wood on his cheek. "Come on, Dany!"

No sound from beyond the door.

"Dany, Dany! Please, Dany. It's Kane." Weakly, he slapped the door again. "It's Kane." He was soaked with perspiration, shaken, throbbing. He felt sick. "Let me in, please, please, please, please . . . He held his temples, gasping and retching. He sucked for breath. It was so hot. He went to the window again, but couldn't force it. "Got to get some air. Feel sick. Got to get some air," he said to no one.

He reeled out of the room in his shirt sleeves, his collar open, his trousers crumpled, his bedroom slippers clomping on the carpet. He had to breathe fresh air. He didn't notice the amazement of the elevator operator, the horrified glances of the clerk and the bellhops in the lobby. Then he was aware of noise around him. Noise. Talk. A dog was barking. He was on the dark street. The air was damp; and the sky had a ghostly pallor.

He turned away from the staring doorman, breathing deeply, holding his head up. Got to get out of here, he told himself. Where? He shuffled now, slowly. Cross with the light. Have to go home now. Back to Washington. They wouldn't beat him without a fight. He'd fight. He clenched his hands and turned back toward the hotel. No, he reasoned. Can't go back there . . . can't.

He leaned against the display windows of a haberdashery, thinking, forcing his muddled, drunken mind to help him. Lenore! Oh, dear God in heaven, why didn't she come? . . . When she promised . . . promised. Then he'd go to her. . . . He'd said he would . . . and he kept his promises. . . . A cab. . . . First a cab. He walked to the curb. Holding to a mailbox, he retched. This is best, he assured himself. I'll feel better. No cab. . . . Where's a cab? Hell with cab. On the side street behind the hotel he saw a sign, and hazily recalled that the hotel garage was somewhere . . . Through the fog of his distempered brain, he oriented himself. That's right . . . over there.

It took him ten minutes, ten minutes of head-bursting retching and a fall in which he bruised his shin and an endless wait in a darkened store lobby while a couple passed by, before he reached the garage.

"You better take a taxi, buddy," the attendant said as they waited for his car to come down on the elevator.

"I . . . was sick," Kane said, and had to force himself to control the violent cramp that tore at him. "All right, now. Thanks."

He got into the car, worried frantically when he could not remember how to start it, tried the key, and relaxed as the motor turned over. Get to Lenore's, he told himself. Feel better. And think. Got to think. . . . That's all. . . . Not through. Licked them before. Can't prove anything . . . nothing. He was dizzy; and he shook his head, as if he could clear his mind. Then he turned the car into Park Avenue, shuddering as a taxi whipped by.

Plenty of people for me. Who's been destroying Reds? God, I'm so sick! Sick . . . Sick . . . Just in time, he saw a red light, and jammed on his brakes. The car lurched and screeched to a stop. Beside a corner newsstand, he saw the morning edition of the Brider paper. Lucy and Mel would help. They'd know what to do. Sick cramp . . . hot . . . nausea. The headline swayed and melted. . . REDS LEAD FIGHT AGAINST O'CONNOR. . . Against me. . . . They're against me. . . . All against me. . . He rubbed his eyes, and leaning forward, tried to focus on the words, REDS LEAD . . .

Horns were sounding behind him, and he pressed the accelerator, sending the car forward. He turned the no-draft window, allowing the wind to rush at his face. Feels so . . . better. Better . . . And the faster he moved, the stronger the breeze that promised to revive him. He went through an intersection, and heard the rubbery shriek of tires as another car jolted to a stop a few feet to his right. He turned up a one-way street, oblivious of the horn that wailed at him, the yell cf a cab driver. Fifth Avenue . . . and across the Park. . . . Lenore's going . . . to help me. . . . Della's going to help me . . . and I'll beat them all. . . . Beat them all, yet . . .

The light was with him when he crossed Fifth Avenue and entered the Park. And the sight of the trees and grass, the glistening towers to his left, and then the great boulders . . . and the lamppost sentinels were invigorating to him. Show her. . . I'll show her. . . Wouldn't come, but I said I'd . . . He barely averted a head-on collision, grabbing at the wheel, fighting the car to stay on the roadway, skidding at the walk, and back on the pavement again. Steady . . . steady . . . steady . . .

A sharp-toothed spasm gnawed at him. And he tried to fight it, tried to slow the speeding car. But he couldn't stop it. . . Nothing worked . . . couldn't find the brake, couldn't turn the wheel. And a wall was in front of him . . . a wall . . . and then, he saw the wall no longer.

For one anguished moment of awareness, he lay on the pavement, saw flashing headlights that grew and grew . . . and were upon him . . . saw a Wrigley wrapper clinging to the filth on his sleeve. He felt nothing. Lights. People. A haze of smoke. Or mist? Steam? No. More like glaring sun. Words spoken. Meaningless. Doctor. Wait. Don't crowd. Don't move. Don't touch. Don't. Don't. Don't.

Faces. He did not know them. Not one face? Not even one? There! She was young. And her dress was straight and starched and blue. A cameo brooch. She spoke. Quiet! He could not hear. She offered him something. Fine. Clean. It was a pair of blue serge knickers. With buckles.

"Miss Bessie!" Kane whispered, knowing her name at last. "Miss Bessie! Get me a priest!"

49

ST. MATTHEW'S CATHEDRAL in Washington. Requiem Mass. Mitred archbishop. Altar boys in black cassocks and white surplices. Ivory candles burning above the high altar. The black-robed deacon chanting the Latin gospel. The subdeacon and celebrant listening.

Beneath them the casket of gray-blue steel was shrouded in flowers. There were wreaths from the great, and scattered blossoms sent by the countless unknown, who had believed in Kane O'Connor, who had stood in line for hours to pass before his bier.

And filling the crowded pews were many who had loved him and some who had hated him and others who had feared him; men who believed his death was the inevitable end of all tragedy; men who believed his death was an incalculable loss to the nation. There was the delegation from the House of Representatives, the newsmen who were filing their last O'Connor story, the morbidly-curious, the sightseers, the Mayor of Manton, a priest from Baltimore who had denounced O'Connor's methods from his pulpit, and hundreds of secretaries and businessmen and housewives and students and servicemen and government workers who were certain that Kane O'Connor's name would live as the man who had awakened America.

Laurie, sitting in one of the front pews, stared straight ahead, her eyes fixed on the flickering orange flame that, inch by inch, moved down the candle before her. And she thought of Kane, not as she knew him in Manton, but as he was during that single hour in New York—anguished, beaten, riding the seesaw between gaiety and despondency. His life had been in broken fragments, and he had come to her searching for someone to help him pick up the pieces and make it miraculously whole again. Her hand went out to touch Wesley Barrett's, but the old man's fingers did not respond.

Judge Barrett straightened the flower in his lapel, thinking of his parting with Mady. "Go if you like," she'd told him, "but I won't. Kane'll pollute Hell itself." The judge believed Kane had not been as callous as he appeared when he had taken the nomination from him. Perhaps, he thought, if Kane had ever found time for sober reflection, he would have regretted much of what he had done. But he had climbed so ruthlessly, rushing on without pause or rest, that it seemed he could not wait to reach the precipice from which he had made his fatal plunge. Well, being here was the least an uncle could do. Wesley Barrett no longer held any rancor in his heart.

Across the aisle, Dany, her eyes red-rimmed, her lips quivering, half-heard the droning monotone of the priest. If . . . if only she had let Kane in! But she had wanted him so badly that she had driven him away. If . . . if only he had gotten rid of Roberts! But that was one of Kane's endearing qualities. He was always amazed at duplicity in others. If . . . if only he had fought back with the savage fire and skill and ingenuity he had shown before! But something had gone out of him. . . . She reached into her purse for her handkerchief—a purse he had bought for her in Woody's, a handkerchief he had used to wipe her lipstick from his mouth on that last wild vacation in the mountains. . . .

The visiting archbishop, adjusting his miter, left his throne and walked to the pulpit. "My dear brethren in Christ," he began. "We who unite with all those who oppose the Godless forces of communism are gathered . . ."

June Sands whispered to Tod: "He fooled a lot of people."

"Shut up!" he said harshly. "What do you expect to hear?" What had happened to Kane? Tod asked himself. What was the poison that had been brewed within him? What was the fatal weakness that had made him go to pieces when he was challenged and circumstances closed in on him? Tod's lips curled in a wry smile. I've got all the questions and none of the answers, he thought. In the final analysis, Kane was a schemer with charm. But when had schemes and charm carried anyone so far? So very far...

The archbishop, aware of the conglomerate character of his congregation, looked out over the pews. He had known Kane O'Connor only by a single brief meeting at Hunting Acres on Kane's first evening there, while many of those in the cathedral had known him intimately. But he wanted to make it clear to all that it was Kane O'Connor, a man, God's creature, they must bury, and not simply the Kane O'Connor of the headlines. "Today we pray for the soul of a man who will be remembered by many as a great crusader . . ."

Cy, standing in the shadows beside the pew in which Laurie and Judge Barrett sat, tried again to assess the Kane he had known. It seemed that all his life the thing Kane wanted most was fame. It had been his obsession . . .to be known, to—as Kane said— "be somebody." And Cy could hear that strong, hearty voice saying those words. Well, Kane had made the grade. He would have exulted in the flowers, the turnout, the press coverage, the newsreel and television cameramen outside, the black-bordered front pages of the Brider papers. It all meant—-fame.

"Heir to man's strength and man's weakness, Kane O'Connor labored to expose the enemy at our doors and within our gates," the archbishop said. "Although he was maligned, although he was challenged, no one can deny that he had the courage, the fortitude and the brilliance to serve this nation. He needs no eulogy, no stone memorial. A man's monument is his work. . .

Norman Keller sat directly behind Dany, watching her, his eyes never wavering. He had been wrong from the beginning, he had decided. For he had mistaken Kane's cleverness for brilliance, his calculation for patience, his ruthlessness for determination, his conceit for self-confidence. Kane had not believed in principles. He had believed only in his own destiny. . . "a prophet is not without honor, save in his own country," the archbishop quoted. "He sounded the warning against those who would lay waste Christ's teachings and return the world to darkness . . ."

Lucy Field puzzled over the tragedy. It's just impossible, she thought. The hotel employees had said he was disturbed. And he had been expecting someone in his room. But who? The garage attendant had said Kane had worn bedroom slippers and his clothes had been filthy and he had been in a hurry. . . . She turned to Mel who sat beside her holding Dany's hand. "Hon, do you think it's possible the Reds were after him, that it wasn't really an accident?"

The Air Force major who sat across the aisle from Dany owed his life to Kane O'Connor. But he had not seen Kane since. . . He tried to recall the exact time. Wounded, tangled in the wreckage, he had watched one crewman after another tumble from the plane.

And then Kane had stood there, buffeted by the wind. Unable to speak, the major, then a lieutenant, had fixed his eyes on Kane's back, willing him to turn to him. And Kane had turned . . . had hesitated, cursed, laughed, and gone forward to, somehow, pilot a plane he had never flown. The major, who had caught a hop from March Field two hours after he heard of Kane's death, allowed his mind to dwell on that single moment of unspoken kinship, on that moment when Kane had chosen to gamble his life rather than let a comrade die. Tugging at his mourning band, the major straightened it on his arm, and forced himself to concentrate on the voice from the pulpit.

"I will not presume to list all of his accomplishments," the archbishop said. "I will not praise him for his victories or censure him for his failings. All of us have our own memories of Kane O'Connor. And each of us sees him through his own eyes. All of us have imperfections. And each of us has the breath of God in him. There is enough room in every heart for both love and hatred, generosity and meanness, mercy and malice, greatness and pettiness, sacrifice, selfishness, kindness, cruelty, courage and cowardice . . ."

Matt Fallon leaned against a pillar in the rear of the cathedral and crimped the brim of his hat back and forth in his hands as his gaze wandered over the scene around him. In a few hours he would sit before the television cameras and tell Kane's story. But, despite the time he and his staff had spent sifting and probing Kane's life, Matt knew he had gathered only the high moments which had won Kane his fame. Nothing had yet been distilled and refined from that story that might give it meaning.

Matt reached for the notepad in his pocket and read the lines he had scribbled during his flight from New York, the words that were to close his broadcast:

That's Kane O'Connor's story. It is a tale of a bold hero, a great cause, the sweep of mighty events, the wielding of personal power, the pageantry of war and politics, and—the tragic flaw . . .

When the services ended, Matt allowed himself to be pushed through the doors to the front of the cathedral where the streets were jammed and hundreds lined the steps. In a moment he was herded behind a rope by policemen, and stood with Tod Sands, awaiting the procession that would bear the casket to the hearse.

"Get a load of that," Tod said as Ward Roberts, a swollen eye hidden behind dark glasses, supported one corner of the coffin and began to descend the steps. "I don't know how the bastard worked it, but there he is, outdoing Judas himself! The guy who shot Kane down, carries him off. That's the way it goes. The shysters and the sharks and the men-in-a-hurry are always around."

Matt did not reply. Nodding thoughtfully, he turned away, crossed the steps to the opposite line where Milton Pugh and Abel Garren stood bareheaded, passed them and wedged through the crowd.

A block from the cathedral, he was still intent, his shaggy head bent forward, Tod's words expanding in his mind. Men like Kane O'Connor and Ward Roberts were always around, all right. But then, Matt thought, so were the plodding, honest decent sonsovbitches who managed to be on their own two feet at the best funerals.

A motorcycle escort passed. And Matt, standing on the curbing, looked up and watched the polished gloss of the hearse, the purring black limousines and official cars—all with headlights glaring—sweep past as the mile-long funeral procession moved off to Arlington. There was a momentary whine of sirens and the escort rounded a corner and disappeared.

About the Author

Ernest Frankel

Marine Colonel Ernest Frankel—author of three novels— Tongue of Fire, Band of Brothers and Gateway to Everywhere, is a graduate of the University of North Carolina at Chapel Hill.

In World War II, as a Second Lieutenant in the First Marine Division, he commanded a rifle platoon on Okinawa. At war's end, when the Division was tasked with taking the surrender of all Japanese forces in North China, he was assigned to Division Staff, serving in both Peking and Tientsin.

Recalled to active duty during the Korean War, he attended Amphibious Warfare School, and annually returned to active duty to write, produce and direct a tabled musical production for the Secretaries Conference of the Department of Defense.

While serving as Commanding Officer of his Reserve unit in Los Angeles, he once again received orders to report to the First Marine Division—this time for special assignment in Vietnam.

Colonel Frankel, in retirement, is a member of the Writers Guild and the Directors Guild and has a long list of credits in network television, and is now at work on a new novel.

Made in the USA
San Bernardino, CA
16 September 2017